THE DEMON TRAPPERS

Forbidden Forsaken

Jana Oliver's imagination has always had the upper hand despite her attempts to house-train it. When she's not on the road tromping around old cemeteries, she can be found in Atlanta, Georgia, with her husband and far too many books.

Books by Jana Oliver

The Demon Trappers series
Forsaken
Forbidden
Forgiven
Foretold

2 books in 1

THE DEMON TRAPPERS

⋙ JANA OLIVER ⋘

Forbidden
Forsaken

MACMILLAN

First published in the US as *Forsaken* and *Forbidden* 2011
by St. Martin's Press
First published in the UK as *Forsaken* and *Forbidden* 2011
by Macmillan Children's Books

This edition published 2013 by Macmillan Children's Books
a division of Macmillan Publishers Limited
20 New Wharf Road, London N1 9RR
Basingstoke and Oxford
Associated companies throughout the world
www.panmacmillan.com

ISBN 978-1-4472-4174-4

1 3 5 7 9 8 6 4 2

A CIP catalogue record for this book is available from
the British Library.

Printed and bound by CPI Group (UK) Ltd, Croydon CR0 4YY

Contents

Forsaken

THE DEMON TRAPPERS

To
Gwen Gades,
who opened the door

'Hell is empty, and all the devils are here' –
William Shakespeare

Chapter One

2018
Atlanta, Georgia

Riley Blackthorne rolled her eyes.

'Libraries and demons,' she muttered. 'What *is* the attraction?'

At the sound of her voice the fiend hissed from its perch on top of the book stack. Then it gave Riley the finger.

The librarian chuckled at its antics. 'It's been doing that ever since we found it.'

They were on the second floor of the university law library, surrounded by weighty books and industrious students. Well, they'd been industrious until Riley showed up and now most of them were watching her every move. *Trapping with an audience* was what her dad called it. It made her painfully aware that her work clothes – denim jacket, jeans and pale blue T-shirt – looked totally Third World compared to the librarian's sombre navy suit.

The woman brandished a laminated sheet – librarians were always into cataloguing things, even Hellspawn. She scrutinized the demon and then consulted the sheet.

'About three inches tall, burnt mocha skin and peaked ears. Definitely a Biblio-Fiend. Sometimes I get them confused with the Klepto-Fiends. We've had both in here before.'

Riley nodded her understanding. 'Biblios are into destroying books. Rather than stealing stuff they like to pee on things. That's the big difference.'

As if on cue, the Offending Minion of Hell promptly sent an arc of phosphorescent green urine in their direction. Luckily, demons of this size had equally small equipment, which meant limited range, but they both took a cautious step backwards.

The stench of old gym shoes bloomed around them.

'Supposed to do wonders for acne,' Riley joked as she waved a hand to clear the smell.

The librarian grinned. 'That's why your skin is so clear.'

Usually the clients bitched about how young Riley was and whether she was really qualified to do the job, even after she'd shown them her Apprentice Demon Trapper's licence. She'd hoped some of that would stop when she'd turned seventeen, but no such luck. At least this librarian was taking her seriously.

'How long has it been here?' Riley asked.

'Not long. I called right away, so it hasn't done any real damage,' the librarian reported. 'Your dad's removed them for us in the past. I'm glad to see you're following in his footsteps.'

Yeah, right. As if anyone could fill Paul Blackthorne's shoes.

Riley shoved a stray lock of dark brown hair behind an

ear. It swung free immediately. Undoing her denim hair clip she rewound her long hair and secured it so the little demon wouldn't tie it in knots. Besides, she needed time to think.

It wasn't as if she was a complete noob. She'd trapped Biblio-Fiends before, just not in a *university* law library full of professors and students, including a couple of seriously cute guys. One of them looked up at her, and she regretted being dressed for the job rather than for the scrutiny. She nervously twisted the strap of her denim messenger bag. Her eyes flicked towards a closed door a short distance away. RARE-BOOKS ROOM. A demon could do a lot of damage in there.

'You see our concern,' the librarian whispered.

'Sure do.' Biblio-Fiends hated books. They found immense joy rampaging through the stacks, peeing, ripping and shredding. To be able to reduce a room full of priceless books and manuscripts to compost would be a demon's wildest dream. Probably even get the fiend a promotion, if Hell had such a thing.

Confidence is everything. At least that's what her dad always said. It worked a lot better when he was standing next to her.

'I can get it out of here, no problem,' she said. Another torrent of swear words came her way. The demon's high-pitched voice mimicked a mouse being slowly squashed by an anvil. It always made her ears ache.

Ignoring the fiend, Riley cleared her suddenly dry throat and launched into a list of potential consequences of her actions. It was the standard demon-trapper boilerplate. She began with the usual disclaimers required before extracting a

Minion of Hell from a public location, including the clauses about unanticipated structural damage and the threat of demonic possession.

The librarian actually paid attention, unlike most clients.

'Does that demonic possession thing really happen?' she asked, her eyes widening.

'Oh no, not with the little ones. Bigger demons, yeah.' It was one of the reasons Riley liked trapping the small dudes. They could scratch and bite and pee on you, but they couldn't suck out your soul and use it as a hockey puck for eternity.

If all the demons were like these guys, no big deal. But they weren't. The Demon Trappers Guild graded Hellfiends according to cunning and lethality. This demon was a Grade One: nasty, but not truly dangerous. There were Grade Threes, carnivorous eating machines with wicked claws and teeth. And at the top end was a Grade Five, a Geo-Fiend, which could create freak windstorms in the middle of shopping malls and cause earthquakes with a flick of a wrist. And that didn't include the Archdemons who made your worst nightmares look tame.

Riley turned her mind to the job at hand. The best way to render a Biblio-Fiend incapable of harm was to read to it. The older and more dense the prose, the better. Romance novels just stirred them up, so it was best to pick something really boring. She dug in her messenger bag and extracted her ultimate weapon: *Moby Dick*. The book fell open to a green-stained page.

The librarian peered at the text. 'Melville?'

'Yeah. Dad prefers Dickens or Chaucer. For me it's Herman Melville. He bored the . . . crap out of me in lit. class. Put me to sleep every time.' She pointed upward at the demon. 'It'll do the same to this one.'

'Grant thee boon, Blackthorne's daughter!' the demon wheedled as it cast its eyes around, looking for a place to hide.

Riley knew how this worked: if she accepted a favour, she'd be obligated to set the demon free. Accepting favours from fiends was *so* against the rules. Like potato chips – you couldn't just stop at one – then you'd find yourself at Hell's front door trying to explain why your soul had a big brand on it that said PROPERTY OF LUCIFER.

'No way,' Riley muttered. After clearing her throat, she began reading. '*Call me Ishmael.*' An audible groan came from the stack above her. '*Some years ago – never mind how long precisely – having little or no money in my purse, and nothing particular to interest me on shore, I thought I would sail about a little and see the watery part of the world.*'

She continued the torture, trying hard not to snicker. There was another moan, then a cry of anguish. By now the demon would be pulling out its hair, if it had any. '*It is a way I have of driving off the spleen, and regulating the circulation. Whenever I find myself growing grim about the mouth; whenever it is a damp, drizzly November in my soul . . .*'

There was a pronounced thump as the fiend keeled over in a dead faint on the metal shelf.

'Trapper scores!' she crowed. After a quick glance towards

a cute guy at a nearby table, Riley dropped the book and pulled a cup out of her bag. It had a picture of a dancing bear on the side of it.

'Is that a sippy cup?' the librarian asked.

'Yup. They're great for this kind of thing. There are holes in the top so the demons can breathe and it's very hard for them to unscrew the lids.' She grinned. 'Most of all, they really hate them.'

Riley popped up on her tiptoes and picked the demon up by a clawed foot, watching it carefully. Sometimes they just pretended to be asleep in order to escape.

This one was out cold.

'Well done. I'll go sign the requisition for you,' the librarian said, and headed towards her desk.

Riley allowed herself a self-satisfied grin. This had gone just fine. Her dad would be really proud of her. As she positioned the demon over the top of the cup, she heard a laugh, low and creepy. A second later a puff of air hit her face, making her blink. Papers ruffled on tables. Remembering her father's advice, Riley kept her attention on the demon. It would revive quickly and when it did the Biblio would go into a frenzy. As she lowered it inside the container, the demon began to twitch.

'Oh no you don't,' she said.

The breeze grew stronger. Papers no longer rustled but were caught up and spun around the room like rectangular white leaves.

'Hey, what's going on?' a student demanded.

There was a curious shifting sound. Riley gave a quick look upward and watched as books began to dislodge themselves from the shelves one by one. They hung in the air like helicopters then veered off at sharp tangents. One whizzed right over the head of a student and he banged his chin on the table to avoid being hit.

The breeze grew, swirling through the stacks like the night wind in a forest. There were shouts and the muffled sound of running feet on carpet as students scurried for the exits.

The Biblio stirred, spewing obscenities, flailing its arms in all directions. Just as Riley began to recite the one Melville passage she'd memorized the fire alarm blared to life, drowning her out. A heavy book glanced off her shoulder, ramming her into the stack. Dazed, she shook her head to clear it. The cup and its lid were on the floor at her feet. The demon was gone.

'No! Don't do this!'

Panic-stricken, she searched for it. In a maelstrom of books, papers and flying notebooks she finally spied the fiend navigating its way towards a closed door, the one that led to the Rare-books Room. Ducking to avoid a flight of reference books swooping down on her like a pack of enraged seagulls, Riley grabbed the plastic cup and stashed it in her jacket pocket.

She had to get that fiend into the container.

To her horror, the Rare-books-room door swung open and a confused student peered out into the melee. As if realizing nothing stood in its way, the demon took on additional

13

speed. It leaped on a chair recently vacated by a terrified occupant and then on to the top of the reference desk. Small feet pounding, it dived off the desk, executed a roll and lined itself up for the final dash to the open door, a tiny football player headed for a touchdown.

Riley barrelled through everyone in her way, her eyes riveted on the small figure scurrying across the floor. As she vaulted over the reference desk something slammed into her back, knocking her off balance. She went down in a sea of pencils, paper and wire trays. There was a ripping sound – her jeans had taken one for the team.

Scrambling on all fours she lunged forward, stretching as far as her arms could possibly reach. The fingers of her right hand caught the fiend by the waist and she dragged it towards her. It screamed and twisted and peed, but she didn't loosen her grip. Riley pulled the cup from her pocket and jammed the demon inside. Ramming her palm over the top of the cup, she lay on her back staring up at the ceiling. Around her lights flashed and the alarm brayed. Her breath came in gasps and her head ached. Both knees burned where she'd skinned them.

The alarm cut out abruptly and she sighed with relief. There was another chilling laugh. She hunted for the source but couldn't find it. A low groaning came from the massive bookshelves to her right. On instinct, Riley rolled in the opposite direction, and kept rolling until she rammed into a table leg. With a strained cry of metal the entire bookshelf fell in a perfect arc and hit the carpeted floor where she'd been seconds before, sending books, pages and broken spines outwards in a wave. Suddenly all the debris in the room began to settle, like someone had shut off a giant wind machine.

A sharp pain in her palm caused her to shoot bolt upright, connecting her head with the side of the table.

'Dammit!' she swore, grimacing. The demon had bitten her. She shook the cup, disorienting the thing, then gingerly got to her feet. The world spun as she leaned against the table, trying to get her bearings. Faces began to appear around her from under desks and behind stacks of books. A few of the girls were crying and one of the hunky boys held his head and moaned. Every eye was on her.

Then she realized why they were staring – her hands were spotted with green pee and her favourite T-shirt splashed as well. There was blood on her blue jeans and she'd lost one of her tennis shoes. Her hair hung in a knotted mass over one shoulder.

Heat bloomed in Riley's cheeks. *Trapper fails.*

When the demon tried to bite her again, she angrily shook the cup, taking her frustration out on the fiend.

It just laughed at her.

The librarian cleared her throat. 'You dropped this,' she said, offering the lid. The woman's hair looked like it had been styled by a wind tunnel and she had a yellow sticky note plastered to her cheek that said *Dentist, 10 a.m. Monday*.

Riley took the lid in a shaking hand and sealed the demon inside the cup.

It shouted obscenities and used both hands to give her the finger.

Same to you, jerk.

The librarian surveyed the chaos and sighed. 'And to think we used to worry about silverfish.'

Riley grimly watched the paramedics haul two students out on stretchers: one had a neck brace and the other babbled incoherently about the end of the world. Cellphones periodically erupted in a confused chorus of ringtones as parents got wind of the disaster. Some kids were jazzed, telling Mom or Dad just how cool it had been and that they were posting videos on the Internet. Others were frightened out of their minds.

Like me.

It wasn't fair. She'd done everything right. Well, not everything, but Biblios weren't supposed to be psycho-kinetic. No Grade One demon would have the power to cause a windstorm, but somehow it had. There could have been another demon in the library but they never work as a team.

So who laughed at me? Her eyes slowly tracked over the remaining students one at a time. No clue. One of the cute guys was stuffing books in his backpack. When she caught his eye, he just shook his head in disapproval as if she was a naughty five-year-old.

Rich creep. He had to be if he was still in college.

Digging in her messenger bag she pulled out a warm soda

and took several long gulps. It didn't cut the taste of old paper in the back of her throat. As she jammed the bottle into her bag the demon bite flared in pain. It was starting to swell and made the arm throb all the way to the elbow. She knew she should treat it with Holy Water but the cops had told her not to move and she didn't think the library would appreciate her getting their carpet wet.

At least the cops weren't asking her questions any more. One of them had tried to bully her into making a statement, but that had only made her mad. To shut him up she'd called her father. She'd told him that something had gone wrong and handed the phone to the cop.

'Mr Blackthorne? We got a situation here,' he huffed.

Riley shut her eyes. She tried not to listen to the conversation, but that proved impossible. When the cop started with the attitude, her father responded with his *you don't want to go there* voice. He'd perfected it as a high-school teacher when facing down mouthy teens. Apparently campus cops were also susceptible to *the voice* – the officer murmured an apology and handed her the phone.

'Dad? I'm so sorry . . .' Tears began to build. No way she'd cry in front of the cop, so Riley turned her back to him. 'I don't know what happened.'

There was total silence on the other end of the phone. *Why isn't he saying anything? God, he must be furious. I'm so dead.*

'Riley . . .' Her father took in a long breath. 'You sure you're not hurt?'

'Yeah.' No point in telling him about the bite – he'd see that soon enough.

'As long as you're OK that's all that matters.'

Somehow Riley didn't think the university would be so forgiving.

'I can't get free here so I'll send someone for you. I don't want you taking the bus, not after this.'

'OK.'

More silence as the moments ticked by. She felt her heart tighten.

'Riley, no matter what happens, I love you. Remember that.'

Blinking her eyes to keep the tears in check, Riley stowed the phone in her messenger bag. She knew what her father was thinking – her apprentice licence was history.

But I didn't do anything wrong.

The librarian knelt next to her chair. Her hair was brushed back in place and her clothes tidy. Riley envied her. The world could end and she'd always look neat. Maybe it was a librarian thing, something they taught them in school.

'Sign this, will you?' the woman said.

Riley expected a lengthy list of damages and how she'd be responsible for paying them. Instead, it was the requisition for payment of demon removal. The one a trapper signed when the job was done.

'But—' Riley began.

'You caught him,' the librarian said, pointing towards the cup resting on the table. 'Besides, I looked at the demon chart. This wasn't just one of the little guys, was it?'

Riley shook her head and signed the form though her fingers were numb.

'Good.' The librarian pushed back a strand of Riley's tangled hair and gave her a tentative smile. 'Don't worry, it'll be OK.' Then she was gone.

Riley's mom had said that right before she died. So had her dad after their condo burned to the ground. Adults always acted like they could fix everything.

But they can't. And they know it.

Chapter Two

Forced to wait outside the library, Denver Beck gave a lengthy sigh as he ran a hand through his short blond hair. His mentor's kid had just topped the list for Biggest Apprentice Screw-up. That upset him, not only because of the ten kinds of grief she'd get from the Trappers Guild, but because that had always been *his* honour. Who'd have thought she could outdo his nightmare capture of a Pyro-Fiend in a MARTA train station at rush hour? A disaster that had required not only the fire department, but a HazMat team.

'But somehow ya did it, girl,' Beck mumbled in his smooth Georgia drawl. He shook his head in dismay. 'Damn, there's gonna be hell to pay for this.'

He rolled his shoulders in a futile effort to relax. He'd been wired ever since Paul phoned him to say that Riley was in trouble. Beck was on the way to the library even before the conversation ended. He owed Paul Blackthorne nothing less.

Barred from entering the library by the cops, he'd cooled his heels and talked to some of the students who'd been inside during the trapping. It'd been easy to get information – he was about the same age as most of them. A few reported they'd seen Riley capture a small demon, but none of them had been clear as to what had happened next.

'Somethin's not right,' Beck muttered to himself. A Biblio-Fiend could make a damned mess, but that didn't usually involve emergency personnel.

A pair of college girls walked by, eyeing him. Apparently they liked what they saw. He ran a hand over the stubble on his chin and smiled back, though now was not the time to be making plans along that line. At least not until he knew Riley was OK.

'Lookin' fine,' he called out, which earned him smiles. One of them even winked at him.

Oh yeah, mighty fine.

A campus cop came within range, the one who'd told him he wasn't to move. They'd traded words, but Beck had decided not to push the issue. He couldn't collect Paul's daughter if he was handcuffed in the back of a patrol car.

'Can I go in now?' Beck called out.

'Not yet,' the cop replied gruffly.

'What about the demon trapper? She OK?'

'Yeah. She'll be out pretty soon. I can't imagine why you guys would send a girl after those things.'

The cop wasn't the only one thinking along those lines.

'It's not legal if she's bein' questioned without a senior trapper there,' Beck warned.

'Yeah, yeah. Your rules, not ours,' the man replied. 'Nothing we care about.'

'Not until ya get a demon up your ass, then you're all over us.'

The cop snorted, hands on his hips. 'I don't understand why you don't just cap their asses, like those demon hunters do. You guys look like a bunch of sissies with all your little spheres and plastic cups.'

Beck bridled at the insult. How many times had he tried to explain the difference between a trapper and a hunter? Trapping a demon took skill. The Vatican's boys didn't bother – they went for firepower. To the hunters, the only good demon was a dead demon. No talent needed. There were other differences, but that was pretty much the dividing line. The average Joe just didn't get it.

Beck summed it up. 'We got skills. They got weapons. We need talent. They don't.'

'I don't know. They look pretty damned good on that television show.'

Beck knew which one the cop was talking about. It was called *Demonland* and was supposedly all about the hunters.

'The show's got it all wrong. Hunters don't have any girls on their team. They live like monks and have about as much sense of humour as a junkyard dog.'

'Jealous?' the cop chided.

Was he? 'No way. When I get done with my day's work, I can go have a beer and pick up a babe. Those guys can't.'

'You kidding me?'

Beck shook his head. 'Nothin' like that TV show.'

'Damn,' the cop muttered. 'Here I thought it was all chicks and flashy cars.'

'Nope. Now ya know why I'm a trapper.'

Beck's jacket pocket erupted into song: 'Georgia on My Mind' floated across the parking lot. That earned him a few stares.

'Paul,' Beck said, not bothering to look at the display. It had to be the girl's dad.

'What happened?' the man asked, his voice on edge.

Beck gave him a rundown of the situation.

'Let me know the moment she's out,' Paul insisted.

'Will do. Did ya trap the Pyro?'

'Yeah. I wish I could get away, but I have to finish up here.'

'No sweat. I'll keep an eye on things for ya.'

'Thanks, Den.'

Beck flipped the phone shut and jammed it in his jacket pocket. He'd heard the worry in his friend's voice. Paul was fanatical about keeping his apprentices safe, and even more so when it came to his daughter. It was why he'd slowed her training to a snail's pace, hoping she'd change her mind and pick a safer profession. Like walking the high wire for a living.

Not gonna work. He'd told Paul that countless times, but he wouldn't listen. Riley would be a trapper whether her father approved or not. She had that same stubborn streak as her mother.

Beck's attention moved to the news crew positioned near the building's entrance. He knew the lead reporter, George something or other. He'd covered Beck's catastrophe. The media loved anything to do with demon trapping as long as it went wrong. A quiet catch in an alley would never land on tape. A Hellfiend going berserk in a train station or a law library and they were all over it.

A lone figure appeared out of the milling crowd. It took Beck a moment to recognize her. She clutched her messenger bag to her side with whitened knuckles like it held the Crown Jewels. Her chestnut brown hair was a mass of tangles and she walked with a slight limp. She seemed taller now, maybe five inches or so shorter than his six feet. Not so much a kid any more. More like a young woman.

Damn, girl, you're gonna break hearts.

When the newshound headed for her Beck went on alert, wondering if he would need to run interference. Riley shook her head at the reporter, pushed the microphone out of her face and kept walking.

Smart girl.

He could tell the moment she spied him: her expression went stony. No surprise there. When she was fifteen she'd had a huge crush on him even though he was five years older than her. He'd just begun his apprenticeship with her dad so he'd done the smart thing – he'd avoided the kid, hoping she'd latch on to someone else. She had, but that story didn't have a happy ending. Riley got over her puppy love, but not the hurt feelings. It didn't help that he spent more time with her father than she did.

He flipped open his phone and called Paul. 'She's OK.'

'Thank God. They've called an emergency Guild meeting. Warn her what she's in for.'

'Will do.' Beck stashed the phone in his jacket pocket.

Riley halted a few feet away, her eyes narrowing when she saw him. There was a rip in the leg of her jeans, a bright red mark on a cheek, and streaks of green on her face, clothes and hands where the demon had marked her. One earring was missing.

Beck could play this two ways – sympathy or sarcasm. She wouldn't believe the first, not from him, so that left the other.

He cracked a mock grin. 'I'm in awe, kid. If ya can do that kind of damage goin' after a One, I can't wait to see what ya got in mind for a Five.'

Her deep blue eyes flared. 'I'm not a kid.'

'Ya are by my calendar,' he said, gesturing towards his old Ford pickup. 'Get in.'

'I don't hang with pensioners,' she snapped back.

It took Beck a second to decipher the insult. 'I'm not old.'

'Then stop acting like it.'

Seeing she wasn't going to give an inch, he explained, 'There's an emergency Guild meetin'.'

'So why aren't you there?'

'We both will be, just as soon as ya get in the damn truck.'

Reality dawned in her eyes. 'The meeting's about me?'

'Duh? Who else?'

'Oh . . .'

When she reached for the door handle, she hesitated. Beck realized the problem by the way she held her hand. 'Demon bite ya?' A reluctant nod. 'Did ya treat it?'

'No. And don't bitch at me. I don't need it right now.'

Grumbling to himself, Beck dug in his trapping bag on

the front seat. Pulling out a pint bottle of Holy Water and a bandage, he headed round the truck.

Riley leaned against the door, weary, eyes not really focusing on much. She was shivering now, more from the experience than the cold.

'This is gonna hurt.' He angled his head towards the news van. 'It would be best if ya not make too much noise. We don't want them over here.'

She nodded and closed her eyes, preparing herself. He gently turned her hand over, studying the wound. Deep, but it didn't need stitches. The demon's teeth didn't rip as much as slice. The Holy Water would do the trick and it would heal just fine.

Riley winced and clenched her jaw as the sanctified liquid touched the wound. It bubbled and vaporized like some supernatural hydrogen peroxide, removing the demonic taint. When the liquid had entirely evaporated, he shot a quick look at her face. Her eyes were open now, watering, but she'd not uttered a peep.

Tough, just like her daddy.

A few quick wraps of a bandage, a little tape and it was done.

'That'll do,' he said. 'In ya go.'

He thought he heard a reluctant *thanks* as she climbed inside the truck, still clutching the messenger bag. Beck hopped in, elbowed the door lock and then started the engine. He pushed the heater control to its highest mark. He'd broil, but the girl needed warmth.

'Do you really use that thing?' she asked, pointing a green-tipped finger at the steel pipe that poked out of the top of the duffel bag on the seat between them.

'Sure do. Handy for Threes when they get rowdy. Really good if they sink a claw in ya.'

'How?' she asked, frowning.

'Gives ya leverage to push the fiend away. Of course, that rips the claw out, but that's for the best. Worst case, the claw breaks off inside ya and your body starts to rot.' He paused for effect. 'It's this really gross brown stuff.'

He'd been graphic on purpose, testing her. If she was squeamish she might as well give it up now. He waited for her reaction, but there was none.

'So what happened back there?' he asked. Riley turned towards the window, cradling her injured hand. 'OK, don't tell me. I just thought we could talk it out, figure out where it went wrong. I've been yelled at enough by the Guild I thought I could give ya some pointers.'

Her shoulders convulsed and for a moment he thought she would cry.

'I did everything like I was supposed to,' she whispered hoarsely.

'So tell me what happened.'

He listened intently as she told him how she'd trapped the Biblio-Fiend. The girl really had done almost everything right.

'You're sayin' the books were flyin' all over the place?' he quizzed.

'Yeah, and the bookshelf tore itself out of the wall. I thought it was going to crush me.'

Beck's gut knotted. None of this was right. To calm his worries, he tried to remember how Paul had handled him after the MARTA incident when he was sure his career was over. 'What would ya do different next time?'

Riley's misty eyes swung towards him. 'Next time? Get real. They're going to throw me out of the Guild and laugh about this for years. Dad is so disappointed. I totally blew it. We won't be able to pay the –' She looked away, but not before he caught sight of a tear rolling down an abraded cheek.

Medical bills. The ones left behind after Riley's mom died. From what Paul had told him they were barely getting by. It was why they lived in a dinky ass apartment that used to be a hotel room and why Riley pushed herself so hard to earn her journeyman's licence. Why Paul had to take any trapping job he could find to make money, though it cost him time with his only child.

Troubled silence fell between them as Beck concentrated on the traffic and what the evening might bring. The trappers weren't easy about change and having a girl as one of their own made a lot of them just downright pissy. Riley needed to talk it out, get over the guilt before the meeting or they'd eat her alive.

After honking at a rusty Mini Cooper that cut him off, he took the turn towards downtown. The intersection ahead of them was a tangle of bikes and motor scooters. One guy was pushing a shopping cart filled with old tyres. Another was on rollerblades, his hair streaming behind him, gliding through the traffic like a speed skater. Nowadays people used whatever it took to get around the city. With the ridiculous cost of fuel even horses made sense now.

The biggest problem was the empty air above the intersection – the traffic lights were gone.

'They keep this up and there won't be one damned light left in the city,' Beck complained.

Most of them had been stolen and sold for scrap by metal thieves. It took some guts to climb up on those things in the middle of the night and dismantle them. Every now and then a thief slipped and ended up a grease spot on the road, buried in a tangle of metal.

Like so many things, the city turned a blind eye to the thievery, saying they couldn't afford to replace every missing light. Too many other things to worry about in this bankrupt capital of five million souls.

Beck nearly clipped some idiot on a moped and then made it through the intersection. His hands clutched the wheel tighter than was needed.

Talk to me, kid. Ya can't do this alone.

Riley flipped down the visor and stared into the cracked mirror.

'Ohmigod,' she said. He watched out of the corner of his eye as she gingerly touched the green areas where the demon pee had dyed her skin.

'It'll be gone in a couple days,' Beck said, trying to sound helpful.

'It has to be gone by tomorrow night. I've got school.'

'Just tell 'em you're a trapper. That should impress 'em.'

'Wrong! The trick is to blend in, Beck, not glow like a radioactive frog.'

He shrugged. He'd never blended in and didn't see why it mattered that much. But maybe to a girl it did.

Turning to the mirror Riley began to dislodge the tangles in her long hair. Tears formed as she pulled a comb through it. It took time to get presentable. She put on some lipgloss, but apparently decided it didn't work with the splotchy green and wiped it off with a tissue.

It was only then she looked over at him and took a deep breath.

'I should have . . . treated the doorway into the Rare-books Room with Holy Water. That way, if the demon got loose, it wouldn't have been able to get in there.'

'Dead right. Not protectin' that room was the only mistake I see. Bein' a good trapper is just a matter of learnin' from your mistakes.'

'But *you* never learn,' she snapped.

'Maybe so, but I'm not the one who's gonna get reamed by the Guild tonight.'

'Thanks, I'd *so* forgotten that,' she said. 'Why were the books flying all over the place?'

'I'd say the Biblio had back-up.'

She shook her head. 'Dad says demons don't work together, that the higher-level fiends think the little ones are nuisances, like cockroaches.'

'They do, but I'll bet there was another demon in that library somewheres. Did ya smell sulphur?' Riley shrugged. 'See anyone watchin' ya?'

She gave a bark of bitter laughter. 'All of them, Beck. Every single one of them. I looked like a total moron.'

He'd been there often enough to know how that felt, but right now that wasn't the issue. Why would a senior demon play games with an apprentice trapper? What was the point? She wasn't a threat to Hell in any real sense.

At least not yet.

Riley shut down after that, staring out of the passenger side window and fidgeting with the strap on her bag. Beck had a lot of things he wanted to say – like how he was proud of her for holding up as well as she was. Paul always said the mark of a good trapper was how they handled the bad stuff but telling her that wouldn't work. She'd only believe it if she heard it from her father, not someone she considered the enemy.

They passed a long line of ragged folks waiting their turn to get a meal at the soup kitchen on the grounds of the Jimmy Carter Library. The line's length hadn't shortened from last month, which meant the economy wasn't any better. Some blamed the demons and their devious master for the city's financial problems. Beck blamed the politicians for being too busy taking kickbacks and not paying attention to their job. In most ways Atlanta was slowly going to Hell. Somehow he didn't figure Lucifer would object.

A few minutes later he parked in a junk-strewn lot across

from the Tabernacle and turned off the engine. If there was any way he could take her place tonight, he'd do it without thinking twice. But that wasn't the way things worked when you were a trapper.

'Leave the demon here,' he advised. 'Put him under the seat.'

'Why? I don't want to lose him,' she said, frowning.

'They'll have the meetin' warded with Holy Water. He'll tear himself apart if ya try to cross that line with him in your bag.'

'Oh.' She'd forgotten about that. Before every Guild meeting an apprentice would create a large circle of Holy Water, the ward as it was called, which would serve as a sacred barrier against all things demonic. The trappers held their meeting inside that circle. Beck was right, the Biblio wouldn't cross the ward. She pulled out the cup, tightened the lid and did as he asked.

'One piece of advice – don't piss 'em off.'

Riley glared at him. 'You always do.'

'The rules are different for me.'

'Because I'm a girl, is that it?' When he didn't answer, she demanded, 'Is. That. It?'

'Yeah,' he admitted. 'As long as ya know that goin' in.'

She hopped out of the car, hammered down the lock with her uninjured fist, then slammed the door hard enough to make his teeth rattle.

A green finger jabbed in his direction the moment he stepped out.

Forsaken

'I'm not backing down. I'm Paul Blackthorne's daughter. Even the demons know who I am. Someday I'm going to be as good as my dad and the trappers will just have to deal. That includes you, buddy.'

'The fiends know your name?' Beck asked, taken aback.

'Hello! That's what I said.' She squared her shoulders. 'Now let's get this over with. I've got homework to do.'

Chapter Three

Riley paused on the sidewalk, shaking inside. Her outburst had cost her what little energy she had left. She needed food and a long nap, but first there was the Guild to deal with. She could already imagine their smirks, hear the good-old-boy laughter. Then there'd be the crude jokes. They were really good at those.

I don't deserve this. The other apprentices made mistakes but they'd never rated an emergency Guild meeting.

The sun was setting and for a moment she could believe there was no disappointed father waiting for her inside that building. Her nose caught the tantalizing scent of roasted meat. Smoke rose in thin, trailing columns from multiple wood fires across the street at Centennial Park. The grounds were dotted with multicoloured tents, like some modern-day Renaissance Fair. A tangle of people wandered the grounds as vendors called to them from tables piled high with goods. She could hear a baritone voice announcing that he had fresh bread for sale.

They called it the Terminus Market after the city's original name. At first it'd just been open on the weekends but now it was a permanent thing. As the economy got worse the market blossomed, filling the missing holes as regular businesses went under. You could buy or barter almost anything, from live chickens to magical supplies. If the vendor didn't have what you wanted, by the next night he would, no questions asked.

'Sign of the times,' Beck said under his breath. 'Not that it's right.'

Caught by the deep frown on his face, her gaze followed his. On the sidewalk was a dead guy, loaded down with packages from the market. He wore clean clothes and his hair was combed, but you could tell he was dead – the pasty grey complexion and the zoned-out expression gave it away every time. He stood a few steps behind his 'owner', a thirty-something woman with strawberry-blonde hair and designer jeans. Everything about her shouted money, including the car. No solar panel on the top so she wasn't concerned how much a gallon of fuel might cost. No dents, no rust, just clean and new.

Probably has the dead guy wash it.

From what Riley had heard, a Deader wasn't like a zombie in the movies, just a sad reminder of a past life. For people with money they were the perfect servants. They never asked for vacation and they weren't entitled to wages. Once a necromancer pulled a corpse from the grave it was good for nearly a year, the downside of better embalming techniques. When it ceased being useful it was buried again, if the owner was compassionate. If not, the Deader would be found abandoned in a dumpster.

'They're just slaves,' she said. 'Once you're dead you should be left alone.'

'Amen to that.' Beck cleared his throat. 'Well, ya won't have to worry. If a trapper gets chewed up by a demon, the necros don't want 'em.'

Now that's great news.

Riley watched as the Deader piled the packages into the boot of a car. When he was finished, he climbed into the back seat. They were good for simple tasks, but driving wasn't one of them.

She turned back towards their destination. Built of red brick, the Tabernacle had clocked over a century of use. It'd been a Baptist church, then a concert hall. She'd come here for an Alter Bridge concert to celebrate her dad's thirty-fifth birthday when they'd lived in Buckhead and her mom was still alive. Back when her parents were teachers at a real school and everything was good.

Beck paused at the entrance, leaning against a rope that served as a handrail. The metal ones were long gone. Still holding his duffel bag in one hand he turned towards her, his face unusually solemn.

'It's not just because you're a girl,' he said in a lowered voice, his mind still on their earlier conversation. 'A lot of these guys are gettin' older, and they're not happy competin' with younger trappers.'

'Like you?'

He nodded. 'Don't expect a good time, OK? But don't let 'em push ya around. It was a good trappin' gone wrong.

That's happened to every one of us. Don't let them claim anythin' different.'

Then he left her on the street, putting distance between them like he didn't want to be seen with her.

Creep.

Her dad was waiting inside that building. What would he say? Would he tell the Guild he'd made a mistake, that she wasn't trapper material? Or would he try to defend her?

If he does, they'll roast him.

That thought pushed her forward. Her father wasn't going to face this alone. This was *her* mistake, not his.

Riley limped up the steps and entered the building, closing the street door behind her. Nothing much had changed since the last Guild meeting: cobwebs still hung from the ceiling and the floors were laced with dust and discarded foam cups. A sneeze overtook her. Then another. Pulling a tissue out of a pocket, she blew her nose as she wandered into the huge auditorium. It was a vast space with uncomfortable wooden benches in three sections that rose to the rear of the building, most of it in the dark now. There used to be a pipe organ but it was long gone. Metal was too valuable.

On the floor in front of her was a wet line in the dust that encircled the area where the meeting was being held. Why the trappers bothered to have a Holy Water ward never made sense to Riley. No demon would wander into a roomful of trappers. It'd be a way dumb move. Still, it was tradition and it fell to an apprentice to ensure the ward was properly applied. One day it would be her turn.

This was only the second time she'd been in front of the Guild. The first hadn't been a blast, with lots of argument whether to issue her an apprentice licence or not. Most of the trappers hadn't cared either way, but a few clearly resented her. Not because of her dad, but because she wasn't male. They'd be her foes tonight.

And I gave them all the ammunition they need.

Only the ground floor General Admission section was illuminated. Above her, dust hovered in the bright streams of light pouring down from the floods. The lights doubled as a heat source, which left the rest of the building uncomfortably chilly.

The meeting had already started and her dad was at one of the round banquet tables, arms crossed. It was his *you're standing on my last nerve* pose. He was wearing his Georgia Tech jacket and sweatshirt and faded blue jeans. His brown hair really needed a trim. Just like an average dad – except he trapped demons for a living.

'How'd this simple job go so far off the rails, Blackthorne?' an older man asked. He was grey at the temples and had a deep crescent-shaped scar that ran down one side of his face. His nose had been broken and hadn't healed right. He looked like a cross between a pirate and a convict.

Harper. The most senior of the three master trappers in the Atlanta Guild.

'That's what we're here to find out,' her dad replied, his voice clipped. 'Riley should be here soon, then we can hear the full story.'

'Don't care if she's here or not. She's done as far as I'm concerned,' Harper replied. The sneer on his face pulled the scar out of alignment.

'We've all made mistakes.' Her dad pointed towards a beefy black man at a nearby table. 'Morton destroyed a courtroom trying to trap a Four right after he became a journeyman. Things happen.'

'What did I know?' Morton said, spreading his hands. One of the few African Americans in the Guild, he dressed like he should be selling houses rather than trapping fiends. 'The defence lawyer acted just like a demon. I'm still getting sued over that one.'

There was muted laughter.

Her dad nodded. 'My point is that Riley is smart and she listens to instructions. She'll learn from this and the next trapping will be picture perfect.'

'That's better than your last apprentice,' someone joked. 'He never did listen.'

Beck stepped into the circle of light. 'Evenin' all,' he said.

'Speak of the devil,' the same trapper called out. 'What do you say about this, Mile High?'

From the way Beck tensed, Riley could tell he didn't like the nickname. He just shrugged and parked himself at her father's table, then pulled two beer bottles out of his duffel bag and set them in front of him. Twisting the top off one, he took a long swig and settled back like he was there to watch a stage show.

You selfish jerk. He wasn't going to stand up for her. How many times had her father saved his butt?

So much for gratitude.

Gnawing on the inside of her bottom lip until she drew blood, Riley stepped into the light, blinking to clear her vision. When they spied her, some of the trappers snickered. She held her ground, hands knotted at her side.

'There's Little Miss Screw-up now,' Harper said.

Riley's father glared. 'Keep it civil, Harper.'

'If she can't take it, she shouldn't be here.'

'There's no need to be rude,' another trapper insisted. It was Jackson, the Guild treasurer. He was a tall, thin man with a goatee and ponytail. He'd worked for the city before the first round of layoffs a few years back. In lieu of a response, Harper spat on the floor then dug out another wad of chew.

Though Riley really wanted to run into her father's arms, she took her time crossing to him. She refused to act like a scared little girl in front of these jerks, though deep inside she was freaking out.

Her dad stood and put his hands on her shoulders, looking deeply in her eyes. When he saw the damage to her face, he winced.

'You OK?' She nodded. He squeezed her shoulders for support. 'Then tell them what happened.'

He'd treated her like an adult, not a frightened kid. That simple gesture gave her the courage to face this.

She scanned the circle of men around her. There were about thirty of them. Most were middle-aged, like her dad. They'd become trappers when their other careers had ended, destroyed by an economy that had never found anything but the bottom. Bitterness hung on them like a heavy winter coat.

Riley cleared her throat, preparing herself. Harper snapped his fingers impatiently. 'Come on, spill it. We don't have all damned night.'

'Don't let him goad you,' her father murmured.

Hoping her voice wouldn't quaver, she gave her report. Her words sounded so insignificant inside the cavernous building, a mouse squeaking to a pack of lions.

When she'd finished, Harper huffed and crossed his arms over his chest, revealing a blood red tattoo on his forearm. It was a skull with a writhing fiend in its mouth.

'Demons don't work together,' he said. 'Every apprentice knows that. 'Cept maybe you.'

He made it sound like she was lying.

'How else would you explain all the damage?' Morton asked.

'Don't know, don't care,' Harper said. 'All that matters is that we're the laughing stock of the city and we know who's to blame.'

Murmuring broke out among the men.

'It's not as easy as that,' her dad began. 'If the demons are banding together, we need to know why they've changed tactics.'

'You're just trying to save your brat's ass, Blackthorne. She would never have been given a licence in the first place if she wasn't your daughter.'

Beck stirred and set his beer bottle down on the table with a clunk. 'Why not? She met all the requirements.'

Harper swung his dark gaze towards him. 'Why do you give a damn? Looking to get a piece of that, are you?'

Riley's dad shifted in his chair, his face growing red with anger. Beck, on the other hand, was icy calm. It wasn't what she'd expected of him.

He popped open the top of the second bottle, took a long swig, then smacked his lips. 'Nah, she's too young. She can't buy me beer.'

'Damned straight,' someone called out. 'Nothin' more than jailbait.'

Her father's frown deepened.

'I say we eyeball the library's security tapes,' Beck said in a thick drawl, heavier than usual. 'That'll tell us if there was another demon there.'

'Take too long to get them. We need to vote on this,' Harper argued.

'We don't need the tapes, Master.' That was Simon Adler, Harper's apprentice. He was tall and blue-eyed with bright blond hair that swirled in waves. When Riley was small, her mom bought an angel for the top of the Christmas tree. Simon's hair was the same colour. A couple of years older than her, he wore jeans and a Blessid Union of Souls T-shirt. A wooden cross hung from a thick leather cord round his neck.

'There's already a video of it on the Internet,' he said, gesturing towards a laptop on the table in front of him. Riley was surprised he'd bring it into this dustbowl.

Harper threw him a furious look. 'Who the hell asked you?'

'Sorry,' Simon replied, 'but I thought we'd want to know the truth.'

'You keep your goddamned mouth shut unless I say otherwise, got it?'

The apprentice winced at the blasphemy.

Beck cut in. 'Come on now, Simon's doin' what any *good* trapper would do – keepin' tabs on the demons. That's what you're teachin' him, isn't it?'

Harper's face turned dark with anger, making the scar stand out.

'Let's see it,' Jackson called out. 'Maybe it'll make our report to the Church easier.'

The Church. The trappers only captured the demons: the Church was responsible for dealing with them after that. It was a complex arrangement but it had held together for centuries. The Guild always went out of its way not to piss off the Church.

Simon tapped away on the keyboard as men crowded around. There were too many trappers so it looked like they'd have to take turns watching the screen. A running commentary began at the same time as the video.

'Damn, look at that flying tackle,' Morton said. 'That had to hurt.'

It had.

'She got him!' one of them called out.

'Oh my God, look at the—'

Bookshelves. A tremendous crash came from the computer speakers. Exhausted and shaking, Riley sank into the closest chair. Her dad pushed a bottle of water her way. She twisted off the plastic cap and sucked the cool liquid down, gulp after gulp. Her stomach rumbled, a reminder she'd not eaten since breakfast.

Her dad hadn't hurried over to watch the video. There was only one reason for that. *He thinks I screwed up.*

That hurt more than the burning demon bite.

Finally, Simon set the computer in front of her father. 'Just press this key and it'll play,' he said. He gave Riley a quick smile and retreated.

Trappers moved in behind her, talking among themselves. One of them was Beck. She gritted her teeth at what was to come.

'You ready?' her dad asked.

She nodded.

It was worse the second time around. Like watching one of the *Demonland* episodes on television, only this time she was the star and there was no stunt double. Whoever captured the video did a pretty good job, though the picture would swing wildly every now and then.

This is all over the Internet. People in foreign countries would watch it and laugh at her. Mock her. There would be no hiding from this.

'Look at all that stuff blowing around,' someone exclaimed.

Beck sucked in a sharp breath as the bookshelves committed suicide. The final portion of the video showed Riley limping out of the library, bloody and battered.

'My God,' her father whispered, pulling her into an embrace so tight she couldn't breathe. He wasn't mad at her or disappointed. He only hugged that hard when he was scared. When they broke apart, she saw it on his face, though he tried to cover it. Then he smiled, soft crinkles appearing at the corners of his brown eyes. 'You did very well, Riley. I'm so proud of you.'

Her mouth fell open as the threat of tears returned.

'Ditto,' Beck said as he returned to his beer.

When she looked up, all eyes were on her. A couple of trappers gave her a nod of respect. Jackson looked over at Harper, then back at her.

'That sure as hell wasn't just a Grade One,' he said.

'I agree. That's a Geo-Fiend for sure,' another said.

Harper straightened up. 'Doesn't matter. We can't give this one a pass. Makes us look bad.'

'Oh, go screw yourself, Harper,' Jackson growled. 'You've hated every apprentice we've had. Those you train you treat like dirt. I should know.'

'If you weren't such a jerk-off, Jackson,' the master began.

Her dad tugged on her sleeve. 'Why don't you go outside? It's going to get nasty and I'd rather not have you hear it.'

'But what about my licence?' she asked.

'That's why it's going to get nasty.'

Oh.

Beck tossed his keys on the table in front of her. 'Keep the demon company, will ya? He's probably missin' ya by now.'

She glowered at him.

Her father intervened. 'Wait in the truck and lock the doors. I'll be out soon. Go on. It'll be OK.'

It'll be OK.

It sounded like a curse.

Chapter Four

The moment Riley reached the truck she kicked the closest tyre, imagining it to be Beck's head. It was a stupid thing to do because now her foot ached like the rest of her. Her anger wouldn't make a bit of difference – if Harper bullied the others long enough they'd revoke her apprentice licence. Once they voted her out, she was done. There was no going back.

Then what? She'd have to get a job waiting tables or something. *That's so not me.*

A chittering sound brought her eyes upward as a whirl of bats exploded from under the Tabernacle's eaves. She watched them skitter away into the dusk, envying their freedom. In the distance a thin chorus of howls echoed in the streets. Coyotes. They hunted every night, slinking around in packs, looking for a stray meal to wander their way. The city was slowly reverting to nature's laws.

She eyed Beck's ride. It was so him. Who else would drive around in a battered rust-red Ford F-250 with a Georgia state flag decal in the rear window? Next to that was the official Trappers Guild emblem and underneath the unofficial slogan – *Kicking Hell's Ass One Demon At A Time*. A mass of beer bottles in the truck bed rolled around like bowling pins every time Beck took a corner. He'd be adding more to the pile soon enough.

She unlocked the door and climbed in, eager to get out of the cold. The interior smelled like the owner's leather jacket. Digging under the seat she retrieved her demon and stuck it in her bag, ignoring the offer of a favour to free it and then the upturned middle finger.

How long will this take? 'Just vote me off the island and move on,' she groused. If it took too long she'd have to start the truck to get some heat, but that would be wasting fuel.

To try to keep her mind off all the drama, Riley raided the glove compartment. It was a lot like snooping in someone's medicine cabinet – you learned a lot about a person that way. The first thing she found was the gun. That didn't surprise her: trappers went into rough neighbourhoods. She cautiously pushed it out of the way. Next up was a flashlight. She flicked it on and hit pay dirt – Beck's Trappers Manual.

Apprentices received their manuals in sections as they progressed through their training to prevent them from going after bigger demons before they were ready. All she had was the section about Grade Ones, like the Biblio-Fiends. Denver Beck was a journeyman trapper, one step below a master: this manual had almost all of the good stuff, except the parts on the higher ranking fiends and Archdemons.

Riley hesitated. They were going to kick her out, so why bother?

'But if they don't . . .' She'd never get an opportunity like this again.

She did a mental coin flip and curiosity won. It always did with her.

Riley made sure the doors were locked, then angled her body so the flashlight hit the pages and began to read, lured like the time she'd found her mom's stash of smutty romance novels.

'Grade Three demons are territorial and are best known for their ability to completely gut and eat a human in as little as fifteen minutes.'

Maybe this isn't such a good idea.

She'd just started on the section on how to trap Threes when a knock came at the window. Riley jumped. After frantically jamming the book and the flashlight into the glove compartment, she looked up. It was Simon, Harper's apprentice. Embarrassed at being caught, she sheepishly climbed out of the truck.

'Sorry I scared you,' he said, stepping back a few paces, seeming to understand she needed her space. Not all guys did that. 'I thought I'd check and see how you're doing.'

Here I am with a seriously hunky guy and I'm covered in demon pee. Why does the universe hate me?

She tried to run a hand through her hair, but the bandage pretty much ended that effort. Feeling she should say something, Riley stammered, 'I was . . . was reading . . .'

A slow grin crawled on to Simon's face as he adjusted the computer bag on his shoulder. 'The manual. I saw that. But it wasn't yours. Too thick.'

Busted. She slumped against the truck. 'It's Beck's.

You won't say anything, will you?'

Simon shook his head. 'I pulled the same stunt with Harper's manual, except he was the one that caught me.' His face darkened at the memory.

'Dad doesn't tell me anything. I hate it.' A moment after she'd vented, she wondered if that was a good thing. Could she trust Simon?

'Harper's the same way, and then he yells at me when I don't know something he thinks I should.' Simon frowned. 'I'll make journeyman yet, just to prove him wrong.'

'I won't. They're going to throw me out.'

'You never know,' he said. 'Some of them were pretty impressed.' He paused and then added, 'I think you were awesome.'

That caught her totally off guard. *He thinks I'm awesome?* 'Ah . . . thanks!'

Simon smiled and suddenly she didn't feel so cold any more.

They heard voices – Beck and her dad were headed in their direction, talking animatedly. Neither of them looked happy. Beck was gesturing and she thought she heard a curse word or two.

Simon began to edge away. 'Better go. Nice to meet you, Riley,' he said.

'You too, Simon.' Right before he crossed the street, he looked back at her. She waved. That made his smile widen.

He's really cute.

Riley hopped into the truck to get the Biblio that had

caused all the problems. The flashlight was still on inside the glove compartment, issuing a glow around the edges of the door. She hurriedly fixed that problem, then grabbed the messenger bag.

'I see Simon was keeping you company,' her father said as he walked up. 'I'm glad he checked on you.'

That made her feel even better. If her dad liked the apprentice, then he was probably OK.

'So? What's the verdict?' she asked, clenching her hands into fists to prepare for the bad news. The one with the demon bite promptly throbbed in response. 'They tossed me out, didn't they?'

'You're still an apprentice, for the time being,' her dad announced. 'The video convinced them there was another demon present, one that you weren't qualified to trap. The next time there's a problem, you're out.'

They weren't telling her everything. 'And?' she pressed.

Her dad and Beck traded looks.

'There are also sanctions against me,' her dad replied. 'If you lose your licence I won't be able to take on an apprentice for another year.'

'That was Harper's little roadside bomb,' Beck grumbled. 'Miserable bastard.'

Riley was stunned. Her dad was a born teacher, whether it was history classes in high school or bringing a new trapper up through the ranks. He would lose not only his one joy in life but also the stipend they paid to train new members. That money bought their groceries. No apprentice, no food. It was that simple.

'Bottom line, you're still in the Guild. We'll worry about the rest later.' Her dad put his arm around her. 'Come on, let's get you home.'

'Yeah, I hear she's got homework to do,' Beck chided.

Riley threw him a glare but didn't bother to reply. He was the least of her hassles.

As they pulled out of the Grounds Zero drive-through, Riley's hot chocolate steamed up the side window and made her feel good for the first time all day. It wasn't only the hot beverage – she was with her dad and that always made her feel better. The feeling wasn't going to last. Once they got home he'd take off with Beck for another night of trapping. They'd been trying to capture a Grade Three demon down in Five Points and it kept getting away. Now it was a matter of pride for both of them.

Riley knew it was selfish to be upset that he was gone all the time. She knew they needed the money, but sometimes she craved spending more time together, even if it was trapping demons. But that wasn't going to happen until she learned to trap a Three. Then she and her dad could work as a team and Beck would have to find someone else to trap with. She wondered if Backwoods Boy had figured that out yet.

Riley poked absentmindedly at the rip in her jeans. She wouldn't bother to mend it – ripped jeans were OK, but the green demon pee was another matter. It bleached out the denim. There was no way she could afford a new pair.

When she set her hot chocolate in the centre console, she spied a computer disk next to a pile of crumpled gum wrappers. Probably some of her dad's Civil War research. When he had free time, which wasn't very often, he'd go to the library and use one of their computers. Faster than the one they had at home, that was for sure.

'So what is it this time?' she asked, pointing at the disk. 'Antietam or Battle of Kennesaw?'

He seemed startled at the question and quickly tucked the disk into his pocket. 'How's this for a deal? After I make the rent money I'll take a night off. We'll get some pizza, maybe watch a movie.'

She nodded enthusiastically. 'Sounds good! I'd love that.' *Every night.* Then a thought came to her. 'Just us. No Beck.'

'You really don't like him, do you?'

'No, I don't. On the way to the meeting he said he wanted to help me, but he didn't do a thing. He's a creeper.'

Her dad shook his head. 'You're not seeing the bigger picture.'

'Really? He sat there drinking his beer, acting like it was some picnic. You said his mom's a drunk and the way he's going he's going to end up the same. I don't know why you bother with him.'

Her dad didn't answer, his brow furrowed in thought. Riley cursed to herself. Why did they always argue about *him*?

Feeling guilty, she blurted, 'What do you think of Simon?'

Her father appeared pleased at the change of topic. 'Quiet kid. A lot going on in that brain. He's a methodical trapper.

He'll do well in the business if Harper ever signs his journeyman's card.'

'I like him.'

'And I think he likes you. Just be careful of Harper. He's really hard on the boy.'

Riley's phone emitted a chorus of cricket chirps. She studied the display and smiled. It was her best friend. 'Hey, Peter. How's it going?'

'Hey, Riley. I saw your video. You rock! The stats are off the chart. You're going viral!'

Riley groaned. Just what she always wanted – thousands, millions of people laughing at her.

She could hear the sound of a keyboard. Peter was into multi-tasking so he was probably IM-ing with a couple of his buds while talking to her on the phone.

'It wasn't that much fun in person,' she admitted.

'Yeah, but you nailed that little guy. All that stuff flying through the air looked like something out of *Harry Potter*!'

Peter would love that kind of thing. He'd collected all the books and the movies.

'Hold on,' he said. She heard a voice in the background – Peter's mom finding out who he was talking to. 'OK, I'm back,' he said. 'It was the warden making sure I hadn't escaped.'

Riley looked over at her father and then sighed. She liked talking to Peter, but her dad wasn't going to be around all evening.

'Ah, Pete, can I call you later? I'm with Dad right now and

he's going to have to leave pretty soon and . . .'

'Understood. Call me when you get a chance, OK?' her friend said. 'You still rock, by the way.' Then he was gone.

Her father halted at a stop sign as an old man puttered across the intersection. Tied to his shopping cart was a scruffy dog toting something in its mouth.

'You see that?' her dad asked.

'You mean the old guy?'

'You don't see the white outline around him?'

All she saw was an old guy with a dog.

'He's an angel,' her father explained.

'No way!'

Riley stared at the man. He looked like any one of the other homeless dudes in the city. 'I always thought angels would have wings and wear robes or something.'

'They do. The ministering kind can look like us, unless they want to reveal their true form.'

The man/angel reached the sidewalk, petted the dog and set off again.

'There are more of them in Atlanta now,' her dad observed.

Something in his tone caught Riley's notice. 'Keeping an eye on the demons. That's good, right?'

Her father shrugged. 'Not sure.'

'Do they really do angel sorta things, like miracles and such?'

'So it's said.' He was silent for a while, concentrating on his driving. Then out of the blue he asked, 'You and Peter ever going to date?'

She blinked in surprise at the question. *Where did that come from?*

'Ah . . . no.'

'Why not? He's a nice kid.'

'He's . . . Peter. I mean . . .' She struggled to come up with the best explanation for what seemed obvious to her. 'He's just a friend.'

Her dad smiled knowingly. 'Got it. I knew a girl like you when I was in high school. Never once thought I might have a thing for her.'

Dad rarely talked about his past. She couldn't resist. 'Who was she?'

'Your mom.' He waggled his eyebrows at her groan.

'He just calls me because he's lonely,' she explained.

'Or because he really likes you.'

'Yeah, yeah. Nice try. He's got his eye on Simi.'

'The punk barista at the coffee shop?' her dad quizzed. 'The one with neon hair?'

Riley nodded. 'You should have seen her last month – she had black and white stripes with purple tips. Seriously breathtaking.'

'Don't even think about it,' her dad replied, lifting a warning eyebrow.

'As if.' She had enough problems as an apprentice without looking like a Halloween costume gone wrong.

'How's school going? They still have you juniors sit near the dairy case?' he quizzed.

Riley wrinkled her nose. 'It's OK. The store smells like

mouldy cheese and has all the old signs hanging from the ceiling. It's yucky in there. There are mice creeping around and dead roaches.' She wiggled her fingers in disgust.

Before her father lost his job and started trapping demons, she and Peter had attended a real school. Now, because of budget cuts, they went to night school three times a week in an abandoned grocery store. Most of the teachers had other jobs hauling garbage or selling hot dogs at convenience stores.

'Some of my teacher buddies are saying there are plans to reorganize the classes again,' her dad warned. 'You might be moving locations.'

That wasn't good news. 'Just as long as Peter goes with me, I don't care where they stick us.'

'At least you got a grocery store this time. It could have been an old Mexican joint and you'd come home smelling like stale bean burritos.'

'Euuuu . . .' she said.

'I always figured I'd have a teaching job for life,' her dad admitted. 'I even thought it was a good deal when the city sold the schools to Bartwell, figured it would get us more money for education.' He shook his head. 'I was so wrong.'

Riley knew this story well. Bartwell Industries had leased the school buildings to the city and kept raising the rent. In the midst of a budget crisis and unable to handle the increased expense, Atlanta farmed out their classrooms to uninhabited businesses hoping to pressure their landlord to lower their rates. Bartwell promptly went bankrupt. The result was dilapidated school buildings, classes held in defunct grocery stores and a lot of unemployed teachers.

'At least I can trap,' he said ruefully.

'We both can.'

He nodded, but she could see he wasn't eager to agree.

Her father was usually in a hurry to leave, keen for the hunt, but they took their time walking from the parking lot to the apartment complex.

'I don't expect you to become a trapper just because I am,' he said, his tone pensive.

Riley thought about that as they wove their way through the rusty bikes and the scooters. 'I want to do this, Dad.' She caught his hand and squeezed it. 'I don't want to work behind a counter somewhere. That's just not me.'

A resigned expression settled on his face. 'I'd hoped you'd change your mind, but tonight I knew it wasn't going to happen. You stood up to Harper and that takes guts.'

'Why is he such an idiot?' she asked. 'He acts like he hates everyone.'

'He's had a lot of losses. Everyone has a breaking point, Riley. He hit his a long time ago.'

'But you didn't.'

He smiled and squeezed her hand. 'Because of you.'

Weaving his arm around her waist, they walked up the stairs in tandem.

Someday he'll be home all the time. Then it'll be good again.

Chapter Five

Once her dad had departed, Riley spent a long time in the shower. To her relief it took most of the green out of her skin. With some creative make-up application she might pass for human by tomorrow night. She hoped none of her class-mates had seen the video. Besides Peter, that is.

Right. Dream on.

Every evening she tidied the apartment. Tonight wasn't any different, despite the fact she felt she'd been body-slammed by a sumo wrestler. Cleaning never took very long as the place was Barbie-sized, two hotel rooms kludged together, the walls an industrial beige. The extra bathroom had been divided in half and converted into a closet. There were three rooms total – a twelve by fifteen-foot living room and kitchenette, a bathroom and tiny bedroom. A decrepit wall unit offered minimal heat and air conditioning. They didn't run it very often because it was too noisy.

'When I'm a journeyman . . .' Riley mused, 'we'll move into a nice apartment.' She knew what it would look like – she'd found a picture in a magazine, all wood floors and big windows and gleaming stainless steel appliances. The picture was stuck to the ancient refrigerator. Her dad kidded her about it, but he hadn't taken it down. He had dreams too.

Riley plopped on to the couch and dialled her friend. Peter answered on the first ring.

'Hey, Riley,' he said. There was the sound of rustling paper. 'Our term papers are due tomorrow.'

'Yeah, I'll work on it tonight.'

'Mine's done,' he boasted. She heard a slurping sound like he'd taken a drink through a long straw. 'I tear apart the South's assertion that slavery was necessary for their survival.'

Peter wasn't really a nerd, but he acted like one. He'd been that way since they'd met in fourth grade. With his round face, mouse-brown hair and glasses he looked like an accountant or a computer programmer.

'Sounds deep,' she said. 'You think Mr Houston's going to like it?'

'It's solid. He'll accept it.'

No way. Houston had a Dixie accent as thick as Atlanta's smog and was always talking about the War of Northern Aggression. Peter's paper would not be met with applause, or an A.

'What's yours about?' her friend asked, followed by more slurping. It made her thirsty so she chugged down the last of her hot chocolate before answering.

'General Sherman and why he was actually a terrorist.'

There was a sharp intake of breath across the line. 'Wow! I would never have made that connection.'

'Thought I'd try it on for size. Can I use your printer tomorrow?' she quizzed.

'Sure. I'm getting drilled and filled in the morning, so make it after four. Maybe the ghouls will be out.' The ghouls were the twins, Peter's younger brothers. He'd called them that ever since they'd started to walk. Something to do with the fact that they followed him everywhere, even into the bathroom.

'Dentist in the morning. Got it,' she said, grinning.

'Better yet, send the file over tonight and I'll have it all ready for you.'

'Cool! OK, see you tomorrow night, Peter.' *As long as I'm not green.*

'Later, Riley.'

She settled at the card table that served as a makeshift desk and pulled up the computer file entitled *General Sherman – War Hero or Domestic Terrorist?* Typing proved harder than she'd expected – the bite on her right palm wasn't co-operating. Then the *N* key popped off the keyboard and flew towards the stained carpet.

'Ah, come on!' she groused. 'Why does everything fight me?'

Digging under the card table yielded the key, which she carefully reattached, leaving a trail of n's across the screen. At least the gold star she'd stuck on it made it easier to find when the thing went AWOL.

It was times like this she longed for the computer system she'd owned before the condo fire: a Mac with speakers and everything. Now all she had was leftovers because the insurance company only paid enough for the condo mortgage and to buy some second-hand furniture, but not a new computer.

Her dad had found this one at a second-hand store and the keyboard they'd scavenged from the bin behind a sub shop. It'd taken a lot of time to clean it up, and it still smelt like surgical spirit and onions.

A scratching sound came at the door. She ignored it, studying Sherman's bio. He'd warmed up with the Seminoles and then moved on to scorching large parts of the South, including Atlanta in 1864.

'Pyromaniac. I'm just saying . . .'

An e-mail from Peter popped up. *Check this out!* the subject line read.

It was a hyperlink to another one of her videos. There were more than a hundred thousand hits on it already.

'I'm so viral,' she said, groaning. No way she was going to watch it. She clicked the page closed and went back to Sherman.

More scratching. That had to be Max, Mrs Litinsky's Maine Coon. He was a giant of a cat with a patchwork of thick white, brown, grey and black fur. His sensitive feline nose would be telling him there were demons inside the apartment.

Opening the door, she found Max digging at the threshold. Riley knelt and petted him. She got a throaty purr in response. Some nights she let him in and he'd keep her company, but not tonight.

'Sorry. You'll tear the kitchen apart trying to get to our stash,' she said. Not that the three Biblios currently housed inside the cupboard with the canned green beans actually constituted a stash.

Tomorrow her dad would make a run to one of the local demon traffickers, who would relieve him of the fiends in exchange for cold hard cash. Then Max would be welcome in the apartment once more.

Riley gave the cat a few more cuddles, shooed him out and shut the door, making sure to lock it. Sinking into the creaky office chair, she yawned and cautiously stretched. Something popped in her back and the ache diminished. Considering how hard she'd landed on the library floor it was amazing she wasn't one solid bruise.

When she put her hands on the keyboard, the *N* was missing again. She made a quick check of the floor. Not there.

'Now that's weird.'

Another check of the floor turned up a rusty paperclip and an expired roach, but nothing else. Riley leaned back in the chair, trying to work out what was going on. The missing key's gold star gave her a clue.

Can't be. To test her theory, she checked the top of the battered dresser in the bedroom. The silver seashell earring she'd found in Centennial Park last summer was missing too.

Riley grinned. No other explanation – there was a demon in their apartment. Maybe she could redeem herself by catching it. Besides, the fiend was worth seventy-five bucks and that would take them one step closer to their pizza and movie night.

She returned to the front room, retrieved her Trappers Manual from the bookshelf and thumbed to the second section, the one that dealt with types of Hellspawn. Running a greenish finger down the list she found:

Klepto-Fiend (Magpie, Hell's Cat Burglar). Three inches tall, light brown skin, pointed ears. Often seen in ninja garb toting a small bag of loot. Cannot resist jewellery, coins or shiny objects.

Should be easy to trap. Or not. At least these fiends didn't curse or pee on you. Their demonic activity was confined to stealing bright and shiny stuff.

But why is it in our apartment? That would seem to be the last place a demon would want to be discovered.

Riley slumped on the worn burgundy couch and conducted a visual search around the tiny room. The demon could be anywhere, though most likely it would be hunting something shiny. Nothing near the makeshift bookshelves they'd constructed from salvaged two by fours. Nothing near the family pictures on the top shelf of the bookshelves. One of those frames had sparkles on it, but it was probably too big for the tiny fiend to cart off.

'Where are you?' she called out in a sing-song voice. Nothing moved. Well, she was a trapper, after all. Flipping farther into the manual she found the section that told her how to trap a Magpie. She scanned the text to refresh her memory. She really had to find him – it'd be hard to finish the paper without the full keyboard, especially since the subject's name ended in *n*.

A sharp hiss came from the hallway. Then a growl. Had the

demon slipped out of the apartment? Riley grabbed a sippy cup from the cupboard, one her father had specially prepared with a layer of glitter on the bottom. When she slowly edged the door open, she found Max a few feet down the hallway, his fur on end and his back humped. Every whisker bristled at attention.

The reason crouched on the floor near an air vent. It was one of Hell's cat burglars. Similar to a Biblio-Fiend, the Magpie was the same size with human-like hands and a forked tail. Its eyes were red, but not that hellfire bright that bothered her. Just like the manual said, this one was clad in ninja black, and even wore boots. It was furiously trying to jam a canvas bag through the fins of the air vent. Even though the bag was tiny – demon-sized – Riley could tell it wasn't going to fit. The demon wouldn't leave the bag behind – the pretties were everything to them.

Max took another step closer, his growl deepening now. If this had been a Biblio, the demon would have slammed a fist into the cat's nose or peed in his eyes then made a run for it. Magpies survived by stealth. Unfortunately, this one had nowhere to run.

'Max?' The cat's back rumpled in irritation at her voice, but he didn't break his vigil. 'You can't eat it. It'll make you sick. All your hair will fall out, then you'll go into convulsions. Dead cat, get it?'

The feline growled in response. It was matched in volume by the demon's warning hiss.

'Come on, Max. Let it be,' she coaxed.

In exaggerated slow motion he took one more step towards the Magpie.

A door slammed on a floor below and Max jumped at the sound, momentarily losing eye contact. It gave Riley the diversion she needed. Flailing her arms in the air, she shouted nonsense at him. The feline took off as if she was crazy.

When she turned back, the demon was still trying to cram its loot through the vent. She knelt, tipped open the cup and dropped a few pieces of glitter on the floor. Magpies were wired for bling. All she needed to do was provide the bait.

The demon stopped its frantic attempts to escape. It stared at the glitter and began to pant, fingers twitching in anticipation. More twitching. Faster than she'd expected it zoomed up to the sparkles, despite the danger. She snagged the demon right before it picked up the last one and dropped the Magpie into the cup. Instead of a flood of swear words or the offer of a favour, she heard a long, tortured sigh. Then it sat, sorting the glitter into piles *by colour*.

Now she'd seen everything. She screwed on the lid, grabbed up its bag, and hurried into the apartment before Max had the courage to return.

Before getting back to work on her assignment, Riley sorted through the demon's hoard, reclaiming the earring and the *N* key. It rapped on the side of the container and pointed at the bag with a concerned expression. She understood. It would be like someone making off with her favourite lipgloss.

'OK, Flash, here you go.' Unscrewing the top she carefully dropped the bag inside, then tightly resealed the lid. It promptly pulled out a shiny penny and someone's tie tack. Those earned her a grateful demon smile. The Magpie curled around the treasure and fell asleep.

Pleased at how things had turned out, she sent a text to her dad.

I caught a Magpie in our apartment! Score one for me!

Riley waited, but there was no response. Probably busy trapping that Three. When she finally shut down the computer a couple of hours later, there was still no reply.

'You go, Dad! Movie night, here we come.'

Chapter Six

Whistling 'God Rest Ye Merry Gentlemen' louder than was necessary, Beck waited in the middle of Alabama Street as night settled in for keeps. The steel pipe stuck in the back of his jeans was uncomfortable, but he left it in place. If they were lucky it wouldn't be there much longer. To his right, Paul was hidden behind a dumpster, armed and waiting for their prey.

Beck had to admit that Five Points was one of his favourite trapping locations. *Demon Central*, as the trappers called it, perfect for Grade Three fiends. Threes loved the tangled warren of gutted buildings, seemingly bottomless holes, busted concrete and overflowing dumpsters. Those few buildings still intact had metal gates over every window and door to keep Hell's evil outside. It was the only part of the city that had much metal left. It was too dangerous to try to scavenge down here, though some folks tried. All of them regretted it.

Any exposed concrete sported long claw marks starting at four feet up, the way Threes marked their territory. That and stinking piles of demon crap acidic enough to melt asphalt. At least the cold weather had cut the stench a notch.

Beck was summoning their prey on a couple of levels.

Threes detested Christmas music and couldn't resist rabbit entrails, especially if they were a bit ripe. They had one-track minds: if something moved, they ate it. If it didn't move, they ate it anyway just to be safe. While on the hunt, which was pretty much once it got dark, they ripped apart anything that got in their way. They'd grown so ferocious that most trappers had a buddy along as back-up.

Beck caught movement near one of the countless holes that littered the street. It was a skulking rat, probably the only one within a square mile. That was a side benefit of a Three infestation – the rat and pigeon population dropped dramatically.

Even though he was growing impatient, Beck forced himself to hold his position. Pulling off his Braves cap, he smoothed his hair. It was getting shaggy by his standards, but he didn't have the time for a haircut. The last two girl-friends had liked the look. Not that they hung around long, but there was always another one giving him the eye.

As Beck waited, he swore he could feel the ground set-tling all around him. Built on top of what used to be street level Atlanta in the nineteenth century, this part of town had been sinking for the last decade. Holes developed over the old steam vaults. Then the holes got bigger. And bigger. The last cave-in had been near the Five Points MARTA station. With the city bankrupt, the holes kept enlarging. Only the demons found that a blessing.

Beck shifted his eyes sideways towards the battle-scarred dumpster fifteen feet away. Even in the dim glow of a single streetlight he could see the serene expression Paul wore when on the hunt. How he managed that Beck never understood. It was probably why his partner had outlived his encounter with an Archfiend.

I sure as hell won't.

There was a sound near one of the holes as a Three climbed out of whatever lay below.

'Demon at one o'clock,' Beck murmured. Paul nodded, holding his silence.

The beast should have been solid black but this one had big white splotches like a lethal Holstein cow. Repeated applications of Holy Water did that to a Three, like a bad bleach job. This one had seen a lot of it and was still going strong.

The slavering beast hunkered down next to the bunny bait and gobbled the offering in one gulp. Then it looked up, those laser-red eyes scanning the terrain for the real bait – Beck.

'Trapperrr,' it hissed.

'Deemonn,' Beck hissed back. He waited for it to charge. They always charged, howling and waving those scimitar claws. Instead the thing's paw closed around a beer bottle, arming itself. That was a new tactic. Usually they leaped on you and kept slicing until they had you on the ground.

'Incomin'!' Beck taunted. He ducked as the bottle flew by him. 'Ha! Ya couldn't hit your own fat-assed mama with a throw like that!'

'Chew yourrr bones!' the demon cried, waving its furry arms above its head like a demented orang-utan.

Beck mirrored the gesture and then sneered. 'Yeah, yeah. If you're the best Hell can do, no wonder your boss got kicked outta Heaven.'

'Name not He!' the demon shouted, cringing.

That was a sore point for those who were on Lucifer's leash – they didn't like to be reminded. Beck got an idea.

'Let's see now, what's his name?' He tapped his forehead in thought. 'Yeah, that's it!' He grinned and then started chanting, 'Give me an L. L! Give me a U. U! Give me a C . . .'

Enraged, the demon sent a volley of beer bottles his way. Only one came close. Beck executed an exaggerated yawn, which only infuriated the fiend further. He could sense Paul's disapproval from the direction of the dumpster. The master was never happy when his former student showboated, as he called it.

But, damn, this is fun.

The telltale scrape of claws across the broken pavement brought Beck back to reality. He kept his eyes on the thing as it scrambled towards him. Twenty feet. Fifteen. Ten. Sweat broke out on his forehead. Beck remembered how those claws felt when they'd dug into him. The smell of rancid breath in his face. The click of incisors as they went for his neck.

'Now!' he shouted, brandishing the steel pipe.

A clear globe arced through the air and impacted directly on top of the creature's head. Glass shattered and Holy Water drenched the fiend's fur-covered face. The demon began to dance around as if it was on fire, swiping at unseen enemies. Then it crumpled.

Paul stepped out from behind the dumpster, studying the monster from a respectful distance, another sphere already in hand.

'Damn, you're good,' Beck said, edging closer. 'I can never hit 'em when they're runnin' like that.'

'Takes practice. You be careful,' his mentor urged.

'No problem. I learned my lesson about these things.' Beck gingerly prodded the steel into the side of the demon. It wasn't breathing. Which meant it was getting ready to strike.

'Heads up!' he shouted. The fiend was on its feet in an instant, moving faster than he'd expected. One of its paws clamped on to the pipe. Beck knew better than to keep hold of it – he'd made that mistake before and been pulled into the other set of claws. He surrendered the pipe, but by that time the demon was already lunging for him, hellfire eyes glowing. He kicked with his steel-toed boot and caught the thing on the shoulder. As it spun round, one of the claws ripped the hem of his jeans, pulling him off balance. If he hit the ground he was dead.

As it turned, another sphere smashed into the Three's back full on, causing it to shriek and bat wildly at the soaked fur. Before either trapper could react it raced towards the closest hole, dived into the darkness and disappeared.

'Ah, damn!' Beck spat.

Paul joined him, slipping the strap of the duffel bag on to his shoulder, his face radiating disapproval.

'Go on, say it.'

'What's the point? You never listened when you were an

apprentice – you're not going to now.'

Beck waited him out. There was always more.

Paul shook his head. 'You can't do it straight, can you? Always a hotdog. It's going to get you dead, Den.'

Beck was used to this lecture. He'd heard it often enough.

'It's just . . . never mind.' Skating on the edge made him feel alive, kept things interesting. But he knew better than to try to explain. 'The Holy Water hardly touched the thing. It shoulda been out for at least a couple minutes.'

'It's happening more often now.'

Beck arched an eyebrow. 'Any idea why?'

His companion shook his head. 'No, but I'm working on that.' Paul studied the alley. 'We need to rethink our strategy, at least for this demon.'

Beck reclaimed his pipe. It had four new claw marks on it. 'Yeah, big time.'

They turned and began the walk to the truck, both of them on edge. It reminded Beck of when he was in the Army, out on patrol. Waiting for that first burst of gunfire, or a thundering explosion along the roadside. Here it was teeth and claws, but the effect was the same. If a trapper didn't pay attention, he got injured or he got dead.

'That Five at the library today,' Paul said out of nowhere.

Beck had wondered when that subject would come up.

'Why did it come after *my* daughter?'

'No clue. Any way ya can keep her from trappin' for a while?'

'Probably not, but I can restrict her to being with one of

us. That'll keep her safe until we get this sorted out.'

'Better not send her out with me. She'll feed me to the first Three she sees,' Beck said, trying to lighten the moment.

'She's not got a crush on you any more, Den, if that's what you're worried about.'

'Oh, I know that. Now she just hates me. I don't know which is worse.' A grunt of agreement came from his partner. 'Ya think the Five made itself look like one of the students?'

'That's my guess. They don't change forms very often, but it's possible. As long as it kept its feet from touching the ground, it could work its evil.'

A breeze stirred, kicking up puffs of concrete dust. The hair on Beck's neck ruffled. He shot a concerned look at his companion.

'Just the wind,' Paul said. 'A Five's not going to mess with two of us.'

'Tell him that,' Beck said, pointing down the alley.

A Grade Five Geo-Fiend materialized thirty feet in front of them, hovering a foot or so above the road. Beck estimated it was at least seven feet tall, its coal black face dominated by curved canines and twin horns that sprouted from the side of its head, curving upward like those of a bull. It had a massive chest, like an Olympic weightlifter who'd overdone the steroids. Brilliant red eyes glared at them, flickering in the dim light.

This was one of the big boys. Unless they were very careful it'd turn them into sushi.

'That's one damned ugly demon,' Beck muttered.

Paul palmed a Holy Water sphere.

'Hey, dumbass,' Beck shouted. 'Trash any books today?'

The resulting laugh cut like razor blades. 'Blackthorne's daughter will be mine.'

Paul's legendary composure fled. His voice went low, urgent. 'Circle around to the truck, Den. I'll handle this.'

'Kiss my ass, Blackthorne.' It was exactly what he'd said the first time they'd met in history class.

After a worried frown, Paul called out, 'Demon, this is your only warning.'

Warning? Trappers never warned demons. *What's he doing?*

In response, the Geo-Fiend made slight hand movements like it was flicking lint off its clothes. Blue-black clouds began to form, the warm-up to a full meteorological assault. The fiend laughed again, its eyes glowing bright in anticipation.

'So what's the plan?' Beck asked, his throat turning dry.

'Back up slowly.'

A snarl came from behind them. Beck looked over a shoulder. The Three had returned, drooling and clicking its claws together.

'Not happenin'.'

Paul shook his head. 'This is so wrong.'

'Like they care,' Beck said, slowly rotating until his back was against Paul's, his eyes on the furry omnivore bringing up the rear. 'Got another plan?' he asked, testing the weight of the steel pipe in his hand.

'No,' Paul replied. He hurled the sphere, but a full blast

of wind hit them a second later, like a summer squall, causing the orb to disintegrate in midair. Stinging rain and hail pelted them and a thunderclap shook the air, making their ears pop. Beck yelped and dropped the steel pipe, cursing as lightning sparked off it. Slowly they were pushed towards the slobbering demon. It held its position, its meal being catered.

Paul dug in his duffel bag and handed a blue grounding sphere to Beck. Then he pulled one out for himself. 'You go left,' he ordered. 'Count it down.'

Beck took a deep breath, his gut twisting in fear. 'Three . . . two . . . one!'

He hurled the sphere to his left as Paul slung his in the opposite direction. Glass smashed and the spheres' contents erupted in a blaze of brilliant blue light. The grounding magic began its run across anything metal, making it look molten. It shot along a section of rusty fence, leaped to the battered dumpster, then to a mangled bicycle. If the two portions met and formed a circle it would ground the Geo-Fiend into the earth. Once grounded the fiend lost its ability to use the forces of nature against them.

The Five hesitated, seeing their plan, and then moved higher into the air. It swept its hands upward, creating two new whirlwinds. Pieces of debris sucked into the vortex, like iron filings to a powerful magnet. Nails, shards of glass, slivers of wood and pieces of brick all whirled in a huge circle.

Beck picked up a broken two-by-four, gritting his teeth as the slivers drove themselves into his scorched palm.

'Eyes!' Paul shouted, smashing a shield sphere to the ground.

Even though his were closed, Beck could see the sheet of white light as it bloomed around them. Once he felt the brightness subside, he prised them open. A white veil hung in the air around him and his friend, a defence against the storm. It wouldn't last long.

The twin whirlwinds struck hard against the magical wall, debris attacking from every quarter. It sounded like hail against the magical shield. As the storm intensified, ripples of magic, like long blue tentacles, stretched upward to the Geo-Fiend. It fought the grounding, hurling wind, snow and lightning like a vengeful god.

The white protective shield evaporated. A second later Paul cried out and slammed into Beck, causing the younger trapper to tumble to the ground. Rolling to the side, Beck came to his feet, crouched and ready for battle. Adrenalin pumped through him with every staccato heartbeat. It made his vision clear, each breath deeper. It made him feel alive.

There was a final wail as the weather demon sank into the earth behind them. The grounding spheres had saved their asses. As the wind died, there was the patter of urban debris falling to the ground.

'Sweet Jesus,' Beck murmured, his breath coming in sharp gasps. Edging sideways, he picked up the pipe in his sweaty hand, dropping the two-by-four. Keeping a wary eye on the Three, he moved backwards, step by step, until he was even with his friend. His fellow trapper was on his knees, bent over like he was in prayer.

'Paul?' No reply. 'Ya OK?'

His mentor slowly raised his head, his face a bluish grey. In the fading glow of the grounding sphere's magic Beck saw a coin-sized dot of blood over his friend's left breast.

Paul took a tortured, sucking breath, one that made his whole body shake. 'Lies . . .' Terror filled his eyes. 'Riley . . . Oh God, Riley . . .'

As his mentor crumpled into Beck's arms, the remaining demon charged.

Chapter Seven

Beck began his slow ascent. Right leg. Left leg. Right. Left. He concentrated on the movement up the two flights of stairs, sixteen steps total to the second floor and the apartment where Riley Blackthorne slept. There was one step for each year of his life before it'd been forever altered by the girl's father.

Beck didn't remember much about his first two years – probably for the best. From age three on he remembered too much. Nights alone in a cold room, his mom gone. When she did come home she was too drunk to know who he was. No food, not even a hug. Night after night he curled on the floor in a makeshift bed of dirty clothes, thinking he'd done something to make her hate him. On his fifth birthday he remembered his mother passed out on the worn plaid couch in their living room, the man who'd come home with her zipping up his jeans. When Beck had told him it was his birthday, the guy laughed, tousled his hair and gave him a dollar bill. Beck cried himself to sleep that night, wondering why he hadn't got real presents like the other kids. At ten he knew his father was a phantom, someone who had picked up Sadie's bar tab the night he'd been conceived.

By the time he turned eleven, Beck knew she wanted him to run away. He refused – that would have been too easy for her. As he reached the thirteenth step he recalled the beatings. One of the men who'd moved in had taught him fists were a great weapon. Beck learned that lesson well and used it on the other kids. On anyone who challenged him. He'd spent his next two birthdays in juvenile detention.

In his sixteenth year he'd met Paul Blackthorne. The history teacher hadn't treated him like some of the others at school. Hadn't told him he was a loser headed for prison or an early grave. Instead, Blackthorne talked about the future. In his own way Paul had seeded Beck's desire for revenge – the ultimate revenge – turning out better than his alcohol-soaked mother.

When Beck reached the top step, he moved on to the landing, like his own life at the same age. He'd bailed out of high school early, barely getting his diploma. For three years in the Army he took on an enemy he never understood, watching friends die while they cried out to God and their mothers. Beck didn't believe in either. At twenty he was back in Atlanta. Back with Paul: the only person in the world who ever gave a damn about Denver Beck.

He halted in front of the apartment door, feeling the blood cracking on his face, the pulsing burn on his right hand, the prick of glass in his left knee. Raising his fist, he let it hang in the air, not wanting to take that final step. Finally he hammered on the door. A decade passed. Riley's sleepy voice asked who it was. He told her.

'Dad?' she called out. 'Are you there?' When he didn't answer, she began to frantically undo the locks. 'Dad?'

As she wrenched the door open, their eyes met.

Beck's heart turned to ashes.

'What do you want?' Riley asked. When he didn't reply, she shoved past him, not caring that she was in her nightclothes. 'Dad?' she called out.

There was no one else in the hallway.

She whirled round. 'Where is he? Is he hurt?'

A shudder coursed through Beck's body. 'Gone,' he murmured, then looked down at the floor.

'What do you mean gone?'

'I'm so sorry, girl.'

Confusion gave way to anger. 'Is this some sick game?' she asked, jamming a finger at him. 'Why are you doing this to me?'

'I tried, but there were two of them and . . . He's gone, Riley.'

Her hand was in motion before she realized. He made no effort to block the blow and the slap landed soundly on his cheek. Before she could strike him again, Beck snagged her arm and pulled her up against him. Though she struggled and swore, she couldn't break free.

'Goddammit,' she heard him whisper.

He hugged her so tightly she couldn't breathe, then broke his embrace.

Unable to think of what this meant, she shoved him away.

Her hands came away sticky, imprinted with blood.

It was only then she saw the gouges on Beck's face and hands, the long strips of leather missing from his jacket that revealed a shredded T-shirt underneath. Both legs of his jeans were ripped and stiff with dried blood.

The rational part of her examined those injuries, catalogued them and told her that if Beck was that badly hurt her dad wasn't coming home.

Her heart refused to accept it.

No. He's alive. He'll be here in the morning and . . .

With each passing second the pressure built inside her. It coiled around Riley's chest, forcing itself up into her throat. She wrenched herself away and fled into the apartment, stumbling into the bedroom. Only then did she let the scream loose into the depths of her pillow, let it rend her throat until she had no more breath. Then the tears came, streaming hot, salty. She tried not to let them overwhelm her but it was no use. She choked on her sobs, hammering the bed with her fists.

Images of her father came to mind – teaching her how to ride her first bicycle, comforting her after she took a headlong tumble down a flight of stairs when she was five, holding her hand at her mother's funeral.

Not this. Please, not him.

How long she cried she couldn't tell, her sense of time stripped away. When Riley could finally catch her breath, she wiped her eyes and blew her nose with a wad of tissues from the box on the nightstand. There was the sound of running water in the bathroom. When it shut off, she heard thick sobs through the thin wall.

Beck.

Her father was really gone.

Later, when she rolled over in the bed she found Beck sitting on the chair near the door. His eyes were swollen, dark red and he stared at nothing, unaware that the wounds on his face were still oozing. He only roused when she pulled herself up against the headboard.

Beck hoarsely cleared his throat. 'We tried to catch . . . that Three. It got away. We were walkin' . . . to the truck when –' He broke off and looked down at the floor, his elbows on his knees. His jacket was off and there were claw marks on his chest. 'A Five popped out of nowhere. Then the Three came back. They were workin' together.'

That wasn't what she wanted to know. 'How did he . . . ?'

'A piece of glass got through the shield. Doc said it hit his heart.'

Now she knew. It didn't help.

'Where is he?'

He looked up at her. 'Oakland Cemetery. None of the mortuaries will have anythin' to do with a trapper.'

'I want to see him,' she said, shifting her feet to the edge of the bed.

'Not till mornin'.'

'I don't want him alone.' She bent over to try to find her socks.

'He won't be. Simon's with him.'

She ignored him.

'Riley, please. Simon will watch over him. Ya need to stay here.'

Beck was right, but it robbed her of something to do when every minute promised unbelievable heartbreak.

Riley sank onto the bed. 'I have no one left now,' she said. 'No one.'

'Ya have me.'

She glared him. How could he possibly think he was interchangeable with her father? 'I don't want you!' she snarled. 'If you really cared for him, he'd be alive and you'd be the one –'

Beck took a sharp intake of breath as if she'd broken something inside him. She turned her back on him and let the tears fall. A door closed and then there was silence.

A few minutes later something touched Riley's knee and she jumped. It was Max. He settled next to her, leaning into her body, purring as loud as she'd ever heard him. At first she resented his presence, but he kept rubbing up against her. Finally she gave in and hugged him tight. His thick fur soaked up her tears.

'Riley? I have tea for you, child,' Mrs Litinsky offered. Riley prised her face out of the cat's fur. Her elderly neighbour stood in the doorway, a cup in hand.

'No . . . thanks.'

'It is chamomile. It will help you rest. That is what you need right now.'

Knowing Mrs Litinsky wasn't easily put off, Riley sat up

and took the cup. The herbs smelt fresh and they helped un-stuff her nose.

The old woman settled on the side of the bed in a robe, her pure white hair in a braid that nearly reached her waist. She seemed almost ethereal, like a fairy. 'Mr Beck has left. I urged him to get his wounds treated. They look bad.'

Then what does Dad look like?

Riley nearly choked at the thought. She forced herself to take a sip. It was hot and tasted sweet, as if there was honey in it. She took another long drink, accompanied by the old woman's approving nod.

'Mr Beck said to tell you he took the demons with him. They were making considerable noise.'

'What?'

'The small ones in the cupboard,' the woman explained.

'Oh.' Which was why Max was lounging on the bed rather than trying to tear the kitchen apart. She reached out and stroked his thick fur.

'He will stay with you tonight, keep you safe,' Mrs Litinsky said.

That seemed silly. What could a cat do?

The yawn caught Riley unawares. She finished the drink and handed the empty cup to her neighbour, her hands quaking.

'I'll be out on the couch,' the woman announced. 'Call if you need me.'

Before Riley could protest, there was the soft shuffle of slippers and then the door closed. She fumbled for a photo on the nightstand. It was one of her and Dad from last summer mounted in a picture frame they'd bought at a dollar store. It had orange kittens running around the edge. Dorky, but cheap.

They'd gone on a picnic that day, just the two of them. She'd made sandwiches and cupcakes and lemonade. She could almost smell the fresh lemons and see the blue sky draped like a canopy above them. The picture had been taken by a young man who was there with his new wife. They'd been all over each other. Her dad was embarrassed, but she'd thought it was cute.

Her father looked younger in the picture, content, like all the bills and worries didn't exist. She hugged the frame close to her body, wishing time had stopped that day in the park. Then she and her dad would be together again.

Max moved closer to her, wedging himself up against her stomach, his rich purr reverberating throughout her body. She curled round him, clutching the photo to her chest. The last thing she could remember was him licking her hand and her father's reassuring voice saying that everything would be OK.

Chapter Eight

Riley woke to household noises, the sound of clanking pans and water running in the sink. Her dad was making her breakfast. He often did that, though he was exhausted from being up all night.

She rubbed the sleep out of her eyes, puzzled about why she was so tired. There was a thump as something tumbled to the floor. Bending over, she saw the framed picture. She stared at it, her heart tightening.

'Dad?' she called out. 'Dad?!'

The noises ceased in the kitchen, followed by heavy footsteps in the hall, the same solid clomp clomp her father's work boots made on the wood.

'It was a nightmare,' she whispered. And an ugly one at that. *But how could it have felt so real?*

When Beck's unshaven and scored face appeared in the bedroom doorway, Riley shoved herself up in bed, biting back a sob. Without saying a word he returned to the kitchen. She jammed a hand over her mouth, feeling the tears prickling on her cheeks. It hadn't been a nightmare or Beck wouldn't be here. Her father was dead.

The tears burst free, scorching her throat raw, making her

nose drip and her neck wet. When she finally hauled herself to the bathroom the face in the mirror seemed alien. Hollow, puffy red-rimmed eyes stared back at her. She doused her cheeks with cold water, blew her nose again and then jammed her hair in a clip, not caring that it stuck out like a porcupine. Tugging on fresh underwear and her last pair of clean jeans, she dug in the clean clothes basket until she found a T-shirt. It had a tombstone on the front.

With a sharp cry, she slung it away in revulsion. More digging unearthed a plain one. It had been her dad's. She slipped it on, the thin cotton brushing against her skin like a whisper.

Now came *the firsts*. The first morning without her father. The first breakfast, the first day, week, month. She'd gone through this painful accounting after her mom died. After a few months she'd ceased the mental maths, but this morning there was no way to shut it off.

Her visitor had his back to her. He was being domestic, cooking something on the gas stove despite his bandaged hand. For a moment she wanted to believe it was her father, though he wasn't the same height and his hair was the wrong colour.

Beck looked over his shoulder, ruining her delusion. 'I've got some breakfast for ya.'

'You're not my dad,' she said defiantly.

'I couldn't be if I tried.' He pointed towards the table. When she didn't move, he put the oatmeal in a bowl and set it down, along with a plate of scrambled eggs and some sausage. Mismatched silverware followed. 'Come on, girl, ya gotta eat.'

She stared at the food, wishing it would disappear with the guy who'd made it. When Beck pulled out her dad's chair to join her, she snapped, 'Don't sit there!'

He looked puzzled for a second, then nodded like he understood it meant more than just a place at the table.

'Keep the doors locked. If ya need me, call,' he advised. 'I'll be back at four. The service is at four thirty. Pack a bag for the cemetery. You'll be stayin' there tonight.'

'Why would I stay –'

But he was already out the door. Riley waited until she heard his footsteps on the stairs before she turned the locks. Then she kicked the door for good measure, making her toes ache.

He'd planned the funeral without her. How could he do that? Muttering under her breath she retreated to the kitchen. Her dad's empty chair mocked her. She pushed it all the way under the table so no one would ever sit there again.

Yesterday her father had been so tired after the night's trapping, but he'd sat and talked to her over a cup of coffee as she'd eaten her breakfast. His hair had been wet from his shower and he'd smelled of cheap shampoo.

She'd wasted their last morning together. She'd chirped on about Peter's latest run-in with his dictatorial mom and the dumb *Demonland* television show. He'd listened so patiently, as if everything she said was really important.

When his eyes began to droop, he'd given her a kiss on

the forehead and gone to bed. 'Sleeping in shifts' as he called it. He was a sound sleeper, so yesterday she'd tried to find where he'd concealed his manual. He always hid it too well. Now she wondered if she'd ever find it.

Their last morning together. And neither of them had known it.

When Riley looked down, the food was cold. Grease congealed on the plate. Something beeped and the noise dragged her eyes to her father's cellphone tucked up next to the salt and pepper shakers. Beck must have left it for her. The low battery light was blinking along with an occasional warning sound. Flipping it open she studied the messages. The text she'd sent him about the Magpie sat at the top of the list.

He'd never had a chance to read it.

It was close to two in the afternoon when her other visitor arrived. The woman was a tall brunette, toting a backpack with the Guild logo. Her hair was pulled into a tight braid and her brown eyes were rimmed with red. She was wearing black trousers and a poloneck and one of those thick red insulated vests.

'Riley, I'm Carmela Wilson,' the woman said. 'I'm the Guild's doctor. I was a . . . friend of your dad's.'

When Riley didn't respond, she added, 'Den asked me to check in on you.'

It took Riley a moment to realize she meant Beck.

'I'm OK,' Riley said reflexively. It was easier to say that so everyone didn't freak. She started to close the door, but

Carmela wedged in a booted foot so it wouldn't shut.

'Other people might buy the *I'm OK* line, but I'd say that's bull. I'm not OK with Paul's death, so I figure you're pretty much torn to hell. Am I right?'

Riley nodded before she could stop herself.

'Just as I thought.'

Riley stepped back and the woman strode into the apartment, did a visual inventory of the crowded space and then headed for the kitchen where she dumped her medical bag on the table. She sank into the closest chair – it was Riley's.

'First off, I want to see that demon bite you got yesterday,' she said, her voice not allowing for argument.

I don't need this. Not now. Riley began to back away towards the bedroom.

'I lost my dad when I was ten,' Carmela explained, her eyes meeting Riley's. 'I've been there, so I'm not playing head games with you.'

Riley froze, caught between the need to fill the vacuum inside her and the overwhelming urge to bury herself in the pillow again.

Her visitor shifted uneasily. 'Come on, let me look at the wound. I promise it won't hurt that much.'

Riley reluctantly sank into her dad's chair. The doc immediately went to work, pulling out a fresh bandage, a bottle of Holy Water and some medical tape. After removing the old bandage, she poked, prodded and pinched the area around the bite. Riley ground her teeth against the discomfort.

'Looks good,' she said. 'Den was sure your hand would be rotting off by now.'

'He could have asked me,' Riley retorted.

'Would you have told him the truth?'

'Probably not.'

Carmela nodded her understanding. 'Besides, we can talk girl to girl. Guys don't get half of what we say even when we say it reaallllly slow.'

Riley scrutinized the woman more closely now. 'You don't let him run over you, do you?'

'No way. You're going to be the same. He'll bitch and moan, but he'll respect you for it.'

'Right. Don't see that happening.' *Not in this lifetime.*

Carmela broke the seal on the pint bottle of Holy Water and handed it over. 'This'll sting. The stuff's only a day old.'

Riley took herself and the bottle to the sink and cleaned the wound. The doc was right: the stuff was strong and it made her wince. The trickle of the water down the drain brought back memories. How many times had she treated her dad's wounds? None of them had been that bad – except when he'd first started trapping, and her mom had taken care of those. He'd always joke that no demon would ever best him.

But one did.

When the plastic bottle was empty, Riley returned to the table. There was more poking until the doc was satisfied with the condition of the wound. From what she could tell, it was already closed, only a thin red circle where the demon's teeth had met flesh.

Forsaken

But what does Dad look like?

'You saw him after . . .' she began, than faltered.

Carmela's expression flattened. 'Den called me so I could certify Paul's death.' She let loose a long sigh and blinked her eyes rapidly as if she was trying to hold back tears. 'A glass shard embedded in his heart; that's what killed him. It would have been very quick.' The woman's hands fumbled with the bandage. 'Paul looks asleep, not . . .'

Dead. 'What about the demons? Did Beck catch them? *Kill them?*

Carmela tidied up the table before she answered, buying time. 'No. They only grounded the Five. The Three ripped the hell out of Den, but he wouldn't let it get near your dad's body. Which means you have a decision to make.'

'What decision?' Riley asked, puzzled.

When the woman looked up, there was pity in her eyes. 'Your dad's body is in good shape. In such good shape that he's prime fodder for the necromancers.'

Riley's stomach heaved. She barely made it to the bathroom before the soup from lunch vaulted into the toilet. She kept retching until there was nothing more to offload.

A cool hand touched her forehead, causing her to jump. 'Ah, damn. I'm sorry. I should have said that better,' Carmela murmured.

Riley flushed the toilet, dropped the lid and then flopped down. Her throat burned from the acidic taste of vomit. Carmela handed her a wet cloth and Riley mopped her face.

'Why didn't Beck tell me this?' Riley demanded. 'He was Dad's partner.'

'He couldn't. This is hurting him as much as it is you.'

Like hell. 'What's this decision I have to make?'

The doc sat on the side of the tub, rubbing her arms like she was cold. Her eyes were pointedly fixed on her boots.

'If your dad's body remains the way it is,' she said, her voice barely audible, 'the necros will try to steal it. That is, unless you decide to sell him to them.'

'Sell him? No way!' Riley growled. 'Not happening.' Her stomach tumbled and she swallowed hard.

Carmela's eyes met hers. 'In that case, you'll have to sit vigil every night until the next full moon to keep him safe.'

'What do you mean?'

'You cast a magical circle and it keeps the necromancers from summoning your father. After the full moon, they can't touch him.' Carmela paused. 'Or there's another way.'

Riley waited her out.

'You have one of the trappers –' the woman took a deep breath – 'make your father's body less . . . whole. If he's no longer in one piece, the necros won't come after him.'

Riley stared, horrified. 'You mean have Beck slice up my dad?'

'It won't be Den,' Carmela replied, her voice taut.

'Doesn't matter who it is!' Riley frowned. 'Can't we . . . cremate him or something?'

'State law doesn't allow trappers that option if they've

been killed by a demon. Some nonsense about contamin-
ation or something.'

This was a nightmare.

'So either I sit vigil or have my father . . . dismembered?'
Riley asked. 'That's *so* medieval.'

'No argument there,' Carmela said. 'It's your call. There
are consequences no matter what you do.'

There was only one answer. 'He goes in the ground like he
died. I swear to God if anyone touches him –'

There was a low sigh of relief from her visitor. 'That'd be
my call. Just realize it's going to be a bitch for the next few
weeks.'

'Can't be any worse than now.'

The doc gently smoothed away a strand of hair from
Riley's face.

'You might be surprised, hon.'

Chapter Nine

Riley dug out the black dress and held it to her body. She hadn't touched it since her mother's funeral. It reached just above her knees now. She remembered her father bringing it home for her, thinking at the time how plain it was. He hadn't had a clue about her size and bought it too big. Now it would probably fit perfectly, as if he'd foreseen she'd have to wear it again.

A shiver launched up her spine and wedged at the base of her skull.

No way. He couldn't have known this would happen.

Though she really wanted to curl on the couch, bury herself inside the heavy comforter to forget what this evening would bring, Riley forced herself to get ready. Black tights. Black dress. Black boots. She creaked open the lid of the tiny ballerina jewellery box and found the heart locket her dad had given her on her sixteenth birthday. It had a picture of her parents inside. She kissed the cold metal.

'Thanks, Daddy,' she murmured, her tears soaking into the dress, unseen. Maybe that was why people wore black when someone died.

A knock came at the door.

It was Beck. They gravely studied each other for a few moments, as if they were afraid of what the other might say. She'd never seen him in a suit before. He'd been on leave when her mother died, and he'd worn his dress blues to the funeral. His face was shaved – it must have been tough to work around the cuts. The dark circles under his eyes told her he hadn't slept any better than she had. There was the hint of aftershave – something like pine trees, she thought.

'It's time,' he said, voice low and raspy.

She picked up her mother's wool dress coat and Beck helped her put it on, though she could tell his shoulder hurt him. He took possession of the bag she'd packed for the graveyard. As she shut the apartment door, she swore she could hear her father's voice calling out his goodbye.

Beck's truck didn't look the same as the night before: it had been washed and all the beer bottles in the bed were gone, the inside swept and the console cleaned. It smelled like the new peach air freshener hanging from the rearview mirror.

Why did he do all this? It wasn't like her dad would care.

She solemnly buckled herself in and then stared out of the side window.

'Riley . . .' he began.

She shook her head. There was nothing he could say that would make it better. If anything, he'd only make it worse. Beck took the hint and fell silent. As he drove, the only sounds were the tyres on the pavement and the occasional *click-click-click* of the indicator. Not much different than when they'd

97

driven her to the cemetery for her mom's funeral. On that trip Beck sat in the back seat of the car, his hair so short it made him look bald. Every time he'd moved she'd heard the stiff fabric of his uniform.

They parked outside Oakland Cemetery's main gate, joining other cars and trucks in the parking lot. Most of the vehicles sported the Guild emblem in their rear windows. Riley got out of the truck and tugged her dress in place. She knew the area fairly well. Situated east of the state capitol building, the graveyard was bordered on the south by Memorial Drive and the MARTA tracks to the north. Every few minutes a train would roll in or out of the station with a peculiar whirring sound.

They crossed underneath the brick archway and on to the tarred road that led along the oldest section of the graveyard. It'd been here since the 1850s. Some of Atlanta's most famous people were buried here, like the lady who wrote *Gone with the Wind*.

And now my dad.

Beck cleared his throat. 'There'll be a short service and then the burial,' he explained. 'After that, ya change clothes and we'll set the circle.'

'We?'

'Simon and me. He offered to stay with ya tonight, keep ya safe.'

That she hadn't expected. Rather than dwell on that, she asked, 'How does this circle thing work?'

'Don't really know,' he said, shaking his head. 'The magic

keeps the necros from summonin' your daddy, that's all that matters.'

As they walked past the redbrick Watch House, she asked, 'Why didn't you tell me about the necros?'

He stopped in the middle of the road. 'I couldn't,' he said. 'That's why I asked Carmela to do it. If ya'd wanted him cut up –'

'You know I wouldn't,' she said, stunned that he'd think she'd have her own father mutilated to save a few uncomfortable nights in a cemetery.

'I didn't know,' he admitted. 'If ya'd asked me to do it . . .' Beck shook his head. 'Not possible.'

'For either of us.'

They started walking again, the tension between them draining away like they'd crossed some unseen barrier. Around them, birds settled into the trees and dried leaves rustled as a squirrel bounced its way past a row of graves.

'Your daddy had a life insurance policy,' Beck said as they followed the road to the left. 'It'll take a while for the money to come through. It's not much, but it'll bury him and give ya some to live on.' He paused and then added, 'Oh, and the others took up a collection, bought some flowers for the funeral.'

Riley's throat tightened. 'Thanks. I didn't think of that.'

He gave her a sad smile. 'Me neither.'

The Bell Tower, a two-storey building that held the cemetery's offices, was stark white in its simplicity. As they approached, she saw Simon waiting for them. Like Beck, he was in a suit.

After a quick look at the other trapper, almost like he was seeking permission, Simon stepped forward. 'Riley,' he said quietly. Without hesitation, he embraced her. It felt good.

'Thanks for watching over my dad,' she murmured. She felt a nod against her cheek.

'He's down here,' Beck said, gesturing to a set of stairs that led to a lower level. After a deep breath, Riley followed him, her hands knotted around a bunch of tissues she'd pulled from her coat pocket.

The stench of the Easter lilies hit her nose the moment she reached the door. There was a big vase of them just inside the room. She hated them. To some they spoke of resurrection. To her they meant nothing but death and loss.

At the far end of the room sat a plain pine coffin on a raised stand. The lid was closed.

Dad.

Riley remained rooted in place. She could lie to herself until she saw him in the casket, then all those lies burned away.

Beck cleared his throat. 'Riley?'

'Give me a minute,' she said, though no amount of time was going to make this bearable.

'It never gets any easier.'

She looked over at him, caught by the emotion in his voice.

'I still remember my granddaddy's funeral,' he said. 'I was ten and my uncle came down to Waycross to pick me up. Hauled me all the way to North Georgia so I could be there. I cried like a baby.'

'What was your granddad like?' she asked, curious. Beck never talked about his family.

His face turned thoughtful. 'Elmore was a cantankerous old cuss. Lived up in the hills and made moonshine.' He looked over at her. 'Taught me how to trap squirrels and roll cigarettes.'

'Skills every ten-year-old should know.'

He shrugged. 'Some might not see it that-a way, but he was a good man. He'd tell me I could be anythin' I wanted.' He looked over at the coffin. 'Like your daddy.'

The throbbing ache in her heart grew. 'Dad . . . really liked you.'

Her companion's eyes misted. He swiped at the tears like they were a weakness. 'I never wanted anythin' but to make him proud.'

Without thinking, she took hold of his hand and carefully squeezed it, mindful of his wounds.

'Did he . . . say anything when he . . . ?'

'Your name.'

Oh, God. Riley's shoulders hitched and the sobs erupted before she could stop them. Tears followed. Beck let go of her hand and placed his arm round her shoulder, holding her close. Her tears soaked his suit coat.

When she finally pulled away, they took slow steps towards the coffin. The room pressed in on her, choking her in the stench of those damned lilies. She pressed the tissue to her nose.

On the coffin lid was a brass plaque. The script was fancier

101

than she'd expected, but it was easy to read.

Paul A. Blackthorne
Master Trapper, Atlanta Guild

He was more than that, but she knew there wasn't enough room on that piece of metal to tell the world everything he'd been.

'Ready?' Beck asked.

No. Never. But she nodded anyway and he slowly opened the lid.

Now she knew why Beck had been rummaging through the closet when she was in the bathroom. He'd picked out her father's burial clothes. Her dad was in his best suit and his favourite red tie, the one she'd bought him for Christmas a few years back. He looked like he was asleep, like Carmela said.

Riley bent over and kissed his pale cheek. It was so cold, like kissing stone. She smoothed back a lock of brown hair, the one that always fell into his eyes.

'He's with Mom now,' she said, stinging tears slipping down her cheeks. 'Bugging her about her cooking and those dumb soap operas she used to watch.' *The ones Dad liked too, but he'd never admit it.*

Beck sucked in a jagged breath. His eyes were closed and his cheeks wet. His whole body shook with grief. No matter what she thought of him, her dad had always cared for Denver Beck. It looked like that love went both ways.

*

Riley headed up the path towards her family's mausoleum. It was designed like a miniature cathedral, built of reddish stone with a tall spire at the top. The two bronze doors had lion's head door pulls. The rear of the building was curved and held five stained-glass windows, each with a verse from the Bible.

Back in the late 1880s the family had had money and the mausoleum was ample proof of it. One of the Blackthornes had been a banker and made his fortune before the Civil War. His wealth had left the structure for his descendants. The mausoleum was full, so her father would be placed right next to her mother on the west side of the building where they could watch the sunsets together. That'd been her mother's choice.

Riley turned at the sound of scuffing boots as six trappers carefully manoeuvred the casket towards the grave. It was difficult work and they went slowly. Despite his wounds, Beck was at the head of the coffin, Simon on the other side. One of the men began to sing, and his tenor voice carried throughout the graveyard.

> *Swing low, sweet chariot,*
> *Coming for to carry me home . . .*

Her dad had always liked that song, especially the part about the band of angels. There were no angels here tonight, at least none that she could see, but he wasn't alone. Trappers stood in dignified rows, hands clasped in front of them, the two remaining masters in the front row. Harper wouldn't meet her eyes, but Master Stewart did. He was in full Scottish regalia and cradled a bagpipe in his arms.

Another knot of men stood a short distance away, but none of them looked familiar. Carmela leaned close to her, apparently noticing her confusion. 'Demon traffickers. Fireman Jack is the one in the dark blue suit. He and your dad were good friends.'

Riley found her eyes drifting to the man Carmela had indicated. He nodded to her in response. Now that she knew who he was, she remembered her dad saying that Jack always wore barber-pole braces. She couldn't see them now, hidden by his suit coat.

A hand touched her elbow – it was Mrs Litinsky. She was in a royal blue coat, her hair braided and tucked up on her head in a thick bun. Riley gave her a wan smile. At best there were thirty or forty people here. She'd trade them all to hear her father's voice one more time.

Once the coffin was situated, Beck stood next to her. He awkwardly offered his hand and she took it. His emotions were shuttered again. Riley didn't know how he could do that so easily.

The Guild's priest, Father Harrison, took his place in front of the coffin. He was young, almost boyish in his looks, with dark brown hair and eyes. It was tradition for a Catholic priest to handle the services, even if the trapper wasn't of that faith.

He began by talking about her father, how he was always eager to teach the newer trappers and how he possessed that quiet sense of destiny.

'To lose such a man might make us question God's mercy. I believe that Paul was called home because his work was done. He has fought the army of darkness and fallen in battle, but will always remain in our hearts. O Lord, in Your mercy, grant him eternal rest.'

'Amen,' Riley murmured along with the others.

Father Harrison looked over at Beck. 'We also give thanks, O Lord, that we are not mourning the loss of another this night.'

Beck lowered his eyes as if embarrassed he was still breathing.

What if he had died too?

Riley shivered at the thought. In response, Beck put his arm round her shoulder, thinking she was cold. It was deeper than that.

Harrison turned towards her. 'O Lord, Father of us all, please watch over Riley, as she takes up the fight against all that is evil in this world.'

'Amen.'

As the priest spoke of resurrection and heaven, they lowered her father into the ground. During the final prayer she didn't look down into the grave, but up at the sky. Dad was up there somewhere, watching over her. No demon could ever hurt him now. Once the full moon came, no necro could either. He'd kept her safe all these years, she'd do the same for him.

I promise.

Beck and Simon stripped off their suit coats and handed them to another trapper. Then they began to shovel the earth into the grave.

'It's tradition,' Carmela explained. 'Trappers have a lot of them. Some of them even make sense.'

Beck didn't go for very long, his face radiating pain. Jackson took over as Simon handed his shovel to Morton. And so it went, trapper after trapper, until the entire coffin was covered in red Georgia clay.

Then the gravediggers took over. As they completed the job, the trappers departed in reverse order of seniority. Another tradition, apparently. Stewart's bagpipe stirred to life and the strains of 'Amazing Grace' filled the air. Riley bowed her head. When the final note faded, the remaining mourners drifted towards her.

One by one they introduced themselves – some were teachers who'd known her father from years before, others were former clients. They each had a story to tell. Her dad had removed a demon from their basement, saved their beloved Dobermann from a ravenous Three, captured an incubus that had terrorized a private girls' school.

Her father had done so much, and yet she felt she knew so little about him.

'Riley?'

She turned to find Peter watching her with the saddest expression. His eyes were red and he was wearing a suit that seemed a size too big.

'Peter?' They hugged awkwardly and he stammered how sorry he was.

'Son . . .' a woman standing behind him nudged.

'Sorry. Riley, this is my mother,' he said, looking embarrassed.

So this was the warden. Riley had never actually met the

woman, which she'd counted as a good thing. Keen to make a favourable impression, at least for her friend's sake, Riley politely shook hands.

'You have my condolences,' Mrs King said. 'Who will you be staying with now?'

What? That was a very direct question. 'Haven't worked that out yet.'

'You can't stay on your own,' the woman cautioned. 'Do you have any other family?'

Peter shifted, clearly not pleased by his mother's inquisition.

Her tone rubbed against Riley's raw nerves, though Mrs King probably thought she was being helpful. 'I have an aunt in Fargo.' *Who hates me.*

'Then I suspect you'll be moving, won't you?'

'No!' Peter exclaimed. 'You can't leave Atlanta.'

Riley took her friend's hand and gave it a squeeze. 'Don't know yet. Too much to think about right now.'

That seemed to settle him down. When Mrs King announced they had to leave, he protested, but it got him nowhere. He gave Riley another hug and then was gone.

Beck joined her. 'His momma doesn't like ya.'

'Never has. Thinks I'm a wild child or something.'

Beck snorted. 'Not even close.' He looked over at the mounded grave. 'Your daddy got a good send-off. I think he'd be pleased.' When she didn't reply, he handed her the bag she'd packed for the vigil. 'Best get changed. We need to get the circle in place before sundown.'

And now it begins.

Chapter Ten

As Riley peered through the grille on one of the bronze doors, her fingers traced the cold metal of a lion's head. Those had always fascinated her, unlike the gargoyles high on the mausoleum's roof. Though they had the same lion faces, she'd always thought the gargoyles were creepy. Her dad said they guarded the dead.

Now they'll watch over you.

When she was younger her family would often come to the mausoleum and visit the dead relatives. Her mom would clean the stained-glass windows, then sweep the floor. Her father would tell her stories about some of the people buried there. Then they'd have a picnic on the grass, just like the Victorians who built the cemetery.

Now as she peered inside the structure the sun's final rays poured through a couple of the windows, projecting a mosaic of primary colours on to the stone floor. Riley unlocked the doors and pulled them open with a noisy scrape. As she walked inside, she ran a hand along one of the vaults.

JOHN HARVEY BLACKTHORNE
BORN 17 AUGUST 1823

Forsaken

DIED 4 JANUARY 1888
I WILL NOT CEASE FROM MENTAL FIGHT,
NOR SHALL MY SWORD SLEEP IN MY HAND . . .

Her mom had said the verse came from an old poem. It seemed an odd thing to put on the tomb of a banker. In the back of the building was a raised platform covered in a thin stone veneer, which cleverly concealed a storage bin. She levered the lid open with considerable effort. A tiny spider crawled out and vanished over the side, its rest disturbed.

The interior looked like her father had left it a few weeks before. She took the sleeping bags out of their cases and shook them out one by one. She'd need them tonight.

'Good choice for a bolt hole,' Beck observed from the doorway.

Trappers called them different names: bolt hole, sanctuary, bunker. Most had one in case of a demon uprising. They were always located on hallowed ground and included stores of dried food, spare clothing, water and medical supplies. Some had a weapons stash. Her father had instructed Riley and her mom what to do if the demons ever waged war. Now it would be up to her to keep it stocked and ready.

'Mine's in a church basement,' Beck added. When she didn't reply, he struggled on. 'It's quiet here. I like that. Mine isn't. It's next door to the furnace room.'

It was clear he was going to keep talking no matter what. Maybe it was nervous energy. Whatever the reason, it was bugging her.

'It's too bad your daddy's not in here,' Beck said. 'It'd be easier to sit vigil.'

She shoved the sleeping bags and extra blankets in his arms. 'I'm changing now so you need to go.'

'Oh, sorry.'

Riley swung the bronze doors closed behind him and stripped out of her dress and boots. The bare stones felt chilly beneath her feet. She pulled on the blue jeans, leaving the tights underneath for warmth, then added a heavy sweater. Then the boots, hopping from one foot to the other as she zipped them. Finally a heavy coat because her mother's wasn't going to be warm enough.

As she stepped outside, the sun backlit the capitol's golden dome.

'It's time,' Simon called out. He'd changed too, in jeans and sweatshirt now. He stood inside a large circle of candles that ringed both her dad and mom's graves. Each candle was about twelve inches from its neighbour.

When Riley drew close, both of the trappers looked over at her. Beck's face was set in a determined expression. Simon's was full of compassion.

'You really think they'll come for him?' she asked.

'They read the papers just like everyone else,' Beck replied.

She hadn't even thought about that. How big an article would her dad have rated? Front page? *No way.* Inside the paper somewhere, probably buried beneath notices for lost pets. Trappers only made the front page if they trashed law libraries.

Belatedly, Riley began to think of what this long night

might be like. She wasn't that good with being cold and sitting still. Never could stand camping. Then there was Simon. She really didn't know him. What if he was creepy or something? She shoved that thought aside instantly – her dad had thought he was OK. Then another worry caught up with her.

'What if I . . .' She sighed. 'What if I need to go to the bathroom?'

Beck didn't smirk as she figured he would. 'There's a toilet in the basement of the cemetery office. The door's locked. The code's in there,' he said, pointing at a booklet in Simon's hand.

Oh.

Beck took a deep breath. 'Whatever ya do, don't break the circle. If ya kick over a candle or walk through the circle without doin' it proper, it's history. Ya understand?'

She nodded.

'Do ya really understand?' he pressed.

She glowered. 'I'm not slow.'

Simon's grin quickly vanished when the other trapper noticed it.

'It's not that easy. The necros play all sorts of head games.' Beck looked over at Simon. 'You're in charge.'

Riley ground her teeth. He was treating her like she was four.

'I'll keep them both safe, I promise,' Simon said diplomatically.

'Be sure ya do.' Beck turned on his heel and marched off towards the truck, fuelled by some emotion Riley couldn't fathom.

'Jerk,' she muttered.

'He's OK,' Simon replied. 'He's just worried about you and your dad.'

The young trapper lit a kerosene lantern and set it on a flat piece of ground. 'He says you've never done this before. Is that right?'

She nodded. 'Mom died of cancer. It wasn't pretty.'

His eyes softened. 'I'm sorry.' She shrugged like it wasn't a big deal, but she was lying.

'Everything you need is in here,' he said, gesturing at the booklet. 'There are sample invocations, or you can use one that has special meaning to you.'

'Like?'

'Some people call the circle into existence by invoking the names of the Archangels, others use football teams. It's the intention that counts.'

Intention. 'Ohhkay.'

'A necro's power is strongest at night, so you have to re-set the circle each sundown. Doesn't matter if it's raining or whatever.'

'What happens during the day?' she asked.

'The cemetery has volunteers who sit vigil during the day-light hours.'

'Ah, does that cost anything?' she asked. Money was more of an issue than ever before.

'The Guild pays for it. They don't have enough funds to cover twenty-four/seven. They figure the family will be here at night.'

'Got it.' She puzzled for a moment. 'Why didn't a necro come for Dad before he was buried?'

'From what I understand if a necromancer summons the deceased before the first sundown, the spell doesn't work right.'

'Oh. So, how does this all work?' she asked, growing more nervous by the minute. What if she screwed something up?

Simon looked down at the booklet and then pointed at a plastic jug. 'Run a line of Holy Water just inside the candles.'

Riley broke the seal, twisted off the cap and dribbled the water as instructed. Hunched over like a gnome wasn't a comfortable position, so by the time she'd made the entire circle her back was beginning to cramp.

'Now you do it again in the other direction.'

Riley groaned and did as he asked.

'These aren't ordinary candles,' she said, studying one. The wick looked more like a coiled metal rope than twisted fibre. The candle was short, like a votive.

'No, they're special. The cemetery has more of them if you want to expand the circle. They don't charge for them, but they would appreciate a donation.'

He went back to the instructions. 'Move the candles on to the circle of Holy Water. Make sure they're the same distance apart.'

More bending. When she stopped to rest her back, Simon urged her on. The sun was almost gone.

'Perfect!' he said. 'Now light every other candle, *clockwise*, while I recite the invocation. Once you're done, light the remaining candles in the opposite direction. Don't pause in between. And, whatever you do, don't say a word until I've completed the invocation.'

Riley sort of freaked, trying to remember all the instructions.

He gave her a reassuring smile. 'Don't worry, you'll do OK.'

'What are you going to say?'

'The Lord's Prayer.'

She took a deep breath and began to light every other candle. Her hand kept shaking, the demon bite causing her fingers to cramp. The wicks flamed in a sudden burst, then settled into a clear white light. Behind her, Simon's strong voice filled the night air, slowly intoning the Lord's Prayer in English and Latin.

> *Pater noster, qui es in caelis,*
> Our Father, which art in Heaven,
> *Sanctificetur Nomen Tuum*
> Hallowed be Thy name

He didn't stumble over the Latin, but sounded like he was born to it. After she'd lit all the candles Riley went still, afraid of doing something stupid and ruining everything.

Simon raised his arms to the heavens. 'By the blessing of God, His Son and His holy angels, let all inside this sanctified circle be safe from harm. Amen.'

'Amen,' she whispered, and then grimaced. She wasn't supposed to talk. Had she messed it up?

Forsaken

To her relief, a brilliant flash of light leaped from candle to candle until the entire circle was blazing. The flames shot high in the air like torches, then sent fiery tendrils above her, creating a glowing sphere around them. She felt a strange tightness and her ears popped. The sphere shimmered for a few seconds, then the flames sank to ground level, dimming to a soft ethereal glow.

'Wow! It's like magic!' she exclaimed.

Simon laughed. 'As long as it flashes like that you know you've set the circle. If it doesn't, you redo the invocation.'

'How do I get outside the circle without breaking it?'

'Ah, good question,' Simon replied. 'You walk up to the candles, clear your mind, and visualize yourself walking through the barrier without disturbing it.'

Huh? 'But what if I kick over a candle?' she said.

'That would be bad. Here, I'll show you.'

Simon rose, walked to the circle's boundary, murmured something under his breath and stepped over the candles.

'OK. So how do you get back in?'

'You have to give me permission to enter.' Before she could ask how, he pointed at the booklet. 'Page five, last paragraph.'

Riley found the passage and read, 'If you mean no harm, then pass within.'

Simon stepped across the candles and returned to his place on the sleeping bag.

'And if you were a bad guy . . .'

'The circle would not let me in.'

'How does it know who's a bad guy?'

He shrugged. 'It's a lot like a Holy Water ward. Evil things stay away.'

Sounds really iffy to me. But if Simon and Beck believe in this circle thing there must be something to it.

'What if I accidentally break it?'

'Then you start all over, right after you set the candles. Oh, and every night you have to move the candles away from the original circle of Holy Water. Most folks make it a bit smaller.'

So many things to remember. 'What if it rains?' she quizzed.

'Rain won't break the circle – neither will wind for that matter, though it won't be pleasant. What's important is the circle remains intact and that you state its purpose clearly.' He sat on the sleeping bag, popping his knuckles one by one, clearly pleased with himself. 'Now we wait until sunrise.'

'That was a lot more work than I realized,' she said, plopping down next to him. This would have been way hard if he hadn't been here.

'Once you've done it a few times it's no big deal. It's harder when you're on your own.'

She looked over at him. 'How did you learn all this?'

'I come from a big family. Someone's always dying, so my uncle taught me how to do the invocation. He's a priest.'

A big family. What would that be like? There'd only been her. Her mom had always joked that after you achieved perfection, why try again? Riley had always figured there was something more to it.

'I'm an only child,' she said, then grimaced. He knew that.

Simon didn't act like she'd said something stupid. 'I wanted to be sometimes. I have four sisters and three brothers.'

'What's it like with that many bodies in one house?'

'Like living in a beehive. We had a schedule posted on the two bathrooms. My sisters were the worst.'

Riley chuckled, wondering if that was true. His hair looked too good for a quick shampoo and blow dry. She re-arranged her coat so it would cover her legs. Luckily there was no wind. Or rain. In the distance a pale haze hung over the city. She could see the skyscrapers in downtown Atlanta, at least the few still lit at night. The high-pitched whine of the MARTA train heading east echoed around them.

She waited for Simon to say something. He just stared out into nothingness. It was going to be a long night if he wasn't going to talk.

'How old are you?' she asked, desperate to avoid the silence.

'Just turned twenty. You?'

'Seventeen.'

'You're a little younger than my sister Amy. She got married last summer.' He paused and gave her a quizzical look. 'So what are you going to do now that you're on your own?'

On my own. 'Don't know. There's only my mom's sister left. She lives in Fargo.'

'You could continue your apprenticeship there.'

'She wouldn't go for that. She blames my dad for Mom's death, like he personally planted the cancer in her or something. Nasty woman. I can't live with her. No way.'

'Then who will you stay with?' Simon prodded.

'I don't know. There is no one else.'

'Well, I'm sure Beck will help as best he can.'

A change of topic was vital.

There was the sound of footsteps. The man approaching them was as short as he was wide. His trench coat almost reached the ground and he wore a fedora.

'Is he a necro?' Riley whispered.

'I'd say it's a good bet,' Simon replied. 'Be on your guard. They can be tricky.'

The man stopped just outside the circle of candles and tipped his hat.

'Good evening to you,' he said.

'Good evening,' Simon replied. He was polite to everyone, even someone who sold corpses for a living.

'My name is Mortimer Alexander and I am a licenced summoner,' the newcomer announced proudly.

'Darn. I'd hoped you were the pizza delivery guy,' Riley quipped.

A hint of a smile crossed the man's face. 'No such luck.' He sobered instantly. 'First, I wish to offer my sincere condolences for your recent loss.'

'Ah, thanks.'

'However, now is the time to be practical. Your loved one resides in a better place,' the necromancer continued, vaguely waving towards the sky. 'His . . . earthly shell, however, can be put to use for a better society.' He dug in his pocket and consulted a piece of paper. 'I see that Mr Blackthorne would occasionally donate to charity. Perhaps we can reach an arrangement where I will contribute a sum in his name and in trade he will act as a paid domestic for a specified period of time.'

'Ah, well . . .' Riley began. Why had she been warned against these guys? This one sounded so reasonable. Her dad was always for the underdog. Wouldn't he want to help out even now?

'Riley?' When she didn't respond, Simon joggled her elbow. Then he shook it. 'Riley!'

'What?' she snapped.

'He's using persuasion magic. They'll do anything to get to your father.'

'Got it,' she said. Simon relaxed and his hand retreated. She wished he'd left it there.

The necro shuffled papers. 'I understand your sacrifice and am prepared to make monthly payments into an account to cover the . . . inconvenience of having your loved one exhumed. At the end of a year, we agree to inhume him in a dignified ceremony and pay all expenses required to do so.'

Riley remembered the Deader on the street toting packages for the rich lady. What if that had been her dad? She shuddered.

'No way,' she said, crossing her hands over her chest in defiance.

'Ah, I see that you have some reservations,' the necromancer continued. 'That is to be expected. It is a big step and—'

'Not happening. Now go away.'

'Please,' Simon added. She wondered if he was that nice to the demons when he trapped them.

Mortimer looked crestfallen. 'I understand. You should be aware that I'm the most ethical of the summoners you'll meet before the full moon. It earns me no end of grief from the others, but I feel honesty is important.' He placed a business card at the edge of the burning circle. 'In case you wish to contact me.'

'Not likely,' Riley replied.

'I understand. Thank you for your time. Again, my sincere condolences.'

Then he was gone, walking slowly up the path while consulting his pile of papers. When he passed the cemetery office, he cut west towards the parking lot.

Riley sighed in relief. 'Well, that's over.'

Simon shook his head. 'Like he said, he's the first of many.'

'Why?' she asked, surprised.

'Rich folks like to collect unique things. In this case, it'd be a famous master trapper as their servant. No one else would have one so that would make him very special.'

Damn. 'No wonder people have the corpses cut up.'

Simon shot her a horrified look. 'No! What you did was right. Mutilation is unholy,' he retorted, then appeared chagrined at his outburst. 'Sorry, it's a hot button for me.'

'Really?' she jested.

'Yeah,' he admitted. 'At least you've only got twelve more nights of this.'

Riley rolled her eyes at the thought. Twelve loooong nights filled with lying necromancers, a cold butt and no sleep.

Thanks a bunch, Dad.

Chapter Eleven

'Whatcha want?' the bartender asked, his tattooed biceps announcing to the world he was one of The Few, The Proud.

A Marine. Beck had never really liked the Semper Fi crowd, but at least he knew how they'd act.

'Shiner Bock,' he replied. 'Start a tab.'

'Need to see some ID.'

Beck frowned. 'I'm legal.'

'Don't doubt it, but it's the law now,' the man replied. 'Gotta card everyone, even if they come in here using a goddamn walker.'

Beck fished out his driver's licence and tossed it to the bartender. The guy gave it a quick look and handed it back. 'You look older. I'd have figured you for thirty.'

'Ya can blame the Army for that.'

'Where'd you serve?'

'Afghanistan.'

'Man,' the bartender replied, grinning now. 'No charge for the first beer. I was over there too.'

He placed a bottle of Shiner Bock on the bar, reached for a glass, then changed his mind.

'Good call,' Beck muttered. He raised the beer in the air.

'To those who didn't make it home.' He took a swig and then raised the bottle again. 'And to Paul Blackthorne. Rest in peace.' Then he downed half of it in one long gulp to ease the ache.

'That the guy who died down in Five Points?' the bartender asked.

'Yeah. He was good people.' *Good people always die sooner than the assholes.*

'You a trapper?' the man asked, eyeing him.

No reason to deny it. 'Yeah.'

'I don't hold much with trappers.'

'I'm not fond of jarheads, so we're even,' Beck replied.

The bartender snorted. He picked up a glass of scotch from the back bar and raised it high. 'To those who made it home.'

'Amen,' Beck said, raising the bottle again, then downed the rest.

'No trouble, you hear?'

'None planned. Just wanna get drunk.'

'Sounds good,' the bartender replied. 'You want another?'

'Hell, yes.'

This was his second bar. Beck had started the evening at the Six Feet Under Pub & Fish House, the trappers' favourite watering hole. He'd stayed there for a couple of drinks to honour Paul, as was custom, then decided he didn't want to be there any more. Didn't want to be around if anyone accused him of not doing right by his friend. Not that any of them had. They all knew better, but that didn't mean they weren't thinking it. He was, so why wouldn't they be doing the same?

Forsaken

This bar wasn't one of his usual haunts but they had his favourite beer. By the time he was on his sixth bottle there were two voices competing for his attention: Paul's was nagging about how he should be working, not drinking. How he had responsibilities now, at least when it came to Riley. The other was the skinny girl next to him, giving him *that look*. A few weeks ago he would have taken her up on her offer without thinking about it.

But not now. With a tortured sigh, he downed the last of the beer and left the bar before he changed his mind.

On a scale of one to ten Beck knew he was about a seven when it came to being drunk. Decent buzz, but not too loaded. He'd learned how to handle the booze in the Army. You wanted to be intoxicated enough to feel good, but not too trashed to show up for roll-call.

Except right now the feel-good thing wasn't working out so well. He slammed the truck door and turned the key. The radio blared. He turned it off. A moment before he put the truck in gear he spied an Atlanta cop sitting at the corner in his patrol car, scoping the street.

'Damn.' He didn't dare drive, not in his condition. The police came down hard on drunk driving – it was a lucrative bust what with that new law. Not only did they toss you in jail, but they took your vehicle and sold it to pay the towing and court costs. A $1,000 fine and a $5,000 truck? Somehow the bankrupt city never bothered to pay you the difference.

A few years ago he would have risked it, wouldn't have

given a damn, but now he had Riley to worry about.

Beck groaned. 'Dammit, how'd I get into this mess?'

By not saving Paul. It all came down to that. Now Riley was his responsibility, at least until she was eighteen or one of her family stepped up and took charge of her. Like he knew anything about playing big brother to some girl.

Beck pulled himself out of the truck, locked the door and headed for the nearest Stop 'n' Rob on foot. Once there he scoured the aisles, steering clear of the old guys buying cigarettes. He didn't know how they afforded them, not at a hundred a carton. That had made it easy for him to kick the habit.

He needed to get back in the game tonight, but trapping while buzzed was a sure ticket to joining Paul in the dirt. He grabbed a six-pack of energy drinks and a large bag of peanuts. Salty ones. The peanuts would make him thirsty and all the fluid he'd have to chug would dilute the booze.

Once he was in his truck he started in on the food, alternating energy drinks and peanuts. He could remember when the drinks came in aluminium cans. Now they used thin plastic that cracked too easily, just one of the reasons he usually put the stuff in an empty whiskey bottle.

As he drank, the ache under his breastbone kicked in again. He'd like to believe it was sore muscles, but it wasn't. It was the same feeling he'd had when his granddaddy died. Every time he lost someone he cared for, a bit more of him went with them. In time, there wouldn't be much of him left.

Now that Paul was dead he'd have to trap every night to

keep both him and Riley in good shape, at least until her aunt came for her. From what Paul had said the woman was like a buzz saw. Still, she was family and that was important.

'No more playin' pool,' he said, shaking his head. No more doing what other guys his age liked to do. He'd lost his childhood to his mother's drinking and now he was going to lose even more of his life to taking care of Paul's kid. He twisted off the top of another bottle and took a long swig, followed by a handful of nuts. His stomach rumbled, complaining about the abuse.

By the time the first three bottles of energy drink were gone, he'd thought out a plan. It was a simple one – find the demon who'd killed his friend and waste the thing. It was an insane plan, but Beck didn't care.

'I'm gonna carve ya up, ya bastard. Send a message to Hell.'

To do that he'd have to work the lower ranks of demons until one of them squealed on the Five, gave him an idea where to find it. He knew Paul wouldn't want him looking for revenge, but he didn't care. Beck wanted payback.

And not just for the kid.

In a few short hours Riley knew one thing for sure – she needed earplugs. From what she could tell, each necro had a different sales pitch, like infomercials. As predicted, Mortimer was the nicest. The next four had grown increasingly malicious. All but Mortimer tried to breach the circle and went away with scorched shoes and a bad attitude.

By the final visitor she was so bitchy, so sleep-deprived, she'd told him off even before he'd opened his mouth. That had earned her a profanity-laced rant that would have impressed a rapper. Simon surged to his feet and told the guy to blow off, without using curse words. To her surprise, the necro had done just that.

After his rare flash of anger, her companion went to sleep, curled up in a sleeping bag, his hand thrown over his face like a cat. Every now and then he murmured to himself, though she couldn't make out the words.

Much to Riley's annoyance, she had to wake him a few hours later. It was either that or she'd wet herself.

'I'll stay awake until you return,' he said, still half asleep. 'Be careful.'

She took a deep breath and did exactly as he said, wincing as she stepped over the glowing line. Nothing happened but a brief flicker and that strange popping sound in her ears like she'd crossed some unseen barrier. Riley trudged off to the cemetery office. It was spooky. The Victorians were big into symbols, like weeping angels and obelisks to represent resurrection and eternal life. That only added to the creep factor. It was really dark with no moon. The faint rustle of leaves made her turn round more than once. All that was needed was a thick fog and a baying wolf and it'd be the stuff of slasher films.

After she returned and Simon allowed her entrance, he slipped round the rear of the mausoleum for a quick pee.

Guys have it so easy.

When he returned, he began to talk again. 'Be careful when you're here on your own. Necromancers can pretend to be cemetery employees, cops, you name it. They try to con you into breaking the circle or inviting them inside. Not everyone in the cemetery is after your dad's body, but I've heard tales, you know?'

Riley stifled the shiver. His warnings delivered, Simon curled up and fell asleep. She wished she could. Instead, she snuggled into the sleeping bag and stared up at the night sky. A hunting owl winged by a few times, then perched in a nearby tree to announce its territory. She watched it for a long time. It seemed to be doing the same of her.

When a mouse skittered across the path, the owl was all business. With an expert glide and lethal talons, it collected its startled meal.

Riley's back began to cramp so she rose and walked to her mom's grave. The flowers they'd left a couple of weeks ago were withered now, a victim of the night frosts. She knelt and brushed away the dry leaves that covered the plain granite headstone. It was nearly three years since Miriam Henley Blackthorne had left them. There wasn't a day she'd not been missed. Riley moved to her dad's grave, the smell of fresh earth filling the air around her. The flowers on top of the mounded earth were tipped with a thin layer of frost.

Mom was probably waiting for him on the other side. Riley crinkled up her face. That wouldn't be a good meeting. As her mother had lain dying, she'd made her dad promise to keep Riley safe. Now their daughter was on her own.

Yeah, Mom is going to be severely pissed.

She touched the cold earth, thinking of her father lying underneath it.

They're together now. It didn't help. They were together and she was all alone. No one left to laugh at her jokes, hold her. Love her.

A bottomless pit opened in front of her and a choked sob escaped her throat. Then another as warm tears coursed down her cheeks. She bent almost double, crying for herself more than her parents.

Someone touched her and she jumped. It was Simon. He didn't say a word, but opened his arms to her. She fell into them and continued to weep. He murmured comforting words, but she didn't understand them. What mattered most was that he was holding her. When she could no longer offer up any tears, she pulled away from him and blew her nose, embarrassed she'd lost it in front of him.

'Sorry . . . I . . .'

'They know you love them and that you miss them. That's what important.'

'I don't know what I'm going to do,' she admitted.

'You'll find your way. I know you will.'

Simon took her hand and led her to the sleeping bags. He tucked her in. He climbed into his own bag and wiggle-wormed over until their sides touched. Pulling his arm out, he had her rest her head on his shoulder. She snuggled in, grateful for his kindness.

'Your arm is going to freeze off,' she said in between sniffles.

'You're right.' He took one of the blankets, covered himself and settled back in place. She snuggled close, feeling warm and secure for the first time since her father's death. That she could feel that way said a lot about Simon.

'Thanks. You're . . . really sweet.'

'It's easy with someone like you. Now get some sleep. Dawn is in a few hours,' he whispered.

Knowing he was there to watch over her, Riley drifted into an uneasy dream filled with leering necros, thieving Magpies and dark laughter.

Simon's wristwatch beeped and he sat up and stretched.

'Good morning,' he said.

Riley blinked her eyes open, then wiped the sleep out of them. When she sat up, her hair felt weird. She ran a hand through it. To her relief there were no icicles.

Sleeping outside sucks.

'It'll get easier each night,' Simon said. 'Just be sure you don't sleepwalk.'

He made another trip round the back of the mausoleum to water the grass.

So unfair.

When he returned, he sat Indian style, fingered his rosary beads and began to pray.

Definitely an NCB – a Nice Catholic Boy, as her mom called them. Polite and so not a sleaze. No wonder her dad had liked him.

After a few minutes of prayer he tucked the rosary away.

'Good morning,' he said again, more cheerfully this time.

'Yeah, right . . . morning,' said Riley, struggling into a sitting position.

'You usually this grouchy?' he asked, as if taking notes for future reference.

'I've earned the right – my butt hurts, I'm tired, I'm cold and I want to go home. This has been one of the worst nights of my life.'

'Oh.' There was hurt in his voice.

Riley slapped her forehead. 'Sorry! That was dumb. Thanks for staying with me tonight. I would have been freaked on my own.'

Simon recovered instantly, smiling at her like she hadn't been a completely ungrateful dork.

'Glad I could help.'

Can this guy be for real? If he was, he had to have a girlfriend with six more waiting in line.

'Did you get any sleep?' he asked.

'A little. I had weird dreams about demons who acted like angels. Confusing.' She thought for a moment. 'Have you ever seen them . . . angels, I mean?'

'One or two. They only reveal themselves when they want to.' He sounded disappointed.

'Dad said there's this glowy sort of light round them, but to me they look like everyday people.'

'Maybe someday we'll see them clearly,' Simon replied wistfully. 'I'd like that.'

Forsaken

A voice called out. It was right before dawn so it should be the cemetery guy. At least she hoped it was.

A man walked up to the line of candles and gave a toothy smile.

'Good morning. My name's Rod. I'm here for the day shift. You Miss Blackthorne?'

'Uh huh.'

'Glad to meet you. Don't worry, I've been doing this for years. No body's been stolen on my watch.'

'That's good to hear.' *Really good to hear.*

The volunteer waited until Simon issued the invitation, then stepped over the candles. They flickered and returned to normal.

Riley let out a sigh of relief.

The newcomer chucked off his coat, revealing a heavy sweatshirt. He set up a camp chair and dropped a bag marked VIGIL SUPPLIES next to it.

'Those are for tonight when you reset the circle.'

'Thanks,' she said. She hadn't even thought that far.

Out of his backpack came a newspaper opened to the Sudoku page, followed by a pencil and a big green thermos.

As he was settling in, Riley rolled up the sleeping bags while her companion folded the blankets. By the time she was ready to leave the volunteer was already in his chair, paper on his lap.

'So who showed up last night?' he asked cheerfully.

'One guy named Mortimer and some others who didn't say who they were. They swore at me a lot.'

The volunteer broke out in a smile. 'Figured Mort would stop by. Best of a bad lot.'

'So I noticed.'

'Just make sure you're here before sundown. If there's an emergency, call the office and let them know.'

'Got it.'

Riley gingerly crossed the circle, ears popping once again. She doubted she'd ever get used to that. After she'd stashed the sleeping bags and blankets in the mausoleum, she locked the doors. Out of habit she gave them a firm rattle to make sure they were secure.

Simon fell in step with her as she headed for the parking lot.

'Congratulations. You've survived your first night.' He sounded genuinely proud of her.

'Yeah, I did.' Then it dawned on her. 'Do you have wheels?'

A nod. 'Beck asked me to drop you home. Said he'd be too tired this morning to do it.'

Tired? No way. He'll be hungover. You can bet on that.

In a few short minutes she was headed towards her apartment in a car with a St Christopher's medal hanging from the rearview mirror and a statue of St Jude on the dash. After she'd given him directions, Simon went quiet. She was getting accustomed to her escort's lengthy silences so it didn't trouble her.

It was only when he pulled into a parking lot near the front of the apartment building that he spoke. 'Looks like an old hotel.'

'It was. They converted it to apartments a few years back. It's nothing fancy.'

'At least it's a home,' he said. 'If you need help tonight, call Beck.'

That sounded like he was happy to be rid of her. 'Tired of me already?' she asked, hurt.

'Oh, no, I'm sorry,' he said, embarrassed. 'That came out wrong. I have to trap with Master Harper tonight, so Beck said he'd be able to help you.'

Backwoods Boy? No way. 'I'll be OK on my own. Thanks for showing me what to do.'

She pulled herself out of the car. It took a lot of effort. Sleeping on the ground was for little kids.

Simon rolled down the window. 'Just don't listen to the necros. They're as bad as the demons.'

She put her hand on his arm. 'Thanks for everything. I mean it.'

'No problem.'

Right before he turned on to the street, he gave a wave. She returned it.

What a cool guy.

Riley forced herself across the parking lot and up the stairs. She could still remember when they'd moved into the apartment. It'd been a blazing hot Atlanta day. After they'd finished, they'd gone for ice cream. Her dad had bought her a sundae and laughed when some of it had ended up on her nose.

By the time Riley reached her floor, her hand was shaking,

making the keys rattle. For one last time she could believe that everything was all right. Her dad would be sitting on the couch, organizing his paperwork, a cup of coffee in his hand. He'd look up and smile at her when she came in. He'd make room on the couch and ask how her day had gone. He always did that. Always made time for her. Always loved her.

The door swung open on rusty hinges. The couch was empty. She could hear the soft *plink plink* of water dripping into the oatmeal pan from yesterday's breakfast, the faint hum of the refrigerator. A fluff of Max fur sat underneath the kitchen table. The light on the answerphone was blinking frantically. Probably necromancers too lazy to make the trek to the graveyard.

Her dad had said he was lucky that he had her to come home to, how some folks had no one.

Like me.

Riley swung the door closed and methodically engaged all the locks, shutting out the world that had made her an orphan.

'It's not fair!' she hissed, slamming her fist into the wood. 'Why both of them? You took Mom. Wasn't that enough?'

No answer. No cosmic 'sorry about that'. Just emptiness. The tears came again and she let them fall.

When she'd cried herself out and blown her nose, Riley took a marker and found the date of the full moon on the calendar. She circled it and marked it with a big D. That would be the day her dad was truly free.

I won't let them get you. I swear it.

Chapter Twelve

Beck peeled open his eyes and did a slow scan of the terrain. The parking lot was deserted, unless you counted a pair of rusty shopping trolleys and a pile of old tyres. Quiet, open space. That was the way he liked it. Not that a trapper could park anywhere else since the pair of demons in the truck bed limited his choices.

Morning wasn't his favourite time, especially when his head felt like it was being torn apart by rabid weasels. Energy drinks and booze were a toxic combination, at least for him. Once he'd sobered up enough to trap he'd gone after the first Three he could find. It hadn't been hard as the thing was snuffling around the dumpster behind a butcher's shop. Too busy scoring castoff bits of fat and rancid beef to realize it had a trapper closing in, Beck had bagged the thing without a hitch. But it wouldn't squeal on the Five that had killed Paul. Annoyed, he kept hunting until he found another Three. Same deal. Lots of swearing, lots of threats to tear him apart but no information.

'Honour among demons,' he grumbled. 'That's so wrong.' At least the Threes didn't offer boons for their freedom. The mood he was in now, that would have been hard to pass up

135

if the boon was how to find Paul's killer.

Groaning at his thumping head he flipped the radio off, poured three more aspirin into his palm and gulped them down with some water. The previous dose hadn't done a thing and he figured these wouldn't either.

Sleep. That's what he needed, but that was going to be tough with all the caffeine skulking in his body. If he was lucky, he'd flame out sometime this afternoon. If not, it could easily be tomorrow.

His phone rang and he dug it out of his jacket pocket. 'Beck.'

'Simon. She's home safe.'

He sighed in relief. 'Thanks, man, I owe ya.'

'I didn't mind it a bit.'

Beck flipped the phone closed and frowned. 'Bet ya didn't.'

He wasn't quite sure what he thought of Simon Adler. Just because he was religious didn't mean he might not hit on Riley. Any guy would. She was really pretty. No ignoring that fact.

If things were different, he might have asked her out himself. But he couldn't now, not with her dad gone. It wouldn't feel right. Or at least that's what he told himself.

Beck settled back against the seat and closed his eyes, if nothing more than to keep the increasing sunlight out of them. In the distance he heard a garbage truck pick up one of those big dumpsters and bang the hell out of it. After a long yawn, he did the perimeter scan again. This time the lot wasn't empty.

'Dudes at ten o'clock,' he said, shifting his position. He

moved his steel pipe closer to him on the seat and then did the same with his Sig 9mm. The pipe was the first resort, the gun the very last.

He was in a part of town where people came in two kinds: predator and prey. He knew where he stood, but some of the locals might not have got the memo. Like the three kids who were sauntering towards the truck. *Urban youth*, Paul had called them.

All stupid. He could guess that much from their swagger. They were wearing the latest fashion – their jeans pulled down over their high tops with long red laces woven up the leg and tied below the knee. The colour of the laces was supposed to tell you which gang they belonged to. Beck didn't care. They were all losers to him.

They started laughing among themselves and pointing in his direction. Probably figured he was a drunk snoozing off the buzz. They could score some cash, a truck, and give him a good ass-kicking just for fun.

'Got no sense,' he said, shaking his head.

When they were within twenty feet, he hopped out of the truck, leaving the steel pipe on the seat behind him. If he was lucky, he wouldn't have to go all medieval on these guys.

'Mornin'!' he called.

One of them gave him the finger. Beck's fingers curved round the pipe. He adjusted his grip, keeping it hidden behind the door.

'Now that's not polite. Didn't your momma teach ya manners?'

'What you doin' here, asshole?' the kid demanded. He pulled a knife and the others followed his lead.

'Waitin' for breakfast. Ya got some?'

The kid sneered. 'We ain't no freakin' McDonald's.' They began to fan out, getting into position, watching for a chance to jump him.

'Breakfast isn't for me, dumbass. It's for them.' Beck hammered on the side of the truck with his fist. 'Chow time, guys!'

The demons erupted into snarls as they thrashed around in their steel bags. The noise was impressive in the still morning air. One reared up just high enough for the losers to see him, claws and all.

'No way, man, those are—'

'Demons,' Beck said. 'And boy are they hungry. Can y'all step a little closer, make it nice 'n' easy for 'em?' he asked.

The trio took off in a panicked retreat. One fell, rolled and was back up on his feet without taking a breath. If it had been an Olympic event, Beck would have given him a 9.8 or a 9.9, but the kid lost points for dropping his weapon.

Beck peered down at the demons. 'Sorry, guys. Looks like your breakfast made a run for it.'

Close to nine in the morning Beck wearily climbed the stairs to Fireman Jack's office in the old fire station. The demon trafficker was behind his desk, a steaming mug of coffee in front of him. His barber-pole braces made a nice contrast to the black chamois shirt and blue jeans. A thick stack of papers sat in front him. When he wasn't buying demons, he wore his lawyer hat and handled the Guild's legal work.

'Beck!' he called out. 'How you doing?'

'Jack.' Beck slumped in the closest chair and rubbed his eyes in exhaustion.

'You look like crap,' his host observed.

'Feel like it. Been up too long, I think.'

'Coffee?'

'God, no more caffeine.' He leaned back in the chair and it creaked in protest.

Jack reached into the mini fridge near his desk, then offered Beck a cold bottle of water.

'Thanks. Maybe that'll help.' Beck drained half of it without pausing for breath.

'What have you got for me this fine morning?'

'Two Gastros.'

'Two? You've been a busy boy,' Jack said, smiling. 'Who are you trapping with now?'

'No one.'

'You took those down on your own?' Jack asked, surprised.

'Yeah. I know, it wasn't smart. Don't want to split the money with another trapper. Until Paul's life insurance comes in, his kid's gonna need somethin' to live on.'

Jack rose, opened his safe and counted out the money, then placed it in front of Beck who stashed it away in his jeans pocket. After signing the paperwork, he pushed it across to Jack to finalize the deal.

'Who'll be her new master?' Jack asked, settling back into his chair.

'I'm hopin' it's Stewart,' Beck said, tucking away his copy of the paperwork. 'He'd be good for her. He doesn't yell at everythin' that moves, not like Harper.'

'I'd love to find out what idiot put a burr up Harper's ass all those years ago. I'd personally feed the fool to the first demon I saw.'

'Ya'd have to stand in line,' Beck said.

'How's Riley doing?'

Beck shook his head. 'Lost. Ya can see it in her eyes. She's tryin' to be tough, but it's killin' her.'

'Can't imagine what it's like losing both your parents.'

'Sucks, that's what it's like.'

Before Jack could reply, Beck's phone erupted in music. He flipped it open without looking at the caller ID. 'Yeah?'

'Oh my God, they're going to dig him up!'

'Huh? Riley?' he asked. 'What's wrong?'

'One of the debt guys was here and he said they're going to take Dad and sell him.'

It took a moment for Beck to realize what she was saying. 'What debt guy?'

'The one for Mom's medical bills. Consolidated Debt Collectors. He was really mean.'

Beck's anger ignited. The kid had just buried her only surviving parent and some parasite was harassing her about money.

'Did you sign anythin'?' he demanded.

'Of course not!' she retorted. 'I'm not stupid.'

'OK, calm down. I'll ask Jack what we should do.'

'Fireman Jack?'

'Yeah, he's the Guild's lawyer. Just hold on.' He muted the phone and laid out the situation. Jack listened without interruption, pencilling notes on a legal pad, his brow furrowed. Once Beck was finished, he leaned forward and tented his fingers.

'First thing, she's a minor so she's not responsible for any of her parents' debts. Don't let them guilt her into paying a cent.'

'That's good, but what about diggin' him up? Can they do that?' Beck pressed.

'If Paul's loan agreement had that option, they can. They just need to present the proper paperwork to the cemetery and he's theirs.'

Beck shook his head. 'I can't imagine he'd go for somethin' like that.'

'Probably figured he was going to be in too many pieces for a necromancer to mess with. Unfortunately, that's not the case.'

'So what do we do?' Beck asked.

'I'll request a copy of the contract from the debt company and see if they left us any wiggle room. If not, Paul could be out of the ground in short order and his daughter won't see a penny of that money.'

'That's the best ya can do?' He got a curt nod in response. 'No wonder everybody hates lawyers.'

'Tell me about it.'

Beck relayed the news to Riley. He could imagine her

pacing around the dinky apartment, scared she'd lose her dad . . . again.

'Sorry, I kinda freaked,' she admitted. 'I just got to sleep and he scared me.'

Beck knew how much it took her to admit that, at least to him.

That bastard's lucky I wasn't there.

'Don't worry, your daddy stays in the ground no matter what.' Brave words that he might not be able to back up, but she needed some hope right now.

He heard a weak *thanks* and then she hung up.

'Just keeps gettin' worse,' he grumbled, and dropped his phone into a pocket.

'If they have the legal right to reanimate him, what are you going to do?' Jack asked.

'Too God-awful to think about.'

Their eyes met. 'If you really want to keep Paul from being sold, it may come to that. They won't touch him if he's not whole.'

Beck swallowed, his stomach executing a warning lurch. 'Just do what ya can. Send me the bill. I don't care what it costs.'

'It's Guild business, so I'll bill them.'

Beck heaved a long sigh of relief. 'Thanks.'

'Let's get those demons unloaded. Then you get some sleep. I do not want to attend another friend's funeral any time soon, you got that?'

'Yeah, I hear ya.'

Chapter Thirteen

Peter's voice rose in indignation. 'You're, like, kidding me, right? They want to *sell* your father's corpse?'

'Yeah, that's the plan,' Riley said, cradling her phone against her shoulder as she waited for her computer to boot up. 'The guy said Dad was a . . . fung . . . a something asset.'

'Fungible,' Peter corrected. 'It means interchangeable. In this case he'll act as payment against the money you owe them.'

'Whatever. Beck talked to the Guild's lawyer. He's going to try to stop them.'

'God, Riley, that sucks.'

'Welcome to my new life. One long moment of suckage.'

There was an awkward pause. 'What's it like now?'

Riley thought a moment before answering. 'Too quiet. I always knew Dad would be home every morning so the quiet didn't bother me. Now it's . . . forever.'

'Not forever,' Peter said. 'Maybe you could get a room-mate or something.'

'How many people want to live with someone who stores demons in their kitchen cupboard?'

'Good point.' More silence.

'So what are you working on?' he asked, sounding eager to change the subject.

'My computer is getting weird again so I thought I'd better do a back-up.'

'Weird how?'

'It locks up all the time and I lose stuff.'

'Yeah, definite back-up time. I'll see if I can get over there this weekend and work on it for you.'

You'll come here? Peter had never been to the apartment. *What would he think of it?*

'Will the warden let you loose?' she asked.

A tortured sigh came through the phone. 'I don't know. She's just not that into you, Riley.'

'I noticed. Why doesn't your mom like me?'

'Because I do.'

Riley blinked a couple of times. 'Wow, that's radical.'

'Just the truth. All of us are on short leashes after what happened to Matt.'

Peter's oldest brother, the one who'd mixed a fatal combo of alcohol and automobile. His girlfriend had supplied the brew and walked away from the crash with a few cuts. Pete's mom had never forgiven her.

'But we're just friends, not like Matt and Sarah.'

'She doesn't see the difference. In her mind any girl is a threat to her sons. It's how she copes.'

'Sorry, Peter. That has to be brutal.'

'It is. But don't worry. I'll find a way to get over to see you.'

'Cool.' *Something to look forward to.* Maybe she'd make pizza or something.

Riley spied the yellow computer disk near the keyboard. Apparently her dad had dropped it off before he went trapping. *Before he . . .*

She shoved the thought away, pushing it behind an opaque curtain. It was that or she'd be blubbing tears on the keyboard. She pushed the disk into the slot and its contents appeared on her monitor. There was only one file and it was labelled RESEARCH.

'Password? What's this?' she mumbled.

'Riley?' Peter asked. 'Talk to me. What's going on?'

'This is weird. Dad never locks any of his files. I mean, who would want to read about the Battle of Shiloh?'

'So what's his password?' Peter prompted.

Riley tried a couple – her name, her mother's. Nothing happened.

'No clue. Damn, now he's got me wondering what's on this thing.'

'Bring it to school. I'll hack it for you. I'll need your birthdates, common stuff like that. People use those rather than something harder.'

'Will do.' She popped out the yellow disk, got another out of a shoebox next to the computer and inserted a blue one. That one wasn't password locked. The computer whirred as the back-up commenced.

Riley noted the time on the monitor. 'Gotta go. It's going to take a while to pack for the cemetery. I need *much* warmer clothes.' Tonight there would be no Nice Catholic Boy to snuggle up to. *Drat.*

'Watch out for the big bad necromancers,' Peter said jokingly.

'I will.' *I'll ignore them and they'll all go away.*

Rather than drive the car up to the mausoleum, Riley parked in the lot and proceeded to load herself up like a burro. As she hiked, her breath puffed out in the chilly air. The exercise felt good, but it reminded her that she was still sore from playing tag with library demons.

The cemetery guy from this morning was gone, replaced by a woman sitting in a chaise longue. She was wearing a heavy black dress that came to her ankles and a pair of orthopaedic shoes with really thick soles. On top was a thick black coat. Her bright silver hair pegged her at about seventy. Maybe older.

'Hello!' she called out brightly.

What is it with these people? Do they give them happy pills or something?

'I'm Martha, by the way,' the volunteer explained. Before Riley could reply the woman rattled on. 'It might rain. Did you bring an umbrella?'

Riley waved at the pile at her side. 'It's in there somewhere, I think.'

'Good. You should get some plastic tarps. They work great for keeping you dry and you won't have to sit on the wet ground.'

'Thanks,' Riley said, meaning it.

The old woman's eyes twinkled. 'You learn a few tricks over the years. If the weather really gets bad, just make the circle bigger and sit vigil inside the mausoleum.'

Riley made a note of that one. 'Do you really enjoy doing this?'

'Yes, I do! I'm in the fresh air and I help people,' Martha replied. 'I love this old cemetery. No better place in this world.'

Riley decided not to argue that point.

The volunteer drew herself up. 'If you mean no harm, then pass within.'

Riley cautiously lifted her gear over the candles and walked inside.

'You need help setting up the new circle?' the volunteer asked.

Riley almost said yes, but changed her mind. She'd have to do this on her own eventually. 'I'll be OK.'

'Then have a safe night, dear.' The woman marched up the path like she was half her age, with a folded chair in one hand and a paisley knitting bag in the other.

'OK,' Riley muttered. Now it was up to her. 'This is doable,' she said, although it felt like there was a swarm of monarch butterflies in her stomach trying to migrate in all directions at once. 'How hard can it be? I lay out the circle, do the invocation and I'm good.'

It sounded too easy.

Riley dug through the canvas bag marked VIGIL SUPPLIES.

'How many candles do I need?' She did a quick count of the ones currently in place and added a few more just in case. After a nervous glance at the booklet she began the ritual. Holy Water in one direction, then the other. She carefully set a new line of candles on top of the moistened ground, just inside the existing circle, trying hard to keep the exact same distance between them. Carrying the pamphlet and the fireplace lighter she'd borrowed from Mrs Litinsky, she began igniting the candles while saying the Lord's Prayer in English. She added 'Keep us safe, please,' and waited. All the candles went out at once, including the ones in the old circle.

'Ohmigod! No, don't do that!'

Her dad was totally unprotected.

Riley panicked. It was too close to sunset for mistakes.

I'll call Simon. No, he's trapping. Beck? No way I'm calling him. He'll think I can't do anything on my own.

She took two deep breaths to steady herself and opened the book.

'Oh, Jeez!' Serious Simon hadn't told her one vital bit of information – if there was only one person setting the circle, you lit the candles first, then did the invocation and the intention. From what she could tell, the invocation wasn't mandatory, but ensuring the circle knew who to repel was the most important part.

She relit the candles and then paused. The Lord's Prayer was OK, but it didn't feel right for her. But what to use? She heard a car door slam and jumped. Maybe now was not the time to be picky.

'Ah, God, sorry to bother you but this is Riley . . . Blackthorne. Could you keep my dad safe inside this circle? I mean, don't let the necromancers take him away. I'd really appreciate it if you could.'

The candles didn't flare like they were supposed to. Maybe she hadn't been specific enough. Or put enough force of will behind the words.

Taking a deep breath, she called out, 'If someone wants to harm us, do not let them inside this circle!'

The candles flamed high in a deep whooshing sound, then died down, making her ears snap from the pressure.

'Cool.'

It was only then she realized she was sweating despite the chilly night air.

Riley giggled nervously. 'See, Dad? I did it on my own. Yay me!'

The self-satisfied glow was still bubbling around inside her when Mortimer appeared. He politely tipped his hat and began his sales spiel in the same monotone he'd used the night before. Riley listened, taking time to study him. He was probably in his mid-thirties and the kind of guy who still lived at home with his widowed mom and collected stamps for fun.

When he'd finished his spiel, she shook her head.

Mortimer took the rejection graciously. 'Well, thank you for your time,' he said, placing his business card in front of the circle like the night before.

'So do you work for debt collectors?' she asked, her eyes narrowing.

'No,' he said, shaking his head in disgust. 'I won't reanimate for anyone but the deceased's family.'

A necro with conscience. Now that was refreshing.

'I think I'm starting to like you, Mortimer,' she said.

He looked embarrassed. 'Be careful, will you? Don't trust any of us.'

'Not even you?'

'I have scruples,' he replied proudly. 'As I see it, I am treading far enough off the path by summoning the dead.'

'Then why do you . . . summon the dead?'

'It's pretty much the only thing I'm good at.' Another tip of the hat and he left her alone inside the ring of candles.

'If all the summoners were like you, this would be easy.'

Riley knew better. This was the second time Mortimer had warned her about the others.

Maybe it wasn't so smart being out here on her own.

Chapter Fourteen

A sharp, sparking noise caused Riley to sit bolt upright in the sleeping bag, her heart hammering. For a second she thought it'd been a dream but the candles told her otherwise. The flames were higher now, some twenty feet off the ground like a force field that had repelled something nasty. Slowly the light dimmed to its usual level.

Probably a leaf. But there was no wind. Riley dug for her cellphone, then shook her head. Even if she called someone it would take too long for them to get here. This was her vigil and she had to brave it out.

As her eyes adjusted to the darkness, she saw the figure. It was just outside the circle, clad in a long black cloak, like you'd expect a wizard to wear.

He's just trying to scare me.

'Cool cloak,' she said, pumping confidence into her voice though there was none. 'Is there, like, a Necromancers 'R' Us shop or something?'

A weird laugh came from behind the hood. It reminded her of one of those wraiths in *The Lord of the Rings*. She couldn't see the figure's face, but the ice that ran down her spine told her this one wasn't anything like Mortimer.

'Paul Blackthorne's daughter,' the voice said, 'break the circle. Do it now.'

'No.'

'Break the circle,' he repeated, this time with more intensity.

Her mind began to whisper that she should do it. What would be the harm? After all, her dad was dead. He wouldn't care. She would be able to sleep in her own bed every night. No one would fault her for wanting that.

'That's right,' the dry voice soothed. 'You keep the money for yourself.'

'How much?' she asked before she could stop herself.

'Five thousand dollars. That will be a comfort to you, won't it?'

Five . . . thousand. That was a lot of cash. She could live on that for a long time.

'Your father would want this. Drop the circle and everything will be good again. You know you want to.'

Without realizing what she was doing, she opened the locket her father had given her. Inside was a picture of her mom and dad in Lincoln Park. It was summer and sitting between them was Riley, still a baby.

Their loving faces cleared her mind instantly.

'Not happening,' she said. 'Back off.'

'You will break the circle,' the necromancer commanded.

'You're wasting your time. Dad stays put.' She snapped the locket closed, clutching it tightly in the hope that her memories of her parents were stronger than the summoner's persuasive magic.

'You are not listening to me,' the voice said, deeper now. 'That's a mistake.'

'Not my first.'

If that circle doesn't hold, he's going to toast me.

The figure cocked its head, like he was weighing a number of extremely unpleasant options. 'Perhaps blood magic will do the trick.' He reached inside his cloak and pulled out something small. Something that hissed and wriggled.

It was a kitten, all cute and cream-coloured with black splotches.

'Get real. I'm not into bribes,' she replied. 'Just go away so I can get some sleep.'

There was a glint of a blade, though there was no moon. It seemed to generate its own light. It wasn't like one of those you find in a kitchen drawer. This was a ritual knife, the kind in horror movies. The kind of blade used for some bad-ass magic.

He wouldn't . . . .

The necromancer poised the blade an inch from the kitten's neck.

Riley leaped to her feet. 'What the hell are you doing?'

'Break the circle or I cut its little throat. Your choice. Your father is too valuable to leave in the ground, child.'

'You can't do that!'

'Of course I can.'

The kitten cried piteously, twisting in vain to sink a claw in its captor's hand.

Dad for a cat? He didn't even like them that much.

She couldn't let him hurt it. Could she? If he killed the poor creature, what would he do next? Kill her?

When Riley didn't move, the knife shifted closer.

'Last chance. Break the circle or it dies. You don't want its blood on your hands, do you?'

'You bastard!' she shouted. He responded with that creepy laugh, like it was a compliment.

Riley's toe scraped across the ground towards the nearest candle, then stopped the moment before it reached the circle. She looked over her shoulder at her father's grave and then back at the necromancer. Clenching her fists, she teetered on the edge. The kitten looked up at her, helpless. Only she could save it.

There was a flash of green fire in its eyes.

'No.' Then she jammed her own eyes closed, feeling like a monster. There was a hissing snarl followed by a shrill screech of pain.

'Heartless girl,' the necro called out. It sounded like praise. 'I'm impressed.'

Riley prised open her eyes in time to see him toss the kitten on the ground in front of the circle. It was still alive.

She heaved a thick sigh of relief.

'Your dad's corpse is mine, child. It's only a matter of time.' With a swirl of the cloak worthy of any movie villain, he strode away. Partway up the path he disappeared into a whirl of dried leaves.

Oh, now that's just creepy.

The kitten trembled at the edge of the circle and began to keen.

'Ah, you poor thing,' she said, stepping closer. Maybe she'd been wrong about its eyes. A trick of the light, not that there was much tonight. 'It's OK. He's gone. He can't hurt you any more.' All it needed was cuddling. She could do that at least. It'd be nice to have the company so she wouldn't feel so alone.

Simon's warning filled her mind. *They'll do anything to get to your father.*

Something felt wrong. The kitten should have taken off the moment it was dropped, found somewhere to hide. Instead it was outside the circle, like it was waiting.

Waiting for me. Those eyes again. Now they were fiery blue, glowing in the night. Riley took slow steps backwards. 'I don't think so.'

The beast hissed at a volume ten times its size and shot a claw at the nearest candle. The circle responded instantly, leaping dozens of feet into the air, glowing brilliant white. The kitten yelped and disappeared in a resounding snap of energy. The wind grew, slinging branches and leaves against the barrier. Then it grew deathly still. The candles returned to their usual height.

'Nice try, jerk!' she shouted, retreating to her sleeping bag. The shakes caught up with her almost immediately and she hugged herself to try to stop them. That hadn't been some foul-mouthed dude trying to talk her into some stupid deal for her dad's corpse. That had been dark magic.

And I almost fell for it.

*

By four in the morning she'd had the same number of visitations as Scrooge on Christmas Eve, if you counted Beck in the total. He moved slowly, deliberately, like he'd exceeded tired and moved right on to totally wiped. As usual, he was toting his duffel bag.

Probably sleeps with the thing.

Wary of necro games she watched him approach, fearing this was yet another trick.

'Riley,' he said. When she didn't answer, he added, 'How bad has it been?'

'Just fabulous. The demonic kitten really made my night.'

He didn't act surprised. She intoned the invitation and he marched through the circle without effort. His timing was excellent. A pee break was seriously needed.

'I'll be back,' she said, heading towards the candles.

'Ya got something with ya? A weapon?'

'No. Just going to the bathroom.'

He dug in his duffel bag and handed her the steel pipe. 'Take this.'

Riley rolled her eyes, but took it nonetheless. As she hurried off into the darkness, she heard him flop down on the sleeping bag and yawn. Now he'd spooked her about taking a pee.

Thanks a lot for that.

Clicking on the light in the bathroom, she checked both stalls before finding relief. When she stepped outside, a moth streaked by her face, causing her to squeak in panic. Then she felt dumb. Luckily Beck couldn't see her or she'd never have heard the end of it.

Beck wasn't alone – a heavy-set man stood a respectful distance from the circle. He was dressed rather flashily for a graveyard: blue suit, pink shirt and a glittering phalanx of rings. More like a pimp than a necro.

Riley scooted to the other side of the circle and waited until Beck invited her in. The moment she crossed the line of candles she felt it flash behind her, shoving her inside.

'Lenny,' Beck scolded. Apparently the necro had tried to cross over the circle at the same time, but had failed the *no harm* test.

The necro shrugged. 'Had to try.'

'Yeah, right.' Beck retrieved his pipe and dropped it near his pack.

'You two know each other?' she asked, surprised.

'Sure,' Beck responded, like she was being silly. 'We play pool together at the Armageddon Lounge. Lenny's pretty good.'

The necromancer beamed. 'Thanks. That's a compliment coming from you.' He turned towards her, polishing the glittering rings on his right hand against a coat sleeve. 'I was explaining to Beck that your father needs to earn his keep. Best way to do that is above ground. So how about it?'

'Nope.'

'Pity. A few more nights in the cold and you'll see things in a different light.' He looked over at her companion. 'Later, man.'

'See ya, Lenny.'

Riley settled on the sleeping bag as far away from Beck as she could. He may have been her dad's favourite trapping partner, but something about him made her uncomfortable. Not creepy uncomfortable, like he'd jump her or anything. More like she never knew where his mind was at any given moment.

'You hang with necros?' she asked. 'They're like . . . pond scum.'

'Some folks think the same of trappers.' He lowered himself on the blanket. 'So what happened tonight?'

She ignored him, digging out a bottle of water and taking a long swig.

'Come on, I'm not the enemy. I know ya have a problem with me, but I owe it to your daddy to look after ya.'

'Don't need you helping me,' she shot back. 'I'm fine.'

'Right, kid,' he said.

She glared at him. 'Why do you always call me that?'

'What?'

'Kid. I'm not twelve.'

'I know. It's just easier,' he mumbled.

'Huh?' That didn't make much sense.

A frown flitted across his face. 'Ya remember when I first got back from over there, how goofy ya got?'

Goofy? Riley's temper stirred. 'I wasn't like that.'

'Well, ya had your eyes on me, that's for sure.'

She gave him a stony silence, because he was right. His time in the Army had left him tanned, muscled and way cuter then when he'd left. A total hunk, and she'd fallen hard.

Then you shot me down like I was nothing.

'So why the kid thing?' she repeated, still savouring the anger.

He glowered at her. 'Ya know I couldn't go there, not with your daddy and me workin' together and ya only bein' fifteen and lookin' so fine and . . .' He faded out, his eyes riveted on the ground.

Riley hid the grin. She'd managed to push one of his buttons or that explanation wouldn't have been so long.

'OK, I got it,' she said. If he acted like she was a kid, he didn't have to work through all the emotional stuff, which suited her just fine. The idea he thought she was *fine* wasn't something she could handle right now. 'Just don't call me kid any more, OK?'

'Or?' he challenged, back in control in a heartbeat.

'I'll go all *goofy* on you again, whatever that means.'

Beck seemed to weigh the option and then muttered, 'Deal.'

He dug a bottle out of his duffel bag. The label said Johnny Walker. After a long swig, he smacked his lips.

'What're you doing?' she demanded. 'You keep it up and you'll be a drunk like your mom.'

He snarled at her and her blood ran cold. The flames were taller now, maybe a foot off the ground, registering his anger. Was that even possible?

Suddenly it didn't seem so safe with him *inside*.

'Ya leave that . . . *her* out of it,' he spouted, jamming the bottle into his bag. 'That's none of your damned business.'

Riley curled up in the sleeping bag, feeling sick to her

159

stomach. She shouldn't have said that to him. He couldn't help what his mom was like.

Just apologize. 'Beck . . .'

'What?' he said, his voice muffled. Even in the dark she could see the lines etched into his face. They made him look so much older, like he'd experienced everything bad the world could throw at him.

'I'm sorry,' she admitted. 'It wasn't right for me to say that.'

His shoulders hitched for a second. 'Go to sleep.'

'I can't.' Riley tugged the blanket round her shoulders.

'Just because she's a drunk doesn't mean I am,' he growled.

'Got it. Won't make that mistake again.'

He turned towards her. 'It's an energy drink,' he explained. A long yawn followed. 'Supposed to keep me goin' when I don't have time to sleep. It's not workin'.'

Now she really felt like a dork. 'Why put it in a whiskey bottle?'

'Just do.'

It wasn't that simple and they both knew it.

'What's it taste like?' she asked. He handed it over and Riley took a tentative gulp . . . and nearly gagged. The stuff was a blend of super-strong coffee laced with raw kerosene. 'Yuck.'

'Ya get used to it.'

'Not me. When was the last time you slept?'

'Doesn't matter,' he said.

'Tired trapper equals demon bait. Dad told me that.'

Beck looked over at her. 'Told me the same.'

'Then get some sleep, will you?' she urged.

'Ya need it more than I do.' He took another swig. 'I sold your demons, the ones in the cupboard. The money's under the microwave. Just forgot to tell ya.'

'Thanks,' she said grudgingly. She'd miss the Magpie, but the money was vital. 'Who's going to take over my training now?'

'Don't know yet.' He yawned again. 'I'll try to help ya when I can, but I have to trap or I can't pay my own bills. We need to figure out where ya can live.'

'What?' she said, caught off guard.

'Ya can't stay on your own, and ya sure as hell can't move in with me.'

Got that right. She could imagine what his house was like – probably ankle-deep in grubby old pizza boxes and empty beer bottles.

Then the first part of his statement caught up with her.

'I'm not moving. That's my home,' she protested. It wasn't much, but she couldn't lose the last connection with her dad.

'It'll take time for the Guild to pay the life insurance, and I can't afford to cover both places. Call your aunt, see if she'll take ya in for a while.'

Crap. He'd overheard her talking to Peter. 'I'm not moving,' she repeated, stronger this time.

Beck kept rambling, caught in his own personal minefield about how she'd need clothes and food and how she had to keep going to school.

You're not listening, Backwoods Boy. I belong here.

The power struggle had begun.

Chapter Fifteen

Morning brought Max to Riley's door and more bills in the mailbox. She welcomed the cat, but not the stack of windowed envelopes. At least none of them were marked OVERDUE.

Not yet.

Max promptly sprawled on the couch, licked a paw and then tucked himself into a massive ball like a furry armadillo. He acted like sleep was the answer to all the world's problems.

Only if you don't dream.

Riley grimly studied the pile of envelopes on the kitchen table. 'Welcome to your new life.' From what she could see, it was way worse than the old one. At least her old life had a parent in it. Now there was no dad, no dad income. The first hurt really bad. The second just amped up the heartache.

Max made a snorking noise in his sleep and twitched. At least one of them was happy. In the background the television droned on. It was one of those local talk shows discussing the rise in teen suicides, how the economy was causing kids to hit the wall. Most didn't survive the impact.

Riley had hit the wall and bounced so many times she didn't know any other way. Her mother's death, then the condo fire. Now her dad.

With a tortured sigh, she started with the first bill – the rent. That wasn't optional unless she wanted to move into a draughty refrigerator box under one of the city's leaky bridges. It went into the *life really sucks if this isn't paid* pile. Electric, gas and water. *Ditto.*

She continued on through the rest of them – monthly dues to the Guild Fund, both national and local, cable and cellphone bills. The final one was the biggest – her mom's medical care.

'$54,344.75?' she said, boggling at the amount. She'd known it was outrageous, but not the exact amount. Over the last three years her father had painstakingly whittled it down from a high of sixty-five thousand. The interest was taking a massive bite out of the payment, and there was still another seven years on the loan.

She'd be twenty-four by the time this was paid off. By then she'd be a master trapper. It seemed so far off.

Riley stuck the bill in the *when everything else is paid* pile. 'Sorry, Dad, but that's the way it has to be.'

Using her cellphone to do the maths she realized that even if she ignored the medical bill she was going to be in real trouble in five days when the rent was due. Maybe the life insurance payment would come in really quick and . . .

Life doesn't work that way. Riley had learned that much from watching her dad strain to balance the finances month after month. The urge to binge on chocolate reared its head. After a quick hunt through the apartment she didn't locate any, so she ate a banana instead. No comparison.

While she was rummaging, she found the demon money right where Beck had said it would be, another $225, along with paperwork that said he'd sold the demons to a trafficker named Roscoe Clement. Riley had heard of the guy. Her dad had described him in two words: total sleaze.

Bet Beck shoots pool with him too.

Slumping into the chair, she counted the pile of cash she'd dug out of their makeshift 'bank' inside one of the cushions. Her dad had always joked that they looked like drug dealers with the stacks of fives, tens and twenties on the kitchen table. Keeping money inside a cushion wasn't really a smart idea, but they'd had little choice. If they put anything in the bank the medical bill idiots would siphon it right out as part of the claim. They'd learned that the hard way and lived on ramen noodles for a month because of it.

Riley did the maths again.

'Better, but I still need three hundred dollars,' she said. If she could find that somehow, she could pay the rent and the utilities and leave a bit for food. She'd worry about the rest of the bills when their time came.

Her dad had faced this every day, every week, month after month. He'd remained cheerful, at least around her, but she knew it'd dragged him down. She gazed at the chair. Empty. No smile, no laugh. That emptiness spread throughout the entire apartment, an invisible choking fog.

Riley sprawled on the couch next to Max. The packing-box coffee table received a sound kick, startling the cat.

'Where am I going to get three hundred bucks?' she

groaned. Max's answer was to yawn, exposing a long pinkish tongue. He curled up again.

'Borrow it from Beck?' she pondered. Riley shook her head even before she'd finished the question. He was already trying to take control of her life and owing him money would only give him more power.

She had to find a way to live on her own or Beck would drive her crazy.

Riley's eyes lit on her father's trapping bag near the door. Beck had brought it home for her.

She retrieved it and returned to the couch. The sides of it had small tears and there was dried blood on it. Zipping the bag open, she studied the interior. Her dad had repacked it every night, replacing any supplies he'd used. Since he wasn't here, the job fell to her.

A plan slowly formed. It was pretty bold, crazy even, but if she could pull it off . . .

Paul Blackthorne couldn't trap any more.

'But his daughter can.'

Riley parked underneath one of the few working security lights near the old grocery store. The light was on life support, blinking on and off at random intervals. Farther away from the building were other cars with windows steamed opaque because the occupants were busy making out.

Tonight was going to be a nightmare. By now her classmates would have heard what had happened at the library, maybe even about her dad. She didn't think she could handle false pity right now. Or insults. Somebody would get hurt.

Riley sat in the car for a few minutes, leaving the motor running. It would be so easy to ditch class. Beck would never know. She could be in Five Points hunting demons rather than hanging around here.

She spied Peter by the front door. He was watching for her, like he did every night they had class. He was holding something – her report. She couldn't blow him off when he'd done all that work. And then there was the computer disk mystery. The longer she'd thought about it, the more it had bugged her. Like trying to guess what was inside a Christmas present, except rattling a disk didn't tell you much.

As she stepped out of the car, Peter saw her and waved. Shouldering her messenger bag, she headed towards him.

He'll help me get through this.

'Hey, Riley,' Peter said as soon as she drew near. She noticed he kept his voice muted so it didn't carry across the parking lot. 'Glad you're here.'

'No choice,' she said, then felt bad. 'How're you?'

His smile thinned. 'Worried about you.'

She didn't even think twice when he gave her a hug.

Peter stepped back and opened his mouth. Then he shook his head like he knew nothing he could say would help her heal.

'Here you go,' he said, and handed over the neat stack of paper. 'Your report.'

'You're a great guy, you know that?' she said, all serious.

'Sure am. Destined for fame and fortune,' he joked. 'I still think my paper's better.'

'You would.'

'Hey, Blackthorne,' one of the other students called out. 'Trashed any libraries today?'

Before she could respond, a classmate elbowed the ass, then whispered in his ear. The guy's eyes grew large.

'Sorry, I didn't know about your dad,' he mumbled. Around them, other kids watched nervously, wondering if she was going to lose it.

Riley turned her back on him. No tears. Not here. She felt Peter's hand on her elbow, then a gentle squeeze of reassurance.

'Er, did you bring that computer disk?' he asked. He was trying to distract her, and she loved him for it.

Riley unearthed the disk from the bottom of her messenger bag and delivered it into his eager hands, along with a list of birthdays and other personal information.

'Cool. Now I can hack your bank account,' he said, winking.

'Hack away. We . . . I don't have any money.'

Peter cocked his head. 'How bad is it? Do you, like, have enough for food?'

'I'm three hundred short for the rent,' she admitted. 'I could ask Beck, but he's . . .' She shook her head. 'Not going there.'

'I've got almost a hundred I could loan you.'

She studied Peter anew. He was serious. She knew he'd been laying aside cash for a new hard drive but he was willing to help her without even thinking about it.

'No,' she said, shaking her head. *I have to do this on my own. I can't sponge off my friends.* 'Thanks, but I'll work it out.'

The worried expression on Peter's face didn't budge. 'What do you have in mind?'

A field trip to Demon Central. Instead she said, 'I'm thinking of getting a part-time job.' That wasn't really lying, was it? Peter would never agree to her trapping on her own. Neither would Beck.

So I won't tell them. At least until she'd caught her very first Three.

When Riley dropped the report on Mr Houston's desk, the older man looked up, his pale blue eyes barely focusing on her. He murmured his sympathies then returned to his paperwork. That angered her. She didn't want sympathy, but her dad was more important than a few words that didn't mean anything.

Riley took her chair and fell into tortured silence, despite Peter's attempts to cheer her up. The new curriculum required teachers to teach multiple subjects even if they didn't really understand them. Mr Houston was a good example. He was great with English, but not so hot with the other classwork.

Like maths.

As he droned on about the finer points of calculating the volume of a cylinder, she was light years away from the here and now. Almost everything triggered memories of her dad, like being in class. She'd sat in on some of his history lessons when she was a kid. He was a great teacher, not like Houston, who could put stones to sleep. She'd met Beck in one of those classes. He'd checked her out, then laughed, making fun of her braids and knobby knees, not realizing she was the teacher's daughter.

'You're kidding!' Peter exclaimed.

Riley pulled herself back to the present. 'What?' she asked, wondering what she'd missed. Peter was never that empathic about maths.

'They're closing this school,' he said, angling his head towards the teacher.

Houston had a pile of envelopes in his arthritic hands. 'These are your assignments. Your next class will meet in the new locations.'

'Why are they closing this one?' one of the kids asked.

'Just are,' Houston said. He looked around at the dead bugs and the maze of multicoloured wires protruding from the dairy case. 'Any place will be better than this, guys.'

'Got that right,' Peter whispered.

An envelope landed on her desk. Official news always came in white envelopes with neatly typed labels. This one was no different.

BLACKTHORNE, RILEY A. (Junior)

She looked over at Peter and they ripped open their envelopes simultaneously.

'I've got an afternoon class now,' she said. *How had that happened?* It'd always been at night.

'Where?' Peter asked, leaning over to look at her paper.

'Fourteenth Street. An old Starbucks.'

Silence.

'Peter?'

His face fell. 'Damn,' he muttered, and handed over his letter. The day had just got worse. Peter wasn't in her class any more. Instead, he was going to be somewhere on Ponce de Leon Avenue at a place named *Kids Galore!*

Riley returned the letter, trying not to let this news body-slam her. She failed.

'We've always been together, ever since elementary school,' she said.

'Maybe if I ask them to change it . . .' he began. Then he shook his head. 'I bet Mom's behind this.'

If so, Mrs King had discovered a truly cruel way to separate them.

Peter adopted his game face. 'We'll talk every night after class,' he said, trying hard to put some positive spin on this disaster. 'We'll have twice the stories, you'll see.'

'Yeah.' He was doing the happy-talk thing, but it wasn't working.

'Riley?' he said. She looked over at him. 'No matter what, I've got your back.'

Not if you're on the other side of the city.

Chapter Sixteen

Serious nerves kept Riley rooted to the car seat. She sat just inside Demon Central, near Underground Atlanta. Her dad had said it was a rundown area, but that was an understatement. It hadn't always been that way. When her mom was alive, they'd come down for New Year's Eve. It'd been cool back then. Now it was a dump. If she was going to find a demon, it would be here.

Riley had everything she needed – her dad's trapping gear and the special steel mesh bag to hold the Three after she'd caught it. She'd spent nearly forty-eight dollars for Holy Water and three spheres from a gun shop on Trinity Avenue. Only one thing was missing – guts.

I can do this. She'd been saying the same thing to herself for the last ten minutes, ever since she'd called Beck and lied to him.

Not a total lie. I am tired.

But she had lied, at least about class running late and that she needed to get some sleep and could he watch her father's grave until midnight?

He'd agreed without giving her any hassle. It would have been easier on her conscience if he'd been a jerk. Instead, he'd sounded really concerned and that made the lie turn to rock in her stomach. Would borrowing money from him be the end of the world?

Yes.

Time was passing.

Riley tapped her fingers on the steering wheel. If she was truly Paul Blackthorne's daughter, she'd be out there hunting a Three rather than worrying herself sick in the car. She'd be taking care of herself rather than waiting for someone else to do it for her.

Her hand shook as she reached for the door handle.

'I'll just see what it looks like, then decide,' Riley said, trying to find some middle ground that didn't allow that stone in her stomach to grow any heavier.

After the boot lid popped open, she slipped the straps of her father's trapping bag on her shoulder. It seemed heavier than when she'd hauled it out of the apartment.

'No wonder he lifted weights,' she grumbled, dropping it to the ground. There was the sound of breaking glass.

'Ah, crap!' She'd broken one of the spheres. They were designed to crack easily and she only had three. Squatting down, she rummaged in the bag. One of them had split open and a sea of Holy Water flooded the interior.

She gingerly fished out the broken glass, trying not to slice her fingers, and tossed the shards into the gutter. After removing the bag's other contents, she drained the water onto the ground. It splashed on her tennis shoes and her feet began to tingle. Now she'd have cold and holy feet all night.

Her ham sandwich was soaked. That was OK. When she'd caught a demon, she'd haul it over to Fireman Jack and collect her money. Then there'd be a celebratory trip to McDonald's for supper on the way to the graveyard. She might even supersize the fries.

An odd shuffling noise caught her notice. She leaned round the boot lid. An old black man was making his way up the broken sidewalk, dwarfed by layers of clothes, as if he was wearing everything he owned. He hunched against the cold, shooting glances over his shoulder every few steps like he expected trouble.

Once he was gone, Riley repacked only what she needed into her messenger bag and slipped the strap on to her shoulder. *Better.* After slamming the boot lid and pocketing the keys, she set off into the heart of Demon Central, her heart thudding in her ears.

Fifty feet down the abandoned street she came to a stop.

'There just had to be holes,' Riley muttered. She hated them. Things lived down in those holes. Things that would love to eat her.

She paused and studied the closest abyss. It was jagged and deep, with pieces of metal sticking out from the edges like porcupine quills. She thought she heard water running somewhere underground.

This place was a Three's dream home: loads of rubbish strewn around and hardly any light. What light there was seemed to be timid, barely illuminating the centre of the street and avoiding the corners entirely. She strained to see into one corner, but it was impossible. Anything could be watching her, waiting, choosing the moment to bring her down.

A few streets over a coyote howled, high and throaty. The howl was picked up and amplified into a wild and energetic chorus. Riley began to shiver.

Was Beck this afraid when he trapped his first Three?

She wasn't sure. He didn't seem to be scared of anything, but then her dad had been with him and that would have made all the difference.

As Riley edged forward her shoes crunched on something. Broken glass and white powder spread in a wide arc on the rippled asphalt. Debris had swirled around that circle, like a hurricane does its eye. Edging closer, she found tracks through the powder. She knelt. The powder came from a shield sphere and the tracks were from work boots like the kind trappers wore. Dry rust-brown stains were splattered like a child had shaken out a paint brush. She picked up a strip of ripped brown leather crusted with dried blood and examined it.

It was from Beck's coat, the one he'd been wearing the night her father died. She could remember what it had looked like in the hallway, slashed and shredded, coated with his blood.

Riley lurched to her feet, stumbling backwards. She barely stifled a cry of anguish.

This was where her dad had died.

What am I doing here?

Her dad and Beck trapped as a team. That wasn't to keep

each other company. Apprentices didn't start trapping Grade Threes until almost six months in, and then only with a master at their side. Even then, they still died.

Get the hell out of here!

It was her father's voice, echoing deep inside her head.

Riley executed the turn as slowly as possible, eyes darting from hole to hole, expecting a stinking furry body to be crawling out of every one. She wanted to run, but she kept her movements steady. Demons chased their victims. If she acted like she was in control, maybe nothing would come after her.

Four steps later she heard the sound.

'Just a rat,' she whispered. Not that she'd seen any, but they had to be down here, right?

The sound grew louder. A sort of sloppy snarl. Muscles tensing and heart jittering, Riley looked over her shoulder. Crouched in front of one of the holes was a Grade Three demon. The thing looked like some monster out of a science fiction movie – four feet tall, a patchwork of black and white spiked fur with scimitar claws and horrifically sharp teeth that protruded beyond the lower jaw. The creature rose, stretching like it was limbering up for gym class. It examined her with menacing red eyes.

'Oh . . . my . . . God.'

'Black . . . thorne's daughter,' it bayed. It slicked its thick tongue across its lips. Drool rolled down its chin.

'Niiice demon . . . That's it, just stay there.' Riley fumbled in the bag and pulled out the cow entrails she'd retrieved from the freezer. She slung the package as hard as she could and it landed with a plop on the asphalt. Louder snarls came from the beast. In a move that seemed impossible for its bulk, it leaped on the food and swallowed the entrails and the plastic wrapper in one big gulp.

'Oh, God,' she said, stumbling backwards. That had been her only diversion and it was long gone. Her hand closed on one of the spheres. 'I'm leaving now. No need to get upset, Mr Demon.'

'Chew yourrr bones!' it cried, waving its arms in the air.

A second later, all Riley could see was a whir of black and white, all teeth and claws, moving towards her at frightening speed. She stumbled, nearly falling. Cursing, she tossed one of the spheres at the oncoming fiend. It missed and smashed to bits on the uneven ground close to where her father had breathed his last.

Riley ran, the messenger bag banging into her side. Once she got to the car the thing wouldn't follow her, would it?

The beast had other ideas, growing closer, calling out her name. It snarled and clawed the back of her jacket, spinning her round like a top. Falling hard, the wind knocked out of her, Riley rolled to protect her final sphere. She shrieked as the demon dived at her, claws raking across the asphalt in a trail of sparks just inches from her face. It yowled in frustration when it missed. Riley regained her feet only a second before it dodged sideways, aiming its glistening ebony spikes at her belly. She forced the bag forward, trying to block its lethal reach. It bit at the canvas, snarling and growling as she fumbled for the last sphere.

A thick paw arced round the bag and dug into her left thigh, burying claws deep in her flesh. Riley screamed in agony and slammed the sphere into the fiend's open maw, embedding the glass into the beast and deep in her palm. In slow motion, the Three ripped its claws out of her leg and sank to the ground, bloody and unmoving.

Riley fell to her knees and began to retch, the adrenalin making her heart thud so fast she thought she'd faint. Prickles of light danced at the corners of her eyes. She forced herself to slow her breathing, studying the still form. The demon was taking quick puffs of air through its mouth, its laser-red eyes staring up at nothing. Black blood dripped from its tongue on to its neck. Riley forced herself to her feet and with fumbling hands broke open the seal on the steel bag.

How do I get this thing inside?

In the end, she kept jamming the fiend's legs, body and arms into the bag, like stuffing a pillowcase with foul-smelling fur. The thing stank like sulphur and rotten meat, making her stomach roil and acid singe her throat. She worked left-handed as the right was bleeding, waves of pain telegraphing up her arm.

With incredible effort, she locked down the two clamps that secured the demon inside the bag. She'd actually done it – caught her first Grade Three Hellspawn.

Rising to her feet, Riley wobbled for a few seconds. The adrenalin was gone, leaving a sour stomach and a sick, pounding headache. It was only then she dared look at her thigh. Thick red blood bubbled out from the six holes in her slashed jeans, one for each claw. The leg felt numb, which was weird. It should be hurting like hell.

'Trapper . . . scores,' she said weakly. *Sorta*. Folding out the steel bag's handle, she dragged the dead weight up the street one-handed. It was slow going; the fiend was much heavier than she'd expected.

How am I going to get this thing in the boot? It certainly wasn't riding up front with her.

'One problem at a time,' she said, refusing to admit this was more than she could handle. Riley looked down at her catch. She couldn't wait to see Beck's face.

Hey, Backwoods Boy! Guess what I did tonight?

It was going to be *sooo* sweet.

She heard laughter. For a moment it didn't register as a threat.

'Hey, girlie!' someone called out.

Riley whirled round to find two guys following her. One of them was chunky, like a Beck gone to seed with rolls of flab round his middle. He was wearing a faded baseball cap and his long hair needed washing.

'She looks tasty . . . for a trapper,' the second said. He was short and wiry with an unlit cigarette dangling out of his mouth.

Just a couple of jerks from the Guild trying to psych me.

Riley fired up the attitude. 'I'm with Beck,' she fibbed. 'He's not going to be happy you're messing with me.'

'So where is this guy?' the first one asked. He had a load of gum in his mouth and he kept working it.

'Down there,' she lied, pointing towards the end of the street.

The big man spat. 'Ain't no one down there. You're on your own.'

'Just the way we like 'em,' the second added.

This was bad. These guys weren't trappers. They were too shabby, and neither of them had any trapping equipment with them.

'What do you want?' Riley asked, tightening her grip on the steel bag.

The sick leer that formed on the big man's face sent a frigid shiver to her toes. 'The demon . . . to start with.'

Riley shook her head. 'No way. Go catch your own.'

'Seems we just did. That thing's worth a lot of money.'

'You can't sell a demon,' she protested. 'You have to be a trapper.'

'Hear that, Dodger? She says we can't sell it.' He chuffed. 'Never stopped us before. It'll get us five hundred, no sweat.'

Five hundred? Who's paying that much for a Three?

The wiry guy began to circle her. 'How's about we share, girlie?'

'Yeah,' the big man agreed. 'Get some booze, some blow, and have a party, just the three of us.'

Oh God.

Rage-laced panic exploded inside her. She couldn't escape with the demon – it was too heavy to move quickly. If she dialed 911 it'd take the cops too long to get here, even if they could be convinced to come to Demon Central. By then . . .

The demon or these sick perverts?

Slinging a torrent of hellish curse words at them, Riley dropped the bag and limped off as fast as her injured thigh would let her. The wounds fired to life, sending jolts of pain into her leg. If she only had a steel pipe, anything that would keep them away from her. Keep them from touching her and . . .

'Run, girlie!' Dodger taunted as he started after her. His heavy boots crunched across the pavement, moving closer with each step. He was just playing with her. There was no way she could outrun either of them.

A strange sound filled the street, a combination of a throaty howl and a deep, raspy snarl.

'Oh, damn,' the big man shouted. 'The thing's awake. Help me with it!'

Riley risked a glance over her shoulder. The small guy was still gaining on her. Behind him, the demon clawed and bit at its steel prison like a rabid dog, thrashing so the metal bag rolled around the pavement.

The smaller man was catching up. She scooped up a charred piece of wood, holding it like a club, and turned to face him. A hundred words came to the tip of her tongue, but she was too scared to say any of them.

The big man was losing his battle. 'Dammit, Dodger, forget her! She's not worth the five hundred.'

With a snarl that would have impressed any fiend, Dodger whirled and ran at top speed to help his partner.

Riley limped away, pushing as fast as she dared. As she turned the corner, she saw the two men wrestling with the bag as the Three tried to tear it apart.

'Go demon,' she urged, blinking away tears of anger. Maybe it'd get free and rip those losers apart. Eat them both. 'That'd be so righteous.'

By the time Riley reached the car, she was shaking like a dog in a thunderstorm. The thigh felt like it was boiling from within, shooting pain into her groin and all the way down to her toes. Popping open the boot, she grabbed the pint bottle of Holy Water, broke open the seal and soaked her thigh, jeans and all, making it look she'd wet herself. Instead of the burning pain she'd expected, it only stung a little then eased off.

Maybe the wounds aren't that bad.

Riley swallowed, twice, and took some deep breaths. Her heart still drummed in her ears and her stomach felt seconds away from erupting. At least the claw marks wouldn't infect, though she'd still feel like crap for a couple of a days. Like a bad case of the flu was how her dad described it.

'I have nothing to show for it,' she growled. Tossing the empty bottle in the boot with more force than was necessary, she slammed the lid. There'd been no choice. If she'd tried to fight them, they would have jumped her and . . .

'You asshats!' she shouted, thumping her uninjured fist on the boot lid. She'd bagged her very first Three and they'd taken it away from her like a bully steals a kid's lunch money.

If Dad had been here . . .

Tears welled in her eyes again. If her dad had been here, they'd have that demon in the boot and those two losers would have learned what it meant to tangle with a master trapper. Instead they'd tangled with her, and won.

Epic fail.

'Beck is so going to kill me.' The Three had been her best defence against his anger. He'd have bitched at her, but in the end he would have respected her.

Not now. He's never going to trust me again. He'll just tighten up his leash.

Instead of heading for the graveyard, she drove home one-handed, tears coursing down her face. They felt icy against her skin as a full body shiver cramped her muscles and her teeth began to chatter. She turned off the heater. Sweat bloomed on her forehead, despite the chilly night air.

Once she got home, she'd call Beck, tell him what had happened. Then it would get really bad.

'Someday,' she muttered in between intense shivering sessions. Someday she'd catch up with those guys and make them pay. Someday they'd know what a mistake it was to mess with Riley Blackthorne.

But not today.

Chapter Seventeen

The dial on Beck's watch glowed blue in the growing light – it was a half hour until dawn. With each passing hour he'd talked himself out of dialling Riley's cellphone and rousting her out of her bed. The kid had to be worn out, the shock of her dad's death hitting home about now. He knew how that felt.

There'd always be sadness when he thought of Paul. The man could have easily blown him off, treated him like everyone else, but Paul had told him he'd seen that spark in Beck's eyes, that drive to be something better. Beck had never thought to argue the subject. His teacher had such a reasoned way of explaining things it sounded like gospel.

Beck sighed, feeling that dull ache deep in his chest again. He still expected to see his phone light up and it would be Paul, checking in on him, just wanting to talk. That would never happen again. He was truly on his own now. *Just like Riley.*

It was a still night and the swirl of dead leaves immediately caught his attention. Mortimer had already visited, polite as ever. Lenny had dropped by a little after two and another necro named Christian at three. It was as if they had assigned times. The leaves coalesced into a form outside the circle, causing the candles to flare. It reminded Beck more of a high-level demon than a summoner of the dead.

'Wastin' your time,' he called out.

The form wavered for a moment and then took a more defined shape. Black cloak, carved oak staff, all the theatrical props.

'I can give you what you most want in life,' the voice within the hood said in a sibilant whisper.

'The hell ya say,' Beck replied, too tired to be polite. 'Ya can give me a night in Taylor Swift's bed? Damn, that woman's fine, and she can sing too. Or maybe a new truck. That'd be nice.'

'Nothing so mundane.' A dramatic pause. 'I can deliver the demon who killed Paul Blackthorne.'

Beck's heart double beat, his humour gone. 'Your kind only messes with dead folks, not Hellspawn.'

'I am prepared to make an exception in this case.'

'Why is Blackthorne so important to ya?'

The figure leaned on the staff in a pensive pose. 'Just accept that he is. It's not like Mr Blackthorne will be in service forever.'

The necro did have a point. Paul would be returned to his grave in a year at the latest, and the demon would be dead. There were ways to hide the truth from Riley, especially if she went to live with her aunt. With the grave so fresh, once the body was exhumed and reanimated Beck could smooth over the dirt and she'd never know.

'Certainly you want to see justice done,' the figure

soothed, 'and prevent the chance the fiend will come after the one remaining Blackthorne.'

He played to Beck's greatest fear. The only way to keep Riley safe was to kill that Five and send a message to Lucifer to back off. Beck wanted that more than anything else in the world, even sleeping with his favourite country music singer.

He rose, taking a few tentative steps towards the glowing circle.

The figure fell silent, drawing him closer. Beck slowly turned to look at the mound of dirt. What would Paul think of him if he disturbed his rest? What would Riley say if she knew he'd betrayed her?

'All for a good cause,' the necromancer insisted. 'You must keep her safe. She has a will of her own and it has put her in danger tonight.'

Beck whipped round. 'Whadda ya mean?'

'She went hunting in Five Points. Alone. I hear it went very badly.'

'You're lyin',' Beck retorted.

'And if I'm not?' the necromancer replied, his tone too sure for Beck's comfort. 'What if she's dying right now? Would it make sense to guard this grave when she's heading towards one of her own?'

'No way she'd go to Five Points alone.' The moment Beck uttered the words, he knew he was wrong.

Damn, girl, ya wouldn't. He frowned, the truth hitting as hard as a slug to the gut. *Yeah, ya would, just to spite me.*

First the necro had said the demon might hurt her. Now

he claimed she was already hurt, maybe dying.

Lies.

Beck forced himself back to the blanket. 'I'm not buyin' it.'

The cloak shifted in what passed for a shrug. 'Then it's on your head,' the summoner replied, no hint of disappointment in his voice. 'By the full moon this man's body will be mine. Do not doubt it.'

The form reverted to leaves and scattered in a light wind.

Riley's cellphone went unanswered, rolling over to voicemail again and again. When the cemetery's volunteer arrived a few minutes later, Beck bolted for his truck.

Riley prised her eyes open to find sunlight on the bedroom ceiling whirling like a kaleidoscope. All sorts of colours. It was really pretty. With considerable effort, she pulled herself upright on the bed, wondering what time it was. She hiccupped and the shivering began again as her fever rose. The left thigh was the problem. It was swollen, the denim soaked with something brown. The entire leg pulsated with each heartbeat.

The Holy Water was supposed to neutralize the poison.

'Not so much,' she said, falling back on to the pillow. Time slowed.

Riley knew what was happening. She'd heard her dad talking to her mom about this when he thought she wasn't listening. Her leg would go septic in a few hours and the poison would spread throughout her body. It would kill her.

Maybe that's best. She could be with her parents. Do whatever angels did all day. No worries about money or school or demons . . .

An annoying noise pulled her out of her fevered imaginings. It was her cellphone. She faded out until it started making noise again. With sweaty hands Riley flipped it open. Someone called out to her in a frantic voice. 'Riley? Are you OK?'

'Sick . . .'

'What happened?' the voice asked.

'They . . . stole it.'

'Stole what?'

'Demon got me . . . Sorry. You were . . . right.'

She flipped it closed and let the phone fall next to her on the bed, knowing that Beck would find her body and bury her next to her parents.

No vigil needed.

Violating scores of traffic laws on the way to the apartment, Beck worked his phone, calling in favours. He started with Carmela, rousing the doc out of bed and earning him an earful until he explained the situation. Then he called the Guild's priest. Father Harrison had just stepped out of the shower but promised to come over as quickly as possible.

After making a parking place where there wasn't one, Beck leaped out of the truck and took the stairs two at a time. Hammering on Riley's door got no response. He called out. Nothing. He tried Mrs Litinsky's, then he remembered something about her going to visit her family in Charleston.

For half a second he thought of kicking in the door but discarded the idea – Paul had spent a lot of time reinforcing it, worried about Riley staying home alone at night. He had to find a key.

Swearing under his breath, he ran down two floors to the door marked SUPERINTENDENT. He banged on it. Time crawled by until a scrawny, unshaven face appeared at the door. Beck physically bullied the guy up the stairs, then glowered menacingly while the super fumbled with the keys.

To his relief Riley hadn't engaged the chain lock. The instant the door opened he shoved past the super, calling out her name. She wasn't in the living room or the kitchen. He found her in the bedroom, a tangled mass of sweat and delirium.

It was worse than he'd feared.

She was fully clothed, her hair matted on the pillow and her face deep crimson. The brown sludge oozing out of her thigh was the reason. The necro had been right – she'd tangled with a Three. They loved to hook their prey, drag them in so they could gnaw on them. Their claws were lethal.

Huge sweat rings soaked her T-shirt. Her eyes were closed and she moaned with each breath. The sweet, cloying smell of infection clouded the room. But it was her leg that made Beck nauseous, swollen twice its usual size. He knew all about that. His first Three had clawed him. He'd got sick, but not this bad. Paul had made sure of that.

The super took one look at the feverish body and fled.

Forsaken

Beck threw his jacket in the corner and flung open the rusty window to gain some fresh air. He gulped it in to keep from throwing up. He knew what the sweet smell meant – she was rotting from the inside out.

He heard someone call his name. 'Back here!' he said.

Carmela paused in the doorway. 'Den?' Her eyes went from him to Riley. 'Oh, no.'

'Yeah, big time,' Beck said.

Carmela paused to hit the light switch by the door, then hefted an orange suitcase on to the end of the bed. Flipping it open she tossed out medical supplies like a squirrel unearthing acorns. Bandages, scissors, empty binbags, IV solution and tubing all fell in a disorganized heap on the covers.

'The Holy Water I have is a few days old. We need fresher than that,' she said.

'Harrison's on his way,' Beck replied. He grabbed a pair of surgical scissors and applied the business end to the left blue jean leg, trying to keep his cool. He'd treated soldiers on the battlefield. You worked on what would kill them first. In this case, it was the poison in Riley's system. But this wasn't some young private from Ohio. This was Paul's daughter, the little girl who used to follow him around like a heartsick puppy.

'Hey, don't be stupid,' Carmela said. She tossed him a pair of latex gloves. 'You don't want that crap in your system. All it takes is a paper cut.'

'Thanks.' Why had he forgotten that? His hands shook as he tugged on the gloves, making the job twice as hard.

Get your head in the game! It was Paul's voice and it had

the desired effect. He bent down and began to work on the denim. The jeans leg came free, leaving only an inch or so for modesty at the top. He examined the thigh – six individual claw marks, all of them swollen and draining brown pus.

'Now that is seriously gross,' the doc said. She gently placed an electronic thermometer in Riley's ear and then whistled the moment the numbers appeared on the digital readout. 'A hundred and four point three. I'd expect a hundred and three, tops. Something else is going on.'

Carmela took hold of Riley's ankle, carefully lifting the leg. The girl moaned in response. 'Lay down a plastic barrier, then a bunch of those disposable towels. By the time we get done this place is going to look like an oil slick.'

Beck did as he was told, trying not to wince every time Riley moaned.

'What happened?' the doc asked.

'She went trappin' on her own.'

'Why the hell didn't she treat it?'

He had no answer.

'Beck?' They turned to find Father Harrison in the doorway. He was in his usual black suit and clerical collar, a large backpack in hand.

'Father,' Beck said. 'Thanks for comin' so quickly.'

He could tell the moment the priest saw Riley – Harrison's face sobered and he made the sign of the cross. 'How much do you need?' the priest asked.

'At least a half gallon to start with,' Carmela replied, her back to him.

It took three attempts before the doctor found a decent vein in Riley's right arm. Once the IV was secured, she flipped it wide open, then applied a snug bandage. 'Maybe that'll keep her from tearing the thing out. This is going to get rough.'

'Yeah.' The fresher the Holy Water, the more it hurt when it came in contact with anything demonic. The treatment was going to rip the girl apart.

Carmela studied him. 'I know what you're thinking. Trust me, it beats being dead.'

'Maybe that's what she wanted,' he replied.

'Ugly way to go.'

Beck caught her tone of voice. 'You don't think she'll make it, do ya?'

'Not sure. The one thing she's got going for her is her age.'

'And God,' Father Harrison added from his position near the door. He offered up two quart jugs of Holy Water.

'Him too,' Carmela replied. She took the jugs from Harrison and then handed him a pair of gloves. At the priest's quizzical look, she explained, 'Hold down her legs. You try to keep her on the bed, Den. I'll do the honours.'

As he bent over to pin Riley's shoulders down, Beck whispered in her ear, 'Sorry, girl. This is gonna hurt like a son of a bitch.'

Father Harrison closed his eyes and began to pray, his steady voice filling the room with hope. Beck wondered if it would be enough. He heard the doctor mumble something as she spread wide the first claw mark. The priest changed tone, praying louder now. Beck swallowed hard as the sacred liquid sank inside the wound.

The reaction was immediate. Riley's shriek nearly deafened him as she shot straight up off the mattress. He forced her down as she screamed and cried, her fingernails digging into the flesh on both his arms. He winced at the rush of pain as she found his healing wounds. No matter how bad it hurt, it was nothing compared to what she was feeling.

Come on, girl, pass out, will ya?

But she didn't and continued to tear at him. Carmela moved to the next wound, then the next. The Holy Water bubbled and hissed, sending up a thick vapour that hovered in the air for a moment then evaporated.

Father Harrison continued to pray, his face as white as his collar.

'No! No!' Riley screamed. As she twisted and cried, Beck knew how it felt – like someone was burning her bones from the inside out.

'There's the problem,' Carmela said, sounding relieved. 'A broken claw. No wonder she's like this.' The doc plucked a set of forceps from the bag and turned her attention to the wound.

As the doc removed the hooked claw, Riley painted the room in an ear-splitting scream. Then the darkness pulled her under.

His muscles aching from the effort, Beck slumped against the wall, his stomach tumbling. He swallowed repeatedly to keep from heaving. Riley had looked right at him, cursing him. She would never forgive him.

'Sweet Jesus,' he whispered.

'Yeah,' Carmela muttered.

Father Harrison slowly made the sign of the cross and finished his prayer.

'Hands of God and all that?' Carmela asked, regrouping with that particular resilience that doctors seemed to possess.

'Always is,' the priest replied. His forehead remained furrowed. 'Do you need more Holy Water?'

'I think we've got enough. At least the next time it won't burn so bad.'

Stripping off his gloves and throwing them on the bed, Beck crossed to the window and sucked in deep gulps of air to clear his head. When he turned round Carmela was sitting on the wooden chair near the bed, her mouth a grim line.

'Tell me that was worth it,' Beck said.

She arched an eyebrow. 'Too soon to tell.'

Someone pounded on the apartment door and the priest headed in that direction. Words were exchanged and then Father Harrison reappeared.

'Tenants from downstairs. They were upset that we woke them up. I reassured them that we'd be quiet from now on.'

Beck snorted. He turned and stared out of the window for a long time, listening to the whimpers coming from the bed behind him.

What if she dies? The very thought felt like ice in his veins.

'Den?'

'Huh?' He found Carmela packing her bag. The bed was clean and she had a binbag on the floor by the door. 'You're leavin'?' he asked, feeling an uncharacteristic panic.

'Only for a few hours. I've got some other folks to check on.'

When he didn't reply, Carmela cocked her head. 'You OK?'

He waved her off. No way could he admit what he was feeling at that moment.

'You know how to change the IV, so I can skip that lecture,' Carmela said. 'I bandaged her hand. Looks like she sliced it on something. It should heal just fine.'

'I didn't even see that,' he admitted.

'Easy to miss with the thigh being as bad as it is. I've put one litre of fluid through her and I've set the rate at one-fifty an hour.' She scratched her chin. 'I'll file the tax paperwork for the Holy Water.'

'Yeah, can't have the city not get their tax money,' Beck replied bitterly.

'I'll be here at noon and we'll do it all over again.'

'Noon. OK.' He could make it until then. 'Harrison still here?'

'Gone. He's got Mass this morning so he had to scoot.'

Carmela zipped the suitcase closed, watching him more closely than he liked.

'Thanks. I owe ya,' he said.

The doctor nodded. 'You do.' She glanced over at Riley. 'If the Holy Water works, she'll live. If not . . .'

When Beck heard the apartment door thud closed, he collapsed into a chair near the bed. His eyes shut immediately, the stress and exhaustion pulling him down towards the oblivion he needed.

Riley called out for her dad. Then her mother. It tore his heart to hear her like that. He took her sweaty hand, holding it as gently as possible.

'Sorry, girl, they're gone.'

All ya got is me.

Chapter Eighteen

Riley awoke in semi-darkness. She wasn't boiling hot now. That was good. Her mind felt hazy from the fever and all her muscles ached like she'd run a marathon. It took a while to realize she was in her own bed. There was a creak of wood – someone was sitting in the chair, reading by the light of a dim lamp.

'Dad?'

'No, honey, it's Carmela.'

'Carmela?' Her brain wasn't cooperating. It felt like it was full of week-old pudding.

When she didn't reply, the woman added, 'The Guild's doctor?'

'Oh, yeah, sorry,' Riley said, trying to sit up. 'Where's my dad?'

The doctor didn't answer, but Riley's memory did, slitting through the fog with frightening clarity.

Dad's gone. The tears wouldn't come. *Why didn't I die? I'd have been OK with that.*

More bad memories trooped in like an avenging army – she'd caught a demon and lost it, but not before it had ripped her to shreds. Riley tried shifting her left leg, but she couldn't feel it. Maybe they'd sliced it off. They'd probably give her one of those high-tech titanium legs, like some of the soldiers used.

I'll never find shoes to fit.

'My leg, is it—'

'It's still here. The Holy Water makes it numb. Trust me, it's for the best.' A pause. 'Why didn't you treat your wounds, Riley?'

'I did. It hardly hurt at all. When you guys did it . . .' She shuddered.

'You must have used older Holy Water. Father Harrison was here, so ours was really stout.'

They called in a priest? That was sobering. Riley pulled herself up again. It was hard to move when her leg acted like it wasn't there.

'Here.' Carmela handed her a glass of clear soda and she took a lengthy sip. The cold fluid felt good going down and rinsed away the yucky film in her throat.

'So what happened?' the doc asked as she settled on the edge of the bed. Her hair was in a bun at the back of her head and she was wearing a light orange shirt and blue jeans.

Riley didn't think a lecture was in the works, so she laid it all out. 'I caught a Three all by myself and it, like, got me. Then they took it away from me.'

'They?' Carmela asked, brows furrowed.

'A couple of guys. I thought they were trappers at first, but they weren't.'

'They stole your demon?' There was shock in the woman's voice.

'Yeah. I told them I was with Beck, but they didn't believe me. They wanted . . .' She bit her lip at the memory of the pair of them leering at her.

'Come on, tell me,' Carmela urged. 'Did they hurt you?'

Riley shook her head. 'No. They wanted to party.' She straightened the sheet on her lap. 'I had no choice. I had to leave the Three behind or they would have . . .'

The doctor lightly touched her arm. 'Got it. What did they look like?'

Riley gave her the descriptions, including that one of them was named Dodger.

'I'll tell Den.'

Riley frowned. *Why does everyone think Beck's my baby-sitter?*

'I don't need his help,' she snapped. 'I caught the demon, didn't I?'

Carmela frowned back. 'Not asking for help bought you six claw marks in your leg. Den will handle it. He'll make sure they learn some respect.'

'Why would he even care?' Riley asked. 'He doesn't owe me anything.'

Carmela's frown faded. She leaned closer, pensive.

'Den never had a father. The closest man to fill that role was your dad. I think he sees you as his little sis and he's not going to let anyone jack with you.'

'He acts like he knows everything.'

Carmela chuckled. 'Honey, that's what all guys are like. You should know that by now.'

Riley managed a weak smile, causing her lips to crack. 'How mad is he?'

'In. Can. Descent. Prepare to have your butt chewed. Major league. You scared the hell out of him. I've never seen him that worried.'

'If you say so.'

The doc wasn't reading him right. Beck believed the world should do whatever he said, just because he said it. He was only upset because Riley wasn't playing his game.

Carmela took the glass to the kitchen, refilled it and returned. Riley sucked down half of it in one long gulp.

'So, you got a boyfriend?' the doctor asked, propping her feet on the bed. Then she grinned. 'Enquiring minds want to know.'

Peter came to mind. 'Just a friend who's a boy.' *But then there's Simon.* Riley couldn't hide the smile.

'I know that look. You have your eye on someone. Good for you.'

Riley wasn't so sure. 'I don't think it'll go anywhere. He's Harper's apprentice.'

'Simon Adler?' the doc guessed. Riley nodded. 'Cute. You've got good taste.'

'He's way tightly wrapped,' Riley admitted.

'Well, you won't have to worry he'll paw all over you, that's for sure. Some of those guys . . .' Carmela shook her head in disgust.

Riley's bladder kicked in, sending an urgent message to her brain. 'Um, can I get up and pee and take a shower?

I smell,' she said, wrinkling her nose.

'Yes on the toilet, no on the shower.' Carmela rose. 'That leg's going to feel like dead wood and I don't want your IV to get screwed up. You can wash at the sink if you want, sitting in a chair.'

'How soon will it be out?' Riley quizzed, peering at the clear tubing in her arm.

'Tomorrow morning. The wounds look tons better.'

'Can I see it?'

Carmela reached over to uncover Riley's leg. 'You ready?'

'Is it really gross?' she asked, scrunching her face.

'Sorta. Not as bad as two days ago.'

'Two days?' Riley gasped. 'I've been sick that long?'

Carmela nodded. She pulled off the gauze. 'Ta da!'

Riley gasped again. It looked like a moonscape. The claw marks were encircled by red, puffy skin, but at least there was no brown gunk now.

'No shorts in my future.'

'Hey, I'd show off those scars. How many girls can say they caught a demon?'

'But I didn't get to keep him,' Riley complained.

'That's not the point – you *caught* a Three. That takes chutzpah. Next time have Den waiting in the wings. He'll teach those thieves some manners.'

That sounded like a plan, despite the fact it involved Beck. She could only imagine what Backwoods Boy and his steel pipe could do to Dodger and his fat buddy.

'It's healing so fast,' she said, peering down at the slices.

'The Holy Water does that. Doesn't do much for regular wounds, but get chewed up by a fiend and it's the treatment of choice.' Carmela looked around the room as if searching for something. 'There was a claw in one of them. I took it out. It's here somewhere.'

Ewww . . .

Riley pondered on that as she hopped her way into the bathroom, Carmela holding onto her arm. When she saw herself in the mirror she moaned.

'Medusa hair. That's so gross.'

'But curable.'

Riley pushed a greasy lock out of her face. Then a horrible thought hit her.

'Simon didn't see me like this, did he? I mean, he didn't come over and—'

Carmela's musical laugh filled the small room. 'I wouldn't do that to you. Now hit the can and let's get you cleaned up. You're going to run out of steam really quickly.'

Riley hated to tell her – she already had.

By morning, the IV was out and Riley had experienced a long hot shower. Two, actually, though one had been plenty. The Holy Water treatments only stung now and the wounds were knitting together. Carmela had found some clean sheets in a drawer and when Riley flopped in bed after the second shower it felt like heaven.

It was late in the afternoon when she woke to find Beck parked in the chair, arms crossed over his broad chest as he glared at her like a malevolent gargoyle. He had three days' worth of beard and a powerful frown on his face.

He was clearly over being worried about her.

'Lookin' better,' he said, his drawl thicker than usual. That wasn't a good sign.

'Thanks,' she said weakly. She reluctantly sat up in bed, tucking the sheets round her waist. When he made no move to help, she knew she was in for it.

'So let me get this right,' he began. 'I blew off an entire night's trappin' cuz ya just had to get your beauty sleep.'

Riley remained mute. Experience had taught her that if you jumped in too quick, people only got madder.

'But instead of sleepin', ya decided to play trapper and take your little ass down to Five Points. Demon Central, no less.'

She bit the inside of her lip and tried not to fidget.

'And ya went down there . . . *alone*.'

Riley studied the geometric pattern on the sheets, waiting for the shouting to begin. She hated it when people shouted.

'Tell me what happened,' he barked.

Riley blinked at the demand. 'I caught a Three and—'

'No!' Beck retorted, surging to his feet. He would have paced if the room had been bigger. 'I want it from the beginnin'. Why ya went down there, all of it.'

She took a deep breath and told him the story, including the part about the two jerks who'd taken her prize. When she finished, she looked up at him. His frown was deeper now.

'They didn't touch ya. Is that right?' he asked, his voice cold steel.

'No. But they wanted to.'

'Did that scare the hell outta ya?'

Riley nodded. It still scared her when she thought about it, how things might have fallen out if that demon hadn't woken when it did.

'Well, at least ya got some sense,' he said, his voice thick with derision. 'What about the Three?'

'It moved faster than I thought it would. It clawed me so I rammed the sphere in its face.'

'You're supposed to throw 'em.'

'I did. The first one missed.'

He dropped into the chair. 'Anythin' else?'

When she didn't answer, he repeated the question with more force.

She sucked in a deep breath. 'It didn't look like I thought it would. They're supposed to be black. This one was all spotted.'

'Did it have a big white patch on its neck?' he quizzed.

'Yeah. It was way heavy and it smelt *really* bad.'

'They do, cuz of what they eat.'

She shuddered, realizing it could have been her instead of the cow guts.

'What did ya learn from this dumbass stunt?'

Here's where she was supposed to apologize, promise to be a good little girl and never do anything like this again.

Screw that.

Riley locked eyes with him. 'I learned that the Holy Water better be fresh, that I need practice throwing the spheres, and someone has to watch my back so asshats don't steal my demons.'

Beck's expression alternated between anger and something she couldn't quite comprehend. Almost like . . . pride.

'Ya lied to me and put yourself in danger. If the Three hadn't ripped ya apart, those two bastards would have. Ya gotta listen to me, girl. I've been down this road myself.'

Riley smirked. 'Those guys wanted to party with you too?'

She knew the joke was a huge mistake the moment it left her mouth. Beck's face went dark crimson, the veins popping in his neck.

'Dammit, girl, cut the crap! I owe it to your daddy to keep ya safe. I can't do that if you're jackin' with me all the time.'

His anger ignited hers. 'Guess what? You're off the hook, Beck. I'll take care of myself.'

'Like ya did with the demon?'

'I did OK for my first Three,' she protested. 'I made some mistakes, but I caught the damned thing! *Without* back-up.'

He smirked. 'Yeah, well from now on ya won't be able to do diddle in this city without a master at your side.'

'I have to trap or I can't pay my rent!'

'I'll loan ya the money.'

'No deal,' she said, shaking her head. 'You think you own me now. It'll only be worse if I take money from you.'

The muscles in his jaw twitched. 'I'm too damned tired to argue with ya, girl. I'll have somebody watch your daddy's grave. You're here until I say otherwise.' He held up two key rings. One held her car keys, the other her father's. 'I'll be keepin' these, in case ya think of joyridin' to Five Points again.'

'You can't strand me here!' she argued.

'The hell I can't,' he said, and stomped out of the room. A few seconds later the front door slammed, rattling the pictures on the living-room wall.

'You arrogant son of . . .' She pounded the pillow, but it didn't help. Why was he so mad? Did he really think she was going to let him take care of her like she was some helpless girl?

Riley slid down under the covers, pulling them over her head.

My . . . Life . . . Totally . . . Sucks.

As long as Beck stood in her way, that wasn't going to change.

Chapter Nineteen

Beck's anger began to fade about the time he wheeled his truck into Cabbagetown and made the turn towards his house. Not that he hadn't cursed Riley most of the way home.

She's just like I was at that age – all bad-ass attitude. Except with him it involved too much booze and the belief that if he didn't get his *attitude* adjusted at least a couple of times a week the world was going to end.

He'd not been able to tell her, but he was so damned proud that she'd trapped her first Three on her own. He hadn't even done that. Still, it scared the hell out of him. She wasn't thinking stuff through and that had almost got her killed.

If Harper found out about her little adventure, there would be hell to pay. The master had been jonesing to have her licence revoked and this time he might pull it off.

Might be for the best. But it wouldn't be right. The Three she'd caught was the one Paul and he'd been hunting for the better part of a week. She'd brought the thing down on her own, newbie mistakes and all.

'Damn, Riley girl, ya got stones,' he muttered, shaking his head in astonishment. Problem was this job took smarts as well. You had to think out a situation, not bulldoze your way through.

'God, now I sound like Paul,' he said. That was damned ironic.

After a shower and a quick run through McDonald's, a trip to Five Points was on his radar. Riley had mentioned seeing an old black guy on the street with a strange sort of shuffle. That was probably Ike. The old veteran might know what had really gone down the other night.

Beck had always believed that the homeless guys living around Forsyth Street were more on the ball than the politicians at the State Capitol. Ike was a good example. He was a transient, as the bigwigs liked to call them. As in they hoped Ike and his kind would move on to Birmingham or Chattanooga, anywhere as long as it wasn't Atlanta. None of that bothered the old guy. His family had been here since the Civil War. Once he'd figured out how to work the system, leaving Atlanta wasn't on the cards.

That's not exactly how the city had imagined their social experiment would work. A few years ago they'd put yellow and blue 'donation meters' around downtown so folks would feed the meters rather than whatever panhandler was pestering them. The cash was collected and was supposed to go to the shelters, but with the city short of money who knows where it ended up. Though fewer people donated now, Ike had learned he could score cash for his booze and food if he collected his cut before the city. It just took a crowbar and a little leverage.

Beck wandered up to the guy, slow and easy. It was best not to spook him since Ike had logged his time in hell during the First Gulf War and still suffered nightmares. They shared common ground in that department.

'Ike,' he said politely, setting his duffel bag on the ground.

The old black man looked over and his face broke out in a toothy smile. 'Denver, good to see you.'

Ike was whippet thin underneath the layers of grimy clothing. The clothes were mismatched, whatever he could scrounge at the local shelter, including the Steelers stocking cap. His fingers were gnarled by arthritis and he had a strange shuffle that made it seem as if he was trying to go forward and sideways at the same time.

Beck pulled the McDonald's sack from his bag. 'Figured ya might like some food.'

The smile grew toothier. 'Never turn down chow. Give me a moment, will you? Need to do some banking.'

After a look around to ensure they were alone, Ike placed a hand over the front of the donation meter. A little bit later he lowered it and waited. The hatch at the bottom of the meter sprang open and coins spilled out. He shovelled them into his pockets, tossed a few in for seed and then fished something out of the meter which he carefully placed in the opposite pocket. No crowbar needed.

Ike clicked the meter shut and grinned. 'All done.'

Beck frowned, trying to determine what had just happened.

'Figure it out?' the man teased.

Then it clicked. 'It's a demon, isn't it?'

Ike nodded. 'Found him outside the casino digging through the bins. We made a deal – he gives me the money out of the meters and I make sure he gets lots of pretty stuff for his stash.'

He fished the fiend out of his pocket. The Magpie was wearing the trademark bandanna and holding a little bag of treasure, like all Klepto-Fiends. 'I call him Norton.'

Beck studied the demon, who frowned back, recognizing a trapper when he saw one. 'Hi, Norton.'

The fiend squeaked in return, clutching his bag like Beck was going to snatch it away from him. Little Norton was a problem. Trappers were supposed to capture Hellspawn, even if they were keeping a buddy fed.

Ike scrutinized him, like he'd heard Beck's thoughts. 'You're not going take my demon away, are you?' The fiend issued a worried squeak.

Beck raised his eyes from the infernal thief, knowing what he had to do.

'Demon?' he asked. 'Where? I don't see one.'

Ike chuckled and returned a relieved Norton to his pocket. 'Thanks, man. The priest tells me I'm going to Hell for doing this.'

Beck gestured at the broken city. 'And that would be different . . . how?'

Ike guffawed. 'Let's go up the street. I like to be on holy ground as much as possible, even when I'm eating.'

Smart. The homeless learned that lesson quickly – stay on

sanctified soil or risk being taken down by a Three. That's why there were always scruffy men clustered on the steps of nearly every downtown church.

A block farther on they passed a mailbox. Ike dropped off the demon and the fiend wasted no time scrambling up the side and then diving down the mail slot. Beck could only imagine what sort of fun it would have going through all the letters and packages.

They settled on the stairs that led to the Shrine of the Immaculate Conception on Central Avenue. Beck handed over the supersized cheeseburger, the fries and the large vanilla shake. The more calories the better – Ike was as skinny as a toothpick.

'No onions. Got it right, man,' Ike said, peering under the bun. 'You always remember.'

Beck pulled out his supper, which was pretty much the same, except he went for extra cheese on the burger to up his protein intake. They ate in silence, too hungry to be chatty. It wasn't until the burgers were gone and they were closing in on the last of the shakes that Beck posed his question.

'A few nights ago a trapper got rolled by a pair of losers down here. One of them is called Dodger. Ya know these guys?'

'Yeah, I do. They hang around looking for someone on their own. Then they pick 'em off. Mostly it's the casino folks.' He chuckled. 'They're stupid, though. They hit 'em *after* they've been inside and lost all their money.'

'Have you heard anythin' about them traffickin' in demons?'

'Don't know about that, but I saw 'em with one the other night. It was in a steel bag like the kind you guys use. They were dragging it along the street, bitching and moaning how heavy it was. Man, was that thing howling up a storm.'

'Was that Sunday night?' Beck asked. Ike nodded and took a long slurp of his shake. 'Ya see a girl down here?'

'Sure did. Young thing. She was pulling a bag out of a car, acting like it was too heavy for her.'

'Did you see her later?'

'No.'

'That was Paul Blackthorne's daughter.'

Ike's expression saddened. 'Ah, man, I heard about him. Sorry. I know you were tight.'

'Yeah, we were.'

'Why'd you let her down here alone? You know what it's like,' Ike scolded, shaking a bony finger at him. 'You lost your mind?'

'I was watchin' her daddy's grave. I didn't know what she was up to.'

'She OK?' Ike asked.

Beck shrugged. 'Got clawed up, but she'll make it. Those two assholes took her demon. I wanna let them know that's not polite.'

'I can imagine how that'll go,' Ike smirked, issuing a wheezy chuckle. 'Want me to keep an eye out for 'em?'

'Sure do.' Beck rose, wadding the paper bag in his hands and giving it a twist like it was someone's neck. 'Just be careful, OK?'

'I will,' Ike said. 'She's a good-looking girl. You sweet on her?'

Beck hesitated, not sure what to say. 'She's real young.'

'You looked in a mirror today? You're not much older than her.'

'Way older up here,' Beck said, tapping his temple.

'Yeah, well, that don't count until you been *over there,*' Ike replied. 'The rest of the world don't understand.'

'God, that's the truth.' Beck fished out a twenty and handed it over. 'Thanks for your help.'

'No sweat,' Ike said, palming the bill. 'Could you drive me to the shelter? It's a long walk for my old bones.'

'Sure. I'll go get the truck,' Beck offered. As he walked down the street, Ike descended into a deep coughing fit, one that shook his thin frame like an earthquake.

That'll be me someday.

Chapter Twenty

'You trapped a what?' Peter asked, confused. Riley had called him to complain about Beck, in particular, and about losing her demon, in specific.

'A Gastro-Fiend. Look them up on the Internet,' Riley advised. She'd hopped her way out to the couch and was enjoying a leftover piece of pizza she'd found in the refrigerator. It was all vegetables, which made her think it wasn't Beck's. 'Any luck cracking the password on the disk?'

'Not yet. I've tried all the obvious ones. I'll get it. Only be a matter of time.' More keyboard noises. 'Holy crap! These Three things are wicked!'

Before Riley could respond, there was a voice in the background – Peter's mom asking why he was shouting. It was like the woman lurked outside his bedroom door. He gave her some lame excuse and then came back on the line.

'Sorry, it was the warden.'

'Did she see the demon on your computer?' Riley asked.

'No way. She doesn't like you as it is. If she thought you were hanging with things that look like Abominable Snowmen, she'd freak.'

'Too short for an Abominable. More like a really tall Tasmanian devil.'

'Does it make all those weird noises?'

Riley laughed. 'Pretty close.' *Right before it eats you.*

'So was Beck impressed?'

'Ah, not so much.' She gave him an overview of what had happened, without mentioning how close she'd come to joining her mom and dad.

There was a prolonged silence on the other end of the phone. She thought maybe he was IM-ing one of his buds but there wasn't any keyboard clicking.

'Peter?'

'Are you, like, crazy?'

'I need the money.'

More silence.

'Peter?'

'I always thought your dad would look out for you and now that he's gone it's . . . more dangerous.'

'Stop worrying. I'll apprentice with one of the master trappers and get my full licence. Then I can go after that Geo-Fiend.'

Peter's voice got all strange. 'Ah, I need to go, Riley. Let me know what the new school is like. Anyway . . . later . . . bye.'

Riley found herself listening to the dial tone. He'd never left her hanging on the phone like that, even when pestered by his mom.

'Thanks, dude. I knew I could count on you.' She clicked off the phone and dropped it on the couch next to her. When it bounced off the cushion and hit the floor, she made a gun out of her fingers and riddled it with bullets. No one understood what it was like unless they were a trapper.

Which was how her life was going to play out from now on. She'd put in her time at school until she got her diploma, but her real life was the demons. And, just like Peter, there would always be people who wouldn't understand that. Wouldn't know the thrill of trapping a Three and living to tell about it. She'd never be normal again.

If I ever was.

Leaning back on the couch Riley stared at nothing, letting her thoughts ramble. At least until the nothing moved. Sitting up, she caught sight of something small and stealthy toting a little canvas bag as it crept along the edge of a bookshelf.

The Magpie had returned. At least it looked like the same one she'd caught that night in the hallway.

'How'd you get away?' The demon just grinned and parked itself on the edge of the shelf, legs swinging back and forth. It began to unpack its bag, laying out a variety of shiny objects with studied reverence. One of them was the N key from her keyboard. Riley bet if she checked her dresser the silver earring would be long gone.

She could catch it and that would be seventy-five bucks, money she really needed. If it was that good at escaping, it'd just come back and she could earn another seventy-five bucks. She could make her rent off this one demon.

Riley rose off the couch. In a flash the fiend was gone, along with its bag. It hadn't moved that fast the other day.

'Wow. You're supersonic.' Clearly it'd decided it was going to stay. 'Just don't let anyone see you,' she advised. 'And put my N back right now!'

There was a blur towards the keyboard and then to the shelf. The key was in place and not one foul word had been uttered.

'So not a Biblio.'

Beck had barely walked inside the Tabernacle and settled at a table for the Guild meeting when Simon edged up to him.

'How is she?' the young apprentice asked, keeping his voice low. At Beck's quizzical expression, he added, 'Doctor Wilson told me what happened.'

'She's doin' better.'

'Would Riley like me to visit her?' Simon asked.

Riley might, but I'm not so sure I do. He hadn't quite worked out what he thought of Simon, especially since the guy definitely had his eyes on Paul's little girl.

Ah, what the hell.

'Yeah, go see her,' Beck replied. 'She'd appreciate talkin' to someone who doesn't piss her off.'

Simon brightened. 'I'll call her later.'

'Anyone else know about this?' Beck asked, letting his eyes trail across the other trappers in the room.

'Harper doesn't, if that's what you're asking.' Simon retreated across the open space to take his place behind the master. Harper glared and snapped at him out of habit.

Beck took a chair and went still, like a sniper in a tree.

Besides his usual bottles of beer, in his pocket was Exhibit A, the three-inch claw the doc had excavated from Riley's leg.

Just in case there's Show 'n' Tell.

The first part of the meeting was the usual stuff – Guild housekeeping as Paul had called it. Collins, the Guild's president, announced an increase in dues was in the works to cover the cost of meeting at the Tabernacle for the next year. That earned groans from the members. There were the usual complaints about trappers not filling out their paperwork properly.

'Anyone had any problems with the Holy Water?' Collins asked.

'I have,' Beck replied. 'It didn't take down a Three like it was supposed to.'

'Was the Holy Water fresh?'

'Yeah. One day old.'

'It helps if you actually hit the demon, Mile High,' one of the other trappers jested.

Beck wasn't in the mood. 'Paul hit it straight on, but it didn't matter.' The mention of the dead master's name shut down the joking immediately.

'Speaking of which,' Collins began, 'why don't you tell us what happened the night he died.'

Beck had dreaded this moment. Out of respect for his mentor, he rose. The room fell silent.

'This is hard,' he began, feeling the prickle of tears in his eyes. He blinked them away, took a long, deep breath and delivered the report in measured tones like he was in front of a superior officer. When it was over, he remained standing in case there were questions.

'Ya say the beasties were workin' tagether?' Master Stewart quizzed.

'Timin' was too good to be coincidence.'

'Bull,' Harper said, glaring over at Beck. 'He's just saying that because he screwed up and got his partner killed.'

Beck's heart began to hammer in his ears. Fists clenched, he forced himself to stay put, not vault across the room and take Harper out.

'I didn't screw up. I did every goddamn thing right and he still . . .'

Beck unclenched his fists and put his hands palm down on the table to keep from losing it.

Better tell them now.

When he looked up, all eyes were on him. 'It was the same Five that went after Paul's daughter in the library.'

Harper smirked. 'How'd you know that?'

'I asked it. The damned thing laughed at us, like we were nothin'.' He hesitated, and then let loose the final secret. 'It was the first time I ever saw Paul afraid of a demon.'

Some of the trappers shifted nervously, whispering among each other. If a Geo-Fiend could take out someone as experienced as Blackthorne, then any one of them was at risk.

Even Harper. And the old master knew it.

'Any other questions?' Silence. 'Thanks, Beck. Sorry about Paul.' A pause. 'Jackson, you're up.'

The Guild's treasurer rose. 'Got a report that someone is

selling demons illegally. You guys heard anything?'

'Fireman Jack mentioned something about it the other day,' Morton replied. He still hadn't made master because Harper refused to sign off on his application, which had made for bad blood between them.

'That asshole?' Harper huffed. 'Wouldn't trust a thing he'd say.'

'As long as he treats us fairly, I don't care what church he worships at,' Jackson shot back.

'You wouldn't.'

Beck shook his head. Harper never failed to amaze him. The man was a natural-born asshole.

Jackson cleared his throat, twice, his way of keeping his cool. 'I checked with a few of the traffickers. One of them was complaining that someone paid five hundred for a Three earlier this week. He didn't know who bought the thing and wanted to know why the Guild was allowing that.'

'We aren't,' Harper said testily. 'Any you guys trap a Three this week?'

One of the trappers raised his hand. 'I did. I sold it to Jack for three hundred.'

'Anyone else?' Seven more men raised their hands and all of them had sold the fiends for the standard fee.

'I sold two,' Beck added.

'So we're wasting our time, then,' Harper said. 'Let's move on.'

They don't know about Riley's demon. Beck weighed the situation. He might be able to bury her misadventure deep enough they'd never find out, but it wouldn't change the fact that someone was stealing demons and selling them illegally. That would eventually come back to haunt them.

Pain now. Pain later. Never a good call.

Sorry, girl, it's gonna hit the fan.

'There was another Three caught this week.'

'Who trapped it?' Collins asked.

'Paul's daughter. She took it down in Demon Central Sunday night.'

Harper broke out in a thick laugh. 'Nice one, kid.'

'I'm not jokin'. She was worried about payin' her rent so she loaded up Paul's gear and went huntin'. She took down a Three . . . *on her own.*'

'No way,' Jackson said. 'For real?'

'For real.'

'She tell you that?' Harper asked. Beck nodded. 'Then she's lying.'

Beck's muscles tensed. He moved his neck to loosen them, like a fighter does right before a bout. Harper caught the gesture and sneered at him.

'She's got six claw marks in her leg that say otherwise,' Beck retorted. 'And just in case you think *I'm* lying . . .' He raised the claw fragment in the air so the others could see it. The trapper closest to him winced. 'Doc Wilson dug this out of her thigh.'

'Claws marks don't mean she trapped the thing,' Harper protested.

'Once it hooks you, it only goes two ways: you trap it or it eats you. There's no other options,' Morton replied. He gave Harper a hard stare. 'I would expect a master to know that.'

Harper spat on the floor in disgust.

'I did some checkin',' Beck replied. 'Seems there's a couple of losers down there who like rollin' folks. Riley trapped the Three and then they showed up. They told her they could get five hundred for it.'

'You sayin' they stole her demon?' Jackson asked, astonished.

Beck nodded. 'It was easy. Young girl on her own. They figured they'd score some serious cash and have a party. She had to leave the demon behind if she didn't wanna get jumped.'

'That ain't right!' someone called out from the back of the room. 'Those two need some thumpin'.'

'Amen to that,' another voice said.

Collins looked over at Beck. 'How's the kid?'

'Healin'. And seriously pissed off.'

There were nods around the room. Beck kept the smile to himself. These guys were hardcore, with a simple view of how the world should work. Trapper Rule No. 1 – no one messed with your capture. Rule No. 2 – no one messed with a fellow trapper. Violate either of those rules and serious pain was in your future.

Jackson frowned, his face deep in thought. 'Who's buying these fiends for that kind of money? The legit traffickers know better. The world falls in on them if they deal under the table.'

'What do they do with the demons after they buy them?'

Morton asked. 'They have to go to the Church. But if the buyer's illegal, they can't do that without the paperwork.'

'We need to get a handle on this,' Collins interceded. 'Stewart, can you check in with the archbishop and find out if anything's happening on that end?'

'Aye,' the master replied.

'What about Blackthorne's brat?' Harper asked. 'She was trapping illegally. We can't let that happen.'

Stewart chuckled and rose, supported by a cane. 'Nay, we canna. Paul was one of the best damned trappers I ever knew. If his lass can pull down a Three at this stage, I'd say it'd be in the blood.'

'You willing to take that on?' Collins asked. 'She sounds damned wilful.'

'Aye, I'd be pleased ta train the lass. All she needs is a firm hand.'

Beck allowed himself to exhale. Stewart was a good man. A bit slower now that he'd gotten banged up tangling with an Archdemon, but still a lot kinder than the other choice. *And a lot less prejudiced.*

'No,' Harper barked. 'I'm senior trapper and I get my choice of apprentices. Blackthorne's brat is mine to train.'

Stewart eyed his rival. 'Ya gonna be fair with her?'

'Just as fair as she deserves,' Harper retorted. The unholy smile on his face said it all.

Simon went pale. He gave Beck a desperate look, but there was nothing they could do. Harper had seniority.

Damn. His plan had failed.

Collins gave Harper a long look. 'We'll want regular reports on her progress.'

The smirk grew wider. 'And you'll get them, trust me.'

'OK, let's move on. What's this about not telling mall security when you're trapping in a department store? You guys know the rules.'

Chapter Twenty-One

Riley heard the telltale clomp of boots in the hallway before the knocking started. It was close to eight at night. Simon wasn't due until nine, which meant this was probably Beck returning for another lecture.

'Hey, girl, ya awake?'

Riley muted the television and hopped to the door. With a groan, she flipped the locks and opened the door part way, but not enough to allow her nemesis to barge in. 'What's up?'

Beck waved a bag in front of her face. It sported the logo of the Grounds Zero. 'Brought ya one of their brownies. Thought ya liked them.'

'I do. Just don't like the delivery guy.'

'Sucks, don't it?' he said. 'So do ya let me in or do I toss this in the dumpster on the way out?'

Riley gasped at the thought of such cruelty and waved him in. Beck plopped on the couch, placing the bag on the packing box coffee table. He still looked tired, like sleep no longer held any value for him.

'New coat?' she asked. His old one had been dark brown. This one was a creamy beige and it looked good on him.

Beck nodded. 'Found it at the market. It's used, but I like

'em that way. Not as stiff, makes it easier to move.' He stared at her for a few seconds. 'Ya have any soda?'

Riley hobbled into the kitchen, retrieved the drink and then began to fume. She was the one with the gored leg. Why wasn't he getting his own drink? When she returned to the living room, she realized why. He'd set out the plastic-wrapped brownie and leaning up against it was a coloured envelope adorned with a smiley face.

He bought me a card?

She handed over the drink and then eagerly thumbed open the envelope.

Oh.

The card wasn't from Beck, but from the baristas at the coffee shop. They'd signed their names in different colours, along with more smiley faces. Simi's was in bright orange.

Riley made sure to smile anyway. 'Cool.'

'Thought ya'd like that.' He placed something next to the brownie. It was a demon decal. She'd receive one for each Three she trapped. Most trappers put them on their vehicle like fighter pilots did during the wars. Beck's truck had a lot of them. He'd joked they were what held it together.

She grinned, studying the decal. 'Way cool! Thanks!'

'Ya earned it.' He took a long drink of the soda, gave a distinct burp but no apology. A white envelope landed next to the decal. 'For your rent. Consider it a loan.'

'How much?'

'Five hundred.'

Five hundred more reasons you'll think you own me.

'Thanks,' she muttered. She'd accept the cash or sleep in the streets. No coin flip needed.

Riley peeled off the plastic that entombed the brownie. As long as she had a fix of chocolate, she could handle anything. 'Who is watching Dad tonight?'

'One of the journeymen. Don't worry, nothin' will happen.'

He seemed so sure.

'How'd the meeting go?'

Beck frowned. 'How'd ya know about that?'

'Carmela. She dropped by to make sure I hadn't gone all furry or anything.'

'Ya won't. Not till the full moon,' he said. 'I can't wait to see that.'

'I do, and you're the first one I maul.'

He didn't look worried.

'Meeting?' she nudged. Simon had hedged when she'd asked him about it on the phone, which meant she might not like the news.

Beck took another sip of soda, this time minus the burp. Slouched against the couch, he had one booted foot up on the packing box like he was watching a football game.

'Did ya hear from Simon?' he asked, changing the subject. She nodded. 'He comin' over?' She nodded again.

He fell silent, which made her wonder if he was happy with that bit of news.

'Let me help you here,' she said, reluctantly placing the brownie on her lap. 'I say, "How'd the meeting go, Beck?"

and you say "Well, Riley, it was . . ."' She gestured for him to complete the sentence.

That got her a glower. 'Not terrific. Harper was on his high horse and the Guild knows ya were out trappin' on your own.'

'You ratted me out?' *You couldn't wait to tell them, could you?*

'Yeah,' he said, but his face told her he didn't find any joy in that. 'The Guild's not happy about your stunt.'

'Surprise.' She'd be naive to assume they'd give her a round of applause.

The enticing scent of chocolate wafted into her nose. She closed her eyes and savoured the moment as a tiny moan escaped her lips.

'What is it with girls and chocolate?' Beck grumbled after another swig of soda. 'Tastes like burnt coffee to me.'

Her eyes snapped open, annoyed he'd ruined the moment. 'This from a guy who guzzles energy drinks out of recycled whiskey bottles?'

'Better than that stuff.'

This wasn't getting her anywhere. 'So what happened?'

He sighed, running a hand through his hair. It made it stick up in the front. 'You're not to trap again until you're workin' with a master. Period. The end.'

Better than she'd expected. Riley took a bite of brownie in celebration. The chocolate hit her mouth like a gooey bomb.

Heaven.

'So who's going to train me?' she asked around the confection.

Her visitor didn't answer, suddenly fascinated by the ingredients listed on the back of the soda bottle.

Stall alert. 'Harper?'

A curt nod. 'He's senior. He has the right.'

'But he hates me! He'll make sure I fail. That's not fair.'

Beck walked to the kitchen while guzzling the last of the soda. The glass bottle landed in the recycling bin with a rattle. When he returned, his right eyebrow crooked upward.

'Not fair? If ya want fair, Princess, don't be a trapper.'

Princess?

Beck paused near the door. 'If you're good, you'll survive. If not?' He shrugged like it was no big deal.

So much for sympathy. 'What about my car keys?'

'Take the damned bus. It's good for the environment.'

Then he was gone, combat boots thumping on the stairs.

Riley sighed and scratched her thigh through the denim. The wounds were torturing her in a new way – near constant itching.

'Wait a minute,' she said, a grin sprouting. There was *one* bright side to apprenticing with Bad Ass Harper – and that was his other apprentice. Simon would be training alongside her for a few months until he became a journeyman. 'Maybe this isn't as horrible as I think.'

If she could survive Harper's blistering bitchiness, she'd become the first fully licensed female trapper in Atlanta's history.

'Then I'm gonna kick your ass, Backwoods Boy.'

*

Three outfits later, Riley had finally decided what to wear. Simon had seen her post-library disaster in all her green-hued glory, but this was a chance to look good for a change. She glanced up at the clock on the nightstand – twenty more minutes before he was scheduled to arrive at her door.

'Please don't be early,' she muttered. Beck had taken up more time than she'd realized, though the brownie had given her extra energy.

Riley hopped into the bathroom and donned her make-up. At least Simon hadn't seen her in full rotting mode. There was no amount of foundation or lipgloss that could erase that image.

She scrutinized herself in the mirror. Her hair was back to normal – which meant it had a will of its own – and the pink on her cheeks had nothing to do with a fever. After another liberal dose of lotion to the demon scars in the vain hope they'd stop itching, she dressed: black trousers, red poloneck and black boots.

She fidgeted in front of the long mirror on the back of the bedroom door, adjusting the poloneck's sleeves, her hair, everything. Nothing seemed right, and she was freaking out. Simon was totally cute; there was no way he didn't have a girlfriend. She had to find a way to ask him without sounding pathetic. Then he'd say he was dating and it'd all be over.

Simon was all smiles when he appeared at her door wearing a black jacket, navy blue shirt and blue jeans. The navy went well with his white gold hair and deep blue eyes. As usual, the wooden cross was in plain sight.

For half a second Riley eyed him, soaking in the view. *Yummy.*

'You look very nice,' he said.

'Thanks. It's good not to be green any more.'

Dork! Why did I say that?

'Are you up for a hot chocolate run?'

'Yes. YES! Anything to get out of here,' she exclaimed.

Riley grabbed her bag by the door. Something landed on the floor in a rattle of metal. The two key rings. Beck had returned them and not said a thing.

The moment she locked the apartment door, Simon offered his arm. Way old-fashioned, but thoughtful, especially since her leg could go from fine to crampy in a matter of seconds.

'Too bad the elevator's broken,' he said. 'It'd be easier for you.'

He was always thinking of other people.

'I could carry you down the stairs,' he offered. 'You don't weigh that much.'

He isn't joking.

'Ah, no, that's OK. I have to get used to this. It's feeling better, honest,' she fibbed.

When Riley faltered a few steps down, he moved his hand to round her waist. Not too tight, but enough to let her know he wasn't going to let her fall. She hoped he'd leave it there.

'So what have you been doing since Beck grounded you?' he asked.

'I've tried to find Dad's manual.' Each step made the thigh

cramp, which shot a bolt of pain into her groin. 'I've gone through every drawer, bookshelf and box,' she said, trying to keep her mind off the discomfort. 'No go.'

'You try his car? Like maybe under the spare tyre?' Simon asked.

Riley gaped at him. 'How did you—'

'I saw him put it in there after one of the meetings. He made me promise not to tell you. But now, well . . .'

Now it didn't matter. 'Thanks! I'd never have thought of looking under the tyre.'

His grin widened. 'Duh! Why else would he have put it there?'

She elbowed him. 'What's happening with Harper?'

'I hear he's got a new apprentice,' Simon replied. 'A pretty one.'

'How hard is he going to be on me?'

Simon's good humour withered. 'Way hard. He'll tear you apart. He does that to all of his apprentices and it'll be worse for you because of your dad.'

'What happened between them?'

'No idea,' he said, shrugging. 'But whatever it was Harper's never forgotten it.'

'And now he has another Blackthorne to torment.'

'He's expecting you at nine in the morning. I'll give you directions.'

When they reached his car, Simon opened the door for her. She climbed in, but it proved harder than she'd expected. Finally she realized it was best to sit and then use the centre console as an anchor so she could pivot herself inside.

'Ouch, ouch, ouch,' she said, rubbing the leg to try to ease the cramp.

Simon knelt next to her, concerned. 'Anything I can do?'

'Just get me high on hot chocolate, that's all.'

His worried expression eased. 'For you, anything.'

Her friend Simi changed her hair colour more often than she did boyfriends, which was saying something. Tonight her locks were coal black with brilliant purple highlights. On anyone else it would have looked silly, but Simi's exotic face allowed her to do almost anything and look great. It came with her unique ancestry: a mash-up of Lebanese, Chinese, Irish and Native American.

'Hey, Blackthorne!' the barista called out. Heads turned and Riley inwardly groaned. The coffee shop wasn't that busy, but she much preferred to be anonymous right now. The family name had been in the papers too much recently.

'I escaped!' she replied, holding her hands up in triumph.

'You did. I'm impressed. You get the card?'

'Yes,' Riley said. 'Thanks!'

'It was the trapper's idea. He brought it in and had us sign it,' Simi admitted.

Beck bought the card. Why didn't he say that?

'So is he, like, dating or anything? He's way hot,' Simi remarked.

Beck hot? Well, maybe a little. His serious case of attitude got in the way of his hotness every time. In lieu of an answer, she gestured towards Simon.

'This guy has offered to buy me all the hot chocolate I can drink,' she said, beaming up at her escort.

'Niiice,' Simi said, raising a black eyebrow. She didn't mean the *all the hot chocolate* part either. 'You want the same?' Her eyes remained on Simon.

'Yes, thank you,' he replied.

'Real nice,' she said, then went to work creating the drinks. 'How's your leg doing?'

'Better,' Riley replied. 'Itches a lot. Feels like I've been bitten by a five-hundred-pound mosquito.'

Simi gave a sympathetic nod. 'The trapper said you'd gone after a demon on your own. Is that right?'

Riley nodded. 'Wasn't the smartest thing I've done.' She heard a grunt of agreement from Simon.

Simi's eyes lit up. Since they'd been talking about demons, Riley knew what was coming.

'No, I did not watch *Demonland* last night,' Riley said, hoping to short-circuit the subject. It never worked, but she still tried.

'Oh, man, it was awesome,' Simi proclaimed. 'Blaze took out a Winnebago full of demons with a Walmart shopping cart.'

Any television producer who would put Walmart, demons and an RV in the same episode was just asking for trouble, but then Hollywood's idea of the Vatican's demon hunters was more flash than reality.

'Was Blaze wearing those ridiculous heels again?' Riley

grumbled, leaning against the counter for support.

'Yup. And that skin-tight leather outfit you hate, the one that barely covers her butt,' Simi replied. 'It was a totally kick-ass episode.'

'But the demon hunters don't admit women,' Simon said, perplexed.

Simi gave him a look like he'd just flattened her favourite puppy.

'You've never watched the show, have you?'

Simon shook his head. Riley's estimation of him grew tenfold.

'Then you can't judge it,' the barista said, returning with the hot chocolate. 'You have to admit last season's final episode was truly epic.'

Simon gave Riley a raised eyebrow.

'One of the hunter guys destroy a mega demon on top of St Peter's Basilica,' Riley explained.

'St Peter's is holy ground,' Simon began, 'so no demon can—'

'Are you, like, an authority or something?' Simi retorted.

Riley left them to it, limping her way to the closest booth. She slid in, happy to let her thigh rest. It was doing its dull burn thing now.

Her eyes tracked to *her* booth along the far wall, the one where she and her dad had always sat. A familiar shard of guilt drove itself in a little deeper. How could she be out with Simon when she should be watching over the grave? Not that Beck would let her until her leg healed, but it still felt selfish.

'No, Dad would want me here,' she said resolutely. *He liked Simon.*

Her escort delivered the hot chocolate.

'Who won?' Riley asked, angling her head towards the barista.

'It was a draw. Either that or coffee stirrers at twenty paces.'

For the next few minutes they drank in silence. Riley spent that time savouring the exquisite goodness of the drink and screwing up her courage to ask The Question.

'Ah, thanks,' she said. 'This is really good.'

'There's more if you want some.'

Simon didn't seem like he wanted to be somewhere else and he wasn't checking his phone every few minutes as if he was expecting a call.

Just ask him.

'Are you dating someone?' she blurted. *Oh, that was smooth.*

His forehead crinkled in amusement. 'Maybe.'

'Oh.' She sighed. *Of course he's dating, you idiot. He's way too cool to be on his own.*

'I've just started seeing someone,' he said.

That made it even worse.

Simon touched her hand with his fingers. 'There's this really nice girl. She's got the most amazing blue eyes and an incredibly sharp mind.'

'Oh.' *So not me.*

'And we've got something in common. We both trap demons.'

It took her a second to realize he was talking about her.

'Me?' she asked. He nodded. *Me!* 'Then it's all good.' *Really good.* She gifted him with a smile.

'But we can't let Harper know we're dating or he'll make it worse for you.' He gnawed on his lip for a moment. 'Will you promise me something?'

'What?' she asked, caught off guard by his serious expression.

'Promise you won't go hunting on your own again, at least not until you're a journeyman.'

What? Where was this coming from?

She pulled her hand away. 'I can't make that promise, Simon.'

'Riley, you're real brave, but you're still a—'

'Girl?' she asked, her temper rising.

'Apprentice,' he replied, an edge to his voice.

'Who happens to be a girl,' she pushed back. That was always the bottom line with these guys. She wasn't one of them.

'No!' he said emphatically. 'Not everything is about gender. This is about you being safe.'

Riley's eyes bored holes into her cup. She really liked this guy, and yet here he was trying to box her in, just like Beck.

'Do you think I'm crazy wanting to be a trapper?' she demanded.

Simon frowned. 'Yes.' When she opened her mouth to protest, he raised his hand to cut her off. 'I understand why you could want this so badly. I know I do, even if it makes no sense.'

He's not playing power games. He really cares.

The realization left her breathless. Simon took her hand again and squeezed it, rubbing his thumb over her palm in a gentle motion. 'Just be careful, will you? That's all I ask.' His voice was so gentle.

'Only if you promise the same.'

'Deal.'

They held hands for another minute or so and then he rose to fetch more hot chocolate. After he placed the order, he looked over at her and smiled. The rest of the room faded to grey – there was only him, his brilliant blue eyes and that amazing hair.

Something had changed between them. Whatever it was, it felt right.

Chapter Twenty-Two

It took Riley a while to decipher the peeling sign on the concrete building.

'Ming and Sons Auto Repair.'

The sign boasted Ming could fix transmissions, radiators and CV boots. Now the building housed the most senior trapper in Atlanta, and the one with the shortest temper.

At least it's close to the cemetery. Real close, like down Memorial Drive. Now that she went to school in Midtown she'd have to drive through Atlanta to class, put in her three hours, then drive all the way down here to spend the night watching over her dad.

She yawned at the thought. *Only five more nights.* Despite her tummy being full of luscious hot chocolate and the toasty inner glow Simon had kindled, Riley hadn't slept well. Too worried what today would bring.

Her cellphone began chirping. It was Peter.

At least he's talking to me again.

'Hey, dude,' she said, making sure not to let the relief show in her voice.

'I cracked it!' he crowed.

It took her a moment to realize he was talking about the computer disk.

'So what was the password?'

'Eleven nineteen eighteen sixty-three.'

'Huh?'

'The date of the Gettysburg Address,' he replied proudly.

'Makes sense. Dad wrote his thesis about it.'

She heard a groan. 'You couldn't have told me that up front and saved me hours of hacking?'

'Don't give me that. You loved every minute of it.'

She knew he was grinning. 'Busted,' he said. 'I'm still digging through the files. From what I can tell, it's research about Holy Water. History, folklore, all of it. It'll take a while to get through all this.'

'I wonder what he was up to,' Riley admitted.

'We'll find out. So what's your day like?'

'I'm standing outside my new master's place. Not impressed.'

'Well, have at it. Call me when you get a chance.'

'Later, Peter.'

She put away the phone and trudged across the gravel parking lot to the metal door located at the front of the building. The door was battered and scratched and definitely needed a paint job. She raised her hand to knock, but the door opened before she could do the honours.

It was Simon and he was frowning. 'Riley.'

'Hi. How are you?' she asked, remembering how pleasant last night had been.

'Good,' he said, but it didn't sound that way. 'Harper's inside. Be careful.'

Riley nodded and mustered her game smile. 'It helps that you're here.'

He shook his head. 'It'll only make it worse, for *both* of us.' He pushed past her and headed towards his beat-up silver Dodge.

OhhK.

After he'd pulled away, she had no further reason to stall. The moment she stepped inside the smell hit her. Engine oil. Old tyres. And something else. Raw sulphur.

Demon.

The building was laid out like any garage – twin double doors led to service bays. All the metal lifts were gone and the exposed ceiling rafters sported wires and ropes that ran over the beams like spaghetti. In one corner was a huge pile of plastic jugs and bottles, the kind used for Holy Water. Apparently, Harper's place was some kind of recycling location.

One half of the building had been sectioned off. To her right along the wall were five heavy-duty steel cages, only one of which was occupied. Unlike the demon she'd tangled with, this Three was all black, like they were supposed to be. It slavered and slobbered, reminding her of an overly hairy dog, except this one's long claws raked against the sides of the reinforced steel enclosure like it was sharpening them.

'Blackthorne's daughter,' it growled.

Before she had a chance to reply, a voice bellowed, 'Get the hell in here, girl!'

Forsaken

With a pleading look heavenward, Riley made the journey into what must have been the shop's office. It was small, and crowded with furniture. On one side of the room was an old wooden desk with an equally ancient desk chair. On the other, Harper was sprawled in a tattered dark blue recliner that had been new before computers were invented. His eyes were red and his face unshaven, probably because of the half-empty bottle of Jack Daniel's at his elbow. His shirt was clean but wrinkled, and his jeans had black stains on them. Behind him was a wooden door that led into the rear of the building. Through it she could see an unmade bed and what looked like a kitchenette. Dirty dishes were piled in the sink.

He lives here? She'd expected he had an apartment or a house, like the other trappers.

Riley had never really paid much attention to Master Harper, mostly because he was always busy hating her dad. Now she'd be with him for the next nine months. *Less if he wants to get rid of me.*

'Mr Harper,' she said. No reason to piss him off right off the bat.

'Brat,' he replied, daring her to challenge him. He flicked a lighter on the end of a cheap cigar.

'I'm Riley, sir.'

'No, you're Brat.' Smoke coursed out of his mouth, revealing surprisingly decent teeth.

Establishing the pecking order. Maybe that was as far as it'd go.

'All my apprentices need to know one thing – my word is

law. You screw up and you're gone and no other master in this country will touch you. Got it?'

Annoy you and I'm gone. 'Yes, sir.'

'Just because you're Blackthorne's girl doesn't mean you're going to get any slack. I don't trust you as far as I can spit you, got it?'

'Yes, sir.'

'It's clear to me Blackthorne was doing a piss poor job of training you, so we're gonna start over from the beginning.' He pointed to a battered metal bucket and a scrubbing brush in a corner. 'The floor under the cages needs cleaning. Get to it.'

'Yes, sir.' She looked at the implements, remembering the sizeable piles of demon crap. 'Do you have a shovel and some gloves?'

He took a pull on his bottle. 'Yeah, I do.'

She waited, but he didn't move, didn't tell her where to find them. Then it dawned on her – she wasn't going to be using them.

'You can shovel the crap like I did when I started . . . with your hands. Put it out back. It kills the roaches.'

She opened her mouth to protest, then jammed it shut. He was waiting for her to refuse – she could see it in his bloodshot eyes.

'Out back. Got it.'

As the morning progressed, Riley began to learn a lot about demon scat. It stank like brimstone and whatever the thing had eaten recently, which was just about everything. The crap stained concrete and it stung her skin like scalding water if it was fresh.

She'd started on the furthest cage from the occupied one, kicking at the mound of dried excrement with the toe of her tennis shoe. Mistake. The kicking had no effect on the mound.

Leverage. That's what I need.

Digging around the back of the building revealed a collection of junk and a fairly decent stockpile of discarded metal that included bent hubcaps and broken manhole covers. Since the yard was fenced and secured with a padlock, it made Riley wonder if her new overlord traded in the stuff.

More digging unearthed a tyre iron and a hammer with a cracked handle.

Better than nothing.

After prising, pounding and tugging until her arms ached, the mound of crap broke up chunk by chunk. The outside might have been like concrete. The inside wasn't.

'Oh, gross,' she muttered, her stomach churning as the smell and heat reached her nose. Had her dad started out like this?

Another scrounge around the warehouse turned up a battered garbage-can lid, but nothing to scoop with. That made her think Harper had hidden anything she might be able to use.

Hands or nothing. Before she got them any dirtier, she rolled up her sleeves. At least the wound on her palm had closed and she no longer needed a bandage.

Riley closed her eyes and started scooping the mess on to the lid, trying to imagine it was anything but what it was. Tears formed as liquid heat cooked her fingers, palms, even her nails. Her hands quickly turned an abnormal shade of purple red, even though the demon crap was solid black. She kept shovelling until the mound was gone, then stood. Her thigh cramped, no matter what she did.

This wasn't demon trapping. This was scut work, some form of hazing apprentices had to endure.

No way I'm wimping out.

Riley looked down the line of cages – four more, one of which held its own peril. The demon watched her with the intensity of a snake eyeing an injured bird.

It took most of the morning to make it to the occupied cage. Midway through, Harper stood at the door to his office, watching her, a bottle of JD in hand.

'Not what you thought, huh?' he called out, his voice rough with liquor and cigars.

If she said 'no', he'd gloat. If she said 'yes', he'd dream up some other torment. Riley clamped her mouth shut. It was either that or she'd sling some of this stuff in his direction and she'd be an ex-apprentice in a heartbeat. Once she was out of the Guild, their lawyer would probably bill her for all those legal fees.

Shut up and scoop.

'Bet your dad never had to do that,' Harper taunted. She heaved a sigh of relief when he returned to his office. The recliner creaked under his weight as the television began to drone sports scores.

Doesn't he ever go out and trap anything?

It was nearing noon when she reached the occupied cage. The fiend had eyed her all morning, making those slobbery noises and licking its ebony lips. Knowing its time had come, it called out her name again.

'Yeah, that's me. So who are you, fur bag?'

It seemed surprised, then answered with some long-ass name that made no sense unless you were one of Lucifer's own. Like Argabettafingle something or other.

'Sorry I asked.' She eyed it, testing the weight of the tyre iron in her hand. The only way to clean under the cage was to get within range of those claws.

'Don't even think about it.'

It snarled and swiped a paw in her direction. A second later it howled, that paw held up to its mouth, red eyes blazing.

She waved the tyre iron at it. 'You were warned.'

Bending over, she began to scoop the dung out from under the cage. It was fresh and burned like acid, making her eyes and nose flood like a toddler with a head cold. A claw snicked through her hair cutting off a few strands which floated to the ground, embedding themselves in the pile.

'Hey, stop that!' Pissed, she tossed a handful of the steaming manure at the thing. The stuff stuck in its fur and the demon howled again, batting at it like it hurt.

Maybe it does.

'Don't like that, do you? You keep messing with me,' she said, shaking a mucky finger, 'and I'll bury you in it. Got it?'

The demon hissed and backed into the corner of the steel cage.

'That's better.'

Riley finished digging out the mound under the cage and added the crap to the heap behind the shop. Harper was right: there were dead roaches in a four-foot radius of the pile.

'If the pest control dudes could figure out how to use this stuff, they'd make a fortune.'

Riley swore she could feel the flesh melting off her bones, so she fled to the bathroom. Hitting the light switch with her elbow, she prepared herself for the worst a guy bathroom had to offer. It was like there was an unwritten code that they had to be disgusting.

To her relief this one was better than most, even though the toilet seat was up. The sink was clean, but by the time she'd finished washing her hands and arms with the dish-washing soap she'd found on the top of the toilet tank it wasn't any more. Now her hands smelled lemony fresh, but they still burned. It took another few minutes to return the sink to its previous state. No way was she going to let the guys claim she'd messed up their bathroom.

That left hosing down the floor under the cages. As she worked, the demon jammed its face up against the bars trying to reach the spray. Did the things drink water? Did Hell even have water?

She turned down the pressure and aimed the stream so the fiend could reach it. It drank greedily. Then it issued a lengthy and profound burp.

Riley shook her head. 'You and Beck. Separated at birth.'

There was a chuckle and she turned to find Simon watching from a respectful distance. For half a second, she thought of wetting him down just for the smirk on his face.

'Looks good,' he said encouragingly.

'If you say so.'

He angled his head towards the outside door. 'Got something for you.' She looked towards the office, on the alert for Harper. 'Passed out,' Simon mouthed.

Stepping into the sunlight, Riley gasped when she saw her arms. Blotches of bright red and dark purple covered her skin, making her resemble a plague victim. Her nails were black. Simi would love them.

'No blisters,' Simon observed. 'That's good news.' He retrieved something off the car seat, broke the seal and offered it to her.

It was a quart of whole milk.

Riley blinked at him. 'Ah . . . thanks. I'm thirsty.' Actually she was.

'It's for your arms. The fat in it'll cut the sting. Jackson told me about it when Harper pulled that stunt on me.' He gestured for her to hold out her hands and then did the honours.

It looked stupid, all that white liquid splashing off her and coating the gravel. But it worked. The burning sensation damped down considerably.

'You still may end up with some blisters, but not as bad as if you hadn't treated it.' He handed her the bottle. 'Drink the rest. Maybe it will work from the inside out.'

She gulped down the remainder of the moo juice. 'Good!'

'Just like in the commercials.' He executed a cautious look towards the warehouse. 'Don't tell Harper I did this. He'll be pissed.'

Pissed because you were nice to me? That sucks. 'Why is he such an idiot?'

'Don't know.' He took the empty container and put it in the car. 'You best get in there before he wakes up.'

As he turned away, she touched his arm. 'Thanks, Simon.'

'Watch yourself, OK?' he said, his brow furrowed in worry.

'You too.'

When she returned to the office, Harper was still asleep in his chair, his mouth open, snoring. The whiskey bottle was empty and lay discarded near the rubbish bin. Riley placed the bucket and scrubbing brush in the corner, trying not to make any noise. When he didn't stir, she hurried out into the office. As she saw it, the smelly demon was better company than her new master.

Chapter Twenty-Three

'Déjà vu,' Riley grumbled, pulling into the parking lot near the defunct Starbucks. She'd been here a few years ago on a date when the coffee shop was still open for business. The guy behind the counter had been seriously adorable. Model-level cute. She'd mentioned that and Allan, her then boyfriend, hadn't taken it well. That's when she'd learned that male egos and fruit had a lot in common – both bruised easily.

The moment she stepped outside the car she saw the other kids. There were three distinct groups plus a few stragglers. She'd probably end up being one of those.

Wish Peter was here. He was the one constant in her life, the friend who'd helped her get through the last four school changes. He viewed change as an opportunity. Riley only saw it as a hassle.

Why bother? In a few months the Powers That Be would move all the kids around to new locations, like throwing a deck of cards in the air. The educational types had fancy names for the reshuffling, but in the end it was the students who got the worst of it. Why become friends with someone who'd be gone in a couple of months' time? If Riley didn't play the game, the kids would think she was stuck up or weird or both. But did she really care?

'Nope. I'm sitting this one out,' she announced. With all that had happened in her life, it wasn't worth the effort.

The closest group was all girls about her age. They dressed nicer than she did, but couldn't be from rich families or they wouldn't be going to school in a defunct coffee shop. As she moved closer to the entrance, she studied the pack. The girl in the centre, a tall, stick-thin brunette with large brown eyes and full lips, was surrounded by five others who gazed up at her like androids waiting for instructions. They were all wearing the same colour.

Riley suspected they were not destined to be best buds.

The girl pointed at Riley's car. 'Is that yours?'

Didn't I just get out of the thing? 'No, I stole it on the way over here. Mine's a red convertible.'

One of the other girls giggled but shut down immediately when The Self-Proclaimed Centre of the Universe shot her a dirty look.

'So what's your name?' the girl asked.

'Riley. Yours?'

'Brandy.'

Of course.

'You're new here,' Brandy observed. 'Where'd you go to school before?'

'A grocery store over on Moreland.'

'Sounds gross.'

'It was.'

Before Brandy could throw more questions her way, the

double doors swung open and an authority figure waved them inside. According to Riley's paperwork that would be Mrs Haggerty. It wouldn't be hard to guess what the kids called her behind her back.

Mrs Haggerty looked fifty with silver streaks at her temples. Her hair was cut short at the collar and she dressed in layers. An angel pin decorated the lapel of her cloth coat.

Riley queued up and the moment she crossed over the threshold, she took a deep breath. *Coffee.* The place would always smell like that, even though it had been some time since the last bean had been roasted.

Better than mouldy cheese.

The students clustered towards the front of the store near the big windows, still in their groups. As they settled into their seats, Riley did a quick look around. The counter was gone, as were all of the displays. The benches along the rear wall were still there and all the original tables were still in place, though they looked way worse than she remembered. More tables had been added and lined up in rows facing the front windows. Riley picked one of the smaller ones. The way the thing wobbled told her why no one wanted to sit there. Riley bent over and jammed the strap of her bag under one of the legs and the table became pretty stable. The top wasn't something she could fix – it was covered in graffiti, most involving the 'f' word. In one case it was spelled wrong.

When Mrs Haggerty finally paused behind the card table that posed as her desk, Riley rose and made her way to the front. She knew this drill – hand transfer papers to authority figure, receive acknowledgement of her existence, then return to her seat. Mrs Haggerty eyed the forms, looked up, frowned at Riley then looked down at the name and sighed.

'You were supposed to be here last Monday.'

'I couldn't make it,' Riley said. 'I was ill.' *Like dying from demon cooties.* It was a good bet every single student was listening to this conversation, trying to scope out the new kid. Maybe the teacher would let it drop.

'Attendance is very important,' the woman replied. 'You have to think of your future.'

That's a laugh. Riley nodded obediently. Teachers were less of a hassle if they thought you agreed with them.

'I'll need a parent's signature for your excuse,' Mrs Haggerty added.

'Sure.' *I'll just dig him up.* Luckily she was pretty good at forging her dad's signature.

'Students? This is Riley. Please welcome her to our class.'

Cool. She didn't use my last name. Maybe this was going to work out after all.

Then Mrs Haggerty pulled the pin. 'You can sit down, Miss Blackthorne.'

Crap.

As she headed for her seat, Riley could see her last name rattling around in the students' heads. Their eyes widened when it hit home. If one of them was clueless, another would lean over and whisper in an ear. A couple pulled out their cellphones, no doubt hunting up one of those online videos.

Now that her secret was out Riley wasn't surprised when

the kid sitting next to her, the bony one with the dull brown hair, watched her out of the corner of his eye like she was going to conjure up a fiend in the middle of class.

Sometimes I wish it worked that way.

Mrs Haggerty immediately dug into the classwork. It was the same as at the other school, following the state-mandated curriculum so they started with a half hour of maths, which really wasn't a stretch for Riley. Then a half hour each of English, science and literature. The final hour was history, in particular the Civil War. Riley had that down cold, courtesy of her dad. During Mrs Haggerty's snore-inducing account of the Battle of Lookout Mountain, she thought she could hear whispering behind her.

The three hours moved quickly, despite the smirks and the chatter behind her. Five o'clock came and went. Then it was five ten. Riley began to fidget because class was supposed to be over by now and she had to get to the cemetery. If she wanted something to eat, that would chew up even more time. The cemetery volunteer would stay put, but they'd charge her extra if she wasn't there by sunset.

Money I don't have.

Mrs Haggerty kept talking. And talking. Riley glanced at her watch again. Five fifteen. She began to pack her stuff. That immediately caught the teacher's notice.

'Miss Blackthorne? We're running late tonight. That happens from time to time.'

Riley stood. 'I'm sorry, I have to go. I have . . . something I have to do.'

'Which is?' Mrs Haggerty asked, giving her *the teacher stare.*
Damn. 'I have to sit vigil over my dad's grave,' Riley replied.
The teacher blinked. 'You're *that* Blackthorne?'

Apparently the teacher was the only one in the classroom
who hadn't connected the dots.

'OK, class, we'll call it an evening. Read the chapter on
Sherman's destruction of Atlanta for Sunday.'

Riley shouldered her messenger bag and hurried towards
the door, but it took some time to get outside as everyone
seemed to be in her way. The reason for the delay became
obvious when she reached her car. A message was scrawled
on her windshield.

Demon lover.

The colour of the lipstick looked familiar.

Riley shot a venomous look at the pack of girls. Brandy
grinned at her, waving a lipstick tube like a mini light sabre.

Riley hopped in the car, flipped the lever to clean the
windshield. Bad plan. The lipstick spread itself across the
glass in long, greasy smears. She kept working the lever until there was a clean patch, then drove away using language
only demons would understand.

In her rearview mirror, the pack brayed in laughter.

With only minutes to spare Riley hustled up the road as fast
as she could, clutching her father's trapping manual to her
side. It had been under the spare tyre but so far she'd had no
time to dig into it.

Rod the volunteer issued a welcoming smile as she approached. 'I'd stay and talk, but it's league night.'

'League?' she asked.

He slipped off his coat far enough for her to see he was wearing a red bowling shirt. *Six Feet Under* was embroidered on the back. The Six Feet Under Pub & Fish House sat across the street from the cemetery. On rare occasions her dad would take her there as a special treat when they had a few extra dollars left at the end of the month. The trappers held their parties and their wakes there. Yet another tradition.

'Need any help?' Rod asked. When she shook her head, he hurried off.

Riley set the circle with only a brief twinge of anxiety, then dialled Peter.

The moment he answered, she started in. 'You won't believe what happened at school!'

Her friend wisely listened without interrupting.

'Wow, they sound like complete dogs,' Peter commiserated. 'Sorry I wasn't there.'

Riley sighed. 'It's the usual crap, Peter. They have to pick on someone and I'm it. I'm always it.'

'Not always. Sometimes I am. We're different and that bugs them.'

'I have no clue how I'm going to get the lipstick off my windshield,' she grumbled.

'Hold on.' She heard the clicking keys in the background. 'Ammonia will take the stuff off your windshield.'

'Thanks!' Not that she had any in the apartment, but leave it to Peter to find the answer.

'So what's it like being Lucifer's biatch?' he joked.

'Peter!'

'Just kidding,' he said, then laughed. 'As for your other problem,' he continued, 'if you didn't trap demons those skanks would find something else to hate about you. Like your hair or your nose or something.'

'What's wrong with my nose?'

'Don't get me started,' he replied.

'Peter,' she cautioned, 'you don't want to go there.'

He laughed again. 'Don't let them get you down.'

'I won't, but it's always this way. When I was a kid –' She halted, aware she was about to reveal one of her deepest secrets.

'Go on,' he prodded.

This was Peter. He wouldn't laugh at her. At least not for long.

'You remember how in junior high I never fitted in? I had this thing I did every summer. I tried to be someone new, someone different, so that when I went back to school all the kids would say, 'Wow, Riley's cool.' Of course it didn't work. No matter what I did, all they saw was the old me.'

'So that's why you were so weird the first couple weeks of school. I could never figure it out.'

'Yeah, I probably acted pretty strange.'

'I like the old Riley,' Peter admitted. 'She's cool, even if she's Lucifer's biatch.'

'Enough with that.'

'Oh, we're grumpy. At least you ended up at a Starbucks.

I got sent to a daycare centre. It's still open during the day.'

'So what's that like?'

'It smells of kiddy poop and baby powder.'

She smirked. 'Do you get to sit on a tiny chair?'

'No, but we have to lie down on these little mats and take a nap after our juice and crackers.'

She let the laughter roll free. 'I miss you a lot, Peter. I wish you were in class with me.'

There was a moment's hesitation. 'Could you repeat that?'

'Why?'

'So I can record it. That way I can replay it when you start calling me a butthead again.'

'No way. You missed your chance.'

'So you know, I'm trying to get transferred to your school.'

'Really? Think it'll work?' she asked, her hope surging. Then everything would be fine again.

'Don't know. The warden didn't have a thing to do with the new school, so it was just random bad luck. I figure I might be able to affect that randomness in some way.'

'How?'

'Not the kind of thing we want to discuss on the phone.'

Which meant he was trying to hack the education department's computer system and generate a transfer.

'Be careful,' she said. The more creative the endeavour, the less the educational types would like it.

In the distance she saw Simon approaching. 'Gotta go. It's one of the trappers checking on me.' *The one who just happens to be my new boyfriend.*

'Be careful out there,' Peter warned. 'Oh, and I'll have a printout of all this stuff from your dad's disk ready tomorrow morning. Ring me and we'll set up a time to meet, OK?'

'Sure. Night, Peter.'

'Later, Riley.'

Simon called out his greeting and after she'd invited him in he joined her in the circle. The candles barely flickered.

'Thought I'd see how you were doing,' he said, shielding something behind him.

'I'm tired. Class ran late. I almost didn't make it on time,' she replied. *Whine much?* 'Sorry, I'm a little cranky.'

'Well, this should help. I got you a present.'

He brought his arm round, showing her the object he'd been hiding. It was a brand-new blue tarp still in its clear plastic wrapper.

Other girls get flowers – I get a tarp. And she didn't mind a bit.

'You're awesome, Simon,' she said, meaning every word.

'Aren't I?' he replied, waggling his eyebrows.

Riley quickly tidied the ground. Pinecones and rocks were evil, and became more so as the night progressed.

'Here, let me help,' Simon offered. Together they laid out the tarp, then the sleeping bags, her blanket and other necessities. 'Is there anything left in your apartment?' he asked, waving a hand at all her stuff.

'Yes!' she said, shooting him a mock glower. 'Pop-Tart?'

'Sure! Got strawberry?' She dug inside the box and found one. Treats in hand, they settled on the makeshift campsite, sharing a blanket.

Forsaken

'So what happened to your windshield?' he asked around munches of the tart. 'It's got something red on it.'

Riley gave him the quick and dirty version. To her surprise, his face coloured when she told him what the lipstick had said.

'You're nothing of the kind!' he said, frowning.

'Thanks.' It felt nice to have him stick up for her. 'I haven't decided how to get even yet.'

'That's a waste of time. It screws you up more than it does them.'

She cocked her head. 'You don't lose your cool when Harper's being an asshat; you're polite all the time, even to the demons. How do you do it?'

He tapped his cross. 'It helps me find my centre.'

'Mom used to talk about that sort of thing.' Treasured memories arose. 'I liked going to church with her. She took me to a Latin Mass once. It was all spooky and mysterious,' Riley said.

Simon gave her a sidelong look. 'I didn't realize your mom was Catholic. What about you?'

'I'm not sure. I think God's up there somewhere watching over us, but if He is, He must hate me.'

Her boyfriend slipped his arm round her, pulling her closer. It made her feel good deep inside.

'He doesn't hate any of us,' Simon explained. 'He just tests us. Unfortunately, your tests have been really hard.'

'What about you?'

'Haven't really had any tests yet. Nothing major, that is.'

He leaned closer and then placed a gentle kiss on her lips. Though surprised, she didn't push him away. He was a good kisser. Not that she'd had tons of practice, but she knew she'd be happy if he kissed her again. And he did. This time the kiss lasted longer and tasted of strawberries. He finally pulled himself away, a faint blush on his cheeks.

'You are such a temptation,' he muttered, shaking his head.

He makes that sound like a bad thing.

To her disappointment he suddenly rose, like he didn't trust himself alone with her. 'I've got to go. I promised my mom I'd be home in time for dinner.'

'Must be nice,' she said wistfully. With a family as big as his, it'd be chaos, but you'd never be lonely.

He pondered for a second. 'You should come over sometime. Mom makes incredible fried chicken.'

Did he just invite me to his house?

'I-I'd . . . like that,' she stammered.

'Good. My parents want to meet you. I've told them all about you.'

Me?

She stood and delivered a quick peck on his cheek. Another kiss ensued and this time there was no hurry.

'Definitely a test,' he murmured. 'You call me if you need anything.'

'I will. Night, Simon.'

'Goodnight, Riley.'

As he walked away, she replayed the last few minutes.

He kissed me. He invited me to dinner and his parents want to meet me.

This was moving way faster than she'd expected.

Chapter Twenty-Four

Riley reluctantly looked up from her father's manual, clicking off the flashlight to save the battery. She was deep in the section on how to trap Threes, the part she really should have read before going it alone. Her visitor was Mortimer. He was still in the fedora and the long trench coat.

Riley yawned a greeting.

'Good evening. How are you, Miss Blackthorne?' the necro asked in a husky voice. It sounded like he was coming down with a cold.

'It's been better,' she said. Then she held up her hand before he could make his usual offer. 'If anyone asks, you did your thing and I shot you down like every other night. That way we're not wasting our time. Besides, I'm too tired for it.'

Mortimer smiled. 'You're not like the others. They usually curse at me. I appreciate that.' He paused and then asked, 'Do you really enjoy trapping demons?'

'A week ago I would have said yes because I could trap with my dad. Now? Not so sure. I've got a new master and he's a real asshat.'

'Ah, I know how that works. We have a similar system to the trappers. New summoners are required to work up through the ranks. I was assigned the task of maintaining the reanimates when I first started. They require some care or things get pretty bad after a while.' He held his nose for effect.

'Can't hang an air freshener on them and call it good?' she joked.

Mortimer chuckled. 'No, but if you treat them carefully they look and smell better than when they were first in-humed. It's an art, you see.'

She rose and stretched. For once her thigh didn't bitch about the move.

'How long have you been a necro?'

'We prefer being called summoners.'

'For you, summoner. All the rest of them are necros in my book.'

He gave her a genuine smile. 'I've been reanimating the dead for over five years. It's a living. Before that I worked at a mortuary.'

'So the dead have always been your thing, then?'

'Pretty much.' He looked up the path. When he turned round, there was a frown on his face. 'Time to go. It's been good talking to you. You have a good night, and do be careful.'

'You too, Mortimer.'

'Mort. That's what my friends call me.' He tipped his fe-dora and headed up the walk. As he made the turn towards the entrance, she saw another figure approaching. To her surprise, Mort veered off among the graves rather than passing the newcomer on the road.

'I got ya some food,' Beck called out, holding up a

bulging paper bag as he strode towards her.

Maybe you're not so bad after all.

He paused at the edge of the circle. 'Ah, damn, my boot's untied. Here, take this,' he said, offering the bag. Riley started to reach across the circle, then paused. Something didn't feel right. She looked down at his boots. Beck always double-knotted his. She remembered him saying how he didn't want to fall over his laces and get eaten by some dumbass demon.

She stepped back and checked him out with a more critical eye.

No duffel bag. Beck always had it with him, even at her dad's funeral. And Mort had gone out of his way to avoid this guy.

'Nice one.' If she'd reached across the candles to claim the bag, she'd have broken the line of protection and her dad would be someone else's property.

It didn't surprise her when 'Beck' evaporated into a swirl of leaves, revealing the creepy necro. None of the others attempted such sophisticated magic.

'You are smarter than most,' he observed. 'I'm rather enjoying the challenge.'

'Yeah, yeah,' she said, making talking motions with her hand. 'It's not happening.'

'So you say,' he replied. With a whoosh, the circle flared into the night like he'd touched it, then it subsided. The summoner was gone, a whirl of leaves shooting up the path like a malevolent tornado.

Riley heaved a sigh of relief. She needed to ask Mort about this guy, because it looked like Mr Black Magic Necro wasn't going to quit until he'd scared the living crap out of her.

Morning brought a light frost and a black plastic bag tied to her car door handle. After much fumbling with cold fingers, Riley untied the bag and dumped its contents on the frost-painted hood. A thick manila envelope slid out, along with a wad of paper towels and a plastic bottle of ammonia.

There was a note attached.

Warm car first, then clean windshield or you'll be sorry.

'Peter strikes again.'

While the car warmed, she dialled her friend.

'Got the delivery?' he asked without bothering to say hello.

'I did. Thanks,' she said, watching the heat make small circles on the windshield. The bag's contents sat on the seat beside her. 'How'd you get out here?' Peter didn't have a car and she doubted the warden would let him take off so early in the morning on his own.

'David dropped it by for me as he was headed to work. He thought it kinda weird I was having him make a delivery to a cemetery.'

David. His next oldest brother who wanted to be a pilot but was working at a bakery instead. 'Man, there's a lot of paper here. What is all this?' she asked, hefting the nearly inch-thick envelope.

'Everything that was on your dad's disk. It's all about Holy Water, or at least as much as I got to read. The warden kept checking in on me last night so I gave up.'

'I'll go through it,' she said, 'but I have no idea why my dad was going to all this trouble. He never said anything about it.'

'Definitely a mystery,' Peter replied, and then crunched on something through the mouthpiece. Cereal no doubt.

Rivulets of water ran down her windshield in response to the blast of heated air. Time to break out the ammonia and destroy Brandy's work of art.

'Thanks, Peter, I owe you.'

'Definitely.' He hung up.

Riley leaned back in the car, savouring the warmth. She really wanted a nap, but she had barely enough time to clean the windshield, grab a breakfast sandwich and get to Harper's. If she was late, the master would find another way to torment her. With her luck it would involve more demon poop.

She reluctantly stashed the manila envelope in the glove compartment for later.

The Three was gone – apparently her master had sold the thing to a demon trafficker. She tidied up underneath its cage before he told her to, which seemed to aggravate him. By the time she'd finished Simon was packing his car for a run. He'd barely said two words to her over the last couple of days, at least when Harper was around. All her daydreams about how cool it would be to train with him hadn't materialized.

'We're going trapping,' he explained. She started to ask whether she could come along but stopped at the warning look in his eyes.

Harper lumbered up, clad in a thick coat and a duffel bag in hand.

'I decide who goes and who doesn't go on a run.'

Riley took that to mean she wasn't invited. That changed the moment the two men were in the car.

'So get your ass in here, Brat,' Harper ordered. 'We don't have all damned day.'

No way I can win.

Riley eased into the back seat and slammed the door. Part of her was stoked. She was out of that smelly building and doing what she should be doing – trapping demons. Well, not her, exactly. This was Simon's show and from the conversation in the front seat they were after a Grade Four Hypno-Fiend, or Mezmer as the trappers called them.

Harper supplied the directions.

'What are we getting into?' Simon asked, turning off Memorial Drive and heading north towards downtown. His voice held a hint of nervousness.

The master shoved some paperwork over the back of the seat to Riley. 'Earn your keep.'

Pushing a strand of hair out of her eyes, she skimmed the report. As with all trapping requisitions, the paperwork stated the complainant's name, address and type of suspected demonic activity.

'A Mr Ford says this boy is hanging around his daughter, Carol, and getting her to do things she shouldn't be doing. He thinks the boy is a demon because every time he tries to run him off he finds himself agreeing with whatever the kid says.'

'Sounds like a Mezmer,' Harper said.

'He might just be a creep,' Riley said.

The master trapper gave her a strange look over the seat. 'Been there, have you?'

Sure have.

Riley had met Allan right after Beck had tossed her to the kerb. She'd been vulnerable and Allan had taken advantage of that. It hadn't mattered that her father had disliked her new boyfriend from the moment they'd met. In her mind, Allan was the only thing in her life that mattered and she'd do anything for him to keep him interested in her. And she had. It'd started with the small stuff – lying, sneaking around, stealing cigarettes from the grocery store, though neither of them smoked. It ended the day she'd been one step away from stuffing a $2,000 mini laptop under her jacket. He'd told her it would prove that she loved him.

The instant her hand had touched the computer a shock ran through her entire body. The future unfolded like a bad movie – it wouldn't be him at the police station getting yelled at by the cops. He wouldn't be fingerprinted, thrown in a cell or have to face the judge. He wouldn't have to endure her father's horrified disappointment.

Freaked, she'd hurried out of the store minus the computer. As Riley passed the security guard, he'd given her a nod. He'd known what she was going to do.

'Smart move, kid,' he'd said.

Allan hadn't seen it that way. When she'd admitted she couldn't do what he wanted, he'd shouted her down in front of everyone in the parking lot, calling her awful things. Then he'd hit her.

Riley touched her cheek, remembering the sting of the blow, the taste of blood in her mouth, his furious face only inches from hers as he called her nasty names.

She'd found the courage to leave him swearing in that parking lot. It'd taken three bus rides to get home. When her father saw her, and the growing bruise, his face went crimson in anger. She'd collapsed in his arms and told him all of it. When she'd finally stopped crying, he'd asked her only one question.

'Do you believe you deserved to be hit?'

'No!' she'd said. 'He had no right!'

Her father's expression had melted into relief.

'Always remember that, Pumpkin. *No one* has the right to hurt you.' Then he'd hugged her and taken her out for ice cream to celebrate her lucky escape from The Worst Boy-friend Ever. A few months later she'd heard Allan had broken his new girlfriend's arm during an argument.

I got off so lucky.

'Hey!' Harper called out, snapping his fingers and causing Riley to jump. 'Pay attention, will you? Cos if you think you know all this, you're wrong.'

'Sorry,' Riley said. 'What were you saying?'

'I was saying that Grade Four demons are devious mothers. They sing a sweet song in your ear and next thing you know your soul's got a brand on it courtesy of Lucifer. Sometimes they do it fast, sometimes slow. Doesn't matter which because your soul is what they want, before or after they screw you over. Once they claim your soul they have two choices – harvest it right then and there, in which case you are dead meat, or sell you to a higher-level demon to curry favour.'

'What does the higher-level demon do with a person's soul?' Simon asked, frowning.

'Since you're still alive, they own you. You're theirs for eternity.' He turned to Simon. 'Tell us the difference between an incubus and a succubus.'

Her fellow apprentice sighed, not pleased at having to discuss such matters in front of Riley. 'A succubus seduces males and takes energy from them during the sex act. An incubus does the same with women.'

Harper nodded. 'They're evil. No other way to say it.'

'So how do you stop them?' Riley asked.

'A Babel sphere does the trick,' the master replied.

She wasn't that far in the manual. Maybe she should have read ahead. 'How does it work?'

Harper huffed like she was ignorant. 'Tell her, Saint.'

The so-called Saint, who'd been doing some heavenly kissing the night before, studied her via the rearview mirror. 'The Babel sphere translates what the demon is really saying, rather than what it wants you to hear. It reveals the fiend underneath the illusion.'

'Once we're sure this is a demon, we'll bust open a Babel and then bag the damned thing,' Harper said. 'Piece of cake.'

Riley caught a glimpse of Simon's face in the mirror.

That wasn't what either of them was thinking.

Chapter Twenty-Five

The Armageddon Lounge wasn't busy, but the folks inside eyed the three of them like refugees would a free Sunday buffet.

This is where Beck plays pool. It suited him – a seedy End Times-themed bar with eight pool tables and a big screen television running some college football game. The green felt on the tables was worn and the painted concrete floor needed mopping. It smelt of cigarette smoke, which meant the owner had paid the city extra for that option.

Harper nodded towards a young couple at one of the tables.

'Probably them,' he said. The boy was almost Simon's height, five nine or so, with black scruffy hair and a collection of metal in his eyebrows, nose and tongue. Riley wondered how he could afford all that bling. The boy wore stonewashed blue jeans and a black T-shirt that said *I'm Perfect! Deal!*

No ego there.

As Riley moved closer she examined the girl. The paperwork said she was fifteen but Carol Ford looked older. Her hair was blunt cut and blonde, her face remarkably plain.

Riley couldn't help but notice the dark circles under her eyes. Either Carol was ill, a druggie, or her boyfriend really was an incubus sucking the life out of her. No matter what the cause, no amount of concealer was going to fix that.

Simon unzipped his trapping bag and set it on the floor next to him. Next to it went a bright blue lunch tote.

'Excuse me, are you Carol Ford?' he said. She turned towards him and blinked repeatedly like he'd shone a bright flashlight in her eyes.

'Yes?'

'I'm Simon Adler. I'm a demon trapper. You might have a problem I can help you with.'

Riley envied him: he sounded so in control, except with Simon it came from his faith not years of experience.

'You don't need to talk to them,' the boy said in a commanding voice, turning his full attention their way. 'Your 'rents sent them.'

'Parents?' she asked, like she'd forgotten she had any.

'There's been a misunderstanding,' the boy continued. He put his arm round Carol, who shivered at his touch and not in a good way. 'Her 'rents don't like me, but we're meant for each other. It's not fair that people keep getting in our way. You should leave us alone.'

He sounded reasonable, but so had Allan when he was on his game.

'It's not like we don't care for each other,' the boy continued. 'You love me, don't you, Carol?'

Carol nodded like a puppet.

'I won't let anyone hurt her,' the boy continued, then let his eyes roam to Riley.

The moment their eyes met Riley felt the weight of his attention, like they were the only ones in the bar. She could hear him talking to her, but it didn't seem that anyone else heard him. He was telling her how she was so pretty, how he was sorry she was all alone now, that he'd make it right. How he'd never leave her like everyone else had.

You trust me, don't you? he asked.

There was a loud snap and both apprentices jumped. Harper had busted a pool cue over one of the tables.

'For God's sake, get on with it, Saint!' he ordered.

Simon jerked to attention and clutched his wooden cross, lips moving in silent prayer. A moment later a sphere impacted the floor and exploded in tiny glass fragments. Carol gave a gasp of surprise as the air immediately filled with the smell of raw cinnamon and a mosaic of flickering lights. The lights rose with the scent, then veered directly towards her boyfriend, encompassing him.

'What is that?' she asked nervously.

'Evil . . .' the boy hissed. 'How dare you –' He flailed at the magic as the honeyed voice took on a reedy quality. Higher and higher it went as his face shifted from handsome to hideous in a reverse makeover. His clothes vanished, as if revealing a body that looked like it'd been dipped in mud. The brown layer was cracked in places, revealing sallow skin underneath. His blood red eyes bore into Riley, glowing in the bar's muted light. He had no horns, but a long, barbed tail flicked behind him like an angry cat as his taloned hands clawed the air.

With the clothes gone, Riley caught a glimpse of what no mortal should have to see.

Oh, great. Now that's seared into my brain forever.

Once it dawned on the bar's patrons they had a naked demon in their midst, there was a stampede for the front door. When Carol saw her boyfriend's real form, then looked further south, she shrieked and back-pedalled.

'Her soul I nearly had,' the demon shouted. 'Evil you are!'

Simon ignored him, donning a pair of heavy latex gloves.

'Boon I grant all of you!' the demon offered.

'Get screwed,' Harper replied.

The fiend began to shrink like a child's balloon with a slow leak. As he diminished in size, the demon yowled and swore and flailed his hands, but it didn't stop the magical process.

That is so cool. I wonder how it works.

Finally he was only a foot tall, stuck inside a circle of bright twinkling lights that resembled a miniature force field. Simon scooped up the snarling fiend, dumped it in the over-sized lunch tote, zipped the container closed and padlocked it. The magical charms tied to the handle rattled as he picked it up. Apparently they were supposed to keep the fiend from clawing his way out.

Riley clapped, pleased at Simon's success. 'Trapper scores.' He gave her a modest smile but she could tell something was bothering him.

Harper didn't share her joy. In fact, he glared at the pair of them. 'What the hell were you two doing?' he demanded. 'I told you he'd mess with your head and you stood there like a couple of dummies!'

Riley didn't bother to argue. If the fiend could get into Simon's mind, it could get into anyone's. She turned her attention to Carol. The girl seemed paralysed, staring at the container that held her ex-boyfriend. Copious tears rolled out of her eyes.

'H-he's . . . he's a . . .' she stammered.

'Demon. They happen,' Riley said, trying to sound supportive.

The girl wailed and flung herself into Riley's arms.

'Let's get out of here,' Harper ordered, casting a wary eye around the bar. A crowd of curious locals had formed at the door. 'Don't want to waste my time with the cops.'

As Simon toted the demon outside, the bartender got in Harper's way, bitching about the broken pool cue and all the glass on the floor.

'You want us to turn him loose?' Harper demanded. The guy paled and shook his head. 'Figured so.'

Once they were outside, Riley pointed Carol towards the police station. 'Go over there and call your parents,' she advised. 'Tell them you screwed up.'

'I thought . . . he was . . .' the girl said, sniffling. She blew her nose. 'He was so . . .'

'Wrong for you.'

'But they'll ground me,' Carol cried, totally focused on her ruined love life and not the *what might have been* if the Four had won this round.

Getting grounded or spending forever with a demon?

'Small price to pay,' Riley said, patting the girl's arm in sympathy. 'Trust me on that.'

Simon remained dead silent on the drive to Harper's place.

You caught the demon. That's all that matters. Did he really think the thing wasn't going to try to con him? That he was immune somehow?

Harper was quiet too, so Riley spent time trying not to stare at the lunch tote on the seat next to her. She could hear the demon in her mind offering her a boon if she'd set him free.

'No way that's happening, so just shut up,' she muttered.

Harper gave her a stern look over the seat. 'Is it talking to you?' She nodded. 'Tempted?'

'No.'

'Why not?'

'Because I'm a Blackthorne,' Riley replied before she could stop herself.

He smirked. 'Like that makes a goddamn bit of difference.'

The demon kept bugging her so she took a mental vacation to when Simon had kissed her the night before. Its voice faded away to nothing.

The instant they reached Harper's building, the master was on her case. 'There's some Ones in the office. Take them downtown to Roscoe Clement on Peachtree Street and sell them. You'll get seventy-five a piece for them. Get the paper-work signed, got it?'

'Sir, I don't think that's a good idea,' Simon chimed in, troubled by the order. 'Roscoe is –'

Harper delivered a blistering look at the older apprentice. 'Not your call, Saint.' He jabbed a finger at Riley. 'Be back by the time we are.'

And that will be? She didn't dare ask, not with his black mood. Harper barked orders at Simon and then they were gone, the old Dodge belching smoke. Going somewhere to sell the Four.

But not to Roscoe. Now why is that?

Her dad had spoken about this Roscoe dude, telling her that he sold adult videos and bought demons on the side. How he'd received Church approval to be a trafficker, no one knew. Her dad had warned her to stay away from the sleaze unless he was with her. Now Harper was sending her to Roscoe on her own. It was like throwing a chunk of bunny entrails in front of a Three.

'Bet you didn't do that to Simon,' she groused.

Riley found the four fiends sitting in their individual sippy cups on Harper's desk. They were all Biblios.

One was sleeping, but the others got in the finger before she stowed them into her messenger bag. The paperwork went in next. It was in quadruplicate – a copy each for the trapper, the trafficker, the city and another page for when the demon trafficker delivered the fiends to the Church. Every demon sale was tracked from the time the fiend was captured to the time the Church took control of them.

According to the Trappers Manual the paperwork went all the way to Rome. She could imagine the accountants in the Vatican poring over the reports, tallying them into some huge ledger that dated back to the Middle Ages. Maybe the Pope got to see the ledger with his coffee every morning. Which meant maybe someday he'd see Riley's name and all the demons she'd caught.

How cool is that?

Chapter Twenty-Six

Fewer cars should equal more parking. That hadn't been Riley's experience. The city's predatory search for revenue, including converting the empty parking spaces on Peachtree Street to makeshift shops which had to pay a monthly fee, made it difficult to find a place for her car. As she waited for a blue van to finish unloading so she could scoop up the parking place, Riley tugged out the manila envelope and leafed through the pages. Peter had separated the contents into specific stacks with sturdy binder clips. She studied the first batch, flipping up her eyes every now and then to see how the unloading progressed.

The History of Holy Water

Her father never approached a subject half-assed and he hadn't changed his approach when it came to the sacred liquid. In her hands was a detailed account of Holy Water's legends and folklore in minute detail. He had a list of miracles attributed to the sacred liquid, old wives' tales regarding its use, even a chart that showed how Holy Water was manufactured and distributed in the Atlanta area.

Riley checked the van – still unloading – then returned to the page. The local manufacturer, Celestial Supplies, created the Holy Water in a plant in Doraville. From there it was sent to a licensed distributor who supplied various stores in the city. Every single pint, quart and gallon of the holy liquid was tagged with a sales tax seal and catalogued by batch number.

'And we care about this . . . why?' she said, frowning. Maybe her dad was going to write an academic paper or something. 'But who would read it?' She'd admit that some of the folklore was kind of cool, but the rest was a snooze.

Further on she found page after page of numbers, an inventory from Celestial Supplies that represented every single batch of Holy Water produced in the last six months.

'Whee!' she said, rolling her eyes. This wasn't getting her anywhere. She looked up to see a stocky guy close the van's rear door and lock it. He jumped in and pulled out of the parking spot.

'Mine,' she said, grinning.

Riley trudged past the Westin, one of the few hotels still open downtown. Smokers huddled together outside the front door, puffing away. One of them had a Deader standing near him, holding his briefcase. The live guy in the expensive suit was talking rapid fire on his cellphone, pacing back and forth, leaving a long tail of cigarette smoke behind him.

Riley's eyes met those of the reanimate, a petite Hispanic woman in a black trouser suit and white shirt. The combination did nothing for her grey skin. Her hair was held back by a clip and she looked so sad. Maybe she'd been this guy's secretary before she died and he didn't want to replace her. No matter what, she was his slave now.

That has to suck.

Riley gave the woman a sympathetic nod. The Deader returned the nod. That surprised her. They usually stared at the world through empty eyes. The woman's owner gestured and she came closer, opening up the briefcase and offering its contents for his inspection. He chose a sheaf of papers and returned to his marching, ignoring everyone around him.

Sorry, Riley mouthed. She didn't get a response.

The intersection of Baker and Peachtree lacked a traffic light. Constant bike and moped traffic zipped past her, and one rider nearly clipped her toes. At least horses weren't allowed in downtown any more since no one really wanted to wade through the manure.

A few doors down from Max Lager's, a popular brew pub, sat Roscoe's Emporium. You'd have to be blind not to find the place. It was dripping in obscene neon signs.

The strap on her messenger bag slipped and Riley adjusted it. Tiny voices rose, barely audible. She tapped the side of the bag.

'Knock it off.' Silence fell. It was safe to assume that middle fingers were hoisted in her direction.

Riley stood outside for at least a full minute hoping God or whoever was in charge of the universe would step in and she wouldn't have to do this. When there was a disappointing lack of divine intervention, she shuddered and pushed open the door.

As her eyes adjusted to the dim light, she saw the huge

video screen on the far wall. A knot of customers were clustered in front of the screen, fixated, mouths agape.

My Dad is spinning in his grave.

Roscoe spied her immediately, like he'd been expecting her. He stood behind a lengthy glass counter showing something to a potential customer.

'Be with you in a sec,' he called out, drawing all eyes to her.

Thanks, perv.

While she waited, Riley rooted herself by the front door, refusing to wander through the shop. Not that she was a prude or anything, but a few of the customers looked scary and they watched her every move.

Eventually Roscoe huffed his way over, his big belly arriving ahead of the rest of him. His rusty brown hair was too curly to be natural. He had tattoos on both arms that proved mermaids were *really* into sailors.

Even before she had a chance to say a word, he licked his lips and grinned. 'This way, girlie. We'll do the deal in the office.'

Girlie. She shook her head. Apparently Harper had called ahead so this should go fast. *Anything to get me out of this place.*

It was hard to tell where the store ended and Roscoe's office began. Nude calendars adorned the other walls while a small television featured a truly disgusting video. There was even a framed photo of Roscoe on the wall. The newspaper clipping below it said the adult entertainment tsar – Riley smirked at that – had paid over fifty thousand dollars in state licensing fees and sin taxes in the past five years. Which was why the city tolerated his smut. As her dad would say, they got their cut.

Roscoe crunched down into a worn leather chair. The move made his vast stomach roll over the top of his jeans, fighting a battle against the tight T-shirt. It wasn't an attractive sight

Uck. Riley made sure the office door was open behind her.

With a dry chuckle, Roscoe ran his eyes up and down her body, assessing her like she was a piece of prime beef. 'So let's see the goods.'

The urge to run slammed head on against her assignment. Harper would be furious if she didn't sell the Biblios and she knew revealing Roscoe's sleazy advances wouldn't make a bit of difference. How would Simon handle this? She discarded that thought immediately. He was too polite. Beck? That's who she should be channelling right now.

Riley glared at the porn king. 'OK. Goods it is.' He leered until she removed the Biblios from her messenger bag, lining them up on his desk though she didn't like getting *that* close to him. One of the fiends was working on his lid, feet braced on the sides of the sippy cup in a vain effort to unscrew it. She tightened the lid just in case.

'I'm here for Master Harper,' she announced. 'Nothing else.'

Roscoe looked crestfallen. 'You sure?' She nodded defiantly. 'Damn.'

'Not happening. Now can we get on with the deal *for the demons*?'

Roscoe leaned forward, the grease on his nose shining like a beacon. The expression on his face almost made Riley vomit. 'Ninety a head,' he offered, scratching his belly thoughtfully.

Ninety?

He interpreted her silence as a stall for more money. 'All right. A 'C' note for each. At that price I'll take all of them you can find.'

'As many as we can trap?' she asked, hedging. Harper had said to expect seventy-five. What was she missing here?

'You heard me. A hundred a piece. That's my deal.'

Harper said to sell them and it would be righteous to see his face when she returned with that much extra money. Maybe the Church had authorized higher payments and Harper hadn't got the word yet. Riley pulled out the paperwork and laid it near the cups. 'You'll need to sign for these.'

Roscoe's forehead bloomed in sweat. 'Don't need the Church's paperwork. I've got a new buyer. They pay more, and that's why I'm giving you more.'

'Who's buying them?' Riley asked.

'Not your concern, baby doll.'

Baby doll? Double uck.

'I can't sell demons without the paperwork,' she said. It was the law.

'OK, make it one-fifteen a head,' Roscoe replied. 'That's as high as I can go. Tell that old bastard you got seventy-five each and you lost the paperwork, then you pocket the difference.'

Her cut would be $160, enough to buy groceries for a month. If this was a set-up, Harper was making it really tempting.

It isn't right.

Riley reluctantly shook her head. 'Unless you sign the paperwork, no deal.'

'Don't get a bug up your ass, girlie. I'm doing this as a community service. As far as I'm concerned, you could flush them down the toilet.'

Riley began to repack the demons into her messenger bag, her stomach sour at the way this had played out. *Harper is going to lose his mind.*

'Hey, what are you doing?' Roscoe asked, lurching out of his chair.

'Doing what I'm supposed to,' she said, packing faster now, eager to get away from this weirdo.

'One-twenty,' Roscoe said. 'That's more than you'll make anywhere else.'

The sleaze bled desperation; she could taste it in the air. Something was going on with this guy, but it wasn't her problem. As she tucked away the last demon, his sweaty hand grabbed her arm.

'You can't do that. You have to sell them to me,' he barked.

She jerked her arm away, sickened by his touch.

'You're being stupid,' he growled.

'Not the first time.'

Riley pushed her way through customers and employees. The moment she reached the street the demons erupted into a chorus of raucous cheers.

Even Hell has standards.

Fireman Jack had been fairly easy to find since there weren't that many vintage firehouses left in the city. Riley squared her shoulders and poked at the doorbell located next to the overhead door. No answer. She pushed again and the service door began to open.

'Hello?' A hand waved her in. It was attached to a young guy, probably in his twenties. He was clad in blue overalls and wore black and white checked high top tennis shoes. His hair was a nest of spikes. Simi would love this dude.

'Yes?' he asked, eying her critically.

'I need to do business with Fireman Jack,' she said. 'I'm Riley Blackthorne.'

'Blackthorne?' An eyebrow raised. 'Right this way.'

As she followed him inside, Riley realized a fire station was a good choice for a trafficker. The trappers could pull their vehicles inside the building, close the overhead door and offload the larger fiends. No chance for the things to get loose and maul a passerby.

Her nose caught the brimstone stench of demons before she heard the growls. There were half a dozen Threes lined along a back wall in their individual steel cages. They all slobbered and flashed their claws, fur rippling in waves. The floor beneath them was spotless. She wondered if the guy in the high tops got stuck with clean-up duty.

'Blackthorne's daughter,' one of demons howled. The others picked up the chant and magnified it.

She kept the shiver to herself as she passed by the last cage.

Two flights of stairs got her to Jack's office, though it took some time to get there since her thigh hadn't liked the hike. The office was big and airy with light streaming through four skylights, illuminating the old red brick walls. She liked this place. It felt good. Maybe if she got rich someday she'd buy a fire station. A quick look around proved it wasn't just Jack's place of work – a queen bed sat in one corner along with a tidy kitchenette and on the other wall a flat screen streamed stock quotes.

The owner of the place sat behind a large wooden desk. It wasn't a fancy piece of furniture, but it'd seen years of use. Jack looked near her father's age – mid-forties. Old, but not ancient like Harper. He had dark brown hair with silver streaks at his temples and wore blue jeans, a red shirt and those colourful braces. Not hard to spot him in a crowd. A baseball cap sat on his desk. He was a Yankees fan.

The man was on the phone. He raised a hand to give himself a second, then went back to the call. He was questioning someone about regulations regarding demon disposal.

While she waited Riley checked out the long wall to her left, which was blanketed in pictures and paintings. There was a common theme: famous fires. London 1666. Chicago 1871. Atlanta 1864 and 1917. Even the Lenox Plaza fire just last year. That had been started by a couple of horny Pyro-Fiends. Luckily that didn't happen too often, but when it did the results were way incendiary.

Jack hung up the phone and pointed towards a wooden high-backed chair. 'Riley! Have a seat. How are you doing?'

'OK, I guess. I'm with Harper now.'

Jack made a gagging motion with his finger and it set her to laughing. She could see why her dad liked this guy.

'Actually, that's not fair,' Jack said. 'He may be a platinum-class jerk, but he's a good trapper. You'll learn a lot providing you don't kill him first.'

'So far I've become an expert at cleaning up demon crap.' She raised her chapped hands as proof.

'Gotta start at the bottom,' he said, smirking. The smirk faded as he opened a drawer and dropped a file folder on top of the desk. It was full of legal-size papers. 'I had a look at the contract the debt collectors sent over.'

'And?' she asked, unable to read the news on his face.

'They have a solid claim against your dad's body.'

She banged the back of her skull against the wooden chair, the discomfort short-circuiting the anger and tears. 'No way we can stop them?'

'I've filed a motion asking the court to rule on some specifics of the claim. The best we can do is stall long enough that it doesn't matter.'

'I'd pay the money if I had it,' she said. 'I really would.'

'Since you are a minor, you don't owe them anything. The reason they are going after the body is that's the only money they can hope to receive. Sorry I don't have better news.' He put away the folder. They studied each other for a few seconds. 'Anything else I can help you with?'

'I'm here to sell you some Ones.'

Jack pulled a face. 'Why me and not one of the other traffickers?'

'Harper sent me to Roscoe. We couldn't come to a deal.'

Jack leaned over the desk. 'He sent you to Roscoe? Good God. Does Beck know?'

'No.'

'Make sure he doesn't find out. He'll go ballistic.'

'I know. What a sleaze.' It was her turn to make a gagging motion. 'He offered me one hundred and twenty dollars for each demon.'

Jack gaped. 'One-twenty? He can't be selling to the Church at that price. We only get eight-five a piece for them.'

'Could Harper be setting me up?'

'Maybe. You never know with him.' Jack thought for a moment. 'I don't usually buy anything below a Grade Three.'

'I figured, well, you and Dad were buds and . . .' she said, turning on the charm.

The trafficker laughed. 'Playing me already? Well, you got the face for it. How many?' he said.

'Four. All Biblios.'

Jack leaned back in his chair, slipping his thumbs under those garish braces. 'If you turn out half as good as Paul, you've got a future in this business. I'm not stupid. I don't want to piss off the next generation of trappers.'

She cocked her head and waited. It felt like there was more.

'OK, I admit it,' Jack said. 'I love it when an underdog wins, so I'm pulling for you. You'll get a lot of grief because you're female. Give it right back to them, OK?'

He didn't call me girlie, Baby Doll or Princess. Jack moved up to the top of her Good People list.

'Let's see the little guys.'

She set them out, one by one. The Biblios were swearing again.

'What does the Church do with them, I mean, *really* do with them?' she asked.

'The official answer is that they put them in special containers, ship them off to monasteries in Europe and the monks pray over them. It puts them to sleep. Eventually they disappear. The Church thinks their souls are saved. I think they return to Hell and are recycled.'

'How long does that take?' she quizzed.

'I don't know. I honestly think they disappear so they don't have to listen to the endless chanting.' He studied her intently. 'You sure you want to sell them to me?'

'Yeah, why not?'

Jack hesitated for a second then tightened the cup lids even though she'd just done the same thing.

'OK, it's on your head, then. Seventy-five a piece.'

She nodded, though it was considerably less than what Roscoe had offered. While Jack counted out the money, she thought things through. 'Did my dad say anything to you about Holy Water?'

'No. Why?' he asked, looking up from the vintage green safe behind his desk.

'I found some notes of his. He was researching it, but I don't know why.'

'Ask Beck. He'd know if anyone does.' Jack swung the safe door closed and handed her an envelope. 'Don't put this in your bag. Someone might try to take it. The locals know folks coming out of here have cash on them.'

She tucked the envelope in the waistband of her jeans. They signed the paperwork and the deal was done. He rose and offered his hand and they shook firmly.

'Remember me when you get your journeyman's licence. I'll be interested to see what you catch. I'll buy whatever you bring me.'

Now that rocks. At least someone is on my side.

Chapter Twenty-Seven

Riley laid the cash on the master's desk in a neat stack right next to his box of cigars.

'You sold them?' Harper asked. There wasn't a whiskey bottle in sight and his eyes were predatory, like he was waiting to pounce. It gave her the creeps and she wished Simon was here, not out buying trapping supplies.

Riley dumped the paperwork in front of him. A frown appeared as he flipped the pages. She'd sold the demons for the amount he'd said and brought him the cash and forms. Why was he upset?

'You sold them to the Fireman?' he bellowed.

Uh oh. That's what Jack had meant when he said it was on her head.

'Why the hell didn't you go to Roscoe like I told you?' Harper demanded, his voice echoing off the open rafters. 'Can't you do one damned thing right?'

'I went to the perv. He wouldn't sign the papers.'

'Why the hell not?'

'He said he'd give me one-twenty apiece for the demons as long as I did the deal under the table.' She took a gulp of air. 'He said to tell you I got seventy-five and lost the paperwork, then I could keep the rest.'

Harper's eyes turned flinty black. Faster than she thought he could move, his hand shot across the desk and grabbed her forearm. The fingers dug in like iron. 'You're lying.'

She tried to twist out of his grasp, but he only tightened his hold. 'I'm not lying! Stop it. That hurts.'

The master suddenly released her and she staggered a few steps away, fear coursing through her. Harper was too volatile. The next time he might hit her.

He produced a full bottle of whiskey from a drawer. The amber liquid sloshed into a cracked glass. 'I don't sell to the Fireman. Never have, never will.'

'I didn't know,' she retorted.

'You just did it to make me look bad. You're as twisted as your old man,' he spat.

You leave my dad out of this!

'Get the hell out here,' he shouted, 'or I swear you'll be bleeding.'

Riley barely reached the front door when glass shattered in the office.

'Goddamn Blackthornes!' Harper cursed.

Simon looked up as she fled into the parking lot. When he saw her face, he dropped a box back into the boot of his car and hurried up to her.

'Are you OK?' he asked.

'Don't go in there,' she said, shivering. 'He's crazy. He's throwing stuff.'

Simon studied her for a moment, then after a quick look

at the building he put his hands on her shoulders and gave them a gentle squeeze.

'What happened?' he asked.

If she told him, what could he do? Argue with Harper? Get tossed out of the Guild? That wouldn't help either of them.

Riley shook her head, pulled away from him and hurried towards her car.

It's not your fight.

The shakes finally subsided by the time Riley slumped on her couch. She pulled up her sweatshirt sleeve and studied her arm. Five dark finger-sized bruises stood out against her skin. She tugged the sleeve down. The bruises would eventually fade. Her fear wouldn't.

'He's going to keep doing this. He's going to keep hurting me until I quit.'

Her eyes filled with tears.

I don't know if I can do this any more, Dad. I'm so scared.

Her phone rang and she jumped at the sound. Reluctantly she dug it out of her bag. It was Simon.

'Riley, where are you?' he asked. Behind him she could hear street noise.

'I'm at home.'

'Please tell me what happened. I don't want to walk in on him without knowing.'

'I sold the Ones to Jack. Harper didn't like it.' *And then he hurt me.*

'Did he . . . hit you?'

She sat up on the couch. Apparently she wasn't Harper's only target.

'I'm OK, Simon.'

'I'm so sorry. I was hoping he'd be better with you.'

Not a chance.

She flipped the phone closed. Her fear sheeted off her like a thin layer of ice in the full sun. 'Harper, you miserable . . .' He'd dissed her dad. He'd hurt her and Simon.

Her father's voice asked the question as clearly as if he was sitting next to her.

Do you believe you deserve to be hit?

'No.' And though Harper scared the hell out of her, she wasn't giving up. She'd just stay out of his reach from now on. He'd had his one shot at her and there would be no others.

There was a tentative knock at her door.

She opened it, leaving the chain in place, still on edge. It was Beck, who wasn't known for knocking so softly.

'What?' she grumbled.

She could tell by the way he held himself that he was upset.

'Simon called. He was worried. He thought Harper had hurt ya.'

'I'll handle it,' she said evenly.

'Riley, he's a vicious SOB. That's why I wanted ya with Stewart.'

'I'll handle it,' she repeated. How she'd do that she had no idea, but if Beck got involved he'd end up in jail for assault and lose his trapping licence.

'What set him off?' She told him. 'Oh, God, I thought ya knew Harper didn't like Jack.'

'How would I know that?' she complained. 'I'm an apprentice. I'm not supposed to know stuff, but everybody thinks I do because my dad was a master.'

Beck absorbed her tirade without a twitch.

It wasn't fair chewing on him. He wasn't the problem.

'Sorry.' She unlatched the chain and waved him in.

He didn't budge. 'I thought we might go for a ride. Talk it out.'

'I'm not in the mood for—'

'I'm trappin' this afternoon and I need back-up.'

'What are you after?' she asked, still dubious.

'A Firebug.'

A Pyro-Fiend. He knew what kind of bait to use.

'Well?' he asked, hands jammed in his jeans pockets. It made him look his age for a change.

'Will Harper be pissed off if I trap with you?'

'Count on it, if he finds out. Does that bother ya?' he asked.

'After this morning? No way.'

Riley had barely climbed into Beck's truck before it was in gear and rolling out of the parking lot. She hastily attached her seatbelt. She knew if she let him steer the conversation they'd keep talking about Harper so she headed it in another direction.

'Simon trapped a Four at your pool hall this morning. It was really slick how it got into my head.'

'Hard to ignore 'em, especially if they're comin' on to ya.' Beck gave a dry chuckle. 'There was this succubus who worked the convention circuit downtown. Damn, she was a hottie. I really hated trappin' her, but I had no choice.'

'She didn't get to you?' Riley asked, curious. 'I mean, in your head and all.'

He smirked. 'She got to me every way she could, and then some. The things she was sayin' to me . . .' He whistled. 'It'd make any man fall on his knees and beg to be her slave.'

Riley gave him a long look. 'Then how'd you tune her out?'

'Taylor Swift. Hummed one of her songs. Did the trick just perfect.'

Beck dodged a streetcar and continued north along Peachtree Street.

'So where is this Firebug?' she asked.

'At the law library.'

Riley swung her head towards him, panicking. 'I can't go there! Not after what happened the other day.' He cracked a wicked grin. 'You lie!' She landed a light punch on his shoulder because he deserved it. 'So where *are* we going?'

'It's in a parkin' garage at Atlantic Station.' He eyed her. 'Have ya found your daddy's manual yet?' She nodded. 'How far are ya into it?'

'Grade Threes. Pretty disgusting reading. They even eat fibre-optic cable. How sick is that?'

'Well, that's about as far as you're gonna get.'

'What do you mean?'

'I took out the back section, the parts that covered Fours and up. Don't want ya tryin' to trap an Archfiend or nothin'. Ya made the rest of us look bad enough takin' out a Three, ya bein' an apprentice and all.'

It took a while to register what he'd done.

'You removed the rest of the manual,' she said flatly. No wonder the thing hadn't been as thick as she'd expected.

He shot her a broad grin. 'Just keepin' ya safe, Riley girl. Ya'll thank me one day.'

Not in this lifetime.

It took the better part of an hour of skulking around the parking garage to finally locate the fiend in question. As they'd hiked through the multistory concrete structure, Beck remained on guard the entire time. It felt weird trapping with him but she had to admit she wasn't afraid.

He can handle anything. Her dad had taught him well.

'Not quite what ya thought trappin' would be?' Beck asked. It sounded like Harper's question, except there was no malice in it.

'I figured it'd be more exciting. Less hiking, for one.' She'd managed to keep up with Beck, but it had been a struggle with her sore thigh. 'I've never seen a Pyro.'

'Evil critters. They love fire. It fascinates 'em.'

'Like Fireman Jack.'

'Yeah, 'cept he doesn't go around settin' 'em.' Beck did a

quick one-eighty, surveying the area around them. 'It won't be out in the open on the top deck, so this floor has to be it.'

'Glad to hear it. All this incline stuff isn't feeling good on the leg.'

He shook his head like he'd been stupid. 'I'm sorry, girl. I didn't think of that. Ya wanna wait in the truck?'

Did he just apologize? That had to be a first.

'I'm good,' she said, ignoring the jittery muscles and the cramping as best she could.

Beck scrutinized the area with wary anticipation. 'Ya need to stay behind me. If this goes wrong, run,' he ordered.

'Wrong how?'

'Like if this thing gets a couple cars burnin'.'

Exploding gas tanks. Not good.

'Hold this, will ya?' He handed over his duffel bag. It was so heavy she nearly dropped it. 'Careful! There's spheres in there.'

'You could have warned me it weighs more than I do,' she groused.

'Ya need to build yourself up, girl. Only way to handle a full trapper's bag.'

Muscles. Right. Just what I need. 'Why don't you pack lighter?' she asked.

'Ya need all the gear with ya.'

'Why? You know this is a Two.'

'Higher level demons can act like the lesser grades. Ya think you're trappin' a Three and it turns out to be a Four and if ya don't have the right equipment that's a LLM.'

'Huh?'

'Life. Limiting. Mistake.' He stripped off his leather jacket and tossed it on a nearby car. He was wearing a *Take No Prisoners* camo T-shirt underneath. It was looser than most guys would wear. He wasn't looking to show off his muscles, but making sure he had plenty of room to move. Picking up a white sphere, Beck began his search. Luckily there weren't as many cars as on the floors below. A sparking noise came from underneath an old SUV. It was one of the big monsters, the kind that no one would buy any more what with gas running ten or more a gallon. It was originally black, but now it was covered in a fine layer of dust as if it'd been abandoned here.

Something red, like a giant rubber band, snaked out of the tailpipe. As it reached the concrete floor, it took shape. It looked a lot like an eight-inch-tall red rubber doll with horns and a forked tail. It grinned a mouthful of sharp teeth, then snapped its fingers. Brilliant red-gold fire shot out of its palms.

'Trapper,' it hissed.

'Howdy, demon. Nice flames,' Beck replied.

A second later a bolt of fire went streaking towards him like it had come from a military flame-thrower. He deftly stepped aside and the bolt exploded on the concrete next to him. It'd happened so fast Riley hadn't had time to react. If Beck was frightened, he certainly wasn't showing it.

'Roast you, trapper!' the fiend hissed, snapping its fingers again. Then it caught sight of Riley.

Before her companion could shout a warning, a bolt came

straight at her. She shrieked and cowered as the flames raced over the top of her. There was a sizzling sound as they struck a concrete support. The scorch mark was four feet wide.

Holy crap. Now she *was* scared.

The next fireball went straight at Beck. He weaved, lost his footing on a patch of oil and fell to one knee. The sphere in his right hand shattered and magically charged water burst forth in a rolling wave across the floor. In a few seconds ice crystals sheeted across the concrete like frost on a window pane in deep winter. Beck struggled to his feet and quickly backed off to avoid being trapped in the rapidly freezing pond.

'I need another one!' he called out.

With a high-pitched cackle, the fiend hopped on to a nearby Honda and began to fire incendiaries at the unarmed trapper.

'Throw a sphere!' Beck shouted, dodging and ducking to avoid the flames.

Riley pulled one out without looking, about to dash it to the ground.

'Not that one!' Beck cried out as an arc of flame caught him. 'Get a white one!'

White. She put the duffel bag on the ground and frantically rummaged through the contents. Beck cried out as another arc of flame got too close. The cackling fiend was playing with him.

'White!' she shouted. 'Got it.' She hauled back to dash it on the floor of the garage.

'Up! Throw the thing up!' Beck called out and then rolled between two cars to avoid another burst of flame.

'Up?' She took a huge breath and underhanded the glass ball straight up towards the concrete above them.

The demon turned towards her, igniting a massive fireball on its palm.

'Oh, God.'

The sphere struck the garage ceiling an instant before the demon set the fireball loose. Beck yelled something, but by then it was too late.

Pure white light slammed into her eyes, blinding her. Stumbling backwards, she crashed into a support and landed hard.

Beck shouted again. The demon shrieked.

Then it began to snow.

Chapter Twenty-Eight

Riley pulled herself up against the concrete pier. Nothing was broken as best as she could tell, but she knew she'd have more bruises by morning.

It was snowing in the parking garage. Serious snowage, like somehow they'd moved this battle to Chicago in January. There was already three inches on the concrete and it wasn't melting.

She hunted through the falling white until she found the demon. His fire was out, thin tendrils of grey smoke curling upward from his hands. He stormed and shouted and cursed, but couldn't generate a flicker.

'Beck?' she called out.

He hauled himself out from behind a car. 'Ya OK?'

Ouch. My butt hurts. 'I'm good.'

Carefully he worked himself across the frozen pond and tagged the Pyro. It didn't try to run, its movements slowed by the cold.

'Kiss my ass, demon!' Beck whooped, and shot a fist in the air.

He slid his way over to her, nearly falling. 'Hold this,' he said, and dropped the Pyro into her hands.

It was uncomfortably warm, like a hot rubber ball, and it glared at her malevolently.

'Blackthorne's daughter. We know thee. Boon we grant –'

She ignored it. What she couldn't ignore was the weird look on Beck's face.

'What?' she asked.

'It said your name.'

'They all do,' she said, shrugging. 'Always have. I told you that.'

'They don't do that to me.'

'That's cos I'm special,' she said, winking. Adrenalin flowed out of her body and she felt suddenly exhausted.

'Special, huh,' Beck mumbled. He pulled a lunch tote from his trapping bag. It was large for a tote, bigger than the one Simon had used for the Four, and it had a logo on the side from some Gainesville bait shop. He unzipped it, revealing jagged chucks of dry ice.

The demon began to wail and curse, twisting in Riley's grip.

'Tough break, asshole,' Beck said. He took the demon and dropped it head first into the dry ice. The ice hissed and went white. The cursing stopped as Beck zipped the container closed.

'Do those magical charms really work?' she asked, pointing at a nest of them attached to the handle. They seemed to be made of jade and wood.

'Supposed to, at least that's what the witches claim.'

'Just checking here – I thought I was supposed to watch,' Riley said, unable to resist pulling his chain.

'Ya were,' Beck replied, suddenly serious. 'If anyone asks, I threw both globes, OK? If not, there'll be hell to pay.'

She nodded wearily. 'Whatever.'

It had stopped snowing, though there was at least five inches of the stuff on the garage floor. The giant pond was covered with it.

'Should have brought our ice skates,' Riley said. Then another idea dropped into her head. How many times would she get a chance like this in Atlanta? Turning her back to her companion, she packed herself a snowball.

'Beck?' she called out, all innocence.

'Yes, kid?' he replied, turning towards her.

Kid? That did it. She threw the snowball and it struck centre chest. He oofed, glared and then stalked towards her, intent on his prey. 'You called it . . . *Princess!*' She turned to escape, but a snowball hit her right on the butt. He'd planned a similar ambush.

'That wasn't hard to hit,' he joked.

'Are you saying my butt's big?' she demanded.

His grin grew wider, egging her on.

'Die, Backwoods Boy!' Two more went his way and only one connected, splattering him just north of his belt buckle. She scurried to rearm herself, knowing the battle was heating up.

'Backwoods Boy?' he called out, frowning. 'Ya got no respect, girl.'

He slid on the ice, moving faster than she'd anticipated and swooped in like a basketball star. A mushy snowball dropped down the front of her jacket. It melted into her bra and on to her skin, making her shriek and dance around until the remaining snow fell out of the bottom of her sweatshirt.

Laughing at her antics, Beck was already packing another missile. She ducked at the last minute and it glanced off an expensive sports car.

'Step away from the car!' the auto's alarm voice commanded. 'Step away from—'

'Let's get out of here before someone calls the cops,' he advised.

The Corvette's alarm was still issuing orders when they reached his truck on the first level. He toted the demon and the duffel bag while she took control of his jacket.

'You OK?' she asked, noticing the back of his T-shirt had a sizeable scorch mark.

'A little crisped, but not bad. That's why I took off my coat. It's the third I've bought this year.' He eyed her as he stowed the gear in the front seat. 'Ya really don't know the spheres by colour?'

'Dad wouldn't tell me about them.'

Beck mumbled something under his breath. 'He figured ya'd quit, get a real job.' He thought for a moment and then nodded to himself. 'Let's find some food and we'll work on that.'

'Can we get barbecue?' she asked, suddenly hungry. 'I haven't had barbecued chicken forever.'

A big grin appeared on her companion's face. 'I know this great place on Edgewood. Mama Z's. It's a dive, but damn the food's good.'

'What about that thing?' she asked, pointing at the bait container.

'We'll do a drive-by to Jack's. It'll stay quiet until the dry ice thaws, then it'll get nasty again. Best it's Jack's problem at that point.'

'What's he do with them?'

'Throws them in a bigger canister of dry ice.'

'Doesn't that kill them?'

'No way,' he said, shaking his head.

As Beck drove out of the garage, he gave the parking attendants a big toothy smile and a wave. 'There's some snow on the fifth level. Thought ya might like to know. Y'all have a nice day, now!' he called out.

No wonder Dad liked working with you.

Beck did the drive-by to Jack's. She remained in the truck as he completed the transaction and collected the payment.

'Two hundred and fifty,' he said, shutting the door. He promptly dropped half of it in her lap, mostly in twenties. 'That's your cut.'

'But—'

He raised a calloused hand. 'I know – you're not supposed to be earnin' anythin' unless it's with Harper. So if anyone asks, ya didn't get a cent.'

She looked down at the money. 'Thanks.'

He shrugged. 'Saves me having to loan it to ya. Ya did help out back there.'

'Help out? I totally saved you.'

She expected an argument, but it didn't come. 'Sure did. Thanks . . . Riley.'

An apology and a thank you, all in one day? This has to be a dream.

They'd picked up the food and headed for her apartment. Along the way he'd shared some of his knowledge of Firebugs and how her dad had taught him the ropes. Riley didn't interrupt, hoping this would never end. It was nice not to argue with him. She actually liked the guy when he wasn't going all Big Brother on her. After all, they had a lot in common – they were both trappers and they'd both adored her father.

'I guess it was only right ya followin' in the business,' he said, making the turn towards her place. 'Ya got it in the blood, all the way back.'

She gave him a puzzled look. 'What do you mean? My grandfather was a banker.'

'That was his day job. Your granddaddy and his people were all trappers. It calls to ya no matter what.'

'My grandfather was a trapper?' Her parents hadn't mentioned that, like it was some dark secret.

'Your great-granddaddy too. Blackthornes have been trappin' since . . . forever. Like the Stewarts.'

'I didn't know that.' No wonder she'd had the feeling she *had* to do this. In some ways, that was sorta disturbing, like she didn't have a choice. 'Why didn't Dad tell me?' she asked, her anger stirring.

'Never wanted his daughter to be a trapper. Too dangerous.'

That she couldn't argue. If she worked at the coffee shop like Simi, she sure wouldn't have got clawed up by an espresso machine.

'What about your people?' she asked. 'Were they trappers?'

He shook his head. 'Didn't trap demons, only small varmints. Too busy runnin' bootleg whiskey and tryin' to stay out of jail. I'm the first one in the family.'

'They must be proud of you.'

'Not to hear them tell it.'

When Beck set the takeaway bag on the kitchen table, he hesitated.

'Which chair can I sit in?' he asked.

'That one,' she said, pointing at hers.

He reached for it and then changed his mind. 'I better wash up first,' he said. As he walked down the hall towards the bathroom, he stripped off his T-shirt. He wasn't just singed. There was a big red burn between his shoulderblades, intersected by newly healed claw marks.

'Beck?'

'Yeah?' he called out.

'We need to treat your back.'

'Nah, it's OK.'

She fished a bottle of Holy Water out of his duffel bag, checked the label to ensure it was fresh, and then wedged herself in the doorway of the bathroom so he couldn't escape.

He saw the look in her eyes. 'That bad?'

'Not good.'

He blew a stream of air out of his lips. 'Sink or tub?'

'Tub.'

She used the entire bottle on his back and shoulders as he bent over the bathtub to keep the Holy Water from going everywhere. Some got in his hair, but he didn't seem to mind. From her vantage point she could tell he definitely had muscles in all the right places. Simi would say he was hunkalicious, but this was Beck after all.

'Those claw marks,' she said. 'You got them the night Dad died, didn't you?'

He stood up, swiping damp hair away from his forehead. 'Yeah,' he said softly.

'You kept Dad from being . . .' *Eaten.*

'He'd have done the same for me.'

'Thanks.'

He shrugged as if it was no big deal. She couldn't push it much further or he'd get more uncomfortable and that usually made him surly. She loaned him one of her dad's T-shirts and tossed his in the garbage.

Famished, Riley attacked the chicken, the sweetcorn and the mashed potatoes with a vengeance. It was as good as her companion had promised.

'This is great stuff,' she said, wiping barbecue sauce off her face. 'It's really hot. I like it that way.'

'Best in Atlanta,' he replied. 'I'll take ya there when Mama's workin'. She really likes me.'

'You charmed her on purpose, didn't you?'

'Never piss off the people who feed ya. I learned that in the Army.'

It was an opening she'd not expected, a chance to learn more about him.

'What was it like over there?' she quizzed.

He didn't answer for some time, but his eyes went distant, as if he was seeing things she couldn't hope to understand.

'I felt alive for the first time in my life. Kinda weird, if ya think about it, with all that dyin' around me. Somehow I knew I was supposed to be there to help those guys. Get a few of them home in one piece, not in some body bag.'

'Dad said it was hard on you, that you changed.'

Beck rubbed his chin. 'Ya see so much. I was young and I didn't know how to handle it.'

'You're still young,' she said. 'You're not that much older than me.'

'I don't feel like it,' he admitted. 'Never really had a chance to be a kid.'

'Do you regret going over there?' she asked, wondering what sort of hell he'd endured.

'Some nights, when the dreams won't leave me be.' Beck slowly pulled his eyes up to hers. 'Other times, no. I don't fear dyin' now, not like some. I've seen it too many times.'

'Why trap demons?' she quizzed.

A faint smile came to his face. 'Because of your daddy.'

'Like me, then,' she said.

'It's a good enough reason.'

He rose and headed for the couch. Instead of stretching out as she thought he would, he began to dig inside his duffel bag, carefully laying out different-coloured magical spheres on the seat cushions.

'Come here,' he said, beckoning. 'I'll give ya the quick and dirty on these things. Just act surprised when Harper does all this, OK?'

'It'll be our secret,' she promised.

The spheres ranged in size from a golf ball to a grapefruit on steroids. There was every colour you could think of – white for the snow globes, clear for the Holy Water, blue for the grounding spheres, purple for Babel spheres, and so on. He explained each one in detail, then put them back in the bag.

'That wasn't so hard,' she said, sucking on the last of her iced tea. It was more syrup than tea, just the way she liked it.

'We're not done.' Beck dropped his hand into the bag and pulled out a blue sphere. 'Quick, what is it?'

'Ah . . . ah . . .' she struggled.

'Think! The demon is fixin' to nail ya and you're not givin' me an answer.'

'Babel sphere?' she guessed, then winced. *Wrong!*

'Babel spheres are purple.' He handed it to her. 'This is a groundin' sphere. It pulls a Geo-Fiend into the earth so it can't summon weather or make earthquakes.'

'It didn't work for Dad.'

'It did. The demon got lucky.'

He pulled out another sphere.

This one she knew. 'White. It's for Firebugs.'

'That was too easy.' Another appeared in his hand. *Red.* 'Ah . . . oh lord.' This was hard.

'A shield sphere,' he said.

And so it went until she could pretty much identify each sphere for its properties and use. Whites went up, the rest went down. Blues needed to contact metal. Purples needed to land at the demon's feet. Reds only lasted a short time.

'Did Dad say anything to you about the Holy Water?' she asked.

'Only that he was worried that it wasn't workin' as well as it used to on some of the demons.'

'What kind of demons?'

'Threes. Why ya askin'?'

She waved him off. 'Just wondering.'

He returned the orbs to the bag and zipped it shut. 'Ya still confused about the spheres?'

'Yeah. Were you at first?'

'Got it right off,' he said. 'No sweat.'

'You lie!'

A boyish grin told her she was right. Then he set a small box on the couch between them.

Riley stared at it, then up at him. 'For me?'

When he issued a quick nod, her heart rate sped up. There was no writing on the box, so she had no clue what might be inside. The moment the lid came off, she gasped. A long black demon claw sat inside. The top of it was captured with silver wire and it had a thick chain curled up behind it.

'Is this . . .' she asked with a slight shiver.

'Yeah, it's the one out of your leg,' he admitted. 'I asked a friend of mine to make it so ya could wear it. I hope ya like it.'

In some perverse way, she did. A lot. When she looked up at Beck, concern covered his face. This really did matter to him.

Riley looped it over her neck and then held it away from her body so she could see it. The claw looked scary close up, just like its former owner.

'It's awesome, Beck!'

His expression relaxed. He acted like he wanted to say something more, but then shook his head. Standing, he put the strap of the duffel bag on his shoulder and scooped up his coat with his free hand.

'Take a trip to the market tonight. Introduce yourself to the witches who make these puppies,' he said, tapping the side of the bag. 'They'll tell ya how the spheres work.'

'But what about Dad?' she asked, confused. She'd need to be at the graveyard in an hour.

'I'll watch him till ya get there.'

As he reached the door, she called out, 'Beck?' He turned round, reminding her more of the young man who'd gone to war, not the old one who'd returned. 'Thanks. For everything. I mean it.'

A slow grin edged on to his face. 'You're worth it . . . *Princess*.'

Her tennis shoe hit the door a second after it closed.

Chapter Twenty-Nine

As Riley waited for Simon at the end of Centennial Park, she tried to relax. Her back was sore from playing tag with the concete support and she still felt scorched, though she'd washed her hair and changed clothes. No wonder trappers bought most of their threads second-hand: they had a shelf life of fresh oysters.

Riley returned her attention to the nest of newspapers in her lap. If her father had one weakness it was details, and she only wanted to see the bigger picture, not the complete history of Holy Water since the dawn of time. She wanted to know why he was interested in the topic, but so far she'd not found anything that answered that question. One thing came through clearly in his notes – her dad was worried.

Frustrated at her lack of progress she jammed the papers into her messenger bag. She had called Simon and asked him to join her on her trip to the market, and as she waited for him to arrive her hand trailed up to the chain that secured the demon claw. She'd pulled it out a couple of times to look at it, marvelling how really neat it was, but then hid it again. Metal was valuable and it wouldn't be smart to let anyone know she was wearing some. The silver in the chain and the wrapping was the good stuff, the kind her mom used to have before they had to sell it to help pay for her chemotherapy.

'I bet this was way expensive,' she mused. She still couldn't believe he'd done it. *I guess I really don't know him that well.*

The whole afternoon felt different, like aliens had kidnapped Backwoods Boy and rewired him to be nice. He'd acted like he wanted to be with her, laughed at her jokes, didn't make her feel like she was being goofy at all. He'd even taught her how to trap a Firebug.

Hope it lasts. It'd be good to have him as a friend, maybe even a trapping partner once she made journeyman.

She looked up to see Simon approaching. 'Hi there!'

He shrugged. The Silent Order of Simons was back.

And they think girls are moody.

'Hey, no fair being so quiet,' she nudged.

He looked embarrassed for a second. 'Sorry.'

Riley took his hand and squeezed it. When he didn't return the gesture, she dropped it. For half a second she wondered if she'd done something to tick him off, but she couldn't think of anything. This was just Simon. Sometimes he was fun, sometimes he was silent.

'What did Harper do to you?' he asked in a voice so quiet she almost didn't hear him.

'Yelled a lot.'

'That's it?'

'Yes,' she lied.

A relieved sigh. 'Keep out of his reach. He'll beat you for no reason,' Simon warned.

'You?'

'All his apprentices,' he said, then fell silent again.

As they walked into Centennial Park she forced her mind to happier times as a counterweight to grim reality. When she was little, Riley's parents would tote her downtown to play in the five fountains, which were laid out in interconnecting rings like the Olympic logo. In the summer when it was blistering hot, the park was always crowded. Vendors sold kosher beef hot dogs, vegetable samosas and root-beer floats. This place was all about good memories.

Despite her companion's uncomfortable silence, she couldn't help but share that feeling. She gave him a playful hip-bump.

'My parents used to bring me here when I was a kid. I loved jumping around in the fountains.'

To her relief, Simon roused from his melancholy. 'Mine did too. We'd run around for a couple of hours then pile in the car and fall asleep. Mom and Dad appreciated the quiet since there were so many of us.'

Riley looked longingly at the water spraying high in the air towards the evening sky. The lights were on tonight, making the droplets sparkle like diamonds. As they walked by the nearest jet she pushed Simon closer to it. He yelped in surprise as the water hit him and then charged after her. She tried to run but her thigh wasn't cooperating.

'Got you!' he laughed, and grabbed on to her. He lifted her up and spun her round. When her feet were on the ground, he wore a smile. It made her feel good again.

When they broke apart, Simon caught her hand and held it tight.

'Thanks,' he said. 'I take myself too seriously sometimes.'

'Only sometimes?' she jested. 'You'd make a great monk. You're good with the silent bit.'

'I thought about the priesthood,' he admitted, 'but I decided I'd rather hunt demons. That way I can marry, have kids.' He looked over at her, as if he was judging her reaction.

'How many?' she asked.

'Three, maybe four. More than that is too many unless you have a lot of bathrooms.'

You'd make a good dad.

They paused at the edge of the Terminus Market. It was barely dark and the market was growing more active, like a bear stirring out of hibernation. The lights made the multicoloured tents glow like giant Christmas bulbs. Her dad had claimed it wasn't like it used to be, as if that was a good excuse for not bringing her here.

She remembered mostly baked goods and craft items, but now there was a bit of everything in row upon row of tents, lean-tos and camping trailers. People wandered from vendor to vendor, toting items they'd purchased – used tyres, homemade bread, a basket of apples. There was a white nanny goat and its owner was milking it into a shiny pail. Riley gave Simon a puzzled look.

'He sells the milk,' he said.

'Isn't that against the rules?'

'Yes, but the city ignores what goes on down here. As long

as the stall fees are paid, they're happy.'

As they passed a shop that sold jerky, Simon shuddered. 'I don't trust that stuff,' he confided in a lowered voice. 'The guy says it's beef, but you never know.'

'Well, it won't be rat,' she said. 'The Threes eat all of those.'

'I'm thinking coyote,' Simon replied.

A little farther on she spied a brawny man pounding something out on an anvil. A glowing red fire blazed behind him. A shower of sparks would fly into the night air when his young assistant worked a ragged set of bellows. The man was stripped to his waist, but even in the cold air he was perspiring from exertion, sweat defining the ropy muscles on his arms and chest.

'A smithy?' Riley said. 'Guess it makes sense.'

'Cheaper to fix what's broken than buy new,' Simon explained.

Riley stopped in her tracks and did a slow one-eighty. 'This is like something out of a movie,' she said. 'Like an Arabian market or a medieval fair.'

'With a Southern twist,' Simon said, pointing towards a tent. The menu posted on a hand-lettered sign included grits, collards, fried chicken and sweet potato pie. The pie sounded good, but she was still full from Beck's magnificent barbecue.

Simon paused in front of a tent stocked with different-sized bottles of Holy Water. Riley picked up a pint. It was manufactured by Celestial Supplies, the company her father had mentioned in his notes, and the date stamp said it had been consecrated two days earlier. She rotated the bottle in her hands and checked out the city's tax stamp, which shimmered in the dim light. Since Atlanta couldn't collect money from the Church, they taxed their by-product.

'Always check the date,' Simon advised. 'It has to be fresh if you're treating demon wounds. If you're warding your house, not so much.'

Riley thought about the Holy Water she'd used on her claw wounds. Carmela had said it must have been old, but the guy she'd bought it from had assured her it was fresh. So which was it?

'You're frowning,' Simon said.

'Just confused. I read in the manual that you have to reapply a Holy Water ward at regular intervals, but it didn't say why.'

'It's thought that it absorbs evil and becomes less potent. That's why they sell a lot of it to prisons and jails.'

'And nursing homes, hospitals, schools, government buildings, you name it,' a hefty salesman explained. He was dressed in a blue suit as if he sold life insurance. His hair was patchy at the top, and he clutched a sales pad in his hand. 'It's the only way to keep your family safe from Hell's terrors,' he added.

At that he shoved a multicoloured brochure into her hand that extolled the virtues of Holy Water and its protective properties.

'So how would I know if this is fresh or not?' she asked, thinking back to the demon wound fiasco.

The salesman tapped a fingernail against the pint she was holding. 'Each bottle and every glass sphere has a batch number that includes the date the Holy Water was consecrated. It's state law.'

She already knew that. 'But can some of it be less potent?'

'No,' the salesman said curtly.

Well, that got me nowhere.

'How much is this?' Simon asked, holding up a pint bottle. 'It doesn't have a price.'

'Ten.'

'Whoa, that's high,' Simon protested, his eyebrows rising in astonishment.

'The city raised the tax rate again.'

The salesman spotted another potential customer and took his sales pitch elsewhere.

'Ten for a pint? It used to be that much for a gallon,' Simon muttered. 'That's outrageous. No wonder the price of the Holy Water spheres has gone up so much.'

Riley tucked the brochure into her messenger bag and her hands brushed against the papers inside. They reminded her of her father's research.

'Is there any way a demon could become immune to Holy Water?'

Simon immediately shook his head. 'No way. All Hellspawn react negatively to the concentrated power of divinity.' It sounded as if he'd quoted that from some book.

Then why was my dad so fixated on this?

Simon took her by the elbow and gently steered her to the right. 'The stall we want is this way.'

As they rounded the corner, Riley gasped. The bright

orange tent in front of them was full of dead people.

'They sell them here?' she asked, appalled.

'The necros always have a tent at the market.'

Riley did a quick count – there were seven Deaders and one live guy. He was doing all the talking. The Deaders stared off into space, probably wondering what had happened to them. At least the salesman wasn't hawking them like used cars or that would have really set her off.

'How much do they sell for?' she whispered.

'I've heard as high as five thousand,' Simon replied. His voice hardened. 'It makes me sick.'

She frowned. 'What happens to their souls?'

'I asked Father Harrison about that,' Simon replied, putting his arm round her waist. 'He said the Church isn't really sure what happens, but they believe the soul isn't completely free if the body is walking around. Only the necros know for sure and they aren't talking about it.'

'What if the body goes rogue or something? Starts eating people.'

Simon laughed softly. 'That's only in the movies. These guys aren't good at thinking things through and they're definitely not zombies. They don't eat at all.'

'But they're not mindless,' she said, thinking of the woman on the street with the briefcase.

'No, somewhere in between.' He steered her elbow again. 'Come on.'

As they walked away, she noticed a man watching her from the tent where knives and other sharp pointy things were sold. He was holding a sword. Not holding it actually, but wielding it, as if he knew exactly what he was doing. His sleek black hair was pulled back in a ponytail and tied with a leather cord. A glossy black leather jacket covered his broad shoulders and muscled arms. With a bit of imagination Riley could picture him on the cover of a romance novel. He turned in her direction, then saluted with the blade as a cavalier might salute his queen.

It was an effort not to melt in her tracks.

'Riley?' her companion nudged.

'Ah, sorry,' she said, glancing back at Simon.

When she looked round, the sword guy was gone.

Who was that guy?

'Bell, Book and Broomstick,' Simon announced, unaware her mind was elsewhere. The midnight blue tent was sprinkled with gold and silver stars and there was a long table in front of it laden with amulets, velvet bags and other witchy stuff.

Riley knew Simon well enough not to use the 'w' word. He was way stuffy about anything supernatural and somehow had convinced himself that the spells inside the crystal spheres weren't really magic. No matter what he called it, it *was* magic and the trappers used it or they ended up dead.

And sometimes they died anyway.

Behind the counter was a tall woman in medieval garb, her russet brown hair an unruly mass of curls. A multicoloured dragon tattoo started at her neck and descended deep inside her dark green peasant blouse. When she saw Simon, she leaned over the counter, displaying ample cleavage for his benefit.

'Hey, how's my favourite trapper?' the witch asked. From her tone Riley could tell she loved playing with Simon's head.

Riley's boyfriend noted the cleavage but pulled his eyes away with amazingly little effort. 'Just fine. Ayden, this is Riley,' he said, gesturing. 'She's an apprentice trapper.'

'Paul's daughter?' Riley nodded. 'Goddess . . .' the witch replied. She stepped from behind the table and enveloped Riley in a big hug. Her hair smelt of patchouli incense.

'We all miss him,' the woman said, stepping back, her eyes clouded.

An awkward silence fell between them.

Riley cleared her throat. 'Beck would like you to tell me about the spheres.'

The witch brightened. 'Ah. Sphere Lecture 101. My pleasure.'

'I'll wait here,' Simon said, his hand in the pocket where he kept his rosary.

'I promise I won't turn you into anything that eats flies,' Ayden teased.

Simon stiffened, but didn't move.

The witch waited until they were inside the tent and then leaned close to Riley. 'I love messing with him. He's a real sweet guy, but he hasn't learned that his faith isn't in competition with anyone else's.'

'Did you give him the sphere lecture too?'

She nodded. 'He wasn't that receptive.'

As they walked deeper into the tent, the soothing scent of jasmine enveloped them. Lanterns hung from the tent poles and in one corner someone was having a Tarot card reading. Waving Riley forward, Ayden knelt in front of a large wooden chest adorned with arcane symbols. Some of them Riley recognized: an ankh, the Eye of Horus. The rest was anyone's guess. Celtic maybe.

'We keep them in the chest because they're easily broken,' Ayden explained, opening the lid.

Tell me about it.

The witch dug out three spheres and placed them in Riley's hands. One red, one white and one blue. 'So how do you make these?' Riley asked.

'We buy the glass spheres, blend the ingredients and fill them using a funnel through that little port.' Ayden pointed towards a small cork plug on the side of the sphere. 'Once they're filled, we reseal them. Then we go into the forest on a full moon and charge them with magic,' the witch said.

'Do you dance round a fire or something?'

'Depends on the magic. Sometimes we're skyclad, sometimes not.'

'Sky . . . clad?' Riley asked.

'Nekkid, as they say in these parts,' Ayden said, winking.

'The mosquitoes must be a nightmare.'

The witch issued a rich laugh. 'You should come sometime.'

Not if I have to be nude.

Riley slowly turned the sphere in her hand. 'The Holy

Water bottles have a tax stamp. Why don't these?'

Ayden groaned. 'I hear that's on the legislature's agenda next year, but our lobbyist is trying to push that back. They want to tax all magical items.'

'How much do you charge for these?' Riley asked, tickled to find someone who would give her straight answers for a change.

'We ask for a donation to cover our costs. It doesn't seem right to charge you guys for keeping evil at bay.'

Riley's appreciation of the witches rose even further.

'OK, I admit we have an ulterior motive – besides the good karma, that is. It makes it harder for some of the radical groups to claim we're in league with Hell when we're supplying the means to take them down.'

That made sense.

'First thing I always say about the spheres – think outside the box. The trappers like to believe that a certain sphere should only be used on its primary target. Like a Babel sphere for Fours or a snow globe for Pyro-Fiends. That's short-sighted.'

'Why?'

'Because the magic can be used in a number of ways. Think about the properties of the spheres and match them to the effect that you want to create. You can combine the spheres so they enhance each other's properties. Every time I mention something like that to a trapper he gets all weird on me.'

'Even my dad?' Riley asked. He'd always been open to new ideas.

Ayden spread her hands. 'Paul was beginning to come round, but old habits are hard to break.'

Riley's cellphone chirped. She pulled it out and muted it. Probably Peter checking up on her. After she'd dumped it in her bag, Ayden held up a sphere. White particles swirled inside like a vintage snow globe. The only thing that was missing was an ice skater in the centre.

'So let's start with a white and go from there,' the witch said.

Half an hour later Riley was outside the tent, her head swimming in details. Whites were created using air and water magic. The grounding spheres were a combination of earth, air and fire magic. It went on from there.

I'll never keep all this stuff straight.

She found Simon pacing outside the tent. 'You done?' he asked, clearly eager to be somewhere else.

Riley nodded. 'Want some hot chocolate?'

'No, thanks. I need to get home.'

Oh. So much for making this a date.

Riley checked her cellphone. Three calls, all from Beck. He hadn't left a message.

I knew it was too good to last.

Chapter Thirty

Quit stallin'.

Beck sorted out his trapping bag, which hadn't needed the attention, then did it all over again in a new configuration. If he'd had his gun-cleaning supplies, he would have stripped his Sig and given it a thorough cleaning. None of his efforts helped him forget the Two's voice calling out Riley's name. Lower-level fiends didn't do that. To them all trappers were the same.

In his gut he knew it meant something. He needed advice, but who could he ask without screwing up Riley's future with the Guild?

'Harper?' he mused. 'No way.' The bastard would use the information to throw her to the wolves. 'Stewart?' That was a better choice, but the master might feel inclined to let the Guild know Hell was taking a personal interest in Paul's daughter.

'Ah, damn.' What could he do?

After much thought, Beck decided on a less risky course of action. He waited until Mortimer had made his rounds and then fired up his cellphone, his nerves pushing him along. The call was to an old trapping buddy in New York City who he could trust with a secret.

'Patterson. What kind and where?' the gruff voice asked.

'Jeff? It's Beck.'

'Hey, Den. What's up? Long time, no hear.'

'Got a couple questions for ya. Ever seen demons workin' together? Like a Geo-Fiend and a Three?'

'Nope. That's the only thing that saves our asses. If they ever get smart, they'll nail us. Why?'

'It's happenin' here. That ain't all. Ya ever heard tell of lower-level demons callin' a trapper by name?'

'No, only Fours and above. It's not until they reach that level do they have that sort of knowledge. And an Archfiend, hell, they can tell you the colour of your underwear and when you last cheated on your wife.'

'Good reason not to get married.'

Jeff laughed. 'Why are you asking?'

'We got an apprentice who's bein' called out by every demon from a One on up.'

'Damn. Has Lucifer got his hooks in the guy? That might explain why Hell knows him.'

Could Riley have been rolled by a demon?

'No, the trapper's on the level.'

'You sure? Sometimes you can't tell. It's not like they've got a big brand on their forehead or nothing.'

'No. Both Five and a Three have tried to kill her. Lucifer won't snuff one of his own.'

'Her?'

Patterson he could trust. 'If I tell ya who it is, ya can't spread it around.'

'Doesn't go any further.'

'It's Paul's daughter, Riley.'

'What's she doing in the business?' Before Beck could answer, Jeff added, 'Following her dad, I guess. Anything else weird about her?'

Beck told him about Riley trapping the Three, how she brought it down on her own. 'It was the one that double-teamed us the night Paul died.'

'Blackthorne's dead?' the man exclaimed.

Beck felt a fool. He shook his head at his stupidity. 'Ah, I'm sorry, man. I thought ya'd heard.'

'No, I've been out of town fishing in Canada. You should do that sometime. Get your mind off the job for a few days.' A pause. 'How'd he die?'

Beck made it brief. There was a long silence and then Jeff cleared his throat. 'I've never heard of this kind of thing before.'

'So what do ya think 'bout all this?'

'I think I'm damned glad I'm up here.'

Beck sighed.

'If Lucifer's fiends know her on sight and they've already gone after her, she needs a change of scenery,' Patterson replied. 'Out of Atlanta, for sure.'

'Yeah, we're ass deep in demons right now.'

'We're not. You could send her up here. Course, that doesn't mean they won't track her down, but it might be a local thing, you know?'

Beck had a better idea. 'She's got an aunt in Fargo.'

'Put her on a bus. Those Dakotans are a testy bunch after the fiends caused those big floods a few years ago. Demons don't get too much of a chance up there any more, if you know what I mean.'

'Thanks. I owe ya, Jeff. I mean it.'

'You're buying the first round next time we meet. Later, guy.'

Beck closed his phone and dropped it on the blanket as if it was a live grenade. His gut felt like he'd swallowed a mile of barbed wire.

'Too much weirdness goin' on,' he muttered. Most of it seemed to be centred round Paul's daughter, but that didn't make any sense. Hell was taking too much of an interest in her. The Pyro-Fiend had been the final straw.

No matter how much he'd enjoyed teaching Riley the ropes as her daddy had taught him, he shouldn't have taken her trapping with him. She'd done fine, better than most apprentices, but he was just being selfish. It was hard to admit he liked being around her. She reminded him of Paul in a lot of ways and when they were together the ache in his chest faded, at least for a little while.

There was only one way to handle this – cut her loose, make her hate him like she did when she was fifteen. He had to get her out of town until things settled down. This was a battle he had to win.

If not, Hell would have the last word.

For once Riley wasn't nervous about seeing Beck, despite his numerous phone calls. This afternoon had proved they could get along, have fun together. He'd even given her a present, one that no other girl in Atlanta could claim.

The moment she'd crossed the circle, he was on her.

'Why didn't ya answer your phone?' he groused.

'Because I was busy learning about spheres,' she said, puzzled at his attitude. *Like you told me to.*

'Who'd ya talk to?'

'Ayden. Simon introduced us. She gave me her card in case I had more questions.'

'Simon?' he snapped.

'Yeah, we made a date of it.'

Something passed over his face for a fraction of a second, but she couldn't decipher it.

'Why am I surprised?' he grumbled. 'Here's the word – ya need to call your aunt, see about stayin' with her.'

What? Where's that coming from? 'I want to stay here.'

'Ya need to be with your family,' he said.

'I don't need to be with family that can't stand me. You don't know her.'

He shouldered his duffel bag. 'Doesn't matter. Just make the call.'

This was his 'my way or the highway' tone again. He was worse than any parent. At least the 'rents made the effort to explain after they ordered you around.

'Everything was good with us this afternoon. What happened?'

He huffed but didn't answer, as if she wasn't deserving of a reason.

'Is this because of Simon?'

His face went as tight as his fists, causing the candle flames to shoot heavenward. 'Don't fight me, girl. Ya can't hang round here any more, goin' on dates like this is some sorta picnic. Ya need to be out of this city as soon as possible.'

Ohmigod, you're jealous. Why hadn't she seen it before? No wonder he'd given her a present; he was trying to compete with Simon. *Like you have a chance, buddy.*

Riley clenched her own fists. 'You hate it that I'm dating. That's why you want me gone. You think we'll break up if I go to Fargo.'

'It's not that,' he said, shaking his head.

'Oh yeah it is. You can't stand me being happy. You just want me lonely and miserable like you.'

'Girl —' he began in a warning tone.

'Admit it, Beck. Nobody cares about you because you act like a butthead all the time.'

He took a menacing step forward. 'Cut the lip, girl. You're outta here, even if I have to throw ya in the back of my truck and drive your butt to Fargo.'

'You wouldn't dare!' she snarled.

'Ya got three days. Make it happen or I will.' He spun on a heel and marched out of the circle. It ceased blazing the moment he crossed it.

'You miserable piece of . . . '

Riley bit her lip as he stomped out of sight. She'd been so stupid. Why did she think he'd changed? He'd just tried to soften her up so he could get his own way.

And I almost fell for it.

Even by the next afternoon the hurt still lodged in Riley's throat like a chicken bone she couldn't cough up. She'd spent most of the day doing odd jobs for Harper and keeping out of range of his explosive temper. It had succeeded because the master and Simon went to trap a Three near the casino in Demon Central. Once they'd left, she worked on her demonic curse words. It was amazing how many applied to Beck.

More than once she wanted to pull off the claw and throw it away, but she couldn't make herself do it. It was *her* claw, not his. She'd earned it. She'd just have to forget that he'd given it to her.

Yeah. Like that'll work.

All the while it was hanging there, reminding her of what it had been like when he'd been nice. Now that he wasn't any more. If that wasn't bad enough, she had the ho-bags to deal with at class this afternoon. If they had any sense, they'd know not to get in her face. Her fuse was too short, and if she hit one of them she'd be out of school in a sec. No school equalled no driver's licence. Public transport so wasn't her thing.

This time Riley parked her car close to the coffee shop and in plain view of where she planned to sit. She needed to be outside before the droids to reduce their options for vandalism.

Brandy and her band were waiting near the entrance. At least they weren't all wearing the same colour tonight. That had been too weird. Riley ignored their giggles and pointing, retrieved her messenger bag and then locked the doors.

'Hi,' a voice said. She turned to find one of the boys standing nearby. 'You're the demon trapper, right?'

'Yes.' He was the scrawny kid who sat next to her in class. His clothes were at least a size too big for him and made him look like an emaciated scarecrow.

'So who are you?' she asked, not sure what was up.

'Tim.' He shot a nervous glance towards the pack of girls. 'I . . . well, I got this project I'm working on and I wondered if . . .'

'Geek alert,' one of Brandy's droids called out and made klaxon noises.

Tim stiffened.

'Ignore them,' Riley said, turning her back on the pack.

Her move seemed to spook him and he scooted backwards. 'Ah-ah . . .' he stammered. 'I've been doing some research into the types of demons and I thought, well, you being a trapper and all and . . .'

'Go on,' she prodded. If this took much longer, she wouldn't be able to claim the seat she wanted.

'I'm confused as to the differences between Biblios, Kleptos and Pyro-Fiends.'

The kid had obviously done some research.

'Why do you want to know?' she asked.

'I want to be a trapper when I'm older.'

You've got to be kidding. He was way too skinny. A Three wouldn't even consider him an appetizer.

'Don't bother. It's not that much fun.'

'But—'

She walked round him like he didn't exist and headed for the front door.

'But . . . ' he tried again, and then she heard the pack laughing. When she looked back, Tim was still standing by her car, his face telling the world how devastated he felt.

'Just deal with it – I do,' she grumbled.

When Mrs Haggerty called them inside, Riley pointedly sat in the back of the room. Brandy kept shooting her looks, followed by a knowing smirk.

They've got something planned.

Maths flew by, followed by a short state-mandated course in personal hygiene. That drew a lot of snickers since the info was pretty basic, though a couple of the guys in the back of the class definitely needed the refresher.

At the end of the class, Riley rose, stuffing her notebook into her messenger bag.

'Riley?' the teacher beckoned.

Not good. That would give the droids time to mess with her car.

'Yes, Mrs Haggerty?' she said, walking to the desk. Hopefully this would be quick.

'When they sent over your file, your term paper was in it.' She handed it over. 'I might not agree with your views but at least you had the courage to state them.'

Riley stared at the red letter at the top of the first page. She broke into a grin. 'I aced it?'

'You did. Solid research, sound argument, even though it was preachy at times. Good work.'

Riley's smile grew wider. 'Thanks!' *Wait till I tell Peter!*

She jammed the paper into her bag and headed for the door. A kid was standing in front of it, blocking her way. It was the one who always sat away from the windows and didn't say much.

'You really a demon hunter?' he asked. His eyes looked weird, like he was wearing some kind of special contacts.

'Demon *trapper*,' she corrected, trying to dodge round him. He wouldn't move. 'Look, I've got to go.' What were the droids doing to her car? If they'd lipsticked her windshield again . . .

'You hunt us,' he said with a faint lisp.

'Not unless you're a demon,' she said.

'Some say we are.' The pale kid smiled. His canines were pointed. Add in the pallid flesh, the inky black clothes, the frilly white shirt and suddenly she got the picture.

A vampire wannabe. Give me a break.

'You will not harm us,' he said solemnly, precise weight on each word.

What is it with the plural thing? It wasn't like he was the King of England. 'Look – whatever your name is – I trap demons. Dee-mons. That's it. I don't go after vampires, werewolves, shape-shifters, none of those things.' *Or crazy people who think they are one of the above.* 'I've got too much to deal with as it is.'

'That's not what we hear.'

'We who?' she asked, frowning.

'The Nightkind.'

'The night kind of what?'

The boy's face twisted in a grimace. 'We rule the dark hours and fear no one. Not even a hunter.'

'Trapper. Whatever.' *I so don't need this.* 'Now can you move?'

He swept backwards and let her pass. 'We won't forget this,' he called out as she sailed through the door.

I will.

The car looked fine, at least at first glance, but the expressions on Brandy and her minions told her that might be a false assumption. She checked the tyres. All fine. No way they could get under the hood. They couldn't put anything in the fuel because the fuel cap was locked. Riley's worry faded. They were playing with her head and they'd done a good job of it. She hopped in her ride and heaved a sigh of relief when it started. As she drove out of the parking lot, she checked the rearview mirror. The pack was laughing hysterically.

What's with them?

Chapter Thirty-One

The right rear tyre was flat. As in Riley wasn't going anywhere. Now she knew why Brandy and her bunch were so merry.

I am going to kill them all. Slowly. Painfully. And in public.

Now what? Call Beck?

'No way.' He'd take that as an opportunity to give her more grief.

Simon? That was a possibility, but time was running short. She had half an hour to get to the cemetery and recast the circle.

Putting her to-go hot chocolate on top of the car, she unearthed the spare and jack out of the boot. Her dad had taught her a lot of things, but changing a tyre wasn't one of them.

'This should be fun to watch,' a voice taunted.

Instantly furious, she turned to incinerate the fool. The words died on her lips – it was the romance-cover dude from the market, a bemused smile on his tanned face.

Riley's fury went flat like the tyre. 'Oh! It's you,' she said, feeling like an idiot. 'You're the sword guy.' His smile widened. 'Did you buy it? The sword, I mean?'

'No. The . . . *heft* was all wrong.'

Riley's throat went dry. She swallowed, twice.

'I'm Ori, by the way.'

'Rrriley.'

When he moved closer, her skin started to tingle. 'Need some help?' he asked.

She could only nod, trying hard not to drool.

He handed her the hot chocolate, saying he didn't want to spill it, then jacked up the car. The way his muscles moved made her wonder why he even bothered using the jack. Riley realized she might owe the skanks a big thank you. This guy was soooo nice to watch in action. Despite the scenery, she gave her watch a quick glance. If he was quick about the tyre changing, she'd still make it to the cemetery with a few minutes to spare. Dad came first, hunk or no hunk.

The lug nut things that held the wheel spun off. Spare tyre on, lug nuts tightened, jack down. He tossed the flat tyre in the boot after giving it a once-over.

'Someone mad at you?' he asked.

'Why?'

He pointed at the valve stem. 'This has been tampered with. That's why you had a flat.'

Riley let loose a stream of curse words.

'You're really fluent in Hellspeak.'

She cocked her head. 'How do you know I was swearing in demon?'

'Just well educated,' he said. He slammed the boot lid and then pulled out a handkerchief to clean his hands. It made him look strangely aristocratic.

Her watch beeped, reminding her the world was still in

motion. 'I've gotta get out of here. Thanks for helping out.'

'Not a problem. Maybe we'll see each other again some-time.'

There were a million other questions she wanted to ask but they'd have to wait. After climbing in the car and buckling her seatbelt, she looked up to give her helper a wave goodbye. He was gone. She searched for him on the sidewalk. On the other side of the street. No Ori.

It was like the earth had swallowed him up.

How do you do that?

The moment Riley had everything in order at the grave-yard – setting the circle went off without a hitch – she dialled Ayden. The witch had to know some seriously spooky ways of settling the score with Brandy and the droids.

'So let me get this straight,' the witch said, the noise of the market making her hard to hear. 'You want to bring the wrath of Riley down on these girls, am I right?'

Wrath of Riley. Oh yeah.

'That's it. Plague of frogs, the whole Biblical thing.'

'OK. I'll be there about eleven. What part of the cemetery are you in?'

Witches make house calls? Who would have guessed?

Riley gave her the information and Ayden hung up.

'You hags are so going to eat it,' Riley said, grinning.

From that point on the evening played out like clockwork. She'd spent some quality time with her dad, telling him about her day as if he could hear her, then there was Mort's usual visit. Lenny appeared wearing a new coat that seemed to glow in the dark. He was especially proud of it, but it didn't get him any leverage when it came to her dad's corpse.

'I hear some debt collectors got paperwork in the pipeline to have your dad exhumed,' Lenny said, adjusting his tie. 'Save yourself the grief, girl. Let me take care of him. I'll make sure you get the money.'

'Nope,' she said, slicing up a Fuji apple with a pocket knife from her dad's trapping bag. 'They're not getting him. Neither are you.'

'Stubborn. I have to respect that, even if it's stupid.'

'Stubbornly stupid,' she said. 'That's what I'm good at.'

'You'll change your mind.'

'Nope. Besides, you're nowhere as scary as that creepy guy who does all the dark magic stuff.' At Lenny's puzzled look she added, 'You know, wears a cape and turns into a mass of swirling leaves.'

Lenny's face went pale. 'Oh, man. I didn't know *he* was after your dad.' The summoner took a step backwards. 'If he asks, I wasn't here. Ever.'

'But –'

Lenny was already hustling away as if a pack of Hell hounds was on his tail.

'Whatever works,' she said, and popped a slice of apple in her mouth.

The witch arrived a few hours later and after the invitation she waltzed through the candles like they didn't exist. She placed a small picnic basket on Riley's sleeping bag and sat down. After taking some time to arrange her voluminous purple skirts, Ayden popped open the basket.

'Wine?' she asked.

'I'm under age,' Riley said. 'I might get you in trouble.'

'Not if I'm a witch.'

'How does that make a difference?'

'You do magic, don't you?' Ayden asked, gesturing towards the lighted circle. 'Then that makes you one of us. As long as the witch is at least sixteen, they're allowed to drink during magic ceremonies. You are over sixteen, right?' Riley nodded. 'Good. I hereby declare this a ceremony, so therefore you can drink legally.'

Riley frowned. 'I've never heard of that law. You're making it up.'

The witch raised her right hand. 'I swear it's true. The bill snuck through the last legislature. I think the politicians were trying to throw a bone to the Pagans. We're getting to be a big voting block.'

Riley filed all that away for future reference as Ayden poured them each a glass. The witch raised hers to the sky.

'Hail to the God and Goddess. Keep us safe this night and help Riley Blackthorne find wisdom.'

That wasn't quite what Riley had in mind, but she took a long sip of the wine anyway. It was really good, a blend of cherry and grape and some other fruits she couldn't quite place. She noted the bottle didn't have a label. Her head immediately began to buzz. *Definitely homemade.*

'So tell me what you want to happen,' Ayden said, leaning

back on an elbow. With her long skirt, curly hair and well-rounded figure she looked like an oil painting you'd find in some musty old gallery.

Riley straightened up, her head still buzzing. 'I want to tag those hags. You know – make their hair fall out or get their periods for month. Something like that.'

Ayden raised an eyebrow. 'That would make you happy?'

'It would make them back off.'

'But what would it do to you? Would it make you feel better?'

Riley groaned. 'No,' she admitted. 'I'm so tired of people dissing me.'

Ayden leaned over and put more wine in Riley's glass.

'Goddess, you sound like me at your age. Here's what I've learned – you can't make them like you. All you can do is be stronger than they are.'

'You mean I should screw with their cars?'

Ayden rolled her eyes. 'No! You've got enough problems without inviting more backlash.'

Riley wiggled on the blanket, uncomfortable at the witch's tone.

'Then what can I do?' she asked.

'What you do is build up your inner strength.'

Riley groaned. She'd hoped for a righteous butt-kicking spell and instead she was getting the Yoda treatment.

'You need an example?' Riley nodded. 'OK, we'll take some folks you know. Simon, for instance. His faith is his strength.'

'I know that.' This wasn't getting her anywhere.

'What about Beck? What's his strength?' Ayden quizzed.

'Backwoods Boy?' Riley smirked. 'Chugging beer? Being a control freak? Playing God?'

'Whoa, things not going well between you two?'

'Just peachy as long as I do whatever he commands, but when I tell him to get screwed things get nasty.'

'OhhhK.' Ayden took a deep breath. 'The question still remains – what is Beck's strength?'

'Being a hick.'

'You're sure of that?'

'He was born near the Okefenokee Swamp. You don't get more hick than that.'

'Beck plays the role for a reason. Sure, he's a South Georgia boy, but he's good at being what everyone else expects. If they don't expect much, he can get away with a lot.'

Riley didn't buy that, but she wasn't going to argue. 'I don't see what that has to do with –'

'Beck has found his strength and he uses it. So has Simon. You need to find yours. What is it that makes Riley special? What is it that you stand for? Do you really want to use magic against these silly girls? Are you willing to reap the consequences of be-spelling them, because trust me there is always a cost to magical retribution.'

Damn. 'No,' Riley admitted. 'I just want them to treat me right.'

'That may or may not happen. Sometimes they're going to hate you.'

Now the witch sounded like Peter. 'So what *can* I do?' Riley asked.

'Be yourself. You're an apprentice trapper. You're a girl. That's a cool combo. Don't hide it.'

Riley shook her head. 'That's not going to help with this crowd. They think I'm snogging Lucifer.'

Ayden snorted. 'That's their problem. You've got enough of your own.'

Riley fidgeted with the chain, then pulled out the demon claw. The witch's eyes clamped on it.

'Is that what I think it is?'

Riley nodded. 'It came out of my leg. Beck had it made into a pendant for me.' The expression on Ayden's face told her another lecture was coming. 'Please don't tell me how he's looking out for me.'

'OK. Lie to yourself if it makes you feel better.'

Riley shot the witch a glare. 'Do you have anything that will help me with those hags or are you just here to make me feel bad?'

The witch reached into the picnic basket and pulled out a light brown chamois bag about the size of a playing card. 'Maybe this will help you. It'll boost your self-esteem.'

Now we're getting somewhere. Riley took the bag and opened it. She looked to the bottom to find . . . nothing.

'Ah, it's empty.'

'Of course,' Ayden replied. 'It's up to you to fill it. Find things that mean something to you, that represent times where you've overcome an obstacle, learned something important. Put those items in the bag and they'll help you find your strength.'

'I'm not sure if that's going to help much.' *Unless I put a brick in it and nail Brandy between the eyes.*

The witch suddenly tensed. She pulled an amulet bag from a pocket and clenched it in her hand, her eyes riveted on something outside the circle.

'What's wrong?' Riley asked, trying to see what had spooked her.

'Necromancer,' the witch whispered.

'It's no biggie. They come and go all the time,' Riley replied, and took another sip of wine. Maybe Ayden could come tomorrow night with more. It made all this sitting around totally bearable.

A tornado of leaves whirled down the path and stopped short of the lighted circle.

'Oh, it's just him,' Riley said, shaking her head.

'I see we've added a witch to the mix,' the necro said as his body appeared. He was dressed as always: cloaked with staff in hand.

How does he know Ayden's a witch?

Riley took another sip of wine, boosting her courage, then struggled to her feet. It took a lot of effort. 'Look, I'm getting tired of this. Who are you?' she demanded. 'And why all this Dark Lord crap?'

She heard her friend suck in a sharp breath, like she'd done something unbelievably stupid.

'The little witch understands that remark wasn't wise, but

you're too ignorant to know who you're playing with.'

'So tell me already.'

The hood fell back. Riley half expected to see two burning red eyes in a bleached white skull. Instead, it was a pretty normal face, an older one with winter-white hair that reached his collar. His eyes were deep black and an arcane symbol glowed gold on his forehead. It didn't look like one of those you bought and stuck on yourself. No, this one was embedded in the skin.

'I am Ozymandias,' he said. 'Does that help?'

'Nope,' Riley said. 'Not a bit.'

'They don't teach you anything in school, do they?' He leaned on the oak staff like he was tired of explaining things to simple people. ''My name is Ozymandias, king of kings: Look on my works, ye Mighty, and despair!''At her blank expression he added, 'Percy Bysshe Shelley?'

'I don't do dead poets.' She plopped down on her blanket, the wine definitely getting to her.

'The dead ones are the only ones that count,' the summoner replied. He shifted his attention to Ayden. 'So, little witch, why are you here?'

'Keeping the trapper company,' Ayden replied coolly.

'It is best if *your kind* stays out of the matter. If not, there will be difficulties.'

'Warning noted,' she said evenly. 'And returned.'

So much for the warm fuzzy approach.

'I am surprised you're bothering with a dead trapper,' Ayden said.

'I have no need to explain myself.' Ozymandias shifted

those bottomless eyes to Riley. 'You don't fear me. That is a mistake I shall rectify.'

Riley waited for him to turn into something repulsive, slam himself against the circle, be infinitely creepy. Instead, the leaves swirled off into the night and then vanished in a brilliant flash of light.

That was far scarier than anything else he'd ever done.

'I'll get you, my pretty . . .' she murmured, and then hiccupped.

The witch wasn't smiling.

'Man, has he got issues. So what's with him?' Riley asked. 'Why does he want my dad?'

'I really don't know. He only summons the dead to gain knowledge. That's why he's the most powerful of the summoners.'

'Master trappers know stuff the rest of us don't. Maybe that's why.'

Ayden shrugged. 'Ozymandias controls not only the dead, but the living. He works the dark magics and it is said he knows the paths between the worlds and walks them without fear. He wields the—'

'Stop! In English, OK?'

After a steely glare, the witch dumped the rest of the wine into her glass then took it down in one long gulp.

'In English?' she asked, throwing the empty wineglass into the picnic basket.

Riley nodded.

'You're in serious trouble.'

Chapter Thirty-Two

Riley forcibly extricated herself from her car, wincing on a cellular level.

'This is so wrong,' she mumbled, rubbing her temples. If anyone could brew wine that didn't give you a hangover, shouldn't it be a witch?

Apparently not. Morning had brought a thumping head, dry eyes and a desperate desire to curl up and die.

The aspirin will kick in. Yeah. Any. Minute. Now.

She groaned and made herself take a gulp of bottled water. Maybe that would help. Shuffling inside, she found Simon hosing down the concrete under the cages.

When he saw her, he turned off the water and gave a low whistle.

'Ouch,' he said. 'Hurts to be you.' She nodded. 'Anything exciting happen last night?'

You mean other than pissing off the most seriously evil necro in the entire city?

'It was really quiet.'

Simon eyed her long black skirt, the result of not doing laundry for over a week. 'You've got ankles,' he jested. 'Who knew?'

'I'm not in the mood,' she said. 'Too much of Ayden's witchy wine.'

'Could have warned you. I've heard the witches' brew is stronger than most.'

'That's an affirmative. So what's up today?' she asked. 'Please tell me it's a lot of sleeping and *no* shouting.'

Simon coiled up the hose in a tight circle before he answered. 'We've got a Three running wild in Piedmont Park. Apparently it tried to eat some lady's dachshund.'

No way did Riley want to confront a dog-eating demon today.

As if he'd read her mind, Simon added, 'You're not on the run.'

'Thank God.'

'Harper wants you to clean out all the plastic recycling. I'll show you how to do that. It'll blow most of the day.'

'Then tonight's the Guild meeting and after that I have a date with Dad.' Before he could ask, she replied, 'Three nights and counting.'

'Almost there,' he said, nodding his approval. 'Oh, and Beck called to check in on you. He said to stop ignoring him – it isn't going to change his mind, whatever that means.'

So much for that plan. She turned her phone on. Five voice messages, all from Backwoods Boy. She deleted them.

With a creak of the recliner springs their master appeared in the doorway to his office. 'About damned time you got here,' he said, glaring at Riley. Then he saw her skirt, huffed and shook his head in disgust.

Not going to apologize.

'Come on, I'll show you what you need to do,' Simon said.

The task wasn't awful, just tedious. First she had to sort all the plastic Holy Water jugs and bottles by size then by batch number and enter that information on a form.

'At least it's better than scooping demon droppings,' Simon remarked. He seriously failed to hide the relief that someone lower on the totem pole was taking over the scut work.

Riley gave the ginormous mound of plastic a dubious glower. 'Why would the city care which bottles are going to the recycling plant?'

'They don't, but Harper does. If you're a recycling centre, you have to keep records.'

There was more to it than that. 'He gets paid for these, doesn't he?'

'Fifty cents a piece.'

I knew it. It always came down to cash.

'Let's get a move on!' their master called. After another withering glare in her direction, Harper stomped out of the building followed by his senior apprentice.

He must sleep on a bed of nails. There has to be a reason he's such an asshat.

The weather was chilly, but her head didn't pound as badly in the fresh air so Riley lined up all the jugs and bottles like plastic soldiers in the fenced lot behind the building. She made sure she kept a respectful distance from Mt Demon Manure and all the dead roaches.

Eighty-seven gallons, seventy-three quarts and forty-nine pints.
That would be over a hundred bucks in Harper's booze fund.

'Yeah, this is what trapping demons is all about,' she groused. 'Lucifer's gotta be freaking in his boots.'

Thumbing through the sheets on the clipboard she found that her boyfriend had last performed this operation three weeks ago, then roughly at the same interval over the last eight months. The pages before that were written by Jackson, now a journeyman. Someday another apprentice would be looking at her sheets and dreaming of the day they made journeyman.

And hating Harper with every breath.

Clicking the pen, she filled in a new form line by line. It wasn't easy as some of the labels were hard to read. It was on the tenth gallon she hesitated. There were a number of bottles from the same batch, but they should always have the same consecration date. The one in her lap was a problem. It had a different date than another of the same batch.

Brain fog. She took a bathroom break, swigged more water and then returned to the work. 'Somebody made a mistake,' she said. Slapped a label on the wrong bottle. It could happen, especially if they had a raging hangover like hers.

By the time Riley worked through all the plastic containers she'd found forty-two that had mismatched batch and date information. One pint said it'd been blessed a week ago, while another from the same batch was ten days old.

She flipped back to Simon's sheets. No problems there. Same with Jackson's pages. Whatever had happened was during the last three weeks.

'Why me?' She knew who was going to be blamed for this, even when it wasn't her fault. Would they split the batches, consecrate them separately?

Her gut told her no, and she had a way to prove it. Dropping the clipboard Riley hiked to the car to retrieve her father's papers, the sheets that listed all the batch numbers from the last six months' production. If Celestial Supplies had split the production run it'd be on those sheets.

Right before she slammed the boot shut she saw the pint bottle of Holy Water she'd bought at the gun shop. She picked it up. The label was hard to read after being soaked in her father's duffel bag. Carmela was wrong – this pint had been blessed on the twentieth, one day before she trapped her demon. The gun shop dude hadn't lied to her – the Holy Water should have burned like liquid fire.

But it hadn't.

Riley closed the boot and leaned on the car, wondering if it was time for more aspirin. Leafing through the pages she finally found the batch number that matched the bottle in her hand.

'What the . . .' She retraced her finger across the page to ensure she'd read the right date. The company's records said this particular batch had been produced and consecrated in mid-September, *four months earlier.*

'No, no, no!' she said. 'This can't be happening.' Trappers always chose their Holy Water by the date it was blessed.

If this stuff is four months old . . . No wonder her thigh had gone septic. She swallowed, twice, to ease the pressure in her throat. It did no good. 'What the hell have I gotten into?'

Riley trudged back to the battalion of bottles and scowled at them as if they were personally responsible for this mess. She began a new sheet, this time listing the company's 'blessed on' date and the ones she was finding on the recycled bottles. Most of them matched perfectly, but the forty-two suspect ones did not.

On a hunch, she took one of the proper pints to the bathroom and ran water on the label. No reaction, even when she purposely tried to smear it. Apparently the ink was sealed in some way. She repeated the experiment with three of the suspect bottles – the ink blurred on all of them.

Riley slumped up against the wall, trying to get a handle on this. Why hadn't anyone else figured this out? Was this one of Harper's sick jokes? Could he be tampering with these bottles?

Much as she'd love to believe that, he didn't have a thing to do with the Holy Water she'd bought for her trip to Demon Central. This was a bigger issue.

'Someone's screwing with this stuff,' she said. 'And they almost killed me doing it.'

Riley paused in front of the Holy Water vendor's tent in the market. She needed evidence, bottles that hadn't been opened so no one would say she'd tampered with them. Maybe there was some way to test the stuff, find out if it was the real deal. She'd leave that up to the Guild. All she needed to do was let the trappers know they had a big problem.

Going on the assumption that dodgy labels equalled bad Holy Water, she picked up a random pint and did the wet-finger test. It was kosher. A bit more hunting found two pints that didn't pass muster. Grumbling under her breath at the expense, she dropped money on the counter and stuck them in her messenger bag. It dug into her shoulder with the increased weight.

'That it?' the salesman asked. It was the same guy in the blue suit.

'Not quite.' She removed a couple of Harper's recycled gems out of a paper bag at her feet. 'Batch numbers should have the same consecration date, shouldn't they?'

The salesman cocked his head. 'They always do.'

She handed him the pints. 'These don't.'

The man twitched an eyebrow, but he didn't bother to look at the labels.

'Look, kid, I know what you're up to,' he said gruffly. 'You think you're going to sue us or something. We've seen all the games. We've got lawyers to deal with your kind.'

Get in this guy's face or back down? Retreat sounded good right now. She'd got what she'd come for.

'Sorry,' she said contritely. 'I didn't mean anything by it. I thought you might give me a free bottle or something.' As she reached for the empty bottles, he grabbed them up.

'I'll hang on to these. You're not pulling this scam with anyone else.'

Fine. I have more in my boot.

'Now get out of here, kid,' he ordered. 'Do your shopping somewhere else from now on.'

Riley walked one tent away, then ducked behind a rack of fruit. From between two stacks of apples she spied on the salesman.

Come on, act guilty.

The guy mopped his brow, look around cautiously, then fired up his mobile phone. He spoke too quietly for her to hear him over the market din.

When a customer came near, he stalked outside the tent, closer to her location. Suddenly he barked, 'I told you, we've got a problem.'

Riley allowed herself a smug grin as she scooted out of the other side of the fruit tent and into the heart of the market.

Her crazy discovery had just been validated.

You guys are so busted.

Still glowing from her triumph, Riley made her way to the tent that sold second-hand clothes. A mound of denim called to her and she began her search for a decent pair of jeans to replace her demon-nuked ones. Most of the nicer pairs were several jumbo pizzas away from her size.

'Not good,' she muttered, tossing aside another pair that had held promise.

'How about these?' a smooth voice asked. A pair was offered. Without looking up, she checked the label and then gave them a look over.

'Nice. Good condition. And the right size.' Then she glanced upward.

It was Ori. He wore a long grey leather coat over black jeans and a turtleneck. Her heart did a little flutter kick, making her feel like she was twelve or something.

How can one guy look that good?

'Thanks,' she said, her mouth refusing to go in gear enough to say anything witty.

'Thought I should help out. You seemed to be on a holy quest.'

'A quest for jeans,' she said, smiling. 'I like that.'

He smiled and it made his eyes seem even deeper.

'You gonna take those?' the vendor asked, causing her to jump. She nodded, handed over the ten and got her change.

'How's about some hot chocolate?' Ori asked. 'We can get some at a tent down the way.'

'Ah,' she began. This was the third time she'd run into this guy: twice in the market and once on the street near the coffee shop. That wasn't just coincidence. He didn't feel like a psycho stalker, but you never knew.

'I'll buy,' he offered.

They'd be in a public place. What was the harm?

Riley checked her watch. 'OK, but I've only got half an hour and I have to leave for class.'

'Plenty of time.'

They took their hot chocolate to go and wandered towards her car at a leisurely stroll. Riley couldn't help but notice her escort was attracting a lot of notice, especially from other girls. He had that eye-candy effect.

'You look good in a skirt,' Ori said.

'Thanks,' Riley replied. 'I need to do some washing, you know?'

He laughed, making the dimple in his chin more notice-able. 'Is that why you were questing for jeans?'

'Yeah. My last pair got holes in them when I was trapping.'

'At the library?' At her puzzled expression he added, 'I read about that in the newspaper.'

'Oh.' She felt an intense desire to change the subject. 'Are you from Atlanta?'

'No. I'm here on business.'

Which didn't tell her where he was from. Mysterious had to be this dude's middle name. His voice didn't give her a clue – no accent to speak of. His clothes pegged him for some-one with money, but that wasn't much help either.

Definite need for more info here.

'What do you do?' she pushed. They weren't going to get anywhere if she couldn't get simple information out of him.

They'd reached her car at this point. He hesitated, looked around them as if worried someone might overhear their conversation, then leaned close to her. He smelt different to other guys. Not different in a bad way, just different. Like a crisp fall breeze.

'You have to promise not to tell anyone.'

'Are you, like, a spy or something?' she asked. That'd be awesome.

'No. I'm a demon hunter,' he replied.

He was one of the elite teams they sent around the world to destroy Hellspawn.

'From the Vatican?' she asked, incredulous. Maybe the television show wasn't too far off after all.

Ori shook his head. 'Most certainly not Rome. I'm freelance.'

'Oh.' A Lancer, as the trappers called them. 'I didn't realize there were freelance hunters too. Why not work for the Vatican? Get the benefits?'

'I prefer to work on my own.'

'What are you hunting?' she asked.

'The demon that killed Paul.'

Riley started at the mention of her father's name. 'You knew my dad?'

'We met a while back. He told me about his daughter, how proud he was of you.'

She couldn't remember her dad mentioning this guy, but that wasn't unusual. He only told her what he felt she needed to know.

'He said your middle name is Anora. I've not heard that before. What does it mean?' Ori asked.

'Light,' she replied. 'Riley Anora means *valiant light*. My parents seemed to think that was pretty cool.'

'So do I.'

His gaze weighed on her and she found it hard to think.

'When you find the Five,' she said breathlessly, 'I want to be there. I want to help you take it down.'

Ori smiled at her and for a second she thought he'd agree.

'No. It's best you stay out of harm's way.'

Riley's excitement deflated. 'You sound like Beck.'

'That's Denver Beck, isn't it? Paul mentioned him. What's he like?' Ori asked.

'Oh, where do I start? Beck's mouthy and he lives to tell me what to do.' *In short, he's so not you.* 'Why do you want to know?'

A glimmer appeared in Ori's dark eyes.

'Just scoping out the competition.'

Chapter Thirty-Three

Riley didn't remember much about the ride to class, her brain too busy replaying her conversation with Mr Mysterious. He seemed to know a lot about her, but so far she'd only scored his first name and his profession. And the fact he was after the demon who'd taken out her father.

Of course, she'd be the first to cheer if he could pull it off, but Fives were hard to bring down, especially if you were working solo. *Maybe the hunters were better at that sort of thing.*

The bigger problem was how to convince the good old boys at the Guild meeting that the Holy Water wasn't reliable any more. Harper would be in her face the moment she opened her mouth, but she had to tell them, one way or another.

Riley shoved that worry aside the moment she pulled into the parking lot. She could only stew on one problem at a time and right now she had some grovelling to do. Guilt had gnawed on her like a rabid rat since she'd taken her Beck-induced anger out on Tim, the boy oh so interested in demons.

Get it over with.

She blew a stream of air out of pursed lips and marched up to him. He tensed as she approached, his eyes darting around like a hare looking for a place to run.

'Tim? That's your name, right?' He nodded cautiously. 'Hey, I'm sorry,' she said. 'I was a hag the other day.'

It took a few moments for him to process what she'd said. Then he frowned at her. 'You were.'

She shot a glance at Brandy and her pack. She'd been just as nasty as them, which made her feel bad. 'The best way to tell the difference between a Biblio, a Klepto and a Pyro is by what they do.'

Tim scrambled to dig a notebook out of his pack. Then he hunted for a pen. 'Go on!' he urged, his eyes alight.

Riley gave him a quick peek into the world of the smaller demons, but not so much as to get her in trouble. The Guild would be upset if she told an outsider too much as it was bound to end up on the Internet. As she explained things to Tim, she began to realize how much she really knew and how much of it her dad had taught her.

'That's about all I can tell you or I'd have to kill you,' she jested.

For half a second Tim looked like he believed her.

'Joking!' she said.

'Oh. OK. Thanks!' Then he grimaced. 'I'm sorry about your tyre. They . . .' He angled his head towards the gaggle of girls. 'I was really mad at you, and then Brandy told me to make it go flat.'

Somehow that didn't surprise her. 'How'd you do it?' she asked for future reference.

'Put BB under the valve cap. Gives you a slow leak.'

'Neat. I'll have to remember that.' *But why were you carrying BBs in the first place?*

'Oh. Thanks for all this,' he said, tapping the notebook with a bony finger. Tim took off. The reason for his sudden vanishing act was Brandy and the pack right behind her.

I still want all your hair to fall out.

'You really trap demons?' Brandy asked.

Riley nodded, thinking of Ayden's lecture. If being a trapper and a girl was so cool, why not see how far that got her?

She pulled the claw out from under her sweater.

One of the droids gasped. 'Is that from a . . .'

'Demon, yes.'

'No way,' Brandy said, leaning closer to study it. 'You bought that at the market.'

'No, they dug it out of my leg.'

Brandy's eyes twinkled. 'Prove it.'

Riley's bluff had been called. If she backed down, they'd think she lied and the harassment would escalate.

'See, I told you she wasn't for real,' Brandy said, smirking.

The other girls hooted in unison.

'Bathroom,' Riley said, waving the annoying girl forward. When the others started to follow, she put up her hand like a traffic cop. 'Just me and her. This isn't a public event.'

Once the bathroom door was locked, Brandy continued to smirk until Riley raised the skirt far enough for her to see the six healed claw marks.

'Ohmigod! Those are gross!'

'I prefer the word *dramatic*,' Riley said, dropping the skirt and smoothing out the wrinkles.

'Did it, like, hurt a lot?' Brandy asked, eyes wide.

'Yeah, big time.'

Apparently satisfied, her nemesis retreated to the mirror and fussed with her hair. 'Do you have a brush? I forgot mine,' she said. Without waiting for an answer, she asked, 'How do you get your hair like that? Mine is all over the place.'

Riley looked over at her enemy. They'd just crossed a line or they wouldn't be sharing styling tips. She dug out her brush and handed it over. 'Just lucky, I guess.'

Brandy bent over, then flung her hair back when she stood up. She started working on the stray pieces, blending them in. 'Did you see that weird guy with the teeth?'

'The vamp wannabe?'

'Yeah. He's really into all that. The black clothes, the red soda, the whole thing.'

'Then why is he going to school in the afternoon? A real vampire couldn't do that.'

Brandy hitched a shoulder. 'Do you like this shirt?' she asked, turning round so Riley could get the full three-sixty.

'Yeah. Pink's not my colour, but it's nice.' *For someone like you.*

'I like it a lot,' Brandy said, handing her the brush.

And then she was gone, probably to report to her entourage that Riley had gross scars on her leg and wasn't a lesbian because she hadn't made a pass in the bathroom.

Weirdly, it seemed to have worked. No bad karma either. *Maybe Ayden was right.*

Class was full of maths, sociology, English literature and even more Civil War. When Riley tried to figure out how all that connected, her brain went flatline.

At least I aced my paper.

The kid who thought he was a vampire keep leering at her, revealing those ridiculously pointed canines.

Note to self: bring wooden stake to class.

'Don't forget the field trip on Friday,' Mrs Haggerty called out. 'We're going to Oakland Cemetery to visit the Confederate section.'

A field trip to a cemetery. Now that's special.

Riley found Brandy and the girls leaning against her car. 'I swear, if you've messed with my ride again, I'm going to rip you apart.'

Brandy shook her head. Which meant nothing. 'You heard the news, didn't you?' she asked, breathless.

Which could mean anything. 'What news?'

'*They're* coming to Atlanta.'

'They who?' Riley said.

'*Demonland*. They're taping the show here!' Brandy said, her voice rising in anticipation.

Riley had heard Harper say something about that this morning, along with the words *pansy-assed actors*. When she didn't respond, one of the other girls chimed in. 'Their website said they're going to meet with the local Trappers Guild.'

So that's it.

'Will you get to see them?' Brandy asked, breathlessly.

'If they come to a Guild meeting, I will.'

Brandy squealed in delight. The sound was almost sonic level in intensity. Riley waggled a finger in an ear to ease the pain, wondering how many bats had been stunned senseless.

'Oh. My. Freaking. God!' Brandy shouted, causing heads to turn across the parking lot. 'That would be *so* cool.' Then she reined herself in. 'Can you get Jess's autograph? He's totally hot!'

Jess Storm something or other. Riley thought she knew which one that was. He *was* hot, especially in those painted-on jeans.

'Jess is dog meat to Raphael. Swoon. He's totally awesome!' one of the other girls said.

'Stacy, you're trash-talking my babe,' Brandy argued, hands on her hips now. Apparently this was a longstanding argument. 'Jess has the most amazing eyes.'

Stacy shook her head, her hair whipping around her. 'No way. Raphael's the man. He's got gorgeous pecs.'

'The show is dumb,' Riley said. There was stunned silence as every one of the girls gawked at her like she'd blasphemed God or something. 'But the guys? They're gorgeous. They've got great butts,' she said before she could stop herself.

Brandy giggled. 'Jess's is the best!'

'No way!' Stacy shot back.

It went downhill from there as each girl listed her fave's stats. By the time Riley left she had their numbers so she could send them cellphone photos of the TV guys when they came to the meeting.

If she could get their autographs, she could actually be

their BFF. The thought horrified her, but it was better than having them as enemies.

Maybe there is something to this whole karma thing.

With traffic in her favour for once, Riley arrived at the Tabernacle way early. As she walked into the auditorium, she saw Simon carefully applying the Holy Water ward. It wouldn't do to interrupt him so she headed to the bathroom and changed into her new jeans. No way she was going to endure the abuse from the other trappers because of her fashion choices.

When she returned Simon was still at it, painstakingly ensuring there were no gaps in the ward. Riley set the messenger bag full of pint bottles on the floor next to a folding chair and tried not to freak about what she was about to do.

'I will not wimp out.' No matter how many times she said it, she didn't feel good about this. What if she was wrong and the Holy Water was OK?

Her phone chirped and she mentally thanked the caller.

'Riley! How's it going?' Peter called out.

'Pretty good. I'm at the Tabernacle. We're having a Guild meeting pretty soon.'

'So how goes the Great Holy Water Mystery?'

Riley gave him the rundown, keeping her voice low so Simon couldn't overhear.

'You really think someone is messing with that stuff?'

'Yeah, I do.' *Learned that the hard way.*

'Whoa. That's way illegal.'

'I figured I'd better tell the Guild and they can take it from there.' The idea that the Holy Water might not be so holy was too scary to think about.

'Will they believe you?'

Leave it to Peter to find the one weak spot. 'Not sure. Some of these guys are sorta dense.'

'I hear you. How did class go?'

Riley gave him the report and had him laughing by the end of it.

'At least they're off your back for a while,' he replied.

'I hope so. If I get the photos and autographs, they'll be making me class president.'

There was a long pause. 'How's it really going?'

He knew her too well. 'I'm OK and then I'm not,' she admitted. 'I go along and then – *bam!* – I remember Dad's gone and it all falls apart.' Riley choked up. Her eyes glazed in tears and she fumbled for a tissue one-handed.

'I get real tired of the warden bitching at me, but I don't know what I'd do if she wasn't here. Or my dad, either.'

'Three more nights and I'm done sitting vigil,' she said, wiping her nose. 'Then he'll be safe.'

'We'll celebrate,' her friend replied, his voice lighting up in anticipation. 'Then we can hang together more often.'

That might prove a problem now that Simon was in the picture.

As if on cue, her boyfriend reappeared, empty Holy Water jugs in his hands. He set them just outside the circle. Then he smiled and beckoned her to join him.

'Ah, got to go. The meeting's about to start,' she fibbed.

'Give me call later, OK?' Peter asked.

'Sure.'

When she joined Simon, he dropped a kiss on her cheek.

'Tease,' she said, feeling bubbly and warm inside. Ori was gorgeous and everything, but Simon hit all the right places. She felt whole when she was with him and right now that meant so much when the rest of her life was an empty shell.

'Let's take a walk,' he said. The glint in his eyes told her he had other things in mind.

As they walked by the empty jugs, she paused. 'Hold on.' Kneeling, she wetted her finger and tested the labels. The ink didn't run.

'What are you doing?' Simon asked.

'Just checking something.' She wouldn't share the news, not with Simon or Beck. If somehow she was wrong, she didn't want Harper taking it out on them.

This is my deal. And my dad's. She'd just finish what he'd started.

Simon's hand touched hers as they walked round the side of the Tabernacle. Her worry about the meeting faded. Being with him helped her forget her troubles, made her feel so good.

Is this what it's like to fall in love?

'There's a quiet place back here,' he suggested, heading towards the rear of the building. It *was* quiet, nestled away from the street. He pulled her into the shadows.

'That's better.' Before she could say a word, he kissed

her, a tentative peck on her lips.

'More?' he asked, watching her reaction closely.

'More.'

The next kiss went on longer. Riley felt the warmth in her chest, then even lower. He pulled her closer, sliding a hand under her coat, then her sweater, his palm pressing against the small of her back. It felt wonderful and she didn't want him to stop.

'If Harper catches us . . .' he whispered in her ear.

'We'll both be shovelling demon crap for months,' she replied.

The next kiss deepened, became more urgent, needy. There was no space between them and she could feel he enjoyed their closeness. Riley heard him moan and they reluctantly broke apart.

Simon sighed. 'Such a temptation.'

'But I'm worth it, right?'

The sparkling blue in his eyes told her he thought so. They sat on the steps that led to the fire escape. Content, she nestled herself against his shoulder and Simon placed his arm round her, drawing her close.

'I really like you, Riley,' he said. 'In case you haven't noticed.'

'Good to hear it,' she said. 'Just part of my cunning plan.'

'Whatever that plan is, it's working.'

They fell silent for a few minutes, just being close. She could hear his heartbeat slow to normal. Other guys might have tried to push her into something she didn't want, move too fast, but Simon hadn't.

Which is why I like you so much.

When the quiet became unbearable, she asked, 'Why do you want to be a trapper?'

'Because it's a holy crusade,' he replied without hesitation. 'Like being a priest. I'm fighting against the forces of evil.'

The strength in his voice said he believed every word. That made sense: Simon's world was black and white, right and wrong.

'I've upset you, haven't I?' he asked, quieter now. 'I do that when I go all religious on people.'

'It's just that . . .' She hesitated. 'The demons, for instance. There's a big difference between a Magpie and a Geo-Fiend.'

Simon shook his head. 'They're both Lucifer's minions. It doesn't matter if one's less of a danger than another. They should be destroyed.'

'Even a Magpie? I mean, they're not evil.' The demon flitting around her apartment was kinda cute, actually, in a larcenous sort of way.

'Doesn't matter. They belong to Lucifer and warrant destruction,' he said resolutely.

Suddenly it all made sense. 'You want to be a hunter and work for the Vatican, don't you?'

He pulled back, studying her as if to see whether she could be trusted with a great secret. 'I do, but I'd appreciate it if you don't mention my plans to the others. Especially Harper.'

'I won't.' The rivalry between the trappers and the hunters went way back, centuries even. Trappers caught demons.

Hunters killed them. But that wasn't all. Hunters had the legal right to arrest, charge and execute anyone who made a pact with Lucifer. Sometimes that was a trapper, which didn't make for good relations. It didn't happen much any more, but the hunters still held those powers and all the trappers knew it.

She eyed Simon solemnly, trying to sort out her feelings for him. He seemed so gentle, so thoughtful, but that's not what a demon hunter was all about.

'Could you kill someone if you thought they were working for Hell?'

To her relief she didn't get an 'oh sure, no problem, they deserve to die' answer. Instead, she could see him wrestling with the question.

'Possibly,' he said, brows furrowed.

'Even if it was some young kid? Could you do it?' she asked, fearing the answer. Was there a heartless monster lurking inside of him?

Simon's face clouded. 'I don't know.' He pulled her close again. 'Too many questions. You make me wonder if I really know what I want in life. Besides you, that is.'

Riley's heart did a double beat. They were definitely moving this relationship along at warp speed. As if sensing her bewildered emotions, he tugged her closer and they remained that way until it was time to go inside. Not for the first time, Riley wished the rest of the world didn't exist.

Chapter Thirty-Four

By the time they returned to their seats there were some forty trappers milling around the centre of the hall, trading stories and proudly displaying their latest wounds. It was definitely a guy thing.

Beck gave her a curt nod, but Jackson waved, clearly pleased to see her.

'See, they're accepting you,' Simon remarked.

'Some of them.'

Riley had expected her personal nemesis to stomp over and annoy her right off, but Beck and his two beer bottles kept their distance. If anything, he was pointedly ignoring her.

You are so jealous.

It was Harper that worried her. If she was going to tell the Guild what she'd discovered, her master had to know about it first. That was the way things worked.

She took a deep breath and went to him. 'Sir?'

'Yeah?' he said, his bloodshot eyes telling her it hadn't been a good day. 'What do you want?'

'I've discovered something about the Holy Water. Not all the bottles are the real stuff. Some of it doesn't work like it should and I'd like to tell the Guild what I've found.'

His intense gaze made her itch. 'Why the hell didn't you tell me about this before?'

'I just figured it out this afternoon.'

He thought for a moment.

What if he doesn't let me tell them? What would she do then?

'Ah, what the hell, go ahead. I can't wait to hear this,' he said, leaning back in his chair. The sly grin told her he was looking forward to her public humiliation.

'Thank you, sir.' Right before she moved away, he grabbed her arm, digging in those fingers, causing Riley to grit her teeth. Why had she let her guard down?

He leaned towards her and whispered, 'You make me look bad and you'll pay for it, girl.'

I already am.

When Collins called the meeting to order, she made a point of not sitting near her master, breaking with tradition. Simon weighed his options and sat next to her.

You might regret that.

After roll-call, Collins started the meeting. 'You heard about that TV show coming to town?'

Hoots of derision echoed through the big hall.

'Yeah, yeah, I know,' Collins said. 'The producers want to work with us. They say they want the show to be more *realistic*.'

'They can start by making the demons look like the real deal,' Jackson said. 'I've yet to meet one who wears an

Armani suit and drives a Ferrari.'

'Ah hell, they all do,' Morton replied. 'At least in LA.'

Laughter broke out.

'They asked if a couple of us would show them around the city, let them see what we really do,' Collins explained.

'Why aren't they working with the Vatican?' Jackson enquired.

'The Vatican's reps shot them down, so now they want to slum with us.'

'Setting us up to make us look stupid,' Harper said.

'That's a real possibility,' Collins replied. 'But if we blow them off we might regret it.'

'What about those hotties? Are they coming?' a young trapper called out.

'A few are. And they're paying for our time. Do I have volunteers?'

Hands shot up and Collins took note of the names. The promise of babes and cash tipped the scales. Riley was surprised to see Beck wasn't one of the volunteers.

The president pointed right at her. 'And you too.'

'Me?' Riley squeaked.

'They say they want a female's take on all this,' he said. 'You OK with that?'

She felt Simon stir next her. 'Get Harper's permission first,' he whispered.

Good idea.

'Only if Master Harper is OK with it,' she said.

The old trapper's eyebrows arched upward, like he'd

figured out her game. 'As long as the work gets done,' he said, nodding.

Don't worry, you'll get a cut of the money.

'Then I'll let them know we're good to go,' Collins said, making a note on a piece of paper.

Riley couldn't believe how easy that'd been. Maybe not getting revenge on Brandy and her bunch had been a good thing.

Collins consulted his notes. 'Anything else?'

Her heart jumped when Harper rose to his feet.

What is he doing?

'Blackthorne's kid,' Harper began. Riley winced. 'She ran into some trouble the other day when I sent her over to Roscoe's to sell some Ones.'

Beck's eyes rose from his brew. His reaction was instant: the muscles along his jaw tensed as the knuckles on his right hand tightened round the beer bottle.

Let it go. Don't piss him off. He'll just take it out on me.

'What was the trouble?' Collins asked.

'Roscoe offered her one-twenty apiece for the demons as long as she didn't do the paperwork.'

Beck's eyes snapped to her. She saw condemnation in them.

You think I sold them under the table. You jerk!

'She told him to stuff it up his ass,' Harper explained.

Beck sagged in relief. She glowered at him and he shrugged in apology.

'No trafficker's ever tried to roll one of my apprentices.' Harper's scar tightened along with his jaw. 'It's not going to happen again, I can tell you.'

'You'll handle it?' Collins asked.

'Damned straight.' The master returned to his seat.

Riley let out the air she'd kept pent up.

'Anything else?' Collins asked.

Now or never. Riley pulled herself out of the seat, her heart thudding.

'Yes, sir . . . I . . . have something.'

Out of the corner of her eye she saw Harper's face – it resembled a vulture waiting for something to die so he could feast on its corpse. She ignored him, focusing on the podium so she didn't lose her nerve.

'I have a question about the Holy Water. Is it possible for it to be blessed in different batches?'

Master Stewart shook his head. 'I've been ta the plant. They've got massive tanks, holdin' hundreds of gallons of water. The priest blesses one tank at a time. Then all they do is put it in the bottles.'

'So every batch number should have the same consecration date?' she asked, feeling excitement rising within her. That's what the brochure said, but she wanted to lay the foundation for her radical claim.

'Of course. Why ya askin', lass?'

'I found some of my dad's notes. He was trying to find out why the Holy Water didn't always work right. He was worried that the demons were building up a tolerance to it.'

Collins and Stewart traded looks. 'Go on,' the Guild's president urged.

'This is a master list of all the production runs for the last six months,' she said, displaying the pages. 'These show the batch numbers, which include the date the Holy Water was blessed.' She set them down and took a hasty swallow from her soda.

Now it gets harder.

'I was recycling the Holy Water bottles for Master Harper and I noticed that some shared batch numbers, but the consecration dates were different.'

'You sure?' Collins asked.

Riley nodded and pulled out three of the recycled bottles, setting them in a row on the table in front of her. She put a hand on top of one of the pints. 'This one was blessed ten days ago.' She continued down the line. 'This one seven days ago and this one five. They're all from one batch. According to the manufacturer's master list, this batch was actually blessed and bottled four months ago.'

'Let me see those,' Jackson said, walking over. He compared each of the pints then his eyes rose to hers. 'I'll be damned. She's right, these do have different dates. But why would someone do that?'

'Money,' Beck called out. 'I've got a buddy who works at the plant where they bottle the stuff. He said they're runnin' three shifts and can't keep up. A pint is going for ten bucks now.'

'Twelve,' Riley corrected. 'I bought some before the meeting. Also the labels are different. Some of them don't react to water – some of them smear really easily. The fake bottles have the smeary labels. I wanted you guys to know about this so you can figure out what's going on.'

'This happened in Cleveland sometime back – someone was refillin' the bottles with tap water,' Stewart said.

'So, is it just bad labels or is the Holy Water counterfeit or both?' Collins asked.

'Let's test it,' Morton said. 'Anybody got a demon in their pocket? How about you, Beck?' he jested, but she could hear the tension in his voice.

'No,' Beck replied flatly. 'Wait a minute.' He turned towards her and tapped his chest. When she didn't respond, he did it again.

The claw. They couldn't get a live demon across the ward, but the claw wasn't alive.

'I think we might have something that'll work,' she announced, pulling the silver chain into view. The black talon hung in the air, twisting at the end of the chain.

'Damn, that's nice,' exclaimed one of the trappers sitting near her. 'Never seen a claw necklace before.'

'Is it the real thing?' Jackson asked.

'Totally,' Riley replied.

She picked up a pint of Holy Water. 'I bought this at the market tonight.' She handed it to Jackson and he ripped off the seal. Riley dipped the claw inside. After several seconds there was no reaction.

'Maybe you need a live demon,' someone said.

'It should work,' Collins replied. 'It was once part of a fiend so the Holy Water should recognize that.'

Jackson opened another pint and Riley repeated the test. Nothing.

'So which one do you think is kosher?' he asked. At least he believed her.

Riley tapped on the next one. 'Its label doesn't smear when it gets wet.'

Jackson ripped off the lid and she dropped the claw in.

And nothing happened.

Ah, crap. If this didn't work, she was going to be in big trouble.

'Riley,' Simon began in a worried voice.

The pint bottle erupted in a torrent of bubbling water that shot out of the top and soaked both her and Jackson. She yanked out the claw, fearing it would be destroyed. The talon was snow white. As it dried, it turned black like an overripe banana.

Jackson wiped his face with a sleeve.

Take that, Harper. As she mopped off her face, she caught a glimpse of him out of the corner of her eye. He was frowning, but not at her.

'What about the Holy Water for the ward?' Morton asked, all trace of humour gone. 'Is it OK?'

'It's good,' Riley said. 'I checked the labels.'

'Well, that's a relief,' Beck said. He popped the top of his second bottle of beer and drained half of it in one swig.

While trappers argued amongst themselves, Riley slumped into her chair, head buzzing. They'd actually listened to her. Her dad would be so proud.

Simon touched her arm. 'Good job,' he said. His praise was at odds with the frown. What was bothering him? 'Why didn't you tell me?'

'If it went wrong, I didn't want you in the middle of it.'

He nodded, but the frown remained.

It took the Guild president some time to call the room to order. Nearly every trapper was talking, gesturing at her, then the bottles.

Collins leaned forward on the podium and rubbed his face wearily. 'Well, this sucks,' he said. 'It looks like not all the Holy Water is the real deal. Since some of us are having the same issues with the spheres, I have to assume a portion of those are bogus as well.'

Harper rose. 'This is getting out of hand! We've got traffickers buying demons under the table and Holy Water that's as useless as spit.'

'Is this happening anywhere else in the country?' Morton asked.

Collins shook his head. 'There've been no bulletins from the national office.'

'Maybe Hell is finally getting it together,' Jackson suggested.

'That'd explain a lot,' Harper said. 'Bet there's an Archdemon behind this somewhere.'

'But why here?' Beck asked. 'Ya think it's all connected somehow?'

'That's what we have to find out.' Collins looked over at Stewart. 'Call the archbishop and the CEO of Celestial

Supplies. Set up a meeting. This is priority one. If we don't get this straightened out, we're going to start losing trappers. We need to get a handle on this now before it gets worse.'

Riley relaxed. These guys would deal with it.

At that, Collins glanced over at her, nodding his approval. 'Well done. That's impressive work from an appren–'

Collins's eyes went wide and his mouth dropped open.

Someone touched her shoulder.

Riley figured it was Simon, but both his hands were on the table in front of him. Probably one of the trappers wanting to see the claw. She turned and gasped.

Paul Blackthorne's corpse stared back at her.

Someone had reanimated her father.

Chapter Thirty-Five

'Dad?' Riley whimpered.

'Paul?' Beck called out as he rose, his chair toppling over. Others surged to their feet, transfixed by the spectacle.

'My God, it's Blackthorne!' one of them cried out.

Her dad was dressed in the suit and tie they'd buried him in, his skin a sallow grey. Immense sadness filled his brown eyes. He stood just inside the Holy Water ward.

'Run . . . Riley,' he croaked. 'Run. Too many.'

'Too many what? How'd you get—'

Deep growls echoed through the building, causing heads to turn. Furry bodies lumbered out of the darkness.

'Demons!' someone shouted.

Trappers surged to their feet, all talking at once.

Riley watched in horror as the Threes headed towards them. There were at least a dozen, maybe more. They lined up round the circle, snarling and slobbering, claws flicking in the air.

'Hold your positions!' Harper shouted. 'They can't get to us, not with the Holy Water.'

'Why are there so many of them?' Simon asked. 'This can't be happening.'

What are they waiting for?

The answer came a split second later.

'Pyro-Fiends!'

Red rubbery bodies ran along the sides of the building, leaping and twisting like ballet dancers, leaving bright crimson ribbons of liquid fire in their wake.

A Three launched itself against the ward and then flew back, howling and shrieking. It rose to its feet and assaulted the holy line again. Others joined it as trappers scrambled for their gear.

Beck was next to her, his duffel bag on his shoulder, the steel pipe in his hand. 'Where's Paul?'

She looked around but couldn't see him.

'Dad?' she called. No reply.

Beck shoved her out of the way a split second before a Three broke through the ward. It scrambled to its feet and dived at a trapper. The man screamed in agony as it pinned him to the wooden floor with its claws.

'The ward's down!' Beck shouted.

'Out! Everybody out! Move it!' Collins shouted. Stewart began to herd his apprentices towards the nearest exit.

'Where's your trapping bag, Adler?' Harper demanded.

'In the car,' Simon called back.

'Damn lot of good it's doing there.' The old trapper dumped his into the apprentice's hands. 'Snow globe!' As Simon dug in the bag, Harper gave Riley a shove, causing her to stagger backwards. 'Go!'

Not without Dad. Riley looked around blindly, but she

couldn't see him. A cheer went up as someone lobbed a sphere high in the air. It broke open and snow began to fall. Then more snow globes. A thick blizzard fell into the smoke that crawled across the floor like a grey snake. Shouts echoed around her.

As the snow landed on her, it melted instantly, plastering her hair to her skull. Riley wiped her eyes. She could only see a few feet in front of her, the exit signs completely obscured in the storm.

Bumped from behind, Riley sprawled to the floor, scraping her shins. Something grabbed her leg and she struggled to pull free. There was a cry of pain and then a vicious snarl. She scrambled to her feet, knowing if she stayed down she was dead.

A Three stood between her and Simon, claws clicking, unable to decide who to eat first.

'Go!' Simon shouted to her. 'Get out of here!'

His cry sent the demon his way. She saw it leap on him, rending and snarling. They rolled over and over on the floor, crashing into chairs and upending the tables. Blinded with fury, Riley grabbed the nearest wooden chair, folded it and swung hard at the demon's head.

'Get off my boyfriend, you bastard!'

There was a sound like a cracking egg and the fiend crumpled. Its paws twitched pathetically, then it stopped moving. She'd actually killed the thing.

'Simon?' She dropped the chair in horror.

'Oh, God,' he moaned. 'Oh, God, it hurts . . .'

His eyes wide in terror, he clutched his chest and belly as blood gushed through his fingers. She saw Jackson and grabbed him.

'Help me get him out of here!' she shouted.

They levered Simon to his feet, his face as grey as her dead father's.

'I got him,' Jackson said, taking the weight from Riley. 'Get going!'

A Three swept by her, howling in triumph as it vaulted towards one of the men. The trapper cried out and then vanished under a mass of fur and slashing claws. The demon raised its face, gore dripping from its muzzle.

When she turned to make her escape, Simon and Jackson were gone, hidden in the snow. Around her, demons leaped through the smoke, picking off their confused or injured prey. One of the Pyros hung from the big chandelier, raining fireballs from above.

She finally found Harper – he was hemmed in by a pair of Threes. Crazed with the smell of blood, they tore at anything that came near, even each other. That gave Riley an idea.

She crept to where her messenger bag had fallen. After looping it over her shoulder, she reached inside and her fingers closed around the only ammunition she possessed – a sub sandwich she'd planned to eat at the graveyard.

Harper slammed a Holy Water sphere into one of the demons. It didn't even react.

'Goddammit,' the master swore. The fiends moved closer, knowing they had him.

'Harper?' she called. 'Get ready to run!'

'Get out of here, Brat!' he shouted.

She did a high overhand pitch that sent the plastic-bagged sandwich between the two fiends. It hit the floor and they fell on it like junk-yard dogs, slashing and clawing at each other. One began to tear into the sandwich. Enraged, the other demon attacked it. A battle ensued, the fiends more interested in gutting each other than human prey.

'Come on!' she shouted, scooping up Harper's heavy duffel, the wide strap digging deep into her shoulder. The master trapper cautiously backed away from the fray and joined her.

'What the hell was that?' he demanded, eyes still on the squabbling Threes.

'Demon psychology.' If it was thrown at them, it had to be food.

Harper seemed to accept that. 'Where's Saint?'

'Outside,' she shouted back. Or at least she prayed that was the case.

Harper motioned for his trapper's bag. He dug inside and armed himself with a steel pipe. It made her think of Beck.

Squinting, she tried to see though the falling curtain of snow, but there was no way she could find him.

Beck will be OK. He has to be.

Following Harper's lead, they made their way towards the closest wall, hoping to find an exit. Riley began to see the bodies. Her stomach roiled at the stench of fresh blood and she fought the urge to vomit.

A Pyro-Fiend ran in front of them, cackling as it laid down

a trail of fire. Harper stomped on the flames with his heavy boots as they continued to edge forward. Panicked shouts rose as one of the lights crashed to the floor, sending a spray of glass in all directions. Riley realized she could see further now as the snow globes exhausted themselves. Smoke billowed from the stage curtains as greedy flames inched higher into the building's superstructure.

No matter how hard she tried, she couldn't see her dad or Beck.

'Girl!' Harper growled. 'Get him up!'

Riley found Jackson hunched in agony, his left arm burned to the elbow. She helped him up, seeing the panic in his eyes.

'Collins. They got him,' he moaned. Riley couldn't bear to look at his wounds, but the smell of burnt flesh attacked her nose with every breath. She almost gagged.

'Where's Simon?'

'Outside,' Jackson wheezed.

The flood of relief nearly took Riley to her knees.

'Keep moving. We're almost there,' Harper said, more to the injured man than to her. 'We stay in here and we're done for.'

Beck heard the growl and found a Three in full stalk mode. He'd know it anywhere – it was the one he'd tried to trap with Paul. The one Riley had captured. Its eyes blazed a strange yellow, but the rest of it was like he remembered.

Someone had set it free.

'Trapperrr . . .' it snarled. A sphere shattered against its back. It twitched for a moment, but kept coming. Beck struck it with his pipe and it fell to the ground, then trotted off in search of a less aggressive meal.

Beck found Morton by his side.

'The Holy Water's not slowing them down,' the man said, breathing heavily. 'Riley was right.'

'Damn,' Beck spat. He wiped a line of sweat off his brow.

'Yeah, I hear you.' Morton set off towards a demon that was slashing through a table to get to a trapper.

Beck heard a shout and turned towards one of the exits. Through the billowing smoke he saw Riley. Harper and Jackson were with her.

'Thank God,' he said. 'Get her out of here.'

The old trapper pushed open the door, checked to ensure there was nothing lurking outside, then gestured for Riley to leave. She ignored the master, looking back into the building, searching for someone. Then her eyes found him.

Beck gave her a salute. 'Go!' he shouted.

She shook her head, waving to him to join them.

His eyes met Harper's. The old trapper gave him a nod and shoved the girl outside over her protests. No matter what he thought of the old man, he owed him.

As long as Riley's safe, nothin' else matters.

His heart singing of war and payback, Beck waded into the battle.

Chaos had set up camp in the parking lot. Wounded trappers sprawled on the asphalt, moaning, bleeding and dying.

Riley kept hunting until she found Simon. Someone's coat was jammed behind his head and Stewart was bending over him, using a sweatshirt to staunch the blood pouring from his abdomen. Her boyfriend was unnaturally pale, his hands quaking as his lips barely moved in prayer.

Another trapper knelt to take over from Stewart. He'd stripped off his shirt and applied it as a compress. It was immediately saturated with blood.

In the distance she heard the high wail of sirens, lots of them.

'We need ta get the lad out of here,' Stewart said. 'First ambulance, ya hear?' The other trapper nodded.

More men gathered around them.

'We're too close to the fire,' Harper said.

'Aye. Come on ya lot, we need ta move the wounded now. This buildin's comin' down and we dunna want ta be near her when she does.'

A cold laugh floated across the parking lot, audible even above the fire's roar. Riley had heard it before – in the library.

No.

'Five!' someone shouted, and there was the sound of running feet as trappers scattered.

Stewart gestured. 'Move 'em, now!' Men struggled to pick up the wounded, helping those who could still hobble across the street towards the park.

Harper turned towards her, his face sweaty and scar pulled tight. 'Go with them, Brat. If it breaks through, get to hallowed ground.'

Forsaken

He didn't understand. The Five was after her. She felt it call to her, offering her the ultimate boon: if she gave herself up, no one else need die.

Riley knelt and kissed Simon's ashen cheek, though she knew Harper and the others saw her. It didn't matter now.

'You stay alive, no matter what,' she whispered. Simon's eyes weren't focusing and she wasn't even sure he'd heard her.

With one last look at the boy who meant so much to her, Riley turned and headed towards her father's killer.

Chapter Thirty-Six

Frantic, Beck tried to fight his way through the flames to reach Morton. Threes had cornered him and he was screaming, begging for help. Beck managed to reach one of the fiends and bust its skull, but the remaining demons gleefully tore his fellow trapper apart and fell on his body for the feast.

'Sweet Jesus,' Beck shouted, but his cry was drowned out as a low rumble filled the hall. He broke more demon skulls, but there seemed no end of them. They began to hunt him like a pack of lions does a cornered gazelle.

The final flakes of snow turned black, sucked upward in the rush of air feeding the burning roof. Beck bolted for the closest exit, jumping over corpses and the tangle of furniture.

The door was padlocked.

'Oh hell!' he swore. No wonder none of the others had left this way. He jammed the steel pipe between the lock and hasp, and tried to prise them apart. Behind him he heard snarls as the Threes closed in. It was only a matter of time before one jumped him and he'd be dead.

Slamming his weight against the pipe, he heard the chain snap. As he flung open the door, a steady breeze blew against his face. He sucked in the clear air and ran for it.

Forsaken

*

Riley found the Geo-Fiend hovering above the parking lot next to the remains of a dented Volvo. The demon was more than seven feet tall, its deep ebony skin pulled tight like a wetsuit across a massive chest that any weightlifter would envy. Thick, corded muscles twined round its bullish neck. The face was like the maw of a volcano, glittering ruby fire seething inside the mouth and the eyes. Its horns reminded her of a steer's, jutting out of the sides of its head and then tapering to sharp points above the crown.

Oh my God.

'Get away from it!' Harper commanded, coming up behind her. He grabbed her arm, shoving her behind him.

At odds with its bulk, the demon made a delicate motion with its hand. A second later a sharp gust of wind slammed against them, blowing Riley into a nearby car, the door handle bashing into her hip. She slid to the ground, whimpering through the pain. There was a sharp cry behind her. Harper lay on the ground clasping his chest. In his hand was a grounding sphere. Somehow he'd kept it from being smashed.

Riley pulled herself up. The demon laughed again, making her blood freeze. Its offer boomed through her mind again like a cannon – her life or it would kill all of them.

Riley knelt next to the man she hated almost as much as the demon.

'Ribs,' he said through gritted teeth. 'Help me up.'

She took the sphere from Harper's trembling hand.

'What are you doing?' he grunted.

Riley turned and moved towards the demon.

Harper shouted for her to come back, but she ignored him.

'This is personal,' she said, though she knew he couldn't hear her.

As she moved closer, Beck's voice was her in her mind, telling her how a grounding sphere worked. She let that voice guide her. Riley lobbed the sphere at the Volvo. It smashed, exploded in a brilliant blue flash and leaped to a nearby car. Then it faltered, unable to find more metal to complete the circuit. The magic faded and died, along with Riley's only hope.

Amused at her childish bravado, the demon responded with a twisted laugh that struck her like a blow. Did her dad hear that same laugh right before he died?

'Yes,' it hissed.

With a flick of its wrist the ground in front of the Five began to heave and roll towards her like an ocean wave as chunks of black asphalt flew into the air. Then the wave halted. The thing was toying with her.

She took a cautious step back, then another, her knees still shaking.

The fiend grinned, showing her pointed teeth that gleamed in the flames.

'What about the boon? Do we have a deal? My life for the others.' The demon hissed. 'Swear it. Swear it on Lucifer's name!'

At the mention of its master, the demon shrieked into the night, shattering windows and making Riley's ears roar. She stumbled backwards in panic, cradling her head. The demon wasn't going to keep its bargain.

The wind began to pick up stray bits of debris from the parking lot, and pieces of gravel and broken glass stung her cheeks. This was how it had killed her dad. She blinked her eyes and stumbled backwards a few more steps.

Another grounding sphere landed near her, but it failed as well.

'Get back here!' one of the trappers yelled. 'We can't hold it!'

'Like father, like daughter,' the demon cried.

There was a crack and then a thick pop as a hole blew out of the asphalt behind her, spewing debris like a geyser, isolating her from the others. Steam belched from the hole along with a choking stench of mould, brick dust and tar. Something swirled towards her out of the night – a dust devil. Before she could move, it caught her like a bird in a gale and slung her into the abyss.

Riley screamed and flailed for anything to grab onto. Her hands caught on some broken steel bars. When she found a foothold, she levered herself up so that her chin rested on the asphalt. It dug into her skin, making her jaw ache. Her relief was short-lived – another wave came towards her, throwing debris into the air like someone shaking crumbs off a table-cloth. When the ripple hit she would be gone, tossed deep into the pit.

As the wave approached, Harper shouted for help. There was a *pop-pop-pop* of exploding tarmac. Debris fell like rain.

Riley closed her eyes and prayed.

Something grabbed her arm and she cried out in surprise as she was winched out of the crater. Landing hard on her back, Riley stared upward, fearing it would be the demon come to claim her soul.

Ori?

'You lead an interesting life,' the man said, casually lifting her up and tucking her close to him as if he did this sort of rescue every day. He had no weapon she could see. Still, she could feel the coiled power in his muscles.

A roar of fury erupted from the Geo-Fiend, shaking nearby windows and setting off car alarms.

Ori shook his head. 'Not yours.'

Despite his warning, the ground wave continued towards them. Riley winced, waiting for the impact, but suddenly it evaporated. The demon roared again, shaking its fists like an angry toddler. In the distance she heard a church bell chime.

'Later, demon. We *will* meet again.' Ori tugged on her arm. 'Time to leave.'

'But –' She looked around for Harper: he was being carried towards the street by a couple of trappers. That only left Beck, but there was no sign of him. The building was fully engulfed in flames now. If he was still in there . . .

Ori urged her along despite her vehement protests. The Five continued to generate a maelstrom of debris, moving closer to the remaining trappers, followed by demons queuing up for a final attack.

'I have to stay!' she said, pulling against Ori's grip.

'You stay, you die. That's not happening tonight.'

They'd just reached her car when Ori abruptly halted. Swivelling back towards the fire, he frowned. 'Well, well, now there's a surprise.'

It took time for Riley's brain to process the scene. The trappers were huddled in a bunch, those still able to fight forming a protective ring round the wounded. But just beyond their circle was another one. It shone pure white, every pinpoint of brilliance at least eight feet tall and holding a flaming sword.

'Angels,' she cried in amazement. 'Ohmigod, they're angels!'

'I'll be damned,' Beck said, shielding his sooty eyes from the powerful light. The ring of glowing figures stood wingtip to wingtip, forming an ethereal barrier between the demons and the survivors. When a Three got too close, it shrieked and burst into flames like tiki torch.

With howls of frustration and rage the demons began to fall back, then one by one they fled into the dark alleys around the burning building. Only the Five was left. With an unearthly roar it vanished in a swirl of black dust and mist.

A few of the trappers let out throaty cheers. Others gaped at Heaven's guard dogs.

'Where the hell were they when . . . this started?' Harper grumbled, his sweaty face contorted in pain. He was bent over, working for each breath.

'Doesn't matter,' Beck said, kneeling next to the injured master. 'They're here now and that's what counts.'

Chapter Thirty-Seven

Riley found herself at the gateway to the cemetery. Her car keys were in her hand, but she didn't remember the drive. Ori was gone. Had she come here alone?

Every few seconds another tremor would shake her from head to toe like she had the flu. Digging in the messenger bag she pulled out her bottled water and drained it. She frowned. Where had the bag come from? She didn't remember picking it up. A quick check proved the demon claw was inside her sweater. *At least I didn't lose that.*

Her mind was still dazed. How had the demons got through the Holy Water ward?

I should have checked it with the claw. What if I was wrong and it was the counterfeit stuff?

A profound shiver flashed through her.

Where had Ori come from? *Doesn't matter. He saved my life.*

Which left the biggest mystery of all – was her dad still in his grave? There was only one way to know the truth.

Riley took off at a run down the path towards the mausoleum, the bag bumping against her side. She hadn't gone far before her thigh cramped, forcing her to limp, her lungs burning with each breath. She coughed deeply and tasted soot in her mouth.

He's there. I know he's there.

When she drew close to the mausoleum, she saw the glow of the candles. Riley cried in relief. It was some necro's sick game.

The circle was different. Bigger. It no longer encompassed the graves, but the entire mausoleum. Martha was in her chair facing west like she wanted a ringside seat to the Tabernacle's destruction. As always, she was knitting.

When Riley hobbled up the old woman smiled at her, pushing a row of stitches to the end of a needle. 'Ah, there you are. I'm sorry about your dad, dear, but sometimes these things happen.'

'Dad?' Riley swung her eyes towards the dark corner that housed her parents' graves. The ground above her father's wasn't a smooth mound any more.

The grave was wide open.

'No!' she shouted. 'No . . .' The circle of light burst high into the air, reacting to her anger and grief. Riley averted her eyes from the painful brilliance.

'What happened?' she demanded. 'How did they get to him? The circle's still in one piece.'

Martha looked up, her needles moving at lightning speed. 'This one is. The first circle was breached, so I recast it.'

'Why bother?' Riley asked, dumbfounded.

Martha paused mid-stitch. 'Rod came down with a cold so they sent another volunteer. He's fairly new. Unfortunately, he has a phobia about dragons and that's exactly what came after him. He said the thing was twenty-foot tall and it shot a wall of flames at him. It was too much for the poor dear. He dived for cover and accidently broke the circle.' Martha finished the stitch and tucked the knitting into her bag. 'He's quite upset,' she added.

'Oh, I bet. Just devastated.' Riley coughed and then glared at the old woman. 'Who took him? Was it the debt collection people? Give me a name.' *So I can tear him apart.*

'The volunteer never saw the summoner.'

'Never saw . . .' Riley hung her head in body-numbing despair. 'Dammit! It wouldn't have happened if I'd been here.'

This was as much her fault as the dragon-phobic guy's.

'Why the circle?' Riley asked. 'What's the point?'

'It's for you, dear.'

'The demons can't come here.'

'But the living can and some of the necromancers are sore losers. Best you stay inside the circle tonight.'

Something in Martha's voice made Riley pause. The moment the volunteer invited her inside she scurried across the candles.

'Goodnight, dear. Don't worry, everything will work out,' Martha said in that overly cheery voice of hers. She gave a wave and trudged into the night.

'Oh yeah, things are working out great,' Riley muttered. She glowered up at heaven. 'Thanks for nothing.'

It took some time for her to go to the empty grave. There was no Dad to talk to now. He was wandering somewhere around the city, playing slave to some rich bastard.

Forsaken

She fell on her knees in the red clay, staring into the deep hole. The pine coffin's hinges were twisted and broken like her father had busted out of a prison cell.

Fury roared within her. She shovelled the dirt back into the hole where it thunked inside the open box, bulldozing until her arms ached, her muscles jittered and her palms were raw.

'So which one was it? Mr I'm Totally Harmless Mortimer? Lizard Lenny?' *Or His High Lord Ozymandias?* She'd have to find out.

'We almost made it, Dad. Almost.'

Riley stumbled to her bag and rooted through it until she found the chamois pouch Ayden had given her. She prised open the strings and then returned to the grave. Taking a pinch of clay, she dropped it inside the bag.

The witch had said to collect things that made her feel strong, that defined her as a person. The soil that had covered her dead father would remind Riley never to trust someone to do her job.

They always fail you.

'I'll find you, Dad. I'll get you back here as soon as I can, I promise.'

Then Riley gave in to the much-needed tears, wailing like a lost soul. She didn't bother to wipe them away and they dried on her cheeks, cracking in the cold night air. Salty testimony to the endless ache in her heart.

Knowing there was little she could do for her father or the other trappers, Riley toted the tarp and the sleeping bag to the west side of the mausoleum and arranged them on the hard ground. It was difficult to think so she found herself making trips for single items: one for the bottled water, the flashlight, another for the blanket.

Curling up inside the sleeping bag, she sat upright and watched the fire. In the glow she thought she saw faces. Dead men's faces. She'd seen trappers torn apart, sickened by how much blood had poured from their bodies. Those images would never leave her. *Never.*

Simon. Would he make it through the night? What about Beck? Would morning bring more bad news?

'Please, God. I'll do anything not to lose them.'

There was a stir of wind in the bare trees.

Desperate for something to occupy her mind, to keep her from thinking about Simon dying, she pulled out her phone to call Peter to let him know she was safe. It didn't work, didn't even light up.

She removed the back and found the wiring inside was fused.

'Oh, damn,' she said, tossing it in the messenger bag, no clue as to how it'd become damaged. Her friend was probably watching the news reports, frantically dialling her over and over. *He'll think I'm dead.* So would Simi and all the kids at school. Maybe even her crazy aunt in Fargo.

'I could have been.' She owed Ori her life and couldn't remember if she'd thanked him.

Her eyes finally closed and Riley slid into tortured slumber. She heard someone calling for her. Simon. He kept crying her

name, begging her to save him. She ran through the smoke
and flames, kicking Threes out of her way as if they were
made of straw. Then she saw the pit. Simon was lying at the
bottom, covered in blood. His chest was ripped open and
she could see his beating heart. He kept calling out to her
but she couldn't get to him. His body sank lower and lower,
fires raging beneath him. There were demons down there,
with pitchforks and pointed tails. They howled in laughter
and then pulled him into the depths as he issued one final
pleading scream.

'Riley!'

She jumped and grabbed the flashlight for a weapon.

It was Beck. He stood just outside the circle hunched in
pain and blinking at her as if he wasn't sure she was real.

'Riley?' he whispered.

Is it really him?

She cleared her throat and rubbed away the crusty tears.
'If you mean no harm, then pass within.'

He made a few more steps inside the circle before he staggered and fell into her arms, his duffel bag hitting the ground
with a thump.

'Thank God!' he murmured. 'Thank God.'

He sagged and collapsed in a heap at her feet. Dropping to
her knees, she shone the flashlight on him. Burns on his face,
his right hand. His thigh had taken the worst of it.

'A Three?' she asked, and he nodded numbly, his hands
clasped round the torn denim and ripped flesh.

'I've got fresh Holy Water,' she said, taking off at a sprint for the mausoleum. When she returned, he was still clutching the leg, his eyes closed in agony.

Which was only going to get worse.

She broke the seal. 'You ready?' He nodded. The moment the stuff hit the wound he bellowed, writhing back and forth, making it difficult to keep the fluid going where it was needed. She kept pouring until he sagged against the ground, his breathing laboured.

'I'm so sorry, Beck!' she said. She remembered what it felt like, how her bones had burned deep within. *At least this is the real stuff.*

'Had to be done,' he said through clenched teeth. 'Go on. Do the rest.'

Riley gently took his hand and treated it, then dabbed the Holy Water on his face. He kept his eyes closed the whole time.

As she made them a bed in the mausoleum, zipping the two sleeping bags together for warmth, she could hear Beck moaning with each breath. By the time she was finished her preparations he was sitting up, staring at the open grave. His hands quivered like an old person.

'It *was* Paul,' he said.

'Yeah. He came to warn me,' Riley said. Beck gave her a strange look. 'I know that sounds weird, but he told me to run, that *they* were coming.'

'How did he know?'

She shrugged. Beck was shivering again.

I can't help Simon, but I can help you.

'Come with me. It's too cold to stay out here,' she said.

Forsaken

To her relief he tried to help as she pulled him to his feet. It was hard going; he weighed more than she did and his leg was too numb to be of use, but she managed to guide him inside the building. Beck let her strip off his leather coat and wrap him up in a couple of blankets. Riley lit a candle and placed it on a ledge at the rear of the mausoleum. The dim light fell across his blackened face in a dance of light and shadow. She closed the heavy doors and sat next to him, tucking them into the sleeping bag. When she offered him a bottle of water, he downed it without pausing for air. His fingers tightened round the plastic and it crackled.

'Did you see dad after . . . ?'

Beck shook his head.

'Maybe he didn't get out,' she said.

'No, he's out of there. Any necro worth his salt would have made sure of that.'

'How many dead?' she asked.

'Not sure. Ten at least,' he said in a smoke-roughened voice.

She had to know. 'Who?'

'Morton, Collins, Ethan. All dead.'

'Ethan?' she asked, not wanting to believe it. He was one of Stewart's apprentices and was getting married in a few months.

'He went quick. Not like some of the others.'

'What about . . . Simon?'

Beck didn't meet her eyes. 'I don't know if he made it. They were tryin' to get him to the hospital. I didn't see him after that.' He turned completely towards her now. 'I couldn't find ya. Someone said the Five was after ya and I thought –'

'I'm OK.'

He pulled her into a tight embrace. There was the sting of tears on her cheeks, but they weren't hers. He kissed the top of her head and murmured something. She didn't hear what he'd said, but that didn't matter. He was alive.

Riley wanted to stay in his arms, but Peter would be frantic by now.

She unwound herself. 'Is your phone working?'

Beck shook his head. 'Happens sometimes around the groundin' spheres.'

Crap. Sorry, Peter.

The wounded trapper folded himself into the sleeping bag as Riley covered him with every extra blanket she had. When she slipped in next to him, he pulled her close, his injured arm over her for protection.

'I'll go back in the mornin',' he said faintly. 'I'll see about Simon and the others.'

'Were those really angels?'

'Yeah. Now get some sleep. You're safe. I won't let anythin' hurt ya.'

And she knew he wouldn't.

While Riley slept, Beck fell back on what he knew best. He remembered what it was like right after a battle. Everybody had their own way of dealing with it. Some guys drank, others shot up. He'd always go somewhere quiet and think it through, remember the stench of war, the pleas of the dying. He was doing the same now in the solitude of the old stone building.

Come morning the trappers would have to face a new reality. They'd have to find out who was messing with the Holy Water and how the demons had crossed the ward. Was Hell making its big move? Was this really the end? So many questions that had no answers.

He pushed them all aside. There'd be time to figure all that out down the line. Instead, he calmed himself by listening to Riley's measured breathing, her warm body tucked up next to his. He'd thanked God repeatedly she was alive, and with those thanks came the truth that he'd been trying to deny.

I care too much for ya, girl.

Every person had a breaking point. Losing both Paul and Riley would have been his. How he would have stopped the pain, he didn't know. Didn't want to know.

Riley stirred, crying out. He comforted her and waited until she went back to sleep, gently stroking her hair. Morning would bring her even more hell. He knew what a dying man looked like – he'd seen them often enough in the war. His gut told him Simon wasn't going to make it and that was going to rip her apart.

I'll be there for ya, girl. No matter what.

Beck took a deep breath and released it slowly. He had to stay strong for her, make the tough decisions. It was best Paul's daughter never knew how he felt about her. There'd be less hurt that way, for both of them.

Just keep her safe, God. I can settle for that.

Chapter Thirty-Eight

When Riley finally stirred, Beck was gone along with his trapping bag. Rising on stiff legs she stretched and opened the doors. It was past dawn, the sun higher than she'd expected. She broke the circle, packed her gear and headed for the car. As she drove, the thin curl of black smoke rising from the city drew her like a magnet.

The Tabernacle's burnt-out husk seemed alien in the thin daylight. Two of the brick walls had collapsed inward and the stained-glass windows were gone. Disorientated bats chittered in the air, their roost history. The area was blocked with barricades and the occasional police car. Riley walked towards the smoking ruins. There was a makeshift morgue on the sidewalk closest to the park. She tried not to count the body bags, but couldn't help herself. *Thirteen.* About forty trappers had been at the meeting last night. That meant only twenty-seven had made it out alive.

She crossed the street and immediately encountered a cop.

'Can't go in there, miss,' he said sternly, his hands crossed over his chest. Not knowing what else to do, she pulled out her trapper's licence.

'You were here last night?' he asked, eyes taking in the

bruises on her face, the singed hair, and the apron of dried blood on her jeans.

Riley nodded. He waved her through the crime-scene tape without another word. The parking lot looked like giant gophers had gone berserk. There was a municipal gas crew working on a mass of pipes. Some of the craters had steam rising out of them, like one of those apocalyptic movies.

She found Beck in a small knot of trappers. He held himself stiffly, moving in slow motion. As she grew closer to the group, Riley realized the topic of conversation was her dead father.

'I know what I saw,' one of the men said. He had a bandage on his arm and a deep scowl on his face. 'It was Blackthorne and he was helping those demons.'

'That's bull,' Beck growled.

'Then how the hell did they get in? Someone had to break the ward. It sure as hell wasn't one of us.'

Another trapper jumped in. 'It had to be him. It's too much of a coincidence. Blackthorne shows up and a few seconds later we're ass deep in demons. No other explanation.'

Riley pushed her way forward through the group, furious. 'He came to warn me. He told me to run.' The moment after she spoke, she realized it was the wrong thing to say.

'How he'd know that?' one of the trappers demanded. His name was McGuire and he'd opposed Riley's apprenticeship from the start.

'He wouldn't have broken the ward,' she protested.

'If Blackthorne didn't let them in, who did? You?'

'It be time ta step back, trapper.' It was Stewart. He had a thick bandage on his forehead. His skin was as pale as his hair and he leaned heavily on his cane. 'We'll work it out later. Right now, we need ta take care of our own.'

The irate trapper didn't back down. 'I know what I saw.'

'Did ya ever think that's what the beasties wanted ya ta see?'

Grumbling broke out around them, for and against the argument.

'We gotta know who we can trust,' McGuire replied. 'It's all connected – the Holy Water, the attack, the demons working together.' He pointed at Riley. 'It all went wrong when she joined the Guild. She's to blame!'

Stewart put himself between her and the angry men. 'Go stock yer bags and get back ta work. The city hasta see we're still out there. If not, they'll be callin' in the hunters as fast as ya can fart a tune.'

The group slowly dispersed.

Stewart pointed at Beck. 'Take this one home, will ya, lass?'

'But I was going to the hospital,' Riley began. 'I want to see Simon. See if he's . . .' *still alive.*

The master pulled her aside. 'Yer worried about him. I am too. But Simon has family ta watch over him.' He looked back at the injured trapper. 'Ya hafta be there for Beck. Yer all he's got now.'

Riley sighed. 'I'll get the car.'

*

Forsaken

Other than providing directions to his house in Cabbagetown, Beck didn't say a word. Finally he pointed to a driveway that led to a compact green house with white trim. The mailbox had his last name stencilled on it and a purple clematis vine wound its way up the wooden post. She wasn't sure exactly what she'd expected, but this wasn't it.

Beck climbed out of the car as if it took every bit of energy he possessed, but refused her help up the stairs. Instead of unlocking the door he sank on the top step.

'You OK?' she asked, concerned.

Beck stared into the middle distance. 'It's all goin' wrong. I don't understand.' He looked over at her. 'What did your daddy say to ya?'

'That I should run. That there were too many. I guess he meant the demons.'

Beck frowned. 'Ya sure that Holy Water was good?'

'I thought it was.'

'Which necro took him?'

'No idea.' Riley tugged on his arm. 'Come on.' He didn't budge. 'I've never been inside your place,' she urged. 'I want to see if it's as messy as mine.' *Anything to get you out of the cold.*

Beck seemed puzzled by that. 'I'm sorry. I thought ya'd been here. Your daddy was off and on. He liked it.' A melancholy smile creased his face. 'He said he wanted to buy ya a house like this.'

Riley didn't want to think about what might have been. Not ever.

He finally got the front door open and tapped away at the alarm panel. The beeping ceased, then he limped into the front room.

Riley was greeted by dark hardwood floors and a braided rug to clean your feet on. There were pegs to hang coats and tan walls with pictures of Okefenokee Swamp. He'd surprised her again – the house was way clean by guy standards. There were no mouldy chunks of pizza on the counter or dirty underwear lurking on the floor. In fact, the place was as clean as her own.

She pointed him to a kitchen chair and asked, 'Where's your Holy Water?'

'Hall closet. Get a bottle for yourself and carry it with ya from now on.'

'Why?'

'If ya need a quick ward, pour a circle and get inside it. It's better than nothin'.'

'You're thinking the demons aren't done with us.'

'I'd say they're just warmin' up.'

Other people's closets held stuff they rarely used: ice skates, Christmas ornaments, old pairs of shoes that were long past their prime. Beck's held his trapping supplies. Everything was methodically organized, shelf by shelf, and included several pints of Holy Water, steel bags, coiled rope, spheres, you name it. Even a spare length of steel pipe.

Riley found the freshest bottles, verified the labels with the wet finger test, and returned to the kitchen to stuff one in her bag. Beck still stared at nothing about twelve inches in front of him.

'Time for some more pain,' she said.

'Is it the good stuff?'

'Oh, yeah.'

He slowly stripped off his jacket, then his shirt. He took the pint from her. 'I'll do it.'

Works for me.

After washing her hands, Riley rummaged around inside the refrigerator and found eggs and some sausages. More hunting helped her locate a frying pan, which she set on the gas stove. A sharp yelp came from the bathroom, then a stream of swear words, most of them starting with 'f'. Then another yelp. The shower began to run.

That's the good stuff. Riley turned the heat down under the sausages, suspecting it might be a while before he emerged. While Beck showered, she used his home phone to call Peter's mobile phone.

'Hello?' a wary voice asked.

'Peter, it's Riley.'

'Riley! Where have you been? Ohmigod, you scared me,' he said, his voice thick with worry.

'I'm sorry I didn't call sooner. My phone got fried and I spent the night in the cemetery.'

'They had it on the TV all night. I thought I might see you in one of the pictures and then I'd know you were OK. When I never saw you . . .' His voice trailed off.

'I'm so sorry, Peter.'

'You knew all these guys who died, didn't you?'

'Most of them.'

'What about Beck? Is he OK?' She told him a few details, but left out the worst stuff. Peter didn't need her nightmares.

'So that's it, isn't it? They'll have to close the Guild?' he asked.

He almost sounded hopeful. 'No. They'll have trappers come in from other cities. We'll start over.'

'Oh.'

'Peter, I'm not giving up on this. I want to be a trapper. Even more now!'

'I know,' he said softly. 'It's like watching you play tag with ravenous wolves. One wrong step and they rip you apart and I can't do a thing about it. I don't know if I can take that any more.'

Peter might not have known it, but he'd drawn a line in the sand. On one side was the way their lives used to be – chatting about school, complaining about their parents, all of that stuff. On the other side was Riley's new life. The one that could get her ripped apart.

'We can talk about this later, Peter.' No way could she handle this on top of everything else.

Silence.

'Peter?'

'The point is we never do talk it out. That's not the way a friendship works. I can't take this any more. I mean it.'

Then he hung up on her.

Riley felt sick inside. When she dropped the phone back

into its cradle, she found Beck watching her from the hall-way.

'He hung up on me. He can't deal with me being a trap-per.'

'It's hard for them,' he said, his voice rough. 'They don't understand what we do, why we do it.' He shook his head in regret. 'It tears 'em apart worryin' about us.'

'It doesn't have to be that way. My mom was OK with Dad's work,' she protested.

Beck arched an eyebrow. 'Ya sure about that?'

Riley wanted to argue, but she'd overheard her parents' hushed conversations. Her mother had worried every moment her husband was out of her sight, afraid that one day Paul wouldn't be coming home.

Beck slumped in the doorway. 'When I first started I thought I could have it all. Now all I see is a life on my own, at least until I get too old to trap or some demon makes a meal of me.'

Riley shivered, running her hands up and down her arms. 'God, that's so . . . brutal.'

'It's the price we pay for takin' on Hell.'

Her breath hitched at the thought.

To his credit Beck stayed out of the way as Riley cooked the rest of the meal. He ate what she put in front of him with-out bitching that the eggs were overcooked and the toast too brown. She found herself hungrier than she'd expected and cleaned her plate, wondering how she could eat after what she'd seen the night before.

It wasn't until Beck finished a second helping of toast, lighter this time, that he started to talk. 'Jackson's injured, but should be back pretty soon. Stewart's up and goin', though I don't think that's a good idea. Harper's ribs are banged up.'

'Is he in the hospital?'

'No, he's at his place. He'll need help for a time.'

'What comes next?' Riley asked, sipping on the coffee. It was too strong, but then she'd never been good at making the stuff.

'Funerals. Then we've got to do all that damned paperwork for the national office. They'll have to send us a master to start trainin' replacements.' His voice trailed off. 'It'll be a couple years before we're back to full strength unless other trappers move here.'

'Will they?' she asked, brushing the last of the crumbs off her sweater.

'I sure as hell wouldn't move here, not with what happened last night,' he replied. 'Be lucky if we can keep the ones we got.'

He was probably right. 'I'll keep an eye on Harper, help him if I can,' she said.

That got her a long look. 'Thought ya hated him.'

'Doesn't keep me from looking after him.' *As long as I keep out of range.*

'Well, that makes sense,' he said, indicating the meal. 'Ya did the same for me.'

Why did he make everything so personal? 'Beck, I don't hate you, it's just that . . .' She had no idea how to explain how much he rubbed her up the wrong way, or how good it had been that day when they were trapping together. How much she wished it was always that way. 'I want it to be OK between us, but I'm not giving up Simon just because you don't like him.'

'He's OK.' Beck stared down at his empty plate. 'Truth is, ya were right – I'm . . . sorta jealous of him. He's lucky ya like him so much. Any guy would be.'

I like you too, but you don't see it.

Not knowing how to tell him that, Riley rose and shoved her chair under the table. She reached for the plates, but he stopped her.

'Please call your aunt, let her know you're OK. I'll get ya a bus ticket to Fargo.'

Back to that again. She shook her head, her fingers digging into the back of the chair. 'I'm not leaving, not with Simon the way he is.'

Beck rose, face set. 'I know ya care for him, but he'd want ya safe. The demons shouldn't know your name, but they keep callin' ya out. That Five was willin' to kill every last trapper to get to ya. That's real bad, Riley.'

She heard fear in every word. Fear for her. 'It doesn't matter what the demons are doing, I'm not leaving.'

'Somethin's goin' down in this city, girl, and you're in the middle of it.'

'Doesn't matter if I'm in Fargo or wherever. If the Five wants me, it'll find me. Game over.' When he opened his mouth to argue, she waved him off. 'You're wasting your time. I'm staying and that's the end of this conversation.'

'You're one damned pigheaded fool,' he growled.

'You would know what that's like.'

With a snarl, Beck swivelled on his good leg and limped down the hall. A door slammed. Then there was a loud thump, like someone had struck a wall with a fist.

Buy all the bus tickets you want. There's no way I'm leaving.

Chapter Thirty-Nine

The ICU nurse in the blue scrubs took one look at Riley and went wide-eyed. 'Are you OK, miss?' he asked, rising from his chair.

Riley could only imagine what she looked like. She hadn't taken time to change her clothes, hadn't even thought of it. Then she caught sight of her reflection in the waiting-room window. Her jacket was dotted with scorch marks and one sleeve had a long slit in it. Her hair hung limp, frizzled at the ends from the heat. Both her sweater and jeans were caked with a thick layer of dried blood.

'Ah, yeah, I'm OK,' Riley said. 'I'd like to see Simon Adler.'

Don't tell me he's dead. Please, don't . . .

'Are you family?' the nurse asked sceptically.

'Ah . . .'

'She is,' a voice called out. It belonged to a young woman standing in the waiting-room door.

The nurse still appeared sceptical. 'OK, but five minutes only,' he advised.

The young woman took Riley by the hand and led her farther down the hall. She was blonde with blue eyes, about Riley's height. There was a slight thickness at her waist. A baby bump.

'You're Riley, aren't you?' she whispered. 'I'm Amy, Simon's sister. He told me about you.'

'You got married last summer,' Riley said.

The girl nodded. She put a protective hand on her stomach. 'I'm going to have a baby,' she said.

They walked in silence until Amy paused outside a room.

'How bad is . . . ?' Riley began, then lost the will to finish the question.

'They say he lost a lot of blood, that it hurt his brain. They say he's not there any more. That we have to decide if we keep him on the machine or . . .' Amy's eyes brimmed.

Oh, God.

They hugged, sharing tears.

'He's the greatest brother ever,' Amy said between sobs, her head buried in Riley's shoulder. 'Why did this happen to him?'

The images of lacerated bodies, ferocious demons and all that blood steamrolled through Riley's mind. She could hear the screams, the snarls, the crisp crackle of the flames as if she was inside that building once again.

'Are you OK? You're shaking,' Amy said, pulling away.

'I'm OK,' Riley said, but that was a lie.

Amy took her arm. 'Bro told me how much he liked you. He said you were special. I thought you should know that.'

'Thanks, I . . . he's special to me too.'

After she'd squeezed Riley's hand Amy made her way back to the waiting room.

He's not there any more.

Riley gingerly pushed open the door to Simon's room. A nurse looked up, gave her a nod and then finished hanging a new IV bag. It had blood in it. She left without offering a word of encouragement.

Which means there isn't any hope. Riley had learned that when her mother lay dying.

Simon was so pale he'd qualify as a corpse and the medical equipment seemed to dwarf him. A ventilator kept him breathing. Air in, air out. A long green line sprawled across a monitor, registering every heartbeat. Tubes were everywhere. One snaked out from under the covers and into a bag to collect his urine.

Riley swallowed hard, moving slowly to the side of the bed. Just yesterday they'd been kissing, holding each other, talking about the future.

She slipped her hand between the cool metal rails. Simon's felt like lukewarm marble. He didn't twitch when she touched him, didn't squeeze back. She remembered the soft look in his eyes. How he'd treated her like she was the only girl in the world. Bending over, she pushed a piece of hair off his forehead and then kissed him.

'Hurry and get well,' she whispered in his ear. 'We're getting behind on the kissing.'

No response, not even a flicker of an eyelid. The ventilator continued to push air into his lungs and the heart monitor beeped, but no one was home. Even Riley could tell that.

'You can't be like this,' she said. 'You can't leave me

alone. I don't care what it takes, but you have to get better, Simon Adler. I'll do anything, you hear? Just don't die on me!'

Nothing. Her tender hope began to disintegrate into tiny wounded shards.

Simon had told her his faith had never really been tested.

Now he was serving as a test for those who loved him.

This one I'm not going to pass.

As she cried at the elevator, Riley saw the angel in the hallway. Nobody else seemed to notice it, despite the white robe and the feathery wings neatly tucked behind its shoulders. In fact, a nurse walked right by it, then ducked into a patient's room, intent on her own business.

The ethereal messenger beckoned to Riley, then pointed towards the chapel down the hall. Riley hit the down button again, hard.

'You are a stubborn girl, aren't you?' the angel said. The voice sounded so familiar. So Martha.

The knitting-addicted cemetery volunteer was an angel?

'You're kidding me,' Riley said. 'Why didn't I see you like this before?'

'I didn't want you to,' Martha replied. She pointed towards the chapel again.

'What do you want?' Riley replied, not willing to budge.

The angel puzzled on that, scratching a wing in thought. 'Some fine alpaca hand-dyed yarn would be a good start. Oh, and I'd love to have a pair of rosewood needles.'

Riley tried again, her frustration rising. 'What do you want *with me*?'

'A chat, dear, before it all goes to Hell.'

Feeling really dumb talking to something no one else seemed to notice, Riley gave in and shuffled her way towards the chapel. Pushing open the door, she found Martha in the front pew, but now she was dressed like an old woman, orthopaedic shoes and all.

'How do I know you're not one of *them*?' Riley asked.

Martha spread her hands. 'We're on hallowed ground.'

'Didn't help last night,' Riley retorted. 'We were behind a holy ward and inside a building that used to be a church.'

That got her a pensive frown. 'The bottle of Holy Water in your bag – pull it out.' The angel cupped her hands. 'Pour some for me.'

How did you know I had that?

Riley's own hands were shaking as she did the honours. She waited for the screech, the sprouting of horns, the flick of a barbed tail. Instead the liquid pooled in Martha's hands and started to glow greenish gold. Then it vaporized into a mist and spread throughout the room.

'Wow,' Riley said, watching it float on invisible air currents.

'I love doing that,' Martha admitted. 'Now take a deep breath and tell me what it reminds you of.'

Riley inhaled. 'Summer, at the beach. I can smell the salt-water and fresh watermelon.'

Martha sighed. 'I can't smell a thing. You mortals are so lucky.'

Riley screwed the cap on the Holy Water and dropped it back in her bag. This was God's representative. If she couldn't complain in person, the angel would do just fine.

She drew in a tight breath. 'Who took my dad?'

A shake of the head. 'Next question.'

'How did the demons get inside the ward?'

'Evil neutralizes Holy Water. Too much evil and . . .' The angel spread her hands.

That only made Riley more upset. 'Why did your boss let all those people die? We're on your side, or don't you guys get that?'

'Everything has a reason. You have to trust His divine will.'

'Trust?' Riley shouted, her voice echoing in the small room. At this point she didn't care if she was turned into a pillar of salt or whatever. 'That might work for you but it's been an epic fail for me. I prayed for my mom. She died. I prayed that my dad wouldn't get hurt. He did anyway. Now Simon's . . . Now he's . . .' She sank into the pew, palm clamped over her mouth, tears bursting from her eyes. The shaking started again, making her muscles lock up.

'You really care for him, don't you?' Martha asked softly.

Riley nodded. She found a piece of tissue in her pocket and blew her nose. 'He's . . . I think I . . .' *I think I'm falling in love with him.*

'So you are,' Martha replied. 'We'll ensure your young man recovers from his injuries, provided you agree to help us.'

Riley blinked in confusion. 'I'm already helping. Trapper,

remember?' she said, pointing at her chest.

'We'll need more than that. When the time comes, you must do something for us, no questions asked.'

That didn't sound good.

'Why do I need to make a deal with you? Why don't you just help him? He's your kind of guy. He follows all the rules.'

The angel didn't reply, which only gave Riley time to feel totally selfish. Why would it matter what they wanted as long as Simon was alive? But what if this was a trick and they didn't make him better?

Martha looked upward towards the ceiling and then gave a quick nod as if she'd received further instructions from an unseen superior. She dropped something on the pew next to Riley.

It was a tract, one of those THE END IS NEAR! ones that you find under your windshield wiper at the shopping mall. After last night's horror the crude illustrations of collapsing buildings, earthquakes and billowing flames hit too close to home for Riley's comfort.

With a snort of derision, she pushed it aside. 'This is total crap. They've been saying that for years.'

'Ever since the beginning,' Martha replied gravely.

'So what does this have to do with me?' Riley demanded.

The angel stood, fussing with her cuffs. 'Because if you accept our offer, you're the one who's going to stop it.'

'Me?' Riley sputtered. 'Are you kidding?'

'No.'

'Hello? I'm seventeen. I haven't even got out of high

school yet and you think I'm going to stop the end of the world? What *are* you people smoking?'

The angel raised one silver eyebrow. 'Joan of Arc was your age when she led the French into battle.'

'Wait, don't tell me. I know how this story ends. Roasted martyr. Yeah, that's my dream job.'

'It's your choice,' Martha said. She vanished, leaving Riley in a room that smelt like watermelons with the fate of the world hanging over her head.

Let Simon die or owe Heaven big time?

'That's no choice!' Riley called out.

There was no reply but the sound of the furnace kicking in. No chorus of angels or hisses of demons. Only hot air blowing in her face.

Riley started to laugh. It had a hysterical edge to it. 'You're just messing with my head.'

Any moment now Martha would return, admit that it'd been a big joke.

When that didn't happen, Riley retraced her steps to the elevator and stared at the buttons. Up or Down. Simon lives. Simon dies.

She remembered his calm presence at her dad's funeral, him kidding her about her ankles, them sharing their dreams. She'd fallen for him and there was no way to deny that.

My choice.

'OK, you got a deal,' she said, not sure if anyone could hear her. 'Do whatever it is you do.'

She waited, but nothing happened. Maybe it took a while.

Maybe it was a test and they'd let him die anyway.

The elevator doors opened and she got on. Right before the doors closed, Amy joined her. They shared sad smiles.

'I need to get some sleep,' the girl said. She patted her tummy. 'Growing a baby makes me tired.'

A child her brother might never see.

As they walked out of the hospital along the sidewalk towards the parking garage, music filled the air. Amy dug in her voluminous suede bag and retrieved a mobile phone.

'This is Amy. What? What do you mean?'

And then she shrieked and took off at a run back towards the hospital.

Good news? Bad news? It could be either one. Amy's shriek hadn't been very specific.

'Hey! What happened?' Riley called out.

She didn't get a reply.

Simon's sister made it to the bank of elevators faster than Riley, pregnancy not hampering her speed as much as a demon-clawed leg. The doors closed before Riley reached them.

'Damn!' She bounced back and forth from foot to foot. 'Come on,' she grumbled as she kept punching the button. No elevator.

An older woman watched her and delivered a matronly shake of the head.

'You young kids are just so impatient nowadays.'

Riley punched the button three more times to further demonstrate her youthful impatience. By the time the next elevator arrived she was about to brave the stairs, leg cramp or not.

Pushing through the double doors into the ICU, she found the area in front of Simon's room crowded with family. There was lots of crying and hugging going on.

When she drew closer, they cleared a way for her.

'That's his girlfriend,' one of them whispered to another.

As she stepped inside the room, the first thing she heard was Amy's sobs. There was no mechanical whoosh. The ventilator was off.

Riley closed her eyes, feeling the shakes coming again. She'd given Heaven her word. Had they'd failed her? Like always?

'Riley, look!' Amy exclaimed. 'He's awake! He's breathing on his own.'

Riley whipped open her eyes, desperately wanting to believe it was true.

The breathing tube was gone and the nurse was carefully positioning an oxygen cannula in Simon's nose.

'Simon?' Riley said, putting all her prayers into the one word.

Her boyfriend's bloodshot blue eyes slowly opened and a croak came from his lips. Then he saw her at the end of the bed. 'Ri . . . ley,' he whispered.

Joy burst through her like a lightning bolt. Simon was alive and he had a working brain or he wouldn't have known who she was.

'They did it,' she said. 'Ohmigod, they did it!' She sucked

in the pungent, unforgettable scent of watermelons. The Angel Martha had been here and pulled off a miracle.

As Riley shared a celebratory hug with Amy, the truth hit her.

Her boyfriend was going to live.

Heaven had kept its part of the bargain.

Which means I'm on the hook for the rest.

Forbidden

THE DEMON TRAPPERS

To
Michelle Roper
who taught me to find humour
in the small things

For they both were solitary,
She on earth and he in heaven.
And he wooed her with caresses,
Wooed her with his smile of sunshine

– *Song of Hiawatha*, Henry Wadsworth Longfellow

Chapter One

2018
Atlanta, Georgia

The Grounds Zero Coffee Shop made the most amazing hot chocolate in Atlanta, maybe even the whole world, but it appeared Riley Blackthorne would have to wade through Armageddon to get it.

'The End is Nigh!' a man called out. He stood near the shop's entrance holding a home-made cardboard sign that proclaimed the same thing. Instead of having a scraggly beard and wearing a black robe like some biblical prophet, he was wearing chinos and a red shirt.

'You've got to prepare, missy,' he said, and shoved a pamphlet towards Riley with considerable zeal. The tract looked remarkably like the one she had in her jacket pocket. Like the one the angel had given her right before she'd agreed to work for Heaven to save her boyfriend's life.

'The End is Nigh!' the man shouted again.

'Is there still time for hot chocolate?' Riley asked.

The-End-is-Nigh guy blinked. 'Ah, maybe, I don't know.'

'Oh, good,' she said. 'I'd hate to take on Hell without fuelling up.'

That earned her a confused frown. Rather than explain she jammed the tract in her pocket and pushed open the door to the coffee shop as the man went back to exhorting his audience to prepare for the worst.

The Grounds Zero didn't look any different from the last time she'd been here. The smell of roasted beans hung in the air like a heady perfume and the espresso machine growled low and deep. Customers tapped on laptops as they enjoyed expensive coffee and talked about whatever was important in their lives. Just like every day. Except . . .

Everything is weird now.

Even buying hot chocolate. That used to be easy: place order, pay for order, receive hot beverage. No hassles. That didn't appear to be the case today.

The barista kept staring at her, even as he made the drink, which wasn't a good thing as he nearly scalded himself. Maybe it was the multiple burn holes in her denim jacket, or the ragged slice down one sleeve that revealed the T-shirt underneath. Or the fact that her long brown hair had a frizzled, been-too-close-to-a-flame look, despite two shampoo sessions and a lot of conditioner. At least she'd changed her blood-soaked jeans or the guy would be staring at that. Blood that wasn't hers.

'I saw you on TV. You're one of them, aren't you?' he asked in a shaky voice, brown eyes so wide they seemed to cover most of his face.

On TV? Riley had no choice but to own up. 'Yeah, I'm a demon trapper.' *One of the few lucky enough to survive last night's slaughter.*

The guy dropped the ceramic cup on the counter, sloshing some of the chocolatey goodness over the side and on to the saucer.

It's just one creepo guy. No big.

But it wasn't just him. Other customers stared at Riley as she made her way to an empty booth. One by one they looked up at the television screen high on the wall, then back to her, comparing images.

Ah, crap.

There, courtesy of CNN, was last night's disaster in glorious technicolor: flames pouring out of the roof of the Tabernacle as demons ran everywhere. And there she was, illuminated by the raging fire, kneeling on the pavement near her injured boyfriend. She was crying, holding Simon in her arms. It was the moment she knew he was dying.

Oh, God. I can't handle this.

The saucer in Riley's hand began to quake, dislodging more of the hot chocolate. It'd been bad enough to live through that horror, but now it was all over the television in full and unflinching detail.

She paused near a booth as a picture of Simon appeared on the screen. It must have been his high-school graduation photo, since his white-blond hair was shorter and his expression stone serious. Most people would think Simon was like that all the time, but when they were hanging together he'd let his guard down, especially when they were kissing.

Riley closed her eyes, recalling the time they'd spent together before the meeting. They'd kissed and he'd admitted how much he cared for her. Then a demon had tried to kill him.

Riley sank into the booth and inhaled the rich scent of the hot chocolate, using it to push the bad memories away. The effort failed, though it never had in the past. Instead, her mind dutifully conjured up the image of her boyfriend in his hospital bed, tubes everywhere, his face as white as the sheets.

Simon meant so much to her. He'd been a quiet, comforting presence after her father's death. Losing him so soon after her dad was unthinkable, and Heaven had known that. What else could she do but agree to their terms: Simon's life in trade for Riley owing Heaven a favour. A Really *Big* Favour. Like stopping Armageddon in its tracks.

'Why me?' Riley muttered. 'Why not someone else? Why not Simon?'

He was religious, followed all the rules. He'd be the perfect guy to keep the world from ending. Heaven could have made the deal with him when he was injured.

Instead they chose me.

To Riley's annoyance, the hot chocolate had cooled beyond what was acceptable drinking temperature, but she sipped it anyway. She kept her eyes riveted on the cup's contents, away from the television screen. Someone scraped a chair across the floor as they sat at a table and Riley jumped at the sound, half expecting a horde of demons to pour through the front door at any moment.

The cup trembled in her hands, reminding her how close she skated to the edge. Too much had hit her in a short period of time. Any more and she wouldn't be able to cope.

I have to find my dad. That she could do. Maybe. Still, it was something she could focus on. It was unlikely his body was buried under the rubble at the Tabernacle, not when a necromancer went to all the effort to summon him from his grave. That's what necros did: they reanimated corpses and sold them to rich people as unpaid servants.

Once he was 'owned' by someone it'd be nearly impossible to get him back. She could take his new owner to court to prove the summoning hadn't been legal, but rich people had expensive lawyers and she was barely making the rent. By the time the case reached a judge her father would be back in the ground anyway. Deaders weren't good for much more than a year, even with the best of care.

What is it like to be dead and walking around like you're still alive? Besides the creep factor, it had to be truly weird. Did her dad remember dying? Did he remember the funeral and being buried? Spiky cold zipped down Riley's spine. She had to get her head in the game.

I'll find him. I'll get him back in the ground and that'll be the end of it.

Her eyes wandered back to the television. A different reporter was doing a play-by-play of last night's horror. He had it mostly right – the local Trappers Guild had held a meeting at the Tabernacle in downtown Atlanta just like they always did. In the middle of the meeting the demons had arrived. Then it got bad.

'Eyewitnesses say that at least two different kinds of Hellspawn were involved in the attack and that the trappers were quickly overwhelmed,' the reporter said.

Three different kinds, but who's counting?

Riley frowned. The trappers hadn't been overwhelmed. Well, not completely. They'd even managed to kill a few of the things.

When she went to pick up the cup of hot chocolate, her hands were still shaking. They'd been that way since last night and nothing she did made them stop. She downed the liquid in small sips, knowing people were watching her, talking among themselves. Someone took a picture of her with their cellphone.

Ah, jeez.

In the background, she could still hear the reporter on CNN. 'A number of the trappers escaped the inferno and were immediately set upon by a higher-level fiend.'

The higher-level fiend had been a Grade Five demon who'd opened up deep holes in the ground, spun off mini tornadoes and caused the earth to shake. All in an effort to take out one trapper.

Me.

Forbidden

If it hadn't been for Ori, a freelance demon hunter, the Five would have killed her just like it had her dad.

'We have interviewed eyewitnesses who claim they saw angels last night,' the reporter continued. 'We've had Dr Osbourne, a professor of religious studies at UC Santa Barbara, review the videos. He's with us here today, via satellite.' A solemn grey-haired man appeared on the screen. 'What's your take on this amazing event, Doctor?'

'I've watched the videos and all that is visible is a circle of incredibly bright light, which surrounds the Demon Trappers. I have colleagues in Atlanta who've claimed to see angels in your city. They have appeared throughout the Bible to Abraham, to Jacob. Sodom and Gomorrah rated two of them. In this case, they were actively protecting the trappers from Hellspawn. I'd say that's biblically significant.'

Tell me about it.

Riley dug in her messenger bag, retrieved a pen and began a list on a crisp white napkin.

Find Dad
Bust Holy Water scam
Save the world
Buy groceries
Do laundry

As she saw it, if number three on the list didn't work out, the last two weren't going to be an issue.

Chapter Two

Feeling a tickle in his throat, Denver Beck coughed deeply in an attempt to expel the stale smoke from his lungs. It did little good. In the distance, firefighters moved across the Tabernacle's rubble, working on the hot spots and searching for charred bodies in the mounds of broken bricks and burnt wood.

I should have died last night. In the past it wouldn't have mattered. Now it did. It was his fear for Riley that had driven him out of the smoke and flames.

To his right, Master Trapper Angus Stewart leaned heavily on his cane in the late afternoon sun. His usually ruddy face was nearly the colour of his white hair, pale against the bloodstained bandage tucked under his hairline. They stood near one of the many holes in the Tabernacle's parking lot, the stench of melted asphalt hanging heavy in the air. Beck bent over and stared into the crater's maw, which was laced with tangled wires and debris. It was a good ten feet wide and three times as deep, and a thin column of steam rose from its centre.

'How does a demon do this kind of damage?' he asked in a soft Southern drawl.

Forbidden

'The Geo-Fiend just waved its hands and the abyss appeared. They have some strange power over the earth and the weather,' Stewart said in his rich Scottish accent. It was still noticeable, though blunted by a decade in Atlanta.

As Beck straightened up, the demon wound in his thigh cramped in protest. The dressing was leaking and the fluid had soaked into his blue jeans. He needed more aspirin – his temperature was up and every now and then his teeth would chatter. Like a mild case of the flu with claw marks as a bonus.

Everythin' has changed now. He knew angels were for real; he'd seen them around Atlanta. Most were the ministering kind, the most prolific of Heaven's folk, who came and went doing whatever God wanted them to do. He'd never seen any from the higher realm, the ones with the flaming swords. He had last night.

Beck shook his head again, unable to deal with how eerie the things had been. At least seven feet tall, clothed in eye-blinding white with shimmering alabaster wings edged in grey, their fiery swords had roared like summer thunder and filled the night air with the crisp tang of ozone.

'I've never heard tell of Heaven steppin' in to protect trappers,' Beck said in a lowered voice, mindful of a television news crew on the other side of the parking lot. They were all over the city now, trying to get a handle on one of the biggest stories to hit Atlanta since the 1996

Olympics. 'Why're the demons workin' together now? It feels like a war's brewin'.'

'So it does.' Stewart cleared his throat. 'Seein' the angels make ya a believer?'

Beck blinked at the question. *Had it?* He'd never really thought much about God and he figured the feeling was mutual. 'Maybe,' he admitted.

Stewart huffed in agreement. 'The city will be wantin' action.'

'Master Harper will take care of that, won't he?' Harper was the most senior trapper in Atlanta and Riley's master. From what Beck could tell, he was a serious piece of work, but a good trapper when he wasn't drinking.

'Nay, not with his ribs bein' the way they are,' Stewart said. 'I'll have ta take the lead. With Ethan dead, I'll need yer help.'

Ethan had been one of the master's apprentices, but he'd not made it out of the Tabernacle alive. 'What about your other apprentice? Rollins. Where's he?'

'He quit. Canna handle this sorta thing. I respect that.' Stewart paused a moment, then added, 'I'm pleased ta hear young Simon's gonna make it. That's good news for Riley.'

'Yeah,' Beck replied, unsure of where the old master was heading with that last comment.

'She and Simon have taken a fancy ta each other, did ya know? They were holdin' hands and kissin' before the meetin'. They didn't know I saw them.'

'Kissin'?' Beck felt something heavy form in his chest, like a stone weighing on his heart. Had to be because of the demon wound – they always made you feel sick. It wouldn't do him any good to think of Riley as more than just Paul's little girl.

'Ya didn't know?' the master asked, all innocence.

Beck shook his head. He'd known Riley and Simon were spending time together – they were both apprenticed to Harper and saw each other every day. But he hadn't realized their relationship had gone that far. She was only seventeen, and now that both her parents were dead he felt responsible for her. Sort of like a big brother. Sort of something more.

'Yer frownin', lad,' Stewart observed.

Beck tensed, uncomfortable under the old trapper's scrutiny. 'Simon's better than some she could date,' he acknowledged, 'but he's not what she should be thinkin' about right now. I'll have a talk with him once he's better.' *Let him know if he goes too far with her I'll rip his damned head off.*

The master gave him a fatherly smile. 'Let *them* sort it out, lad. Ya canna keep her in a bubble the rest of her life.'

Wanna bet? It's what Paul would have wanted and, if he was honest, the only way Beck could sleep at night. As he stared at the broken landscape and the savaged building, his mind filled with images from the night before. Of demons and the trappers battling for survival. Of Riley in the middle of the flames and how close he'd come to losing her. Beck shuddered, ice shearing through his veins.

Stewart laid a heavy hand on his shoulder, startling him. 'I know ya stayed inside that furnace until the very last. That takes stones, and I'm damned proud of ya.'

Beck couldn't meet the master's eyes, troubled by the praise.

The Scotsman's hand retreated. 'Ya can't carry it all on yer shoulders, broad as they are.'

He sounded just like Paul: that made sense – Master Stewart had trained Riley's father, who in turn had mentored Beck. From what Paul had said, the Stewarts were some of the best demon trappers in the world.

This man thought he'd done all right last night.

He's just bein' nice.

As if knowing a change of topic was needed, Stewart asked, 'Any idea who pulled Paul from his grave?'

That was the other thing hanging over them. Though he'd been dead for two weeks, Riley's father had appeared at the trapper's meeting, summoned from his eternal rest by a necromancer. He was a reanimated corpse now, money on the hoof, providing he'd made it out of the Tabernacle in one piece.

'Riley did everythin' she could to keep him in the ground,' Beck complained. 'She sat vigil every damned night, made sure there was a consecrated circle round his grave. Then some bastard steals him the one time she isn't there. It just sucks.'

'She have any notion who did it?' Stewart nudged.

'I didn't get a chance to ask her.' Which wasn't quite the truth. Beck could have. They'd huddled together in her family's mausoleum in Oakland Cemetery until dawn, on hallowed ground in case the demons came after them. She'd been so upset about Simon and the others that she'd cried herself to sleep. At the time it didn't seem important to know who'd resurrected Paul, so he'd just held her close, kept her safe, thanking God she'd survived. Trying to work through his feelings for the girl. When he'd left her this morning, she'd still been asleep, dried tears on her cheeks. He hadn't had the heart to wake her.

Stewart shifted position again: he was hurting more than he let on. 'I canna help but believe there's a connection between the demons' attack and Paul's reanimation,' the old trapper mused.

'How could there be?'

'Think it through. Wouldn't he have gone off with the necro who summoned him rather than droppin' in for a wee visit with his old mates?'

'I don't know,' Beck said, swiping a hand through his blond hair in agitation. 'But I'll know soon enough. I'll find the summoner who did it and we'll come to an understandin' – Paul goes in the ground or the necro does.'

Stewart stiffened. 'Be careful on that account. The summoners have wicked magic and they'll not appreciate ya gettin' in their business.'

Beck didn't respond. It didn't matter what happened to him; Paul Blackthorne was going back in his grave and that was that. He hadn't been able to keep him alive, but he could honour his friend's memory in other ways. He'd do it for Paul's daughter, if nothing more than to give her peace of mind.

'I hear that Five went after Riley, in particular,' the master stated. 'I wonder why.'

Beck had no answer to that. Grade Five Geo-Fiends were the big boys of Hell who generated earthquakes and spawned mini storms as easily as he took a breath. A Five had killed Paul and he was willing to bet it was the same one who'd gone after his daughter during the battle.

Beck *was* sure of one thing – the demons were taking too much of an interest in Riley, calling her out by her name. Hellspawn didn't do that as a rule. *Maybe I should tell Stewart. Maybe he would know what's goin' on.*

But if he did it'd only add to Riley's long list of troubles. Before Beck could make a decision, the master's phone began to buzz inside a coat pocket.

He pulled it out, frowned and opened it up. 'Stewart.'

Beck turned his attention to the hole in front of him. One of the trappers told him that the Geo-Fiend had thrown Riley into this very pit. That same trapper hadn't known how she'd managed to escape, said there'd been too much smoke to see what had really happened.

Why didn't the Five kill ya, girl? There was one possibility, but he didn't want to think about that. No way Riley would have sold her soul to Hell to stay alive.

What if she'd fallen into that hole and never come out again?

Before Beck could admit to himself what that loss would mean to him, Stewart ended the call.

'That was Harper. The Guild's representatives are ta meet with the mayor in two hours. We need ta be there.'

'We?' Beck said, caught off guard. 'Me too?'

'Certainly. Ya gotta problem with that?'

Hearing the challenge, Beck shook his head. 'Can't the city at least wait till we bury our dead?'

Stewart huffed. 'Of course not. Politicians wait for no man when they can lay the blame on some other poor bastard.'

Chapter Three

Riley knew that finding a parking place near the Terminus Market was never easy, but today was worse since the market was so close to the site of last night's tragedy. She wouldn't have gone near the place if she didn't need to reassure a friend she was still alive and collect advice on how to find her missing father.

After trolling up and down the street for what seemed an eternity, she finally caught sight of a scooter pulling out leaving a thick blue cloud of exhaust in its wake. She edged her car into the open space, nervous she might clip the stall ahead. It was full of knitted hats and scarves, most sporting Georgia Tech or Georgia State logos. The owner, an older black man, kept a wary eye on her progress. Once she'd turned off the engine, the knitted-hat guy relaxed and gave her an appreciative thumbs up. She returned it.

When Atlanta joined the growing list of bankrupt cities across the country, the city planners mined every possible way to make money. They'd sold off the school buildings, put a tax on cigarettes, alcohol, day-care centres, Holy Water, homeschooling, almost everything. As the parking spaces went empty because of the excessive price of fuel, the city turned them into 'retail opportunities', which meant there was a cluster of mini shops where once there were cars. Each store lived within the white lines of a parking spot, like the guy with the knitted hats and scarves. Some vendors rented more than one, which was why there was a music shop on Peachtree Street called The Five Meters.

Riley crawled out of the car at half speed, her denim messenger bag in hand. It felt like her body had been ambushed by a particularly sadistic army of karate experts. When she'd showered this morning, she'd been astounded at all the bruises. Holy Water was only good for demonic wounds so she'd be a patchwork of yellow and brown spots in a few days. Luckily most of them were hidden by her clothes. The one on her left hip was particularly painful, courtesy of the malevolent Grade Five demon and the door handle of a Volvo.

Riley trudged into Centennial Park on the wide brick path, favouring her sore hip. When she was a kid, this place was just a park, though pretty cool as far as green open spaces went, especially one in the centre of a major city. It had the five Olympic Ring fountains to play in and vendors sold ice cream and other yummy goodies. It was still a cool place, but there was a lot more to it nowadays. Over time, vendors moved into the market with portable campers and a small city sprang up inside the bigger one. Now the Terminus Market, as it was called, was a year-round thing.

Right before she entered the market, Riley paused on the walkway, allowing the past to catch up with her. Closing her eyes, she swore she could hear her mom's voice, jesting with her father about his need to buy *just one more book* on the Civil War.

'I miss you guys,' she whispered. *Wish you were here.* Then she continued into the chaos of the marketplace.

Originally there had been a plan to all this – food vendors in one section, crafts in another and so on. That plan was ignored as the market sprawled in every direction. The tents came in all different colours, ranging from deep black to brilliant red; some were plain, others were adorned with flags and streamers. All had some form of lighting since the merchants were usually open until after midnight.

Riley paused in front of a tent where a dead animal hung from a spit over a large wood fire. A boy was in charge of turning the spit and Riley could tell it took all his strength, his muscles straining with every rotation. The sign on the tent said it was pork, but you never knew. Sometimes they sold goat. It smelt good, whatever it was. Her stomach complained, reminding her there hadn't been a lot put in it all day, besides the hot chocolate.

Later.

A bit further on was a guy selling used furniture – chairs, tables, dressers. Some of it was in worse shape than the third-hand stuff in her cramped apartment.

'Riley?' a voice called out.

She turned, knowing that voice anywhere. The body too. Clad in a black T-shirt, jeans and a steel-grey duster coat that swept the ground, the man striding towards her was over six feet tall with shiny ebony hair and bottomless dark eyes. Definitely yummy. What she liked best was his attitude – it told the world to take a number and wait its turn.

What am I doing? She really shouldn't be checking out other guys when she was dating Simon, especially when he was in the hospital. *Still, it can't hurt to look . . .* That wasn't being unfaithful.

'Ori,' she called out, 'what are you doing here?'

'Still trying to find a proper sword,' he said.

Riley smiled at that. The first time she'd seen him he was at the tent that sold all sorts of sharp pointy objects. He'd been holding a sword, looking like a hero out of a romance novel.

'How are you doing after last night?' he asked, his full attention on her now.

'I'm OK.' It was her default answer.

Ori's jet-black eyes searched her face. 'Try again,' he said softly.

She sagged. 'The truth? Life sucks. There're lots of dead trappers and, just to make things really special, my dad's been reanimated.'

Her companion looked surprised. 'By whom?'

'No clue,' Riley said, holding up her hands in defeat.

'I'm truly sorry.' Ori moved closer to her, sending little

tingles through her skin. She never understood why that happened, but it felt good. He sounded genuine, which caused her conscience to nag at her. Many of her memories of the previous evening were hazy, however one in particular was crystal clear: Ori pulling her from the crater and threatening the Grade Five demon, making it back off. If he hadn't, she'd be lying next to her parents now. One of them at least.

Feeling awkward, she dug the toe of her tennis shoe into the dirt. 'Did I . . . thank you for . . . well . . . saving my life?'

'No, but you just did,' he replied, like it wasn't a big deal.

'Don't go all modest,' she protested. 'You saved me. I owe you.'

A twinkle appeared in his eyes. 'You do.'

'I know it sounds weird, but I don't remember what happened after I reached the car. Next thing I knew I was at the cemetery.'

'It happens. When the mind is confronted by something too big for it to deal with, it shuts down.'

'Wish it worked that way with the nightmares.'

His hand touched hers. It was warm and she could feel the heat radiate through her skin. It wasn't a grabby sort of gesture, more a gentle one.

'Not many apprentice trappers would challenge a Geo-Fiend,' he said.

'I just wanted it to stop killing the others.'

'Which was really brave. Don't sell yourself short.'

She felt a rush of warmth on her cheeks. *He thinks I'm brave. How cool is that?*

'Don't worry, the next time I will kill it,' Ori said, his voice rougher now.

'Do you think it'll come after me again?'

A determined nod. 'I'm counting on it. So don't be surprised if you see me hanging around a lot.' He delivered a sexy grin. 'The only thing I'm stalking is the Hellspawn.'

She couldn't stop the smile. 'Why didn't you just nail it last night?'

'I wanted you out of harm's way,' he replied. 'And I won't show off in front of the trappers. It'll be *my* kill, on *my* terms.'

'I know you don't like them, but the Guild is short-handed right now. I bet you could get a job really easy.'

Her companion shook his head. 'I work alone.'

Which was what she expected he'd say since Ori was a freelance demon hunter, a *Lancer.* Trappers couldn't stand Lancers because they didn't play by the Guild's rules. Rome's demon hunters didn't like them as they wouldn't pay homage to the Vatican. They were a force all their own, each Lancer his own master, and they dealt with demons as they saw fit.

In a few years maybe she would go out on her own. The trappers didn't like her anyway – she might as well work for herself.

'How is your boyfriend doing?' Ori asked.

Riley blinked. 'How did you know Simon and I are dating?'

'I saw you with him right before you went after the Five. You weren't crying over any of the other trappers, so I assumed there was something between you.'

She couldn't argue with his logic. 'Simon's much better today. He's going to make it.' *Because of me and the angel.* A warm glow fluttered through her chest at the thought.

Ori paused near a book stall. After a moment's hesitation, he reached on to a display and removed a paperback. It was *Dante's Inferno.* He glanced at a few of the pages and frowned.

'He got it wrong; the Ninth Circle of Hell is *not* a skating rink.' He thumped the book closed in disgust and returned it to the rack.

'Have you ever seen angels before?' Riley asked.

'Lots of times.'

'Oh.' Maybe it was just her. She'd only seen one her entire life.

'You're talking about the ones from last night, aren't you?' Ori asked, sombre. When she nodded, he explained, 'Those were the . . . ' He paused and searched for a word. 'Warrior angels. It's been a long time since they've been deployed.'

Deployed? Military guys used terms like that. Had Ori been in the Army?

He glanced away at that very moment, frowning as if something had distracted him. 'I'd best be going. It's good to see you again, Riley,' he said.

It was like he was suddenly keen to be somewhere else. Had she said something stupid?

'Thanks . . . again. I won't forget what you've done for me.'

'It was my pleasure.'

Riley watched him head down the row of tents, his coat flapping behind him. Women turned and watched him pass; he had that kind of magnetic pull. She had a lot of questions about this guy, but there was no one she could ask. She'd promised Ori not to tell any of the trappers that he was in Atlanta, which seemed odd since he'd definitely been right in the thick of the action last night.

'I'll think about that later.' Her dad came first. Then she'd figure out Mr Hunky Mysterious Dude.

Riley kept moving towards Bell, Book and Broomstick, the witches' store. It was easy to find, the gold and silver stars on the midnight-blue canvas glittering in the late-afternoon sun. To her relief, Ayden was arranging bags of incense at the end of the counter. The witch wore her usual Renn Faire garb – peasant blouse with a laced bodice, a full skirt and a heavy emerald green cloak in acknowledgement of the chilly January weather. Most prominent was the large dragon tattoo that began at her neck beneath her russet-brown hair, and went all the way down into her ample cleavage. In the midst of the market, she seemed ageless, like a fairy queen.

'Ayden?' Riley called out, stopping a few feet away.

The witch looked up, then raced out from behind the counter, springing at her like a mother does a missing child. The embrace wasn't a quick one, but the kind that tells you the embracee is thrilled to see you're alive. Riley returned it with just as much fervour.

'Goddess, you had me worried,' the witch said, releasing her.

'Sorry. My cellphone got toasted so I didn't have your number. I'm using my dad's phone now.'

'And you lost my business card too?' Ayden chided.

'Ah . . . no.' It was at the bottom of her messenger bag somewhere under all the other stuff. 'I didn't think of that.'

'It's OK,' Ayden said. 'You're alive. That's what counts.'

'Dad's gone. Someone pulled him out of his grave last night. He was there, at the Tabernacle and he . . .' Riley's shoulders began to heave.

There was another embrace and this time her tears soaked her friend's shoulder. When they broke apart, Riley fumbled in her messenger bag for a tissue.

'Come on. There's a guy down the way who sells hot spiced tea. I think we both need some.'

Riley blew her nose while following her friend through the winding paths of the market. The tea merchant's tent reminded Riley of a Turkish bazaar. Red fabric, silk possibly, hung underneath the traditional canvas and it was shot with gold threads. An incense burner sat in the corner wafting something aromatic into the air. The vendor was dark-skinned, Middle Eastern maybe, and she could tell he had his eye on her friend by the way he smiled at her. Ayden returned the smile, but not quite as warmly, collected the drinks and herded her towards the back of the tent, away from the other patrons. They sat on large, plush pillows near an electric heater. The tea tasted wonderful and warmed Riley from the first sip. Not quite as luscious as hot chocolate, but still good.

'Tell me what happened with your dad,' Ayden said.

Riley settled the thick mug on her lap. 'I had to go to the meeting so the cemetery had this new volunteer sit vigil. A necro sprang a huge magical dragon on the guy. He was dragon-phobic, so he freaked and broke the circle. The cemetery people don't have any idea who did it.'

'It was probably Ozymandias, especially after you dissed him.'

Riley groaned. A couple of nights earlier Ayden had been sitting vigil with her at the graveyard, watching over her father's grave while they shared a bottle of the witch's potent home-made wine. Riley had got tipsy, and when Ozymandias, the creepy necromancer who resembled one of the evil dudes in *The Lord of the Rings*, showed up she'd got up his nose. She was inside a protective circle – what could he do?

Steal my dad, that's what. 'I was sooo stupid,' Riley admitted.

'No argument.'

461

'Hey, it's partly your fault. I blame your wine – it was wicked strong.'

'I blame your mouth,' Ayden retorted. 'Either way, your dad's on the loose for the next year. There's not much you can do about that.'

'I'm not letting him stay above ground.'

'Don't even think you can tangle with a necromancer and come out ahead,' the witch scolded. 'Especially if it's Ozymandias. I wasn't joking when I told you he's into the dark stuff. Just let it be, OK?'

Not OK.

Riley fell silent to avoid an argument. Ayden took that silence as acceptance and turned her attention to the remainder of the tea in her mug.

'Do you want to talk about what happened inside the Tabernacle?' she asked in a low voice.

Riley shook her head immediately. How do you explain what it was like to see people you know being ripped apart and eaten? What it felt like to think you were going to die the same way?

Ayden's comforting hand touched her arm. 'When you're ready, I'll listen.'

'I don't know if I'll ever be,' Riley admitted. 'It was too . . . horrible.'

'Is Beck OK?' her friend asked.

'He got clawed up, but he's alive. Simon . . .' Riley jammed her lips together. Just thinking of him made her want to cry.

'Is he going to make it?' Ayden's hand was still on Riley's arm, warm and reassuring.

'I . . . yeah. They didn't think he was, but now he is.'

Ayden frowned, like she didn't understand the verbal gymnastics. 'Anything else you want to tell me?'

Riley couldn't hold it back. Someone had to know her secret. 'Ah, well, you see I made a deal with this angel and . . .'

The witch's frown deepened. After a quick glance around to ensure they weren't being overheard, she leaned closer. 'What do you mean by *deal*?'

Riley told her about the agreement with Heaven.

'My Goddess,' Ayden murmured. 'You sure it was an angel?'

Riley nodded. 'And she came through. Simon's getting better.'

'Once Hell finds out you're on Heaven's team, things could get complicated,' her friend warned.

Riley snorted. 'More complicated than last night? That Five was after me. It was the one who killed my dad and the same one who tried to flatten me at the law library.'

'Which happened before your deal with Heaven,' Ayden said. 'Oh, Goddess, you are in trouble, aren't you? Have you told Beck any of this?'

'No, and I'm not going to. I'll work it out on my own.'

'It's not showing weakness to ask for his help.'

'No way, not from Beck,' Riley retorted. 'End of subject.'

*

Ayden walked with her as far as the witches' store. 'Try the Deader tent two aisles over,' she suggested. 'The man there might have heard about your dad.'

'But you said I shouldn't go near the necros.'

The witch raised an auburn eyebrow. 'I know you're not listening to my sage advice, so I might as well steer you in the right direction.'

'And if that guy doesn't know anything?'

'Then work through the summoners who were hounding you at the cemetery. Minus Ozymandias. Do not go near that man – do you understand?'

'Got it.'

'Really got it or just saying that to make me happy?' the witch pressed.

'Don't know yet.'

Ayden rolled her eyes, then reached for something on the counter. After giving Riley another hug, she handed her a small plastic bag full of herbs. 'Brew yourself a cup of tea with this right before bed – one teaspoon should do it. It helps clear your head and might keep you from having nightmares. I'm thinking you need that right now.'

Riley smiled. 'Thanks, Ayden, for everything.'

The witch traced something in the air between them. It looked like a complex symbol.

'What was that?'

'Just waving away a mosquito,' Ayden replied.

In January? You are so lying.

Chapter Four

The Reanimate Palace, as it was called, wasn't doing much business. Four Deaders stood in a row, staring at nothing, a greyish tint to their wan faces. From what she'd heard, if their bodies were treated carefully, they could remain outside the grave for almost a year.

If her dad's body had been in pieces after his battle with the Five, no necro would have wanted him. Instead he'd died from a single shard of glass driven into his heart by the demon's windstorm. A pristine Dad meant a potential reanimate. Her father was one of a kind: it was rare any trapper ever made it on to the reanimate market.

Riley cocked her head, studying the four forlorn figures – two males, two females. One of the guys was about her age. One minute he was dead, then he was standing inside a tent while people decided whether to buy him or not.

That has to suck.

The government outlawed slavery in 1865; that date had been drummed into her head by her father the history teacher, but the dead were another matter entirely. Recent court cases had ruled the deceased had no civil rights, so there was a bill in Congress to rectify that big hole in the law. It was stalled in committee, the victim of a well-financed lobbying campaign by the necromancers. Meanwhile people like her dad were stolen out of their graves and trafficked to those who could afford to buy them.

Riley took a deep breath to calm her nerves and walked into the tent. The salesman immediately moved forward with oily ease.

'Good afternoon. Can I help you?' he asked, sounding as if he sold bootleg designer purses. Anything but dead people.

'My dad was reanimated last night and I need to know who did it.'

'The summoner should have left a notice at the gravesite, if it was a legal reanimation.'

'It wasn't,' she said. 'I didn't give anyone permission to do that.'

'Ah . . .' the fellow said, moving back behind a folding table that served as a makeshift desk. He riffled through a stack of cards and then offered her one.

'Contact this guy. He's the summoners' ombudsman in Atlanta. He handles all complaints about ripped-off corpses.'

The card was familiar. A number of them had been left just outside the circle that once protected her father's grave. Of the necromancers she'd encountered, Mortimer Alexander had been the nicest, always polite. He'd claimed he wouldn't reanimate a corpse without the family's permission. If that was true, then he'd be her best bet to find her dad.

Riley studied the address on the card. 'Little Five Points?

The sales dude grunted. 'Necros like it there. They say it has a kind of magical vortex or something.'

'Is that so?'

The guy shrugged. 'If Mort can't help you . . .' He handed over another card.

> Gone Missing Detective Agency
> You lost 'em, we find 'em.

'They charge for this?' she asked dubiously.

'Sure. There's always money to be made in death,' the guy remarked, smirking.

Riley hurried out of the tent before she hit him.

Ori followed the girl's movement through the market from his position near the five fountains. After they'd talked, Riley had gone to the witches' tent where she met someone who apparently was a friend given the intensity of their greeting. Then they'd moved to the tent that served drinks. Now she was speaking with someone at the tent where they sold corpses. Others might not see it, but he could tell she was hurting, both inside and out. That wasn't a surprise after the death of her father and last night's battle.

'Too close,' he muttered. By the time he had realized what was happening at the Tabernacle, he'd almost lost her to the demon. 'Won't happen again.' He would be following her from this point on. It was only a matter of time before the Five came after her and he'd be waiting.

At least her boyfriend was out of the way for the moment. *One less complication.*

Ori scratched his chin in confusion. Higher-level Hell-spawn were always on the lookout for souls to harvest. Why hadn't the demon made her a deal – her life for her soul? Then the fiend could use that valuable bargaining chip to buy favour with others of its kind. That was how Hell operated, an endless line of favours owed all the way up to the Prince of Hell himself.

Riley was on the move again. Ori tracked her to her car and watched as she pulled away. No sign of the Geo-Fiend. Sometimes he couldn't get a break if he tried.

Riley's hope that she could zip into the hospital, spend some time with Simon and then retreat without anyone else seeing her was just not on the cards. Her father had once remarked that after every disaster there is a time of reckoning. After the smoke cleared and the bodies were toted off, the survivors and their families needed time to come to terms with what had happened. Put things into perspective.

Since Riley was one of the survivors, her boyfriend's

family wanted to hear her story. Before she'd realized what was happening, she was shepherded into a private waiting room set aside for the Adler family. There were ten of them and they all looked like Simon – lanky and blond.

Someone whispered, 'She's a demon trapper?'

Riley was getting used to that. It came with the territory.

Simon's parents didn't rise from their seats. Their faces pale and lined, they appeared more exhausted than when she'd met them this morning. The others settled in around the couple, talking quietly among themselves and shooting furtive glances at Riley. One of the women carried a sleeping infant. In the midst of the group was a toddler who wandered from person to person showing them his stuffed dog. It had big blue eyes just like the little boy. As he made his rounds, he received lots of hugs and kisses.

I could so use a hug right now. Ayden's had worn off.

When the little one stopped in front of her, Riley smiled and touched his blond hair fondly. 'He looks so much like Simon,' she said.

'Just like him when he was little,' a young woman replied. It was Amy, one of Simon's sisters. 'He used to drive me crazy following me all over the house.' She had her hand placed protectively over a noticeable baby bump that pushed against her blue knitted top.

'Come here, son,' the child's mother urged. The

toddler wandered in her direction, babbling and waving his little toy.

Mrs Adler stirred. She had a kind face. 'When Simon first mentioned a trapper named Riley, I thought you were a boy. You look so young to be catching demons.'

'Lots of people think that,' Riley replied.

'I'm sorry about your father,' the woman added. 'You must miss him deeply.'

Riley could only nod. She took a long sip of water from a plastic cup. She didn't remember where she'd got it, but there it was. The Adlers didn't press her for answers as she organized her thoughts. She appreciated that.

How do I tell them that everything went wrong? That the demons weren't supposed to get across the line of Holy Water. That they had coordinated their attack like an army.

Just get it done.

'Ah . . . we didn't see it coming,' she began.

Her boyfriend's father leaned forward in his chair, brows furrowed.

'Simon and I met before the meeting. He'd just put down the ward, you know, the Holy Water circle we do to protect ourselves from the demons. Then we went out-side for a while.' And that was about as much as she could say about that. It'd been his idea to go round the back of the building. His idea for them to kiss and hold each other close and talk about the future. She remembered how good it had felt, how she'd never wanted it to end.

'Riley?' Mr Adler prodded.

'Sorry.' She cleared her throat. 'We went back inside for the Guild meeting.' Riley hesitated. This was where she'd told the trappers about the Holy Water, how some of it was counterfeit. The Adlers didn't need to know that. 'The demons just appeared out of nowhere.'

'How did the fire start?' Simon's father asked.

'Pyro-Fiends. There were a lot of them. They just went crazy. It was the Threes who broke through the Holy Water ward.'

'Threes?' Amy asked, perplexed.

'They're . . .' How could she explain these things? They were so a part of her world now. 'They're Grade Three demons. They're about four feet tall,' she said, indicating their height, 'and all teeth and claws. They eat . . . everything.'

There were gasps around her.

'That's what hurt my son?' the man asked, his voice edged with a quaver.

She nodded. 'They broke through the ward and one of them got between us. Simon shouted for me to run and it went for him. If he hadn't said anything . . .'

It would have come for me instead.

That would have been OK. Better than watching the thing tear into him like a big cat, shredding and clawing, Simon's blood spraying into the air in a fine red mist.

She shuddered at the memory, the cup shaking in her hand. 'I hit it with a chair and then one of the trappers carried Simon outside and they took him to the hospital.'

Which wasn't all that had happened. She wasn't telling them about the others – the ones that were burnt or torn to pieces. Ethan, Morton, Collins . . . so many.

Mr Adler touched her hand gently, jarring her out of her dark thoughts. Riley looked into the eyes of her boyfriend's father. Simon would look like this in thirty years or so. He would age well, as long he stayed alive long enough to do it.

'It is not your fault,' he said softly.

Wish I could believe that.

'The Guild's doctor said someone treated my son's wounds with Holy Water and that's why they're not infected,' his mother said. 'The surgeons sewed up all the damage and, from what we've been told, he's healing really quickly.'

'Holy Water does that.' Providing the wound was caused by one of Hell's fiends.

'They don't know what to make of the fact that his brain is working again,' his mother continued. 'Father Harrison said it was a miracle.'

That's the truth. Her boyfriend's family would be making funeral arrangements if Riley hadn't agreed to Heaven's terms.

'He was so brave last night.' Riley's heart swelled at the memory. 'He didn't back down at all.'

'Sounds like our son,' his dad said, smiling faintly at his wife, a glint of tears in his tired eyes.

'He's a really nice guy,' Riley said, then felt foolish. They knew that.

'He likes you a lot,' his dad replied. 'He smiles whenever he says your name.'

Riley didn't reply. If she said anything more, she'd start to cry, and she wasn't sure she'd ever stop. The energetic toddler wandered over again. He patted her knee with a chubby hand.

Riley bent and hugged him, feeling his warm breath on her shoulder. The tears came anyway. Then she got hugs from every member of Simon's family. All of them said they were praying for her.

Like I'm one of them.

Simon's hospital room was less crowded with equipment than it had been in the morning. The machine that had helped him breathe was gone and in its place was the soft hiss of oxygen.

Her boyfriend's wavy blond hair held flecks of dried blood. His gorgeous blue eyes were closed and he was breathing deeply just like the night he'd fallen asleep at the graveyard. The same night he'd held her as she wept for her dead father.

Would Heaven have let him die if I'd said no?

There was a slight moan from the bed. Both of Simon's hands and arms were bandaged and the image of him trying to fend off the demon's slicing claws returned before she could block it.

As Riley carefully took one of his hands in hers, Simon painstakingly prised his eyes open.

'Hey there,' she said. His gaze finally settled on her face and he gave her a bewildered look.

'Water?' he croaked.

Riley hunted around until she found a glass of ice on the bedside table. She remembered this from when her mom was sick, and after fumbling with the electronic controls to help him sit upright she gingerly placed a piece into his mouth. He sucked on it, but his bloodshot eyes never left her. After three more pieces, he pushed the spoon away and she returned the cup to the table.

'Riley,' he whispered.

'You scared me. You can't do that again,' she said, smoothing back a lock of hair. It refused to stay in place. Dried blood wasn't a great styling product.

'You're alive,' he said. It sounded like he hadn't been entirely sure on that point.

'Because of you,' she said.

'No.' Then he grimaced, extracted his hand from hers and slowly pulled down the blanket. It was hard going with the thick bandages that covered his arms. He wasn't wearing a gown, but a pair of drawstring pyjama bottoms. Riley barely suppressed the gasp – his chest and stomach were a patchwork of bandages.

'Itches,' he said, wincing, carefully scratching near the edge of a piece of adhesive tape.

'Tell me about it,' she said, pasting a false grin on her

face. Her demon-clawed thigh still demanded a lot of lotion to keep it from driving her nuts. 'It means you're healing.'

It hurt so much to see him like this. He'd be marked for life.

Like me.

'You killed that demon,' he said simply, letting his arms fall on the bed as if the scratching had depleted his energy. 'You saved my life.'

'I didn't like seeing my guy getting chewed on.'

Simon shivered in memory. 'Its claws burned like fire,' he said, not looking at her now. 'I thought it was going to . . .' His voice trailed off.

You thought it would eat you alive. Like the Three that had attacked her a few weeks back. She still had nightmares about that, still felt its claws embedded in her thigh and its rancid breath in her face.

Riley gently squeezed his hand again, waiting for the questions that were sure to come.

'How many . . .' he whispered.

He'll have to know eventually. 'Thirteen that we know of. There're probably more in the rubble they haven't found yet. Another four are in bad shape.'

'Who died?'

'Simon, I—'

'Who?' he demanded, his attention returning to her.

Riley gave him the names, and with each his face grew more solemn. He closed his eyes when she told him about Ethan, one of their fellow apprentices.

'He was so happy,' Simon whispered.

Ethan had a reason to be happy. He and his fiancée were looking for an apartment and were planning a wedding sometime in the summer.

Now he was dead.

'Who else?' Simon asked, his voice so quiet she almost didn't hear it.

'That's it. Both of the masters are hurt – Stewart has a concussion and Harper's got a couple cracked ribs.'

Silence. Not the good kind.

She offered him more ice and he took it. Once it was gone, he sucked in a thick breath. 'I must have put down the Holy Water wrong.'

'No way. You did it perfectly. The demons shouldn't have got through.'

But they had. It was a good bet he would carry that horrendous guilt forever, no matter who said he wasn't to blame. Simon would always second-guess himself.

More silence. She held his hand, knowing he needed to think things through.

Eventually Simon closed his eyes and she took that as a hint he wanted to be alone. After a kiss on his forehead, she whispered, 'You get better. You hear?'

No reply.

When she reached the door, Riley paused and looked back at him. A single glistening tear rolled down his pale cheek.

It was a match to her own.

Chapter Five

When he was young, Beck had spent time in the high school principal's office, hauled in for swearing, roughing up bullies, threatening teachers and vandalizing a skinhead's truck. Same drill in the Army, though most of the time that had been on account of his drinking. Even now, at twenty-two, he knew what it was like to be called to account for his sins, and that's what this felt like.

As they waded through the throng of newshounds outside Atlanta City Hall, he shot a look at Stewart. From the expression on the master's face he could see the man agreed. They were going to be held responsible for this disaster.

Reporters churned around them, shooting questions at them like bullets. As the pair made their way towards the massive building that housed Atlanta's civil administration, Beck did his best to clear the path in front of Stewart, knowing the master's leg was troubling him. Truth was, his was just as bad but at least he had youth on his side.

Once they reached the top of the stairs, they turned as one and were greeted with an amazing sight: Mitchell Street awash with satellite trucks, their masts high in the air like overzealous daisies. Across the street, in the park, the police had formed a viewing area for the curious citizens of Atlanta. Placards were everywhere. *Prepare to Meet Your Maker!* one said in bright red lettering. Others cited Bible verses. Then there was the *Demons Have Rights* group with fake horns on their heads. They even carried plastic pitchforks and wore pointed tails. That bunch was separated from the rest, probably to keep them from getting beaten up.

'So what ya seein' here?' Stewart asked.

'A whole lot of crazy people,' Beck replied sourly.

'A few, maybe. Frightened people do stupid things, lad. Keep that in mind in the days ta come.'

Beck didn't reply. He knew the old trapper was right. As long as the Guild stood between the dark, scary things and the public, the good folks of Atlanta had been OK with that. Now it looked like the trappers were losing the battle, and that scared their fellow citizens out of their minds. *Hell, it even frightens me.*

Beck caught a glimpse of flaming red hair billowing around a woman's shoulders, stirred to life by a light breeze. She wore a chocolate-brown suit and stood near a news van. From this distance it was hard to tell the colour of her eyes, but he'd bet they were vivid green to match her blouse. She stood out like a fiery beacon in the midst of a monotone crowd.

There was a nervous cough from behind them. It came from an earnest young man in a suit. 'Sirs?' he said. 'If you would follow me. The council is ready.'

Stewart waved their escort forward. 'Lay on, Macduff, and damn'd be him that first cries, "Hold, enough!"'

'What?' the young assistant asked, bewildered.

'Never mind, lad. Show us the way, will ya?'

'Yes, sir.'

As they walked into the building, Beck wondered aloud how the solid metal doors had managed to remain in place. 'These must be worth a fortune.'

'The last three fellows who tried to steal them were given a one-way trip to Demon Central,' Stewart explained. 'Word gets around.'

They were shepherded into one of the smaller meeting rooms. It wasn't fancy, nothing more than a long table, a few padded armchairs for the council and folding chairs for the audience. The master trapper sank into a chair near the front, his forehead sweaty.

'Ya OK?' Beck asked, worried.

'Nothin' that a little whisky won't cure,' the man replied gamely. Stewart's eyes met his. 'Ya keep that temper on a leash, ya hear?'

That was going to be difficult. Beck was dog tired, he had a raging headache and his body ached like he'd been in a mosh pit. With demons.

Keep it cool, a voice said inside his head. It was Paul's voice, guiding him like he had since Beck was sixteen.

Ezekiel Montgomery, the mayor of Atlanta, entered from a side door. The politician sported a noticeable paunch and was accompanied by a few council members, a couple of assistants and a pair of Atlanta cops. The officers positioned themselves on either side of the long table, facing towards the audience like they expected trouble.

'They brought back-up,' Beck murmured. He heard a snort from his companion.

'This isn't all of them,' Stewart observed. 'The council president is missin'. I wonder why the others aren't here.'

As the council settled themselves, Beck took a seat next to the master and waited, drumming his fingers on his knee to work off some of his tension. When he brushed a hand over his forehead, it came away wet. He wanted to peel off his leather jacket, but then everyone would see the sweat rings and how his shirt clung to him because of the fever. He'd changed clothes before this meeting, taking care to tightly bandage his left thigh in an effort to keep the jeans clean. The way the leg throbbed he suspected the bandage was a waste of time.

God, I feel like crap. At least in another twenty-four hours he'd be better. Until then, he just had to tough it out.

'Which one of you is Harper?' the mayor asked without looking up from the paperwork in front of him.

Stewart cleared his throat. 'He's out with an injury. I'm Master Trapper Angus Stewart. I'm empowered ta speak for the Guild.'

'Could you stand when you talk?' the mayor

asked. 'It makes it easier for us.'

'But not for me,' the Scotsman said, remaining in his chair. 'Tell 'em why, lad.'

Beck pulled himself to his feet. 'Ah, what Master Stewart means is that he's injured. It's best he sit.'

The mayor frowned, then gave a curt nod. Beck's attention moved to the young man right behind Montgomery. He looked like any other young political assistant, but something about him felt off. The guy wouldn't meet his eyes, but kept his full attention on his boss.

'So who are you?' the mayor asked, scrutinizing Beck like he'd just discovered him breaking into his house.

'I'm Denver Beck. I'm a journeyman trapper.'

'Mr Buck,' the mayor began. 'We offer our condolences for the losses the Guild has incurred.'

That's just fancy talk for: 'As long as it isn't my ass that's hurtin', I'm good with it.'

'The name's Beck,' he said. Grudgingly he added, 'Thank you.'

The councilwoman sitting three seats down from the mayor issued a faint smile. She was African American, with caramel skin and bright eyes. There was no nameplate in front of her so Beck had no idea who she was.

'I want to know what you intend to do about these demons,' Montgomery demanded.

Beck looked over at Stewart, who waved him on. *Why am I doin' all the talkin'?*

'Master Harper called the National Guild and they're

sendin' us a master so we can train new apprentices.'

'How does that solve the immediate problem?' the councilwoman asked.

'It doesn't,' Beck admitted. 'We've put out a call for other trappers to move to Atlanta for the time bein'.'

'How many were in the Guild to start with?' the councilwoman asked.

Beck gave Stewart a quick look and the master whispered the answer.

'Fifty-six,' Beck said, feeling like a talking puppet. 'Not all are active. Right now we have about twenty trappers who can work.' He'd never felt so out of place in his life. What did he know about all this political stuff? He hadn't even voted in the last election.

'What about the demon hunters? Why can't we have them take care of this?' a balding councilman asked.

Stewart finally spoke up. 'I talked with the archbishop about that this mornin'. The Church's position is that we can handle it.'

The mayor's assistant leaned forward and whispered in Montgomery's ear. The mayor shook his head, causing the man to repeat whatever he'd said. This time there was a nod.

'I must respectfully disagree with the archbishop,' Montgomery replied. 'The governor has been in touch with the Vatican and they've offered to send a team of demon hunters to Atlanta. I think we should move forward on that offer.'

The muscles in Beck's jaw tensed, causing him to weigh his words carefully. 'I'm sure the big boys are good at what they do, but they don't know Atlanta, or her demons. Our fiends aren't the same as the ones in New York City or LA . . . or Rome for that matter.'

'So you're saying that your knowledge of the city will be better for this situation than the Vatican's expertise?' the councilwoman asked.

The lady was feeding him the right questions and Beck loved her for it. 'Yes, ma'am. We got ambushed last night, but that won't happen again.'

'If last night was an example of how the trappers work, we're in deep trouble,' the mayor sneered.

One of the other council members nodded. 'I agree. We should request the hunters come to Atlanta. They'll get the job done.'

'The trappers have dealt with our demon issues for as long as the city has existed,' the councilwoman protested. 'Bringing in an outside force will only make things worse. The hunters aren't locals, and they don't have to answer to anyone but the Church.'

'We need to get this behind us,' Montgomery replied. 'We've got major industries looking at moving to this city. Unless we get this settled as quickly as possible, those opportunities are going to dry up.' The mayor began to shuffle papers in front of him, clearly agitated. 'We're having this problem because of the Guild. The trappers had their chance and they blew it. We need professionals, not amateurs.'

Stewart's face turned puce at the grave insult. His mouth opened, but no words came out. Beck was sure the man was going to have a stroke.

After a quick motion, which was seconded, the vote went in favour of the demon hunters. Only one nay vote was cast: the councilwoman had held to her principles.

'Motion passed.' The mayor gavelled the meeting to a close and then rose from his seat. 'Go bury your dead and call it a day, gentlemen,' he said. Behind him, his assistant wore a sly smile like he'd just won a major victory.

Beck's temper burst out of its restraints. He took a step forward, his fists clenched, but he was immediately blocked by the cops, hands on their firearms.

'Don't, lad,' Stewart said from behind him. 'Give it up. They're not listenin'.'

Once they'd waded through the crowds and were inside the truck, the master produced a silver flask from a pocket and took a long swig. He offered it to Beck, who did the same. The whisky burned his raw throat as it went down. 'Thanks,' Beck said, and handed the flask back. As he pulled away from the kerb, he asked, 'Why did ya let me do all the talkin'? I'm just a journeyman.'

The old trapper took another swig of his flask, then smacked his lips. 'Who'll be a master someday. Ya might as well learn the ropes now. It's not gonna get any easier, that's for damned sure.'

Forbidden

'But I'm not . . .' *what ya think I am.*

Stewart glared at him. 'Paul Blackthorne only trained the best. Ya wouldn't want ta be insultin' his memory, now would ya?'

The master had him by the throat: no way Beck could diss his friend. 'No, sir.'

'Good. First thing, take me home. I need sleep. Pick me up about eight tonight and we'll go ta Harper's. We need to find a new meetin' place, start the insurance paperwork, all that.'

'But if the hunters are comin' to Atlanta . . .'

'All the more reason ta get our own house in order.'

Chapter Six

Oakland Cemetery. It was the *last* place Riley wanted to be, but here she was, trudging along the asphalt road that led into the bone yard. The cemetery sat east of the city and had been there since the mid-1800s. Since the Victorians had a thing about graveyards and designed them like parks, Oakland was known for its massive magnolia trees and stately mausoleums.

Over the last couple of weeks Riley had spent almost every evening here, safely tucked inside a sanctified circle of Holy Water and candles, guarding her father's grave from the necromancers. As long as the circle had remained intact, no one could have touched him. Once the moon was full, he'd have been safe from any summoning spell.

But he never made it to the full moon.

'I should have been here,' she grumbled, her breath puffing out in a thin white stream as she tromped deeper into the graveyard. Nothing would have scared her into breaking that circle.

She turned left on to the road towards her family's patch of ground. The air was still at the moment, the moonlight draped across the ancient gravestones like thin silver icing. Beneath each of those stones was some-one who'd lived in this city, walked its streets. Now all they had was a bit of red clay to call their own.

Back when the Blackthornes had money – one of her relatives in the 1880s was a banker – they'd constructed the family mausoleum. It was one of the finest in the cemetery. Sitting on an island between two roads, it was built of red stone, so solid it had withstood a tornado. In true Victorian fashion the builders had really pimped out the place – heavy bronze doors, stained-glass windows and lurking gargoyles on the roof.

Now Riley thought of the mausoleum in terms of hours and hours of sitting vigil for her father. Of last night with Beck after the trappers had been killed. She'd fallen asleep inside the building, nestled in his arms, safe on holy ground. She didn't think he'd ever closed his eyes. He'd smelt of smoke and blood and righteous anger. Denver Beck was a stick of dynamite waiting for a match, and she hoped she wasn't anywhere near when he exploded.

Riley halted in front of the mausoleum and peered up at the gargoyles. Their bizarre lion faces glowered down at her as if she was an intruder. They had always creeped her out.

Since the building was full of dead relatives, her parents' graves were on the west side looking towards the state capitol dome. Though it hurt too much to think about, Riley knelt in front of her father's grave. It was still a mess, like a giant mole had dug itself out, mounding dirt on either side in its frantic effort to escape. The damaged coffin was gone. Apparently the cemetery people had taken it away.

She took a deep breath, feeling the cold saturate her lungs, causing her to cough. Her mouth still tasted of soot. Blinking to clear the tears, she whispered, 'Sorry, Dad. It wasn't supposed to be like this.'

He was supposed to be alive, teaching her how to be a trapper, laughing at her jokes and taking her out for pizza. Calling her a sleepyhead when she woke up late. Being there for her. Now there was just an empty hole in the ground that matched the one in her heart.

Riley remained silent for a time, pulling memories from the corners of her mind like someone might detangle yarn. She never wanted to forget her father's gentle voice, his face, how his hair refused to behave. As long as she held those memories close, he wasn't really gone.

Then she began to talk to him. Though his body was missing, maybe somewhere his spirit would hear her. It wasn't like she hadn't been close to her mom, but her father had been a trapper so she told him what had happened over the last twenty-four hours. She knew he couldn't answer, but somehow the talking seemed to help.

'I saw some of them die,' she said, shuddering. 'Beck's OK, but pretty beaten up. Simon's . . .' Her voice caught. 'He's going to make it, but only because, well . . . just because.'

Forbidden

There was a sigh of wind in the trees around her, like her father had heard her and was offering his sympathy. His calm voice floated through her mind. *It'll be OK.*

When she was a child, she'd believed him. Not any more.

Once she'd talked herself out, Riley rose, dusted off her knees and headed back down the road to the Bell Tower where the cemetery had its office and gift shop. She would wait there for the volunteer who'd failed her and her father so spectacularly.

Boredom quickly took hold and she dialled her best friend. She didn't have many friends, at least none like Peter. He was more like a big brother than a buddy. Unfortunately, the last time they'd talked they hadn't parted on good terms.

'Hello?' her friend asked, his voice hesitant.

She'd forgotten she was using her dad's phone and he wouldn't know the number.

'Hi, Peter. It's me.'

'Hey. Where are you?'

'The cemetery.'

'Still grave-sitting?'

Peter didn't know. They'd last spoken when she was at Beck's place the morning after the Tabernacle fire. Upset that she'd nearly got herself killed, Peter had hung up on her and she'd never had a chance to tell him about her dad.

'No, I'm done with that.' Then she told him why.

'That bites. You go to all that work and . . .' He swore into the phone. 'I'm so sorry, Riley.'

'Yeah, it sucks. I'm trying to find him, but none of the necros are talking.'

More silence on the other end of the phone.

'So what's up with you?' she said, hoping to spark more of a conversation.

'Not much. It's tense here right now. I really should go.'

'Ah, OK. Maybe we can talk tomorrow.'

'Sure. That'll work.' He hung up.

Was he upset because of her nearly dying at the Tabernacle or was it something else? No way she would know unless he was willing to talk, which didn't seem to be the case. She shelved that away as another potential problem.

A quarter of an hour later – Riley kept checking her watch every few minutes – the cemetery dude arrived. He was younger than she'd expected, about twenty-five, and wore glasses. His heavy coat hung off a thin frame. He moved up the road like someone who'd been viciously mugged and expected to be a victim again.

This was the volunteer who'd failed to keep her father safe. Last night she could have happily thrown him to a demon and tonight wasn't much better. Still, she'd almost broken the circle twice herself, only catching Ozymandias's clever ruses at the last moment.

The guy stopped a good ten feet from where she was sitting on the steps that led to the cemetery office. It was easy to see the look of devastation on his ruddy face. He was a walking apology. They stared at each other for a time, neither willing to speak first. At any little noise, he jumped, casting a worried glance in the direction of the sound. What had it taken for him to come here tonight?

This was too painful. 'Tell me what happened,' she said.

He winced. 'I . . . did everything like I was supposed to.'

Oh, God. He sounded just like her after the disaster at the law library. She'd used those exact words when Beck had demanded an explanation.

The volunteer kept fidgeting and finally she beckoned him to sit next to her on the stairs. He did so with great reluctance, as if it was physically painful to be anywhere near her.

'What's your name?' she asked.

'Richard.'

'I'm Riley,' she said, keeping her voice neutral. This was hell for her and it couldn't be any different for him. 'Tell me what happened.'

He sighed and adjusted his leather gloves before answering. 'I set the circle like I always do. No problems. Necros came and necros went, and—'

'Which ones?' That could be important.

He pondered on the question. 'Mortimer and that guy who dresses all flashy. I think his name is Lenny.'

'Anyone else?'

He shook his head. 'I was reading a book and then the wind picked up. I ignored it. That happens sometimes and usually it's a summoner playing with my head. Then the ground in front of the circle began to glow like it was a pool of lava. It was a real strange red and gold.'

'And?'

'Then *it* blasted out of the dirt like a rocket,' he said, throwing his arms wide like an explosion.

'It? You mean the dragon?'

'Yeah. I've always been afraid of them, ever since I was little. My parents bought me a stuffed one because they thought it was cute. I was sure it was going to eat me so I hid it in the back of the closet.'

She'd expected him to blame someone else, but this guy was shouldering it all.

'Did you tell anyone that you were afraid of dragons, I mean like one of the necros?' she asked. Maybe that might give her a clue.

'No,' Richard replied. 'It's not something you go around telling people.'

He had a point.

'What did it look like?'

He rubbed his face, his fingers making a scratchy noise on the stubble around his chin.

'It was huge, at least twenty feet tall. It had these thick mirrored scales that changed colour when it moved. I could see all the candle flames in them. It was really eerie.'

'It didn't fly into the graveyard,' she said, more to herself than him. *Like you'd think a dragon would.*

'No. It came right out of the ground. You should have seen its claws. They had to be at least three feet long. It kept staring at me, hissing. I could hear it in my mind, telling me to break the circle or it'd roast me alive.'

'And you did?' she asked, working to keep her anger out of her voice.

'No!' Richard retorted, shaking his head instantly. 'I closed my eyes and tried to think of anything else but that damned thing.'

'So how did the circle get broken?'

'When I didn't do what it wanted, it leaned back on its rear legs and roared,' he said. 'I saw tombstones shatter and the roof exploded off the mausoleum. Then this wall of flame came right towards me.'

Richard was shaking, and at this point Riley hesitantly put a hand on his arm. It seemed to comfort him.

There was no evidence of destruction near the mausoleum. 'All illusion,' she said.

Richard took a deep breath and then pushed on. 'When the flames hit the circle the candles began to rock. It got so hot I thought I was being baked alive. I dived under a blanket and tried to hide, but somehow I must have kicked over one of the candles.'

Once the circle was broken nothing kept the necromancer from summoning her father.

'What was it like when my dad . . .' she began,

tucking her hands into her lap.

Richard looked over at her. 'The dirt flew everywhere and there was the crack of wood. I think it was the coffin lid. Then your dad just rose out of the ground. I tried to stop him, but he shook his head and pushed me away.'

'Did he . . . say anything?'

'Yes, and that was *really* creepy. Your father walked up to the dragon, stared at it and said, 'It just had to be you.' Richard swallowed hard. 'Then the thing just vanished, taking your father with it.'

'But you never saw the necromancer?'

'No.'

'How about a swirling bunch of leaves?' That was Ozymandias's favourite disguise.

'No.'

Richard was no longer shaking, as if telling the story had somehow exorcized a portion of his fear.

'I'm really sorry,' he said. 'I feel really bad about this. If I hadn't been so frightened . . .'

She could blame this guy for everything or let it go. Hating him for the rest of her life wasn't going to help. Well, maybe just a little hating, but he didn't need to know that.

'I understand. I almost fell for the "Let's sacrifice a kitten" trick.'

At his puzzled look, Riley explained Ozymandias's brilliant scheme, how he'd threatened to cut a kitten's throat if she didn't break the circle. Luckily the cat wasn't real, nothing more than a bit of his dark magic.

'Wow. I've heard about him. You think he's the one who took your dad?'

'Maybe.'

Silence fell between them for a time. Finally Richard cleared his throat and rose. 'Thanks for listening. I was afraid you'd be too angry to talk to me.'

'You did what you could.'

The young man shook his head. 'All I did was let your dad's body be stolen. I don't deserve your gratitude.'

He slumped down the road. Riley watched him until he took the turn towards the entrance. She wondered if he'd guard anyone else's grave or whether Paul Blackthorne had been his last gig.

'*It just had to be you.*' Her father had known who had summoned him. Was it Ozymandias?

'Doesn't feel right,' she said. Ozy would want her to make the mistake, not a cemetery volunteer. *So he could gloat.*

Her phone rang deep inside her messenger bag. She was tempted to ignore it, but it might be Amy giving her an update on Simon. It was Beck. She groaned.

'Ya on hallowed ground?' he asked without bothering to say hello.

'Yes.' She was, though she wouldn't be once she crossed under the cemetery archway.

'Stay there.' It wasn't a request.

'You know, I'm glad I never had brothers.'

'Why?' he asked, clearly puzzled.

'If they'd been like you, I'd have run away from home.'

'Go ahead. Just make sure it's to Fargo,' he shot back.

Jeez, you just don't quit. He'd been on this 'move in with your aunt' kick ever since he'd found out she had a relative in North Dakota. It didn't seem to matter that her aunt had hated her dad and disliked Riley by default. Once Beck got something into his brain, it was as immovable as a lump of dried concrete.

Time to change the subject. 'I'm sleeping in my own bed tonight,' she announced, knowing that would set him off.

'I'm sure your neighbours will really like that when they get barbecued.'

'Huh?' He wasn't making any sense.

'Nothin' would keep a couple of Pyros from torchin' your apartment buildin' just so that Five can get ya.'

She hadn't thought about that. It seemed pretty far-fetched, but fiends attacking the Tabernacle hadn't seemed like a possibility either.

'I want to be in my own place, Beck. I'm tired, I need a shower and I hurt all over.' Maybe that way she wouldn't feel so alone.

'I hear ya, girl, but that's not the most important thing in the world.'

He was lecturing her again like he knew all the answers to life's questions.

'Goodnight, Beck.'

'Riley . . .' he said in warning.

'I get the message,' she said, hanging up.

And I'm so ignoring it.

Though she hadn't seen anyone when she'd climbed into her car at the cemetery, she was unnerved when a motorcycle fell in behind her. It followed her until the next intersection, then it pulled level with her driver's side door.

Oh, crap, now what? The motorcyclist flipped up the helmet's visor. *Ori.* He replaced the visor and fell in behind her again once they cleared the intersection. It felt strange having an escort, but she had to admit he totally owned that bike. Absolute bad boy. The kind you dreamed about but really shouldn't date because you know it would never work out.

They couldn't have been more different: saintly Simon of the most holy kisses, and Ori who stirred primal emotions she didn't understand. Riley shook her head again.

'Can't go there. Simon's perfect for me. And he's *all* mine.' Even her dad had liked him. She suspected that wouldn't have been the case with the hot guy on the bike.

When Riley parked in the lot near her apartment, Ori pulled into a slot next to her.

'Hopefully I didn't frighten you,' he said, walking over to her car.

'A little. I'm not used to having guys follow me around.'

'I'm surprised to hear that,' he said smoothly.

Riley felt the warmth creep on to her cheeks. Luckily

the parking lot wasn't well lit, so he probably didn't notice. 'Only demons follow me around.' How many guys could handle that statement? Only trappers and most of them weren't that cool.

'Ah, well,' Ori replied. 'I'll just have to deal with that problem,' he said.

'You know, you don't carry a duffel bag or anything. How do you kill fiends without any weapons or Holy Water?'

He gestured towards the saddlebags. 'I've got a few things tucked away.'

But you don't carry them with you all the time, not like Beck.

'So this is where you live?' he asked, like he wanted to change the subject. He did that a lot.

Riley went along with the shift of topic. 'This is it. It used to be a hotel. Now it's an apartment building with lots of dinky rooms.'

Ori studied her home. 'It's got a roof and four walls, so that's all you need, right?'

No. It wasn't all she needed. There was so much more to it than just a place to live.

Somehow her escort was closer to her now. 'Sorry, I didn't mean to upset you,' he said softly.

She looked up into his dark eyes. 'Not your fault,' she replied, shrugging. 'Just the way it is now.'

'Maybe that will change,' Ori said. He gently brushed a strand of hair out of her face. 'In fact, I'm counting on that.'

Forbidden

Her cheeks heated up again. *What is it with this guy?*

A moment later he was rolling out of the parking lot. Apparently his idea of watching over her didn't mean camping underneath her window.

Probably a good thing. Or she might be tempted to invite him inside.

When Riley eased open the apartment door, it creaked on its hinges. The place felt wrong – it suffered from a severe lack of Dad. Her father's clothes still hung in the closet, his electric razor sat in the bathroom and all his books were still here, but he wasn't. That was why it felt wrong. She'd hoped to find solace here, but the emptiness just made it worse.

There was a solid bump at calf level and she jumped in surprise. The neighbour's cat.

'Hey, Max.' She knelt to give him a scratch as he leaned against her, purring. His front paws stood on her tennis shoes, the claws kneading into the fabric as his whiskers tickled her hand.

Max was a Maine Coon, a solid mass of feline that weighed in at close to twenty pounds. He was Mrs Litinsky's and seemed to think Riley's apartment was just an extension of his owner's.

'Sorry, you can't come in tonight.' Normally she'd enjoy the company, but now all she wanted was a shower and a good night's sleep. Max would expect a great deal of human fawning and she wasn't up to it.

After another thorough scratch under his furry chin, she managed to get through the door without him following. She heard a petulant meow from the hallway, but didn't allow the guilt to get to her like it usually did.

She dropped her messenger bag on the secondhand couch and joined it a second later. The timer had turned on the one light in the living room and it illuminated the compact space. Since the building was originally a hotel they'd made this apartment from parts of two separate rooms. Between the drab beige walls and carpet and the jigsaw layout, the end result lacked anything resembling coolness.

At least it's mine as long as I keep paying the rent.

Riley pulled herself up off the couch, yawned and then eyed the answering machine on the table near the old computer. The message light was blinking red urgently. She needed an incentive to tackle whatever waited for her on that machine, so she retrieved a strawberry yogurt out of the refrigerator.

'Last one.' She dutifully added that item to the grocery list. The three entries before hers were in her dad's handwriting. Her heart constricted and she was forced to swallow a thick lump in her throat that had nothing to do with the yogurt. Yet another reminder that someone she loved used to live here.

She sank into the chair in front of the computer, and pushed the *play* button on the machine. Five of the messages were from the CDC – the Consolidated Debt

Company. Her father had taken out a loan to pay for her mother's hospital bills, the ones the Guild insurance policy didn't cover. Now the CDC wanted their money back. The first message was polite, but they became less pleasant with each subsequent call. By the last one the caller was shouting into the phone about how she had to pay the debt she owed them and if she didn't they'd exhume her father. The date on that one was yesterday morning.

'Too late for that, guys,' she said, pausing in her enjoyment of the yogurty goodness. 'Someone else beat you to it.' For half a second she actually liked the necro who'd screwed these guys over.

The rest of the calls didn't require her immediate attention, which she took as a blessing. The moment the yogurt was finished, a yawn erupted.

Shower. Bed. Sleep. In that order.

It wasn't to be a good night. Apartment buildings generate ambient noise and though these sounds weren't any different to normal – someone on the floor above flushing the toilet and the occasional cry of the new baby down the hall – all of them woke her up.

'Thanks, Backwoods Boy,' she growled, pounding her pillow into shape. Beck had seeded the idea that the demons would come calling and now she couldn't get that out of her mind, even with Ori doing sentry duty. With a sigh, Riley rose and walked to her window, pushing back the curtain. The moon glared off the car windshields in the parking lot below. No sign of Ori.

'Watching over me, huh?' If he was, he was invisible.

After staring at nothing for some time, she trudged back to bed and flopped down. 'Maybe I should have let Max in tonight.' He would have curled up against her and purred her to sleep.

A slight shifting noise came from her dresser and she remembered why an overnight cat wouldn't be a good idea – her fellow lodger. As demons went, he was not the scary kind, just the larcenous kind. Max would destroy the apartment just to get the thing.

More movement, or at least the faint hint of movement. 'I hear you,' she said quietly.

The sound halted abruptly, followed by a minute sigh.

There were a number of things a demon trapper was supposed to do: Riley was expected to trap fiends, keep the proper paperwork, protect the public and prevent Hell's minions from making a real mess of the world.

She was not supposed to be sharing an apartment with one.

This was a Grade One Klepto-Fiend, or Magpie, as the trappers called them. He was about three inches in height, with brown skin and dressed like a ninja. He even carried a little bag like a cat burglar. He wasn't dangerous, just prone to ripping off shiny items such as bright pennies or pieces of jewellery. Sometimes she'd find them in bizarre places in her apartment, like in the silverware drawer. Often they'd be stuff that wasn't hers.

Riley had trapped and sold this fiend to a demon trafficker, but it had promptly returned, like one of those missing dogs you read about in the paper, the ones who travel hundreds of miles just to find its owner. Not that she owned this fiend. He was definitely one of Lucifer's critters. She wasn't even sure if it was a 'he' but, as she saw it, girl demons probably dressed better.

Riley rolled over, thumped her pillow and tried to shut down her mind. Instead she heard a teeny voice, the demon talking to himself. Probably counting his stash of goodies.

At least you don't start fires.

And with that in mind she drifted into an uneasy sleep.

Chapter Seven

Morning felt as cruel as a dull knife slicing across her throat. To Riley's annoyance her head ached as much as her body, like she'd overdone it with some of Ayden's highly potent witchy wine. Every little noise made her think of crackling flames and the taunting cackles of the Pyros. As a result, she'd slept poorly, bouts of being awake interspersed with seriously bad dreams that had featured fountains of blood and lots of screaming.

'I should have had Ayden's tea,' she grumbled, but she'd completely forgotten that remedy until this morning.

It annoyed her that Backwoods Boy might have a point – if Hell really wanted her dead, the fiends wouldn't care how many people they killed to get to her even if the mysterious Ori was nearby. No way could she admit that to Beck's face. His flurry of unwanted advice would become an avalanche.

Riley sat at the kitchen table, face propped up by an elbow, watching the microwave carousel rotate her dad's favourite cup, the one that said STUPIDITY CAN BE HABIT-FORMING.

Forbidden

Forty more seconds and there'd be hot chocolate.

She felt miserable, partly because of the poor night's sleep, but mostly because of the calendar. Today's date was circled and marked with a big D. She'd marked the calendar that way because this was *Dad is Free* day, the day of the full moon. After today no necromancer would have been able to touch him.

'Yeah, that really worked, didn't it?' she mumbled. She rose and turned the page to February even though it was a day early. Anything to keep from staring at that D.

Just as she returned to her chair and resumed the microwave vigil, her cellphone jarred her out of her misery. She answered it without looking at the display.

'Riley?' a gravelly voice asked.

'Good morning, Beck,' she said, not taking her eyes off the cup. Thirty seconds. First the hot chocolate, then oatmeal. Maybe she'd be adventurous and make toast.

'I told ya to stay at the cemetery, but ya didn't,' he said accusingly. 'I was outside, watchin' your place all night, that's how I know.'

'You've got to be kidding me.' *You sat out there in the cold? What kind of idiot are you?*

That was why Ori was nowhere to be seen. He wouldn't want Beck to know he was around.

'What are ya thinkin, girl?' her caller demanded.

'I'm thinking my hot water is almost ready and I don't want to talk to you any more if you're going to be a stalkery butthead.' She hung up on him. He immediately rang back and she ignored it.

'I'll so pay for that,' she mumbled, but right now breakfast was the only thing she wanted to think about.

Ding!

'About time.'

As she stirred the hot chocolate mix into the cup, she realized Beck wasn't going to give an inch. He'd sit out there, night after night, watching her place like a vigilant bloodhound. If he kept it up, he'd be so tired a demon would make a meal of him. And, if he was out there lurking, it would be harder for Ori to do his job.

'Ah, jeez,' she grumbled. Why was everything so much hassle?

What she needed was a bolt-hole, at least until Ori caught up with that Five. Every trapper had a safe place on hallowed ground just in case the demons went to war. When her father had first told her about that, she'd thought he sounded really paranoid. After the Tabernacle, not so much. Beck's bolt-hole was in a church so it was heated and had a bathroom, both of which would be a major improvement over the Blackthorne mausoleum, her family's 'sanctuary'. Besides, if she could find a place to stay, that would get Backwoods Boy off her case.

Until he comes up with something else to complain about.

The phone rang again, but it wasn't Beck's name on the Caller ID. This wasn't someone she could blow off.

'Lass?' the Scotsman asked, his voice tight.

Forbidden

'Master Stewart.' *Why is he calling me?*

'I'm hearin' that yer givin' Beck a hard time. Now, let's be clear – ya *will* be on hallowed ground after sundown, till I tell ya different.'

'But why not during the day?' The Five had come after her in the late afternoon. Or it might have been right after sundown. It was easy to lose track of time inside a library.

'The beasties are stronger at night. Ya might be thinkin' that ya'll go about yer business and I'll not know if yer followin' my orders. That would be wrong.'

'Yes, sir. I'll be on hallowed ground at night.'

'Glad we got that sorted. Good day ta ya, then.' Stewart hung up.

Riley dropped the phone on the table like it was red hot. 'Cute, Beck. Bring in the big dog,' she said, shaking her head. 'You're such a jerk.'

A sharp series of raps came from the apartment door. She ignored them. Mrs Litinsky didn't knock that loud and she was the only person Riley was willing to see this early in the morning. At least until the hot chocolate was history.

'Miss Blackthorne?' a voice called out. It took a moment for her to recognize it – it was the guy from the collection agency.

'Go away,' she muttered under breath, continuing to stir the hot chocolate. Almost all the little clumps were gone now. A few more stirs and . . .

'Miss Blackthorne? Your car is in the parking lot so I know you're here.'

Well, at least she could see what this idiot knew about her father's summoning.

Riley opened the door, leaving the chain lock in place. The guy promptly wedged a highly polished shoe inside to keep it from shutting. He wore a black suit, white shirt, grey tie and carried a black briefcase. His hair was so glued down it didn't budge when he moved. It made him look like one of those dress-up dolls she used to play with as a kid.

He offered his card and she took it.

ARCHIBALD LESTER, CLAIMS ADJUDICATOR

'What do you want?' she asked. Her hot chocolate was cooling.

'I would think that would be obvious,' the man replied, an eyebrow arched. He pulled a sheaf of legal-size paperwork out of his briefcase. That was never a good thing.

'If you'll just tell me where I can find your father's body and where the funds from his sale are located, we can get this taken care of without any unpleasantness.'

Her sleepy fog vanished. 'You think I sold my own father?'

'Maybe. Maybe not. It doesn't really matter who did the selling as long as we receive the money and the asset in question.'

'Asset?'

'Your father's body.'

Her stomach twisted. 'No way.' She tried to shut the door, but the guy's foot prevented that.

'You're not helping matters, Miss Blackthorne.'

Riley jammed a finger in his direction. 'Why don't you go find the necromancer who stole my dad and ask him for that *asset.*'

'We'd rather deal with you. You don't wield magic. If you refuse to cooperate, I'll be forced to file a complaint with the police.'

A giggle escaped Riley's mouth before she realized it. Then another. She wasn't a giggler, but this was just too stupid to think about. After everything that had happened, this guy was worried about money.

The man's face clouded. 'You're not taking this seriously, Miss Blackthorne.'

The giggles ended abruptly. 'I watched people die the other night. Do you think I give a damn about your money?'

'You should. It's your debt.'

'No, it's not. I'm seventeen so I'm not responsible for anything my parents did. You people are totally hosed and you know it.'

He glowered. 'Then we'll play hardball. We'll confiscate your father's life insurance payment.'

Can they really do that? 'Whatever,' she said. She just didn't care any more.

'You'll regret this,' he called out.

'The regrets line forms to the right,' she said.

The CDC guy retrieved his foot microseconds before she slammed the door.

In Riley's search for the Guild's priest, the church secretary used the words *temporary* and *mortuary* in the same sentence and sent her to a location just west of downtown. After a bit of hunting, she located the building, a music shop that still had sun-faded posters in the windows announcing the latest albums from several years back. Now it was home to the Guild's fallen as no mortuary would touch a trapper if the cause of death was demonic in origin. Another weird superstition, as if *death by demon* was somehow contagious. Apparently Father Harrison had found a sympathetic soul who had agreed to let them use the location until the trappers were buried.

Eight pine caskets sat in a neat row down the centre of the store, their lids closed. Each had an index card attached with the name of the coffin's occupant. These eight were just the start – not all the bodies had been identified by the coroner yet and others were still buried under the rubble at the Tabernacle. Standing near the head of the coffins was a trapper about her father's age. That was tradition – a member of the Guild remained with the dead until they were buried. It had been Simon's choice to perform that duty for her dad. Riley didn't know this particular trapper's name, but he gave her a solemn nod, which told her the man wasn't an enemy. She made sure to return the gesture.

Father Harrison was attempting to comfort an older woman. 'I didn't want him to do this,' she said in between sobs. 'I told him it'd get him killed.'

The man next to her, probably her husband, mumbled something reassuring, but it didn't seem to help. The woman only sobbed louder. As they left the building, Riley stepped aside to give them space.

Father Harrison joined Riley in the doorway. About thirty with brown hair and eyes, today he appeared older, dark circles beneath his eyes.

'Ethan's parents,' he explained. 'He was their only son.'

Riley dug for tissues as tears began to burn her eyes. The priest held his silence until she'd pulled herself back together. He'd probably been doing that all day.

'I heard about your father's reanimation,' the priest said. 'I'm so sorry.'

'Yeah, I thought I had it covered.' She blew her nose one more time, jammed the tissues in a pocket, then leaned against the building. 'You know about the Holy Water problem?'

The priest nodded. 'The archbishop called me. He said you'd discovered the consecration dates were incorrect and that some of the Holy Water was counterfeit.'

'I bought some from the vendor at the market and took it to the meeting last night so we could test it. Some of the bottles didn't react right.'

'Tested? How?' Harrison asked. He too was leaning against the building now.

'I put my demon claw inside the bottles.' Riley pulled the item out from under her shirt, all three inches of ebony lethalness. Its former owner, a Grade Three Gastro-Fiend, had not so kindly left it in her thigh as a souvenir when it had tried to kill her. Beck had made it into a necklace, and now she wore it with perverse pride.

The priest leaned closer to her, studying it intently. 'Wicked thing, isn't it?'

'Totally,' she agreed as she tucked the talon away. 'The real Holy Water went nuts when it touched the claw. The fake stuff didn't do a thing. And I found out that the fake bottles have labels that smear when they get wet so that's a quick way to check them.'

Harrison swiped a hand over his face. 'I'd heard rumours that the Holy Water wasn't working as it should, but I never thought someone might actually be counterfeiting it.'

'I checked the labels on the bottles Simon used for the ward, and they were good.' There was more to it than that. Riley lowered her eyes, not wanting to see the priest's face when she made her confession. 'But I didn't check what was inside those bottles. Maybe if I had those trappers would still be alive.'

She waited for the condemnation. Instead she heard a profound sigh. 'It wouldn't have mattered, Riley,' Harrison murmured. 'It's not your fault. There were a lot of demons in that building, am I right?'

Her eyes rose. 'They were everywhere. It was *so* scary.'

'Holy Water loses its potency in the presence of sustained evil, unless it's consecrated by the Pope.'

'So if it had just been one or two of them they might not have got through?'

The priest nodded. 'Even if the Holy Water Simon used was counterfeit, he'd created a ward for the previous meeting, and the ones before that. The effects wouldn't fade that fast unless there was an immensely evil presence, or all the Holy Water was bogus.'

'The trappers aren't going to believe that. They're going to think he made a mistake, or that I did something wrong.'

'Or that your father let them inside the ward.'

Her eyes veered upward. 'He didn't! He was trying to save me, not kill all of us.'

'I know,' the priest said, gently touching her arm. 'Your father was an honourable man, but that doesn't mean others might not want to make him a scapegoat. Or you, for that matter. You have to prepare yourself for that possibility, Riley.'

'It's already started,' she admitted.

'I feared as much.'

For one wild instant she felt the need to tell the priest about her deal with Heaven. Then her eyes shifted to the trapper standing vigil over the caskets. She didn't dare, not with him here. He might overhear her and then he'd tell the others, who'd make fun of her, accuse of her being crazy. Master Harper might find a way to use that to force her out of the Guild.

I don't want Simon to know. He'd feel like he owed her something and that wasn't the way she wanted their future to play out. She'd tell Father Harrison her secret someday. *Just not today.*

When Riley left a few minutes later she felt better for having talked to the priest, and she'd received his permission to use Beck's bolt-hole at the church for her temporary living quarters. No more cold nights in the graveyard.

One problem solved. That left countless others. On impulse, she dug out the list she'd made at the coffee shop and studied it. Nothing to cross off yet. The least she could do was buy her groceries.

If Harrison was right and concentrated evil had taken out the Holy Water ward, then neither she nor Simon had caused the deaths of their fellow trappers. That was a profound relief. *Simon has to know he isn't to blame.* It was what the priest *hadn't* said that weighed on her mind.

If the Holy Water isn't strong enough, how do we stop the demons?

Chapter Eight

Riley knew she should be at Harper's place by now, but dealing with her master rated a negative five on a scale of one to ten. The feeling was mutual. So she'd bought groceries, one thing off her list, and now she was savouring a big cup of hot chocolate at the coffee shop and wasting time by staring at nothing. If she stared hard enough, she couldn't hear the sound of roaring flames. Or the cries of the dying.

'Hello?' a voice called out. 'Earth to Riley.'

Riley glared up at the unwelcome interruption. Her barista friend, Simi, was clad in a criminally short jean skirt, black tights and blood-red T-shirt that said PHREAKS ARE PHUN, her hair a wild mishmash of electric blue and hot pink. It all looked good because she was a potpourri of Irish, Native American, Lebanese and Chinese. Simi had never really explained how all that global DNA had connected, which was probably for the best.

Her friend pulled out a chair and took a seat. Her bag, a plush vampire bat with huge purple fangs, dropped on the table in front of her.

'Why are you here? You're not working today,' Riley muttered.

'Looking for you. I think it's time for a Simi intervention.'

Riley groaned. The last intervention had been two years ago right after Allan, the soon-to-be ex-boyfriend, had socked her in the jaw. It'd been Simi who'd figured out how to apply enough make-up to cover the massive bruise so there'd be no questions from her classmates, but not so much that Riley looked like a zombie.

'No one has hit me today,' Riley retorted. 'Just go away. I'm busy brooding, OK?'

'Not OK. You're coming with me,' Simi said, jumping up from her chair so fast it spooked a couple of customers nearby. Maybe it was because the girl lived on coffee. 'I'm going to take care of your follicular issues.'

'My hair is fine.'

'No, your hair is fried, toasted and shrivelled. It needs help. Just like you.' Simi leaned over the table. 'You know I'm right. You don't want your trapper boyfriend to see you like this.'

'He already has.'

'And he's probably praying he won't see you like this again.'

'I don't want—'

But that was the problem with her friend – the world ceased to exist until Simi got her way, which she usually did by sheer force of will. Riley continued to protest as she was pushed and tugged out of the coffee shop and on to the street. She gave her friend the glare that always worked on her other friends. No response. Apparently Simi was immune so Riley gave up.

'Where are we going?' she asked.

'You'll see,' her friend trilled.

As they threaded their way through the city's streets, Simi kept up a running conversation about the club she'd been to the night before. Some place called the Decadent Vampire.

'Let me guess, they wear fake teeth and lurk a lot,' Riley said, conjuring up an image of her faux vamp classmate who lisped and wore overly frilly shirts.

'Some. Not all. It's a mixed crowd. I really liked the band last night and –' She lost track of what she was saying, distracted. 'OMG! Hunk at two o'clock.'

Riley wasn't in the mood so she didn't bother to check the guy out. What was the point? There were more important things to worry about than handsome guys, at least in her world.

'He's coming this way!' Simi said, primping. 'Could you, like, fake a heart attack or something so he'll stop and talk to us?'

Riley scowled at her friend. 'Are you kidding? No way.'

'Come on. Just for me? He's amazing.'

Riley finally eyed the oncoming hunk and then smiled. It was Ori, dressed to kill. Literally, if you were a demon. *Simi is going to be so jealous.*

Actually, her friend fell speechless when Ori stopped in front of them, which had to be a first.

'Riley,' he said in a voice that would melt steel.

'Ori,' she said. Somehow the day felt better already. 'How's it going?' At her side, Simi had fallen into full-stare mode.

'You . . . you know this guy?' she asked breathlessly.

'Sure. Ori and I met at the marketplace. He was trying to buy a sword.'

'Occupational hazard. You slay dragons and you go through a lot of swords,' he jested, turning those bottom-less eyes on Simi and playing the rogue. Actually, it was more the default setting with him.

'God, you're so cute,' her friend blurted.

Riley did a mental face palm. 'Simi works at the coffee shop. And lives on caffeine.'

'Ah, that explains it,' Ori replied politely. He didn't seem the least bit troubled by her friend's adulation. 'Glad to meet you.'

'So if dragons did exist, you'd really slay them for a living?' she asked, her eyes locked on him.

'Certainly. And rescue damsels,' he said, winking at Riley.

For a second she thought Simi was going to tackle this guy.

As if Ori sensed the danger, he said, 'I best be going. Good to meet you, Simi. I'll see you later, Riley.' Then he walked off, coat flowing behind him.

The barista grabbed Riley's arm. 'You have been holding out on me, girlfriend. Give me the deets, now!'

'No details. He's got business in Atlanta and we see each other every now and then.'

'See each other? Has he kissed you yet?'

What? 'Pleeease. I'm dating another guy. You think I'm a skank or something?'

'A kiss wouldn't hurt. I mean, you'd probably explode from the ecstasy, but, hey, it'd be worth it. You just don't see guys like that very often.'

Simi was right: Ori was top-shelf material. Which meant he wasn't in their league.

'True, but he's not in Atlanta for that long. Once his job is done, he's outta here. Simon is not going anywhere.'

Simi herded her down a side street. 'Don't be an idiot. This Ori guy likes you or he wouldn't be hanging around all the time.'

'Not going there.'

'You're too stuffy, girl. You need to be wild every now and then.'

'You do wild. I'll do sane.'

Luckily the conversation ended as Riley was shepherded into a salon. The hair stylist had colours even crazier than Simi's, which didn't do a thing for Riley's confidence. But after the shampoo, scalp massage and deep conditioning, she began to relax. The woman seemed to know what she was doing, deftly removing the frizzled hair, shaping it as she wielded the scissors.

'You are overdoing the curling iron,' she said. 'I've never seen hair this badly damaged.' In the mirror Riley could see her friend gesturing frantically, trying to derail the conversation. The stylist kept on. 'Just what are you doing anyway?'

Before Riley could figure out a way to avoid talking about just why she was in this state, Simi tugged on the stylist's arm and then drew her aside for a private talk.

When the woman returned she was repentant. 'Sorry, I didn't know. We'll make your hair look good and there's no charge.'

'But—' Riley said.

'No. I should have recognized you from the television. Don't worry – you'll look great when I'm finished. You deserve that for all you've done for us.'

Twenty-three minutes later Riley stepped out of the hair salon minus the fried ends, and with hair that *moved*, according to the stylist. And it did. Move, that is. She had talked the stylist into a generous tip, but Simi insisted on paying it.

'Better?' her friend asked, beaming like a sun at high noon. She always did that when she got her way. Riley tried her glower again, but couldn't muster the proper level of aggravation.

'Yes.' She had to admit the new haircut, which kept most of the length but had cool layers, looked awesome. Even better, her hair no longer smelt like burnt Tabernacle. That in itself was a blessing.

After a time, they sat on the steps in front of the Suntrust building, soaking up the sunshine like a pair of human solar panels.

'You'll have to keep it trimmed or it'll look awful,' Simi advised as she fussed with her lipstick, some deep purple shade called Nameless Sin. 'You need to look hot now that you've got three guys giving you the eye.'

'Three?' Apparently her friend's maths was different to Riley's.

Simi capped the lipstick with a click and dropped it back into the bat bag.

'Sweet blue-eyed blond trapper,' she said, raising one finger. Her purple nail polish sparkled in the sunshine. 'Muscled blond trapper number two who gives you demon claw jewellery,' she said, adding another finger. Finger number three rose. 'And that gorgeous, "Where have you been all my life?" dude with the raven-black hair and dark eyes.'

'You read too many romance novels,' Riley replied sourly.

'You don't know how good you have it,' Simi countered. 'Any of those guys are great. Me, I'd go for the dark and dangerous one. He's smoking.'

'You would.' Simi was an on-the-edge kinda girl. 'Simon's just fine for me, thankyouverymuch.'

'Of course. You go with safe and secure every time, but no guy's really that way. Might as well go for a wild one once in your life.'

'Simon is right for me,' Riley argued. 'Ori isn't.' It was pushing the envelope to even think in that direction.

'What about Beck?' Simi asked, wrinkling her brow.

'Backwoods Boy? Are you crazy? It'd be a threesome – me, him and and his overbearing ego. Definitely doomed to failure.'

Simi laughed, then a few seconds later her brilliant smile faltered. She took Riley's hand and squeezed it. 'You know, you're doing incredible and dangerous stuff, but I don't want you to forget who you really are.' She perked up. 'With your new hair, you're going to kick demon butt and look awesome doing it. That's the Riley Blackthorne way.'

A lump formed in Riley's throat. 'Thanks.' They hugged and when they broke apart there was a film of tears in Simi's eyes.

'I do not want to see any more pictures of you on the television,' her friend commanded. 'Unless you're winning an award or something.'

'They don't have those for demon trappers.'

'Not yet,' Simi said, hooking her arm round Riley's. 'Now you tell me all about this babelicious blue-eyed boyfriend of yours . . .'

Like most places in Atlanta, Master Harper's place was on its second reincarnation. Once a car repair shop, now it was his home, an ageing single-storey concrete-block building with twin overhead doors that led to what were once the repair bays. Harper had made a few changes, adding a small apartment behind the original office, but it was still a dump that stank of old tyres, grease and demons.

No matter how Riley looked at it, her time with Master Harper hadn't been good. He'd hated her dad for some unknown reason, was a drinker and had a volatile temper. He was too quick to strike out at his apprentices if he wasn't getting his way, often leaving bruises. She'd not seen him since the Tabernacle. What kind of mood would he be in? If she was lucky, he'd be drunk and asleep, then she could do a quick walk-through and take off.

No such luck – Harper was awake in what had been the tyre shop's office, perched in a ratty recliner that gave used furniture a bad name. There wasn't a bottle of booze at his elbow, which had to be a first. Instead there was a bottle of pills that sported a thick red sticker on the side warning against taking them with alcohol. Who knew keeping the old guy sober would be so easy?

His usual frown was in place, along with a sheen of sweat on his forehead, though it was cool in the room. The long scar that ran from his left eyebrow down to the corner of his mouth was pulled tight, like he was in pain. She kept her distance from him. He was vicious on a good day.

The old television was on, tuned to CNN, with yet another talking head standing in front of the smoking ruins. They pulled up a file shot of the body bags lined along the street like long black cocoons.

Her master scowled up at her, hitting the mute button.

'What are you doing here?' he growled.

'Bringing you food,' Riley replied, hoisting the bag of groceries on the desk. *Though you so don't deserve it.* 'I didn't know what you wanted, so I just got what sounded good.'

When she placed a McDonald's bag on the arm of his chair, he glowered at it like it held a bomb. The smell must have got to him because he opened the bag and rummaged through it. The cheeseburger came out first.

'None of this adds up,' he said around a mouthful of burger. 'Demons don't work together.' He frowned, opened up the sandwich and discarded the pickles into a nearby trash can with considerable disgust. 'Every fiend wants to suck up to Lucifer. If that means screwing over another demon, that's the way it is.' Harper's sour expression diminished. 'You got something for me to drink?'

She dug into the grocery bag and then handed over a cold bottle of soda, one of a six-pack. Harper twisted open the top and after two big gulps he put it down. He didn't say another word until the burger was gone, then he started on the fries. As he ate, Riley put away the groceries in the small kitchenette that shared space with his bedroom. Harper's bed was unmade, and from its condition it looked like he'd done a good bit of thrashing around in it. A stack of books sat on the floor and the titles all had something to do with Hell or demons. The image of Harper curled up in his bed doing his homework just didn't compute.

Forbidden

Her master fixed her with a smirk as she exited the kitchen. She figured it was for her new hairstyle.

'You sure that Holy Water for the ward was good, not that fake stuff?' he asked.

He hated her already, so the truth couldn't make it any worse. 'I only checked the labels, not the Holy Water itself. Father Harrison said it wouldn't have made a difference, that there were too many demons for the ward to keep them out.'

She expected a blast of fury from her master. Instead there was a thick huff of air.

'The priest's right. No matter how careful Adler was putting that stuff down, we were hosed.'

Adler. Usually their master just called him Saint because of her boyfriend's religious habits.

'But that don't answer why your old man showed up,' Harper said, eyeing her.

'He told me the demons were coming. He was trying to save us.'

Harper's attention momentarily flickered to the television. 'What about Adler?'

'He's going to make it.'

Then his eyes swung back to her. 'I told you to stay away from that Geo-Fiend. Why in the hell didn't you listen to me?'

'It was the one who killed my dad.'

'Jonesing for revenge, were you?' he sneered. 'You just had to go up and introduce yourself?' He shook his head. 'Stupid move.'

That angered her. 'It said it wouldn't kill any of the others if I gave myself up.'

Harper's bloodshot eyes searched her face. 'And you believed the damned thing?' he chided. 'God, you're a fool.'

'It was worth the risk,' she admitted. 'After Simon . . .'

Harper slumped back in his chair, wincing at his cracked ribs. 'In the future, you listen to what I tell you.'

'Yes, sir,' she mumbled. 'What do you want me to do until you're better?'

Her master rubbed his fingers over his thick chin stubble. 'Get yourself in here every morning. If there're Grade Ones to trap, you'll do 'em. If not, I'll find something to keep your ass out of trouble.'

That she wouldn't doubt.

'I've had enough of you for one day,' he said, running up the volume on the television with the aged remote. 'Get lost.'

If it were only that easy.

It was late afternoon when Beck hiked into Demon Central, his trapping bag fully stocked. He was eager for the hunt and he wasn't too fussy about how many of the demons he caught were still alive when they were sold to the traffickers. If the fiends gave him a reason, he'd kill them without thinking twice, especially after what had gone down at the Tabernacle.

Beck knew he shouldn't be in this part of town on his own, but time was running out. When the demon hunters came to Atlanta, they'd kill every demon they could find, big and small. If he wanted to build up enough money to tide himself over until the hunters cleared out, it was now or never.

There were two problems with his *catch as many demons as possible* plan. First – he wasn't in peak condition, not with the healing leg wound. Second – no demons. He'd usually spot at least one or two fiends in Demon Central during every visit, sometimes as many as five of the things in one night. Tonight all he'd seen was a mangy limping cat and a few scraggly pigeons. Those were usually scarce when Threes were on the prowl.

Demon Central was the trappers' name for Five Points, a section of south Atlanta that never got any breaks. Even the casino they'd constructed a few years back wasn't doing that well, not with the depressed economy. Time and neglect had opened up numerous holes over the old steam vents in Five Points' streets and sidewalks. Since the city didn't have the money to repair them, this area was now home to Grade Three demons. The Gastro-Fiends lived in the holes and ate everything they could gulp down, even fibre-optic cable. Didn't matter if it was a stray dog, a rat or a trapper, if something looked like it could be eaten, the Threes were all over it.

Beck pulled his attention back to his surroundings: daydreaming down here was a one-way ticket to a fiend's belly. He wrinkled his nose at the stench from an overflowing dumpster. To avoid paying the city's exorbitant collection fees, people brought their trash down here and dumped it, even at the risk of becoming dinner for a ravenous Three. The only plus was that the rotting garbage was prime Gastro-Fiend bait.

But there were no demons to be found. At least not down here. He'd heard scattered reports of sightings elsewhere in the city, but they sounded like tall tales. Demons had certain behaviour patterns and some of the stories were too bizarre to be true, like how a Three had broken into a dress shop and had eaten some of the mannequins, clothes and all. Gastro-Fiends would devour anything, but they usually didn't break into businesses for a quick snack.

As Beck hiked down a street littered with abandoned tyres, broken hunks of concrete and boarded-up buildings, his thoughts slipped to Riley. They did that a lot nowadays. It troubled him that he hadn't seen her today, despite his early-morning phone call that had earned him an earful of aggravation. He liked talking to her, even if she gave him grief all the time. It wouldn't hurt to call her, would it? Check in and see how she was doing? See if she needed any help? That's what Paul would expect him to do.

He wavered for a time, then flipped open his phone and dialled. Maybe one of these days he'd feel good about using that text thing.

'Hey, girl, how ya doin'?' he asked as soon as Riley answered.

'I'm OK. What's up?' Her voice sounded neutral, like she wasn't looking to pick a fight. Maybe they could keep it that way.

'Well, some of the funerals are tomorrow afternoon. I was wonderin' if ya could pick me up at my place and drive me down to the cemetery. The services are at South-View.'

'OK,' she replied. 'You know how to get there?'

'Yeah.' He'd been there for another trapper's funeral about a year back. 'Make it about one-thirty.'

Beck shifted the phone to the other ear, keeping an eye on his surroundings. Just because it seemed quiet didn't mean he'd let down his guard. That was usually when you got nailed.

'How's your leg? Is it healing OK?' Riley asked.

'It's better. So what'd ya do today?' he asked, trying not to sound like he was conducting an inquisition.

'A friend made me get my hair cut. It looks better now. And I checked in with Harper,' she said. He heard the sound of a car door closing. 'He's still a jerk, but at least he's not drinking. I'm in Little Five Points. I'm going to talk to Mortimer to see if he has any idea who took Dad.'

Beck opened his mouth to tell her that might not be a good idea, then changed his mind. Riley needed to be doing something useful, keeping her mind off Simon and all the other bad stuff. Besides, she couldn't get into too much trouble in Little Five Points. It was mostly necromancer and witch territory and because of that the demons usually steered clear.

'Sounds like a plan,' he said. 'Let me know if ya learn anythin'.'

There was a momentary pause like Riley had expected a lecture and was astonished when she didn't get it. 'So where are you?' she asked.

'Demon Central. No luck so far.' He did another slow three-sixty. No threats.

'Someone with you?'

He smiled at the concern in her voice. 'Nah. I'll be OK.'

'Beck . . .' she began, the worry clearer now. 'You're still getting over those demon wounds. You need someone watching your back.'

'I'm fine, Riley. No action down here anyways. I'm about to pack it in, maybe go to the lounge and play some pool. Haven't done that in a long time.' *Not since your daddy died.*

Her deep sigh of relief caused his smile to widen.

'Tough life you got there, Backwoods Boy,' she jested.

'Yeah, it's a bitch. Ya gonna be on holy ground to-night, right?'

'You know, I don't appreciate you ratting me out to Stewart. I owe you for that one.'

'Happy to help out, as long as it keeps ya safe.' He did another perimeter check. Other than a rat crawling along a ledge of broken bricks about ten feet to his right, there wasn't anything to worry about. He noted she hadn't answered his question. 'Yer at the cemetery tonight, right?'

'No, I will not.'

'Damn, girl, don't make me call the Scotsman again.'

'You don't have to. I'm staying at St Brigid's, in your bolt-hole.'

'What? Oh. Why didn't ya tell me that right off?' he grumbled.

'Because you'd just bitch at me about something else.'

She had him there. 'Well, then, that's all good,' he said, pleased he'd not have to pull guard duty outside her apartment again. Last night hadn't been that much fun, not with his fever and feeling like death warmed up.

'Now do me favour – get out of Demon Central!' she ordered. 'And don't you dare go down there until someone is watching your back.'

'I'm fine with—'

'If you don't leave right now, I'll call Stewart on you. I swear,' she threatened.

He grinned at how neatly Riley had turned the tables on him. She *was* worried about him.

'Yes, ma'am. I'm outta here. Say hi to Mort for me.' He flipped his phone closed before she said goodbye. He'd always hated *that* word.

Beck adjusted the strap of the duffel bag and headed for his truck. 'Why the hell didn't I think of her stayin' at the church?' he muttered. It was the obvious solution to the problem. Stewart hadn't thought of it, either. 'Too much goin' on. We don't have a handle on this and that's not good.'

But for now, he'd gladly follow Riley's advice: the best therapy he knew was a few games of pool.

Chapter Nine

Little Five Points sat east of the city, a strange mix of New Age shops, tattoo parlours and retro clothing stores. Unlike Five Points, its downtown cousin, L5P's natives wore cruelty-free cotton, adored health food and sported dreadlocks or emo garb. They spoke of auras and ley lines and cosmic karma. Riley liked this part of town. It felt good here, like there was positive energy running under the streets.

Unlike downtown Atlanta, horses were welcomed here as a way to get around the cost of fuel. Like keeping a horse fed and stabled was somehow cheaper. Of course every practical idea had its downside and in this case it was the outlandish carriages. It was a status-symbol thing: the more money a family had, the more ornate the carriage. There was even a television show that went around the country showing the transportation choices of the rich and famous.

From the looks of the open-top carriage in front of her – solid white with gold accents – this family had serious bucks. The gold had to be paint, real gold too expensive to waste on a wagon, but the effect was almost the same. The coach came with a uniformed guy in a blue velveteen coat, short pants, white hose and ruffled shirt. He even had black shoes with big brass buckles.

That has to be embarrassing.

Two girls trotted over and after helping them up to the plush burgundy seats, the uniformed servant placed their packages inside the coach. Riley drummed her fingers on the steering wheel, in anticipation. This was the first parking place she'd found in the last ten minutes and she wasn't about to let it escape.

As she waited, she checked out the passengers. They appeared to be about her age, but their clothes were definitely not secondhand and the plethora of brightly coloured bags at their feet spoke of a monumental shopping experience. One was showing the other a new pair of heels, the four-inch, ankle-snapping kind. They were brilliant orange. Four-inch heels weren't her thing, but Riley felt envious anyway. How long had it been since she could shop and not worry about every penny?

Not since Mom got ill.

Her mom's cancer treatment sucked up every spare dollar and when that money was gone, her dad had taken out the huge loan to cover the bills. For Riley that meant no more new clothes, no more new shoes, at least until the old ones didn't fit any longer. Every penny was hoarded and it hadn't changed now that her father was dead.

It's so not fair.

Riley winced, the envy waning quickly. Cool shoes

and new clothes would be really nice, but she'd trade all of it to get her mom and dad back.

The coach rolled out of the parking spot, the fine black horse clopping its way down the street as the fashionistas engaged in purchase worship, extracting clothes from the bags and comparing them. Riley pulled into the parking place and sighed in relief, happy the fashion show was over.

It wasn't a surprise that Enchanter's Way was different to any of the other streets around it. For one thing, there was a copper archway at the entrance and it was adorned with the symbol of the Summoners' Society – a jagged lightning bolt striking a granite tomb. Underneath it were the words:

Memento mori
Remember that you must die

Riley puzzled on that – not because of the depressing Latin phrase, but because the copper was still there. Why hadn't someone stolen it? Any piece of metal that could be stolen and sold for cash was history. Curious, she touched the archway and immediately yelped in pain, snatching her hand back. The copper was scorching hot, like it'd just come out of a blast furnace. A queer prickly feeling skittered up her arm and across her shoulders, making her muscles twitch, though there were no burns on her fingers.

Magic.

If someone tried to tear it down, it'd make them believe their flesh was roasting off their bones. Apparently summoner magic wasn't just for stealing corpses.

Enchanter's Way was paved in cobblestones and dried ivy clung to the brickwork in twisted brown ribbons. Doors lined either side of the street and some displayed the distinctive summoner's seal. Just ahead, on the right, was a cafe with stained-glass windows and a menu taped to its open door. A little further down the street, on the left, was a weathered sign: *Bell, Book and Broomstick*. She'd always wondered where the witch's store was located, the parent of the stall at the Terminus Market. The closer she got to it, the better she felt, the prickles of magic no longer dancing across her skin. Was that some kind of witch thing?

As she moved forward, the street narrowed until a solid brick wall blocked her passage. It was dotted with metal mailboxes set at random intervals, ranging from only a foot off the ground to near the top. Half bricks stuck out of the edifice like a climbing wall. Apparently the higher level boxes required their owners to ascend to claim their junk mail.

Bet the postal dude loves that.

Every box was different. The one for Bell, Book and Broomstick had an iridescent fairy perched on the top holding a miniature wand while another box had a black-and-white cat with a wooden tail and gleaming yellow eyes.

Forbidden

Riley rubbed her temples to try to ease her growing headache, then took a swig from her water bottle. Any other time she would have enjoyed this weirdness, but she wasn't in the mood. As she sucked down the liquid, she pondered the twin alleys that branched on either side of her. Right or left? Mort's card didn't indicate which one. Riley had just decided to ask for directions at the witch store when a dead woman stepped out of the left passageway. She had silver hair, curled neatly at the collar, and was dressed in a pale ivory top and navy slacks.

The woman paused, then she moved forward, her pumps clicking on the uneven stones. She popped open a mailbox with a pinwheel on top and extracted the contents, but as she turned away a slick magazine escaped her grip and landed on the cobblestones. Riley picked it up. It was a *Summoner's Digest*. The label said its owner was Mortimer Alexander.

Found you.

The deceased woman attempted a smile when Riley handed her the magazine, but the effort failed as the facial muscles didn't work quite right. At best Deaders were half-imagined copies of their real selves. Some of their personalities carried over, but none of the joy.

Dad's like this now.

Riley waited a few moments before she followed the woman to a bright purple door near the end of the alley. To the right of the door were two plaques: the Society's lightning bolt symbol and one that read:

The Demon Trappers

Mortimer Alexander, Summoner Advocate of Atlanta

Screwing up her courage, Riley knocked. Eventually the door swung open and the dead woman peered out at her.

'Yes?'

'I'm Riley Blackthorne. I need to talk to Mortimer about my dad,' she said, displaying the business card the man at the market had given her.

The dead woman waved her inside.

Now I just have to convince him to help me.

Because of Mort's appearance – he was short, wide and wore a trench coat and a fedora – Riley had always assumed he was unmarried and lived with his elderly mother. This place didn't have a silver-haired mom feel about it. The entryway featured a gleaming white tile floor, a black ceramic umbrella stand and an old-fashioned wooden coat rack. Mort's coat and hat dangled from it.

'This way,' the woman said, moving noiselessly down a hallway to the left. As she followed, Riley's imagination fired up. A summoner's place should have all sorts of arcane symbols on the walls, huge oak bookcases full of ancient leather tomes and at least one black cat skulking around. Maybe even a cool wand and a pointy wizard hat.

Which wasn't what she found. The room they entered was totally round, at least twenty-five feet in diameter with painted white brick walls that rose to a vaulted wood ceiling and a series of skylights that offered a dramatic view of the sky. From somewhere nearby water ran in a delicate trickle, but Riley couldn't find the source.

The space smelt faintly of woodsmoke. Not fresh smoke like something you'd expect out of a fireplace, but an aged scent like it'd been baked into the bricks.

I could so live here.

A redwood picnic table and two benches sat in the very centre of the room under the skylights. On the right side of the table sat an ink pot and a black pen, the old kind that you had to fill yourself. A neat stack of books sat to the left. A quick scan of the titles revealed that Mortimer liked C. S. Lewis and books with German and Latin titles.

Riley's escort made her way to a dark wood counter that curved round one portion of the room, filled a kettle from a faucet and plugged it into an electrical outlet. Then she left the room. Riley took the hint and stayed put, tapping her fingers on the side of her messenger bag. Near the picnic table she noticed smudged chalk marks and rusty brown splotches dotting the plank floor. The rust spots reminded her of dried blood.

He's probably a serial killer. The nice ones always were.

'Riley?'

She turned and stared in astonishment as Mort seemed to pass through the curved brick wall. *More magic.*

'You should see your face,' he said, exhibiting a mischievous smile. Mort wore a crisp white shirt and blue jeans, not at all what she'd expected. He seemed thinner somehow, like the trench coat had added thirty pounds.

Riley didn't appreciate the joke, but she needed his help.

'I'm so relieved to see you're in one piece,' he added. 'When I heard about what happened, I was afraid you were gone.'

'I was thinking the same thing.' To change the subject, Riley gestured towards the odd pieces of furniture. 'Why do you have a picnic table inside?'

'It's easy to move when I want to do a ritual,' he explained. 'Big desks require strong backs, and my people aren't that sturdy.'

People? 'You mean the Deaders?'

Mortimer grimaced. 'I prefer reanimates. Deader is so disrespectful.'

'Sorry.' He shrugged like it was no big deal, but she could tell it was. 'I'm here about my dad. He was reanimated without my permission.'

'I heard. Word travels fast in our community.'

'Then you know who took him.'

Mort shook his head, then gestured for her to sit. As she settled on a bench seat a shrill sound filled the room, causing Riley to jump. Then she felt really stupid – it was the teakettle.

Mort dealt with the kettle and returned to the table with a tray bearing two china cups, a matching teapot and a plate full of goodies. 'Cookie?' her host asked, offering the plate.

Forbidden

Riley took one to be polite, wondering if all murderers gave their victims treats before they sliced out their livers. She took a test nibble. Then a bigger one. The cookie was really yummy, home-made and chewy, the best kind.

'This is so good,' she said, around bites.

'Emalee makes them. She stays in the kitchen most of the time because she's rather shy. Right now she's working on strudel.'

He has dead people baking for him?

'About my dad . . .' she said, hoping to get something out of this meeting besides the image of a dead woman pottering around a kitchen in an apron.

Mort didn't reply until he sat on the bench opposite her and poured the tea. 'I don't know who summoned your father. Nobody's talking, which is odd because if I'd pulled off that reanimation I'd be bragging up a storm, at least to my fellow summoners.' He took a thoughtful sip from his cup.

'Could it be Ozymandias?' she asked.

Mort shuddered at the name, making his tea slosh in the cup. 'Maybe.'

'So why would Mr Creepy want him?'

Her irreverence caused a faint smile to appear. 'Lord Ozymandias doesn't bother to tell us lesser mortals what he's up to. In general he treats us like we're annoying pests. It's very irritating.'

More than irritating if the death grip Mort had on the cup handle was any indication.

'Why would a summoner want my dad? Is it so he can trap demons?' she queried.

'I don't think so. Master trappers have certain demonic knowledge that would be of interest to a summoner who doesn't keep on the straight and narrow.'

'Huh?'

'A summoner might require a master's expertise if he intends to call forth a demon.'

'Whoa. Get out of here. You guys summon demons too? Are you crazy?'

'I don't go there,' Mort said flatly. 'Too much downside. Most of the time the summoner ends up being the fiend's lackey, not the other way round.'

Riley shuddered. 'But Ozymandias does?'

'There are rumours to that effect.' Mort offered her another cookie, and this time she took it without hesitation. Oatmeal. With a hint of cinnamon. *Nom.* Even if a dead lady had made them.

'How do you guys do a summoning?'

The necromancer seemed to be weighing his answer carefully. 'Unless you are at the level of someone like Lord Ozymandias, spells require preparation. He can do them on the spot, but then he's not like the rest of us.'

'So how do you do it, the summoning spell, I mean?'

'I collect something of the deceased's – hair, clothing, a favourite book, some part that I can focus on. If I can't obtain an item, it's harder. Then I do a ritual invocation and request that the dead person arise to rejoin the living.'

'Request?'

Mort looked chagrined. 'Well, I request. Most just order the deceased to comply, which I think lacks respect.'

Respect was a big thing for this guy. Riley leaned an elbow on the table, intrigued. 'Which is why you only do legal summonings?'

'Exactly. It's bad enough to lose a loved one and then have a pirate come along and rip that person out of their grave. As you well know, the heartbreak is unimaginable.'

The passion in his voice told her this was personal. 'It happened to you?'

Mort's eyes lowered to his teacup. 'My wife. She was only twenty-five when she died, and within a week she was serving as a maid at a rich household here in Atlanta. I would see her sometimes, on the street.' He took a tortured breath. 'Then they moved to New York City and I couldn't afford to follow them.'

'Can my dad's owner do that?' she asked, horrified.

'It's not against the law to transport reanimates across state lines, at least not yet. Or sell them to someone else, for that matter.'

'Were you able to get your wife back?'

'Not until her year was up,' he replied, his voice torn with emotion. 'By then she was just a . . . husk.'

God. It was hideous enough to bury someone you loved, but to see them like that and have no way to help them pushed Hell into a new dimension.

'It's why I became a summoner,' he admitted. 'In the case of your father, I will file a report with the Society of an unauthorized summoning,' he said. 'Unofficially I'll ask around and see if anyone knows who raised him.'

'If I can get him away from whoever bought him, can you put my father back in the ground?'

'Break a summoning?' Mort executed a low whistle. 'That's asking for serious trouble. We had a magical . . . feud a few years back when two summoners interfered with each other's reanimates. It was a really bad deal.'

'So all you can do is ask questions?' she demanded, sharper than she'd intended.

'There is only so much I *can* do, Riley. Your father has no civil rights,' Mort explained. 'When the time comes for him to be inhumed, we will need his summoner's assistance to reverse the spell. If that summoner is angry at you . . . ' He spread his hands.

'What happens if my dad isn't returned to his grave after a year?'

'The body disintegrates while the living consciousness is still in it. That's *not* what anyone wants to endure – him or you.'

The cookies in her stomach were no longer playing nice. 'So you're saying I'm pretty much screwed?'

'No,' he replied, sighing. 'I'm saying you don't have many choices, but that shouldn't keep you from trying to find him. If whoever has bought him has compassion, they should let you visit him during his term of service.'

'Like he's in jail or something,' she said. That was a depressing thought. 'Is there somewhere they sell them, besides at the market?'

'Yes,' her host said. He toyed with the half-eaten cookie in front of him. 'I'll go to the *vendue* and see if he's there.'

'The what?'

'The *vendue*. It's a French word meaning "auction". The next one's on Friday night.'

'I want to go with you.'

He shook his head instantly. 'You won't be welcome.'

'Don't care,' she said, pushing her cup of tea aside. 'I want to be there.'

Mort's eyebrows knitted together. 'My fellow summoners are a testy bunch. They won't like you asking questions.'

'I want to be there,' Riley repeated. Then she tried the magic word. 'Please.'

Mort sighed. 'All right, just as long as you know this could get unpleasant.'

Only if I don't find my father.

As Riley walked along the alley to the street, she tried to get a grip on her turbulent emotions. Did she really believe that once she'd talked to Mort everything would be OK? That her dad would be waiting for her, ready to return to his grave? If she did find her father and the summoner reversed the spell, she'd have to bury him again. Another funeral.

Oh, God.

As she walked past the mailboxes, a figure caught her notice, a boy spray-painting something on the brick wall ahead of her. He looked about thirteen and his hood had fallen back to reveal a shock of hair the colour of ripe wheat slashed with black stripes. The smell of wet paint stung her nose as he made broad swipes, leaving dripping red letters in his wake. When she moved closer, he jumped in surprise, giving her a panicked expression. He bolted for freedom, and the spray can fell from his fingers, rolling across the uneven ground and bumping the toe of her tennis shoe.

The crimson paint began to change colour, first becoming pale red, then pink and finally white. It slid downward brick by brick, as if someone was wiping it away with a squeegee. When it reached the ground it crackled and then disappeared in a bright cloud of pale dust. *More magic.* It took a moment to puzzle out what the guy had written, spelling errors and all.

NEKROS SUK!

No argument there.

Chapter Ten

'Home sweet bolt-hole,' Riley said. She stood in the doorway to the room in the basement of St Brigid's Catholic Church. The room wasn't fancy, but she hadn't expected it to be. All of about fifteen-by-fifteen feet, there were two stacked wooden bunk beds, a table, a pair of kitchen chairs and a mint-green couch. There was a small television, a mini refrigerator, microwave and a counter with a deep sink. Down a narrow hall she saw a bathroom. If not for the white walls and the crucifix hanging by the door, it would have felt like a bunker.

After dropping her messenger bag on the table, Riley retreated to the undersized bathroom to change into her favourite PJs, the ones with the frolicking pandas. The PJs were totally dorky, but her mom had bought them for her and they held good memories.

If Beck sees these . . .

But he wouldn't, not unless something went really wrong and he had to take refuge here. In that case panda PJs were going to be least of their worries. After scrubbing her face and brushing her teeth, Riley placed her folded clothes on one of the chairs. A blast of hot air ruffled her hair from a vent in the ceiling. She glared up at it.

'Too warm,' she said. Hunting around for a thermostat proved fruitless. That wasn't good news. It was either freeze at the cemetery or roast here.

After ensuring the door's lock was engaged, Riley tried the lower bunk. That rated a definite thumbs up. After some determined pillow thumping to get it into the proper shape, she lay on her back and stared at the underside of the mattress above her.

The furnace turned off. Then on again. Then off.

She was dead tired, but sleep wasn't in the same room with her. It wasn't the heat that was keeping her awake – it was just that this time of day things hurt the most. She'd replay her dad's voice in her head, then her mom's. She'd remember bits of Blackthorne family history.

Eventually Riley sat up in bed, barely clearing the top bunk by a mere two inches. Apparently tall people took the top bunk. She hadn't brought anything to read, sure that she'd be asleep almost instantly. To kill time, she dug out her cellphone and scrolled through the texts. Brandy, her nemesis at the new school, was wondering if she was going to be at class on Friday. Riley ignored that one. Three texts from Simi about a Gnarly Scalenes concert in March and asking if she'd like to go. *Maybe.* Nothing from Peter. She should text him, but what would she write? *Stuck in a church so demons won't eat me.* That wouldn't work for someone who'd always been there for her.

Forbidden

Instead, she dialled his number. 'Peter?' There was a lengthy pause.

'What's up, Riley?' he asked. She processed his tone – upset and exhausted.

'I needed someone to talk to,' she admitted.

'You know, so do I.'

Maybe this would work after all. Riley tucked the comforter around her legs and leaned back against the wooden framework of the bunk bed. It creaked in response. She told him of her new location and what it looked like. 'Master Stewart wants me on holy ground at night. He's worried some demon will come after me.' Actually just one demon in particular, but Peter didn't need to know that.

'Is Beck there with you?'

'No. He's shooting pool.' *At least he'd better be.*

Silence. She tried to wait him out, but finally she gave in. 'Look, Peter, if you don't want to talk to me—'

'It's not that. There's been . . . stuff going on here.'

She shifted positions on the bed, caught by the lost sound in his voice. 'Like what?'

'Mom and Dad are getting a divorce.'

It took time for that to sink in. 'Oh, man, Peter, I'm so sorry. I thought they'd worked through all that after your brother's death.'

'No. It was never the same. They've been acting like it was, but Dad finally cracked. He just couldn't take Mom's Nazi control tactics any more.'

Her friend wasn't exaggerating. After his older brother's fatal car accident, Peter's mom became *the warden*, as he called her. She'd monitored all her kids' moves like they lived in a federal prison.

'She's been doing the same with Dad,' Peter confided. 'If he's a few minutes late, she freaks and hounds him with phone calls.'

'I thought they went for counselling or something.'

'They did. It didn't help,' he said sadly.

'What happens now?' she asked.

'Mom wants to go back to Illinois. She thinks Atlanta's too dangerous for her kids.' A tortured groan filtered through the phone. 'They told us the news tonight. Then they asked who we wanted to live with.'

If her parents had asked her that question, how could she have decided? No matter who she chose, the other would be hurt. 'God, that's brutal.'

'Totally. David said he'd stay here with dad. I wimped out and said I had to think about it. Mom was really upset. I guess she thought I'd just go with her automatically.'

'What about the twins?' she asked, thinking of Peter's two little brothers.

'The ghouls go with her no matter what. Too young to be with Dad.' There was a sigh down the phone. 'So what are you doing tomorrow?'

'I have to check in on Harper, then I need to visit Simon and go to the funerals.'

'So who's this Simon dude? Is he the guy I've seen on TV?' Peter asked.

'Yes. He's an apprentice trapper. We're . . . dating.'

'Cool.'

'It feels right this time, Peter.'

'Well, that's something, at least.'

More awkward silence. 'I'm really sorry for you.'

'Yeah, so am I. For a lot of things. Goodnight, Riley.'

She disconnected the call.

'Don't you dare move away, Peter King,' she whispered. 'You're my best friend. I can't make it without you.'

Ori leaned against his motorcycle across the street from the church, arms crossed over his chest. Riley had chosen her sanctuary well: no demon could tread on holy ground and not pay the ultimate price. This church was old and even from here he could feel the raw power of the Creator pressing against his skin, saturating everything around him. He sucked it in as if it were a breath of tantalizing spring air after a cruel winter.

'You are such an addict,' a craggy voice said.

Ori failed to curb his displeasure at having the peaceful moment disturbed. 'Sartael,' he said acidly. 'Slumming, again?'

A wry chuckle came from the angel standing next to him. Unless you were Divine he appeared unremarkable, a plain man who always managed to blend into the background. A Divine would see the real Sartael – that dark hair, those immense wings and the sword strapped to his back, its hilt protruding just above his shoulders. The blade was dormant at the moment, but once he pulled it free from the bindings it would flame like the desert sun at midday. As always, there was a hint of madness in the angel's eyes.

I wonder if some say that of me.

'I do not like it in this realm,' Sartael replied, gesturing contemptuously at the church.

'So you have mentioned on more than one occasion.'

'Why are mortals so ignorant?' He shook his head in supreme disgust. 'They believe their faith is made of bricks and mortar.'

This was an old argument between them, one of many. 'To them it is,' Ori replied earnestly. 'Mortals need tangible proof of the Creator.'

'*They* are tangible proof that He exists. How soon they forget that little detail.'

'It is easy to become distracted when you're not eternal.'

Sartael gave him a sidelong look. 'Not only mortals have that issue. You have a task to perform and yet here you stand gaping at an old pile of bricks.'

'I am going about my duties,' Ori said, stiffening at the rebuke.

'Is that rogue demon no more? I have not heard its death cries,' Sartael chided.

'The girl is alive and she is the key to finding the rogue.'

'Ah, yes, Blackthorne's child.'

Forbidden

Ori did not like hearing Sartael speak her name, but he hid his frown. 'Is there a point to your presence?'

The other angel turned to him. 'Time passes and you are needed elsewhere. Cease being amused by the mortals.'

'Is that *His* order?'

'Not officially. However, He will ask of your progress and I must answer. I cannot believe you are unable to find a mere weather fiend.'

'I believe it is being shielded by its demi-lord.'

'And who might that be?' Sartael asked, leaning closer, his eyes lit by some internal fire.

'I have no idea.' He and Sartael had always been rivals, so the admission stung.

'Ah, I see. You make excuses to cover the lack of progress,' Sartael said, nodding his understanding. 'To be honest, I did not expect such weakness from you.'

Ori squared up to him, his anger growing. 'Then do you know who is behind this rogue demon?'

'That is not my problem. You know what is expected. Get it done. Fail and there will be a reckoning.'

'Advice noted,' Ori replied crisply, turning back towards the church.

'And ignored, I wouldn't doubt,' Sartael replied. 'Oh, well, it's not my pretty head on the block.' At a wave of his hand, the angel vanished into the night air.

'No, it never is,' Ori grumbled. 'But someday it will be yours, and I'll be wielding the sword.'

Chapter Eleven

Beck pushed open the twin flame-embossed wooden doors that led to the Armageddon Lounge. As was his custom, he paused a moment and gave the place the once-over. Old habits die hard, especially when one of the worst beatings he'd ever experienced was delivered by a jealous husband in a pool hall.

But not this pool hall. The Armageddon Lounge was neutral territory for him and he meant to keep it that way. For that reason he didn't usually pick up girls here. No need to invite trouble.

The Armageddon Lounge's décor was trashy, even for this part of town. Garish flames decorated almost all the walls, except the far one with the black-veined mirror tiles. Figures writhed in those flames, most of them female and nude, someone's idea of what the end of the world would be like.

Fewer mirrors, more screamin'. At least that's how Beck envisioned it.

When he was assured that nobody was in the mood for trouble, he headed for the bar, intent on enjoying his first beer of the day. A couple of years back that wouldn't have been the case: by this time of night he would have already gone through at least a six-pack. It was Paul who changed that early in Beck's apprenticeship.

'There's a time to drink and a time to trap Hellspawn,' his mentor had advised. 'You get those confused and you're demon food.' When Beck had protested he could do both, Paul had summed it up with one question. 'Is it worth dying for?'

The answer had been easy – much as Beck loved a few beers he preferred to remain above ground. He'd cut back on his drinking that very night. It was a sad fact that the booze wasn't the solution; it just wanted you to think it was.

Zack, the bartender, acknowledged him with a wide smile. Stocky and broad-shouldered, his sandy hair was so short you could see his suntanned scalp.

'Hey, Beckster, how you doing?' he called out.

'Good,' Beck said, though that wasn't the truth by a long shot. By the time he reached the bar the beer was waiting for him.

'Quiet tonight,' Zack observed, leaning on the bar. 'Usually Saturday evenings are totally packed. I'm thinking it's because of what went down the other night at the Tabernacle. Folks are scared.'

Beck nodded his understanding. There were only about a dozen patrons in the lounge and he knew most of them by name, though none of them were trappers. Those were probably on the streets trying to take down a demon or two.

And gettin' nowhere fast.

'Lenny was in a while ago,' Zack added. 'He said he'd be back later.'

Lenny the Necromancer. He was one of the summoners who'd been jonesing to pull Paul's body out of the grave so he'd be a good one to pump for information.

'Heard ya had a Four in here the other day,' Beck observed, leaning against the bar.

Zack snorted as he dried a highball glass. 'And some trappers. Seems one of them broke a pool cue and didn't bother to pay for it. Really pissed off the boss. Gave me an earful about how you guys are all arrogant jerks.'

'He'd be right,' Beck replied, taking another sip. 'At least when we're after demons.'

Another snort came his way. 'Boss said the trappers had a girl with them. You guys allowing that kind of thing now?'

'Yeah, we are. The world is changin',' Beck said.

'Tell me about it.' Zack's voice changed tone, went lower. 'So how are you doing after the other night?'

Beck turned back towards the bartender, hearing the concern. 'Breathin',' he said. 'Better 'n some.'

'That's for sure. When I heard about it, I prayed for you guys.'

'That's good of ya.'

'Sounds like it's getting ugly,' Zack remarked. 'I had a regular in here this afternoon telling me he saw a couple demons downtown, right on Peachtree Street.'

'Is this guy on the level?' Beck quizzed.

'Yup. He's a cop.'

Some of those crazy stories just might be true.

Using his bartender radar, Zack headed down the bar towards a couple and refilled their glasses the moment they were empty. The girl was plain to look at, but they were totally into each other.

Beck had been that way once. Her name was Louisa, and they'd been in the same class in Sadlersville, their hometown. The other kids had known not to mess with them: it was always Den and Lou from the time they met in ninth grade. Then Louisa decided she could do better than a poor loser who had an alcoholic for a mother. He still remembered what it felt like to have someone think you were less than human just because of your family. From what he'd heard, Louisa moved from guy to guy after that, never finding what she was looking for.

Beck gave himself a swift mental kick, annoyed at wasting time dwelling on the past. Picking up his beer, he toted it to the back of the bar where one of the pool tables was open. He selected a cue and took his frustration out on the balls. One by one they went into the pockets like remote-controlled robots, just an extension of his hands and brain. When he'd finished running the table, something he'd been able to do since he was thirteen, he racked the balls again.

Part of his frustration was Stewart's insistence he talk

to the press and to the city bosses, that he learn the ropes before he became a master. Beck knew those same ropes could turn into a noose with very little effort. Then there was that flame-haired babe he'd seen at the city hall. No surprise, she was a reporter and she just *had* to talk to him. She'd even got his cellphone number, courtesy of the Scotsman. Beck had dodged her so far, but the master had warned him to just get on with it. That it came with the territory.

'Not a good idea,' Beck mumbled under his breath. He knew what his mind was like when he had a pretty lady in front of him: he said things he shouldn't, but in this case those words would end up in the newspaper, maybe even on the Internet. One slip of the tongue and he might lose his chance of becoming a master trapper.

The double doors pushed open and a man entered the lounge. The newcomer was a little taller than Beck, decked out in black jeans and T-shirt. A grey duster coat hung from his broad shoulders like a hero in an action movie. His midnight-black hair and eyes gave him a *screw with me at your own peril* look.

Trapper? Probably not. Freelance hunter? That was a possibility. Still, he should have some form of defence on him and Beck didn't see one. Their gazes met, sizing each other up, then the dude headed to the bar. After a short conversation with Zack, the bartender began pulling a beer from the tap.

Though this was more of a locals bar, every now and

then someone new wandered in. Beck's mind chided him that he was just being paranoid. When the newcomer settled behind a corner table near the front of the lounge, Beck went back to his game.

Lenny was the next one to arrive. The summoner's biggest sin was that he dressed like a pimp with a limitless credit card. Tonight he was wearing a particularly unholy purple velvet jacket, black leather pants and a frilly black shirt. He really needed an adult to dress him.

'Let me get a beer,' the necro called out.

Beck nodded, then racked the balls, buying time until Lenny joined him.

When the man returned, brew in hand, Beck asked, 'Ya playin' for the exercise or the money?' Best to establish that right up front.

'Exercise. At least when I'm playing with you,' Lenny replied, stripping off his coat and carefully draping it over a stool. His shirt glistened with silver threads. Beck shook his head at the sight, but Lenny ignored him and chose a pool cue. He tested the weight, chalked the end and stepped forward.

'Go ahead and break,' Beck said. It wasn't going to matter either way.

'So who's the new guy?' Lenny asked in a lowered voice, angling his head towards the action hero in the corner.

Beck shrugged. 'No clue.' He could feel the guy's eyes on him since the moment the dude had entered the bar.

'Doesn't look like a local,' Lenny said.

'No. Definitely not from here.'

The necro leaned over, lined up the shot and then straightened up again like he had something on his mind. 'I didn't have anything to do with Blackthorne's reanimation,' he said, a thin sheen of sweat on his brow. 'I wanted you to know.'

'If I thought ya had, ya'd be in a world of hurt right now,' Beck replied.

The summoner nodded and broke.

As Beck walked round the table to choose his shot, he asked, 'Any idea who did it?'

Lenny sagged against the mirrored wall behind them. 'No. I warned the others not to jack with Blackthorne's corpse. I told them you'd rip them apart if they did anything. A summoner's bones break just as easy as anyone else's. Not that you heard that from me.'

Beck grinned. He'd spent a lot of effort building that reputation.

'Someone didn't give a rat's ass what I'd do,' he said.

'That's for sure,' Lenny said.

Beck made sure not to sink the next ball. 'What about Mortimer?' he asked.

A chuckle came his way along with a quick shake of the necro's head. 'Mort's totally by-the-book. He won't reanimate a corpse without the family's written permission . . . in triplicate.'

'How's about Christian?' Beck asked, recalling the

necros who'd been visiting Paul's grave over the last couple of weeks.

'Don't think so. From what I heard, the spell was one serious mother. Christian doesn't have that much juice.'

'So who does?'

Lenny's eyes rose to Beck's, then made a quick circuit around the pool hall. He straightened up again, leaning on the pool cue. 'Only one summoner I know of.' He went back to his shot and blew it.

'And does this bastard have a name?'

'He does, but I'm not saying it aloud.'

'Why would a necro want Blackthorne?'

'It's said your masters have hidden knowledge about every kind of demon there is, even the Archangels and the Fallen. That knowledge could be incredibly valuable if you wanted to summon any of the above.'

Beck blinked in surprise. 'I thought your kind was just into dead bodies.'

Lenny gave him a sour look. 'Magic can be used for other purposes, but most of us are smart enough to stay away from the dark stuff.'

'But not *him*.'

His companion shook his head and leaned his pool cue against the wall. 'Another beer?'

'Yeah, thanks.'

Lenny headed towards the bar. The necro wasn't telling him everything, but Beck had got more out of him than he'd expected.

'You're scared, aren't ya?' he whispered.

And it had nothing to do with Beck's badass reputation.

They were three games in when Beck heard the bar go quiet behind him. He had his back to the door, but felt a gust of cold air strike the back of his neck. A faint tingling began in his limbs, then a peculiar dizziness. *No way.* He took a sip of his beer as a quick test and was rewarded with a heady mixture of hops, grain and alcohol, tenfold what it should be. There was only one thing that could magnify the senses like that.

His favourite pool hall had just rated another Grade Four demon.

Beck carefully set his beer aside while scanning the room through the uneven reflection in the mirrored wall. Many of the other patrons stood slack-jawed, eyes glazed, except the dude in the corner wearing the hero clothes. He was leaning back in his chair, arms crossed behind his head like he didn't have a care in the world.

So what gives here?

When a low voice began to whisper to Beck, he hunted for the source in the mirror and found it standing just inside the lounge doors. 'She' was dressed in thigh-high boots, a tan leather micro miniskirt, a black bustier and a red fake-fur jacket. Her hair was wavy brown. But then that would be what the demon wanted you to think.

This was a Mezmer. They were known by a lot of

names – Jezebels, Tempters, Seducers – and they came in a few different varieties, but all of them sucked out your life essence and then took your soul if you gave them half a chance. As they did you'd thank them for every minute of hellish torment.

Beck wasn't immune to her power and raw desire struck him head on, then migrated further south. He heard her talking to him, promising delights that might be his if he'd just let her do her thing. The tingling grew stronger as the demon wove its spell, slowly encompassing all the men in the bar. The three women in the place just stared around, confused about what was happening. One jostled her date, but he didn't react.

That was actually good news. If the demon was more experienced, all the customers would be under its spell. That meant this one was a younger fiend, less powerful, and by casting such a wide net it was looking to suck up energy to grow.

Beck began to hum under his breath, trying to break through the allure of the demon's seductive message as it trickled through his mind. The humming worked, allowing the dizziness to ebb long enough for him to kneel like he was tying a bootlace. Instead, he cautiously opened the zipper to his trapping bag where it sat underneath the pool table. When he rose, still facing the mirrored wall, he had both hands full: a purple Babel sphere in the right and a Holy Water sphere in the left.

When he turned towards the threat, the demon's eyes

locked on him immediately. He couldn't see beneath the illusion, not until he used the Babel sphere, but there was no doubt this was Hellspawn.

Beck hummed louder, one of his favourite Taylor Swift songs.

The Jezebel wrinkled her face in what passed for demonic annoyance. 'You resist me,' she said.

'That's for damned sure,' he said. That took his attention off the song just long enough for her to send another message to his brain, one that would make a prostitute blush.

'No way,' he said, shaking his head to clear it. He began to sing to himself. The song was a sad one, about a love lost, and it proved stronger than the fiend's seductive message.

'Trapper,' she warned, moving closer to him. 'Come to us . . .'

Beck waited until the last moment, then slammed the purple sphere at the demon's feet. It burst open, setting off a fountain of flickering lights and scenting the air with cinnamon. The magic inside the sphere veered at the demon and the transformation began immediately. The girl's voice went from sultry to rasping as her features melted away and the body contracted. Smaller and smaller she shrank, her clothes vanishing. Left behind was a short, squat body that looked like it'd been coated in brown mud. Hellfire-red eyes gleamed at him and a long, barbed tail thrashed back and forth. The claws were black and razor-sharp.

The other patrons' dull expressions rapidly changed from seduced to shocked.

'Oh my God, that's a demon!' one of them yelled, tripping over himself to get out the door.

'No shit.' Beck caught a glimpse of the bartender; Zack was shaking his head in dismay. Beck shrugged and turned his attention back to the fiend. It was gnawing on one of its claws in agitation and glaring up at him.

'Well done, trapper,' Lenny said.

'Thanks,' Beck said, pleased. 'This one doesn't have much power to it.'

He didn't have a proper container to put the thing in, but he'd find a way of getting it to a demon trafficker and then he'd collect his money. Not a bad deal – shoot some pool, drink some beer and collect four hundred dollars for his trouble. To think he'd wasted all that time in Demon Central when the action was here.

A bizarre chuckle issued from the demon. Then it started to laugh. That wasn't right: it should be angry at being captured, spouting off a bunch of curse words, offering a boon for its freedom. Instead it was laughing like he was the joke.

'What's so funny?' he demanded.

'Ah, trapper,' Lenny said, pointing at the entrance.

Beck swore under his breath. Another figure stood in the doorway, clad in black leather with silver-white cropped hair and a fortune in body piercing. In her right hand was a whip and she was grinning like she'd just won the lottery.

That was why the first one had said '*come to us*'. There were *two* demons and the younger one was the weaker of the pair, an apprentice learning the ropes while the master waited outside in case of trouble. And Beck had proven to be that trouble.

The demon flicked the whip and allowed her barbed teeth to show, causing some of the patrons to knock over their chairs and scramble backwards.

'Time to play, trapper,' it called out.

He had no choice but to bluff. Beck raised the Holy Water sphere. 'Back off, demon. Ya don't wanna go there.'

A sharp crack filled the air as the end of the whip caught the orb and shattered it in his hand. Cursing, he pulled his steel pipe from the trapping bag.

He sized up the situation and it sucked. 'Lenny,' he said, 'get the others outta here.'

'But I can—'

Beck shook his head. 'Don't try it. This one's too dangerous. Just get outta here.'

'If that's what you want,' the summoner whispered, then edged closer to the others in the bar, urging them to follow him to the rear exit. Beck wished he could join them.

'What the hell are you?' a man called out, staggering towards the Four. The way he was moving, the guy had more booze in his system than blood. That made him prime demon bait. 'This is our bar and we don't take kindly to some skanky bit—' He was on his knees a second later, clawing at his throat for air. It was the only reason he wasn't screaming.

'Stop it!' Beck ordered. The Mezmer's eyes swung in his direction. 'This is between us, demon. The rest aren't worth your time.'

The fiend took a step closer. 'Trapper,' it said, sizing him up. It scented the air and smiled. 'You are nothing,' it said.

'Oh, but I *am* somethin'. I'm a journeyman trapper, not just some apprentice.' He paused a moment for effect. 'I was Paul Blackthorne's partner. My soul would win ya serious points with your boss.'

'Blackthorne?' the older demon hissed and in response the whip began to grow flames along its length.

Apparently that was the magic word. The drunk started to bellow, his ability to breathe restored. Two of his buddies pulled him away towards the back of the building.

Beck kept his attention riveted on the more dangerous of the two threats. As he watched, the female form vanished to reveal a Hellspawn as tall as he was with pale beige skin, blazing crimson eyes, long talons and a wickedly barbed tail. Unlike the lesser fiend, this one had horns.

Ah, damn. This demon was close to making the leap to Archfiend. Some of them did that, working up through Hell's ranks, slaughtering rivals with every step. Those that survived were the really evil ones. That it would show him its true form so easily told Beck he was in serious trouble.

'Killing you would be a pleasure, trapper,' it said, licking its lips. 'Harvesting your soul . . . priceless.'

Beck didn't have the experience to tackle one of these things and right now there wasn't a master in the city healthy enough to bail him out. Not that any of them would get here in time anyway. He swallowed his fear, like he had so many times in battle.

'So, demon, ya gonna just stand there lookin' damned ugly or are we gonna dance?'

Chilling laughter burst from the fiend's mouth. 'You will be perfect for my amusements, trapper. I wonder who will buy your soul from me?'

Then it began to whisper dark words. Beck hummed, louder this time, then started singing at the top of his voice. Nothing had any effect. He could feel the demon sifting through his mind, looking for his weaknesses. It uncovered his hidden fears, his dreams, the future that could never be.

The fiend laughed, lower this time, knowing it had hit pay dirt. 'That future is yours. *She* can be yours . . .' it purred.

Beck felt his will cracking like an old piece of china exposed to the bitter cold. It would be so easy to let go. Why be a hero? He didn't owe any of these guys an ounce of his blood. He could have his secret wish. *Forever.*

'No,' he said through gritted teeth. Once Hell had him in its grasp, it'd use him to destroy Riley. She would trust him even as he was leading her to eternal servitude or death. In a last-ditch effort to break the demon's hold, he rammed the steel pipe down on his injured thigh, sending a burst of agonizing pain through his body. Though the pain made him cry out, it wasn't enough to break the demon's spell.

'Your soul, trapper,' the fiend urged. 'Swear it to me and I will make your dreams come true. I'll bring her to you and she will be yours this very night.'

Beck knew he'd lost. He felt the words forming on his tongue, the ones that would commit his soul to Hell for eternity. The words that would doom Riley at the same time.

God, no!

There was more laughter, but it sounded different. It hadn't come from the senior demon because the fiend was hissing now, low at first, then louder, like a cat threatened by a pack of feral dogs.

'Interference,' it growled. 'He is mine!'

Another voice cut through Beck's fog, one he didn't recognize. It sounded male and very, very old. He couldn't understand the words, but whatever they meant the pull on his mind snapped like an overextended rubber band. The sheer force ricocheted him back on top of the pool table, scattering balls in all directions. Tears ran down his cheeks as his head pounded like someone had clubbed it with a sledgehammer.

When Beck finally opened his eyes, Lenny was staring down at him, concerned.

'You OK?' the necro asked. Around them Beck could see other faces, all as worried as Lenny's.

The blazing pain receded. 'Don't know,' he mumbled. 'What happened?'

'Something spooked the demons and they took off,' Lenny reported.

'There was someone talkin'. Sounded really weird. Ya heard it, right?'

'No,' Lenny admitted. 'At least you're OK. Damn, I figured you were history.'

You're not the only one.

Beck closed his eyes for a moment and then smiled. He might not understand how it all happened, but the bottom line was that his soul was still his. The bad news was that Hell knew his greatest weakness now and it was a safe bet they'd use it against him every chance they got.

As the bartender and the guy in the garish clothes saw to the prostrate trapper, Ori slipped through the double doors in search of the fiends. Normally he wouldn't have interfered, but the elder fiend had invoked Riley Blackthorne's name. That made it his business. Having the trapper's soul in the clutches of Hell would only complicate Ori's job.

It didn't take him long to find the pair – they

stood in a smudge of sulphured air in the parking lot, arguing.

'You had almost the trapper,' the younger one snarled in that particularly convoluted Hellspeak younger demons employed once their true forms were revealed. Parts of that form still peeked out from around that of the young woman, a nightmarish mash-up of bared flesh, clothes, sagging breasts and talons. 'Why us leave?' it demanded.

The older demon raised its hand for silence and sniffed the air. 'Divine,' it spat in warning.

Ori halted about ten feet away, not bothering to reveal his true form. They knew what he was and he could get to his sword quicker than the Hellfiends could move.

The twin horrors spun to face him. Power ripped across the skin of the elder fiend. A succubus rarely had the chance to become this powerful as the Archdemons killed them to ensure they didn't have any more competition. That meant this one was particularly vicious.

'I thought I smelt you,' it growled.

'I'm surprised you could over the stench of the brimstone,' Ori said, waving his hand to clear the air.

'Interfere you, why?' the younger demon demanded. It was a mere pup or the trapper wouldn't have been able to shut it out of his mind. And stupid, or it wouldn't have challenged a Divine so openly.

Ori issued a casual grin in response, though all he really wanted to do was cleave these two in half for their arrogance. 'Who set you on the trapper?' he asked.

'Why want you to know?' the younger one asked. The older one snarled and promptly cuffed it on the ear, causing it to whine in fear.

'We work for the glory of Hell,' the senior demon responded, trying to regain the upper hand.

Too late. The younger Hellspawn had confirmed Ori's suspicions – someone had deliberately targeted the trapper in an effort to get to Riley.

Ori made sure his gaze met that of the older demon. It winced at his power and averted its eyes. 'Stay away from Blackthorne's child. If you tempt her, I will execute you like the cockroaches you are.'

The elder demon hissed again and stepped backwards, feeling the seething power of Ori's anger. The younger demon began to protest, but after another blow from its superior the pair hurried away, changing into human form as they moved.

Ori watched them, curious whether they'd go back after the trapper. To his relief they didn't, but instead they encountered a young man on the street. His eyes glazed over as the elder demon put her hand on his heart and began to drink his life essence.

Ori wasn't about to interfere. They had their job. He had his.

And mine is the girl.

Chapter Twelve

The sound of church bells brought Riley out of her vivid dreams. Waking up in a new place was always strange, but the bells calling the faithful to Mass sounded surreal. She rubbed her eyes, yawned and sat up. Another yawn. The bells continued and they made her think of Simon. After a quick trip to the bathroom, Riley crawled back under the covers and dialled his sister.

Please let him be better. She'd uttered that prayer right before she'd fallen asleep, along with requests to find her father and one that Peter would stay put in Atlanta. The prayer list was getting longer every night.

To her relief, the news was positive: Simon was improving, though still not talking much, and there was a chance he'd get to go home in a day or two. Amy said it was a miracle. She was right, but it had a lot to do with the fact that the wounds were demonic and being treated by freshly blessed Holy Water courtesy of Father Harrison. Between Heaven's intervention and the priest, Simon had no choice but to survive.

Riley disconnected the call with a broad smile. Once he went home Simon would loosen up. His family would see to that and, if not, his girlfriend sure would.

A cold morning greeted her as she stepped outside the church. A few cars along the street exhibited a layer of alabaster frost on their windshields. As she walked round to unlock her ride, she found a pure white rose stuck in the driver's side door handle. She carefully pulled it free, mindful of thorns, and sampled its fragrance. It was amazing. More surprising was the fact the hard freeze hadn't affected it.

Must not have been out here that long.

Riley's first thought was of Simon, but he was in the hospital. Beck didn't seem to be the romantic type. That only left . . .

Ori? But why would he give her a rose? After a quick look around and finding no sign of him, she decided not to tax her brain and just enjoy the gift. *Maybe today isn't going to suck after all.*

With no time for a trip home and oatmeal, she drove through the closest fast food place and bought what her father called *death in a bag.* High-fat, high-carb food. She was completely awake by the time she walked into Harper's place where there was the scent of fresh coffee layered on top of the old automotive smells. Apparently he'd felt good enough to use the coffeemaker.

As she entered the office, she braced herself. Harper liked to yell at her just for breathing. No shouting this time – in fact, he barely gave her a second glance. To her relief she found he was still sober. Despite that improvement, she kept out of range and spent time cleaning up, washing dishes and emptying the trash cans, none of which had anything to do with trapping. It was expected that an apprentice would take care of their master, even if he was an asshat.

'Anything else?' she asked, hopeful she could blow out of there.

He shifted in his recliner as if no position was comfortable, which was probably the case.

'Get those Holy Water jugs out into the parking lot. A recycling truck should be coming by to pick them up this morning.' Another shift in position. 'I want every one accounted for. I'll need the money since I can't trap.'

'Shouldn't we keep some of the counterfeit ones for evidence?' she hedged. 'The ones I had were destroyed in the fire.'

'Hold back five of them.' Then he frowned. 'Why didn't Saint see that those bottles were wrong the last time he did the inventory?'

'Because none of them were. The screwed-up consecration dates just showed up in the last three weeks.'

He huffed in disgust. 'I'd love to find the bastard behind that scheme. I'd throw him to a Three and watch the thing gut him.'

Riley shivered: she knew exactly what that looked like. Harper caught her reaction, but he didn't chide her about it like she figured he would.

'There's an order on the desk,' he said. 'It's a Magpie.

You've trapped them before, right?'

She nodded. Grade One demons came in two flavours – Klepto-Fiends, who stole bright objects, and Biblio-Fiends, who chewed up books and swore like rappers. If she had her choice of what to trap, the Klepto-Fiend was it. They weren't malicious, just obsessive and stealthy.

'When you've trapped it, sell it to that new guy . . . Dan what's-his-name,' her master ordered. 'Don't go anywhere near the Fireman, got it?'

That would be Fireman Jack, one of the demon traffickers. Harper had a real hang-up about homosexuals.

'I understand. Where is this Dan guy's place?'

Harper jabbed a finger at the desk. 'His address is next to the trapping order.'

Riley ignored the paperwork for the time being and concentrated on moving the plastic Holy Water bottles to the parking lot. After the first trip she devised a way to run a piece of rope through the handles so she could carry more of them at one time. As she made the trips back and forth she noted that Harper's collection of scrounged metal in the fenced yard behind the building was diminishing.

Selling it off to pay the bills. The Guild's disability fund wasn't very generous.

Once she'd finished the recount, Riley leaned against her car and waited. As long as the bottle count matched the paperwork, Harper would have no reason to bitch at her. At least not about this.

Forbidden

Riley heard the truck from a block away as it ground through gears and eventually pulled up near her car, brakes screeching in protest. The truck bed had a substantial mound of plastic containers held in place by tall wooden racks on all four sides. When a couple of guys hopped out of the vehicle, she handed over the clipboard with the required forms.

'Hey, I saw you on the TV. You know, at the Tabernacle,' the younger of the two men said as the other one checked the count. 'Damn, that was one helluva fire.'

'So what happens to these bottles after you guys get them?' she asked, in an effort to change the subject from one that fuelled her nightmares.

To her relief he took the bait. 'These?'

'Yeah, those,' she said, indicating the bottles. That hadn't been a trick question.

'They go to the recycling plant,' the other man said, his tone guarded.

'Then what happens?'

'Don't know. Don't care,' he said. He counted out the money, then dropped it and one copy of the paperwork into her hands.

Riley pointed to the sheet. 'Sign it, will you?'

'Don't need to,' the guy said, frowning now.

'Please?' she wheedled, turning on the charm. 'Master Harper will be all over me if I don't get it signed.'

The two men traded looks and the younger one scrawled something on the page and handed it back to her. The signature was unreadable. Her thanks yielded no reply as they backed out of the lot in a cloud of exhaust fumes and tormented gears.

While Riley rearranged the paperwork on the clipboard, something nagged at her. She stared at the driver's side door. There was no logo, no lettering, no nothing. All the city's vehicles had Atlanta's official logo on their doors, the image of a phoenix rising from the flames.

So who just picked up those bottles?

Beck didn't like hospitals. He'd spent some time in one during his stint in the Army so he knew how they worked. They harboured weird smells and seemed too sterile for his liking, so finding himself *makin' the rounds*, as Master Stewart put it, didn't do a thing for his attitude. In Beck's way of thinking this was the priest's job, but here he was trooping around the different floors, talking to bedridden trappers and their families, acting like all Hell wasn't breaking loose. Why Stewart had insisted he do this he hadn't a clue, but he could take orders like any good soldier.

Beck had purposely made Simon his last stop, partly because he felt bad he hadn't kept the apprentice from being hurt, and mostly because Simon was dating Riley. He still hadn't sorted out his feelings about that. Not that he had anything against Adler, but it just didn't feel right to him.

Better'n some she could be seein'.

Like that Allan something or other, the abusive dick she'd dated a couple of years back. Beck knew he was to blame for that – Riley had been totally hot for him when he'd returned from the Army. Anyone could see it. That would have been OK if she hadn't been Paul's daughter and only fifteen. He'd pushed her aside, hard. On the rebound, she'd immediately taken up with that abusive loser who had her steal stuff for him. That relationship had lasted right up until Allan had hit her.

But that's the point, isn't it?

Simon would treat Riley right. He wouldn't beat her or talk her into stealing things, but every time Beck tried to tell himself that it stuck in his throat. Did that mean he was jealous?

He shoved that unnerving thought aside and entered Simon's room. He found the patient awake, watching something on television. Beck's eyes flicked towards the screen – it was a talk show about what had happened at the Tabernacle. Every now and then a picture of the inferno would pop on the screen.

Just what ya shouldn't be watchin'.

'Simon.' A weak nod returned as Beck slowly approached the bed. 'How's it goin?' he asked, keeping his tone conversational. Just like a priest would.

A shrug returned.

'I hear the wounds are healin' good.' A nod. It appeared that Beck would have to do all the talking. 'I've been visitin' some of the others. Looks like they're gonna make it, though Barton needs more surgery on his leg.'

'Good,' the patient mumbled, his eyes not meeting his visitor's.

Beck hadn't figured Simon was going to be all perky, but he had to talk this out or it'd eat him alive. Beck knew about that first-hand.

He tried another approach. 'Did ya see the angels?'

Simon's expression saddened. 'No, I didn't.'

'Well, they were truly awesome. I've seen the ministerin' kind before, but these were the big boys. They were seriously kick-ass.'

'Jackson told me about them,' Simon replied. 'He said they had fiery swords and you could feel this sort of power around them.'

'Ya shoulda seen the demons. They ran for it.'

Silence.

Beck leaned on the bedrail. 'Ya know, it's real hard after a battle,' he said. 'Ya can't believe half of what happened and part of ya is too damned frightened to deal with it. Just know, it'll take time.'

Simon swallowed heavily. 'I thought I was going to die.'

'Same here.'

The apprentice's eyes met his. 'Were you frightened?'

'Hell, yes.'

'I shouldn't have been. I knew God was with me.'

'That don't keep ya from bein' afraid. That's natural,' Beck explained. 'Nothin' to be ashamed of.'

'I saw on the TV that the demons are all over the city now.'

'A few. They're actin' strange, but we'll get 'em, don't worry.'

Simon frowned. 'Why hasn't Riley come to see me again?' he demanded, his voice harsher now.

That wasn't a question Beck had expected. 'She's helpin' Harper out and she's tryin' to find Paul. I figure she'll be along directly.'

'That's no excuse. She should be here.'

Oh, lord. 'I'll let her know you're askin' for her.'

That seemed to mollify the patient. When Simon spoke again, his voice was quieter. 'They're going to blame me for this.'

'No one's blamin' anyone,' Beck said. 'There are too many things we don't understand yet.'

Simon's eyes swung in his direction. 'You mean like why Master Blackthorne was there.'

'Surprised the hell outta me, that's for sure,' Beck replied. 'We're tryin' to work it all out.'

The frown returned. 'What's to work out? Either the Holy Water was counterfeit or someone broke the circle and let the demons in.'

'Riley said the Holy Water was good. I trust her on that. No one would break the circle. It'd just get them dead.'

'Not if they were dead already.'

Beck straightened up, knowing that the next words out

of the young man's mouth would be condemning Paul. That he wouldn't tolerate. 'I'd best be goin',' he said.

Simon's eyes closed, his mouth a grim line. 'I think you should,' the apprentice retorted.

He thinks Paul sold us out. That didn't promise a rosy future between Riley and her new boyfriend. She would stick up for her father no matter what.

Ya sure know how to pick 'em, girl.

Chapter Thirteen

Peter hopped into her car and slammed the door the moment Riley pulled to the kerb near the Grounds Zero. He was in his usual jeans and sweatshirt, the one with the picture of a guy taking a sledgehammer to a computer keyboard. The caption said *Commence Reboot*.

He set his computer bag on the floor, then stared at her. 'Your hair. It's different.'

'It needed a trim. It got really frazzled in the fire.'

'I like it. It looks good.' Her friend handed over an insulated cup. 'Hot chocolate with whipped cream,' he announced, then swiped at his brown hair to get it out of his face.

'You brought me hot chocolate. You rock, Mr King.'

'I do, and your timing's excellent. I've only been here a few minutes.'

'You take the bus?' she asked.

'No, David dropped me off. He wanted out of the house as much as I did.'

No doubt. 'I've got a trapping run.'

Peter swivelled in his seat, eyes widening. 'What kind of demon is it?'

'It's just one of the small guys, a Grade One Klepto-Fiend. I figured you'd want to stay in the car.'

'Why? This could be fun.'

This wasn't the Peter she knew. He was always playing it safe to avoid getting grounded by the warden. Now, with his parents divorcing, it looked like he had decided to branch out a little.

Riley gave him a dubious look as she pulled up to an intersection. 'You sure?'

'Yeah, unless that Five is going to be there.'

'It shouldn't be.' *Not during the day at least.*

At the next intersection a man stood in the middle of the chaos clad in an orange vest and white gloves, like a cross between a butler and a traffic guard. Since most of the city's traffic lights had been stolen by thieves, he was part of the city's new scheme of HTLs: human traffic lights. For a little over five dollars an hour he had the privilege of standing in the intersection and trying not to get squashed.

As she waited for her turn to move forward, Riley asked, 'Is it getting any better at home?'

Peter slumped in his seat. 'No. Mom's still guilting us and Dad's not saying much at all.'

'Who do you want to live with?'

'Dad, for sure. He's cool. He has rules, and some of them are kinda stupid, but he's nothing like Mom.'

'What will happen if you tell her that?'

Peter shook his head in despair. 'Cue total meltdown.

If I tell her the truth, she'll just throw Matthew's death in my face.'

'Sounds seriously hideous, Peter.'

'It is,' he murmured. 'She hasn't been right since the twins were born.'

Riley remembered the day her friend had announced that his mother was pregnant. He'd been thirteen at the time and majorly grossed out to think that his parents were having sex.

'I feel sorry for the ghouls,' he said, his term for the twins. 'They just don't get what's going on and so they're really fussy right now.'

A pair of cranky three-year-olds. No wonder her friend wanted out of the house, even if it was to trap a Magpie.

'Well, I'd just tell her and get it over with, Peter. It's tearing you up – I can tell.'

He nodded, but didn't reply.

At least my parents never stopped loving each other.

With a gloved wave from the human traffic light, she edged through the intersection and continued east to the jewellery shop in Poncey Highlands. Peter's sharp eyes spotted the sign before she did. Riley glided to a halt in front of the store, one of those family-owned kind of places that looked like it'd been at the same location for decades.

As Riley turned off the engine and scooped up her messenger bag, Peter appeared to be having second thoughts.

'Is this dangerous?' he asked.

'No way. These guys are all about stealth. That's why we call them Hell's cat burglars. They're just into bling.'

'What kind of bling?' he asked.

'The shinier the better.'

He thought that through. 'OK, I'll see what it's all about. If it gets weird, I'm outta there.'

That was fair.

Right before she exited the car, her cellphone pinged – a text from Mortimer: the vendue was on and if she really wanted to be there she needed to be available tomorrow night. Time and directions followed. A second message arrived before she could reply.

If you attend, don't wear jeans.

She was supposed to be on hallowed ground after sundown. Did she dare risk it?

'Riley?' Peter nudged. 'Something wrong?'

'No, just trying to decide something.' What if the Five came after her at this vendue thing? Then she remembered who would be there: summoners who wielded magic for fun and profit. She couldn't imagine a demon would take that on when it could wait for another time when she wasn't protected. Besides, Ori would be on her tail. She sent Mort a quick text telling him she'd be there.

Riley found her friend studying the contents of one of the store's display windows. It was full of sparkle. 'How do you catch this thing?' he asked.

She dug in her bag, pulled out a sippy cup and handed it to him.

'You're joking, right?' he said. 'You trap demons with cups that have dancing bears on them?'

She glowered at him. 'See the glitter in the bottom? Klepto-Fiends can't resist it.'

He held up the sippy cup and compared it to the exquisitely cut diamonds in the store window.

'Wanna bet?'

And I brought him along why?

He returned the cup. 'The 'rents can't know about this . . . ever.'

'Got it.'

Riley pushed open the reinforced door and looked around for someone who might be in charge. The paperwork said the complaint came from a guy named Abe Meyerson. There were two employees, but the elderly man near the watch case seemed to be the best choice. He had some serious wrinkles and was probably at least eighty, if not older.

After a deep breath to build her confidence, Riley put on her professional *I know what I'm doing* face and approached the glass counter.

'Mr Meyerson?' she asked. The old gentleman nodded. 'I'm Riley Blackthorne and I'm here to deal with your *theft* problem.' Her dad had always insisted that she not use the words *demon trapper* in a retail store until the owner indicated he was OK with his customers knowing what was going on. In case the old man wasn't making the connection, she offered him the paperwork.

Mr Meyerson took the trapping request out of her hand, held it closer to his nose than would have been comfortable for her and then nodded again. Then he looked at her, squinting. 'They're sending young ones now!' the man said with a spry grin. He looked at Peter. 'Are you a trapper too?'

'No, sir. I'm just watching, if that's OK with you.'

'Fine by me. These little thieves are just the nature of the business, but this one only likes loose stones. I think it's a little off in its skull, you know what I mean,' he said, tapping his temple for emphasis.

Not good. That meant this one would be harder to capture. She so needed something to go right for a change, especially with Peter watching her every move.

'How long has it been here?' Riley asked, refusing to let the disheartening news sidetrack her.

'A week.'

'Does it have any particular time that it steals stuff?'

'Just whenever it feels like it.'

She'd have to go through this place inch by inch to find the fiend rather than just waiting it out. With the funerals this afternoon she really needed to make this happen. Taking a deep breath, Riley recited the warnings and precautions that came with removing a demon from a public location. Mr Meyerson had no questions, mostly because he'd been through this numerous times over the years, and he readily signed the form to indicate he knew the consequences.

'Good luck,' he said. 'Let me know if you need anything.' The old man puttered off to sit at a desk that had to be as ancient as he was. Pressing a jeweller's loupe to his eye, he bent over a watch and began poking at it with a little screwdriver.

Cue demon trapper.

Riley retreated to the door and began a visual tour of the showroom, a technique her dad had taught her during one of her first trapping assignments. *Assess the surroundings. Look for obvious hiding places.*

'What are you doing?' Peter whispered.

'Trying to find where a three-inch-tall demon could hide.'

'Ah, that's about everywhere,' he said. 'I don't think your glitter-in-a-cup trick is going to work.'

Unfortunately, Peter was right. There were a lot of nooks and crannies in a building this old. Her usual bait was worthless with all those gems in the cases, each lit with their own internal fire and by carefully positioned high-intensity lights. She could put Holy Water at each of the exits and along the windows to flush the fiend out. But then it'd go nuts and tear the place apart. She already had a reputation for trashing libraries – no need to add jewellery stores to the list.

What am I going to do? She could call Beck and maybe he'd have an idea, but that would make her look like she couldn't handle things on her own. Calling

Harper was *so* not an option.

As she thought it through, Peter parked himself at a chair near the watch case, laptop out, surfing an online gaming site. She looked over his shoulder; he was checking out pictures of dragons. He pulled one of the images into a program and then upped the size so he could see it easier. It made the thing look huge on the vivid eighteen-inch colour screen.

Her eyes went to the closest glass case. The problem was that all these jewels were about the same size. Nothing really screamed BLING! What she needed was a humongous gem.

Peter's dragon now sat on top of a mound of gold and jewels, short puffs of smoke coming out of its nostrils. It looked menacing, but not the twenty-foot-tall, pull-her-dad-out-of-his-grave kind of scary.

The idea that popped into her brain was crazy. She would bet no trapper had ever tried such a stunt, but she was out of options. Either she gave it a go or she had to call Harper and say she couldn't handle the job.

No way. He'd never let me live that down.

Riley cautiously ran her lunatic idea past Mr Meyerson and to her astonishment she received a vote of approval.

'Can't hurt,' Mr Meyerson said. He opened the vault and returned with a large emerald. It was marquis cut and two carats in weight, he said, though Riley had no idea what all that meant. She took a picture of it with her cellphone, emailed it to Peter and then explained exactly what she wanted him to do. To her relief, he didn't tell her she was totally whacked. As her friend worked, the jeweller returned the emerald to the safe, made a quick check to ensure there wasn't a demon inside and then locked it tight.

Luckily there were no customers at the moment as it took time to set the trap. Mr Meyerson turned off all the interior lights, including those in the display cases. There was still light coming in the front windows, but not so much as to ruin her plan.

Peter positioned his laptop on one of the main glass displays, clicked a key and the image of the emerald appeared on the big screen. He'd done something to it so the image rotated, sparkled and shone like it was lit from within by a solar flare.

If the gem could talk, it would be screaming, STEAL ME!

'You think this will work?' Peter whispered as they backed away.

'It better,' Riley whispered in reply.

The jeweller and his assistant hovered by the front door, watching the show. They seemed amused by her high-tech trap.

'Kids are so smart these days,' the old man said.

Only if this works.

Time passed. Peter nudged her with an elbow. 'And this is going to happen . . . when?'

She gave him a dirty look. 'Patience, dude.'

Then she heard it, that pitter-patter of boot-clad demon feet racing across glass. A moment later the Magpie stood transfixed in front of the computer, its bulging bag of loot at its side. It looked like the one in her apartment, about three inches tall, except this one wasn't wearing a black bandana. In the glow of the screen she could see its tiny fingers twitch in nervous anticipation.

That's right. It's all yours. Just don't move.

Riley slowly approached, making each step as quiet as possible. If she spooked it, it wouldn't fall for this ruse a second time. The moment before it leapt at the screen she caught the fiend. She dropped the demon into the transparent sippy cup and slapped a hand over the top.

'Lid!' she called out. Her friend just stared at the cup in her hand, wide-eyed. 'Peter! I need the lid. Now!'

'Sorry,' he called out, and hurried over. Between them they sealed the cup.

'Wow. That's really a demon. I mean, you can see pictures of them on the Web, but . . .'

The fiend in question rose on its feet, pointed at the bag and then began to wail, pulling at its clothes like it was in mourning.

'What's he doing?'

'Freaking. He thinks I'm stealing his stuff.' Riley brought the cup to nose level. 'Hold on, I'll get it for you. I won't take it away,' she said.

Mr Meyerson opened the bag's drawstring and the contents slid across the glass countertop.

'Look at all that,' Peter said in awe. There were at least a dozen loose diamonds and sapphires, but no emeralds.

They'd offered the demon the perfect bait.

The old jeweller separated out the merchandise with a wizened finger. 'That's all of the gems. The rest is just glass. Who knows where it came from,' he said with a toothy smile.

Riley put the remaining loot back in the bag and, with Peter's help, dumped it inside the cup without losing the demon. The Magpie clutched his hoard to his chest and sighed in profound relief.

'Wow, he *is* obsessed,' Peter said, staring at the fiend.

'Totally. Get rid of the emerald. He's forgotten it for the moment, but that won't last.'

'Gone,' her friend said, punching a key. The image vanished and in its place was a thunderstorm rolling over Atlanta's skyline.

'Well done,' the old man said, beaming through a sea of wrinkles. 'Ingenious.'

Riley grinned. 'Thanks.' She looked over at her friend and shot him a thumbs up. 'Who knows, maybe this is the future of demon trapping.'

'Tech rules,' Peter replied.

They left the shop with one demon in a sippy cup, signed paperwork and two free coupons for lunch at a downtown deli courtesy of Mr Meyerson. He'd also promised not to tell anyone about Peter's part in the job.

'Trapper scores,' Riley said, feeling really good for a change.

This is how it's supposed to be.

Chapter Fourteen

It was nearly one thirty when Riley pulled her car up to Beck's house in Cabbagetown. His place wasn't very different to its neighbours' other than it looked better maintained. The trim and porch railing were stark white and the house itself a pleasing shade of light green. She could almost imagine him out there on a ladder slinging paint all over the place.

How does he find the time? She was still behind on her laundry.

Beck sat on the porch in a wooden rocking chair clad in his black suit. From the dour expression on his face all he needed was a shotgun and something to fill full of holes and he'd be just fine.

She'd first heard about the new kid from South Georgia over the dinner table when her father had told them about this smartass sixteen-year-old in his history class, a troublemaker sprinting full speed towards a brick wall. 'Serious lemming potential' was the way he'd described Denver Beck. Now her father was dead and the former troublemaker had taken it upon himself to watch over her so she wouldn't go all 'wild child' on him.

It was a plan doomed to failure.

As she parked the car in the driveway, Beck rose with considerable effort. She didn't think it was because of his injuries – the Holy Water would have started to heal those. What hurt was way deeper and most likely permanent. She carried some of those same scars herself.

Beck climbed in her car, placed his trapping bag on the seat behind them and then clicked the seat belt without so much as a 'hello'. Like it was expected she'd haul his butt around town.

Maybe he doesn't want to be on his own.

She asked the question anyway. 'Some reason I'm driving you to the funeral?' she said.

'Don't need a ticket.' At her puzzled look, he explained, 'After the service we'll go to the Six Under for the wake. Don't want to lose my truck if the cops pull me over on the way home.'

Another trapper tradition – bury your dead and then get drunk. There were a lot of traditions and the Demon Trappers Manual didn't say much on the subject, which led her to believe they'd evolved over time. Anything that involved an excuse to drink was automatically trapper approved.

'I'll drive you home after the wake,' she offered, heading back towards Memorial Drive.

'No, I'll walk. It's not that far.'

'You could still get arrested for that,' she said. 'I'll drive you.'

He eyed her. 'You're not comin' to the bar with us. You're not legal.'

'They serve soda. Besides, it's only right: I was at the Tabernacle when they died; I want to be there for their wake.'

He ignored her from that point on. The silence held for longer than was comfortable and finally she relented. She needed to talk to someone and Beck was the only option.

'The collection agency jerk visited me yesterday. He said they'll go after the life insurance money since they didn't get to steal Dad's body.'

Beck huffed. 'Don't worry, they won't get it.'

Easy for you to say.

More silence. She almost turned on the radio, but the music she liked would only earn her hassles from her companion. 'Trapped a Magpie today. At a jewellery store,' she said, figuring that was a safe topic.

'It go OK?'

'Real well.' She was about to tell him how she'd pulled it off, then changed her mind. He might not like the idea of Peter being there.

They made it through four more intersections before he gave in. 'Ya see Simon today?'

'No. I'm going to stop by tonight.'

'Good, he's askin' for ya. It's gonna take him a while to get over what happened.'

'Same for all of us.' She heard a grunt of acknowledgement. Time to move to more sunny topics. 'Mort's trying to help me find Dad.'

'Does he know who took him?' Beck quizzed.

'No. He thinks it's odd that no one's talking. I'm just hoping it's not Ozymandias. Ayden says he's into dark magic.'

Beck looked pensive. 'That must be the guy Lenny was talkin' about. I'll pay him a visit.'

'He's not like Mort or the others. This one's evil.'

'Evil I can do,' Beck said as if the problem was solved. 'I'll go with you.'

'Not happenin', so don't even think about it.'

Why is everything a battle with you? Why can't you let me make my own decisions?

In response to the tension, Beck began to rearrange the contents of his duffel bag. From what she could tell it didn't need the attention, but he focused on that rather than talking. A nervous habit. She had a few of her own.

He finally stopped fussing with the bag. 'There were two Mezmers at the lounge last night.'

'What?' she said, giving him a quick glance before returning her eyes to the highway. 'Did you get them?'

'No,' he said. 'I tagged the first one, but before I could get it secured the second one showed up. It was . . . more than I could handle.'

She pulled up to a stop sign, jamming on the brakes. 'Beck! You're OK, aren't you?' He nodded. 'How did you get away from it?'

Her passenger shrugged. 'Don't really know. It was workin' me over somethin' fierce and then both of them just took off.'

'Did you tell Stewart?' she asked, more worried now that he didn't have a solid answer.

'Not yet. I will, once everythin' settles down.'

Riley could tell there was more here than he was admitting. What if that thing *had* got his soul? Would she be able to tell? A sick knot formed in her chest. 'Beck . . .' she began, her voice quavering.

'I don't want to talk about it,' he ordered. 'It's over and I'm still in one piece.'

But you might not have been.

Beck had been planning his move from the moment the funerals had ended. As Riley pulled into the pub's parking lot, he hopped out of the car as soon as it stopped, hoping to avoid a confrontation. 'Thanks, girl. Call when ya get to the church so I know you're safe.'

There was no way he could ignore the expression on Riley's face. He knew it well enough: it promised defiance so it wasn't any surprise when she turned off the engine, undid the seat belt and climbed out. Beck watched her walk across the street towards the pub, her hair swinging back and forth, boots clicking on the pavement.

Ya shouldn't be here. It wasn't dangerous or anything, but it was a guy thing.

'We're gonna get drunk, we're gonna swear and tell a

lot of war stories,' he called out. 'That's about it.'

Riley paused at the entrance to the Six Feet Under Pub and Fish House. 'I know. Dad told me about these things.'

'It's no place for a . . . girl.'

'But it is for a trapper,' she said, and left him standing there like a moron.

'Why do ya fight me on everythin'?' he snarled. He had no choice but to let her have her way. Dragging her out of there by the hair would just make both of them look stupid.

He found Riley at the bar, ordering a glass of Pepsi. Just like he figured, the bartender was giving her the once-over.

'You're new,' the guy said, turning on the charm.

'Uh huh,' Riley replied, laying a five on the counter and looking around. 'Where are the trappers?'

'Oh, you're here for that, huh? They're upstairs, on the roof,' he answered, pointing at a set of stairs near the entrance. Then he plunked the glass down and gave her the change. As Beck approached, Riley picked up her drink and headed for the stairs, acting as if he didn't exist.

'Hey, man,' the bartender called out. 'I heard about the Tabernacle. Sorry.'

'It was a bitch, that's for sure,' Beck said. 'Thank your boss for the flowers. The families really appreciated them.'

'Will do.' The bartender stacked a couple of glasses as he watched Riley climb the stairs. 'Now that's a total hottie.'

'Don't even think about it,' Beck warned.

'Oh, sorry,' the guy said, raising his hands in surrender. 'I didn't know she was spoken for.'

Beck realized he'd been a jerk. 'No, not your fault. I'm kind of, well . . . She's a trapper. She's Paul's daughter.'

'I thought she was a groupie or something. Thanks for setting me straight.' He went into bartender mode. 'The usual?'

'Yeah. Make it a pitcher this time and start a tab.'

'You got it.'

The rooftop portion of the Six Feet Under was open to the air, so Riley made sure to sit near one of the radiant heaters. She selected an empty chair at the end of a long wooden table. Three tables, actually, all nosed together to accommodate the trappers. As she sat, heads turned. A few faces frowned. She was pleased to see not all of them did.

'Hi there, Riley,' Jackson called out. He was drinking coffee instead of a beer, probably in deference to his wounds.

'How are you doing?' she asked.

'Not bad. Hurts like hell, but the doc said I don't need grafts so I'm not going to complain.'

'That's really good news.'

'Amen to that. Where's Den?'

'Here!' Beck called out as he walked up. He set his pitcher and pint of beer on the table next to Riley's glass.

Shooting her a snarky grin, he said, 'Now don't ya get those mixed up, ya hear?'

Riley gave him a scathing look, which was a complete waste of time. The group had gone quiet, except for Beck, who took a long gulp of his brew.Then he looked down at the others.

'What's the problem, guys?'

McGuire angled his head towards Riley. He was in his early forties, tall with narrow hips, and thin brown hair that covered his collar. If the deep crease lines on his face were any indication, a scowl was his default setting.

'Apprentices are always at these things. How else are they gonna learn anythin'?' Beck asked.

'But she's . . .'

'A trapper,' Jackson said.

'Not in my book,' McGuire replied.

'You can bitch all you want, but I saw her take down a Three with a *folding chair*,' Jackson replied. 'We would have been burying Simon tonight if it hadn't been for her, so I think maybe you should just can it.'

'The hell I will. First it'll be her, then there'll be more of them. We'll have to take anyone who wants to be a trapper,' McGuire complained.

'I'd say the more the better – we could use the help right now,' Beck said.

McGuire rose to his feet. 'No disrespect to the dead, but I can't be here if she is.' He slugged down what remained of his beer and then stomped down the stairs.

Riley shook her head. *Another enemy. Like I don't have enough already.*

One of the trappers pounded the table enthusiastically. 'Good deal. McGuire's such a downer.' He gave Riley a hundred-watt smile. 'I'm Lex Reynolds, by the way. Pleased to have you here, miss.'

She nodded in reply. Reynolds had a full beard and hair that went below his shoulders. He looked like a surfer, muscled, with a deep golden tan. He wasn't a good ol' boy, that was for sure.

The trapper rose and lifted his glass. With a nudge from Beck, Riley stood like the others.

'Rest in peace, guys,' Reynolds called out, and then everyone took a long drink. 'You keep those Pearly Gates open for us and we'll bring the beer.'

'Amen!' a few of the trappers shouted.

Chairs skidded on the floor as the group returned to their seats.

'Collins owed me twenty bucks,' Jackson announced. 'I'm never going to see that, am I?'

'Twenty? He owed me fifty,' another trapper called out.

'Y'all are screwed,' Beck laughed. 'I bet he's laughin' his ass off right now.'

'God, I miss him. He was so much fun,' Reynolds said. 'Remember when he went after that Four at Georgia Tech right after he became a journeyman?'

'I don't know that story,' one of the trappers replied.

Forbidden

He was an older guy with a waxed handlebar moustache.

'Well, there was this Four eating up fraternity boys like candy. So Collins gets the job. He goes up to this chick and she offers him a good time, so he drops a load of Holy Water on her.'

Jackson chortled. Apparently he knew how this story played out.

'You see, she wasn't a demon.' Reynolds grinned. 'She was an undercover vice cop. Man, did they bust his balls.'

Riley laughed along with the others.

'Sounds like something I'd do,' Beck joked.

A trapper named Thomas jumped in with a tale about Morton catching a Three in a meat locker at a grocery store. Then someone related the joke they'd pulled on Stewart involving a goat in Demon Central. It was only then she realized the masters weren't here.

When she asked Beck why that was the case, he replied, 'So the guys can say anythin' they want and not worry they'll get in trouble. They can blow off steam that way.'

Riley settled back in her seat, letting the stories surround her. This wasn't about remembering the dead, but honouring those that were still alive. These trappers were the real deal, and for a moment she felt a strong sense of pride at being one of them. *This was why Dad did this.* It wasn't just bringing in the demons, or earning a pay cheque. It was about being one of the guys.

But I never will be one of the guys. She didn't have the

right equipment and that made all the difference. Even if she rose to the rank of master, she'd never really belong. Depressed, Riley finished off her drink and stood. All eyes went to her.

'You're not leaving, are you?' Jackson asked. 'The night's young.'

'I need to get some sleep,' she admitted, then wondered if that made her sound weak. It was a better explanation than having to stay on holy ground after dark.

''Night, Miss Riley,' someone called out from the group, though she wasn't sure who it was. She called out her own farewell and headed down the stairs. Beck quickly fell in step with her, following her out to the car.

'I thought ya were gonna drive me home,' he chided.

'Changed my mind.'

'Glad to hear it.' He hesitated and then added, 'I need help with somethin' tomorrow. Will ya be home around noon?'

'Help with what?'

'Just somethin'.'

OK, be mysterious. 'I'll be home then.'

'Good. I'll bring barbecue for lunch.'

'That works.'

They'd reached her car. As Riley pulled out the keys, he said, 'Call me when ya get to the church.'

'Why do you do that?' she demanded, turning on her heel to face him.

'What?'

'You go all old on me, like you're a grandad or something.'

'Ya don't understand,' he said, running a hand through his hair.

'What don't I get, Beck? That you had a craptastic childhood? That you can't change what happened to you so you're going to micromanage my every waking hour?'

His face hardened. 'Yeah, that's part of it. I had to take care of myself since I was little. I know what it's like.'

'You keep it up and you're going to be like Harper, a sad old guy who hits people and bitches about everything.'

'Ya don't understand,' he repeated.

'Then tell me why you have to be like this. One good reason.'

'Because . . .' He slumped against the car. 'I don't know any other way to be.'

Finally the truth. And from the expression on his face it looked like she'd carved it out of his heart.

She leaned against the car next to him, hands crossed over her chest. 'Promise you'll stop going all senior?'

He looked over at her. 'Will you call your aunt?'

Here we go again. 'I won't be any safer in Fargo. If the demons want me, they'll find me.'

Beck put his hand on her arm. 'Please,' he pleaded.

Riley stared at him. That word just wasn't one of his favourites. For him to use it meant he was desperate. When she didn't reply, he removed his hand in defeat.

'I just need to know that there's someone who'll take care of ya . . . if . . . somethin' happens to me.'

Without another word her companion walked back towards the pub. At the last moment, he looked back over his shoulder. This time his emotions were unmasked and she could read them easily.

Fear. For him and for her.

What aren't you telling me? What really happened at the pool hall?

Chapter Fifteen

It took some time for Riley to find Simon: he'd been moved out of ICU. As she drew closer to his room, a man passed her in the hallway. He wasn't hospital staff so for a moment she thought maybe he was a priest, but he wasn't wearing a clerical collar.

Probably a friend of the family. At least someone was visiting Simon besides her.

Riley paused for a moment outside the room to gear herself up for this. It shouldn't be this way. She should be really looking forward to seeing him, but something wasn't right between them. *I'm overreacting. He's just scared like the rest of us. He'll come out of it.*

She cautiously stuck her head in Simon's room and found him in the bed closest to the door. The curtain was pulled, shielding him from his roommate, who was watching television.

Her boyfriend was staring at nothing, hands tangled around a rosary, his face as pale as it had been the last time she'd seen him. She moved to his side, set her messenger bag on the chair and waited for him to acknowledge her. When he did, he frowned like she wasn't welcome.

'Where have you been?' he demanded, scowling. 'I called your house over and over. You didn't answer. Are you blowing me off on purpose?'

Riley counted to ten so as not to buy into his anger. *He's just frustrated. He has to vent.*

'I'm not home much any more,' she explained. 'Call my cell.' Then Riley remembered why that wouldn't work. 'I'll get you the new number. My phone got toasted so I'm using Dad's.'

If she expected that to mollify Simon, it didn't work. 'Why weren't you here this morning?'

'I've been busy. I've had our master to take care of, a Magpie to trap, funerals and a wake to attend. That doesn't leave much time for sitting around the house waiting for your call, Simon.'

'Wake?' he replied. 'Why would *you* go to that?'

Because I'm a trapper? 'Don't start,' she replied. 'I had to listen to McGuire complain about me being in the Guild. I don't need to hear it from you.'

Simon looked away, but no apology was forthcoming.

'Look, I'm really tired, so I'm kind of bitchy,' she said, trying to salvage the conversation. 'Let's start over, OK?'

When he didn't respond, she reached over one of the side rails and touched his hand. Simon flinched and pulled away.

'What is going on with you?' she asked.

'I would think that would be obvious,' he replied, scowling again.

No, or I wouldn't have asked. 'Look, just hang in there. You'll be getting out of here soon. You'll be coming back to work and maybe in a couple weeks we can go to a movie or something. Spend some time together. I'd like that.' *I really need your strength right now.*

'A date?' he retorted, his knuckles white as he clenched the rosary. 'How can you think about that? How can you be oblivious to what is going on in this city?'

Riley's temper reared its head. 'I know what's happening, Simon. I know better than anyone, but—'

'I never realized how shallow you are,' he said, staring at her like he'd just learned her darkest secret. 'Don't those dead trappers mean anything to you?'

'Now listen,' she retorted, trying hard to control her voice so that she didn't disturb his roommate. 'Don't give me this "you don't care" crap. I'm not oblivious, Simon.' *I just want to get things back on track with us.*

'That's not what I'm seeing,' he said, waving a hand. 'We have to find out what happened at the Tabernacle. We have to find out who betrayed us.'

Betrayed? Riley forced herself to sound calm, though her emotions were seething. 'No one betrayed us, Simon. You know that as well as I do.'

'Do I?' he asked, a strange light in his eyes. 'This is a battle for our very souls, Riley. Nothing is like it seems. We can't trust anyone until we know what happened.'

Riley gave up. She was too tired for all this drama. 'Then you work it out. I've gotta go.'

When she dropped a kiss on his cheek, Simon's jaw tensed underneath her lips.

'I'm not giving up on you,' she said defiantly.

'And I'm not giving up until I find the truth.'

Instead of dragging herself into the solitude of the church's basement and listening to the furnace do its on-and-off dance, Riley sat on the stone steps that led to the building's front entrance. It was after dark now, the streets alight with cars and busy with pedestrians heading home for the night. Right now the Five seemed a remote threat. A bigger worry was Simon and what was happening between them. The possibility of losing him weighed on her heart.

'Heaven can't be that cruel,' she whispered.

A slight breeze made her tuck her coat tighter. She heard the light footsteps before she saw him. Ori. He settled on to the steps next to her, dressed in his black leather jacket and jeans. He said nothing for a long time, as if he was respecting her need for silence. Finally Riley knew she had to say something.

'I didn't see you following me from the hospital,' she said, looking over at him.

'I'm very good at what I do,' he replied. 'Something happened there, didn't it?'

'It's more what didn't happen.' She twisted the strap on her messenger bag in agitation, then realized what she was doing and shoved it away. It was a stupid habit. 'My boyfriend's gone weird. I know he's been really ill and all that, but . . .'

'But?' Ori nudged.

'Simon's changing. He used to be so sweet and kind. Now he's nasty, even to me, like it was my fault he got clawed up.'

'Do you think it's your fault?'

Riley rubbed her face in thought. 'Maybe. What if the Five brought those other demons just so it could get to me? What if I'm the reason all those guys died?'

Ori placed his hand on her arm, giving it a gentle squeeze of reassurance.

'If the Five wanted you, it just had to wait for the right time to kill you. It did not have to orchestrate an attack on the Tabernacle.'

Riley searched his face and found only compassion. She needed that support right now. Simon certainly wasn't giving her any. 'You really believe that?'

Ori nodded. 'The demons are not acting normally. Something, or someone, is driving them to this grotesque behaviour.'

'Lucifer?'

'No. Not his style. The Prince of Hell likes order above all things.'

'But who . . .' Riley let it drop, too tired to try to work through it. Stewart and others would take care of it. She had her boyfriend and her dad to worry about.

'I thought that Simon's faith would help him through

this. I mean, he's really religious. I thought we'd deal with this together, but he's not moving on, all he's doing is looking backwards.'

'While you're looking forward?'

Riley nodded. 'That's what I do when it goes wrong. If I slow down, I don't think I can handle my screwed-up life, so I just keep moving, hoping it'll get better. It never does.'

Ori put his arm round her, drawing her close to his body, which allowed Riley to rest her head on his shoulder. She inhaled the crisp, cool scent that was him. Though it made no sense, her worries seemed to fade when he touched her. Maybe if she just stayed in his arms forever, everything would be fine again.

'Simon's journey is his own,' he said. 'If he's foolish enough to push you away, then that's his loss. Don't give up on him just yet.'

'I hope he gets his head straightened out. I really like him.'

'Then he's a lucky boy.'

She straightened up, uncomfortable with how close they'd become in such a short time. She knew so little about this man, and it was a good bet once he'd caught the Five he'd be gone.

'Do you ever look back and regret things you've done?' she asked wistfully.

Ori stared into the middle distance before he answered. 'No,' he said, shaking his head. 'I don't have that luxury.'

As he rose, he looked down at her with a sad smile. 'And neither do you, Riley Blackthorne.'

In Ori's experience it was quite easy to find a demon, especially the ones that ate everything. All you had to do was pitch your ears towards the snarls and home in. He'd already found two of the older, more feral ones, but they hadn't been helpful. He'd left their corpses in the murky dark of this place the trappers called Demon Central.

Now he'd found another, a younger one who hadn't developed its second row of teeth yet. It was rounder, more bulky. It almost looked harmless, but in a few months it'd thin down and become a dedicated killing machine.

It had just caught itself a large rat. The rodent's head was already gone, but this fiend, unlike most of its kind, wasn't a gobbler. It seemed to be savouring the meal.

Ori moved quietly to a position about five feet from the thing. Then he let it see his true form, wings, sword and all.

It shrieked and jumped back in terror, clutching its bloodied meal to its chest. Its black hair stuck out like a porcupine. After a quick look around, it realized it had no place to run.

'Hellspawn,' Ori said, 'you know what I am.' There was a whine of fear from the abomination. 'And you know what I want.'

The demon began to shiver. Gastro-Fiends, or Threes

as the trappers so quaintly called them, weren't very intelligent, all their brains geared towards acquiring food. This one had enough smarts to know that if it pointed Ori in the direction of another demon that might mean its death. Especially when the other fiend was a weather worker capable of killing a master trapper.

'Where is the rogue demon called Astaring?' Ori demanded.

The fiend's face scrunched up in what passed for thought, then it cautiously extended the rat towards him. A bribe for its life, perhaps?

Ori sighed and shook his head. 'No. That is not what I want.' He took a menacing step forward. It got the reaction he'd hoped for – the Hellspawn cowered in fear.

'Tell me, pitiful one,' he ordered, putting power behind the command.

The creature began to babble in Hellspeak. Most of what it said was a list of complaints about how badly it was treated by the other demons, but at the very end it gave Ori a glimmer of information.

'Thank you. Enjoy your meal.' Finally he had a lead on the rogue that had killed Master Blackthorne. Ori turned on a heel and hiked down the alley. He knew not to check on the Gastro-Fiend – it would be down the closest hole by now.

A short time later, he stood in the middle of a street that looked like a war zone. It wasn't his doing, at least not yet. His quarry was close. He sensed the thing. Felt its power.

'Show yourself, Astaring,' he shouted.

A second later he leaped upward to avoid the rush of brilliant flames that blew out of the ground at his feet. He twisted in the air, spreading his wings, sword ready for battle. The flames vanished, leaving a crater rimmed with smoking asphalt. If he had been a few seconds slower, he'd have been a pile of smoking feathers.

'You're a cunning one,' he said. 'Now stop hiding like a silly child.'

A laugh cut through the air, cold and cruel, but the demon did not materialize. 'The War comes, Divine,' it said. 'On whose side will you be?'

Then the fiend was gone, its power fading away in the night air. Ori hovered in the air, studying his surroundings, trying to determine if it was a trick.

'Coward,' he grumbled.

He floated downward, tucking his wings behind him as his feet landed. Demons always spoke of war. They craved it. Like they had a chance of winning against Heaven.

But this time the demon spoke the truth. 'The war comes.'

Chapter Sixteen

The only reason Beck was out this early in the morning was sitting in the booth near the restaurant's front windows. At 7 a.m. the red-haired reporter had called him and then sweetly, but firmly, refused to let him off the hook. The interview just had to happen *this morning*. Beck had finally agreed so he could get this woman off his back.

When the reporter saw him, she smiled warmly. 'Good morning, Mr Beck.' She had an accent he couldn't place. Something foreign, maybe French or Italian.

'Ma'am,' he said, sliding into the booth across from her. He'd shaved and showered and put on the best work clothes he owned, but he was still uncomfortable. There was no good reason for him to be talking to this lady, especially after the wake last night. He'd not got drunk, but it'd been close, and now his body was making him pay for that bar tab.

The reporter daintily offered a manicured hand across the table. 'I am Justine Armando,' she said. 'I wish to speak with you about Atlanta and her demons.'

Bottomless emerald eyes held his gaze.

He gently shook the hand and forced himself to relax. This babe was a knockout, and the way she said *deemons* was cute. She looked like a model, not a reporter, but then that probably worked in her favour. Her light olive skin glowed in the morning light streaming in through the windows, which also set fire to the gold highlights in her hair. It made him wonder if she'd chosen that location on purpose. He also noted she wasn't wearing a wedding ring.

As the waitress poured him a cup of coffee, Beck pulled his head back to business. 'What can I do for ya, ma'am?'

'Justine, please. I am not old and grey-haired,' she said, her green eyes twinkling.

'All right, then, Justine. What is it ya wanna know?'

'I want to tell the story of an Atlanta demon trapper. Your Master Stewart said you were one of the best – that is why I asked to interview you.'

She was shovelling the crap pretty high. He took another slug of coffee to buy time to sift through the mixed signals he was receiving. Usually if you didn't talk the other person would fill in the silence and you'd learn something. The reporter was a pro: she sipped her tea and waited him out.

'Who do ya write for?' he asked.

'I am freelance. I sell my stories to newspapers all over the world,' she said.

'Must be a nice job.'

'It has its benefits,' she replied, flicking a switch on a

sleek microrecorder that sat near a notebook and a gold pen. Then she smiled, pointing at the recorder. 'Shall we begin?'

'Yes, ma'am.' *Let's get this done.* Not that he minded the scenery.

'I have researched you, Denver Beck,' Justine said. 'You were born in Sadlersville, Georgia, moved to Atlanta and then you were in the military. You were awarded medals for bravery in Afghanistan.'

'Yes, ma'am.' That was as far as he was going on *that* topic.

'Why did you want to become a trapper?' she asked.

'Because of Paul Blackthorne,' Beck replied. 'He gave me a future.' He knew that sounded hokey, but it was the truth.

'He died recently. You were with him when that happened,' the reporter said, her voice softer now. 'I understand that his corpse has been reanimated and that he was at the Tabernacle the night the demons attacked.'

'Yes, ma'am.'

She put down her pen and gave him a pleading look. 'I really need more than just a *yes, ma'am*, Mr Beck.'

'Just Beck. That's what folks call me.'

'Well, then, *Just* Beck . . .'

He opened his mouth to tell her she'd gotten it wrong, but then saw the corners of her mouth curve up in a smile. She was pulling his chain.

'You're messin' with me,' he said.

'I am. So why don't you tell me what happened that night at the Tabernacle and I will tell the world.'

'I think they already know.'

'But they haven't heard *your* story,' she said, leaning across the table. 'I know it's a good one.'

'Why?' he asked, frowning.

'I can tell by looking at you. You are not like the others.'

She's right about that. He got another cup of coffee and told her what he remembered about the demon attack, leaving out a few details the world just didn't need to know. She listened intently, taking notes. Only when he'd finished did she put more questions to him.

'How did the demons break through the Holy Water ward?'

'I think it was because there were too many of them.'

She seemed to accept that explanation. 'Do you believe in Armageddon, Beck?' she asked.

'I would have said no a few days ago, but after I saw those angels . . .'

'Then they were really there.' At his puzzled look, she added, 'The photographs and videos don't show them in detail, only a ring of intense light.'

'I was inside that light. They were angels all right.'

Justine seemed to shift mental gears. 'Do you believe the hunters will have better luck subduing the demons?'

'I'm not sure,' he said cautiously, knowing this would be going on the record. 'We know the city better than they do and, from what I hear, once the hunters arrive more demons will show up.'

'More work for you,' she said.

He shook his head. 'They'll cut us out of the picture. We're the locals, the hicks. We don't have the money or the flash equipment.'

'However, you are permitted to kill demons in certain circumstances.' He nodded. 'Is this one?'

'Hell, yes.' They hadn't received the official word from the National Guild, but he didn't care. Everything from a Pyro-Fiend on up was fair game. If he could trap it, fine. If it fought back, it was toast. He'd get paid either way.

'I have an appointment with the mayor in an hour,' she explained. 'I want to hear his side of all this and then I will follow up with you if I have more questions.'

Beck grunted. 'The mayor's all talk, no sense.'

Justine grinned, revealing perfect white teeth. 'May I quote you on that?'

'Better not,' he said, shaking his head. He'd let his mouth get the best of him.

The woman pushed a business card across the table. Her name was written in a flowing script and there was a cellphone number beneath it. 'Keep in touch, Beck. I'm sure I will have more questions.'

He looked into those deep green eyes and decided this hadn't been as bad as he'd thought. Actually, a pretty nice way to start his day. 'I'll do that, Justine.'

As she strolled out of the restaurant, he put the card

in his jacket pocket and signalled for a refill on the java.

'Not bad at all.'

To keep her mind off Simon and his infantile behaviour, Riley dug into the pile of bills that seemed to have grown overnight. Paying bills was like doing laundry and grocery shopping – never-ending. With Beck's help the rent had been paid, along with a few of the other monthly debts, but she would run short of cash again in about a week. That made her eyes stray to the trapping bag by the door. It still had the claw marks from her last solo adventure.

'Been there. Done that,' Riley grumbled, scratching the now healed demon wounds through her jeans. Instead, she made a list of the debts so she could prioritize them. She was nearly finished when a series of knocks echoed throughout the apartment. It was exactly noon.

When she opened the door, Beck held up a large bag from Mama Z's, his favourite barbecue joint. 'Brought ya lunch, as promised,' he said.

Her nose homed in on the piquant scent of spices. 'Yum,' she murmured, her mouth watering instantly.

As Riley set the table, she waited for his usual Spanish Inquisition, in particular, 'Have ya called your aunt in Fargo yet?' But none of that happened. Instead he draped his leather jacket over the couch and headed for the bathroom. Water ran, then he was back and removing the food from the bag, placing the sandwiches and the coleslaw on the plates she'd pulled from the cupboard.

He noticed the stack of bills. 'How ya doin' for money?'

Riley rolled her eyes. 'I paid the cellphone bill, the utilities and the rent. There's more bills due in about a week and I'll be short by then. Peter knows a place where I can sell a few of my old CDs for cash.'

Beck nodded and then fell on his sandwich like he'd not eaten breakfast.

Maybe he hadn't. 'How late did you stay last night?' she asked.

'Until about one. I had to get up early and talk to some reporter.'

'How did that go?'

'It went,' he replied.

Rather than ruin what was going to be a good meal with talk that she might not like, she focused on her own sandwich, savouring the amazing taste. Mama Z's had the best barbecue in the world. Mid-lunch her cellphone pinged in response to a new text. She wiped off her hands and checked it. Then grinned.

'Yes!' she crowed. 'Simon's at home now. They cut him loose from the hospital.'

'That's good news,' Beck said. 'He sure healed quick.'

'On the outside, at least.'

Her visitor gave a huff of understanding. 'Ya see him last night?' At her nod, he added, 'How'd that go?'

'It went,' she said, parroting his words about the reporter.

'Not good?' She shook her head. 'Sorry.' He cleaned his mouth with a napkin, crumpled it up and dropped it in the middle of the plate. 'I'm hopin' the food was a fair enough bribe for this.'

Here it comes. He's going to use the meal to guilt me – I just know it.

'Stewart wants me to fill out the papers for the National Guild.' At her puzzled look, Beck added, 'They're for the dead trappers so their families can get their life insurance.'

'Oh.' Now it made sense why he didn't want to do these alone.

After she'd cleared the table, Riley dropped back into her chair. Beck placed a thick pile of manila folders in front of her. Each one had a name written in block letters.

'How many pages are there to these things?' she asked.

'The form's only got two. The rest is their files.' She studied the first folder and deemed it a blessing the name wasn't one she recognized.

The form was pretty straightforward: a notification to the National Demon Trappers Guild that one of their members had shuffled off this mortal coil and a request to release insurance funds to the listed beneficiary or beneficiaries. Riley opened the folder and found a picture of the deceased. It had been taken when he joined the Guild, which according to the paperwork was six years earlier. She didn't know the man.

Her visitor opened a folder and issued a tortured sigh.

He'd know these guys: probably trapped with some of them, drank with all of them at one time or another.

She let her eyes skim over the paper in front of her. Russell Brody was forty-three, just about her dad's age when he died. He had a wife and two children. Riley forced herself to pick up the pen and begin filling in the form, though it was almost physically painful. His family needed the money and someone had to do this. She moved from section to section entering name, address, social security number, birth date, rank in the Guild, membership number and then the hardest part: how he'd died.

'Ah, what do I put for cause of death?' she asked.

'Hellspawn,' Beck replied. 'They'll add the coroner's report when they send it in, so you don't need to do more than that.'

'Hellspawn,' she said, filling in the blank. It seemed too black and white for her liking.

After she'd completed the first one, she took the next folder and opened it. She didn't know this trapper either. The same thing happened with the next two files. *He did this on purpose.* She thought to thank him, but he might not take it right.

When she'd finished her fifth one, she set it aside and stretched. Beck was still working on his second form, hunched over the paperwork like a gnome. When he wrote a word, he did it slowly, forming each letter with a lot of effort. Like he was having to think really hard.

'You go much slower and I'll end up doing all these,' she said, not pleased at the thought.

'I'm going as fast as I can,' he shot back.

'Fooled me.'

His eyes rose to meet hers and flashed in defiance. 'I'm not good at this, OK? But don't ya dare say I'm dumb.'

Where did that come from?

Beck dropped the pen on the table. 'Sorry. I'm tired and I'm not good company today.'

Riley resisted the temptation to tell him he wasn't good company on most days.

'So what hot button did I push?' she asked, wanting to know for the future.

Beck winced. 'I don't read or write good. Never had anyone show me, not at home at least. Teachers tried, but they couldn't do much because I wouldn't listen to 'em.'

'You listened to my dad.'

'He knew how to teach me. None of the others could.'

It slowly dawned on her why he'd asked for her help. 'Stewart doesn't know about this, does he?'

'No,' Beck said, shaking his head. 'I don't dare tell him, not if I wanna make master trapper. That's why I came here.'

He'd put his inflated guy ego on the line, trusting she'd not make fun of him. That made Riley feel really good inside.

'That's why you don't send text messages, isn't it?'

'Yup.' Beck looked down at the form in front of him.

'I'm better than I used to be,' he said. 'The Army helped me a lot. It just doesn't come easy for me.'

'You get around town without any hassles. I've seen you do it.'

'I know the city,' he said, his eyes meeting hers now. 'I don't have to read the street signs to get where I need to go. It's when I'm doin' somethin' new I get into trouble.'

'Like these forms.' A nod. 'You've been doing OK,' Riley said encouragingly. 'Your writing's a lot neater than most guys, and you're getting the stuff on the right lines.'

'I watched ya so I know where it goes.'

She didn't dare pity him. That would make him furious.

Riley spread her hands. 'Hey, I had it lucky. Both parents were teachers. It was hardwired in.'

'I had a . . . ' He stopped short, but Riley knew what he was thinking.

A drunken mom who didn't care how you turned out.

'Do you read books?'

'Some of the kid ones,' he said. 'I get 'em from the library, that way folks don't know what I'm readin'.'

So nobody will make fun of you. 'How did you get through the Trappers Manual?' she asked, intrigued.

Embarrassment formed on his face. 'I didn't. Your daddy read it to me.'

Which meant all those hours Paul Blackthorne had spent with Beck weren't just about trapping demons or hanging together. *My dad was teaching him to read and write.*

She'd always loved her father, but now she loved him even more.

'How did you pass the journeyman exam?' she asked.

'I didn't cheat,' Beck said, instantly defiant.

'Hello?' she said, rapping her knuckles on the table. 'Did I say that?'

He half shrugged. 'I knew all the answers. I just couldn't read the questions that good, so Paul had me learn 'em in order.'

Which was OK since they gave the test questions out in advance to help increase the odds the apprentice might actually pass.

'I couldn't do that,' she admitted.

'What?'

'Memorize all the questions. That would be way hard. You might not be able to read and write that well, but you're smart in other ways.'

'Not sure of that.'

I am. That's why her father had gone to such effort. *Now it's my turn.*

A thought twitched in her brain. 'Do you have a computer?' she quizzed. A nod came her way. 'My buddy Peter has a program that takes text and makes it into speech. You could listen to stuff off the Web and read along. Newspaper articles and things like that.'

'That sounds cool. Is it really expensive?'

'I don't think so. I'll ask him about it.' Beck instantly tensed. 'Without telling him why I want to know.'

'Thanks.' He looked down at the form and then back up again. 'I mean it.'

The next folder in the stack was Ethan's. She took it.

'I'll do that if ya want me to,' her companion offered.

Riley shook her head, feeling the prickle of tears. She flipped it open and studied the apprentice's picture. He was so young and now he was gone. If things had been different, Beck would be filling out Simon's sheet. Maybe even hers. She went to the bathroom to hunt up tissues, wiped her eyes and returned to the table.

Beck dropped another file into the completed stack. 'Only a few more,' he said. She could tell this was hurting him as much as it was her.

Riley nodded and returned to the work. It wasn't until near the end of the stack that she actually read the fine print on the second page of the claim form. Under the name of the beneficiary was a place for a signature and an address, so the cheque could be sent directly to them.

'Beck?'

'Hummm?' he said, not looking up as he painstakingly formed a letter.

'Why didn't I have to sign a form for my dad?'

He kept his eyes down, but he wasn't writing any longer.

'Beck?'

He set the pen down deliberately and leaned back in the kitchen chair, face pensive. 'I signed it.'

'Why?'

'Because the money comes to me.'

'I'm not my dad's beneficiary?' she asked, totally side-swiped.

'If Paul left ya the money, the debt collectors might take it. With it comin' to me, they can't touch it. Don't worry, I'll have Fireman Jack figure out how to get it to ya.'

'Why should you? It's your money. You can buy yourself a new truck with it. Nobody could say a thing.'

Beck's face twisted in hurt. 'How can ya think I'd—'

'I don't what to think any more. Nothing is like I thought it would be. I figured I'd get my licence and then Dad and I would be together all the time and – '

She spun out of her chair and found herself near the big window, the one overlooking the parking lot. Below, someone was lugging groceries towards the entrance. It was proving difficult as their poodle wanted to anoint every car tyre it passed.

Beck was right behind her now. 'I won't keep any of that money, girl. It's yours. Your daddy wanted it this way, I swear.'

'He didn't trust me.'

'No, he didn't trust the debt collectors. He didn't want ya to lose the only thing he could leave behind.'

Beck hesitantly put his arm round her shoulder and drew her close. She could feel him shaking. 'I won't let ya starve,' he whispered. 'I'll do whatever it takes.'

They stood there for a few minutes, just looking out of

the window, neither of them talking. Finally, Beck pulled away and returned to the table and the paperwork. Riley forced herself to join him and they worked through the remainder of the files in silence.

Once they were done, he placed the files into his duffel bag, picked up his jacket and offered his thanks. Riley locked the door behind him, feeling she really needed to say something, but wasn't sure what.

It wasn't until later that she found the thick white envelope tucked underneath the pile of bills. The envelope was stuffed with twenties and she counted them into one-hundred-dollar stacks. There were ten.

One thousand dollars.

Beck must have put it there when she'd gone in search of the tissues. Riley bowed her head in despair. She'd practically accused him of stealing her money and all the while that envelope had been sitting there. He'd never said a thing.

She remembered him standing at the window, deep in thought. How defensive he'd become because he could barely read and write. How her father had trusted him to do the right thing.

Denver Beck was a hard guy to like, and even harder to understand. One thing was clear – his word was golden.

Why can't I accept that?

Chapter Seventeen

'What is it about this place?' Riley grumbled as she drove past Oakland Cemetery and then cut down one of the side streets in search of a parking place. 'Why do I spend most of my life here?' The universe had no answer for her, so she kept driving up and down the streets. This field trip would be her first day back in class after the Tabernacle disaster. Her classmates would want to know what it was really like, badger her with questions, because she'd been there when it all happened.

It wasn't like talking about it made it go away. It was just the opposite – the hellish images were too fresh in her mind, searing deeper every time she thought about them. If she could hold her classmates off today, maybe something else would have caught their interest by the next time. *As long as it has nothing to do with me.*

The schools made these mandatory historical education trips three times a year, dividing up the classes across different days. There'd probably be two hundred kids here today and the school district didn't bother with buses any more. Though the classes were designed to arrive at thirty-minute intervals, that hadn't lightened the number of bodies tromping towards Oakland's entrance like a herd of well-dressed zombies.

Riley finally found a place to park three blocks from the cemetery. As she approached the brick archway that led into the graveyard, a familiar face caught her notice. 'Peter?' she murmured. Her best friend stood by the main gate, scanning the knots of students as they passed by. He brightened up the moment he spied her, and waved.

'Hey!' he said as she joined him. 'I was worried you'd blow this off.'

'No way. Mrs Haggerty will do roll-call and I don't need detention.'

He shoved a package at her. 'A reprint of your father's Holy Water research. I read it this time. Your dad was amazing.'

'Yeah, he was,' she said, taking the package. 'I think I might have a lead.' She told him about the unmarked truck that had collected the recycled Holy Water bottles. 'Maybe if I follow those guys around I might be able to figure out who's stealing the bottles and refilling them.'

'Sounds like a plan,' Peter said, nodding his approval. 'Let me know if you need someone to ride shotgun.'

Cool. 'It's a deal.' They passed underneath the brick arch into the cemetery. 'I thought you were supposed to be here tomorrow.'

'I've been transferred to your class,' Peter replied, grinning.

Riley stumbled to a halt and a student behind her

swore when he almost ran into her. 'Sorry,' she said, then turned back to her friend. 'Do you mean that you hack—'

Peter clapped a hand over her mouth. 'As I was about to say, I'm happy to report that our educational overlords have decided I shall be in your class.' He lowered his hand and winked. 'Imagine my surprise.'

Surprise. Right. Peter had managed to hack the computer system that housed the student data and set up a transfer. If he was caught, he'd be expelled, exiled to darkest Illinois with his unglued mother.

'Are you insane?'

'Of course. It wasn't that hard, not once I figured out I had to transfer two or three others at the same time to cover my tracks. It's all about camouflage.'

'You moved other people to our class?'

'Sure did.' He smiled, clearly pleased with himself. 'Easier than I'd thought, actually.'

'But –'

Someone stepped in front of them on the road, blocking their way.

Oh, jeez. As if life wasn't absurd enough, the obstruction was her class's vampire wannabe, the kid with the jet-black hair and the alabaster skin. Today he had on a black frock coat and a blood-red shirt with decorative lace at the collar. A cameo sat at his neckline. The face on the cameo sported fangs.

You've got to be kidding.

'You live,' he lisped, glaring at Riley, his dark eyebrows

furrowed. The fake pointed canines were definitely causing the speech impediment.

'Yeah, I'm alive. And your point is?' she asked, annoyed at the interruption.

'We will not be thhhwarted,' he replied. The lisp really came through this time, along with some spit.

Gross. 'Can you move, please?'

The fake vamp didn't budge, but continued to glower and display his plastic teeth. Riley strode round him, shaking her head.

As they moved further down the road, Peter asked, 'Ah, what was that?'

'That is our vamp wannabe. He drinks red soda and uses the royal *we* all the time. He's harmless. Just ignore him.'

Peter looked over into the graveyard. 'Kind of hard to do,' he said, pointing.

The kid darted among the graves, skulking behind trees and the larger monuments. Every now and then he'd leer out from behind a stone obelisk or angel.

'What's he got against you?' her friend asked.

'He thinks I hunt vampires. I told him I only trap demons, but he doesn't believe me. He has this need-to-be-a-victim thing going on.'

Peter gave her a confused look. 'Ah, correct me if I'm wrong, but that's so not a vamp's operating system, you know? They don't do victim.'

'Tell him that.'

'So what's his name?'

Riley shrugged. 'I was afraid to ask.'

Out of the corner of her eye she saw her vamp stalker trip over a headstone and do a total face plant in the dirt, fake teeth and all.

Why me?

There'd been no communication from Simon during the time she and Peter had traipsed all over Oakland Cemetery, cataloguing graves for their class assignment. Once that was completed, Riley headed for her boyfriend's place. Now, as she stood at the kerb in front of the Adler family home, she adjusted her hair and clothes for what had to be the fifth time. At least the black denim jacket she'd found at the back of her closet fitted. She'd forgotten it was there until the blue one had been fried, sliced and peed on. Black would hide the stains better.

The house was big, two-storey and covered in pale peach stucco. Curtains hung at every window and there were flowerpots full of pansies on the steps that led to the front door. This should not be a big deal, but it was. It would be the first time she'd been in their house, the first time she'd seen Simon since he'd left the hospital. Would he be better now that he was home?

He just has to be. She visualized what Simon had been like before the fire, before he'd been so badly hurt. The warm smile, the loving kisses. That was what she wanted more than anything.

Mrs Adler opened the door wearing a pair of sweat-pants and a worn Bon Jovi T-shirt. Her blonde hair was in a ponytail and sweat glistened on her forehead. Riley had managed to catch her mid-exercise regime.

'Come to see the fair-haired boy?' Mrs Adler asked.

'If it's OK.'

'Sure. He's had a few visitors, but he certainly needs the company.' She waved Riley into the house. The entryway was paved in ceramic tile and there were family photos along both walls. With a family as numerous as the Adlers, they'd need all the wall space they could get.

Riley followed the woman through what looked to be a living room into a small room at the back of the house. The shades were drawn giving the space a dungeon-like gloom. There was a flat-screen television and the kind of chairs you sink into and never come out of again. Simon was on the leather couch.

'You've got a guest,' his mom called out. She left Riley standing at the door and headed towards the front of the house.

Riley drifted to the couch and sat next to her boyfriend, putting her messenger bag on the floor. Simon was in sweatpants and a long-sleeve T-shirt. The wooden cross he always wore was missing. Had he lost it at the Tabernacle? In his hands was the rosary and he twisted it back and forth like a set of worry beads.

'Riley.' The way he said the name didn't convey any meaning. No 'gee, I'm glad you're here' or anything personal. It was flat, just a word.

'So how are you doing?' she asked, trying to fathom where his head was at the moment. If he was in the same crappy mood as the previous night, there was little she could do for him.

'I'm home.' Again that flat tone, like it didn't matter.

Riley took hold of one of his hands and squeezed it. 'Simon, come on. What's going on in your head? Talk to me.'

His deep blue eyes met hers. 'Not sure what's going on.'

'Having trouble sleeping?' A nod. 'Nightmares?'

Simon seemed surprised she'd know that. 'I see the demons and the blood and feel the flames . . .' He kept rubbing one of the rosary beads between his fingers. 'My dad says they'll get better, that they're the mind's way of dealing with what happened.'

'He's right. How are your wounds?'

'Almost healed. The doctors don't know what to think of it. They've never seen anything like it.'

Bet they haven't. Not unless angels routinely make hospital calls.

Simon's hand gripped hers tighter, then released it. 'I knew I was dying. I could feel it. I wasn't afraid – I was just sad,' he said. 'I thought I'd never see you again.'

'Well, pretty soon you'll be healed and we'll go trap some of those demons. Teach them a lesson.'

She expected a PC version of 'Hell, yes, let's kick

some demon ass.' But there was no reply. Simon's fingers continued to worry his rosary as his blue eyes stared at nothing.

'You saved me,' she said. 'The demon came after you instead of me. I won't ever forget that.'

'I did everything right,' he retorted, frowning now. 'The demons should not have been able to cross the ward.'

'Of course you did it right. No one's blaming you.'

He wasn't listening. 'I put the Holy Water down in one direction, then repeated it in the other. There were no gaps. The demons should not have been able to get to us.'

'Father Harrison says there were too many of them, that they overwhelmed the ward.'

'No!' Simon replied, shaking his head vigorously. 'Demons cannot cross the power of God.'

'But you told me that Holy Water absorbs the evil. If there's too much . . .'

'When did I tell you that?' he asked, confused.

'When we were at the Holy Water vendor in the market.'

'No, that's not possible. If demons can destroy God's power, then what's the point?' he argued. 'We're doing His holy work and He let us be ripped to pieces.' He took a sudden breath as if a memory had just hit him full on. She knew what it was – the demon's claws ripping at him, the smell of its rancid breath in his face. The certain knowledge that he was going to die.

When Simon began to shiver, she tried to hold him

Forbidden

but he pushed her away. He ceased talking after that, refusing to meet her eyes. Not knowing what else to do, she dropped a kiss on his cheek and left him in the gloom. He had to find his own answers.

Just don't lose yourself when you do.

Chapter Eighteen

It took Riley less time than she'd expected to drive from Simon's house to the old theatre in Buckhead where the vendue was being held. By the time she arrived it was just after dark and the bright lights of the marquee had been easy to spot. She located a parking place in the lot just north of the building, sliding in next to a Mercedes with tinted windows. Then she just sat there trying to work up the courage to take this next step.

What if her father was here tonight? Could she handle seeing him again? It was one thing to say goodbye when he was lying in his coffin, but another to watch him wander around like he was still alive. He'd remembered her at the Tabernacle, but what if those memories were gone now? What if . . .

The keys made a harsh, jangling sound, her hands shaking as her heart rate accelerated. Her vision tunnelled as each breath became more difficult than the last.

Panic attack. She'd had them after her mother had died and thought she'd outgrown them. Riley forced herself to conjure up images of frolicking puppies and days at the beach, trying to think of anything but Simon, demons and her reanimated father. Then she began to sing to herself. It was just nonsense words because she couldn't remember any songs at the moment, but it seemed to work. Finally her heartbeat slowed and she could take a deep cleansing breath. When Riley looked down, her hands were no longer quaking.

'Let's not do that again, OK?' she mumbled, as if her body would actually listen to her for a change. 'It so doesn't help.'

As Riley pulled herself out of the car, she paused. Was Ori somewhere nearby? She let her eyes search the area and quickly spied him leaning against a shiny black motorcycle across the street, arms crossed over his broad chest. He gave her a nod in acknowledgement.

My own personal bodyguard. That rocks.

Which left Riley no excuse not to go to the vendue.

She sucked it up and headed for the front of the theatre. Mort was waiting for her clad in a necromancer's cloak, light brown, without his trademark fedora. The cloak halted just above the tops of his polished shoes and seemed to have an energy all its own, like magic was woven into the fabric. It made him look mystical, which she suspected was the desired effect.

'This isn't going to be easy for either of us,' he warned.

'I know. What if my dad's not here?' she asked.

'Then I'll ask around to see if anyone's heard who re-animated him. Just let me handle this.'

Riley hesitated. 'What's this like?' If it was like the

Deaders in the market, that wouldn't be so bad.

The summoner puzzled over the query for a moment. 'It's a cross between a fashion show, a Roman slave auction and a theatrical production.'

'You're kidding.'

'No. If you're a buyer, it's one big party. If you've lost someone recently, it's pure hell.'

Riley sucked in a deep breath. 'Does it involve hordes of man-eating demons?'

Mort looked surprised at the question, then shook his head.

'Then it's doable.'

The old theatre's marquee announced that the place was closed for a private event. *Private* seemed to be the key word. There was only one line to get in, marked by a pair of red velvet ropes like you'd find at one of the trendy Midtown bars. The two men at the door looked like bouncers.

A woman at the head of the line was waved away. When she protested, a third black-suited guy appeared at the doorway and herded her back in the direction of the parking lot. He held her arm tightly and as they walked he was saying something to her. The woman's eyes widened. She shook her head and then skittered off into the night, clearly frightened by whatever he'd whispered in her ear.

Riley shot a questioning look at her escort.

'She's probably looking for a loved one,' Mort

explained. 'The management can spot those a mile away.'

'How can they tell?'

'Her clothes weren't expensive and she seemed ill at ease.' He nodded towards the favoured ones in line. 'They think they own the world. That's the difference.'

Riley looked down at her black slacks and scuffed shoes. She'd worn the best she owned. 'Then why will they let me in?'

'Because you're with me,' he replied, though she heard uncertainty in his voice.

Apparently necros had no DNA for queuing because Mort didn't join the line, but walked right up to the door like he owned the place. The moment they saw him, the bouncers perked up. The heavier of the two beckoned them forward. There were grumbles from the well-dressed, but no one outwardly challenged them. Why annoy someone who could drop a magical cluster bomb on your head?

'Good evening, Summoner,' the heavier bouncer said politely. He eyed Riley. 'Your companion is . . . ?'

'An apprentice,' Mort replied. 'We're here on Society business.'

That was smooth. She *was* an apprentice, just not with the necromancers.

One of the man's bushy eyebrows ascended. He turned away, holding his hand to his ear, talking to someone through a tiny microphone. When the man turned back, he was all false congeniality. 'You are always welcome here, Advocate.'

'Thank you.'

The two heavies parted to allow Riley and her escort to pass through the shimmering curtain that divided the real world from the obscene. She let out a puff of air in relief once they were inside. It was matched by Mort's.

He didn't think they'd let me in.

It began to dawn on her the risk the summoner was taking on her behalf. Clearly bringing a Deader's daughter to one of these things wasn't business as usual, even though he was the Advocate.

'Thanks,' she murmured. He didn't seem to hear her.

The lobby wasn't full, but it felt that way and it took Riley a moment to realize why: every person in the room acted as if they were bigger, more important than their physical bodies. As if every ego took up space of its own. Older, immaculately dressed women stood near a portable bar, chatting to each other. They glistened in the overhead lights like aged fairies on a summer's night. It was the jewellery. It had such weight that on anyone else the bling would be wearing them.

The next group was younger women in their perky dresses, wedge sandals and cascading hair extensions. They sipped champagne from crystal glasses held in manicured hands and laughed in high tones. It was a safe bet they didn't have demon claw marks on their leg or have to worry if they'd be able to pay the gas bill this month. Why did they have it easy and she had to struggle for every dime? Why was she an orphan and they had everything? Nobody would dare steal one of these princesses' fathers. They would have professional vigil sitters and armed guards to ensure nothing happened.

Riley pushed aside the anger. It wouldn't do her any good and if she tried to tell one of the princesses how she felt, what it was like to lose her father to some necro – it would be a waste of time. She'd just drawn a different lot in life and no amount of envy was going to change that.

On the other side of the lobby a knot of men clustered together. They ranged in age from twenty- to sixty-something, from casually dressed to suit and tie. She heard words like *gross metric tonnage* and *FOB* being thrown around. To her surprise, a couple of the younger ones gave her the eye.

'How much money do you have to have to get into this place?' Riley whispered.

'More than you or I will ever see.'

Figures.

Mort beckoned her towards a set of highly polished wooden stairs where a plush red runner greeted their ascent as brass banisters and ornate crystal wall sconces led the way to the first level. He caught her elbow right before she reached the top stair.

'Don't do anything rash or we're both in big trouble.'

The moment they reached the first floor she realized why he'd delivered the warning. There were only summoners up here, their voluminous robes ranging from pale white to black. Most of them were male, though a few females were present. One of the women wore a carmine robe, which stuck out like a bright robin in a flock of dull pigeons.

A necro spied Mort, smiled and walked forward to greet him. The greeting died on the fellow's lips when he saw Riley.

'Sebastian, good to see you,' Mort said warmly, taking the last few steps as if he hadn't noticed the man's reaction. 'This is Riley Blackthorne.'

'Ah . . .' Sebastian shot a look at her and then back to Mort like he didn't know what to say. He was older than her companion, maybe in his late forties, with a gleaming bald patch at the top of his round head.

Riley deployed the charm. 'Nice to meet you, sir.'

Sebastian frowned, then shook his head. 'You really do like stepping on toes, my friend,' he said, addressing Mort.

'Riley has asked for the Society's help. As Advocate, I am obligated to assist her.'

'By bringing her *here*?' the man retorted. 'Are you mad?'

'Her father was illegally summoned,' Mort replied evenly. 'I think it's best we solve this quietly before some reporter gets hold of the story. The name Blackthorne *is* newsworthy at the moment.'

Sebastian's already pale complexion went a shade

lighter. 'But *he's* here tonight!' the man hissed. 'By all the stars, have you no sense? The Eldest will not tolerate this infraction.'

The pale and sweating necro had to be talking about Ozymandias, and this time there was no protective circle between Riley and that monster.

Ripples of goosebumps flooded across her forearms, followed by the sting of magic.

'Summoner Alexander?' a smooth voice enquired.

Mort turned stiffly and gave a low bow. 'Lord Ozymandias. How good to see you.'

A dry chuckled returned. 'Somehow I doubt that.'

Riley took a deep breath. She could cower or meet this obnoxious asshat head on. If he was the one who'd taken her dad, she wasn't going to let him do whatever he wanted just because he was the most powerful of the bodysnatchers.

Riley turned towards the necromancer who had terrorized her throughout her dad's vigil. Ozymandias was in his usual black cloak, but the oak staff was nowhere to be seen. That funky tattoo on his forehead gave off a faint sheen like it was radioactive. Now that she was so close, she could see his eyes were pale green with odd brown flecks.

He won't do anything here, not in front of the others. That was her edge.

She gave a nod in his direction, trying to keep her fear in check.

'Are you sober this evening, Miss Blackthorne, or can I expect a repeat performance of your juvenile belligerence?' he asked.

'No witchy wine tonight,' she said. 'Just the real me.'

'And no little witch to guard you. You are foolish.'

Mort cautiously cleared his throat. 'My lord, Miss Blackthorne is seeking her father.'

'I heard he was among the walking again.'

'Did you yank him out of his grave like you said you would?' Riley demanded.

A collective gasp came from those around them.

Oops.

Ozymandias was suddenly closer to her, though Riley could have sworn she hadn't seen him move. 'So ignorant.' The tattoo glowed brighter now. 'The Society would never allow you to become an apprentice. You're only fit for that collection of scum in the Guild.'

You . . . How dare he diss the trappers? All these necros did was rob graves and wear stupid robes. When she opened her mouth to reply, Mort's trembling hand on her arm cut her off.

'I think it is time for us to find our seats. By your leave, Lord Ozymandias.'

The High Lord of all things necromantic delivered a gracious nod, but in his eyes she saw contempt.

Wait until I'm a master, you jerk. I'll teach you some manners.

As they entered the theatre and walked down the

ramp, Mortimer grumbled, 'Which part of "Don't do any-thing rash" didn't you get?'

'No one disses the trappers, not even His Creepiness,' she retorted.

'Sometimes being humble keeps you alive.'

'He's not going to go after me here. Too many wit-nesses.'

'Who would say they never saw a thing.'

'You would.'

He eyed her. 'Not if I'm dead.'

The expression on Mort's face told her he was totally serious.

Riley was still seething when they reached their row, but at least her escort had removed his death grip on her arm. They'd no sooner sat in the wide, plush seats when a cocktail waitress in an extremely short dress and heels hurried up to them. Riley wondered how she got up and down the stairs without falling.

The waitress handed Mort a piece of paper. He glanced at it and then stuck it under his robe.

'Champagne? Canapés?' she asked in a cheery voice that sounded rehearsed.

'Ah, no, thank you,' Mort replied.

'What about you?' the woman asked Riley.

'No, thanks.'

Mort produced a ten-dollar bill and dropped it on her tray. 'We're good. You won't need to check on us again.'

'OK, thanks!' She headed off.

Riley took the opportunity to look around. No one was sitting near them, and even Mort's friend Sebastian was pointedly keeping his distance. She didn't bother to try to locate Ozymandias. He was here: those goosebumps were still in place.

There was the sound of someone settling in a seat behind them: it was the woman in the carmine robe. She had wavy dark hair that touched her shoulders and laugh lines around her eyes. She looked like the kind who could tell a really good joke and not screw up the punchline.

The necro leaned forward and placed her palms on Mort's shoulders. 'You brought a reanimate's daughter to the vendue? I'm impressed. So what do you do for an encore?'

Mort noticeably relaxed. 'Don't know yet.' He allowed himself a pleased smile, then seemed to remember they weren't alone. 'Riley, this is Lady Torin, one of our senior summoners.'

'Glad to meet you,' the woman replied. 'Sorry to hear about your father. I'm hoping Mortimer can find him for you.'

Riley studied the woman. She didn't seem to be blowing smoke just to be polite. The way her hands were resting on Mort's shoulders indicated she was fond of him. Or was she giving him her blessing in some way, telling the other summoners that she approved of Mort's actions and that screwing with him meant crossing her?

'Thank you,' Riley said. *No matter what you're up to.*

'Just be very careful, dear Mortimer. You're treading into uncharted waters.'

Lady Torin leaned back in her seat, rearranging her cloak. When the cocktail waitress appeared at her elbow, she put in an order for a Scotch, neat.

'Do all the necros come to this thing?' Riley whispered to her companion.

'Don't call us that!' Mort pleaded. 'At least not where *they* can hear you. You don't want one of us to download a spell on you, trust me.'

'OK, then the same question but with summoners.'

Mort shook his head. 'You are only required to attend if you have a reanimate in the vendue.'

'Then she . . .' Riley began, aware that the *she* in question was probably hearing every word.

'Has someone on offer. Lady Torin doesn't like this any more than I do,' Mort replied.

'How do you get to become a lord or lady in your Society?'

'The rank is awarded according to magical ability.'

Which didn't tell her much. *Probably the point.* Trappers were equally cautious about discussing their trade. Since Mort and Riley were located in the front row of the balcony, she took the opportunity to peer over the wood rail into the rows below. There weren't any. Instead it looked more like a club than a theatre. Tables sat at discreet intervals from each other, covered in fine white tablecloths and in the centre of each one was an iced bottle of champagne. A tuxedoed waiter approached one table and replaced an empty bottle with a fresh one.

'Champagne?' When Riley glowered at Mort, he had the good sense to look embarrassed.

'The auctioneers know how to cater to those who have money,' he explained. 'Each auction has a theme. Tonight it's . . . gothic. Better than the last time. That was a salute to Hawaii. The luau was over the top.'

Riley groaned under her breath. *This better not be totally stupid or I'm out of here.*

The overhead lights flicked on and off a few times and then darkened causing the crowd noise to die down like this was some popular Broadway show. A single spotlight appeared on stage showcasing a man in a tuxedo and a black satin cape.

'Good evening, ladies and gentlemen,' he said in a deep, resonant voice, employing the same false smile as the waitress. 'Welcome to our second vendue of the new year.'

He walked a few paces, the spotlight following him. 'Tonight we have a lovely collection on view. Do not hesitate to enjoy the refreshments and remember that a small portion of tonight's sales will be sent to this month's designated charity. And now, without further delay, the show,' he said, his hand gesturing towards the centre of the stage.

The spotlight faded to nothing as the curtain rose with

a soft mechanical whir. The low, ominous tones of a pipe organ filled the space, causing Riley's back teeth to hum. As her eyes adjusted, other details began to reveal themselves. A full moon hung over the stage like a huge silver eye. The skeletal branches of a gnarled oak tree draped over tombstones that rose out of a white fog sea like weathered teeth. A wolf howled and Riley shivered at the sound.

Mort sighed deeply. 'I'm sorry you're going to see this,' he said.

The fog parted in front of the largest tombstone as a man's head appeared like an oversized mushroom just above the stage floor. Bit by bit the rest of him rose until he was completely exposed. The guy was about her father's age and he held a skull in his right hand. His blinked his eyes rapidly in the bright lights. After an awkward pause he began to speak in a halting and raspy voice.

'Alas . . . poor Yorick.'

Mort groaned.

'I knew him . . . well . . .' the dead man intoned, misquoting Shakespeare, his forehead wrinkled in thought as if it was taking every brain cell to remember the words. 'A fellow of . . . of infinite, ah, jest. Ha! Ha!' Then he hoisted the skull up into the air and glanced nervously at the tables closest to him. Someone laughed and the poor guy heard it.

The master of ceremonies moved across the stage. 'This, ladies and gentlemen, is Herbert. In his previous life he worked for the Internal Revenue Service as an auditor. His knowledge of corporate tax matters is his biggest asset. If you wish to avoid tangling with Uncle Sam over a few million dollars, this is the reanimate for you.' Their host paused and then called out, 'Do I have a first bid?'

'Ten thousand,' someone shouted.

'Eleven,' another said immediately.

They are really buying this guy. Riley had known this moment would happen, but seeing it in person was too much. When her stomach rolled over, she gripped her abdomen with both hands.

'Restroom?' she pleaded.

Mort pointed and she fled up the stairs. She could still hear the bidding as she pushed through the door to the women's toilet.

'Eighteen thousand!'

Riley's stomach opted not to revolt, so she wet her face with cold water and let it air-dry. As she examined her face in the mirror a gruesome thought hit her.

How would they sell her father? *Own the city's most legendary demon trapper! Learn the secret mysteries of Hell.* Would they want him for his Civil War knowledge or maybe as a tutor to their kids?

There was a thrum of organ music and a clash of thunder. Applause followed. Herbert's auction was over. Riley made her way back to her seat, apologizing when she stepped on Mort's toes. The final sales price was displayed on the tombstone in bright red LEDs. Eighty-five thousand dollars.

There's always money to be made in death. The guy at the Deader tent had been right.

'So who gets all that?' she snarled. 'You guys?'

Mort shook his head. 'The family will receive eighty-five per cent, tax free.'

'They agreed to this? How could someone do that?'

'Herbert wanted it this way,' Lady Torin's frosty voice said from behind them. 'He wanted to ensure his wife and children had as much financial security as he could provide, even after his death.'

'That's what life insurance is for,' Riley retorted.

'Yes, but he wanted to go the extra mile. I just wish this could have been a private sale. Far more dignified.'

'So what happens in a year? He ends up in a dumpster?'

The necromancer moved so close Riley caught the scent of whisky. 'My people *do not* end up in dumpsters, Miss Blackthorne. My people are given all the respect they are due. Don't you dare accuse me of not caring – do you understand?'

Riley nodded numbly. 'Sorry. I'm . . .'

'You're not using your head or you wouldn't be challenging me like this.'

'Hey, why not? I already dissed Ozymandias. Why not make it a full sweep?'

What is it with my mouth tonight?

She tensed, waited for the searing blast of magic. Maybe she'd end up with a furry tail. It would be a good bet it wouldn't be the same colour as her hair.

Instead, there was a wry chuckle. 'You *do* like to live dangerously.'

The next reanimate was a young man just a few years older than Riley. He held a sword like he had no idea what to do with it and stomped around the stage misquoting more Shakespeare. He went for five thousand, sold for his gardening skills. By the time they reached the seventh Deader, Riley had begun to wish she was legal age. Anything with booze in it would be great right now.

Three more Deaders crossed the stage, all sold for their various talents. Riley fidgeted in impatience. 'Is my dad here?' she asked. She frowned when Mort shook his head. 'How do you know that?'

'The server showed me a list of those up for auction,' he replied.

'So why in the . . .' She counted slowly to five. 'Why did you make me sit through this?'

'Because you have to know what you're up against.'

The current offering, a middle-aged housewife whose rendition of a tune from *The Phantom of the Opera* had scarred Riley for life, went for considerably less. Thankfully the MC called an intermission.

'Now what?' Riley quizzed as she and Mort filed out of the balcony.

'Now is when I get to ask questions.'

Chapter Nineteen

The summoners didn't hang with the moneyed elite, but had their own reception room, complete with crustless sandwiches and tuxedoed servers toting silver trays loaded with drinks.

Mortimer made his way through the group, Riley trailing behind. She knew everyone was staring at her. She was easy to spot – other than the catering staff she was the only one not wearing a cloak.

Lenny walked up to them. 'Miss Riley,' he said. His usual pimp suit wasn't in sight, hidden by a light grey cloak. His cheeks were flushed red, probably because of the half-full cocktail glass in one hand and the empty one in the other. 'How goes it?'

Lenny was pretty harmless so chewing him out wasn't going to get her anywhere. Besides, he was friends with Beck. 'Not going that well, Lenny. It'd be better if I could find my dad.'

'Ah, I heard about that. Sorry, girl. I had three buyers lined up and you would have got the money. I warned you it could get nasty.'

You did. 'Any idea who took him?'

Lenny narrowed his eyes, then announced, a bit too loudly, that he needed to get his drink refilled. She watched him head for the bar.

'Better let me do the asking,' Mort counselled.

Riley had come to a few conclusions by herself. 'The guy who did this had a lot of power. That's not Lenny, right?'

'Right. To conjure up that sort of illusion requires something more than an entry-level summoner.'

'So where are you on the scale between newbie and Dark Lord?' she quizzed.

Her escort didn't reply, suddenly uncomfortable.

'Mortimer is about three-quarters of the way there,' Lady Torin said as she joined them. She held a plate full of cheese wedges and crackers. 'Of course, he won't admit that. He likes to appear harmless.'

Mort gave her a gracious nod and held her eyes a second longer than was needed. Was there something between these two? As if he realized he was showing more than he wanted, Mort headed towards another summoner, one who had made the mistake of getting caught with his hands full of food and drink and no place to run.

Riley turned her attention to the other necromancer. 'So how about you? How close are you to being Dark Lord?'

Torin's mouth twitched in a grin. 'I'm about seven-eighths of the way. Except in my case it would be Dark Lady.'

'And Ozymandias?'

Torin's eyes met hers. 'He doesn't even register on the scale any more.'

Whoa. 'Who do you think took my dad?' Riley asked.

'Someone Mortimer level or above,' the lady replied. 'That's his mistake, you see. He's asking questions of every summoner, rather than focusing on those at Theta level and up.'

'But one of those lower dudes might know something.'

'A lower-level summoner is not going to tattle on someone higher on the food chain.'

'Out of respect?' Riley asked, curious.

'Out of fear.' Torin finished demolishing the cracker.

Riley and the lady talked to five summoners before the lights flickered and it was time to go back into the theatre. With absolutely no results. Mort joined them and she could tell from the expression on his face he'd struck out too.

'You might as well go home,' he conceded. 'I'll talk to the others, but most of them are too scared to say anything.'

'Thanks anyway,' she said, her heart sinking. As Mort and Lady Torin began to converse in lowered voices, Riley tromped down the stairs, her mood as dark as a senior necro's cloak. Ozymandias stood near the front door, like he was waiting for her. There was no one else around except for the bouncers outside. The only way to get to her car was to pass by him.

She halted and stared up into his really weird eyes. 'If you took my dad, just tell me. I have to know where he is.'

The summoner regarded her solemnly. 'Stop hounding Mortimer to find your father. You're going to get him hurt if you keep interfering. Is that what you want?'

'No. I just want what's mine.'

Ozymandias raised a silvery eyebrow. 'As do I.' He swept back into the theatre, but the magic still danced across her skin. *How is that possible?*

Riley pushed her way out of the door, past the bouncers and into the night. In the parking lot the woman who'd been turned away looked over at her, forlorn, her hands full of tissues. Was this Herbert's wife? Was she regretting his decision to support their family by making the ultimate sacrifice?

Riley had just made it to her car when her cellphone chimed. It was Mort.

Wait for me. I have an idea.

After one particularly lengthy yawn, she saw the summoner hurrying in her direction, his cloak flapping behind him. When he joined her, he gave a wary look back the way he'd come.

'I hesitate to say this, but there is another way to find your father,' he said. 'It's risky, but it might be worth a try.'

A sharp tingle of hope shot through her. Riley straightened up. 'Go on.'

'A certain type of summoning spell will call forth your father's spirit,' Mort explained. 'If he appears, maybe he can tell you who took him and where he's located, providing he can reveal that information.'

Now we're getting somewhere. 'Can you do this spell?'

'I can . . .' he started, 'but I won't. It will put me on the wrong side of the Society and I'm pushing the envelope as it is.'

'What would they do to you?' she asked.

He sagged against her car, apparently not worried his cloak would get dusty. 'The Society doesn't solve its internal problems by kicking someone out. In my case, I'd probably be found dead, just an overly large pile of ashes. It's not like I'd get a slap on the wrist.'

'Oh.' That *was* serious. 'OK, who else can do this location thing?'

'Anyone who is a magical practitioner.' Their eyes met. 'Like a *witch*, for instance. But you didn't hear that from me.'

'Gee. I know one of those,' she said, grinning.

'I figured you might. Most trappers do.'

'So what keeps the Society from turning my friend to a pile of ashes if she gets in their face?'

'For all their New Age beads and incense, witches pack some serious power and they protect their own. The last magical war we had with them ended in a draw so we're not eager to repeat that mistake. There's still bad blood between us.'

Riley had seen that animosity first-hand when Ozymandias had threatened Ayden and the witch had returned the threat without batting an eye.

'OK, Mort, I got this covered,' she said. Mindful of the High Lord's warning, she added, 'You've done enough for me as it is.'

'Just be cautious,' he said. 'Whoever took your father isn't going to appreciate you nosing around, especially if it's done with witch magic. It could get really unpleasant.' He looked towards the theatre. 'And if it's Lord Ozymandias . . .' With that Mort trudged back to the building.

Now it was time for Riley to move the ball forward on her own. She sent a quick text to Ayden with the unusual request. Now she'd have to wait and see what the witch thought of the plan.

As Riley turned to open her car door she became aware of someone standing near her. A second before she realized it was Ori, she gave out a squeak of surprise. And then felt really dumb. 'Whoa, warn a girl, will you?' she complained.

A stunning white rose came her way. 'Will this serve as an apology?' he asked.

Riley stared at the offering. Why was he doing this? 'Where do you get these? They're way expensive.' She knew that because she'd bought one on the anniversary of her mom's death to place on the grave and they'd cost her two weeks' worth of hot chocolate purchases.

'I have my sources,' he replied.

She accepted it and inhaled its rich fragrance. It was just as amazing as the previous one.

'Where to next?' Ori asked, lounging against the car. 'Shopping? The coffee shop?'

All of that sounded good, but . . .'Time to go to the church, I guess.'

'No reason to go there. I'm watching over you.'

'You're just hoping the Five makes its move on me.'

'That, and I enjoy your company.'

Give this guy points for knowing the right thing to say. 'Thanks, but I am tired. It's been a long day.'

'Your call.' Ori straightened up. 'Mind if I ride with you?'

'What about your bike?'

'I'll come back for it.'

'Aren't you afraid someone will steal it?'

'No,' he said. 'No one will touch it.'

He seemed so sure, and Riley had no objections to the company. Ori waited until she'd unlocked the passenger side door and then slid into the car. She set the rose between them, careful not to damage any of the petals. Part of her felt guilty for accepting it – she *was* dating someone else – but it was so pretty and had the most intoxicating scent.

As she pulled on to the street, she looked over at him and frowned. 'Seat belt, dude.'

'I'm sure you're a safe driver,' he replied.

'Doesn't matter. The city wants money so the cops will

ticket you. And me, for letting you be in the car that way.'

Grumbling under his breath, Ori fumbled with the thing, then clicked it home.

'Don't you get tired of following me all over the place?' she asked, heading south into the city.

'No, you lead an interesting life. Today you went to class at a cemetery, visited your injured boyfriend and then came to the theatre and hung with a bunch of stuffy necromancers. That's not boring.'

'You *have* been following me.' *Everywhere.* It bordered on the creepy if she hadn't known he was trying to kill the Five. 'But I thought the Geo-Fiend would only come after me at night.'

'It's strongest then, yes, but I don't like to take chances.' He turned towards her. 'So what was it like, the summoner thing?'

Riley told him how awful it had been. How her dad wasn't there and how afraid she was of never finding him again. Tears blurred her eyes and she cursed under her breath. As she blinked them away, she felt his hand on her arm, warm through her jacket. He didn't say anything, but just his touch made her feel better. That's what she'd been wanting from Simon.

What is it about this guy? Why do I feel so completely different when I'm with him?

When Ori's hand retreated, she missed it immediately. Her passenger was frowning now and the temperature inside the car seemed to drop a degree. 'I thought I had a lead on the Five last night, but it didn't work out,' he admitted.

'What kind of lead?'

'I convinced a Gastro-Fiend to tell me where the Five is hiding. The silly thing tried to bribe me with a half-eaten rat. Absolutely pathetic.' He sighed. 'Unfortunately, someone else tipped off the Five and it disappeared before I could kill it.'

'Why would someone do that?' Riley asked, puzzled.

'Hell has its informers, just like Heaven.'

'So I'm still bait?' she said glumly.

'I'm afraid so.'

Chapter Twenty

Usually Beck slept in until at least noon after a night of trapping, but for two mornings in a row he'd had to crawl out of bed early. Too early by his way of thinking. Now, as he stood in front of the Atlanta City Hall, he muffled a yawn with the back of his hand, earning him a bemused look from the Scotsman. The bandage on the master's forehead was gone, replaced by a neat row of transparent strips across a healing wound. He was dressed in a colourful kilt, which seemed odd, but maybe there was a rule about what a master wore when you met the hunters. Beck had opted for a clean pair of jeans and a blue shirt, topped off with his leather jacket. He felt naked without his duffel bag but Stewart had insisted he leave it in the truck.

Where they stood gave them an excellent view of the street below. The street itself was clear, but the sidewalks on either side were jammed with people eager to get a look at the Vatican's boys. It reminded Beck of the day after the Tabernacle attack. Some of the same sign-wavers were back and a new group insisted that Atlanta was doomed because of the gays and the unbelievers. Another yawn overtook him and this one he couldn't stop.

'Late night?' Stewart asked.

'Trapped a Pyro near Lenox Station. It was setting dumpsters on fire.' He had tried to convince the fiend to tell him where to find that murdering Five. No luck. So he'd hauled the thing to Fireman Jack and sold it. At least that part of the evening was a success.

The master pointed to a large sign with bold letters and blood-red flames around the border. *Kill Every Demon. Make America Safe for Our Kids*. He shook his head in despair.

'What would happen if we *did* kill all the demons?' Beck asked. He knew that was impossible because Lucifer had an endless supply of the fiends. Still, it was something to think about.

'No demons and ya got no balance,' the master replied solemnly. 'I'll tell ya how it all works when yer ready ta become a master.'

'Another year then,' Beck replied. *At least.*

Stewart gave him a sideways glance. 'I'd say sooner.'

Before he could follow up on that comment, there was the sound of sirens in the distance. Beck perked up.

Stewart grunted. 'That'll be hunters. They do love a show.'

'So what's gonna happen here?'

'In front of the cameras they'll be all friendly-like,' the master replied. 'Behind the scenes it'll get dirty. The Vatican knows how ta pull strings with the best of them.

Comes with centuries of practice.'

'Ya sound like ya know them pretty well.'

'Aye, lad. My family's been trappin' fiends for over eight hundred years. The hunters are the reason for that.'

Beck looked over at him, confused. 'What?'

'It's a tale best told over whisky.' Stewart shifted his weight from one foot to the other. 'I want ya ta trap with Riley every chance ya get. Whilst I respect Master Harper, I'm not fond of his methods.'

'No way he's gonna let me work with her.'

'As long as he gets a cut of the money, he'll be happy.'

Beck doubted that, but decided not to argue the point. If they did trap together, he could keep a closer eye on Paul's daughter. Maybe keep her from getting hurt again. 'Yeah, I like that idea,' he said, but for an entirely different reason to the master's.

Sirens wailed and rose in intensity. The sound abruptly cut off as two police cars turned the corner on to Mitchell Street, lights flashing like they were leading a parade. Right behind them came four sleek vans followed, in turn, by a white limousine. The black vans were identical and displayed the papal coat of arms on the side doors.

'Where'd they get their rides?' Beck asked.

'Airlifted them in from New York City. Money isn't a problem for these folks, not like it is for us.'

The lead van halted in front of the building, the others quickly lining up behind it. Flashbulbs lit up as bystanders began to push against the barricades. Some were crying. The lead van's doors slid open and two men hopped out, one on each side of the vehicle. Both were clad in black military fatigues and combat boots and they carried specially modified assault rifles. The men scanned their surroundings, then beckoned to their comrades. Five more men exited the van, remaining on alert. Once the first vehicle was empty, the third van in line followed the same drill, then the fourth.

'Smart,' Beck said, impressed. These guys weren't mugging for the cameras, but eying the terrain for potential trouble, human or demonic. They were a mixed lot – white, black, Asian and Latino. One thing was for sure: they'd all be Roman Catholic. That was a job requirement.

Only when the area was deemed secure did the side door on the second van slide open. A man stepped out. He was taller than Beck, six foot two or so, with a Mediterranean complexion and a goatee. Inky black hair ended at his collar. He was wearing a dark navy turtleneck with epaulettes, navy trousers and combat boots, armed with a pistol at his waist. Over his left breast was the demon hunters' emblem – Saint George slaying the dragon.

'Head dude?' Beck asked.

'Aye. That's Elias Salvatore, the team's captain,' Stewart replied. 'He's thirty-two, the youngest leader they've ever had.' Another man hopped out of the van. 'That's Lieutenant Maarten Amundson, his second-in-command.'

Beck scrutinized the hunter, watching his body

language. He was older, beefier than his superior. 'He doesn't like his captain. Not one bit.'

'How can ya tell?' Stewart asked, intrigued.

'The way he looks at him. It isn't respect – it's something else.'

The master trapper nodded his approval at the assessment. 'Amundson figured he'd be top dog by now and he's none too happy about Salvatore takin' his job. What else are ya seein', lad?'

'Their men are well trained. They're on alert, like they expect to be ambushed. Can't think that's just for the cameras.'

'It's not. They were attacked in Paris by a pair of Archdemons a few years back. Got five of them dead and they've not forgotten that humiliation. They're tired too. It's not jet lag, but somethin' deeper here. They're bein' pushed too hard, I think.'

The master was right: Beck could see it in how the hunters held themselves. They were still deadly, but not totally in peak condition.

'If they were trappers, I'd say they need some R & R. Get drunk, get laid, get their attitudes adjusted,' he said.

Stewart chuckled. 'Well, that's not gonna happen and the reason is in that limo.'

Beck hadn't noticed the vehicle until the master pointed it out. As if on cue, one of the hunters marched back to the car and opened the rear door. A priest stepped out. He was older, maybe sixty, his dark hair lined with silver and his eyes sharp like a hawk. He was wearing a cassock.

As the priest approached, a wave of tension passed through the hunters' ranks, as if a wolf had just entered into their midst. 'They can't stand this guy,' Beck observed.

'He's nothin' like our Father Harrison. This one's the Vatican's man – Father Rosetti. He's here ta make sure the hunters stay on the straight and narrow and don't embarrass the Holy See. He's known ta be overzealous. Even Rome thinks so.'

Beck turned to the Scotsman, astounded at the man's inside knowledge. 'How do ya know all this?'

'I have contacts here and there. Comes with bein' a master. It opens up all sorts of doors.'

The captain and his lieutenant had their photo-op with the governor, the mayor and a few of the city council members, all eager to be shown with the Vatican's team. Then it was the trappers' turn to meet the men who might turn this city into a war zone.

To Beck's surprise, the lead demon hunter made the first move, striding past the mayor and the governor, extending his hand towards the older trapper. 'Grand Master Stewart. It is a pleasure. I've long wanted to meet you.'

'Captain Salvatore. Welcome ta Atlanta.'

Grand Master? Beck had never heard of that title before. He'd have to ask Stewart about it sometime. Hell, he had a lot of things to ask once everything died down.

'I believe you met my father many years ago,' Salvatore said.

'Aye, I remember it well,' Stewart replied. 'It was in Genoa. He'd killed an Archfiend that day and ya'd just been born. We shared a bottle of whisky ta celebrate.'

'He recalls that occasion very fondly.' Elias's face sobered. 'The hunters are truly sorry about your men.'

'Thank ya for that.' Stewart looked over at his companion and gestured. 'This is Denver Beck, one of our journeymen. He'll be yer contact while yer in Atlanta. He knows the city and her demons better than anyone.'

Flustered by the compliment, Beck shook hands with the captain and murmured his greeting. The priest didn't look happy. Was it because Salvatore was being too friendly with the good ol' boys? Father Rosetti said something in Italian that caused the captain to stiffen like a dog at the end of a leash. Salvatore said something back and the priest frowned.

'Gentlemen, if you'll excuse me,' the lead hunter said. He returned to the podium where the mayor, never one to miss an opportunity, shook the captain's hand again, knowing it would set off a flurry of flashbulbs.

'The citizens of Atlanta will sleep easy in their beds tonight knowing the Church's demon hunters are here,' Montgomery proclaimed.

Beck gritted his teeth. Atlanta's citizens hadn't realized they'd been sleeping easy for all these years thanks to the trappers. As the mayor droned on, Beck's eyes skimmed over the crowds at street level. Funny how you can't resist trying to find someone you know in a pack of people. The red hair caught his notice immediately. Justine waved and smiled and he resisted the urge to wave back. Then suddenly it was all over: the hunters loaded back into the vans and the motorcade drove off.

Stewart didn't budge. 'A wee word of advice, lad. Be verra careful with the hunters. They're not a bad lot, but it'll get ugly if they think they're being made fools of.'

Beck nodded his understanding. 'What do ya want me to do?'

'Just try ta keep them from burnin' the city to the ground. That's all I ask.'

For a moment Beck thought the master was messing with him. Then he saw the expression on the Scotsman's face.

Oh, God, he's serious.

'I do believe this qualifies as torture in most civilized countries,' Peter groused. He was hunched up in the passenger seat of Riley's car, staring mournfully at the other side of the street where the recycling guys were loading Holy Water bottles into the back of a truck.

Riley took another lengthy slurp of her soda. 'Yeah, this is a snore, but I have to know how this all works. Somewhere there's a break in the chain.' Which was why they'd been following this one collection truck all over the city for the past two hours.

'You sure the counterfeit water dudes aren't just buying new bottles?' her friend quizzed.

'I don't think so, not with a tax stamp on them. Those are specially made and you can't buy them anywhere but from the city.'

Peter gave her a dubious look. 'How do you know that?'

'I went to the city's website and checked it out.'

That response earned her a nod of respect. Any interaction with the Internet was righteous according to Peter. 'Can we get food after this?'

'Sure.' She wasn't hungry, but her buddy seemed to eat his own body weight every day. Apparently he was in another growth spurt. She wondered how his dad could keep enough food on the table with two boys in the house.

Bored, Riley checked her phone for something to do. Not a word from Simon. She had the volume as high as it would go so she wouldn't miss his call, but that only worked if he actually made the effort.

'He's not talking to anyone,' she grumbled.

'Your dude?' Peter asked.

'Yeah. He's all caught up in himself.'

'Maybe you're not giving him enough time to pull his head together,' Peter said. 'You can be impatient, you know.'

Harsh as it sounded, her friend was correct: she often expected things to happen faster than they did in the real world. Maybe she was pushing Simon too hard. He'd admitted he'd never had any serious trials in his life and then he'd landed a huge one. He needed time to get a grip on it all. *But his mom wants me to get him talking.* Riley typed out a text message to her boyfriend. *Thinking of you!* If he replied, she'd back off for a while. If not . . .

There was a resounding lack of a response as the minutes crawled by.

Riley growled under her breath: Simon the Silent was definitely getting a visit this afternoon. She would not let him stew in his pool of depression any longer. It was time to move forward, even if he was confused and scared. *We can be that way together.*

'Ah, here we go,' Peter said with exaggerated relief.

When the recycling truck pulled into traffic, Riley fell in two car lengths behind. Being big and loaded with plastic bottles made it easy to follow.

'So how many stops was that?' she asked.

'Four. No, five,' Peter said, consulting his notebook.

'The thing's full.' *So either they go to the plant or . . .*

But they didn't go to the Celestial Supplies plant. Instead Riley followed the truck to a large brick warehouse near East Point.

'So what just happened here?' Riley demanded as she manoeuvred the car on to a side street. 'This isn't the Holy Water plant. That's up in Doraville.'

'Seems to be some sort of recycling centre,' Peter said, unbuckling his seat belt. 'I'll go get a closer look.' Before she could protest, he was out the door and hiking up the street.

This is a waste of time. Even my dad couldn't figure it out and he was way smarter than me.

Her cellphone pinged. A text from Peter. *In position.* She rolled her eyes. At least her friend was enjoying himself. Then another text. *I'm going inside.*

No! she typed back.

I'll be OK. Just hang tight.

It was a long fifteen minutes. Riley thought of sending him another text, but that might ruin whatever he was up to. Every minute increased her worry.

I shouldn't have brought him with me. He's going to get into trouble and his dad is going to go nuclear and . . . Every possible scenario ended with Peter hurt or exiled to Illinois.

When her friend sauntered back to the car in no particular hurry, he sported a pleased expression on his face, which meant he'd learned something.

The moment Peter climbed into the car, Riley unloaded. 'You're crazy, you know? You shouldn't have gone in there on your own. Who knows what they might have done to you.'

'Crazy? This from a person who traps demons for a living?'

'This isn't about me!' she retorted. 'So give it up. What did you find out?'

'I told the guard I had a report to do for school. I made

sure to look like a nerd so he wouldn't think I was any threat.'

Channelling a nerd wasn't really hard for Peter. 'And?'

'This place is the city's only official recycler, at least for the Holy Water bottles. They collect them, strip off the labels and tax stamps, clean them out, then load them into trucks and haul them to the Celestial Supplies plant to be refilled, where they're relabelled and stamped before they're sent to the distributor.'

'They're being stolen from here?'

'Don't know yet. The guard says they count every bottle that comes in and out. But if someone can find a way to smuggle a few out before they're cleaned and stripped, all they'd have to do is put a new label on them and fill them with tap water.'

'And as long as the new label has the original batch number and it matches the tax stamp number, it all looks kosher.' Then she shook her head. 'But they'd have to fake the paperwork to make up for the missing bottles.'

'That's the problem with this theory,' he admitted. 'But once we figure out how to do round-the-clock surveillance, we'll nail them.'

'And you'd do that with me?'

'Sure.' Peter interlaced his fingers and cracked his knuckles. 'Tech rules. I'll find a way.'

Her friend was beginning to plumb new depths of self-assurance. 'You're really awesome, you know that?'

'I may be awesome, but I'm hungry.'

'I'll buy you lunch, how's that?' She saw him open his mouth to protest, but cut him off. 'I have money.' Then she explained how she'd got it and just how much.

'Beck left you a thousand bucks?' Peter said, astonished. 'And you think he's a butthead because . . . ?' He gestured for her to fill in the blank.

'Don't start.'

Her companion checked something on his phone. 'There's a Vietnamese restaurant four point three miles north of here. I want pho.'

'Noodles it is, dude.'

Chapter Twenty-One

Though they'd been 'invited' to meet with the hunters at the Westin, Beck and Stewart were stuck in the hallway, ignored. The longer they waited, the more pissed off Beck became. When it appeared they weren't going to be ushered into the hunters' presence any time soon, Stewart sweet-talked a maid into finding them two chairs, gave her a tip for her service, and then settled back in one.

'Sir . . .' Beck began.

The Scotsman waved him into a chair. 'Don't let them psych ya, lad. It's all on purpose. We'll give them five more minutes and we're outta here. And then I'll be talkin' ta the archbishop.'

They'd just risen to leave when one of the hunters appeared in the hallway and waved them inside. To Beck, the hotel room seemed huge, like three rooms in one. There was a galley kitchen to the right, a small bathroom to the left and a big open area in front of them. In that area was a conference table and six chairs.

The smell of fresh coffee caught his nose, reminding him he was a few cups short for the day. Next to the coffee-maker was a plate of doughnuts. It appeared the hunters liked the frosted ones with the little sprinkles.

Sitting in padded chairs around the table were three men – Captain Elias Salvatore, Lieutenant Amundson and the priest. Behind them was a massive window – Atlanta from a bird's-eye view. And another hunter. His eyes weren't on them but on the city below, an assault rifle in hand.

Vigilant bunch, that's for sure.

Captain Salvatore rose from his chair. 'Grand Master Stewart, please excuse the delay.' His tone told Beck he wasn't happy about it, either.

'No trouble, Captain,' Stewart replied, choosing a chair at the end of the table near Salvatore. The priest gave them a cursory glance and then returned those dark eyes to the paperwork in front of him.

'Gentlemen, this is Father Rosetti and my second-in-command, Lieutenant Amundson,' the captain said, unaware that Stewart had already given Beck a complete rundown.

Amundson delivered a crisp nod, but the priest pointedly ignored both of them. That didn't sit well with Beck. He could understand the priest blowing him off – he wasn't important – but Stewart deserved respect. To his credit, the Scotsman ignored the slight like he'd expected it. Uneasy, Beck sat next to him, which put the priest on his right.

'I'm actin' in Master Harper's stead,' Stewart explained. 'We're here ta help ya in any way we can.'

Without looking up, the priest thumbed open a thick file folder stuffed with documents. 'We have opened an investigation into the events at the Tabernacle,' he said, his English heavily accented. 'In particular what role Paul Blackthorne or his daughter played in that tragedy.'

Stewart frowned, but didn't reply.

'Tell us what happened that night.'

As the master delivered the report, Beck could hear the increasing tension in his voice. All the while Father Rosetti made notes on a sheet of paper.

'Who is the necromancer that reanimated her father?' the priest asked.

The Scotsman looked over at Beck.

'We don't know that yet,' he replied. 'The summoners aren't talking.'

More notes went on the paper. Beck found it interesting that Rosetti was asking all the questions while Salvatore and his lieutenant watched from the sidelines. That meant he was really in charge of the operation, not the captain. *Wonder how that sits with him.*

'You are convinced the Holy Water used at your meeting was genuine?' Rosetti quizzed.

Stewart hesitated momentarily, then nodded. 'Aye.'

'I was not aware the Guild admitted females to their midst,' the priest remarked.

'It's a recent change,' Stewart admitted.

'This girl, what is she like?'

'I don't get your meanin',' the master replied.

'Can she be trusted?'

'Absolutely,' Stewart replied, his tone prickly now. 'The Guild is investigatin' the problem, and I've kept the archbishop in the loop. It'll take some time, but we'll find the source of those bottles.'

'That is not important at the moment,' the priest said dismissively.

'On the contrary, it is verra important. The public must trust the Holy Water will keep their homes safe. If not, there'll be citywide panic.'

The priest put down his pen. 'The more I look into this matter, all I see is one person in the very centre of it all: the girl, Riley Blackthorne. Her father's papers only indicate he *felt* something was amiss, yet she claims the Holy Water isn't genuine.'

Beck jumped in. 'She tested the bottles. Some of them didn't react.'

The priest studied him, then flipped a page. 'Yes, and for that test she employed the claw of a demon. A symbol of Hell.'

How do ya know about that claw? Who told ya that?

'Why not? It came from the Three she caught.'

Rosetti's eyebrow rose. 'You cannot possibly have me believe such a young child could capture such a Hell-spawn by herself.'

What's goin' on here? All of this was about Riley, not about how to stop the demons.

Apparently Stewart was thinking along the same lines.

Forbidden

'So what is the offiicial agenda, Father?' the master demanded.

The pen went down again. 'We are here to take control of the city's Hellspawn problem. We cannot allow Lucifer to obtain a foothold in our world. To that end, if we find that anyone has sided with our enemy in this battle, they will be arrested and tried. That includes Paul Blackthorne's girl.'

'Now wait a minute—' Beck began.

'Easy, lad,' Stewart said. Then he addressed the priest. 'Why are ya so interested in her?'

'Often there is a nexus, a specific individual that Hell uses to lay its plans. Usually that is someone young and impressionable. In this case, perhaps it is Riley Blackthorne, especially since she was at the Tabernacle the night of the attack.'

'She had nothin' ta do with that,' Stewart replied.

'Either way, we need to speak with her on these matters.'

'Not unless her master agrees,' Stewart said, drawing the line in the sand.

'Master Harper's approval has little to do with the matter. We *will* talk to the girl,' the priest replied, his face set.

'Not unless Harper agrees,' Stewart retorted. 'We don't throw our people ta the wolves.'

The priest tensed. 'You are impeding our investigation, Master Stewart. I shall be filing a formal complaint with the mayor . . . and the National Guild.'

'Ya misunderstand me, priest. We came here ta offer our assistance, not have ya make one of our own a scapegoat.'

'Your protest is noted,' the priest replied. He shuffled his papers in an agitated manner. 'We have nothing further to discuss.'

That was as cold a dismissal as Beck had ever heard.

'Mind you,' Stewart added, his voice rougher now, 'somethin's afoot in this city and it would be a mistake ta think it's all Hell's doin'.'

The priest studied him gravely. 'Which is exactly what I would expect a trapper to say. Come now, Master Stewart, we both know who guards your kind, where your loyalties lie. That was so plainly evident the other night.'

'That's not the issue and ya know it,' Stewart retorted. 'We'll not have this city destroyed just ta make yer boss happy.'

The priest bristled. 'This is about evil, Master Stewart, not currying favour with His Holiness.'

'Just as long as ya remember that.'

With a curt nod to the captain, Stewart rose to leave the room, Beck in tow. Amundson had taken a position near the door. The master passed without incident, but the hunter purposely bumped Beck hard, bouncing him off the door frame. Beck whirled, eager to take on this jerk, but never got the chance as Stewart's cane shot between them.

'Stand down, lad!' With an oath, Beck stepped back,

furious that he'd lost control in the first place.

Stewart stared up at Amundson's gloating face. 'Another time, hunter. Mark you, that time will come, and I'll be damned happy ta turn this lad loose on ya.'

Beck seethed all the way down the hall, wanting to hit something. He tried to chill, but the anger wouldn't fade. There was a showdown coming with the hunters – it was going to be bloody and he was going to be in the middle of it.

As they waited for the elevator, the Scotsman called Riley's master and related the news. 'Aye. I agree.' He hung up, still frowning.

'Sir . . .' Beck began. 'Harper isn't goin' to give her up, is he?'

'Not without a fight, that's for sure.' The elevator dinged its arrival. 'Let's head ta my place. It's time ya know what's really goin' on.'

As Beck waited for the master to climb out of the truck, he checked out the man's house. It was three storeys, fancy in an old-fashioned sort of way, and painted in different shades of blue. It even had a small tower off the front. His host led him into a room near the back.

Beck liked this place. It felt like a home, from the big fireplace to the little crocheted things on the backs of the chairs.

Stewart took a position near a large cabinet and studied his extensive liquor collection. From what Beck could see of the labels, most of it was Scotch.

'Ya got a favourite?' his host asked, peering at him over his shoulder.

'No, sir. Never drank much whisky except for my grandaddy's.'

The master poured a hefty amount in a tumbler, then something for himself from a different bottle. 'Have a seat, lad,' he said, handing over the liquor.

Beck settled into a red stuffed chair near the fireplace. Once the master had taken his place in a matching chair across from him, Beck gave the whisky a cautious sniff. *Not bad.*

'*Slàinte mhath!*' the Scotsman proclaimed.

Beck had no idea what the man had said, but he smiled and raised the glass anyway. The first sip told him he liked this stuff a lot, which meant it cost more than he could afford.

The master propped up his left leg on an ottoman. After another lengthy sip, he smacked his lips in appreciation. He seemed in no hurry, though he'd been the one to issue the invitation.

'Stewarts weren't the first trappers, but we're some of the best,' his host began. 'The Blackthornes were the same until they came ta America and got too much into earnin' money rather than trappin' the beasties. At least Paul came back ta the fold.'

'That took some doin', I imagine,' Beck said, hoping to hear a bit more about his mentor.

'Paul had the Blackthorne tradition ta uphold, though he didn't see it that way. In times past, his family would send their sons ta Scotland and we'd train 'em.'

'He never said a word about that.' But then there was a lot Paul hadn't told him. 'So what's this Grand Master thing? I've never heard tell of it before.'

'It's just a title we use in Europe. It means I'm one of the more senior masters.'

Bet there's more to it than that.

'It made for hard feelings with Harper when I first came here,' Stewart confessed. 'Ten years ago, he was barely holdin' his own against some of the other masters here in Atlanta. They were a bad lot. Takin' bribes in a protection racket. If ya didn't pay their price, they'd set a Pyro-Fiend loose.'

'What?' Beck spouted, horrified. 'That's damned evil.'

'Aye,' Stewart said, nodding sagely. 'One of the masters went after Harper and cut him up bad. That's how he got that wicked scar. While he was healin', the National Guild asked me ta come over and clean the house.'

'So that's how he got to be senior master, by ya kickin' out all the others?'

'Pretty much. Truth be known, he wasn't happy when I showed up. Felt like National hadn't given him enough time ta straighten things out.'

'And now?' Beck asked.

'We've learned ta tolerate each other,' the Scotsman said with a wry smile. 'I tried to recruit Paul when I first came, but he turned me down flat. Then his teachin' job was gone and he was willin' to listen.'

The master rose slowly from the chair and refilled his glass. 'More?' he asked.

'Not yet, thanks.' No way he'd keep up with the Scotsman.

Stewart recapped the bottle with a thwack of his palm, then returned to his chair. 'Back in the day most demons were dealt with by the Church. The priest would exorcize them. Some began ta hunt them, mostly as sport. The bishops encouraged that, partly because those men could be used as muscle when the Church felt the need.

'As time passed,' Stewart continued, 'the hunters gained a reputation for bein' damned ruthless. There was a dispute between one of my ancestors, a Malcolm Stewart, and one of the local hunters. Somethin' about a bit a' land. The hunter claimed that Malcolm and his family were conspirin' with Hell so the local bishop gave orders ta solve the problem.'

'Solve it, how?' Beck asked. He suspected it didn't involve a lot of praying.

'A team of hunters descended on Malcolm's home in the wee hours and butchered everyone they could find. Hacked them ta death, even the bairns. Malcolm they burned at a stake, claimin' he was a warlock.'

'Sweet Jesus,' Beck said, his gut twisting at the thought.

'Aye,' Stewart replied. 'Malcolm's son, Euan, had the good fortune ta be in Edinburgh that day. Knowing he'd be next for the stake, he came up with a brilliant scheme. He ordered the rest of the family ta trap demons and deliver them ta their priests, as many as possible in the shortest period of time.'

'Smart,' Beck said, seeing the plan clearly. 'The Stewarts couldn't be workin' for Lucifer if they're trappin' demons.'

Stewart nodded. 'Euan was a canny one. After he'd trap a demon, he'd leave a few coins behind. Word got around. It was better ta get some brass for yer demon rather than havin' the hunters burn yer house and put yer family ta the sword.'

Beck couldn't stop the grin. 'Way smart.'

'Aye. Because of that, the trappers became verra popular. That's why there's always been demon trappers in our family, even when some went Protestant.'

Beck retraced to the beginning of the story. 'What happened to the hunter who led the raid?'

A wolfish smile filled his host's face. 'He vanished a short time after the massacre. They found him up in the heather. It took four men over an hour ta gather enough pieces to bury.'

'Righteous,' Beck replied. He took another sip of the whisky, surprised at how things were playing out. Stewart wouldn't be sharing this knowledge unless Beck was going to make master. That stirred a rare feeling of pride.

'So that's why the hunters don't like us much,' his

host said. 'That hasn't changed in over eight centuries. If anythin', it got worse once they came under the Vatican's thumb.'

Beck's cellphone rang. He swore at the interruption and flipped it open. 'Yeah?'

'It's Justine,' a light voice said.

He didn't bother to hide the smile. 'How ya doin'?'

'Very well, thank you. Is it possible for us to meet to-night?'

He shot a look at Stewart and then said, 'I'm kinda busy.'

'I am about to finish the article and I have a few more questions.'

'A reporter?' the master mouthed. Beck nodded. 'Just get it done, lad,' was the reply.

He gave in. There was a triumphant lilt in Justine's voice as they worked out a time and a place to meet.

After the call ended, the Scotsman eyed him intently. 'More whisky?'

'Yeah. I think I'm gonna need it.'

Chapter Twenty-Two

Riley was met at the door by one of Simon's younger brothers, but which one she wasn't sure. Like his elder sibling, he had the trademark blond hair and deep blue eyes of the Adler clan. He said *the grump* was in the den and that no one could watch the television because of it.

'Have some of the other trappers been here?' she asked. Maybe they could get through to Simon, help him get back on track.

'A few. You just missed one guy, but I don't think he was a trapper,' the boy said.

'Who was it?' Riley asked, curious.

The boy shrugged. 'He visited him at the hospital too. I wish he wouldn't come here: Simon just gets weirder after he talks to him.'

'What's this guy look like?' Another shrug. *Maybe it was McGuire. He'd make anyone grumpy.* 'So Simon's still not himself?' Riley asked. She got a sullen shake of the head. 'Then it's time to change that.'

'Good luck,' his sibling muttered, and then disappeared into the kitchen to raid the refrigerator.

Riley took a moment to check herself out in the hall

mirror. She'd spent extra time on her hair and make-up and wore the nicest sweater she owned. It was bright blue and did good things for her complexion. She paused again outside the room, unusually nervous.

Please let him be better. She'd do anything to see that golden smile, know that everything was right between them again.

To her relief she found he had the lights on and the curtains open, but a tense frown settled on Simon's forehead as she entered the room. In his lap was a Bible, its pages dog-eared and thin strips of ribbon bookmarking different sections. On the table next to him was his rosary, an uneaten sandwich and a can of soda. A bright red afghan lay over his lap, the fringe tickling the carpeted floor. Probably his mother's handiwork.

'Hey, Simon,' Riley said, 'I brought you cookies from the coffee shop. I thought you might like some.' She placed the bag on the couch near him. He ignored it as his blue eyes flickered in irritation.

'What's going on?' he demanded. 'No one is telling me anything. I want to know what the Guild is doing.'

So much for the *How are you, I've really missed you* part of this conversation. Riley gave in and delivered the news bulletins. 'Beck and I did the paperwork so the life insurance policies will be paid. Harper is healing pretty well. He's wondering when you're coming back to work. Oh, and the demon hunters arrived today. Downtown traffic's a mess because of it.' She'd have been down there too, just out of curiosity, but Simon took precedence.

'That wasn't what I asked,' her boyfriend retorted. 'I want to know how the demons got through the Holy Water. I want to know what the Guild is going to do about it.'

Back to that again. She'd tried to explain this before and he'd blown her off. *One more time.* 'Father Harrison says there were too many of them, that they overwhelmed the ward. It's been known to happen.'

'He told me that too. I don't buy it.'

He doesn't believe his own priest? 'You saw them – they kept pushing until the ward broke.'

'I didn't see that. I saw them swarm us. I saw them kill and . . .' He looked down at the Bible in his lap, his hands quivering now.

She knew how that was. Did he get panic attacks too? His blue eyes rose to meet hers. There was no tenderness in them, not like in the past.

'Why did the Five come for you?' he asked in a low voice.

Simon had been too badly hurt to see the Geo-Fiend himself. *So who told you it was after me?*

'I don't know,' she admitted. 'It's the same one that killed my dad and tried to destroy the library. It must have this thing for Blackthornes.'

There was a long pause as Simon shifted in his chair, his face suddenly flushed. He leaned over the side of the chair and picked up a pint water bottle, but he didn't take a drink from it. When he finally spoke, his voice was acidic, full of accusation. 'Lucifer has sent his devils after you. What have you done, Riley?'

'Huh?' she spouted. 'I haven't done anything.' *Except save your life.*

'You're lying. Hell has you in its sights. Why else would your father be at the Tabernacle?'

'Whoa, what are you saying? My dad has nothing to do with Hell.'

'Your father was summoned by evil magic. That you can't deny. He was researching Holy Water. Why? Was he trying to find a way to break the ward for his unholy master? Did he tell you how to do it?'

Riley gaped at him, astounded at the venom coming from her boyfriend's mouth. 'You're accusing my dad of killing those trappers? How can you say that?' She sucked in a hasty breath. 'I don't even know if he made it out of that furnace.'

He sneered. 'Why would it matter? He's dead, or have you forgotten that?'

Riley's mouth fell open, astounded at his callousness. 'What is *wrong* with you? You were never like this before. You actually cared about people. Now you're just . . . mean.'

'I'm seeing things for what they really are. You, for instance,' he said, his hands gripping the water bottle tighter. 'If you've sold your soul to Lucifer, just admit it.'

Sold my soul?

Riley pointed an accusing finger. 'You know, I've cut you a lot of slack, but are you listening to yourself? You're totally paranoid.'

'He said you'd say that.'

'Who have you been talking to? Is it McGuire?'

'It doesn't matter. All I can think of is what you told me before the meeting started.'

'What did I say?' She just remembered the kissing.

'You said it was all part of your plan. Now I'm thinking that's really true, that Lucifer is destroying the trappers from within, using you and your father as his weapons.'

She'd only been joking with him that night; there was no plan other than falling in love with this guy.

Riley grabbed the bag of cookies off the couch. 'I'll keep these. You'll probably try to exorcize them or something. When you decide to be the old Simon again, give me a call.'

He shook his head, resigned. 'That Simon is gone. My eyes have been opened to the battle that lies before us. You have sold your soul or you're a . . .' He took a shuddering breath that hitched at the end. 'I have to know the truth.'

A second later she was drenched in water, launched at her from the bottle Simon held in his hands. Riley shot to her feet, stunned, liquid dripping off her face, chest and hands. It tingled in a way she knew so well.

'That's Holy Water!' He'd just tested his girlfriend to see if she was a demon.

Immense sadness filled Simon's eyes, like he knew

he'd crossed a line from which there was no return, but he wasn't willing to admit the mistake. 'It's best we don't see each other from now on. I can't be with someone I don't trust.'

'What?' *He's breaking up with me? He can't do this. I saved his life.* Maybe if she told him about how she'd saved his life, about the deal she'd made with Heaven . . . *He'll never believe me.*

'How can you do this to us?' Riley demanded. 'I thought we had something special.'

'We did, but now you're different. You're not the girl I once loved.'

He loved me?

Simon waved her away. 'You need to leave now, Riley. You're not welcome here any more.'

Tears broke loose and she didn't bother to wipe them away as they threaded down her already damp cheeks. Dropping the bag of cookies, Riley fled the house.

The demons had killed more than just trappers that night. They'd destroyed her future with the boy she loved.

Beck worked on his second cup of coffee, trying to burn off the Scotch before he met Justine in an hour. He had one final question to put to the old trapper before he left, the one that had been nagging at him since the meeting with the hunters.

'What did the priest mean?' he asked. 'Who guards our kind?'

Stewart was silent for a long time. Finally, he nodded to himself. 'It's only right ya know.' He took a lengthy gulp of his liquor. 'More history,' he said. 'Sorry.' Another long sip, like he was preparing to deliver bad news. 'Some of the angels weren't happy when man was created, not likin' the competition for God's affection. Lucifer, in particular, refused to bow his knee ta somethin' made of clay.'

Beck nodded encouragingly, hoping to keep the man talking.

'God doesn't like someone challengin' Him, so He cast out Lucifer and all of the Divine who'd opposed man's creation. I've heard it was over a third of them, some say over two hundred, others believe it was in the millions.'

Beck whistled. 'That's a lot of damned angels.'

'Aye. The demons first appeared when Adam and Eve gained the knowledge of good and evil. Not too many to start with, but as we moved ta the cities they came with us and grew in number. The fiends serve a purpose, they're part of God's plan.'

Stewart shifted his weight in the chair, gathering his thoughts. 'Back at the beginnin', God told Lucifer, "If ya think these humans are so awful then test them for me, winnow out the wheat from the chaff. Find those whose faith is unshakeable." So He made Lucifer His adversary, His *hasatan*. It's the Prince's job to test our love of God, like a prosecuting attorney.'

Beck took a deep breath to try to clear his mind. It had

to be all the whisky. Stewart couldn't be saying that Lucifer was on the level, could he? 'But he's the Devil.'

'There'd ya'd be wrong,' Stewart said. 'Now, mind ya, there *is* a Devil and he's damned evil, but Lucifer is under God's thumb . . . more or less.'

Beck worked on his coffee for a time, thinking things through. This was so confusing and made his head buzz worse than the whisky. 'Then what did the priest mean?'

There was another lengthy silence as Stewart stared into the fire. 'Even Harper doesn't know this, and it's best none of the others do either.'

'Know what?' Beck asked, his patience wearing thin. Would this man ever answer the question?

'Hell didn't want us ta die the other night.'

'No way,' Beck retorted.

'It's all part of the Grand Game, the one that keeps everythin' in balance. Hell does somethin', Heaven retaliates. Back and forth across eternity. The trick is not ta push the other too far, or there's war.'

'But—'

Stewart held up his hand for silence. 'Neither God nor Lucifer want Armageddon. They both know it'll go badly and the balance will be upset. Now a few of the Archangels and the Fallen, they're hot ta fight. So there's always tension, in Hell particularly.'

Beck ran his hand through his hair, frustrated. 'I respect ya and all, but there's no way ya can say Hell wasn't tryin' its best to slaughter us.'

Forbidden

Stewart locked eyes with him, his face sombre. 'Those angels, the ones that kept us alive. Who do ya think sent 'em?'

Damn silly question. 'Heaven, of course. Who else would bother savin' our butts?'

'No, lad,' Stewart replied, his voice almost a whisper. 'Those warrior angels were sent by the Prince of Hell himself. I swear it on the Stewart name.'

The old man is serious. He really thinks Hell saved our butts. Beck's mind fought against the obvious question.

If those were Lucifer's folk, then who sent the demons?

Chapter Twenty-Three

Driven by some internal autopilot, Riley found herself at St Brigid's. She parked and turned off the car's engine. Blowing her nose again, she flipped down the visor. Her mascara had realigned itself into vertical smudgy trails down her face. She mumbled a caustic swear word and mopped off as much as she could with a tissue. Hopefully the stuff would come out of her sweater. Not that she'd probably ever wear it again – it'd just remind her of *him*.

I was such a fool. She'd daydreamed of their future, what it would be like if she and Simon had married, how many kids they'd have. She'd fallen hard for him and now all that was gone, washed away by his irrational paranoia and a lukewarm bottle of Holy Water.

'You self-righteous hypocrite. How could you do that to me?' He'd really cared for her – she knew it. She'd felt it when they were together and yet he'd thrown it all away as if it was nothing.

Once inside the room, she sat at the table. This was her life from now on. Once Ori killed the Five she wouldn't have to spend her nights on hallowed ground, but not much else would change. She would never find a boyfriend who would understand what she did, what she had to do. Beck had been right – there was a huge price for keeping Hell in line and she was going to pay it for the rest of her life.

The twin roses sat in a glass in the centre of the table – the one she'd found on her car and the one Ori had given her the night before. She pulled the glass closer and tested the fragrance. Still strong. The scent seemed to calm her. She closed her eyes and tried to remember Simon before he'd been injured. The memories were there, but too painful to address.

Her cell lit up. If it was Mr Righteous and he thought he could just apologize . . .

It was Beck. 'Yeah, what?' she snarled.

'I just got a call from Simon. He's carryin' on like a crazy person, says you're workin' for Hell. What's goin' on?' he demanded.

Oh, no. She hadn't wanted Beck to know her love life had imploded.

He didn't wait for her reply. 'Here's the deal, girl: I got too damned much on my plate as it is. I don't need this silly kid drama right now.'

Kid drama? 'Gee, you're all heart.'

'Your boyfriend issues are not my problem. Ya steer clear of him.'

How's that's going to work? We have the same master.

And, right on cue, her caller added, 'Maybe now's a good time to call your aunt.'

Riley hung up on him. To her relief, he didn't call back.

There was more crying over the bathroom sink, choking sobs that felt more like she was standing in front of Simon's coffin than just breaking up with him. Then the doubts came to call, dark, insidious, like nightmares that never give you a moment's peace.

Maybe it's my fault. Maybe if she'd done something different and—

'Stop it!' she shouted at her reflection. 'It's not your fault. You did what was right. You saved his life.'

And lost him forever.

Riley crawled into the bed, her nose stuffy from crying. Simon's ugly words kept throwing themselves at her like missiles. How could he turn away from her so quickly?

Her phone rang, vibrating across the table and bumping into the drinking glass vase. She ignored it. It rang a few minutes later. She turned to face the wall, unable to talk to anyone right now without melting down into an emotional mess. Then a text came through. Then another.

Maybe it was something really important. Maybe something had happened to Beck.

It was Peter. His final text message read: *Call me now! I have to talk to someone!*

That sounded ominous, so she gave in and dialled his number. 'Peter? What's wrong?'

'Hold on.'

There was the sound of footsteps across wood, a door opening and then closing.

'OK, I'm outside now.' His voice was as rough as hers, like he'd been crying.

Peter was never like this and it scared her. 'What's happened?' she asked.

'I finally told Mom I wasn't going with her and the ghouls to Illinois.'

Riley winced as she climbed back into the bunk bed.

'She totally lost it. She cried a lot and accused my dad of brainwashing David and me. They had a big fight. It was totally nuclear here.'

'That sounds absolutely ugly.'

'Yeah. Maybe I was wrong, you know? Maybe I should go with her and . . . '

Her friend sounded so confused. 'Where do you think you should be?' Riley asked.

There was a long pause. 'With Dad. It's way less tense when I'm with him.'

'Then you made the right decision. Your mom is going to have to straighten herself out and you aren't going to be able to help her do that.'

'Dad said the same thing. He wants me to stay here. He says it's time I had space to make my own mistakes.'

'Well, if you're anything like me, they'll be stellar,' she muttered.

He sighed heavily into the phone. 'This is the part

where you're supposed to tell me it's going to work out just fine,' he said.

'No way I'm saying that.'

'You sound weird. What's going on?'

'Simon and –' Her sigh matched his. 'He . . . we broke up this afternoon.'

'But I thought you two were doing really well.'

'We were until he lost his mind.' She blurted out all the gory details, including the 'You Sold Your Soul to Hell' accusation.

'Damn,' Peter said. 'Is there, like, something in the water? First my mom goes crazy, now your . . . ex-boyfriend.'

'Seems like we're the only sane ones,' she said.

'Always have been,' he agreed. 'Don't worry, one day you'll meet some cool dude and he won't be an asshat.'

Her mind drifted to Ori, but she yanked it back immediately. Two roses did not equal someone who wouldn't break her heart.

'You hold it together, OK?' she urged. 'Your mom will be better once she's with her family. Maybe they can get her help.'

'That's Dad's hope. Call me in the morning, will you?' Peter asked. 'My uncle is going to be here with a van and I'm helping Mom pack. I'll need the sanity break from the serious guilt trip she's going to lay on me.'

'I'll call. Don't worry – you did the right thing, Peter.'

'Then why does it hurt so much?' he murmured.

*

Beck pushed open the doors to the Armageddon Lounge, did his perimeter check, then moved into the bar. If he was going to talk to the press, it would be on his home turf. As a peace offering, he placed a quart jug of Holy Water on the counter.

'That what I think it is?' Zack asked, drying his hands on a bar towel.

'Sure is. Put a line outside all your doors. It'll keep the evil things out. I'll bring more when ya need it.' He didn't like the expense, but he didn't want to have to change bars. Not when he had this one broken in.

Zack nodded his gratitude and asked, 'Beer?'

'Soda,' Beck said. That earned him a raised eyebrow. 'Been hitting the whisky heavy tonight, don't need to put beer on top of that.'

'You go sober on us and we'll have to close.'

'Ha, ha.' Beck leaned against the bar, waiting for the beverage. 'What did your boss say about the other night?'

'He swore a lot. Thought about banning trappers from the bar.'

'Not our fault they were here. Maybe he should change the name of the place, ya know?'

'I suggested that. This –' Zack tapped the gallon jug with a finger – 'will help settle his nerves.'

Beck paid for his soda and took it to a booth. An open pool table called to him, but he ignored it. A couple of the regulars gave him nods and he returned them. They seemed at ease with him here. He still couldn't wrap his mind around what had happened with those Fours. He'd have to tell Stewart about them once all the other hassles died down. Maybe between them they could take the fiends out.

Beck sipped his icy soda, deep in thought. He respected the old master a lot, but the Scotsman's claim that Hell had saved the trappers' bacon was just too far-fetched. Stewart had said the rest of the tale would have to wait for another time, which meant Beck had no clue who was fielding those demons. *Gotta be Hell. The old guy must have hit his head harder than we thought.*

At least the thing between Riley and Simon was over. He'd been hard on her, but right now his head was full of more important issues than her boyfriend hassles.

Beck groaned. *That's no excuse.*

He remembered what it'd felt like when Louisa had ditched him, and now he'd been stone cold with Riley when she was going through the same thing.

Sorry, girl.

If he could talk her into visiting her aunt for a while, maybe Simon would get his head together. Not that she'd ever go back to him – once you dissed a Blackthorne you were done for life. Simon had been all lined up and he'd managed to throw away the best girl he'd ever meet.

'What a dumbass,' Beck muttered. 'No way I'd have done that.' *Like I'll ever have a chance.*

The twin doors to the lounge pushed open and all his

thoughts about Riley evaporated.

'Well, damn,' he said, smiling at the sight. Justine scanned the room, then her eyes lit on him. Her smile appeared genuine, like she really wanted to be here.

As she headed for the booth with long, sure strides, every eye riveted on her. It was easy to see why: Justine was dressed in a pair of skintight blue jeans, a cream sweater that hugged her figure, black boots and an ankle-length black leather coat that flapped open as she moved.

Mighty fine. He rose. 'Justine.'

'Good evening, Beck,' she said.

Remembering his manners, he helped her out of the coat. After stashing the coat on the bench seat, Justine slid in and placed her phone on the table.

Beck realized he should buy the lady a drink. 'What would ya like?' he asked.

'Something fruity,' she replied. 'With alcohol.'

He wasn't particularly sure what that might be, but he went to the bar and put in the order anyway.

'So who's the hottie?' Zack asked, keeping his voice low enough so the lady in question wouldn't hear him.

'A reporter.'

'Niiice,' the bartender said, then jammed a slice of orange on the rim of a tall glass and slid it across. Beck paid for it, grimly noting that the more fruit there was in the drink the more it cost.

As he approached, Justine delivered a smile that would have knocked a lesser man to his knees.

'Thank you,' she said. A quick sip of the drink, a nod of approval and then the notebook, pen and digital recorder appeared on the table.

Those implements of torture brought Beck back to earth. 'So what do ya want to know?'

'I have talked to some of the other trappers,' she said. 'Is it true that you remained inside the Tabernacle longer than any of the others? That you saved lives that night?'

Beck felt an uncomfortable twitch crawl over his shoulder blades. 'Not really.' No need to have people thinking he was better than any of the other trappers. 'I just did what I had to do.'

'Some might call you a hero.'

He frowned. 'No. Don't go there,' he retorted with more force than he'd intended. 'I know what heroes are like; I fought beside them in the war. I'm not one of 'em.'

Justine dipped her head in concession. 'Then I will not use that word in my article.'

'Thank you.' He let his tension drain away. 'Sorry. Sore subject.'

'No, I understand.' She took a long sip of her drink. 'Why do you think the demons are acting this way?'

'Maybe Lucifer's testing our defences. He does that every now and then.' That made more sense than Stewart's weird-assed notions of some game between Heaven and Hell.

'You have met with the hunters. What is your impression of them?'

Beck hedged, sensing a trap. 'They're pros,' he said. That was a safe reply.

'Is that all?' she pressed, smiling at his discomfort.

'Yup.'

'They have an impressive track record.'

'And one helluva body count,' he said before he could stop his tongue.

'Can I quote you on that?' she asked, pen poised over the notebook.

There was no safe answer, so he decided to take the plunge. 'Go ahead.'

Justine took another long suck on her straw. He found himself watching her more closely than was warranted. *Might as well ask.* 'Your accent isn't anythin' I can place. Where are ya from?'

'I was born in Italy, raised in Ireland, France and then America. I've been all over the world so I'm a bit of everything. My Irish friends say I sound American. My American friends say I sound like I can't make up my mind what I am,' she said, a full smile gracing her lips. 'What about you?'

'Good old Georgia stock,' he said. 'Lived here and in the Middle East and that's about it.'

'At least you know who you are.' The reporter looked down at her pad and then up again. 'Master Blackthorne's daughter is a trapper now. Does it bother you to have a female in the Guild?'

Sure does. He'd served with women in the Army, knew

they could hold their own like any of the guys. He didn't care if a female wanted to be a trapper. His problem was that it was Riley.

'Not really,' he lied.

Justine studied him intently. 'You put a lot of thought into that.'

'She's young and I'd hate to see her hurt.' Which wasn't a lie.

'Are you two . . . ?' she asked, delicately raising an eyebrow.

Damn, you're nosy. 'No, there's nothin' between us.'

'So you like your women . . . older?' she asked.

The come-on slid across the table so smoothly he almost didn't catch it. Maybe there was more going on here than he'd figured. 'I like women who know what they're doin',' he said.

Justine began to run her slim fingers up and down the side of her glass in a way that made his head spin. 'You're staring at me,' she said, a touch of a smile at the corners of her mouth.

'Just enjoyin' the view,' he said.

'So am I. I don't usually get to say that.'

He reluctantly pulled his mind back to work. 'Can ya tell me what the hunters are gonna do here?' When she didn't reply right off, he added, 'Come on, I've been answerin' all your questions.'

'True,' she replied. She reached over and clicked off the recorder. When their eyes met, he nodded in understanding. This was off the record. 'They begin by surveying the most infested areas of the city.'

'Demon Central, then,' he said. 'That's where the Gastro-Fiends like to hang out.'

'Where is this Demon Central?' she asked.

'It's called Five Points. It's got lots of holes and abandoned buildin's. The Threes love those.' He leaned closer, pushing his soda aside. 'What will they do after this survey?'

'Once they know the types of demons and their locations, they'll move in and clear them out.'

'And if folks get in the way?'

She shrugged. 'They try to minimize the collateral damage, but sometimes that isn't possible.'

'So who's this Father Rosetti?' he asked. 'Are all of Rome's priests such tight-asses?'

A red eyebrow arched. 'Father Rosetti was originally an exorcist for the Vatican. The other priests are not as ardent in their duties. I find it odd – he usually doesn't go out with a team, but remains in Rome.'

'Then why is he in Atlanta?' Beck quizzed.

'I asked that question, but I did not receive an answer.'

The lounge doors swung open and four guys entered, stepping right over the top of the still wet line of Holy Water. Not demons, then. By the noise they were generating, they already had a significant buzz on. Beck frowned. These guys weren't regulars so they wouldn't know not to jack with him. Since he was with the hottest woman in the place, this might not go well. Especially with four of them.

He caught Justine's eye. 'We gotta go. Now.'

To his relief she didn't argue, but scooped up her belongings. As they reached the doors, one of the guys called out from his place at the bar.

'Hey, where ya goin', babe? Come back here. I'll buy ya a beer.'

Justine kept moving, Beck right behind her. When they reached his truck, he set his trapper's bag on the hood.

'Sorry about that,' he said, his eyes still on the lounge's entrance. The quartet was still inside, the lure of more booze stronger than chasing tail.

'I am accustomed to it,' Justine said as she ran her hand over the demon decals on the side of the truck. 'What do these mean?'

'A trapper gets one every time they take down a Three.'

She counted them. 'Very impressive. Hell must hate you.'

He chuckled. 'I do my bit. Can I drop ya somewheres?'

She turned towards him and he could smell her perfume now. Something flowery. When the reporter leaned forward and kissed him, it set his blood on fire. He didn't need a steel pipe to the head to see how this night might play out.

Why not? All he'd done recently was fret over Paul's daughter and work long hours to pay the girl's bills and the only thing he'd got was grief in return.

I deserve some fun.

'I am thinking,' Justine began, running a hand through his hair, 'it would be nice to talk to you about something other than . . . demons.'

Beck didn't hesitate – he pulled her tight against him, enjoying the feel of her body close to his. She felt even better than she looked. 'I'm game as long as this *talk* is off the record.'

'I wouldn't have it any other way,' she purred.

Chapter Twenty-Four

It's never a good sign when your ex-boyfriend's mom calls you at seven in the morning and asks to meet you after Mass. Though Riley was still enduring Category Five break-up grief, she didn't have the heart to turn Mrs Adler down. Rather than just trudging around to the front of the church to meet the woman after services, Riley set the meeting at the Grounds Zero. She needed food and knew that standing on the church stairs talking about how Mrs Adler's son was a crazed religious lunatic probably wouldn't be good for anyone.

Riley ordered a salmon-and-cream-cheese bagel, took it to a booth and ate it without much enthusiasm. Food didn't taste good now, and though this coffee shop made the best hot chocolate she hadn't ordered it as it would bring back too many memories of Simon. Like the night he'd said he wanted to date her. Riley closed her eyes, trying to erase that moment, but it didn't work. She could still hear his gentle voice, feel his hand stroking hers. How great it had felt to know someone cared for her.

'Riley?'

She found Mrs Adler standing nearby. Her purple dress,

matching coat and hat looked really nice, but the outfit didn't disguise the dark circles under her tired blue eyes.

'I'm sorry I'm late,' Mrs Adler said, sliding into the booth. Her bag clunked on the seat next to her. 'I wanted to talk to Father Harrison after Mass.'

All the pain and brutal rejection from the day before slammed into Riley like a shock wave. She bit her lip, not wanting to shout her fury aloud, reveal to the world how badly this hurt.

How could you let him do that to me? Why can't you convince him he's wrong? That he made a mistake?

Riley felt the prickle of tears and brushed them away with the back of her hand. 'Why is he doing this?' she said, her voice cracking. 'He used to be so nice. That's why I liked him so much.' *Why I was falling in love with him.* 'Now he's . . .'

'Lost,' Mrs Adler replied, her eyes drifting down to her folded hands. 'Father Harrison is finding us a therapist, one familiar with post-traumatic stress disorder. Maybe we can help Simon get past this.'

There was only a slim thread of hope in the woman's voice.

'You don't think he's going to get better,' Riley said before she could stop herself.

Mrs Adler jammed her lips together while fumbling for a tissue from her purse. After she'd wiped her eyes, she took a deep breath. 'Simon has always been different to the other children, so serious about everything. When he met you, he started to . . .' She struggled for the right word.

'Lighten up?' Riley suggested.

A weary smile came back to her. 'That's it exactly. He smiled more and talked about you at dinner. He's never spoken of his girlfriends before. That's when we knew you were right for him.'

'Not any more,' Riley said, feeling the tears massing for another assault. 'He thinks I'm evil now, that I'm part of a grand hellish conspiracy.' She sniffed and rubbed her nose. 'I thought if he had time to get over what happened, he'd be better. He's just got worse.'

Mrs Adler reached across the table and gently took Riley's hand, much like her son had done the night he and Riley had begun dating. The woman's skin was cool, despite having been in contact with the coffee cup and its heated contents.

'We didn't know what Simon had done to you until last night. He didn't tell us. Then some men showed up at our house. One of them was a priest, so I thought maybe Father Harrison had sent them.' Mrs Adler's hand retreated. 'They were from the Vatican and Simon had called them. He told them that . . . you and your father were the reason all those trappers died.'

'He called the demon hunters down on me?' Riley cried. Heads turned in their direction. She lowered her voice, but outrage still owned her. 'How could he do that to me? What is wrong with him?'

Forbidden

Mrs Adler shook her head, more tears in her eyes now.

Don't yell at the psycho-ex's mom. It's not her fault. Riley counted to ten very slowly. She made sure her voice was steady. 'My dad had *nothing* to do with the ward failing. Neither did I. There were too many demons. Period.'

'I know,' Mrs Adler admitted, 'but my son is fixated on this. He needs someone to blame instead of God.'

That pretty much summed it up.

'Did the hunters believe him?' Riley asked. *Please say they think he's nuts.*

'I'm not sure,' Mrs Adler admitted. 'I just thought you ought to know.'

Riley mumbled her thanks, but her mind kept screaming: *He called the hunters!* This was way bad news for both her and the Guild.

Mrs Adler rose from the booth, clutching her bag tightly. Mournful eyes blinked tears away. 'I'm so sorry, Riley.' The woman swallowed heavily. 'Please pray for Simon, pray that he might see the truth and be himself again.'

Riley watched as her ex's mom made her way out of the coffee shop, each step laden with worry. *But I did pray for him. Then everything went wrong.*

Justine was already up and in the shower by the time Beck came to full consciousness. It took some time to realize he was in a hotel room at the Westin. He didn't remember much sleep overnight, but that was OK. It hadn't bothered him that she'd asked him a lot of questions about

Atlanta and her demons and about the demon traffickers. Some girls did that – at least she was interested.

He rolled out of bed and used the toilet. Luckily it was one of those separate from the shower because the running water was getting to him. He moved to the sink and splashed water on his face. Then smirked. Justine had left marks on his neck.

You're a fireball, that's for sure.

Beck dressed. He'd just finished tying his boots when Justine entered the room wrapped in a large white towel. Her hair was still damp.

'Are you leaving already?' she asked reproachfully.

'Got to. I'm meetin' with Master Stewart.'

'Will I see you tonight?'

He'd be with her whenever she wanted, but he just couldn't admit that right out. He had his pride to think of. 'Maybe.'

'So it's demons first, then me?' she teased as she sank on to the bed next him.

'Yes. No . . .' *Ah, hell, I don't know.* He kissed her again. Finally, he let go of her, but it took a lot of willpower. Claiming his jacket from a chair, he headed for the door.

'Beck?' He turned at the sound of her soft voice. She was curled up on the bed, sending him invitations he didn't dare accept. 'If you speak to Elias Salvatore, don't mention you've been with me.'

'Why?' he asked, curious.

'Elias and I were once together,' she said matter-offactly. 'He is very jealous. It could go badly for you if he finds out about us.'

I slept with the top hunter's woman? Part of him was jazzed, but the other part wasn't happy at the news. Without knowing it, he'd done the one thing Stewart had warned him against: he'd made a demon hunter look like a fool.

'Feels strange not having to run home and check in with the warden,' Peter said as he and Riley walked towards her car after class. Students streamed out of the old Starbucks, calling out to each other and hopping into their rides.

Riley unlocked the driver's side door and dropped her messenger bag on to the front seat. 'You'll get used to it.'

'I called the city today to find out who picks up their empty Holy Water bottles, in case the guard at the recycling place was lying.'

'Any luck?' Riley asked.

Peter leaned against the side of the car. 'I got blown off. The secretary chick said it would be a breach of security to tell me that information because someone might want to sabotage the shipment.'

'Why would someone sabotage a shipment of empty bottles?' Riley asked.

'I pointed that out, but she wouldn't budge.'

'Damn,' Riley grumbled.

'Don't worry, we'll find a way to get the info. I'll be

able to help more now that I don't have to be chained up in my room.'

Riley eyed her best friend. 'Think you'll be able to cope?'

'Totally. It's like I've been pardoned from a life sentence. I'm worried someone will realize they've made a mistake.'

'They didn't.' *Neither did you.* 'So what are you doing tonight?'

'The house is just going to be a dead zone. I was thinking of going to the library, start on my homework. What about you?'

'No, I'm doing witchy stuff,' Riley said. 'A friend of mine is going to summon my dad's spirit so maybe we can figure out who stole him.'

'Wow. Ah, can I come along?' Peter asked, his face alight.

'It could be kinda weird,' Riley hedged.

'I'm good with weird. Come on, how about it? I need a little excitement right now.'

'I'm not so sure, Peter. If something goes wrong . . .' Maybe she was being selfish, but Riley really wanted him to come along. Still, he had to know what he was getting into. 'When I say weird, I really mean it, Peter.'

He debated for a moment, then extracted his cellphone. 'I have to let Dad know where I am. It's part of our agreement. So how late and where?'

What would Ayden think if she brought him along?

Forbidden

Riley gave in. 'Little Five Points and . . .' She consulted her own phone for the time. 'I'm thinking we'll be done by eight.'

'You'll drop me home?' When she nodded, he stepped a few paces away and dialled his father. As Peter pleaded his case, which did not include mentioning that they were going to visit a real live witch, Riley took the opportunity to check her text messages. She'd heard one arrive during class but she knew not to check it. Mrs Haggerty was not into modern technology.

It was from Ori.

> Meet me at the Market at nine?

Her fingers sent a *Yes* before she had time to think, then wondered why.

Peter gave a thumbs up. 'Good to go,' he announced, rejoining her. 'Dad says I shouldn't get arrested or I will end up in Illinois sharing a bed with the twins.'

'That's a brutal threat,' Riley replied.

'Totally brutal. The ghouls have been known to wet the bed.'

Chapter Twenty-Five

Riley had expected she'd have to do a lot of explaining about Peter's presence, but Ayden only arched one eyebrow when they were introduced.

'Cool phoenix tattoo,' Peter said, admiring the colourful artwork that spread from the witch's neck downward into her cleavage. Unlike Simon, he did allow his eyes to linger.

Phoenix? 'Ah, what happened to the dragon tattoo you had?' Riley asked.

'I changed it,' Ayden replied, still studying Peter intently as if she was weighing his soul. 'It's easy when you wield magic.' She shifted her full attention to Riley. 'You sure about this summoning?'

'I'm good. It might get some of my questions answered. If this doesn't work, I'm out of options.'

'So be it.' The witch led them on a journey through the interior of the Bell, Book and Broomstick where they walked past displays of crystals, spheres and all sorts of metaphysical goodies. The store reeked of incense. It was hard to pick out which scent was stronger than another so it all became a nose blur. Once they reached the back room, Ayden loaded them up with boxes of candles and other paraphernalia. Peter got to carry a sword, which pleased him immensely.

'Is this real?' he asked, gripping the scabbard tightly.

'No point in owning any other kind,' Ayden said, her head deep in a closet. Out came a velvet cloak in rich purple. She draped it over her arm and then herded them towards the rear door. As they exited the building, their escort flipped a switch, illuminating a large courtyard with flood lamps.

'Do you know Mortimer Alexander?' Riley asked as her eyes adjusted to the garish light. 'He lives down the street. He's the summoners' advocate.'

'I've heard of him,' Ayden replied. 'Witches and summoners don't socialize.'

'Because of the magical war?'

Ayden gave her a look. 'How'd you hear about that?'

'Mort mentioned it. He said there'd been bad blood between you guys.'

'Still is. Some of the necros are pretty decent, but their leadership has their heads up their butts. But then so do some of us witches.'

Peter had wandered ahead and now stood transfixed by a circle of stones. There were twelve of them, old, stark white and sticking upward about two feet out of the red Georgia clay. The whole circle was about thirty feet in diameter. Inside was a fire pit and a stone altar.

'This is so unreal,' he explained. 'Like out of a movie or something.'

While Ayden began her preparations, Riley took the opportunity to check out the courtyard. The windows in the building to the left were bricked up, the roof too steep for anyone to climb up to see what the witches were up to. The buildings to their right and in front of them did have windows. Not a private site, but still better than most inside the city. A wall of concrete blocks, probably about six feet tall, surrounded the entire courtyard. Three-quarters of the wall was covered in a giant mural.

Riley wandered over to the closest section and studied the images. At first it just looked like an ordinary forest scene, then she spied the figures.

'Fairies!' she said. 'There's like a zillion of them!' There were tall, stately fairies riding magnificent horses with flowing silver manes. There were tiny fairies peeking out from under mushroom caps and leaves. Some held swords and others chalices filled with golden nectar. Everywhere she looked there was a little face peering back at her. They were all different. Further down the wall the scene changed to marshy grassland. She soon found the fairies amongst the grasses and reeds, though they looked different to the ones in the forest scene.

Peter joined her at the wall and she pointed out her discoveries. 'Aren't they amazing?'

'You really think they exist?' he asked.

'They do,' Ayden replied as she placed a goblet

and a ritual knife on the altar.

'You've seen them?' Riley asked.

'Sure,' Ayden replied, in the same tone of voice as if Riley had asked if she'd ever seen a UPS truck.

'No way. They're just make-believe.'

The witch cocked an eyebrow. 'You mean like demons?'

'Oh.' Maybe there was a lot more to this mystical world stuff than Riley realized. 'Are they really cool? I mean, like Oberon-and-Titania cool?'

A Midsummer's Night Dream was one of her favourite Shakespearean plays, mostly because of the fairies. Most of the Bard's other plays seemed to have a horrifically high body count.

Ayden didn't reply until the brazier came to life, flicking pillars of flame into the air. 'The Fey are a lot like us. They can be arrogant and vindictive or kind and helpful, if they're in the mood. The problem is you never know which mood they're in until it's too late.'

'Are we going to see any of them tonight?' Peter asked hopefully.

'Not likely. If we were out in the country, maybe.'

'Who painted this mural?' Riley asked, trailing her fingertips over the painted wall. The images seemed alive.

'I did, along with a couple of the others in my circle.'

'*Your* circle?'

'I'm the high priestess,' Ayden replied.

You never told me that.

'So what's going to happen here?' Peter asked as they

moved to join the witch in the centre of the circle.

'I raise a cone of power and call up Paul Blackthorne's spirit.'

'So no big deal, huh?'

'It could get lively,' Ayden replied.

Peter chewed on that for a time. 'Define lively, please.'

Ayden continued her preparations, setting a green candle on the ground, then about ten feet away she put down a yellow one. 'It all depends on what type of magical landmines I trigger.'

'So we could get hurt?'

'Perhaps, but if you remain inside the circle we should be OK.'

'*Should* . . .' Peter frowned. 'If you were me, would you stay or take off?'

'Depends on your freak factor,' Ayden said, rising to her feet and dusting off her hands. 'If you can handle creepy stuff, then I'd say it'd be worth staying. If not, best to wait inside the building. It's warded so you'll be safe there.'

'Warded,' he murmured to himself.

'Peter, you don't have to do this,' Riley said.

He screwed his face up in thought. 'Yeah, I do. Count me in.'

'Then let's get this done,' Ayden replied. 'First, I will honour the four elements, lighting the candles that represent those elements.' The witch adjusted the white tapers in the centre of the altar. 'Then I'll light two which represent the God and Goddess.'

'Is that where we do the ritual sacrifice?' Peter joked uneasily.

'Volunteering, are we?' Ayden asked.

Peter clamped his mouth shut. The witch turned and frowned at the building behind them like she'd forgotten something.

'Could one of you turn off the outside lights? The switch is just inside the door.'

Riley took care of the problem. As she returned to the circle, her nerves kicked into high gear. Her very best friend in the whole world was here. What if something went wrong? What if Peter got hurt?

'It'll be OK,' she whispered as she crossed through the stone circle. 'It has to be.'

Ayden wore the velvet cloak now, her russet-brown hair flowing over her shoulders. A circlet nestled amongst her curls, braided silver with delicate leaves.

In a fluid movement born of practice, the sword slid out of its scabbard. The witch raised it reverently towards the sky like an ancient queen from an Arthurian tale. The light of the brazier threaded a thin, molten line of fiery gold along the blade's edge.

The witch turned, pointed the tip of the sword at the yellow candle at one of the four corners. In a clear voice, she said, 'I call forth the Element of Air. Protect all within this circle from those who would do us harm.'

Riley blinked when the candle burst into life. Ayden

hadn't struck a match. She couldn't with the sword in her hands.

How did you . . .

Peter waggled his eyebrows and mouthed, 'Cool!' Maybe it was good she'd brought him along. He hadn't acted this happy about anything for a long time.

The witch turned towards the south and the red candle. 'I call forth the Element of Fire. Guard us and warm us in our journey.' That candle blazed. When Ayden completed the invocation with the remaining two candles, there was a weird popping sensation, like they'd been enveloped by some sort of force field. Riley knew how this worked – it was like when she'd set the candle circle at the graveyard to protect her father's grave.

Ayden carefully laid the sword on the altar, then lit the two white candles with a match, invoking the presence of the deities in a clear voice. If Simon was here, he'd be having kittens by now. Raising her arms in the air, the witch called for protection, for wisdom and for knowledge. Then she waved Riley and Peter forward.

Edging close to the altar, Riley shot a quick look up at the window above them. Gazing down at them was a white-haired lady, her elbows resting on the windowsill.

'She likes to watch,' Ayden explained.

'Is she a witch?'

'No. Just curious about what kind of mischief we might be up to.'

Knowing Ayden, there wouldn't be any. She took this stuff very seriously.

'I'm going to cast the spirit summoning now. I want you to visualize your father. Try to pick a happy memory. That might make it easier to call him.'

Riley's mind returned to one of the last moments they'd spent together. They'd been in the car after the emergency Guild meeting. They'd talked about a movie night, just the two of them. It wasn't her best memory, but the strongest right now. A sharp pang of loss cut through her, but she pushed it aside, focusing on her father's voice, his smile. How good it felt when he was around and how much she missed him.

As she held that single memory close to her heart, she could hear Ayden chanting something. There was the smell of aromatic herbs, then more chanting.

The air around them shifted as a strange prickle danced across her face and hands.

Magic.

'We ask that Paul Blackthorne's spirit come to us,' Ayden called out. 'Come to his only child so that we may know he is safe.'

The prickling sensation increased, almost to the point of discomfort. Riley blinked open her eyes. The stone circle round them glowed a soft white. Peter's eyes were wide in amazement and his mouth had dropped open.

'Riley?' a voice said. It glided across her mind like a soft breeze.

'Dad?' she called out. *Is he really here?*

Paul Blackthorne stepped out of nowhere, as if through a hole in the air. He wasn't in the suit he'd been buried in, but in his Georgia Tech jacket, jeans and a sweatshirt. The clothes he'd been wearing the night he'd died.

'Welcome, spirit of Paul Blackthorne,' Ayden said solemnly. 'You are much missed.'

He gave a grave nod, then turned those sad brown eyes on his daughter.

'I miss you, Riley,' he said, his voice dry and thick.

Riley began to tremble. This was as bad as when Beck had come to her door to tell her she was an orphan.

'I want to get you back, Dad. Who took you? Was it Ozymandias?'

No reply.

Maybe he doesn't understand. 'We're being blamed for breaking the ward at the Tabernacle. The hunters are in town now. You've got to tell them the truth.'

'Not yet,' he replied.

'Is there anything you *can* tell us?' the witch urged.

Her father's eyes flicked to Ayden and then back to his daughter.

'I love you, Riley. You're stronger than you believe. I'm sorry for what has happened, and for what will happen. It is my fault.'

Then the spirit of Paul Blackthorne began to fade.

'Wait! No, don't go!' Riley shouted. *After all this and he's taking off?*

Ayden chanted again and the vision stabilized. The air just behind Riley's father began to boil in a red-and-gold maelstrom. Then something materialized in that very spot.

Towering over them was a dragon, at least twenty feet or more. Probably the one from the cemetery.

'Oh my Goddess.' Ayden latched on to Riley's arm and then did the same with Peter's. 'Don't move. Don't break the circle!'

There was a screech of shock and their spectator slammed her window shut, as if a single pane of glass would be any protection against this monstrosity.

'Can you make it go away?' Riley whispered.

Ayden didn't reply, murmuring under her breath. Riley caught the word *protection* more than once.

A low growl issued from the thing's cavernous mouth, sending a trickle of brilliant iridescent flames into the night air. 'Cease!' the creature bellowed, and the witch fell silent.

Ayden clamped her eyes on the beast. 'What do you seek, dragon?' she asked, her voice firm and level.

The creature ignored the witch, its glittering eyes only on Riley. 'Blackthorne's daughter,' it said. 'Do not fail us.'

'Who are you?' Riley demanded. 'Why did you take my dad?'

It wrapped its powerful forelegs around her father's form. 'To protect him from those who would use his power for their own gain.'

'I love you, Pumpkin,' her dad called out. 'I'll see you soon.'

The summoning vanished with a loud clap of thunder that reverberated throughout the neighbourhood, rattling windows and setting off car alarms.

'That was a bit over the top,' Ayden grumbled, releasing her grip on Riley's arm.

'Oh . . . dammit!' Riley shouted. 'We didn't learn a thing!' She had failed. Again.

She felt the panic attack coming, but couldn't stop it: her lungs collapsed and she began to shake, her vision constricting to the section of the courtyard where her father had disappeared into nothingness.

Her friends began whispering to each other, but she didn't understand what they were saying. Darkness crept in from the corners of her vision like twilight in a forest. Her breath hitched and she struggled to pull air inside her chest. The next breath was worse and she slumped to her knees.

'Riley?' It was Peter. He was close to her now, touching her hand. His fingers were trembling. 'You remember the first day we met at school? How you didn't have a pencil so I loaned you one? Do you remember which one it was?'

Why is he asking me this? My dad is dead and that thing has him and I have to stop Armageddon and—

'Come on, Riley, you should remember this. It's easy. You gave me crap about it for ages,' Peter urged. Then she knew what he was doing – he was recalling a good memory, trying to exorcize the fear that rode her like a fully-armoured warrior.

'Gollum,' she panted, pulling her eyes to meet his.

Peter smiled through his worry. 'Yup. You told me that any guy who had a *Lord of the Rings* pencil just had to be your friend for life.'

Between the shallow breaths, she tried to match his smile. 'I'm afraid, Peter. God, I'm so afraid.'

'So am I,' he whispered, then his arms went round her and he embraced her.

Riley hadn't lost everything. She still had her friends. Sometimes they were the only thing that kept you going. Her breathing eased and he loosened his grip.

'I promised you weird,' she said.

Peter chuckled. 'And you delivered.' He only let go of her when she took a deep, full breath.

'Thanks, Peter.'

He nodded, but didn't say anything that would make it harder for her. Ayden gave a relieved sigh, then turned towards where the dragon had been. She stared at the spot for some time, unmoving.

'Ah, Ayden?' Peter asked.

'Give me a moment,' she said. She took a deep breath like she was scenting the air, then blew it out a few seconds later. 'And the verdict is: not a necromancer.'

'What? It has to be,' Riley blurted as she scrambled to her feet.

The witch turned and faced them now, perplexed. 'That's what you'd expect, but it's not the case. I'm sensing older, more . . . primeval magic. Necromantic sorcery has a certain feel to it. This magic I've never felt before.'

'Which means?' Riley asked.

'Which means there's a new player in the game. Remember what the dragon said – your father was raised from his grave for his protection.'

'But from who?'

'Whom,' Peter corrected automatically. When Riley gave him a glower, he shrugged his shoulders in apology.

'Ozymandias is my favourite candidate,' the witch replied, 'but who wields the kind of power needed to cross the Eldest of the Summoners?'

'I don't want to be a buzzkill here,' Peter began, 'but are you sure it was your dad?'

'It had to be,' Riley said. 'He called me Pumpkin. I always hated that nickname, but he thought it was cute.'

Ayden was still pensive, her brows furrowed. 'So what is the message here?'

'Dragons are damned scary, even if they are made of magic?' Peter quipped.

Ayden's frown diminished. 'I am beginning to like you, Peter King.'

He grinned in response.

'*Do not fail us*,' Riley said. 'Whatever I'm supposed to do, I'd better not blow it.'

Riley and the witch traded looks. Then Riley shook

her head: no way was she going to tell Peter about her bargain with Heaven. His life was complicated enough without him worrying about the end of the world.

Silence fell between them as Ayden released the magic and broke the circle. They helped her pack up the witchy supplies and tote them back into the store. When she'd stowed away all the gear, she unlocked the front door and they all stood there awkwardly, like no one knew what to say.

Peter sniffed the air. 'Food. I'll . . . catch up with you in a moment.' Without waiting for her response, he headed down the alley towards the cafe.

'He eats like there's no tomorrow,' Riley observed.

'He is a good friend to have,' Ayden said. 'Tell him what's going on. *All of it.* He has a role to play.'

Riley gaped at the woman. 'Was that a prophecy or something?'

'I just know things.' The witch looked in the opposite direction, down the alley that led to Mort's house. 'You should talk to the summoner tonight.'

It wasn't a suggestion. 'You think he knew what we were up to?'

'He'd have felt the magic. I'd be interested to hear where he thought it came from.'

Mort's housekeeper admitted her to the house without comment, like Riley had been expected, and led her to the circular room that smelt of woodsmoke. Mort was at his desk, stacks of books mounded around him like a fortress of words. A plate of strudel sat at his elbow.

He rose. 'What the hell was that?' he said.

The evening had been so outlandish, so scary, that Riley couldn't help herself; she started to laugh. What else could she do? When she finally regained control, she said, 'I have no idea. My witch friend doesn't either.'

Mort sank back on to the bench, his fingers tented in a thoughtful pose. 'What I felt was old magic, so old the summoners don't have a name for it. Tell me what happened.'

Riley sat opposite him at the table. 'Well, we got a dragon,' she began, and then related the rest of the tale. Mort didn't interrupt. 'I've run out of things to try,' she said.

Mort nodded in sympathy. 'Ozymandias has a reward out for your father's corpse, but no one has come forward to claim it.'

'Everybody wants my dad,' she said bitterly.

'So it seems. A loan company has filed suit against the Society, claiming we're preventing them from reacquiring their *asset*, one Mr Paul Blackthorne. Apparently you owe them money,' Mort said.

Riley groaned.

'Just so you know, I've issued a magical invitation. If for some reason the summoner loses control of your father's spirit, I've invited it to take shelter here.'

Riley stared at him. 'You mean my dad might make a break for it?'

Forbidden

'Sometimes that happens, but in this case whoever conducted the summoning seems quite powerful so I doubt we'll have any luck.'

And if it wasn't a necromancer . . .

Riley stared down at her hands. There was dirt under her fingernails, probably from when she was having her panic attack in the courtyard. 'What if I never find him?' she asked.

'Then in a year we'll just hope he's back in the ground and at peace.'

That wasn't the answer she wanted. No, she wanted her dad's kidnapper to bleed, to hurt as badly as she did. After thanking Mort for all his help, Riley left the way she'd came. Behind her, she could hear the summoner mumbling under his breath, the thump of books falling open. He wasn't giving up, no matter what he'd said.

Neither am I.

Her friends waited for her in front of the witch shop. Peter handed over a paper bag.

'Food. You need it. You get any skinnier and you can model in New York.'

'Thanks,' Riley mumbled. She opened the bag and found it contained a turkey sandwich and a supersized chocolate-chip cookie. *Yum.* 'Thanks,' she repeated, this time with more enthusiasm.

Ayden lightly touched her shoulder. 'What did the summoner say?'

'He had no clue who it was either.'

'As I figured. I think it's best you remember what your father said – you're stronger than you believe. That's important. Spirits don't usually lie.'

The witch had spaced off the other thing her father had said. *I'll see you soon.* Since it didn't look like Riley was going to retrieve him from whoever had ripped off his corpse, that meant only one thing.

This might be the last cookie I ever eat.

Chapter Twenty-Six

The sensible part of Riley knew she should be at the church, but she was tired of hiding like some scared little kid. Everyone reached their breaking point, and she was way past it. If Ori was right, her being out like this might lure the Five closer and he could kill the thing.

Then I'll be free.

She heard someone call her name and found the freelance demon hunter striding across the open field at the edge of the market. No way round it, Ori was made of awesome, yummy on so many levels you just didn't know where to start. Simon was handsome, but Ori redefined the word.

Just thinking the name of her now ex-boyfriend made her wince, like someone had jammed needles under her fingernails. This should be Simon at her side, hanging with her, laughing and being with her. *But it isn't.*

When Ori reached her, she murmured her hello, trying to sound upbeat. He examined her for a moment, as if he was trying to see behind her mask.

'You were up to something tonight in Little Five Points. Very noisy. And magical. I almost thought it was

739

the Five for a moment. What were you doing?'

'A witch friend of mine summoned my dad's spirit. I thought we could find out who stole him.' She hitched her shoulders. 'Not so much. He wouldn't tell us anything.'

'I'm truly sorry about that,' Ori said. 'I know how much you miss him.'

'This whole thing has been an epic fail. I promised him I'd keep him safe in his grave. Didn't do that. Promised him I'd find his body. Blew that one too.'

'Well, you're not the only one failing,' he admitted, his tone darker now. 'The Five is hiding, biding its time.'

'So someone really is helping it?' Riley asked, puzzled.

'Hell *is* known for its alliances. Archfiends do not like to work together, but they will make pacts with lower-level Hellspawn, gathering in souls and power. The Five could owe its allegiance to another, one who wanted your father dead and is now sheltering his killer.'

'Great. The manual never mentioned that whole *dealing in souls* part.'

'I'm thinking there's more weight on your shoulders tonight than just your father. What else is troubling you?'

Might as well unload it all. 'My boyfriend and I broke up.' On impulse, she told him the gruesome story. Including the part with the Holy Water bath.

Ori glowered. 'Paul would not have harmed his fellow trappers. It was not in his character. Or yours, either.'

Riley felt a surge of joy that someone believed in her

dad. Believed in her. She slowed her pace, then stopped altogether. 'Thank you. That means a lot to me.'

To her astonishment, Ori cupped her face with his hands and carefully placed a kiss in the very centre of her forehead. The merest brush of his lips sent heat racing through her veins.

'I will destroy that Hellspawn and then you will not have to be afraid ever again,' he said, his midnight-black eyes inches from hers.

'You would do that for me?' she whispered.

'For you . . . and your father,' he said, then removed his hands. Before she could think of what to say, someone else called out her name. Riley knew that voice anywhere.

'Oh, no! What's he doing here?'

A familiar figure tromped towards them, the scowl on Beck's face promising trouble.

Riley hated to suggest it, but . . . 'He will be furious if he finds you're here with me. He won't understand.'

'That would be his problem,' Ori replied simply. 'I'm going nowhere.'

Riley groaned. She took a deep breath and waited for the trapper to reach them.

'Beck.' *Don't make a scene, please?*

That unspoken plea was wasted.

'What are ya doin', girl?' Beck demanded. 'The sun's down. Why aren't ya at the church?' He ground to a halt a short distance away, his hand knotted round the strap to his duffel bag. She could see the knuckles whiten.

He eyed her, then turned his full attention to Ori. 'Wait a minute, I know that face. Ya were at the Armageddon the other night.'

Ori hangs out at a pool hall? He didn't seem the type.

'I remember you,' her companion replied. 'You were playing pool with a summoner. You were letting him win.'

The trapper puffed up. 'Who are ya? What are ya doin' with Riley?'

'Beck!' Riley retorted. That was just rude.

Ori moved closer to her, like he was claiming her in some way. His hand gently touched her elbow and gave it a reassuring squeeze.

'I asked ya a question,' Beck said.

'The name is Ori and I'm her date for the evening. Why is any of this your concern?'

Date?

Beck blinked a couple of times before his eyes narrowed. 'I'm the guy ya have to deal with if ya think you're goin' out with her.'

'You didn't tell me you had a brother,' Ori said, looking over at Riley. When he winked, she had to struggle to keep the smile off her face.

'Look, dumbass,' Beck growled, 'I don't know what your game is, but you're not playin' it with her.'

'Hey!' Riley said, stepping forward and snapping her fingers in front of Beck's face. 'I'm not invisible. If I want to go out with someone, I'll do it, and you don't have any say in the matter.'

He scowled. 'Like you're a great judge of character. Your first boyfriend was an abusive bastard and the last one was a self-righteous prick.'

'So where do you fall on that scale?' Ori enquired.

Riley almost choked.

Beck's shoulders tightened in response, like he was ready to charge into battle. 'So what's your story?'

Ori's good humour disappeared. 'I'm a freelance demon hunter.'

She was surprised he'd let that one slip.

'That figures.' Beck smirked. 'Here's the deal: lancers aren't welcome here, not unless ya decide to become a trapper and join the Guild, do honest work for a change.'

'You're very cocky for someone who almost lost his soul to a Mezmer in a pool hall.'

Beck's face went pale. 'Now look here, ya son of a—'

'Did he tell you about that?' Ori cut in. 'Apparently not. I'd be ashamed too.'

Riley cringed. 'Enough, guys,' she said, tugging on Ori's arm.

'Girl . . .' Beck, his voice a low growl.

She stepped between them again, though it was a dangerous place to be with all the testosterone in the air. 'I don't care what you think, Beck, so just leave me alone. It's time I made my own decisions.'

'Then don't come cryin' to me when it all goes to hell,' Beck replied.

'Deal.'

She turned her back on him and walked away, Ori at her side. Behind them she could hear Beck swearing in both English and Hellspeak.

'Colourful fellow. Do you think he's watching?' Ori whispered.

'Count on it.'

He ran his arm round her waist and pulled her so close their hips bumped. 'Good. I hope he gets an eyeful.'

'You're wicked,' Riley said, grinning up at him.

'You don't know the half of it,' Ori replied.

When the adrenalin from the encounter wore off, Riley found herself more tired than she'd expected. It'd been a long and pretty much fruitless day. The only positive part was walking next to her. She felt good around Ori, much like she had when she'd been with Simon. She wasn't sure what that meant.

Abruptly Ori slowed his pace, then he stopped and scanned the area around them.

'Is Beck following us?' A shake of the head. 'Is the Five?' she asked. *Would it come for me here? Of course it would.* Being in the market wouldn't mean a thing to a demon.

'No.' He mumbled something under his breath, and then began walking again, faster now, forcing Riley to catch up with him.

What's got him spooked?

As they turned the corner towards the road where

she'd parked her car, someone bumped her from behind. Her head spun for a second and then her vision cleared. When she looked around, whoever had bumped her was gone.

A sharp, stinging sensation came from her left hand. 'Ouch,' she said, shaking it to clear the discomfort. There didn't seem to be anything wrong with it, but it still stung. From the way it felt she'd expected to see a big welt or something.

Ori swore in Hellspeak.

'I'm OK,' she said, rubbing the sore area. That only seemed to make it worse.

'Let me see.' Ori took her hand in his and the pain eased.

'Wow, how did you . . .' Riley looked up at him as she spoke, then all the air fled her lungs.

Ori shimmered in a harsh pulsating light. She might have been able to ignore that, but the immense wings behind him pretty much sealed the deal. They sat tight against his back and were pure white, each feather shimmering in the lights from the tents around them.

As she stared in wonder, a woman walked by them, toting a basket and humming to herself, failing to notice that Riley's date glowed like a supernova.

I've been holding hands with an angel? Having hot thoughts about one of Heaven's peeps? 'You're an—'

Ori shook his head in dismay. 'Not here,' he said. He flicked his hand and the scene changed.

*

Riley found herself surrounded by a deep green carpet of grass, blades bending in the faint breeze. Nestled within the green were bluebells and, in the distance, white clumps. The clumps moved.

'Sheep?' she asked, surprised.

Every now and then one would raise its woolly head, move a few steps and start grazing again. They didn't have sheep in the market and there wasn't grass like this, or a big blue sky.

'What is all this?' A scent tickled her nose and she placed it immediately. *Watermelon.*

Riley found Ori under a broad oak tree that had to be at least a century old. His wings weren't visible now and a dark blue blanket lay on the ground, along with a wicker picnic basket. On the blanket was a white china plate piled with slices of succulent watermelon, the black seeds dotting the firm flesh.

'I thought we needed privacy,' he explained.

It was all so real. 'Where is this place? How did we get here?'

'It'd take too long to explain. Just accept this as a gift from me.' He waved her closer.

A picnic with an angel? Her mind finally completed its reboot. And went suspicious.

'You're not here to have me stop Armageddon or anything, are you?'

'No,' he said, smiling.

'How do I know you're not a demon playing games with my head?'

'You don't,' he said. 'You just have to trust me.' He smiled and beckoned to her again. 'Come on, the watermelon is really good.'

Riley groaned to herself as she hiked up the hill. She paused at the edge of the blanket, arms crossed over her chest. She still wasn't buying all this. 'Why haven't I been able to see your . . . angelness until now?'

'Because the timing wasn't right,' he replied. 'Unfortunately, one of the other Divines thought it would be amusing to alter that situation in the middle of the marketplace.' From the low rumble in his voice it was clear he wasn't pleased by the prank.

'You mean whoever bumped into me? That was an angel too?'

A nod. Ori gestured at the plate of watermelon. 'Your favourite, I believe.' Then he knelt next to the picnic basket and a plate of cheese, sliced peaches and frosty grapes appeared.

'How do you do that?' she quizzed.

Ori's face lit with a smile. 'Divines are allowed small bits of creation,' he said, as if it was nothing.

She took another look around, inhaling the fresh air. 'This isn't small, Ori. This is amazing!'

Finally Riley gave in to the moment. What else could she do? It beat being bored to tears in a church basement. Besides, the smell of the watermelon was getting to her.

*

'Why does it feel different when I'm with you?' she asked dreamily. 'Is it because of what you are?'

'That's why.' He seemed at ease here, not tense like he'd been at the market.

'So are you like my guardian angel or something?' *That would totally rock.*

'No, I'm not.'

'Oh,' she said, sincerely disappointed. 'But you kept the Five from killing me.'

'It wasn't your time to die,' Ori said simply.

Which meant he knew when her time *was* up.

She couldn't ask that question. 'So what do you do as an angel?'

'You mean besides giving pretty girls roses?' he said.

'Yes, besides that.'

'I'm a problem solver. I handle difficult situations.'

'Like . . .' she quizzed, beckoning with her hand for further information.

'Like that Geo-Fiend who killed your father. It's a rogue demon. It must be destroyed.'

'So that's what you do all the time?' she asked, sneaking another piece of watermelon.

'I told you I was a demon hunter,' he said, brows furrowed. 'I didn't lie.'

'You just shaded the truth, a lot. You so didn't mention the *I've got wings* thing.'

'I didn't want to scare you,' he said, his voice softer now.

Forbidden

'Do you always hang around pool halls?' she jested.

'Not usually. It was lucky I was there that night or the Mezmer would have had your friend's soul.'

Riley stilled. 'Was it that close?'

'Yes. He was at breaking point. I made sure it didn't happen.'

She let out a whoosh of air in relief. 'I wasn't so sure if he was OK. Beck wouldn't say much about it. Pride and all.'

'He is his own master. Pride and all.'

Riley cocked her head. 'Why did you save him?'

'Because he's important to you so that makes him important to me.'

She opened her mouth to protest, then realized it would be futile. 'I do like Beck, at least when he's not being a jerk.'

'I thought so,' Ori said, then popped a grape into his mouth. 'Besides, you've lost too much already.'

'Like my dad,' Riley said. 'Do you know who summoned him?'

'No, I don't. It might shock you to know that Divines aren't all-knowing.'

'Of course. That would be too easy.'

Ori put his arm round her, drawing her close. Initially she wasn't sure if she wanted that, but eventually she snuggled next to him, her emotions stilling. She knew from the post-Allan experience that rebound romances weren't a good idea. A rebound with an angel? That didn't even register on the cosmic scale of *not a good idea*.

'I disagree,' Ori said. He delicately tipped her chin up with a finger. His eyes told her what he intended. And then he kissed her, without waiting for her verdict on the subject. Like everything else around them, the kiss was beyond what it should be. Every nerve in Riley's body tingled, a Simon-level kiss on steroids. They kissed again, this time more deeply. Her body began to hum, like it was lit from within by a strange fire.

Riley pulled out of his arms, her head swimming.

Ori leaned back against the tree, one foot propped up. A scoundrel with that black hair skimming over his shoulders and those bold, dark eyes.

Get a grip, girl.

'Why are you are doing this? Spending time with me, I mean. You could have just followed me and I would never have known you were there.'

'I feel alive when I'm with you.'

She barely subdued the snort. 'You're an angel. You hang with God and all those other Divine guys. I'm just . . . me.'

'You're Riley Anora Blackthorne,' he replied, as if that settled the matter. 'You deserve better than what you've had.'

Her mind traitorously returned to Simon and how he found more comfort with his rosary than he did with her. And Beck, the constant annoyance in her life. What would they think if they knew she was hanging with an honest-to-God for-real angel?

Forbidden

Riley felt a faint touch on her arm.

'Neither of them can know the truth.'

'OK, that's way freaky,' she replied. 'You know what I'm thinking.'

'Only when there's a lot of emotion behind the thought.'

Then Ori was near her again, looking in her eyes, his lips barely brushing her cheek.

'One more kiss,' he said, 'then I'll take you home.'

They took their time, and when they finally broke apart Riley could feel her heart hammering. *Amazing.*

'Amazing?' he said, that wicked grin blossoming.

He'd read her mind. Again. 'Stop that,' she chided.

'You'll get used to it.'

'Only if I can hear your thoughts.'

'Maybe that's possible. Let's find out.'

The angel pulled her close. His skin felt warm, toasty even. There was nothing at first, then the silent brush of wings against her mind.

Hello, Riley.

She yanked herself away, blinking in surprise. 'I heard you!'

He nodded, satisfied. 'It is said if a mortal can hear an angel's thoughts, they were meant to be together.'

Together?

He pulled her close again, putting his forehead against hers. She heard him as plain as if he'd spoken the words.

You will be my downfall, Riley Blackthorne.

She surrendered to another kiss, one that seemed to stir something deep inside her, like a flower unfolding in the glorious sunshine. For the first time wild, impossible futures began to form in her mind.

'Goodnight, Riley,' he said, and then she was standing next to her car just outside the market, keys in hand. Ori was nowhere to be seen, but she could still taste his kisses on her lips, the brush of his fingers on her cheek, the warmth in her belly.

Then it all faded, like a dream. Even the watermelon on her tongue was gone.

Like it had never existed.

Beck felt like an idiot. He'd been sitting in his truck for the past hour, waiting, playing the same country song over and over until it sawed across his nerves. It was now close to eleven and Paul's daughter wasn't at the church yet.

'Where the hell are ya?' he snarled. 'If you're . . .' He clenched his teeth, trying hard not to think of what might be happening between that slick bastard and Paul's little girl.

One moment Beck knew what he was doing was right, then the next he felt like a damned stalker. She wasn't a kid, even if he tried to act like she was. He'd not been fair when he'd said all her boyfriends had been jerks. There were a couple of boys between Allan and Simon who had treated her decently. But deep in his gut he was sure this Ori was a bad move.

During his hour's vigil he'd come to one conclusion – he was losing his mind when it came to Paul's daughter. He was jealous. No way to deny it. When he'd seen that man put his arm round her, he'd wanted to rip the dude to pieces.

I gotta get a grip on this. Can't keep goin' down this road.

Beck blew out a lungful of air in relief when Riley's car pulled to the kerb and she stepped out. She had a strange look on her face and wasn't paying attention to her surroundings, so he tracked her until she entered the church and the door closed behind her. At least he knew she was safe.

And alone.

He started his truck, then just sat there. After a moment's consideration, he headed towards the Westin. By now Justine might know something about this Ori guy and, besides, she had her own brand of magic, the kind that would help Beck forget the one girl he'd never have.

Ori found his nemesis in the old cemetery near the master trapper's empty grave. The earth had been returned to the hole now, but it had settled, causing cracks to form along the edges where it met solid ground. He made no effort to cover his approach, but landed squarely in front of Sartael, wings unfurled and prepared for battle.

'What were you playing at?' he shouted, his hands

fisted. 'Why did you reveal me? You nearly ruined everything.'

Sartael observed his anger with cool detachment. 'You know why.'

Ori's fists unclenched and he ruffled his wings in agitation. 'The rogue demon will come for her and I will kill it. I will not allow anything to happen to her.'

Sartael eyed him gravely. 'I have heard all this before. *He* is not pleased with your progress. If that does not spur you on, then you are a fool.'

'I will speak with Him—'

'That is not necessary. You are to use your *special talents* this time.'

Ori studied his foe, unsure if he could trust him. 'Is that His order?'

'You would question Him?' Wings beating in unison, Sartael rose into the sky, sending decaying leaves billowing underneath him in a whirlwind. 'If you do not prevail, I shall. And I promise you will not like the outcome.'

Chapter Twenty-Seven

As the morning newscast droned on the television in Harper's office, Riley worked on the record-keeping. It put her in the unpleasant position of having her back to her master, but he seemed less likely to leave bruises these days, what with his injured ribs.

'Done yet?' he asked, muting the sound.

'Yes, I got it. Between the money for the demons we've trapped, the disability payment from the Guild and the scrap-metal sales, you've got one thousand, two hundred and eighty-seven dollars coming in over the next three weeks.' She turned in the squeaky office chair. 'Is that enough?'

Harper gave a slow nod. 'Better than I thought it'd be. I'll be able to take you and Saint out next week sometime. In the meantime, you trap with Beck.'

Trapping demons with Beck? That had been OK in the past, but after last night she wasn't sure if she wanted to be anywhere near him.

'OK,' she replied. There wasn't any other answer she could give.

The front door to the warehouse pushed open, causing

Riley to take a deep breath and hold it. Was it the hunters? What would her master do if the Vatican came calling?

'Master Harper, good morning,' Simon said, moving slowly into the office. She noticed he didn't bother to include her in the greeting.

'Saint. How you doing?' their master called out.

'Better.'

'Simon,' she said. Only then did his crystal-blue eyes move in her direction.

'Riley.' His voice was as cold as a tray of ice cubes dumped down her back.

More drama. Just what I don't need.

She moved out of the chair and let her former boy-friend sink into it. His face was as pale as his white-blond hair and he had one hand placed on his abdomen like he expected his intestines to fall on to the floor at any moment.

The fact he was up and moving at all was astounding. Heaven really delivered on their promise, even if it did have unintended consequences.

'You sure you're good enough to be here?' Harper asked, rising from the recliner.

'For a little while. Thought I could do the paperwork.'

'Give him the reports, then,' Harper said, and shuffled off towards the bathroom.

Riley moved the stack of papers in front of Simon. 'I haven't got to these yet.'

A nod. Then he picked up a pencil and began to work

through the trapping reports. The moment Riley heard the bathroom door shut, she knelt down until her face was level with his.

'You sicced the hunters on me,' she accused, keeping her voice low.

Simon's eyes bored into her like fiery blue lasers. 'If you're innocent, no problem,' he said levelly.

'How could you do that? I thought we had something, Simon.'

'We did, until you showed your true colours.'

'I haven't changed,' she said. 'You just think I have.'

'Don't try to reason with me,' he retorted. 'I know what you are and I know who you work for.'

'And just how can you tell that?' she demanded. 'Is there, like, some mark on my forehead or something?'

'I just know,' he said, his voice less sure now. 'I'm not the only one who's figured it out. He told me all about—'

When Harper exited the bathroom, Riley lurched to her feet.

'If you don't need anything else, sir,' she said, wanting to put distance between herself and the cold-hearted monster sitting at the desk. This time it wasn't her master.

Harper waved her off. 'Keep your phone on. If a call comes in, I'll need you to take care of it.'

As she left the building, she could hear them talking. She bet Simon would waste no time telling Harper all about her deal with Hell.

And he'll believe every word of it.

*

With time to kill before class, Riley flopped into her own bed and stared up at the ceiling. She'd consulted her list and managed to cross off two items: groceries and laundry. The really big things were still undone, looming over her head like some ancient curse.

Though the tenant upstairs was vacuuming the floor and every now and then there would be a thump as the machine bumped into a piece of furniture, it felt good to lie in her own bed. The sounds of domesticity comforted her. She conducted an inventory: the ache in her chest was still there, aggravated by seeing Simon in all his cruel and unrepentant glory. He really did believe she was evil. Maybe Heaven hadn't healed him as well as they thought. Maybe the lack of oxygen to his brain did do some damage.

Either way, Riley knew from past experience that this loss would eventually contract to a hard knot, but never disappear. She still had one for Allan after all these years and a much smaller one for Beck. Simon's would be the biggest.

The sweeping ended and there was relative silence. Riley's eyes closed, and for a brief moment she swore she could taste watermelon on her tongue. She smiled at the memory as the soft brush of wings in her mind lulled her to sleep.

The knock at her door roused her out of a totally X-rated dream that involved a certain hunkalicious angel. 'Oh, wow,' she said, fanning herself. It was good she was at home. Having that kind of dream at the church was probably a mortal sin.

Another series of knocks. 'Miss Blackthorne?' It was a female voice, one with a strange accent.

Riley relaxed. It wasn't the demon hunters – they didn't have women on their crew. Maybe they'd decided it wasn't worth the hassle to check her out.

I'll be winning the lottery any day now.

She dragged herself out of bed and cautiously opened the door, leaving the safety chain in place. Her visitor was taller than Riley, probably five-nine or so. She was a complete package: a sculpted nose, perfectly arched eyebrows and thick hair that tumbled over her shoulders in a red riot. Her suit had to be custom made the way it moulded to her figure. It was green tweed with an asymmetrical collar and the trousers ended at just the right point above her black heels. Her fingers matched her hair. Even worse, the vivid green eyes weren't from contacts.

Riley instantly disliked her, an automatic response of one woman to another when the other looked this good. Especially when Riley had opened the door clad in stained and ripped blue jeans and a T-shirt that had been tie-dyed by demon pee.

'Miss Blackthorne?' the woman asked. Her eyes flickered across Riley's clothes. To her credit she didn't gag.

'If you're here from the collection agency, don't bother. My dad's long gone and I have no idea who has him.'

'I am not from any collection agency,' the woman

replied. Something floral wafted into the apartment as she offered up a business card with a delicate hand. 'I'm Justine Armando.' She stated the name as if everyone would recognize it instantly.

Riley studied the card.

Justine Armando
Freelance Journalist

'I don't talk to the press,' she said automatically. That was one of the first lessons drilled into an apprentice's brain – talking to the media was a big no-go.

'I am aware of that, but Beck said it would be fine,' the woman replied.

That didn't sound like Backwoods Boy. 'I doubt that.'

'On the contrary, I've already interviewed him . . . extensively,' the woman added.

The words *interviewed* and *extensively* had a certain weight to them, like the reporter meant something entirely different.

Riley eyed her visitor again, assessing the package. 'Stroke his ego, did you?'

Ms Armando's mouth curved into a knowing smile.

Ah, jeez. You're knocking boots with a reporter? Come on, Beck. That's just wrong.

'I thought it would be interesting to hear your perspective on trapping with the men,' the woman explained. 'That cannot be easy for you.'

Forbidden

As much as Riley would have loved to tell her side of the story, if she talked to the press without Harper's permission, he'd be all over her. She just didn't need the hassle.

'Sorry, I can't do it, not without my master's OK,' she said, and shut the door before she lost her nerve.

The reporter knocked again, calling out, but Riley ignored her. She curled up in bed, trying not to conjure up the image of Backwoods Boy and the reporter chick doing what she and the angel had been up to in her dream. She thumped the heel of her hand against her forehead, hoping that might dislodge the slide show. It didn't work. In fact, the images only became more graphic.

'Eww!' she said, grimacing. 'La la la la la . . .'

If they were hooking up, there was only one reason that woman would pick Beck as a lover – the red-haired stick chick was using him to further her career.

'I mean, look at her. She's *so* not your type.' Not that she knew what Beck's type would be, but Riley suspected it would be someone into country music and who liked to hang at the Armageddon Lounge and shoot pool all night. That was not Ms Perfect Size Eight.

Riley finally drifted into an uneasy sleep. Seconds later, or so it seemed, someone pounded on the door. She sat bolt upright, glowering. It was like there was a neon sign on the top of the apartment building that said: *Riley is Trying to Sleep. Visit Her Now!*

'If this is the stick chick again . . .'

This time it was all guys, two of whom were in

military garb, wearing side arms and sporting a special patch on their vests depicting a dude slaying a dragon. Behind them was a priest, clad in solid black like an aged crow. It wasn't Father Harrison.

Simon's call to the demon hunters had borne fruit.

'Miss Blackthorne?' one of the men asked, his accent thick and hard to understand. He was tall, Nordic blond, and pretty scary. 'We are demon hunters, here by special permission from the Vatican.'

Here being Atlanta, she hoped, rather than on her doorstep in particular.

'I can only talk to you if my master is present.' It was a good response to just about anything she didn't want to do.

'Those rules don't apply to us,' the man insisted.

'They do for me.'

'We have the power to detain you for questioning,' he replied, his voice taking on a harder edge. 'We will use that power if needed.'

I so don't need this right now. 'This is because of Simon Adler, right? What he said about me?'

The priest nodded. 'Mr Adler has concerns about your loyalties.' He moved closer to the door at this point. Maybe he thought he had a better chance of convincing her to play along.

'Did he tell you we used to date?'

'He stated that you had coerced him into a romantic relationship.'

'Co . . . erced?' she sputtered. Simon had been the one

to ask her out, not the other way round.

'We need to speak at length about this issue, Miss Blackthorne,' the priest replied. 'Please let us in.'

'I don't know what else Simon told you, but I didn't break the ward. Neither did my father, who is dead and has been reanimated, just in case you haven't heard. I have no idea why the demons came after us and I have class in an hour,' she said in a rush of words. 'That's all you're getting from me unless my master is present.'

'These charges are serious: you have been accused of working for Lucifer,' the priest replied.

'Not a chance. Now good afternoon,' she said, pushing the door closed.

The big blond man slammed his palm against the wood, straining the chain lock. With only a little more effort the chain would snap and they'd be inside.

Panicking, Riley backed off, grabbing her cellphone from the coffee table.

'You stay outside or I'll call the cops,' she warned, brandishing the phone like a weapon.

'You let us in and the door stays in one piece,' the big man replied.

She had no other option but to dial Harper, gambling that he hated the hunters more than he hated her. As the phone rang, there was rapid-fire conversation between the priest and the Nordic guy, all in a language she didn't understand. When her master answered, she unloaded the situation in a whisper.

'What do I do?' she asked, crossing the fingers of her free hand behind her back where the hunters wouldn't see it. *Please don't make me talk to them.*

'Let me talk to the priest,' Harper ordered.

Riley handed the cellphone to Father Rosetti through the wedge of open door. There was a brisk exchange and then it came back to her.

'Sir?' she asked, her fingers still crossed.

'You're not to talk to them unless I'm with you. If they arrest you, call me and we'll take it from there,' Harper said. 'And don't think you're out of it. If you're working for Hell, I'll kill you myself.' The phone went dead.

All right, then.

The priest issued an order and the big man backed off. 'You will talk to us eventually,' the cleric said, giving her a thin smile. If it was supposed to reassure her, it did the opposite.

'The Guild won't let you touch me,' she said defiantly.

'They will if we find evidence of your guilt. They will throw you to us just to clear their name. It is better to plead your case now. Our mercy is not limitless.'

'I haven't done anything,' she insisted. 'So just go away and leave me alone.'

Riley pushed the door closed, then leaned against it, stomach churning. There was the thump of combat boots on the stairs and then silence.

They want a scapegoat and I'm it. Next time I won't be able to stall them.

764

Chapter Twenty-Eight

The big blue tent at the far edge of the Terminus Market seemed an unlikely place to hold a trapper's meeting, but according to Jackson nobody else in the city would rent them space.

'Can't blame them,' the trapper said as he parked himself in a folding chair next to Riley inside the tent. His arm was still bandaged, but he seemed able to move it without much pain.

'Do you want me to do the Holy Water ward?' she asked. It was usually Simon's job, but she doubted he could handle it right now.

'One of the others is doing it.'

Riley knew why. 'You don't trust me to do it right,' she said, hurt more than she cared to admit.

'If it was me, you'd be doing the ward, but Stewart suggested a journeyman handle it for the time being. That way, if anything happens, you won't be blamed.'

'So will it always be this way? Nobody trusting me, that is?' she demanded.

'I honestly don't know,' Jackson replied.

'We didn't do anything to the ward,' she insisted.

'I know that. Sometimes the truth is harder to accept than a lie.'

Jackson was trying to make her feel better, in comparison to other trappers who kept frowning at her and muttering *Blackthorne* under their breath like it was a curse word. *Asshats*. How could they believe she'd let the demons in? All her father had done was protect his daughter.

When Jackson moved to the front of the tent, she looked over at her master. Harper hadn't said a word to her about her phone call this afternoon, like his apprentices were visited by the demon hunters every day. Which meant he thought she was good for it. So did Simon, who sat next to him, his face grim. When one of the trappers said hello, the apprentice only nodded, his mind stuck in some dark mire of conspiracy theories.

Why is everything so wrong now?

Someone called out Beck's name, and a moment later he appeared at the tent flap. He looked like he hadn't slept in days.

Bet it wasn't because you were hunting demons. Not with the arrogant smirk on his face.

He took a seat next to her, placing his trapping bag on the ground. 'Riley.'

The faint hint of something flowery caught her nose and she reacted instantly. 'How's the reporter chick?'

Beck gave her a startled look. 'What do ya mean?'

She took an exaggerated sniff. 'The reporter chick, the

one with the red hair? Unless you're letting your inner girl show, you smell just like her.' When he began to protest, she waved him off. 'She was at my apartment this afternoon trying to interview me so I remember her perfume.'

'Did ya talk to her?' Beck asked, suddenly worried.

'Was I supposed to?'

'No way. Ya know that. Everythin' goes through Harper or Stewart.'

The stick chick lies like a pro. 'You're always giving me advice – here's some for you. She's playing you. She lied to me, told me you said it was OK if I talked to her.'

'That's what reporters do,' he said, but his frown told her he wasn't happy with the news. 'I thought ya knew that.'

'I know a lot of things, Beck, and she's not your type.'

'Ya sayin' I'm not good enough for her?' he said, his voice harsher now.

'No. I'm saying she's not on the level.'

A scowl formed on his face. She knew what was coming. 'Ya called Fargo yet?'

'No, I've been too busy trying to destroy the Guild and corrupt Simon's soul. Being evil is a full-time job.'

Beck snorted. He angled his head towards where her ex-boyfriend sat at the other side of the tent. 'No need to hang around for him any more. He's moved on. That sure didn't last very long, did it?'

Ouch. Riley knew they should step away from this

before someone went too far, but the need to retaliate became overwhelming.

'I'm not staying at the church from now on,' she announced. 'Ori's watching over me. He won't let anything happen. He'll get that Five, you wait and see.'

A chuff of disgust came her way. 'Bull . . . shit. Pretty boys like that don't know jack when it comes to demons. They're just flash.'

Riley leaned closer to her father's favourite trapping buddy, eager to spear his insufferable arrogance in its heart. 'Ori was the one who saved me from the Five at the Tabernacle.'

'What?' Beck spouted.

'You heard me.' She let three seconds pass before delivering the verbal knife-thrust between his ribs. 'He was there for me when it counted, Beck. So where were you?'

The trapper's mouth flopped open in astonishment.

Jackson's timing was perfect – he called out for silence. As trappers settled into their chairs, Beck continued to stare at her in disbelief.

'I'm calling this meeting to order,' Jackson said, waving his hands to gain attention. 'We lost the gavel in the fire so we'll just have to deal. The masters have asked me to be acting president until we have an election. Is that OK with you folks?'

There were murmurs of agreement.

'Fine. First thing, Pritchard is the only one still in the hospital. He'll be going home in a couple of days, but he's done trapping. That's bad news for us, but at least he's still alive.'

'Thank God,' someone called out. Riley thought his name was Remmers or something like that. He was the only African American in the Atlanta Guild now.

'I second that,' another said.

'The remainder of the funerals will be out of the area so I need volunteers to attend those services.' Hands shot up and Jackson made note of the names. 'Thanks, guys. Master Stewart, you want to give a report on the demon hunters?'

The Scotsman rose from his chair, leaning heavily on his cane. 'As we expected, they're gonna do their own thing. My advice is ta stay outta their way. They'll kill a few demons and then leave, if we're lucky.'

'And if not?' Jackson asked.

'Then it could get ugly. We don't want any more casualties so don't cross these guys. Just back off and live for another day.'

'You saying we should just let them do whatever they want?' someone called out.

A wily grin settled on the Scotsman's face. 'No, I'm not. Ya have a problem with them, call me or Beck. We'll get it sorted.'

'Anything from the archbishop about the Holy Water problem?' Jackson asked.

'Not yet. He's checkin' his sources, but so far the city claims there's no problem at all.'

Riley held her tongue. No reason to let the others know she'd been investigating on her own, at least not until she'd figured out the whole scam. Then she'd be happy to drop it in their laps.

'Anything you want to say, Harper?' Jackson asked.

Riley's heart began to thud. *What if he tells them about the hunters? What if he demands they toss me out of the Guild?*

The older trapper shook his head. 'Not right now.'

What? He'd had the perfect opportunity to ruin her career and he'd passed on it. *What's he up to?*

'On to other business, then,' Jackson continued. 'It seems like we've got more press in this city than we have demons, at least that's what it looks like. Be careful what you say to these folks. We need to present a solid front.'

'Better tell Mile High about that,' a trapper called out. Riley didn't recognize the voice.

Beck shifted uneasily in his seat. 'I know how to handle 'em.'

'So we noticed,' was the swift response. Crude jests flew through the tent, followed by laughter. *Even they think you're sleeping with her.*

Jackson shuffled papers. 'The National Guild is requesting trappers to come to Atlanta to help us out, at least in the short term. They're also trying to line up a master for us. It'll be a while before that happens.'

'What about that television show?' Reynolds asked. 'They still coming?'

Forbidden

'I haven't heard anything to say they're not,' Jackson replied. 'Let's talk about what happened the other night,' he added, opening the floor to whoever wanted to have their say.

There were different schools of thought: the Holy Water was neutralized or the bogus Holy Water was to blame. The third explanation cut too close to home: *someone* had purposely broken the ward.

'Riley?' It was their temporary president and he was looking right at her. 'Could you tell us what your father said to you that night?'

She rose, nervous when all eyes turned to her. 'He said I should run, that *they* were coming. That there were too many of them.'

'He was inside the ward, wasn't he?' Jackson asked.

'Yes. He was right behind me.'

Voices erupted from the back of the tent as she sank into her seat.

'I told you he did it!' McGuire shouted.

Harper rose, a hand pressed against his sore ribs. 'That's not what I saw. The ward was still up when Blackthorne was talking to his kid. It didn't break until it was overwhelmed by the demons.'

Harper doesn't blame my dad? She had to be dreaming.

'What's yer theory on all this?' the Scotsman asked.

'Same as yours – too much evil in one place,' her master replied, and sank back into his seat.

As Simon rose to his feet, all eyes went to him. 'How

can you . . .' He paused to suck in a tortured breath. 'How can you believe that God's holy essence can be destroyed?'

'Not destroyed . . . neutralized. There is a difference,' Stewart replied.

'Not to me,' Simon shot back. 'Either you believe Heaven has ultimate power to destroy evil or you believe that Lucifer can win this war. There is no middle ground.'

The silence within the tent became oppressive. No one wanted to challenge him, not after what he'd been through.

It was Harper who finally spoke. 'No one is claiming that Heaven can't kick Hell's ass. What we're saying is that the Holy Water did what it was supposed to do, but there was just too much evil.'

'I refuse to accept that,' Simon replied, glaring at Riley as he lowered himself into his chair. 'Hell had help that night. That's the only explanation.'

She lurched to her feet, eager to tell him how wrong he was about her dad, about her. How much Simon had hurt her and how that agony would never go away.

'Anythin' ya want to say, lass?' Stewart asked.

Her anger made her visibly tremble and she cursed herself for that weakness. 'My dad loved being in the Guild,' she protested. 'He wouldn't have done anything to hurt you, Simon. Or any of those guys.'

'So if it wasn't him,' McGuire called out, 'how about you, girl? Did you break the ward?'

She turned towards her accuser. 'And get myself

eaten by a demon? Do I look stupid?'

'Maybe they said they'd let you go. Hell makes some powerful deals.'

'Talking from experience, McGuire?' she snapped.

'Riley, he's a journeyman and you're—' Beck warned.

'I know. I'm just a damned apprentice,' she retorted. 'I'm so tired of people blaming me for everything. I'm tired of the lies, the sick jokes, all of it. I should just . . . just . . .'

Quit. The word teetered on the tip of her tongue. If she just pushed it out, it'd be over. No more harassment, no more fingers pointed in her direction. She could be Riley Blackthorne again, high-school student and hot-chocolate enthusiast, not some trapper wannabe.

Just tell them I'm out of here. She bit the inside of her lip, drawing blood. *If I do, they win.* The next female will have it twice as bad.

Riley swallowed the words. 'But I'm not giving up,' she said, staring right at McGuire. 'I'm a trapper, from a family of demon trappers. And Blackthornes don't quit.'

'You tell them, sister,' Remmers called out.

Her anger exhausted, Riley folded into her chair, intertwining her hands in her lap so no one could see how badly they were shaking. Her muscles had knotted from the tension and she had a dull headache thumping right behind her eyeballs.

Harper rose again. 'If we fight each other, we can't beat the demons,' he said simply. Then he shot a look at

McGuire and some of the others at the back of the tent. 'And, just for the record, if anyone's going to run Blackthorne's brat out of the Guild, it's me. Got it?'

There were murmurs in the crowd: message received.

'OK, so let's move on,' Jackson said, clearly relieved that was over. 'Anyone know a church where we can meet?'

'The Tabernacle *was* a church,' someone protested. 'Helluva lot of good it did.'

'It'd been desanctified,' Stewart replied. 'No services had been held there in years.'

'We could meet in a cemetery,' Beck suggested.

Riley groaned. *There's a plan.*

'We'll work it out,' Jackson replied. 'Let's get together Friday night at eight. We'll hold elections, try to get back on track.'

'We meeting here?' Remmers called out.

'Sure am,' Jackson replied. 'Look at it this way – at least the rent's cheap.'

Riley waited until Beck was deep in an animated conversation with Master Stewart to make her escape. It felt cowardly, like she wasn't brave enough to face him.

She'd just stepped outside the tent when she heard her name. *Harper.*

'Sir?' she asked, turning towards him.

The moment her master exited the tent a piece of paper came her way. 'Need some food. Drop it by my place. We have to talk . . . *tonight.*'

'Ah, I'm supposed to be on holy ground after dark.'

'Won't take long.'

At least Ori would watch over her. 'Why didn't you tell them about—'

'Later,' her master retorted, cutting her off abruptly. 'Now get going, brat.'

Confused at his behaviour, Riley studied the list as she walked to the car. There was nothing out of the ordinary, just food and supplies, all of which could have waited until tomorrow morning. Which meant he wanted to talk about the hunters and their interest in Paul Blackthorne's daughter.

Jamming the list in a pocket, she rubbed her temples to ease the headache that had struck her the moment she'd been so cruel to Beck. *Guilt.* That was what she was feeling. Industrial-strength guilt. She'd acted mean and childish, just as nasty as Simon, and Riley knew how that felt on the receiving end.

Why did I do that to Beck? Why did I cut him down like that?

There was an answer and she didn't like it one bit: the stick chick. Justine Armando just made her feel mean. It wasn't jealousy, not the usual kind, anyway; it was because the reporter was out of Beck's league. He was simple, plain-spoken, no-nonsense, the kind of guy who always watched your back. The reporter was all bling and abundant money. And she was really pretty. No wonder Beck had homed right in on her.

The Demon Trappers

She's going to hurt you, Backwoods Boy. For all his bluster Denver Beck had deep insecurities, and Justine was using those to get what she wanted. When she finally threw him away he wouldn't know how to deal, not with his history of one-night stands. It'd cut him deep. Riley knew how bad it felt. No matter how much he annoyed her, she didn't want to see him hurt. *He's too good for that.*

Chapter Twenty-Nine

When her headache didn't improve, Riley gave in to the craving for mood-altering chocolate. A short time later she pushed open the door to the Grounds Zero and was instantly cocooned in the lusty aroma of fresh-brewed coffee. The place was busier than usual and she noticed that some of the patrons wore name tags – apparently there was a woodworkers' convention in town.

A couple was just leaving 'her' booth and Riley hurried to claim the space with her coat. Then she joined the line behind two old guys discussing orbital sanders. Simi was at the counter and gave Riley a wide grin. Tonight her friend's hair was brilliant orange, with black spikes.

'Wicked,' Riley said. 'I bet they can see it from space.'

'That was the plan,' the barista replied. 'The usual?'

Riley nodded. Simi always made sure the hot chocolate was topped with loads of whipped cream and chocolate shavings.

'So where's the boyfriend, the one with the gorgeous blue eyes?' the barista asked. 'He's *totally* hot.'

'Simon's history.'

'That sucks. How about the trapper?'

After what I said to him? 'Also history.'

Simi gave her a concerned look. 'You're going through these guys like I do coffee filters, girl. Better slow down.'

When Ori came to mind, Riley made sure to hide the smile from her friend.

Simi set the cup of hot chocolate on the counter and rang up the purchase. Riley automatically dropped the change in the tip jar: that would earn her a refill if she wanted one.

The trip to the table wasn't easy with all the conventioneers wandering around, but she made it without a spill and slid into the booth. While she waited for the drink to cool, Riley nibbled on some of the chocolate shavings.

I so deserve this.

A chiming sound came from her bag, barely audible in the midst of the boisterous coffee house. She dug out her phone, accessed the text message and promptly smiled. Ori.

Missing you. See you later?

She typed the *Yes* before she could stop herself.

What harm could it do? Maybe he'd take her on another angelic picnic. And, unlike Martha, he hadn't expected her to save the world or anything. As she reread it, his text disappeared like it'd never existed.

How does he do that? Angel mojo apparently. She didn't

even think Ori had a phone, but then sending a text without it was no big deal to someone with his job description. Making it disappear – just as easy.

Riley put her cell on the table and tested the hot chocolate. The whipped cream deposited a white moustache on her upper lip, resurrecting good memories. The coffee-house run was a Blackthorne tradition. Riley would always have hot chocolate and her dad would drink coffee, but in a real cup – he couldn't stand the paper ones. Now as she sipped the hot drink she could visualize his mussed brown hair, the laugh lines at the corners of his eyes, that shy smile. This booth was his favourite, in the back, quieter than others. She wouldn't share this spot with anyone, not even Ori.

Riley closed her eyes, allowing the background noise to recede. In its place she heard the clink of a spoon against a ceramic cup as her dad stirred his coffee. She could smell his aftershave, hear him talking about his day. About her mom, about anything. It didn't matter. She could feel his presence and that comforted her. As long as she could hold that moment, preserve it, he would always be part of her even if he was slaving away for some rich creep.

The bench seat across from her creaked and she heard someone say her name. Riley's eyes flew open, her heart wanting to believe in miracles. It was Beck. A quick look around told her they'd have to stay put – there were no other places available.

He peeled off his Atlanta Braves cap, dropped it on the

table and ran a hand through his hair to tame it. It was longer now and it looked good on him. For an instant she saw something in his eyes, but whatever it was disappeared in a heartbeat, like he'd realized he was showing more than he wanted.

'I figured I'd find ya here.' Then a nod of approval came her way. 'Ya look pretty tonight. I like your hair that way.'

Riley hadn't expected the compliment, and she fought the blush. She'd just put on make-up, nothing special. 'Thanks.'

'It's for him, isn't it?' he replied, his tone darkening.

She knew who he meant, but decided not to go there. 'Harper? No way.' That got her a puzzled look. 'I'm going to his place after I finish my cocoa. He wants to chat.'

'About what?'

Riley did a mental coin flip and this time Beck won. She told him about Simon's chat with the hunters and how they'd shown up at her place this afternoon.

'The little bastard,' he said, shaking his head. 'Do whatever Harper says. He won't let the hunters hurt ya, no matter what.'

'Glad you're so sure about that. I'm not.'

'I'll to talk Simon,' he offered. 'Let him know just how much of a prick he's been.'

'No, don't bother. It won't do any good.'

Beck prised the lid off a paper cup and stirred the contents with one of the little sticks. It looked to be coffee, no creamer. 'This stuff costs twice as much as it does at the stop-and-rob. I just don't get it.'

You wouldn't. 'What are you doing here, Beck?'

'Ya ran out of the meetin'. I wasn't done talkin' to ya.'

That sounded for real, but she could never tell with him. One minute he was totally worried about her, giving her money to live, the next he acted like she was an idiot.

You have to be angry at me. Why aren't you yelling? That she knew how to handle. Instead he seemed morose. Lost even.

'You need to stop worrying about me,' she said. 'I'm doing OK.'

'Then you're doin' better than me,' he murmured. 'I miss Paul real bad.'

His stark honesty caught her off guard. She felt tears forming and blinked to keep them in check. 'I keep thinking Dad will be in the kitchen when I get up in the morning,' she admitted. 'He always made me breakfast. His way of showing how much he cared, I guess.'

Beck took a hoarse breath like something stabbed him deep inside. 'I miss trappin' with him. He was always so cool. He never yelled at me. Well, only once.'

'What did you do?' she asked, curious.

'I flipped off a cop,' he said, shrugging like it was no big deal. 'Paul gave me ten kinds of hell for that. Said I had a problem with authority.'

'Duh.'

Beck eyed her. 'You're the same or ya wouldn't

be givin' me all this grief, girl.'

He'd done it again. Just when she'd got a peek of what lay beneath that protective armour, he'd blown it.

'Girl?' he pressed.

'The name is Riley,' she shot back. 'Learn it. Use it!'

Beck's nostrils flared. Backwoods Boy never could stand being dissed. 'I asked around. Seems no one knows this Ori guy.'

'Ori's a Lancer.' *And an angel.* 'End of story.'

'Seems too handy,' Beck said, his face furrowed in thought. 'Guys say anythin' to get laid.'

'He's not like that.'

Beck leaned over the table and lined his eyes up with hers. 'Get a clue, *Riley*, we're *all* like that. We see a pretty girl and we've got only one thing in mind.'

'Like you and the reporter chick?'

He gave her a feral grin as an answer.

Riley felt her cheeks flame. 'She's gonna screw you over – can't you see that?'

'And this Ori guy is any different?'

'Yes, he is.'

'Then he's a damned saint,' Beck grumbled, leaning back.

Weary of the sparring, Riley shoved her way out of the booth and headed to the counter.

'Refill?' Simi called out as she approached.

'Make it to go.' She'd had more than enough of Beck for one evening.

Forbidden

When the barista handed her the cup, Simi angled her head towards the booth. 'He really likes you.'

'Beck? No way.' *Where did her friend get that idea?*

'Oh, yeah. I can tell by the way he looks at you.'

'If that's the case, why is he such a jerk?' Riley asked.

'Some guys don't know any better.'

Riley wasn't buying it. She wasn't surprised that the instant she returned to the booth, Beck started in again just like she'd never left.

'Ya have to be careful. This guy could be a Mezmer. They're way clever.'

Riley shook her head. 'Ori's not Hellspawn. He stood up to a Geo-Fiend, Beck.'

'So? A lower-grade fiend will back off from a top-level demon.'

'He sat on the church steps with me, Beck. He's not a demon.' She knew the problem and it had nothing to do with Ori. 'You're just pissed because that Four didn't get into his head like it did yours.'

Beck's scowl deepened. 'Yeah, I am. And I wanna know why. Until then, I don't want ya seein' him. He's out of your life, as of now.'

'You're just bullying me to feel important. It's not working.'

His face went crimson. 'Call your aunt or I will.'

'You don't have the number.'

Beck grinned. It wasn't a nice one. Then he pointed at her phone. 'I do now.'

Riley's jaw dropped. He'd gone through her cellphone address book while she'd been at the counter. 'How dare you?' she growled, trying hard to keep her voice lowered. People were already staring at them.

'I promised Paul I'd keep ya safe,' he said. 'If that means packin' your ass out of town so it doesn't get screwed by a smooth-talkin' loser, that's the way it's gonna be.'

Stunned at the menace in his voice, Riley pulled herself out of the booth. This was a different side of Beck and it frightened her. Scooping up her phone, she pushed her way out of the coffee house. As she hurried towards the car, a street vendor called out to her, but Riley ignored him. All she wanted to do was run away.

Within a half block, Beck fell in step with her. She didn't dare look at him. Maybe he'd leave her alone if she ignored him.

'Wait,' he said, grabbing on to her arm.

Riley yanked herself free and kept going. It wasn't until she reached the car that she realized he was still following. Her hands shook so hard she couldn't fit the key into the lock. Drained, she slumped against the car door.

In the distance she saw Ori leaning against his bike, on the alert. Probably trying to figure out if the trapper posed a threat. Riley shook her head and he nodded in return, still vigilant.

Unaware she had back-up, Beck halted a few feet away from her. 'Riley, please listen to me,' he pleaded.

'Why are you doing this? You're scaring me, Beck.'

He recoiled, like she'd punched him in the face.

'We could just be friends if you'd stop being a total butthead.'

He sagged. 'I don't know why I'm like this. Too much is happenin' I don't understand.' She waited, knowing there was more. His eyes rose to hers, pleading. 'I can't face losin' ya, Riley. You're all I got left in this world.'

That brutal honesty again. He'd peeled away more armour, and this time he'd exposed his heart.

'Ori's not the bad guy here,' she said wearily.

Beck opened his mouth to argue, then shook his head in defeat. 'That might be true, but that doesn't mean he won't hurt ya.'

'It's still my choice,' she said. 'Just like Justine is for you.'

'I know,' he admitted. He took a few steps away, then turned back towards her. 'I'm sorry it didn't work between us.'

What? 'Beck, I—'

'No. We'll leave it at that. Just be careful, girl.'

As he walked away, his shoulders slumped like he'd taken a vicious beating, gone was the overbearing bully in the coffee house, the arrogant man who thought the world should dance to his tune. In his place was someone she hardly knew.

It was late when Beck headed deep into Demon Central, in search of the hunters. He'd already talked to his buddy

Ike, the old war veteran who lived down here, and had learned the team was scouting the area. There was gunfire now, which meant the Vatican's boys had grown tired of scouting and were reducing Atlanta's demon population one by one.

Beck adjusted his course through the darkened streets, keeping his eyes on the surroundings. It was hard to concentrate: he kept thinking back to what had happened between him and Paul's daughter tonight. The harsh words that had been said.

No matter what he did, Riley only pulled further away. Beck knew it was wrong to push her so hard, but he just couldn't stop himself. He cared too damn much. He hadn't lied – he was afraid of losing her to a demon. Or to someone else.

It sucked, but as he saw it there wasn't much he could do but run interference for her. Besides, he had his own problems: Elias Salvatore for one. If Beck was lucky, no one had told the hunter who his ex-girlfriend was hooking up with. If someone had, hopefully the hunters weren't looking to add a trapper to their kill stats tonight. Beck could just see the news report: Journeyman Trapper dies in tragic accident in Demon Central. Vatican issues formal apology.

Now that would suck.

He made it as far as Broad Street when he caught up with them. He counted six of the Vatican's boys all decked out in their commando gear and there'd be more in the surrounding streets. From the five furry bodies lying in the street, they'd been busy. The single shot to the Threes' skulls did the trick, at least when the bullets were hollow points loaded with papal Holy Water. Fifteen hundred dollars' worth of demon carcasses had bled out on that pavement, and no trapper was going to get a bit of that money.

'What a damned waste,' he grumbled.

Beck had expected to be challenged right off, but he was waved through the perimeter by one of the hunters. He found Salvatore near one of the high-tech black vans. He had a map spread out on a portable table and he was talking to his second-in-command.

'Good evenin',' Beck said politely. He got a nod from the captain and a glower from his subordinate.

'What are you doing here?' Amundson demanded.

Beck set his trapping bag down by the table. 'Wanted to see how the big boys work.'

Amundson opened his mouth, probably to order him to take a hike, but his superior waved him off. 'It's OK, Lieutenant. Go check on Chavez and Rimsky.'

From his frown, Amundson didn't like the order, but he obeyed and headed down the street, his assault rifle in hand.

Beck pointed at the line of dead demons. 'Ya know, ya don't have to kill those things,' he said, just to stir up trouble.

Salvatore carefully refolded the map. 'If we don't kill

them, they'll just come back and eat more of your people.'

'I thought y'all had that handled. Something to do with monks and a lot of prayin'. I heard the demons just disappear.'

'They do disappear,' Salvatore replied. He levelled his gaze with Beck's. 'Then they return to this realm and start killing again. Hell has the ultimate recycling plan.'

Beck wasn't sure if the guy was messing with him or not. 'You're jokin', right?'

The captain shook his head. 'If we kill them, they don't bother us again.'

'That don't track,' Beck argued. 'Hunters have been wastin' demons for centuries and we're not runnin' out of them. Maybe Lucifer gets 'em either way, livin' or dead.'

The captain gave the theory some consideration. 'That'd be a bitch, wouldn't it?'

Beck cracked a grin. *Maybe this guy isn't such a tool after all.*

'So why are you here, Beck? It's not to see how we do our work.'

Busted. 'It's about Riley Blackthorne. I heard that one of our apprentices told ya a wild tale about her and her dad workin' for Hell. That's not true.'

'Of course you'd say that,' Salvatore replied. 'You wouldn't turn on the man who trained you, or his daughter.'

Beck frowned, shifting his weight. 'If they were workin' for Hell, I would, in a heartbeat. I saw too many of our guys ripped apart that night to let somethin' like that slide.'

Salvatore gave a cautious nod. In the distance they heard the sound of a gunshot and then a low, mournful wail.

'And another one bites the dust,' Beck muttered.

'You sure the Blackthornes are on the level?' Elias asked.

Beck nodded. 'Paul was straight as an arrow. Same with his daughter.'

'Grand Master Stewart says the same thing. So if Riley is not the nexus of demonic power in this city, who is?'

'Don't know. The demons have changed their tactics, gotten bolder. They're acting weird now.'

'Not the first time,' Salvatore replied. 'In Moscow in '93—'

The earth began to shake beneath their boots. It paused and started up again, triggering car alarms that howled into the night like electronic wolves.

'That's a Five,' Beck said, his throat tightening. He grabbed his duffel bag and began scanning the area. There were shouts from the streets around them as the hunters sprinted towards their captain.

Salvatore stepped to the van's open side door. 'Where did that come from, Corsini?'

A dark-skinned man stuck his head out. He was holding some sort of electronic device. 'South-east of here, Captain, nearly two kilometres.'

The Demon Trappers

Two kilometres. That was near Harper's place.

Beck turned on his heel and sprinted up the road, his trapping bag slapping into his side. Behind him, he heard the captain calling out his name, but he kept running as if his life depended upon it. Because it did.

Chapter Thirty

To Riley's relief there were no demon hunters waiting at her master's place. Harper was in his office, in his recliner, eyes closed. The television was off. That had to be a first.

Riley set the grocery bag on the desk. 'I found the soup you said you liked.'

No reply. She took that as a hint and put away the food. When she returned to the office, Harper's eyes were open. She'd expected a smirk on his face – there was none. That made her more nervous. What if he trashed her apprenticeship because of Simon's allegations? She had no way to prove her innocence.

Instead Harper went in a direction she'd not anticipated. 'Saint's going to be a problem,' he said in a gravelly voice. 'I don't trust you any further than I can spit you, but I *will not* have an apprentice who is working with the hunters.'

For some bizarre reason, Riley felt the need to defend her ex. 'Simon is really confused right now and—'

'Don't alibi for him!' Harper shouted, his voice echoing off the open rafters. 'He sold you out, called the hunters down on one of his own. What the hell is he thinking?'

'He's not. That's the problem.'

She got a grunt of agreement. 'His crisis of faith is pissing me off,' Harper said.

'Not doing much for me, either.'

Another grunt. 'I'll be talking to him about this in the morning. Then as soon as possible he and I'll go trapping. We'll catch a Three and see if we can get Saint back on track. I don't want to lose him.'

'You think Simon can handle a Three after what he's been through?' she asked, unsure.

'He has to or he's done. It's that simple.' Harper eyed her. 'Then it'll be your turn.'

Riley figured that was coming. Could she face one of those slavering monsters again?

I have to or it's all over.

'I've seen this before,' Harper conceded. 'Until Saint settles his argument with his God, he's going to doubt everything and everybody.'

'Just as long as he doesn't blame my dad for what happened.'

'Blackthorne knew what was going down or he wouldn't have warned you.'

Riley frowned, putting her hands on her hips. 'Oh, right, he gave me, what, *five seconds* to be out of there before it became a death trap? If he'd really wanted to kill all of you, he'd have made sure I wasn't near that building.'

Harper's face sagged. She could see that simple fact was bugging him. 'I talked to the priest right after they left your place. They're going to keep digging, seeing what they can find on you and your father. If you have sold your soul to Hell, you will bring down the Atlanta Guild, do you understand?' he demanded.

Riley shivered at the thought. She didn't like a lot of the guys in the Guild, but destroying it would put them out of work. Put the city at risk.

'Got it.'

Harper sighed. 'Stewart thinks something else is up. I don't buy much of his mystical crap, but he knows what he's talking about. We'll get with him and see what we can do to settle things down. I want the hunters out of this town as quickly as possible, for all our sakes.'

That was the longest conversation they'd ever shared. Since her master seemed to be listening to her for a change, she decided now might be a good time to tell him about her fruitless *following recycling trucks all over Atlanta* investigation. Maybe he'd have some suggestions.

'I've been working on that Holy Water problem.' The man's eyes swivelled in her direction. At least they weren't bloodshot like before. She told him about the unmarked truck and how the drivers hadn't been good with her questions. 'I checked out the recycling place,' she said, cautiously editing out Peter's part of the investigation. 'The bottles go there for stripping and cleaning. Then they're sent to the Holy Water plant. I think they're being stolen somewhere along the way.'

Harper's brow furrowed and she waited for the

smack-down. It didn't come.

'You might be right,' he said. 'Used to be the city would send their own truck to collect the bottles, then I'd have to wait for the cheque. Now they've made some deal with the distributor to pick 'em up and pay me right then and there in cash.'

'When did that change?'

'About three weeks ago.'

'Just about the time the consecration dates went weird.' She knew that much from the paperwork she'd had to complete. When Harper's previous apprentices filled out the forms, all the bottles had proper consecration dates.

'So if I want to steal a bunch of empty bottles that just happen to have the city's tax stamp on them,' she mused, 'I make a deal with the city to collect them, skim some off the top, fudge the paperwork and no one knows the bottles are missing. I fill those with tap water and sell them just like they're the real thing.'

Harper gave her a hard look. 'You've got a twisted mind, brat.'

She couldn't argue with that. 'So we just have to talk to the distributor, see if any bottles are missing.'

'Might not be that simple. The distributor could be kosher, but someone is stealing from them or getting their bottles from some other place. Buying new ones, maybe.'

'But they'd have to have a tax stamp.'

'No reason someone inside the city isn't selling them under the table.'

Riley hadn't even thought of that. 'Now who's got a twisted mind?' she said. A second after she'd made the comment, it hit her what she'd said. Harper didn't seem upset.

'Maybe once we get this figured out the Guild will stop blaming my dad and me.'

Harper snorted in disgust. 'Don't count on it, brat. You're not out of—'

The ground shook, a tremor so light Riley could almost believe she'd imagined it. She locked eyes with Harper. He sat up in his chair, flipping down the footrest, on alert.

Riley held her breath. *Please, God, not here.* Another tremor followed almost immediately, rattling the plates in the kitchenette. She had to hold on to the desk for support as items jittered across the top and tumbled to the floor.

'Oh, hell,' Harper said, jumping to his feet. 'It wouldn't dare . . .'

A blast of straight wind rammed into the front of the building, shattering the windows in the two overhead doors.

'Down!' Harper bellowed. A second later the doors exploded, converting the wood into lethal missiles.

Riley had barely hit the floor before debris speared the room, burying wooden shards deep into the back walls like jagged spears. Then came the laughter. Low, chilling and totally demonic.

The Geo-Fiend had come for her.

Rolling waves coursed across the ground, causing the building's remaining windows to shatter and its masonry to crack. Dust poured down on Riley in a choking fog.

'Pit!' Harper shouted, catching her by the arm and dragging her out of what remained of the office. Another tremor slung them to the ground. Harper crawled back on his feet, hampered by his injury. Above them, the metal supports shrieked in protest as the joints began to fail.

'Help me!' he called, scrabbling at something with his fingers. Through the swirling dust, Riley realized he was trying to pull up a piece of plywood covering a section of the garage floor. Putting her back to the wind and dust storm, she dug into the crevice between the concrete and the wood, attempting to gain leverage on the warped plywood. Lifting it proved impossible with the force of the gale, so with incredible effort they shifted it sideways.

Grimacing in pain, Harper pushed her into the pit. It stank of old oil and dirty rags.

'Cover your head!' he cried. Above them the building twisted on its foundations as concrete blocks ground into each other, then dislodged themselves to tumble to the earth.

Riley beckoned for him to join her, but her master shook his head. 'Stay here!'

With his trapping bag in hand, he wove through the falling debris, then crawled out of a gaping hole in the side of the building.

What is he doing? The demon will rip him apart.

The other trappers would come to help them or maybe the hunters. He could not take on a Five by himself.

Harper had told her to stay here. That's exactly what she should do. Riley hated him, hated how he treated her and her dad. She remembered every bruise he'd given her, every insult.

But he's my master.

With a cry of anguish, she hauled herself out of the pit and ran to join him.

The moment she exited the ruined building the wind died, causing an eerie silence to beat against her ears. She found Harper in the parking lot thirty feet from the towering Geo-Fiend. He was guarding his injured side and his face was sweaty, coated with a thick layer of dust like a coal miner.

The demon was the one from the Tabernacle, the one who had killed her father, and that knowledge kicked her desire for revenge into high gear. The thing was tall and huge, deep black skin stretched over a thickly muscled chest and bulky arms. Muscles rippled in its bull-like neck and adorned the sides of its head, tapering upward into wicked points. Brilliant crimson flames seethed inside its maw and its eyes.

The demon observed her with blazing crimson eyes. 'Blackthorne's daughter,' it cried.

Harper turned, then glowered at her. 'Get back in there!'

Riley shook her head, taking her place next to him.

This was the demon who had killed her father – she would not hide from it.

Without asking permission, she reached into the trapping bag hanging off her master's shoulder and retrieved two grounding spheres. When she handed one to Harper, he studied her for a moment, then nodded grimly, his pale scar stretched tight.

'You know what to do?' he croaked.

'Yes.' Her fear felt so real she swore it was pouring out of her skin like water from a faucet.

Harper angled his head, indicating she should move to the right. As she took the first few steps, she heard the demon chuckle in amusement.

Where is the angel? Or Beck and those damned hunters? Why is it just the two of us?

'Now!' Harper shouted, but his command came a second too late. A solid wall of air hit them like a jackhammer causing Riley to tumble backwards. As she rolled, she cradled the sphere so it wouldn't break. Hail and rain slashed at her body like needles, the wind coming in unpredictable gusts so there was no way to brace herself against the onslaught. Through the torrent she saw Harper regain his feet. He didn't wait for her, but threw his sphere towards the old mangled fence. Enough of it was metal for the sphere to catch hold and begin to run its blue magic towards the demon.

Lightning slashed out of the sky and struck the ground near Riley's feet. She yelped and jumped back, the smell of scorched earth filling her nose. She launched her sphere at the stretch of fence to the right of the fiend.

Abruptly, the wind shifted direction, coming from behind her now. It slammed her on to the ground, then relentlessly pushed her towards the demon. Riley skidded along on her belly, gravel embedding itself in her knees and palms. She saw the demon's outstretched hand, pulling her towards it. Wicked spikes extended from the fingers. Spikes that would impale her before it ripped her in half.

'Die, you bastard!' Harper yelled, and threw another sphere. It was luminescent gold and it exploded with ear-splitting concussion underneath the Five. The demon roared and then began to flail in agony. The wind propelling Riley vanished. She clambered to her feet and cheered.

The joy was short-lived.

Beneath the demon the gold magic spread across the ground, separating it and its source of power. The demon struggled and rose higher in the air. Then it waved a hand, bellowing in pain, and a deep pit yawned open. The spreading gold sank into its depths. With a mighty effort, the fiend forced the hole closed, sealing the magic beneath the earth.

They had failed.

The fiend turned its fiery eyes towards Harper. 'Die, trapper,' it cried, and with a flick of a wrist, a blast of wind flung Harper backwards to the demolished building, rolling him over and over in the dirt. When he finally came to rest in a crumpled heap, the master didn't move.

In the distance Riley could hear the sound of sirens. The cops wouldn't get here in time, not that they could do anything with a Geo-Fiend. There were no hunters, no angels and no Beck. It looked like her dad was right: she'd be seeing him real soon. At least she'd be able to tell him she'd done her best.

The demon turned its hellfire eyes on Riley. 'Blackthorne's daughter,' it called, 'your time has come.'

Hands quaking, Riley armed herself with two Holy Water spheres. They would do no real damage to the fiend, but at least she'd make a fight of it.

No way I'm dying without knowing why.

'Is this because of the Armageddon thing?' she asked.

The demon's reply was a roar that rivalled a jet engine. It filled her with such terror that her body went numb and the spheres tumbled from her hands to smash at her feet. The will to stand drained away and she slumped to her knees. 'Why?' she demanded. 'Tell me why!'

'You stand in the way,' the demon replied. With great effort, she forced herself to look at it. It was closer now. She could feel heat radiating off it and the acrid stench of brimstone made her gag.

'I'd better take it from here,' a voice said.

Ori?

He stood a few feet to her left, clad in light silver armour that seemed to generate its own light, his wings arched behind him. With a deep laugh that spoke more of revenge than mirth, he unsheathed a sword from the scabbard at his waist. The blade ignited in white-hot flames, crackling in the darkening air.

'Ohmigod.'

Riley pulled herself to her feet and backed off as the demon and the angel squared up to each other. She hurried to her master's side and knelt, touching his chest. Harper was breathing. She smiled, despite their turbulent history. He was like her – hard to kill.

The demon stirred, rising higher in the air, gaining strength as winds whirled around it. It laughed its derision. 'You challenge me, Divine? Your bones break as easily as any mortal's.'

'So do yours, Hellspawn.'

The demon sneered, revealing razored teeth among the flames. 'We shall destroy all of you at the End of Days.'

Ori sighed. They were always like this, all hellfire and retribution. He didn't understand how Lucifer tolerated them. 'You have violated the Eternal Covenant. You know the punishment, Astaring.'

The demon snorted flames at the use of its true name. 'I shall feast on your corpse, Divine, then I shall destroy Blackthorne's child.'

'Not tonight,' Ori said, raising his blade. 'Not ever.'

With a tremendous shout that even Heaven would have heard, the angel charged into battle.

A ferocious wind caught him mid-leap, but he used it to his advantage and spun in the air, landing a slicing blow to the fiend's left shoulder. It shouted in pain, then slashed at him with its claws. One caught the trailing edge of a wing, ripping deep into the feathers and tendons.

A second before the other claw would have hooked him, Ori spun out of its reach. A sudden downdraught pulled him towards the earth. His wings acknowledged it, but the injured one didn't have enough lift to counteract the plunge. As he fought to regain altitude, the demon cast a torrential rainstorm against him, drenching his wings and driving him hard into the red clay and gravel. Ori managed to scramble away to avoid being flattened by the fiend's taloned foot.

Killing a weather-worker should have been nothing for a Divine, yet this one had more power than he'd ever seen. 'Who is helping you?' Ori panted. 'Name your demi-lord!'

'I shall tell you as you draw your last breath,' the demon promised.

A bolt of lightning sheared down from the sky, hitting Ori's blade. He reeled back from the blow, but did not drop the weapon. Instead, he channelled the power of the storm upward, gathering the wind, the rain, the hail and the lightning into one massive strike. Then he threw himself at the demon with every ounce of power he possessed.

As the fiend fought against the onslaught, Ori drove his blade deep into the beast's chest. He carved through the ribs until its heart burst free, smoking black, like hot tar. The demon's eyes widened in fear.

'Boon . . .' it cried. 'Boon I grant thee.'

'Death is thy boon,' the angel replied. He unsheathed his sword from the demon's chest and fell to his knees some feet away from his foe. The rogue was whispering, gathering in power, probably trying to heal itself.

The power around the demon shifted, grew stronger. With a final dying breath, the fiend cast forth that energy in a shockwave that blew across the parking lot like a hurricane's winds. Ori cried out a warning, but it was too late.

Riley woke in someone's arms. A soft voice told her she was safe, that the demon was dead. She blinked, trying to clear her vision. It didn't work. Everything was fuzzy, like she was looking through gauze.

'Hold very still,' he said. Ori gently touched a finger above one eye, then the other, and a tingle spread across her face. Riley blinked again and everything became clear. Then the angel took her hands in his and performed the same miracle. The gravel embedded in her palms dislodged as the wounds healed.

'That's serious angel mojo,' she said, trying to smile.

'Better be.'

Then she saw his wounds. 'You're hurt!' His one wing

bled, a brilliant blue fluid leaking from between the feathers. She forced herself to sit up.

'It is already healing. Do not worry,' he said. And as she watched the wing knitted together and the feathers grew back in place.

'Wow,' she said. That was the only word that seemed to apply. She turned to look at where the demon had been. There was just a smoking crater now. 'Please tell me it's dead.'

'Dead and buried, just as I promised.' He paused, as if hearing something she couldn't. 'Time for me to go. Your master killed the demon. You understand?'

'Why should I lie?'

'It's for the best. They cannot know what I've done here.'

'But when will I see you again?'

'At the cemetery, tonight. Come to me when you can.'

'But what about—'

He touched a finger to the middle of her forehead and white light sent her into oblivion.

Chapter Thirty-One

Someone held Riley, calling her name. The voice sounded so worried, frantic even.

'Ori?' she asked. When she opened her eyes, she realized it wasn't the angel. From the expression on the man's face, he wasn't happy she'd called him someone else's name. Especially *that* name.

'Beck,' she said. His worried expression diminished.

'Thank God,' he said. 'When I felt the earthquake, I thought ya were done for.'

Not yet. 'Harper?'

'Bitchin' up a storm. He'll be OK.' Beck looked around. 'Must have been a helluva show,' he said, his voice thick. 'Sorry I didn't get here in time.'

She swallowed and then grimaced. Her mouth felt like it was full of dirt.

'Water?' she croaked.

He laid her back down and dug in his duffel bag. Then she was back in his arms sucking down the cool liquid. It felt so wonderful. She struggled to sit up, cradling the water bottle between her palms.

'Easy,' Beck warned.

Riley nodded, but sat up anyway. Her palms tingled. She inspected one – the skin was pink but there was no sign of the gravel burn.

No doubt about it. Angels are awesome.

She drank more of the water to clear her throat. 'Harper went after it,' she said. 'He told me to stay in that pit thing inside the building.'

'But you didn't stay, did ya?'

She shook her head. 'I had to help him.'

A tortured sigh. 'Well, you're alive and ya got the bastard. I just wish I'd been the one to take it down,' he said.

She realized it was more than just scoring a Five – it was all about Beck extracting revenge for her father's death. 'If you'd been here, you would have, I know it,' she said.

He gave her a nod, telling her he appreciated the gesture.

A paramedic knelt next to her. 'How about you lay back down and I'll check you out, OK?' the woman said.

Riley did as ordered, though she didn't think anything was broken. She answered the paramedic's questions until the woman was satisfied Riley wasn't badly injured.

'I think it would be wise if you went to the hospital, just in case.'

Riley shook her head. 'I'm fine.'

'Your call.' The woman repacked her case and took off.

Riley sighed in relief and sat up again. Beck was near what was left of the building, talking to Jackson and a couple of the other trappers. Firemen milled around and there were a few cops as well.

Her eyes skimmed across the parking lot to the smoking hole where the Five had been. Ori said he'd get the thing, and he had. He'd kept his word.

But why did he wait so long to show up?

She heard Harper's voice, sharp and sarcastic. For some reason that made her smile. He was sitting upright, holding an ice pack to his head, growling at the paramedic who kept fussing with him.

You're just a tough old dude, aren't you? But when the time came he'd protected her.

Riley stood with considerable effort. Her head spun, so she waited until she regained her balance, and then walked across the debris-strewn parking lot to her master.

He looked up at her with bloodshot eyes. 'Brat,' he said.

'Master Harper.'

His paramedic tried the same *you should go to the hospital* spiel with him and failed just as miserably. Once the fellow had cleared off and they were alone, Harper eyed her.

'So where the hell's the demon?' he asked so quietly only she could hear him.

She knelt next to him. 'Dead,' she said. 'You killed it.' *Please don't ask me how.*

He frowned. 'I don't remember doing that.'

'You could have let that thing flatten me, but you didn't. Why?'

'I could ask you the same question.'

She was too tired to edit her mouth. 'You're my master. I couldn't let that thing kill another trapper even if I think he's a total asshat.'

Harper looked at her for a long time, then cracked a toothy grin. 'And you're one mouthy brat, but you're my apprentice. I don't need the reputation that my people die because I don't protect them.'

That was fair.

He slowly turned towards the building and the grin fled. She followed his gaze. The back wall was still intact, but the front was a mound of concrete blocks and protruding metal. Steam rose from a couple of the piles, curling up into the air. Papers fluttered in a light breeze and the office chair's legs stuck up in the air like an overturned turtle.

'Damn, I really loved that place,' Harper murmured.

How could anyone love an old, smelly garage?

'My dad was a mechanic,' he replied, as if he'd read her mind. 'I used hang around and watch him work on cars. He could fix anything.'

'So this place reminded you of him?' Riley asked, intrigued.

'Yeah.'

'Was he a trapper?'

A nod. 'He died taking down an Archdemon when I was sixteen.' Harper swallowed and then coughed, hard. He looked up at her, no hint of arrogance in those ancient eyes. 'It's why I became a trapper.'

He'd suffered a loss just like hers. She never would have guessed.

'Riley?' Beck called out.

She welcomed the interruption. It felt strange having a regular conversation with Harper and she suspected his next move would be to destroy this touchy-feely moment with a caustic remark.

Riley rose. When her balance faltered, Beck caught her elbow. They both turned as four black vans pulled into the parking lot, one after another, throwing gravel as they screeched to a halt.

'Took them long enough,' Beck grumbled. Of the hunters, one stood out immediately. His body language told Riley he was in charge. He ordered his men to fan out, then headed her way.

'Who's that?' she asked.

'Elias Salvatore. He's their captain. Just be careful what ya say to 'em.'

That was a given. At least the priest wasn't with them tonight.

'Next time, tell us where you're headed,' Salvatore growled, his frown aimed at Beck. 'We could have been here sooner.' Then he turned his attention to Riley. 'You OK?' She nodded. 'So what happened here?'

'It was a Geo-Fiend,' her master replied, looking up at the man, his face stern.

'Grounded?'

'Dead,' Harper said. His eyes met Riley and the message was passed. No matter what really happened, the hunters weren't on their side.

The captain signalled to two of his men. 'Check out the crater.' He turned back to the master trapper. 'Any other demons besides that one?'

Harper shook his head. 'That was enough.'

'You have my admiration, Master Harper,' the captain said, tilting his head in respect. 'They are very difficult to kill.'

Harper coughed up more dust. 'I noticed that.'

Salvatore crossed the lot to join his men near the smoking crater, talking back and forth in what sounded like Italian. There seemed to be some debate going on, with lots of gestures.

Harper dropped the ice pack and then extended a hand to Riley. 'Get me up off this damned ground.'

Once she and Beck had helped him up, he hobbled into the rubble, his shoulders bent and his gait uneven. Jackson joined him and they talked quietly among themselves. Then Harper pointed at something. The other trapper began to unearth it.

'So where the hell's your fancy boy?' Beck asked. 'Why wasn't he here keepin' ya safe?'

He was fishing for information and she wasn't going to take the bait.

'Whatever,' she murmured. It didn't matter what Beck thought.

Any doubts she had about the angel had perished with the demon.

It was close to eleven when Beck finally made it to Stewart's place. Harper had refused to leave his scrap metal unguarded so they'd loaded it into one of the trapper's trucks and stored it in Beck's garage. The rest of Harper's stuff was headed for a storage unit in the back of another truck. At least they'd been able to salvage his filing cabinets and business records, though his personal belongings were pretty much history.

Exhausted, Beck sank into the same chair he'd occupied during his last visit.

'Scotch?' Stewart asked.

'Yes, but not much.' He didn't need to get drunk; he needed to sort out his feelings. When he'd seen Riley lying in that parking lot, he was sure she was dead. He'd run to her, praying to a God that he wasn't sure existed, praying for a miracle. Then he'd cradled her body in his arms. When her soft breath had touched his face, he'd almost lost it in front of her.

'Lad?'

Beck jerked out of his thoughts. A tumbler half full of amber liquor sat on a side table next to his chair. He took a long suck on the Scotch.

'Yer not lookin' good,' Stewart said, settling into one of the chairs. 'What's wrong?'

Beck shook his head. He wasn't ready to talk about it.

'Where'd Harper end up?'

'He's upstairs, in bed.'

'No, I'm not,' the older trapper replied. He shuffled into the room and chose a seat near the fireplace. The way he eased himself into it told Beck the man was hurting bad.

'What would you like to drink?' Stewart asked. Beck noted he'd not offered the man liquor.

Harper fumbled in a pocket and produced a bottle of pain pills. 'Water.'

Beck did the honours, though it took some time to hunt through the kitchen cabinets to find a glass. Once he was back in his chair, they all stared at their drinks. None of them wanted to talk about what had happened tonight.

No choice. 'How'd ya kill the Five?' Beck said.

The master shook his head. 'I didn't. The last thing I remember is being rolled across the parking lot like a bowling ball. The Five was still kicking when I went down.'

'But how . . . '

'Riley know how to take down a Geo-Fiend?' Stewart asked.

Beck and Harper shook their heads at the same time.

'Then it appears we have a mystery, gents.'

More silence.

This wasn't going to be easy, but Beck knew it was time to come clean. 'I think I know who took out the demon.'

Both masters' eyes shifted to him.

'There's a Lancer in town named Ori. He's been hangin' around Riley. She told me he was the one who saved her from the Five at the Tabernacle. Maybe he was the one that killed it tonight.'

'Why wouldn't she just say so?' Harper asked.

Beck shrugged. 'This one's an arrogant bastard, and I think he's got more on his mind than just killin' demons.'

'Which means yer opinion of him might be biased,' Stewart replied, a slight smile on his lips now.

'Yeah, maybe,' Beck admitted. *Just tell 'em. If it kills my chances at bein' a master, so be it.* 'This guy was at the Armageddon Lounge a few nights back. A couple Fours came in, working as a team. The older one had me dead to rights. Next thing I know the demons blew out of there like their tails were on fire.'

Stewart scowled and Beck knew his next question. 'My soul's still my own. But this Ori guy just sat there and watched the whole thing go down. They didn't seem to bother him at all.'

'Why didn't ya mention this earlier?' the Scotsman demanded.

'Too much hittin' the fan. And I wasn't proud I'd almost been taken down. That's the truth of it.'

The master took a big jolt of whisky. 'Next time, ya tell me, ya hear?' he said gruffly.

'Yes, sir.'

'Did those demons know he's a Lancer?' Harper asked.

'Don't think so,' Beck replied. 'They didn't act like they knew he was there.'

'A pair of Fours and this guy doesn't make a move on them? That's not right,' Harper said. 'Freelancers are always after money.'

'Same thing tonight: if he'd killed that Five, he'd have stayed behind to make sure he got credited with the kill,' Beck replied. *And to make me look bad in front of Riley.*

Stewart's face was pensive now. 'Push yer personal emotions aside, lad, and do a gut check about this fella. What are ya feelin'?'

Beck tried, but it was difficult. Too much of Riley was tangled up in him now.

'This guy's really smooth, makes the hairs on the back of my neck rise. Somethin' about him's not right and it's not just because of . . . well . . . her.'

'Could he be a Four?' Harper suggested. 'Is that why the Mezmers ignored him?'

'I'm thinkin' not. A Geo-Fiend wouldn't back down from a Four,' Stewart murmured.

'No, Riley said he'd been on holy ground. He's not a demon.'

Stewart sat straighter in his chair as if he'd realized something. 'Is Riley stayin' at the church tonight?'

'No, she's at home, now that the Five is dead,' Beck replied.

'Call her and have her come here.'

'But . . .'

Forbidden

'Just do it,' Stewart ordered, his voice unusually crisp.

As Beck dialled the number, he saw a look pass between the two masters.

'What are you thinking, Angus?' Harper quizzed.

Stewart gave a quick shake of his head. Which meant he didn't want to talk about it in front of Beck.

The call rolled over to voicemail. Same thing with her home phone. 'She's not answerin'.'

'Find her. Bring her here.'

'I'll have to give her a reason.'

'She doesn't need one,' Stewart said curtly. 'She's stayin' here until we know exactly who this Ori fellow is.'

'What's goin' on, sir?' Beck asked. 'Why ya so worried?'

'Just an old Scotsman's paranoia. Get it done, lad.'

Beck left his whisky behind, heading for the front door. Behind him he heard lowered voices – Stewart telling the other master just why he was paranoid. Beck couldn't catch the words, and part of him didn't want to.

Chapter Thirty-Two

True to his word, Ori leaned against the red brickwork of the cemetery gate, arms folded over his chest. He looked like he had the first time Riley had seen him: hair slicked back into a ponytail and wearing that black leather jacket. No sign of those wings, no hint that he took orders from Heaven. Just a hunky guy hanging around a graveyard.

Waiting for me.

It seemed silly, but after she'd called Peter to let him know she was safe just in case CNN covered the Harper thing, she'd showered and put on make-up again. She'd worn her best pair of jeans and her favourite shirt. She'd tried to tell herself it was just something you did, but that's not the way it felt.

As she climbed out of the car, her fingers involuntarily brushed her lips, remembering Ori's kisses, how they'd made her feel. Those had been real. Maybe Simi was right, sometimes you needed to be a little wild, even if it was with an angel.

Moving towards the gate, everything else but Ori faded from view, his lazy smile drawing her in. She offered him one of her own.

'Riley.' His smile widened as he took her hand, twining his fingers with hers. They were warm, though he wasn't wearing gloves.

'I wasn't sure you'd be here,' she said, then regretted it. It sounded needy. 'I mean, you've probably got better things to do now that the Five is dead.'

'I have no other task but you at the moment.'

As if to reassure her, the angel slid his arm round her waist, pulling her closer. She hesitated for a second, then nestled into his side as they walked into the graveyard. Leaves skidded along in front of them. As they passed the empty guard house, a gust of wind pushed against her, whipping her hair forward. Ori paused and looked back towards the main gate, his brows furrowed.

'What is it?' she asked, turning.

A slight frown crossed his face, then vanished. 'Just someone trying to tell me how to do my job. It's nothing.'

'I didn't figure angels had that sort of thing.'

'You'd be surprised.'

Ori squeezed her hand and they began moving again, but she could feel his tension. It hadn't been there when she'd first arrived.

'I don't know how to thank you,' she said. 'It feels weird not having to worry any more.'

'Enjoy your freedom – you've earned it,' he said.

'That was an awesome battle. I just wish you hadn't been hurt,' she said.

'Part of my job,' he replied. He wasn't looking at her now, like he had something on his mind. 'I should have been watching you closer. I am truly sorry about that. I was . . . detained.'

Then he fell silent, like that topic was off limits. Riley's stomach felt like a pretzel. The only way to find out more about this guy was to ask questions. She decided to start with one of the simpler ones.

'What do angels do all day?'

That pulled his attention back to her. 'Divines are given a number of tasks,' he replied. 'For example, this cemetery has its own angelic caretaker who ensures that everything is as it should be. Most places have their own Divine.'

'Are you talking about Martha?' she asked, surprised.

'I know her by another name, but, yes, that's her. Have you never wondered why all this metal is still here?' he said, gesturing to encompass the graveyard. 'She makes sure it doesn't get stolen.'

'So that's why.' Riley looked up at him hopefully. 'When we made the deal, all Martha told me is that I have to stop Armageddon. Do you have any idea how I'm supposed to do that?'

'If I did know, I couldn't tell you.'

'Surprise,' she murmured. 'What she *didn't* tell me is that my boyfriend would go all nuts.'

'Would you have let him die if you'd known what was going to happen between you?' Ori quizzed.

'Ah . . . no,' she replied. 'Simon has a family who love him. I'll get over what he did to me.' *In a few centuries.*

'Maybe sooner,' the angel promised. A lock of dark hair had fallen forward on his face, making him look like a bad boy. A tingling sensation lodged in her chest.

Totally hot. And he's with me. Even if it was only for a short time.

She realized he'd probably read her mind, so she changed topics.

'What's Heaven like?'

Ori put a single finger to her lips. 'So many questions.' He gently caressed her cheek. When he drew her in for a kiss, Riley's world collapsed to only those points where their bodies met.

When the kiss ended, she swore she could see infinity in his dark eyes.

'Why are you doing this?' she whispered.

'Kissing you?' he asked, smoothing back a strand of her hair. 'Because I want to. Because I find you so amazing.'

Amazing?

She took a step back, though it proved harder than she'd anticipated.

'You're frowning. Are my kisses that bad?' he teased.

'No, it's just . . .'

'You do not think yourself worthy of love.'

'No, it's just that I've not had a great track record.'

'Then why blame me for it?' he said, his voice cooler

now. 'I have been nothing but honest with you.'

'Mostly because you haven't told me that much.'

'So if I told you exactly how the cosmos works, how long an angel can withstand a star going supernova and that I was there when it was all created, you would trust me more?'

Riley shook her head. 'Then I'd think you were lying.'

'Exactly. Accept that I enjoy being with you. Accept that when I'm with you I see Heaven in your eyes.'

'It's hard for me to believe that.'

'I know.'

They'd reached her family's mausoleum. Things had been too heavy between them, so she asked, 'Where are we going tonight? On another picnic?' *That would be so cool.*

'Tonight we shall stay here.' He waved his hand and the twin mausoleum doors swung open of their own accord. No key needed when you were an angel. Riley stepped to the threshold and gasped. The interior was lit from within by a myriad candles, like a great cathedral. The flames' reflections flickered off the stained-glass windows, igniting the vibrant colours of blood red, royal blue, yellow gold.

Ori brushed past her and settled into the niche at the back of the mausoleum. Riley hesitated – something felt weird, which didn't make much sense. He was one of Heaven's own. He'd saved her life. If you couldn't trust an angel, things were really bad.

He studied her with those deep eyes. 'I wish you didn't know what I am. It has changed things between us.'

'No. It's not that.'

But it was. He'd probably met God in person, polished His throne or something. It was like one of those books she'd read when she was a kid – the girl would meet an immortal guy, fall in love, and then everything went wrong until they saved each other from a hideous fate. The books always had a happy ending, but she knew that was bogus. There was never a happy-ever-after in real life.

With a sigh, Riley closed the heavy bronze doors, troubled by her conflicted emotions. Behind her there was a whooshing sound. She turned and couldn't stop the gasp.

Ori's leather jacket and T-shirt were gone, revealing his muscled chest. A pair of white wings hung in the air behind him. They weren't fully extended – the mausoleum was not large enough for that – but still they were incredible. There was no evidence of the damage he'd sustained in the battle.

Entranced, Riley walked to him. Each iridescent feather glowed as the candlelight touched it. She carefully ran a finger down the length of one. It felt like fine silk.

Pulling her to the floor, Ori laid her head on his shoulder, curving a protective wing around her. Outside the wind gusted around the building and leaves pattered against the metal doors. All she heard was her heart beating in time with his.

'I could stay here forever,' he said.

'But you won't,' she replied.

Ori tilted her chin upward, looking deep into her eyes. 'Maybe I will.'

She wanted him to kiss her, keep kissing her until nothing else mattered. His lips delicately touched hers, like the brush of a dove's wing. The second kiss was more insistent. A fire ignited in her belly. She felt his fingers brush her neck, gently grazing an ear as he leaned closer and kissed her cheek.

As good as it felt, she was roasting. 'Your wings are really warm,' she said. He helped her out of her coat. She felt naked in front of him, exposed in ways she didn't understand. The fire in her belly burned hotter.

Taking her hand, Ori placed it on his naked chest. Riley could feel his heart beating strong underneath her fingertips. 'You stir my blood,' he whispered. 'It's been a long time since that has happened.'

When they next kissed, she found herself leaning into him, wanting him to touch her. Then she pulled back and shook her head.

'This is . . . crazy. This kind of thing only happens in books.'

'You're sure of that?' he asked, wrapping her in those magnificent wings again.

'Angels can't, like . . .'

'Of course we can,' he whispered into her ear.

At his urging, she skimmed her fingers through his dark satin hair, pulling it out of the ponytail. The pool of heat in her belly spread downward. Without thinking, she kissed his ear. He murmured in appreciation, pulling her closer. This wasn't Simon or one of the other boys at school. This was for real.

Too fast. With a groan, Riley pulled out of his arms. She needed time to think this through, to let her head clear.

'I'm not sure I'm . . . ready for this,' she said. It was a huge step, even with a mortal. She couldn't be the only woman he'd been with all these ages. What would keep him from getting tired of her?

Ori gently pushed a strand of hair off her face. 'It's your choice.'

He'd read her mind again. He was right – this was her choice. 'I've never been . . .'

'I know.'

He knows I'm a virgin? What doesn't he know?

'How to win your trust,' he replied so sincerely it tugged at her heart. He gently kissed her forehead. 'So much sadness for one so young.'

Riley curved into the hollow of his wing, feeling his breath across her skin like a whispering breeze. Outside, the wind skittered dry leaves across the path. She could hear the beating of their hearts.

'Tell me what you want,' Ori urged.

Riley teetered on the edge. She was seventeen, not some kid. She could be with him, but what would happen after that?

'You will set our future, Riley. I surrender myself to you, body and soul.'

His next kiss was surprisingly tender. It felt like a lover's kiss.

'Tell me what you want,' he repeated.

Her final doubts melted away. 'You,' she whispered. 'I want you.'

'Then I am yours, Riley Anora Blackthorne, and you shall be mine.'

Ori curved his wings around her, lifting her face, her body to melt against his. Raw desire surged between them. It surrounded her. Overwhelmed her.

Love me. Forever.

Nothing else mattered.

Riley woke sometime later, covered by a wing that was toastier than any blanket. When she rolled towards Ori, he stirred, those dark eyes searching her face.

'You look content,' he said.

'I am.'

Did she feel different? Not really. Other than an intense heat that surged through her veins, she hadn't changed. Other girls had told her what it was like their first time, but hers hadn't been like that. There'd been no fumbling, no uncertainty. Ori was a born lover and now he was hers.

'I want this forever,' she said, tracing one finger across his full lips. Then she sighed. 'But that's a very long time and I haven't even finished school yet.'

Ori chuckled. 'You worry too much, my *valiant light.*'

He'd remembered the meaning of her name.

She snuggled next to his body. Underneath them was some sort of padding, almost like a sleeping bag only far richer in texture and comfort. *More angel mojo.*

Ori bent over her, running a line of tiny kisses down her forehead to her nose. 'Morning comes soon. Let's not waste the night with talk.'

'What happens in the morning? With us, I mean?'

His answer was a breath-stealing kiss.

Chapter Thirty-Three

When Riley woke, she was lying on the floor of the mausoleum fully clothed. The comfy padding was gone, so were the candles and the angel. For a few seconds she wondered if it had just been a dream.

No dream could have been that good.

Then she saw the rose. It was blood red, lying next to her. She sampled its fragrance and, like Ori, it was heavenly. After some time, Riley finally moved into a sitting position. So where was the angel? Doubts seemed to crowd her when he wasn't near. She wanted him here, holding her, telling her she'd made the right decision.

How long can this last? He was a Divine and he probably wasn't supposed to be doing things with mortals, at least not the kind of things they'd been doing. What would Heaven say if they found out?

She pulled on her jacket and then combed out her hair. A quick check of her pocket mirror generated a sigh of relief. Her make-up wasn't trashed. While she reapplied her lipgloss, Riley tried to recall every moment with the angel, but it seemed too magical to capture in mere memories. Still, something kept nibbling on her like

Forbidden

a tenacious bug. She couldn't quite sort it out. Riley gave up and pushed open the mausoleum doors.

She found him a short distance from the mausoleum. His wings were tightly cramped against his back, a barometer of his mood. Something was wrong.

'Ori?' she called.

He turned towards her with an expression so sad it almost brought her to tears. He beckoned her over, but when she asked again what was wrong he shushed her.

'Enjoy the sunrise,' he said, intertwining their fingers.

They faced east. The sun had just poked over the horizon and it made the feathers on his wings glow as if they were absorbing the light.

'I always love the sunrise,' he said. 'It reminds me of Heaven.' Then a tremor ran the length of his body.

'Ori, what's going on?'

He turned towards her again, taking both her hands in his. His expression hadn't changed. If anything, it was even sadder. 'You have a decision to make, Riley. It is the hardest of your life and I am so sorry you must make it.'

'What are you talking about?' He was spooking her.

The angel hesitated. 'I need you to pledge yourself to me. If you do, then I can keep you safe for as long as you live.'

For a second she swore she felt the earth shake, but it was just her body.

'I have made my commitment by being with you,' he explained. 'I have placed my future in your hands, Riley.

Do not think that was a light decision. In the past, any angel who lay with a mortal woman was punished.'

'Punished? But isn't God all about love?' she asked. 'I mean, wouldn't He want us to be together?'

'There are rules.' Ori let go of her hands. 'Your soul is . . . *in play*, as we call it. It happened the moment you made the arrangement with Heaven. That agreement attracted notice in the lower realms.'

'That makes no sense,' she said, stepping away from him. 'The demons have always known my name. You're saying that, just because I agreed to help Heaven, now I've got all of Hell after me?'

'Not all, only those who are truly ambitious.'

Riley drifted up the path towards the mausoleum, troubled. She hadn't expected this, not after the night they'd spent together. She turned to face him. 'What is this decision I need to make?'

Ori sighed deeply, his expression still troubled. 'The measure of a mortal is their soul. Yours is very powerful, Riley. That is why you must pledge it to me. That is how Hell will know we have a bond, one that is lasting and true. Only then will you be safe.'

He wants my soul?

'Yes,' he said, reading her mind. 'Nothing less will do.' He was a few feet from her now. The wings were gone and he looked like any mortal. Harmless, if you didn't know what lay beneath. Riley hesitated, so many questions pounding at her at once. *Why would an angel want my soul? Martha didn't.*

'That was different,' Ori responded.

'It doesn't make sense. You're saying Hell's after me, but the Five first tried to kill me *before* I did the deal with Heaven.'

'The rogue wasn't after your soul, Riley. It just wanted you and your father dead.'

'Why?'

Ori stepped closer, offering his hand. 'Please trust me. I only do this to keep you alive.'

He sounded so sincere, but she took a step back anyway. 'I have trusted you. I slept with you, remember?' She'd given him something truly precious – her virginity. You could only do that once. Did Ori think so little of her that it meant nothing?

Something stirred inside her. She wasn't sure what it was, but it seared like a live coal in the pit of her stomach. She'd felt this before, in the parking lot with Allan right after he'd punched her.

'What does this soul-pledging mean to me?' she quizzed.

'It means that we are bound together.'

'That was a vague answer,' she muttered. 'You seem to be really good at those. Does that talent come with the wings?'

Ori frowned. 'This is best for both of us. I'm the only one who hasn't hurt you.'

'Give it time,' she said, surprised at her bitterness.

What was feeding that? Maybe the fact that almost every guy had lied to her.

Ori began to pace in front of the mausoleum, his moves disjointed, a mirror to his turbulent emotions. 'I killed that demon for you, Riley. I have saved your life more times than you know. What else can I do to earn your trust?'

The coal in her stomach was a blast furnace now. She felt the tears slip down her face and she swiped them away with the back of her hand. 'Tell me the truth. How many mortals have you been with? Am I the first? The tenth, the thousandth? Or is this just the first time you were caught?'

'This is for your own protection,' he retorted. 'You have no notion of how much danger you are in from both Heaven and Hell.'

'So God's going to smite me too?' she replied. 'If that happens, how am I supposed to stop the end of the world? You guys really need to get your stories straight.'

'If you deny me, others will come for you, others more evil than you can imagine. Please, Riley, I am your only hope,' he insisted.

'They can't get my soul unless I give it to them,' she said, crossing her arms over her chest.

'Oh, Riley,' he murmured, 'there are countless ways to lose your soul, most of them genuinely noble.'

'You're lying. Why did I ever believe you?'

His wings reappeared, snapped tight against his back,

vibrating with anger. 'Clear your head, girl!' he shouted, his fists clenched now. She winced at the power behind the voice. 'I am your last chance! Do not deny me!'

'Oh dear, now you've upset him,' a smooth voice said. 'That is never a good thing.'

Riley jerked in surprise. A figure leaned against one of the gravestones. He was in a black shirt and slacks, his collar-length ebony hair shot with silver. His eyes were bottomless midnight blue.

Ori started, then gave a deep bow. 'My lord, I did not expect you.'

My lord?

The newcomer laughed at the angel. 'Of course you didn't. No one ever does.' His eyes fell on Riley again. They had a depth to them beyond anything she'd experienced.

'Who are you?' she whispered.

'I'm his boss,' he said, angling his head towards Ori.

He sure didn't look like her idea of God.

The figure straightened. 'You work it out, Blackthorne's daughter. You're a very smart girl.'

Blackthorne's daughter. Demons called her by that name. Maybe Heaven did too. They were on holy ground so no way this could be Hellspawn. Ori had called him *my lord* which meant he was an angel, at least.

'You have that right,' the figure replied.

Great. Mr New Guy could read her mind just like Ori.

'I'll give you a huge clue,' the newcomer said.

Something flared in the air and then a crimson doorway appeared next to him. The air seethed inside the portal, buoyed by unseen currents. Something waddled to the threshold, bouncing and giggling. It was round, black and white like a soccer ball, and about three feet tall. It had two feet tipped with claws, horns that spouted out of the top of its head and pincers at the end of its arms. The moment it stepped across the portal and its clawed foot touched the hallowed ground, it shrieked and disappeared in a puff of black, acrid smoke. The unmistakable scent of brimstone stung her nose.

The newcomer rolled his eyes, snapped a finger and the portal vanished. 'Demons are *so* stupid.'

'Ohmigod, you're . . .' she began. 'HIM?'

'Oh, indeed. I'm Lucifer,' he said. 'You'd be surprised how many mortals insist on using the S word. Or the D one for that matter.' He shook his head in disgust. 'I am neither. I am the Light Bearer, the Prince of Hell, the Chief Among the Fallen and *The* Adversary. Accept no substitutes.'

Oh, shit.

'That's a very common reaction,' he replied.

'You can't be here!' Riley protested. 'This is hallowed ground. This has to be a trick.'

'Hallowed ground is death to my Hellspawn, but not to one who was created by the Light. Fallen can tread here as easily as you, child.'

Another one of those things someone forgot to tell her.

Forbidden

Lucifer wandered over to the other angel, eyeing his servant intently. 'So how goes it, Ori?'

'My lord, I am fulfilling my tasks, as you commanded,' Ori murmured. 'Allow me more time, I beg of you.'

'Tasks? And what were those?' his superior quizzed. 'Refresh my mind.'

Ori swallowed uneasily. His wings were no longer pure white, but showed a thin line of ash grey at the tips. 'I was to utterly destroy the rogue demon, which I have done.'

'And?'

'I was to secure this girl's soul by any means necessary.'

'About that *second* task,' Lucifer said, 'I note you have not fulfilled it. Losing your touch?' When Ori didn't reply, the Prince leaned closer. 'Or is there some other reason?'

The fire in Riley's stomach grew hotter, spreading into her chest now, threatening to consume her heart.

'You lied to me,' she shouted, pointing an accusing finger at him. 'You said you loved me.'

'I said I cared for you and that was not a lie,' Ori said, stepping closer to her.

'Right. Try that one again,' she snarled. 'You're just sucking up to *him*.'

'Besides being one of the most arrogant of my servants,' Lucifer began, 'Ori is incredibly talented at seducing mortals. Male, female, doesn't matter. They're all the same to him.'

'My lord, please,' Ori began, like he was embarrassed

to have his sins paraded in front of her.

'Yes, this one is different for you,' Lucifer chided. 'But she is still at risk unless you finish what you've started.'

Riley shook her head. 'No go on the soul,' she said. 'No go on any of this.'

'He was not lying,' Lucifer replied. 'Your soul *is* in play now. You can blame Heaven for that. We offer security. If you do not pledge your soul to Ori, others will seek it and they will use every means to secure it.'

'You can just tell them to back off, right?'

'I can, but free will isn't just for mortals. Demons and Fallen are allowed to make their own mistakes. Like my servant Ori, here.' He clapped a hand on the angel's shoulder, causing her seducer to grimace. 'But we'll get back to that in a moment.'

'Why is this about me?' Riley demanded.

She saw a flash of anger in the Prince's eyes. 'Do not assume you are the very centre of the universe, Blackthorne's daughter. There is more at stake than just your little skin.'

'You know, I don't care any more. I do one good deed and it all goes to—'

'Hell?' Lucifer quipped. 'That's often the case.'

'It'd be family tradition,' Ori said in a bitter voice.

Lucifer gave him a sharp look, followed by a frown. 'Careful, my servant.'

'What do you mean, family tradition?' Riley demanded.

'Why do you think your father lived as long as he did?' Ori questioned. 'Luck?' The smirk on his face made her queasy.

'My dad was an excellent trapper,' she retorted. 'One of the best.'

'He was good, but he wasn't invincible. When that Archdemon was about to rip out his heart, Paul Blackthorne begged to stay alive. How could I ignore such a heartfelt plea?'

'No, you're wrong. My dad killed that thing. That's how he became a master.'

'He did, after we made the deal,' Ori said. 'From that point on no Hellspawn could harm him. In exchange, he would remain alive until you had become a master trapper.'

These were more lies. That's what these monsters did. They twisted the truth until you couldn't tell day from night.

Lucifer bent over and picked up a withered leaf, examining it like he'd never seen one before. 'Your father feared you being an orphan,' he explained. 'A very noble gesture, which cost him his soul.' He blew on the leaf and it turned green, alive from the top to the stem. The moment it left his hand it returned to the dead, shattered fragments floating to the ground.

Ori started to say something, but his master waved him silent.

The lies had a kernel of truth to them. Her dad had changed after he'd captured the Archfiend. Quieter, more thoughtful. He hadn't shown any fear of demons from that point on.

'You understand now,' the Prince of Hell said.

She did. Her father, the man she loved so much, had sold himself to Hell for his only child.

'I will do the same for you,' Ori coaxed. 'No Hellspawn will harm you. You'll do well in this life, and at the end there's just a small payment.'

Like I believe that. 'And what about you? Do I get your soul in return?' she chided. 'You said there was risk for you as well.'

Ori wouldn't meet her eyes so it was Lucifer that answered. 'If he does not take your soul, his power is diminished. Power and status is everything in Hell, much like Heaven. He will suffer for his failure.'

She could trap and not get hurt any more. She'd be as good as her father and none of the other trappers could best her. She probably wouldn't even miss her soul. There was one glaring problem. 'So if this is such a great deal, why is my dad dead?'

The Prince of Hell shrugged. 'Shit happens.'

Riley adjusted the messenger bag on her shoulder, dredging up the last bit of courage she possessed. It was pathetically small compared to the evil arrayed in front of her. 'Well, this Blackthorne isn't playing ball. You had me once, you're not having me again. I'm out of here.'

With her body shaking so hard it was difficult to walk, she turned her back on the two fallen angels. *This is in-*

sane. How many steps would she take before they killed her? Five? Ten? Would they let her think she'd reached safety and then rip her apart? Throw her to a bunch of demons so they could eat her alive?

'Riley, stop!' Ori called out. 'Your soul has to be mine. If you align with one of the others, there will be—'

'Enough!' Lucifer commanded.

A shrill cry of protest filled the air and then there was silence. When Riley looked over her shoulder, Lucifer was leaning against the base of a statue, grinning that maniacal grin of his. Ori was gone. Her eyes tracked up the plinth, then to the statue. At the top was a stone angel, his bare chest exposed to the air. Wings stretched behind him and both fists were raised towards the sky in righteous anger.

It was Ori. In sculpted marble.

Lucifer cleared his throat, bringing her eyes back to him. 'My order to my servant was for one task only – destroy the rogue demon.'

'But he said there were two tasks.'

'Indeed. He made the mistake of trusting another, one who lied to him. One who told him what he wanted to hear.'

It hit her. 'Ori wasn't supposed to sleep with me, try to take my soul,' she said.

'No. This was a test. You both failed.' A pensive frown settled on Lucifer's face. 'Ori had no idea he was being used, and now he is paying the price.'

'Did you turn Simon against me?'

'That was the other's doing, not mine. However, it did push you into Ori's arms, which served my purposes.'

One by one the pieces fell into the convoluted puzzle. She'd been herded like a sheep and never had a clue. 'You test angels too?'

'It is my job,' Lucifer said solemnly. His expression changed to one of determination. 'If you agree to act on our behalf, I will give you certain assurances.'

'You're not getting my soul. That's just not on the table, no matter what you do to me.'

A shrug. 'Right now, you're more valuable as a free agent, though it does put you at greater risk.' Lucifer peered up at the stone statue. 'If you wish to keep those you value safe, you will owe me a favour. Should I set Ori free, he will not remember you with love and tenderness, not after this disgrace. He has pride, one of the Seven Deadly Sins, and you have damaged his reputation in Hell.' Lucifer pulled a face. 'Now just who would he destroy first? Maybe your little friend Peter, or how about that annoying trapper who takes my name in vain so often? You know, the one who loves country music so much?'

Beck.

'I'll even sweeten the deal,' the Prince of Hell added. 'You do what I want and I'll grant you one wish. Oh, and I can't bring the dead back to life, so don't bother with that one.'

It all came back to her dad and his sacrifice. 'Who summoned my father from his grave? Ozymandias?'

A snort came her way. 'A dabbler in the dark arts? Hardly.'

'Then who?'

'Me, of course,' he said, beaming. 'Who else would be the dragon?' It'd been right in front of her all the time. Even the hunters had the dragon on their patches, symbolizing the battle between good and evil.

'Why did you do that to my dad?'

'To keep him out of the hands of those who would use his knowledge against us.'

'Where is he—'

The Prince waved her off. 'Do we have an agreement?' he demanded.

The fight went out of her. 'What do you want me to do?'

'A little task when the time comes,' he replied. All pretence of good humour vanished. 'Fail me,' Lucifer said, jabbing a finger upward at the marble Ori, 'and I'll set the avenging angel free. Trust me when I say that his wrath has been known to level cities.'

My friends' lives. Atlanta. That's what hung in the balance. It was no longer just about her or her father. 'No on the soul, yes on the deal.'

Lucifer's blue eyes sparkled. 'Excellent. Don't worry, it balances out the one you made with Heaven, and just might keep you alive.'

A second later the Prince of Hell vanished in a flash of brilliant light, followed by an overly dramatic clap of thunder. Riley slumped against the nearest gravestone. Her eyes took the tortuous journey from the bare toes to the handsome face of the enraged angel who had betrayed her. God help her, but she still half believed what Ori had said, that he really was trying to protect her. How much of what he and Lucifer had told her was lies? How much was the truth? And why hadn't Heaven warned her she was in danger?

Riley had gone too far now to take this back, not after she'd slept with a Fallen and made a deal with the Prince of Hell himself. The longer she looked at it, the more certain she was that Lucifer had set up his tests to ensure she'd fail. How else would he get her on Hell's payroll?

Harper was right, she was twisted.

Just like my father.

Chapter Thirty-Four

Riley sat in the wooden rocker on Beck's front porch, working up her courage. It was ironic she'd come to him for help, but she had no place else to go. He wasn't home, but if the number of calls on her cellphone was any indication, he'd frantically been trying to find her until at least four in the morning. The messages had a common theme: stay away from Ori.

'Too late.' She hadn't heard her phone ring last night, but it was a safe bet the angel had made sure no one could find her until he'd finished with her.

Beck answered on the first ring and he sounded sleepy. 'Riley? I've been callin' ya all night. Where were ya?'

'At the cemetery. I stayed in the mausoleum.'

'Ya weren't there. I looked. I walked all over the damned place.'

More angel mojo courtesy of Ori. 'It doesn't matter now,' she said. 'I'm at your house, on the porch.' She blinked away tears as the final admission came forth. 'I need your help, Beck. Something bad's happened.'

When he asked what was wrong, she refused to tell him. No way she'd tell him over the phone. He gave her the alarm code and told where to find the spare key. 'I'll get there as soon as I can,' he said, and then hung up.

Once she was inside and had turned off the alarm, Riley stood rooted in the entryway. If things played out like she suspected, this might be the last time she'd ever be allowed in this house.

The morning sun poured in the front window, sending beams of light on to the wood floor. The house smelt like fried chicken. Probably takeout. Riley made it to the couch, tucked herself into a ball and pulled the crocheted afghan over her, even though she was too warm. The afghan's faint pine scent reminded her of its owner's aftershave. She tucked it closer to her chin. Of all the people she could have run to when things went bad, she had come to Denver Beck, even though she knew he'd be the one most hurt by the news. From this moment on, nothing would ever be the same. She had made the ultimate mistake and now she needed to find a way to survive it.

The minutes crept by like a furtive mouse skulking along the baseboards. Soon Beck would pull into the driveway and she'd tell him what had happened. Tell him all of it. Well, not everything. He didn't need to know she'd made a bargain with Lucifer to keep him alive, or that her father's soul belonged to Hell.

All along Beck had watched out for her. 'He warned me. Why didn't I listen?'

Because Ori said all the right words.

Riley ground her teeth in frustration. It would be easy to blame it all on angel mojo, but that wasn't right. She'd been so desperate for someone to love her, not to challenge her every decision, she'd walked right into the Fallen's feather-lined trap. She could blame the angel for what had happened – and Ori was good for a lot of it – but that would be lying to herself. She'd done the same rebound thing after Beck had returned from the Army and ignored her. That had earned her Allan's abuse.

Why do I do this to myself? Am I stupid or what? Why was it so important that someone love and care for her? It wasn't like she'd come from a broken home. She'd been loved, knew what it felt like. And that made her want it even more.

Riley adjusted the afghan, sending another wave of Beck's woodsy aftershave into the air. There was a further reason she'd gone for Ori, and she couldn't deny it any longer.

I was so jealous. Beck's new girlfriend had turned Riley totally green from the moment the reporter had knocked on her door. That envy had coloured almost every decision from that second on. Simon's betrayal had opened the wound and Justine had poured acid into it.

Now I'm in a world of hurt and I have no one else to blame.

She heard a truck door slam and the sound of boots pounding up the front stairs. Her heart clenched, knowing what was to come. Beck was through the door and at her side in only a few steps. His duffel bag clunked down on the wooden floor and then he was kneeling in front of her, his face wreathed in worry.

'What's wrong? Are ya sick? Should I call the doctor?' he panted.

'No.' *He'll hate me when he knows what I did.*

'Riley? Tell me what's happened. You're so pale.' He reached out to touch her face. The tender gesture pushed her over the edge.

Tears burst out of her in torrents, her body shaking to its core. He wrapped his arms round her and that made it even harder. Ori had stolen so many precious things from her and Beck's friendship was one of them.

She heard him murmuring in her ear, telling her it would be OK.

No, it's only going to get worse.

Finally, when she'd cried herself out, she pulled back. Beck was still kneeling in front of her. There was a wad of tissues in her hand and she had no idea how it had got there. She blew her nose, wiped her tears and then cleared her throat. 'Ori . . .'

Beck's face went stony. 'That bastard? Did he hurt ya, girl?' When she didn't answer, he demanded, 'Did he force ya to . . .' His voice faded and she could see the dread in his eyes.

Riley shook her head and laughed bitterly. 'No. He didn't force me. I gave it to him.'

The thick intake of breath told her she'd been right. Beck was going to hate her for this.

'Oh, God,' he muttered. 'Ya let him . . . Why the hell would ya do that? I told ya he was no good.'

She couldn't meet his eyes. 'He said I was special. He said that he loved me.' Even now, as she spoke the words, she could hear how weak they were. 'He said . . .'

'Ya were one of a kind, that he always wanted to be with ya. We all use those lines, girl.'

And we always believe them.

'Goddammit!' he shouted, jumping to his feet. His sudden motion frightened her and she cringed back against the couch. 'Why him? Why not . . . someone who cares about ya?'

Someone like you.

She had never considered that Beck might be interested in her in that way, but from the expression on his face it was true. It was knowledge gained too late.

'So why the hell are ya here? Ya pregnant?' he snapped.

Am I? 'That's not the problem.'

Beck dropped into the chair across from the couch like he had no more strength in his legs to keep him upright. 'Then why come runnin' to me?'

'I made a mistake, I know that, but there's more to it. I need your help because Ori . . . isn't human. He's an angel.'

'Angels don't screw mortals, girl. He's lying to ya again.'

She grimaced at the barely contained fury in his words. 'He showed me his wings.'

Beck smirked. 'Bet that isn't all he showed ya.' Then a frown came. 'What would an angel want with ya?'

Riley had asked herself that a hundred times, but now she knew the answer. 'Because I'm Paul Blackthorne's daughter. Because he wanted my soul.' *So he'd have a matched set.*

'Angels don't want souls. Only Hellspawn pull that kinda . . .'

She could tell the moment the truth hit him.

'Sweet Jesus, he's a Fallen?' Beck retorted.

'Yeah.'

'How could ya be so stupid?'

Her anger finally stirred. 'I made a mistake, OK? I trusted him. You're doing the same if you believe everything the stick chick tells you.'

'Leave Justine out of this,' he said, face growing crimson.

'Ask yourself why she wants you. Is it because you're good at knocking boots or is it because of something else? You sure she's not after your soul too?'

Beck grabbed up his duffel and surged to his feet, a feral snarl erupting from his throat.

'I'm not gettin' lectured by some dumbass girl who puts out for demons,' he shouted. 'I always thought ya were different to the others. I was such damned fool.'

He was out of the door in only a few steps. Seconds later his truck roared to life. She stepped to the window, knowing this was the last time she'd see him. She'd have to go to Fargo now, get out of Atlanta. Get as far away from this city as possible. Leave Denver Beck, the Guild, all her friends behind.

The truck peeled rubber out of the drive and on to the street. As Beck drove away, he was talking to someone on his phone, gesturing towards the house. Probably telling Stewart how badly she'd screwed up.

Her mistake, her BIG mistake, was already rippling outward like a tsunami. Her apprentice licence was gone. No way they'd let someone who'd been with a Fallen stay in the Guild. Beck would hate her for life. That hurt the worst.

Damn you, Ori, you've ruined everything. And I let you.

Riley bent over the sink in Beck's small bathroom, splashing her face with cold water. No matter what she did, she felt like she was burning up inside, as if the lump of coal in her stomach had spread heat throughout every single cell of her body. Was it because she'd been with a Fallen? Would it ever stop? She stared up at her reflection in the mirror. Sweat beaded on her forehead and her face was flushed, despite the cold water.

God, I look old. As if one night with Ori had subtracted three decades of physical payment. The dark circles under her eyes were more pronounced now and her skin seemed translucent, but not in a good way. Riley plucked at a silver strand of hair that poked out at her temple. She was only seventeen. How could she have grey hair? She yanked it out, glowered at the strand and washed it down the drain with extreme prejudice.

A sharp rapping noise brought Riley upright. The noise repeated – someone was banging on the bathroom window. It wouldn't be Ori. He'd just appear out of nowhere, grab her and disappear with her to a remote location where he could torment her. Like Hell, where those stupid soccer-ball demons lived.

The banging continued, more frantic now, and she thought she heard a familiar high-pitched voice. Riley pushed aside the window curtain and started in surprise. The Magpie from her apartment was gesturing frantically, jumping up and down on the sill.

'What are you doing here?' He shrieked something. 'Settle down. What are you trying to say?'

'Deeemon hun . . . ters!' he shouted.

'Where?'

'Here!' the Magpie shouted back. 'Coming for you!'

Ohmigod.

Riley bolted from the bathroom, grabbed her messenger bag and fled out of the back door. A few seconds later she was in her car and careening down the back alley. As she slowed to make the turn on to the street, she saw a black van roll into Beck's drive. Then another. Their side doors opened and armed men burst out of them, heading for the front and back of the house in a coordinated assault.

How could they know about Ori? How did they know I was here?

Forbidden

The answer struck her like a brick to the forehead. Beck had been on the phone when he'd driven away. He hadn't called Master Stewart. He'd called the hunters down on her because she'd chosen Ori over him.

Riley's hands shook so hard she found it hard to drive. The bile rose in her throat, but she forced herself to swallow it down. He had said he'd always look after her, honour her father's memory, but once his guy ego got bruised, Beck was all about payback.

Her phone rang. It was him. She tried to ignore it, but the fury was too much.

'Riley?' Beck said as she answered the phone. 'I—'

'You sold me out, you hick bastard!' she shouted. 'You're no better than Simon or that damned angel. I should have known you'd screw me over.'

'What are ya—'

Riley jabbed the button on the phone, cutting him off. When it rang seconds later, she turned it off and threw it into her bag. With her luck the hunters could track her by it. Who knew what kind of crazy technology the Vatican possessed.

The shakes caught up with her seconds later, causing her to pull into an abandoned parking lot and lean her head on the steering wheel. This time her lungs didn't constrict, didn't fail to pull in the air she needed. If anything, they expanded. The blazing anger inside her fuelled her desire to survive. She would never let anyone hurt her again. *Never*.

The Demon Trappers

But where could she hide? *My apartment?* No, they'd look there for sure. She didn't dare go to either of the masters – that would just make trouble for the Guild. Same with Ayden and the witches. Peter wasn't an option without causing a bunch of hassle with his dad. She had to disappear, make them think she'd left town until she'd had time to do just that. There was only one person who might be able to help, providing he was willing to accept the risk.

Chapter Thirty-Five

It took only a few minutes to make it to Little Five Points. It took longer to locate a parking place. Finally she stashed the car behind a health-food store, away from the main street. Maybe that would buy her time in case the Vatican was working with the local cops.

Paranoid much?

It seemed that just about everyone was out to get her. Well, except the Five and that was because Ori had killed it. Or had he?

Absolutely everything she'd believed was up for grabs. She'd thought Simon was the perfect boyfriend, that they had a future together. That relationship had gone down in flames. Beck would always be there for her. That was a lie. The only thing she could be sure of was that her dad was dead and that she'd slept with a Fallen. The rest was pretty much smoke and mirrors.

Riley hurried down Enchanter's Way, moving past the cafe, the witches' place and then left into the alley that led to Mortimer's house. She kept turning round every few steps to see if she was being followed. After she'd knocked on the necromancer's door, she fidgeted with the strap of her messenger bag.

What if he won't take me in? Then she'd have nowhere to go.

The door slowly opened. She had expected Mort's housekeeper. Instead it was the summoner himself. 'Hello, Riley.' His smile looked genuine. 'It's good to see you.' Then he frowned. 'Are you OK?'

'I . . .' She looked around nervously. Any minute armed men might storm down the alley to arrest her. 'I'm in deep trouble. The demon hunters are after me.'

Mort's eyebrows rose in tandem. For a second she was sure he'd slam the door in her face. To her amazement, he beckoned. 'Then you'd better come inside.' He shut the door behind her, bolted it. 'What's happened?'

She couldn't tell him everything, but at least she could give him the short version. He deserved that if he was going to help a fugitive.

It came out in a rush. 'I've got a fallen angel who wants to steal my soul, I owe Heaven a big favour and the demon hunters want to arrest me because they think I'm working for Lucifer, so I need a place to hide until I can get this worked out.'

'That all?' the summoner asked, quirking a smile.

Riley stared at him. How could he be so calm about all this?

'What are the hunters up to?' he asked.

'They're raiding Beck's place. They could come here too.'

'Wouldn't do them any good,' he stated. 'They won't find you, even if they come inside the house. Magic has its benefits, you see.'

'You could get in big trouble taking me in,' she cautioned.

'Most certainly. Where did you park?' She told him. 'Give me your keys. I'll hide the car.'

Riley handed over the key ring, along with the vehicle's description, knowing she had to trust him.

Mort pointed down the hallway towards the circular room. 'I'll have my housekeeper bring you some food. You look like you could use it.'

'Thanks, I really mean it. I didn't have anywhere else to go,' she admitted.

'I don't get to play the good guy very often. It's kinda fun.'

Not if the hunters arrest you.

Mort opened the front door, then looked back at her. 'He said you'd come.'

Before she could ask who he meant, the necro was gone.

Riley walked down the hallway and into the big room, each step feeling like it was a mile long. The smell of woodsmoke tickled her nose as she dumped her messenger bag on the bench. She issued a heavy sigh. It was answered by an odd sound, like the shifting of dry leaves. It reminded her of Ozymandias's illusion at the graveyard. Had Mort sold her out too?

Then she saw the figure as it rose awkwardly from a chair in the corner, a thin scarecrow in a suit and red tie. It slowly shuffled into the brighter part of the room, a strand of brown hair dangling across its forehead in a way that was so familiar.

'Pumpkin?' the figure called out.

'Daddy?' she cried.

Riley flung herself at her father, nearly knocking him over. As they embraced, the scent of cedar chips and oranges filled her nose.

'My beautiful daughter,' he murmured, hugging her tight. 'I've missed you so much.'

'It's all gone wrong, Dad. I've made so many mistakes.'

'It'll be OK,' he soothed. 'We'll get through this . . . together. I won't let you down.'

She was with her father again. The whole world might be looking for them, but that didn't matter now.

As Riley's tears soaked into his jacket, she made one final vow:

I swear that Hell will not have this man. Even if it means I take his place.

Acknowledgements

First a heartfelt thank you to my friend P. C. Cast, who kept murmuring 'young adult' in my ear when I was first thinking about this series. All this effort would have been for naught if my savvy literary agent Meredith Bernstein hadn't believed in my stories and found them a home. My editor Rachel Petty ensured my books were all dressed up and ready for their UK debut, and the talented folks at Blacksheep created the incredible covers. Also my thanks to Lisa Grindon and Kate Green for touting my books to the world.

My deepest gratitude to fellow author Ilona Andrews, who shared writing tips, and Gordon Andrews, who helped me establish Denver Beck's military background. William McLeod made Master Angus Stewart sound like a Scotsman, and Oakland Cemetery provided the perfect backdrop for my series. A round of applause is needed for my long-suffering beta readers and critique partners Nanette Littlestone, Aarti Nayar, Dwain Herndon and Jeri Smith-Ready, along with Jean Marie Ward and Michelle Roper, who supplied me with manuscript advice and all those 'no, your book doesn't suck' pep talks.

Since the beginning I've had one man in my corner, and that's my husband Harold. I wouldn't be here without him. Dreams are always richer when they're shared.

The end is most definitely nigh . . .

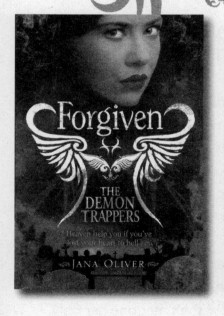

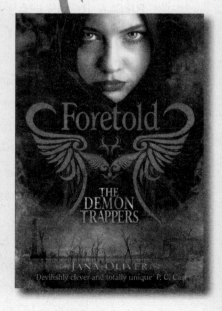

JANA OLIVER

BRIAR ROSE

JANA OLIVER

**BRIAR ROSE HAS ALWAYS BELIEVED
IN FAIRY TALES . . .**

But now, because of a family curse, she's living one.
Doomed to fall asleep for one hundred years on her
sixteenth birthday, Briar has woken up in the darkest,
most twisted fairy tale she could ever have dreamed
of — miles away from the safe, boring small-town life
that she has left behind.

Now Briar must fight her way out of the story,
but she can't do it alone. She never believed in
handsome princes, but now she's met one her only
chance is to put her life in his hands, or there will be
no happy ever after and no waking up . . .